SILENT SUBVERSION

World Wide Web

Hyrum Jones

Silent Subversion II: World Wide Web

Copyright © 2025 by Hyrum Jones

First edition: March 2017

Second Edition: March 2018

ISBN (Print): 978-0-997-21077-4

ISBN (eBook): 978-0-997-21070-5

Interior Artwork: astrosense.net/astrology-fonts

Cover Design: nickcaldwellcreations.com

Anxiety Publishing

Thanks again to Jim, Carlene, Diane, and Bernard for helping prepare the final draft, and to everyone else around me for tolerating my obsessive queries for their opinions.

Summary of Book 1

Here is a little recap of the story before continuing with this book.

After Taylor shared her invention with Gerald and he helped her devise a plan, he introduced her to Cesar, Doroteo, and Dominga. She liked them instantly. Cesar and his friends joined the effort and invited Taylor to live with them in Seattle, Washington. While Cesar helped develop her invention, Gerald went on a quest to discover if there was any truth to the cold fusion story and if anyone had secretly developed it. Gerald ultimately acquired a prototype fusion generator from a group of rogue scientists in Utah.

They were all excited about the new power source, except for maybe Doroteo, and then decided to continue with their original plan to show the world what they had created and make an escape vehicle, just in case they had to flee for some reason. So far, they have kept it a secret, and not even the FBI agent, John Pratt, who was spying on them, knows about it. He figured out that someone had kidnapped and drugged him for information, but he does not know who did it. He's pretty pissed and the incident further motivates his goal of making Gerald Foster suffer for making him look like a fool, previously.

Gerald wanted a few more people involved with the group, people with different backgrounds, so he recruited his friend, Gerda, a botanist. She agreed to help and referred her son's friend, Sadi Jacobsen, a microbiologist. After Gerald met with Sadi, her old friend from childhood, Freddy Carlson, contacted her and told her about some strange things happening to him. She learned of his spider in the crystal and his visions of the woman who told him to contact her.

Shortly after their reacquaintance, Sadi's daughter, Helen, was kidnapped. With the help of his extrasensory perception, given to him by the woman on the plane, Freddy rescued Helen from the child-sex organization. Sadi took Helen's fellow captive, Daryn, to live with them. For the time being, they are safe from the kidnappers, but Freddy and Gerald know they have to prevent the authorities from linking their group to the deaths of those involved in the illegal sex trade organization.

Freddy is left wondering what the woman from his vision wants, why she gave him the spider in the crystal that can put people in a trance, and why he can feel the emotions of those around him. Gerald and Sadi want to know why this strange woman connected Freddy to Gerald's group. Gerald still needs to tell the others about Freddy and Sadi, and what happened. He's afraid of Taylor's reaction, but she has also not told him about what she, Cesar, and Doroteo did to the FBI agent.

CONTENTS

PART I

REDDER AND THICKER

No matter how vile

Always appeal to the gods

With a bow and a smile

ONE

Taylor

May 2009

At 12:34 in the afternoon, Taylor felt her iPhone vibrate, a text message from Gerald. After pausing to stare at the digital readout of the time, she quickly read the message.

Gerald: *Want to go to the Winterhawks game this weekend with Cesar and me? Your new boyfriend, Ryan Johansen, will be there:)*

Very rarely did Taylor allow herself the luxury of attending a sports event, and only if it was hockey. Fortunately, Portland had a good team, the *Winterhawks*. Taylor usually despised watching sports, considering it a waste of her precious time. But in hockey, she enjoyed the intense conflict between the players and how they often resorted to violence to achieve their goals. In many social situations, she fantasized about employing the same tactics.

She especially liked Ryan Johansen, one of their newest players for the season. She once made the mistake of joking with Gerald about having a fantasy relationship with him, and Gerald never forgot.

In his text, Gerald was using the reference as code for her to log onto the website, not immediately, but in the next hour and with

Cesar. After waving to get Cesar's attention, Taylor tossed her phone to him.

"From Gerald," she said.

Cesar turned off the lathe and read the message then tossed the phone back to her.

"You can just tell me what he wants to tell us."

Cesar returned to his work.

Thirty minutes later, Taylor walked into Cesar's office and opened his laptop. While waiting for their website to load, she twisted back and forth in Cesar's leather chair then clicked on the *About* menu option placed above the drawing of the rocket. Another of Gerald's many contacts had made their website, some young guy in his early twenties whom Taylor had not yet met. He intentionally made the chat room difficult to find by hiding the link. Random visitors could discover the link by accident, by clicking randomly all over the screen, or by selecting all the text with the mouse, or hitting *Control-A*. Whenever she rediscovered the link, she had to snicker at all of Gerald's security precautions.

After she entered the site, her icon of a pixelated stick figure began to blink, indicating her online status. Gerald's message quickly appeared.

Gerald: *Is Cesar with you?*

Taylor: *No, he's busy.*

Gerald: *Go get him, I'll wait.*

Taylor ran her hand over her scalp and considered pretending to be Cesar, but something in his abruptness convinced her to obey his demand. As she expected, she had to pull Cesar away from his work.

"Can't you just fake it?" Cesar asked.

"He wrote to get *you*, and I think he means it this time."

Taylor: *OK, we're here. Proceed.*

Gerald: *Have you heard of Max Garner, son of Henry Garner?*

Taylor looked at Cesar, hoping to see recognition of the name, but she saw only a look of confusion. She had heard Henry Garner's name somewhere but could not remember where.

"Henry Garner?" she asked. "You know who that is?"

Cesar scratched his head and suggested the same course of action as her initial thought. "Google him."

Wikipedia appeared at the top of the list of sites. Although she despised using that website, she clicked on it to save time. It would be the quickest way to get some of the basics. The online encyclopedia was too diluted and simple for her taste. Its politically correct spin on everything usually ignited her impatience. Taylor only wanted to find information and not opinion or speculation, but almost every website, especially Wikipedia, interpreted the information for her. She preferred to interpret information herself.

After clicking on the article link, she and Cesar read about one of the most well-known bankers in the world, Henry Garner, and his lesser-known son, Max. More information existed about Max's sister, Audrie, than him, but she skipped the information about Audrie to read about all of the CEO positions their father had held.

They looked at pictures of Henry Garner with President Obama, Bush, Clinton, and even one of the former Federal Reserve chairman, Alan Greenspan. The article did not have a separate link for Max and only mentioned his birth and mother's name, but knowing that his father worked with the biggest thieves in the country became enough for Taylor to know all she cared to know about him.

"Ahh," Cesar said, and he tapped the table with his thumb. "I do remember a little about Max's grandfather. He's a successful businessman, built his company from scratch, supposedly. It was quite the success story. My father told me about it once. This man was one of my father's idols."

The computer made the sound of a bell, indicating another message from the website, and it brought their discussion to a halt.

Gerald: *Hello?*

Taylor: *We're here. Just reading about him on Wikipedia*

Gerald: *Then you know about TerraWatch?*

Taylor decided to answer his question with a lie and her fingers clicked over the keyboard like a hailstorm.

Taylor: *Yes, we read about it. Why don't you just get to the point?*

Gerald: *Max Garner contacted me this morning. He wants to meet with us.*

Taylor: *When you say us, who do you mean?*

Gerald: *He contacted me directly at the office and wants to meet with me and whoever else from the group I feel appropriate to bring. I've been kind of busy with a few cases today and could not contact you until after I did some research on this guy. Before we meet and talk about this, you should read more about his company, TerraWatch.*

Taylor began to write even more furiously.

Taylor: *Exactly how did this guy learn about the group? u need to be more careful about who u talk 2.*

Gerald: *One of my good friends works at Max's company. I contacted him, and he's pretty interested in what we're doing. They're in the aerospace industry. This could be our next break!*

Taylor could feel her pulse continue to accelerate. Why did Gerald insist on being so secretive about their communication when he was talking to all his old buddies about their group? She took a deep breath and hoped to calm her nerves in front of Cesar. He seemed to have one eye on her and one eye on the computer screen.

Gerald: *He's an old friend from college. I've kept in touch and told him to keep it a secret.*

Taylor: *So how did his boss, Max, find out about us?*

While waiting for Gerald to type the rest of his reply, Taylor and Cesar performed an internet search on the company's website. After reading a bit, Cesar said a few words quietly in Spanish that Taylor could not understand, but his tone conveyed a mixture of excitement and anger.

"Damn it," Taylor said under her breath as she read about TerraWatch, one of the leading satellite-communication developers in North America. She could feel her stomach knot up, and the veins in her temples begin to throb. Despite her efforts to stop herself, she kept fantasizing about how the company's resources would be of use to them and at the same time how soldiers would be raiding the machine shop.

A ding on the laptop notified her to switch back to the group website tab and view the next piece of Gerald's text.

Gerald: *I'm sure you can see the implications of this. It could be exceedingly bad or one of the boosts we need. You're probably a little scared right now, Taylor, but Max gave me reason to believe that only he and my friend are aware of this and I doubt he even knows much because I didn't tell my friend much.*

Gerald: *We need to think about this positively, meet with him, and see what he has to say. Max wants to meet within the next two weeks, but the earlier, the better. I'm tied up the rest of the day, but tomorrow after lunch I can meet you guys at the shop, and we can discuss it.*

Taylor turned to Cesar and shook her head in anger. "Why doesn't Gerald just bring a news crew to the shop and show them the fusion reactor and my generator? Damn it, Gerald!"

Cesar seemed to look straight through her, too deep in his own thoughts to appreciate her psychological state. Behind all of her anger, Taylor fought the temptation to feel excited about catching the interest of such a prominent person. She could not bring herself to believe that good things just happened. She had faith in entropy. Taylor always had to struggle for every single step forward.

"We don't know anything yet," Cesar said in an attempt to make her feel better, but she could see the same anxiety in his eyes.

—❋—

They worked the rest of that day without talking about Gerald's announcement again. But every time she thought of it, her anger at Gerald returned. More than once, she found herself imagining Max Garner entering the shop and telling them what to do. Thinking of all her possible retaliations gave her some pleasure, but she hated how the man had already entered her head. She would never take instructions from an everything-handed-to-him-on-a-silver-platter-big-shot. She used the anger as motivation to work harder so they could move on to the next task.

They had been working on optimizing the power output of her momentum generator, and she was almost satisfied with their results. Cesar wanted to move on, but Taylor thought they could still get five percent more output without any significant hit on efficiency.

Cesar never attempted to completely redirect her decisions and seemed to respect her role as instigator and inventor of the NMG, and even referred to her as the head engineer. On a few occasions, he even expressed his feelings, how he considered the opportunity of working under her direction a very high honor. In his life, he'd had enough experience taking the lead and being the boss, so he lacked the need for more personal validation. He silently let her take the lead and the consequences of her decisions.

She felt immense excitement at their next step, transforming something into a two-person plane or spacecraft even, to test their engine and fusion reactor. If she let her emotions become too intense, they could easily weaken her judgment and make her prone to mistakes. She had to proceed carefully.

At the end of the day, they returned to Cesar's house and attempted to act as if nothing out of the ordinary was happening, other than working on a forbidden fusion reactor and hiding their activities from the military. Dominga played the role of the stereotypical housewife, greeting them with a smile and a hot meal. After washing the grease and metal filings off their hands, Taylor and Cesar joined the others at the dining room table as though they were one happy family.

Cesar sat opposite the two women and next to Doroteo, who had three days' worth of stubble on his face. He usually shaved every three to four days, and Taylor had been there long enough to grow accustomed to the cycle of clean-shaven to scraggy and then back again. One night, Dominga referred to it as the shave cycle and explained how his general appearance followed the same sequence. At the start, he could pass as an average human, if not a little intimidating, but the longer he went without shaving, the more his appearance seemed to say, "Get out of my face!"

At first, when he hit the end of the shave cycle, Taylor had been hesitant to make eye contact with the man. On this particular night, his hard outer shell failed to intimidate her. Consequently, she began thinking of ways to try and break him.

During dinner, they had empty and trite conversations. Dominga used several conversational devices to awaken the discussion, but each attempt failed to produce more than single-word responses. Taylor usually did her best to help Dominga keep the conversation flowing at a comfortable pace and only had to use a small amount of her limited social energy, but with thoughts of the day's news filling her head, she had less of her usual available energy. For better or worse, a member of the Western aristocracy she so much hated was again attempting to trespass on her ambitions.

"Teo," Taylor said, hiding her pleasure at the use of his nickname, the one he expressly told her not to use. "Can you pass the salt?"

He passed it without saying anything, and she silently shook it on her enchiladas.

A few seconds later, Dominga fixed her black eyes on Taylor and swirled the red wine in her glass as if trying to hypnotize her. Taylor waited until she could no longer endure the obsidian-black gaze burning a hole in the side of her head.

"Tell me, dear," Dominga began sweetly. "What turned you and Cesar into mindless zombies this evening?"

Doroteo paused momentarily while lifting his fork to his mouth, in expectation of Taylor's answer. Cesar glanced at her and looked away before their eyes could meet. Did she notice a hint of a smile on the corner of his lips?

"Gerald called us this afternoon," Taylor began while picking up her glass of wine and taking a sip. "There's someone who wants to meet with the group, and we're just a little worried about it. That's all. If you want, Cesar can tell you all about it."

If the woman wanted to know the rest, Taylor would rather have Cesar explain the situation. Over the past few weeks, while Taylor had lived with them, Dominga had managed to extract all of her secrets, and she decided not to give the woman another opportunity. Besides, if Taylor started to talk about the subject, she would just get angrier, and she would lose her temper in front of them all again. That would just give Dominga more cause for concern.

"This man who wants to meet with us," began Cesar and then exhaled. "Has connections in high places. We're hoping he does not pose a threat of exposure."

"Hmm, I see," Dominga said and put her glass of wine on the table. "And you thought you could keep this concern away from me? How nice of you to consider my delicate and fragile emotional state."

Cesar ignored her sarcastic tone and explained the entire situation with all of its implications, giving both Dominga and Doroteo every detail. He showed slightly more optimism about the situation than Taylor felt. Dominga also took the positive view of the situation. Doroteo scowled and shook his head but said nothing. The information seemed to put him in deep thought. Cesar told her later that he was mentally preparing for negative consequences. Surprisingly, Taylor felt better to have it out of her head and in the open, as though the others could help share the burden.

—※—

The next day, Gerald canceled his meeting with them, saying that an emergency had come up with a member of the group. He refused to give more details but explained how he had scheduled a meeting with Max Garner and his friend for the next Friday, May 15th, in Seattle. At first, Taylor thought he invented the excuse to avoid her wrath, but she had a bad feeling about the situation. In an uncharacteristic move, Gerald left the chat session without defending his actions.

For the next few days, while finishing their engine optimization, Cesar and Taylor often talked about the upcoming meeting with Max Garner. He would be flying to Seattle on his private jet just to meet with them. Before the meeting, Taylor expected to have a bloody confrontation with Gerald about her presence at the meeting, but she did not doubt who would prevail. She would be attending.

TWO

Taylor

On Thursday, May 14th, a long and thrilling day for Taylor and Cesar, they officially declared the completion of their goal for optimizing the NMG engine and fusion generator. At least for the time being, they felt satisfied with the efficiency and power output. They had wanted to finish before they met with Max Garner, scheduled for the next day.

Taylor spent a few hours that day rewriting the algorithm controlling the nuclear reaction power feedback system, and Cesar was extremely impressed by her programming skills. On a few occasions, he suggested they request advice from Ammon at Cerametrics, but Taylor insisted she could do it on her own. In the end, they increased the efficiency by twenty percent from its original performance.

Taylor did her best to avoid thoughts of the military discovering their intensely energetic fusion power source, not to mention the NMG device. The possible consequences seemed to exceed her comprehension, events only found in books and movies. When she looked at their creations from a distance, she saw nothing remarkable. If anyone were to see them, they would not be suspicious at all. She felt as though living in a dream, an illusory and dark fantasy. She could only move forward and hope for success.

That felt like the true definition of faith, not some religious fantasy where an unknown being watched her every move and she only had to worry about pleasing it. Taylor made her own plans and remained loyal to them, no matter what happened in the end. For all she knew, they might end up in some military prison, tucked away from society for the rest of their days, or killed after the military extracted all of their knowledge. Despite all the undesirable possibilities, she had to keep looking ahead and focus on her goals.

They spent the last part of their day arguing about what to convert into their prototype spacecraft. Cesar suggested they purchase an old aircraft and make it space-worthy. Taylor liked the idea but doubted their ability to maintain an inconspicuous cover. The Federal Aviation Administration tracked all aircraft and their travel logs, and she worried that they could be found too easily and their aircraft searched. She considered a car as a more convenient and easier project. They would be able to fit the reactors and engines, and most importantly, no one would suspect a car of traveling into space.

"We have to assume that our test flights will be noticed," Taylor said. "I think a car would be the best option. If we get on their radar, we can just land and be driving on some road. It will be harder to find us."

"You are probably right, Taylor," Cesar said. "Hmmm, a car. No one would suspect it, and I have just the idea."

When Cesar suggested to use his new BMW 535xi as their prototype spaceship, Taylor inhaled in shock.

"You'll ruin the warranty," she said, aghast, but then laughed at how ridiculous her response sounded.

Cesar just shrugged, his lips curving into a wide smile.

"If we're going to make a test flight in space, we might as well go in style."

While staying with them, Taylor admired the vehicle's engine and construction several times, and the thought of gutting it almost made her physically sick. Sure, she was excited at the thought of her invention, her baby, being part of such a beautiful machine, but coming from an underprivileged background, she could not understand how Cesar could thoughtlessly abandon a fifty thousand dollar engine and drive system. In the end, Taylor accepted his decision. The high-quality construction might be easier to make space-worthy. They definitely could not use one of the beater cars she had been driving her whole life.

Near the end of the day, Taylor's excitement climaxed when they pulled the vehicle into the shop. Making a prototype spacecraft was almost intoxicating enough to eliminate her anxiety about the next day's meeting with Max Garner. Hundreds of tasks needed to be done beyond incorporating their devices. They would need to make the car vacuum-tight, add radiation shielding, install dozens of environmental controls, and above all—make it safe. While thinking of all the redundant systems the craft would need, she felt the beginnings of a migraine.

She felt alive!

—※—

The next morning, Taylor spent very little time deciding on how to handle the discussion with Gerald, who had expressed a desire to meet with Max alone. She understood his desire to keep her away from their meeting. He feared her undiplomatic and abrupt way of interacting with people. She accepted her weakness for one simple reason. She had no interest in being tactful. If people had a problem with her method of communication, they had a problem with themselves and needed to fix themselves. She had no time to fix people or custom-fit her actions.

Gerald had planned to meet them around ten, before his rendezvous with Max Garner, so she and Cesar went to the shop to work until then. At the shop, Taylor needed something to calm her nerves, so they listened to Beethoven's first, third, fifth, and ninth symphonies. Gerald arrived at the beginning of the fourth movement of the ninth and Taylor thought of the timing as an omen. She lowered the volume to talk to him and made a feeble attempt to smile.

"About time you showed up," she said with a slight sneer.

Gerald coughed and cleared his throat. As usual, he wore a dark blue suit.

"Sorry about that. Work's been busy." He walked away from her to take a look at the BMW parked in the back of the shop, in front of the huge garage door. He looked under the open hood to an empty space where the engine should have been. Then he laughed. "Amazing, not a scratch."

"So what's your plan, Gerald?" Taylor asked, ignoring his attempt at distraction.

"I know you think you should come," he said while walking around the vehicle. He kept his eyes on it, instead of her. "I really think it would be better if just I went. We stick to the original plan of me being the face of the group. It really is better for everyone else to have minimal exposure. There haven't been any problems yet."

"Up until now," Taylor began with an obvious tone of sarcasm. She could not believe he left himself so wide open. "Where are we meeting him?"

"He wanted to meet at some place where we would attract the least amount of attention. I agreed. I'm going to meet him at Discovery Park, at Fort Lawton."

Taylor had expected they would meet at a high-priced hotel or restaurant.

"Don't think you can avoid the inevitable, Gerald. I'm coming with you."

"Just hear me out, Taylor, please."

Taylor stepped in between him and the car. "Why don't I just tell you so that we can get it over with. You don't want me to come because you think I'll scare this guy off. If I can guess correctly, this is exactly how you wanted it to work out, for this guy to find out about us. It fits in perfectly with your plans. Recruit the biggest fish with the most money. Well, I get to call the rest of the shots on this one. You are unfit to have an unbiased opinion about it."

"I understand, really—" he began with an apologetic tone in his voice, but Taylor interrupted him.

"I have not complained about your other recruits so far, have I?"

"No, but this guy is exactly the type of person you hate," Gerald said with a frown. "It's impossible for you to have an unbiased opinion about him. That's why you should not go."

Cesar stepped toward them both and smiled.

"Listen," he began and appeared to be holding back amusement. "Gerald, she's right. This is too important for one person to do alone. I'm sure Taylor can see the situation from a clear viewpoint, and she will behave perfectly rational."

Taylor shot Cesar a look of annoyance, intending to convey her lack of desire for assistance. Gerald did not need convincing. Taylor could make the decision, and now that she knew the meeting place, she could go without him.

Gerald looked from Taylor to Cesar and back again and finally sighed in resignation.

"Two against one. I knew it would be hopeless to reason with you." Gerald smiled unexpectedly, and Taylor had a strange impression that he was keeping important information from them. She decided to look for signs of concealment later. For the first time, she felt a moment of distrust for her friend.

"I need to go get dressed, and then I'll be back to pick you up around two. He plans to meet us at the trail at two-thirty."

After he left, Cesar turned to Taylor.

"It's probably a good idea to send Doroteo separately, to keep an eye on things."

"So he'll be at the place but out of sight?" Taylor asked.

"Yes," he said. "Besides, it will give him something to do. A hike seems like a good choice. You should wear sunglasses and a hat. No one would recognize you later."

She had no idea what to expect, but the thought of a small hike made her feel relaxed about the situation. She might feel more comfortable ripping apart the junior oligarch in a more natural setting. Since words were the only thing she could use against him, she would not waste the opportunity to tell their lone representative precisely what she thought of them. She would try to avoid negative statements but would not stop herself if she felt as though the man deserved her wrath. She felt a little like a grasshopper wanting to get noticed by a guy with steel-toed boots.

When Gerald returned, he wore blue jeans with a red and black North Face windbreaker. Taylor had so rarely seen him out of a suit that she had to look twice to confirm his identity. His dark hair appeared intentionally disturbed, not the usual professional look. He reminded her of a younger, college-age Gerald, back when she knew him as a student.

THREE

Taylor

When they arrived at Discovery Park, the air was a crisp eleven degrees Celsius, and dark clouds coasted above them like a vast river. Taylor exited the car and breathed in the salty ocean air. Several vehicles populated the parking area with large gaps between each one. She looked around, hoping to see Max Garner, confident she could recognize him, but she saw only a short, pudgy man with his equally pudgy wife standing at their car with two skinny children. The parents fought to get the kids in the car, but the children apparently wanted to stay there. Other than a couple of other women off in the distance, Taylor saw no one else.

Gerald got out of the car and put on some tan sunglasses. She thought he looked silly with them. He probably purchased them recently for his recruiting efforts. As Cesar suggested, she wore a baseball cap and light sunglasses, so her eyes were still visible.

"We're going to take the footpath loop off to the west," he said, sounding like a frequent visitor to the park.

"So, you've been here before?"

On the car ride, Taylor had forgiven him for wanting to go alone. As she predicted, their natural surroundings made the idea of Max

Garner less menacing. On a more fundamental level, they were all the same creatures, just in different circumstances. Maybe if she focused on that thought, the meeting would go more smoothly.

Gerald smiled at her with some relief at the friendly tone in her voice.

"I've been here a couple of times. It's got some amazing views."

Taylor imagined him walking the trails with his suit and tie. The thought made her smile again.

"That's funny. I thought you forgot that nature existed."

He frowned and began walking to the trailhead next to the parking lot entrance.

"I told Max that we'd meet him on the trail to the west of the parking lot, at 2:30. If he starts walking on it, he'll run into us."

They found the trailhead and started walking down the path. They walked for a few minutes in silence. Taylor spent the time breathing deeply.

"Did it occur to you, Gerald," she said after a pair of female runners passed them, "that he'd want us to run into him and not the other way around? He could have gotten here early like us, to scope out the place."

Gerald turned to watch the women. "I don't think it really matters, as long as we run into each other. It's not a game of cat and mouse."

"You know," Taylor said while Gerald continued to watch the runners. "It's considered rude to lust after other girls when you are with one."

"I think that's them," he said, ignoring her comment and turning back to her. "Two men are coming our way."

She turned to follow Gerald's gaze and saw two men in casual attire walking toward them. Her heartbeat accelerated when she recognized the shorter one as Max Garner. Before leaving the shop, she had reviewed his photograph on Wikipedia so she could easily identify him.

Due to her shopping experiences with Dominga, Taylor noticed their expensive clothing, which fueled her irritation and reminded her that the two men lived in a vastly different financial world. Max stood as tall as Gerald and had blond hair secured under a dark gray ivy cap. He wore an expensive leather jacket and yellow sunglasses with black rims. The taller man next to him had maybe twenty kilograms more muscle with short blond hair, military cut, and he looked the more serious of the two. She experienced an instant physical attraction to him, but she quickly abandoned the feeling and returned her focus to his shorter companion.

When they arrived almost close enough for a conversation, Max raised his hand in acknowledgment. Both Taylor and Gerald did the same. But before stopping, Max turned to his companion and spoke quietly. The man stopped on the trail like an obedient dog. Max continued by himself.

"Gerald Foster?" asked the man tentatively after stopping in front of them and extending his right hand.

"It's good to meet you, Mr. Garner," Gerald said with a genuine smile while shaking hands.

When Max turned to Taylor, she forced a smile. She attempted to see the color of his eyes, but they were drowned in the yellow tint of his glasses.

"This is my friend Taylor," Gerald said simply.

"Max," he said and shook her hand then turned back to Gerald. "You didn't say you'd be bringing anyone else?"

Before Gerald could reply, Taylor answered.

"That was his plan."

"Well," he said with a smile. "I can't say I'm disappointed."

"I thought Mark would be here," said Gerald.

"Then who is that?" Taylor asked and nodded toward the man standing just out of earshot. She did not like the sudden change of plans.

"That is my assistant," Max said and kept his eyes on Taylor. "He goes where I go, but you have nothing to worry from him. I apologize for Mark's absence. He had family matters. His two boys keep him very busy."

"That's disappointing," Gerald said.

Max took a step forward and lifted his chin a bit to indicate they begin moving. "Shall we walk this beautiful trail? I want to see all of it."

They started walking forward, slowly at first then finally to a brisk pace that began to return warmth to Taylor's bones. Max's assistant walked at the same pace, maintaining his distance at about ten meters.

"I'm glad you like it," Gerald said.

Gerald seemed unsure about how to start the conversation. Taylor felt as though Max had the responsibility since he instigated the meeting. While waiting in the uncomfortable silence, she realized that Max intimidated her, but she had already determined not to show or allow it to affect her. She hated the feeling of intimidation maybe more than anything else. It made her feel weak.

"When Gerald told me about your call," she said before anyone else could speak, "he neglected to mention how you came to know about us. Could you fill me in?"

Max looked down at Taylor and smiled again.

"Well, Miss...?" he asked and paused.

"Just Taylor," she answered.

"Well, Taylor," he began again, and his smile grew even wider. "Gerald happens to be friends with our director of guidance engineering, Mark Salmon, who is also a close friend of mine. He and I graduated from MIT together, and after I received my MBA at Yale, I started TerraWatch then asked Mark to come work for me. Even though I'm the chairman of the board, he allows me to be his friend."

Oh, my God, Taylor thought, trying desperately to hide her exasperation. He obviously meant his comment to be funny, but she hated the way he stressed his position and exactly where he received his esteemed education.

"And what exactly did your friend tell you about us?" Taylor asked, hoping to hide her irritation behind the question. Gerald seemed uninterested in participating in the conversation.

"Nothing, Miss Taylor," he said with pride. "A few weeks ago, I caught him looking at your website. He, of course, refused to acknowledge the level of his interest in it, but the fact that he dismissed it intrigued me. I remembered the site name and went to it later. After looking through the site for a while, I realized that something was not quite right. It lacked any significant content, and I couldn't imagine a valid reason for Mark being so interested in it. I liked the rocket ship on the homepage, by the way."

"So," Taylor said impatiently. "If you found nothing significant, why did you contact Gerald?"

His smile turned into a small laugh. "Taylor, you know how to wring all the water out of a sponge, don't you? Well, once I get interested in something, it becomes like an insect bite, and I have to satisfy the itch. I had to find out what he was up to. For fun, I looked up the site registration information and found that it was registered to a guy named Franklin Harvey and not an organization. He could have chosen to have that information blocked, but he didn't, probably because he knew if someone really wanted to know the registration information, they'd be able to find out, especially the government. You're too clever. Hiding that information for something so benign might cause suspicion."

"I found some information about this kid on the internet, which led to another interesting clue. This kid used to leave comments in Google groups, publicly available comments, and he told his friend once about how he hated the astronomy geeks at his school."

"You spent your time reading his comments, and then based your opinion on what he told some friends?" Taylor laughed back at him. "He might have hated the kids, and still liked astronomy."

"True," Max said. "But I followed that line of thinking until it either led somewhere useful or a dead end. Those comments made me question why he created a website about astronomy. I knew it was a cover for something. That's what led me to you, Gerald."

"And how was that?" asked Gerald with suppressed curiosity.

"At that point, I cheated," Max said and shook his head. "I hired a private investigator to follow this kid and discover who might be paying him money under the table for the site. It took about a week to find this interesting bit of information. A picture is worth a thousand words eh?"

He pulled out a picture from under his leather jacket, a picture of Gerald in his car with their website administrator, a young man about twenty, wearing a backward cap on his head and a vinyl jacket.

When Gerald saw it, he grabbed the picture and looked at it carefully. After a moment, he started laughing.

"Here I've been worried about the FBI, and I get caught by a private investigator."

"Can I have that?" asked Taylor as she snatched the picture from Gerald's grip. The private investigator took the picture from across a street from Gerald and Franklin about twenty meters away in a car of his own with the window down. She did not see the situation as funny as Gerald saw it.

"On the phone, you said you were interested in learning more about us," Gerald said, and his voice tore her attention away from the photograph. "We're working on sensitive projects, and I was only asking for Mark's possible help. No offense intended, but I'm not ready to trust you with that information, and Taylor is definitely not ready to trust you with it. It really would have been better to have brought Mark."

Taylor kept her eyes on Max and waited for his answer, but she was relieved at Gerald's boldness. She had begun to fear he would let Max intimidate him into revealing their secrets. She had prepared herself to jump into the conversation and stop him.

"I expected that," Max said confidently. "Trust is always the key. The only way to help you feel better about me is by telling you about myself, and we can go from there. You probably know about my father and therefore need to know how I am not like him, or at least how I can be trusted."

"Sounds good to me," Gerald said.

"No one can be trusted," Taylor said before Max could continue. "Unless they respect the individual and I don't mean Gerald or me, but any individual. What evidence can you provide that you can be trusted?"

Taylor could feel Max's gaze on her, but she kept her eyes on the ground in front of her. He took several steps before continuing. "I admit completely, that I have had a much easier life than most people. Everything was handed to me, and for a long time, I basically took it for granted."

—※—

Hearing him admit to his unfair and privileged life helped Taylor feel vindicated about her feelings of resentment toward him. She felt a little regret for judging him since she hardly knew enough to justify her assumptions. She could only proclaim judgment on individuals and not groups of people. Her prejudice against him might have been unfounded, but she still had difficulty listening to his story impartially.

Growing up under financial hardship provided her with resentment of people who had everything handed to them. Just to pay for her education, she had to work during college, even with her scholarships. She had friends with many thousand dollars of student loan debt to pay even after several years of leaving school. People like this man went to an Ivy League school, financed by mommy and daddy, and he could focus entirely on learning and networking. Deciding what frat party to attend was probably his only difficulty.

All the paths in her life seemed to be uphill with thick undergrowth at every step. He had a million unobstructed paths open to him. A babbling brook ran alongside each one with clear water and fat fish. With his advantages and connections, a completely average person might have made the same accomplishments. With his money, he could hire people like her to keep him on top. None of his experiences seemed remotely like hers. They might as well have been raised on different planets.

For the next thirty minutes, Max disclosed the story of his privileged life. She listened as he talked about his father and how he had failed to participate in his life. His mother ran out on them soon after his birth, and he and his older sister never knew her, but he neglected to say how that experience had affected him.

While listening, Taylor began to feel reassurance that he knew nothing about her secret activities. The story also gave her time to more fully understand the cause of her fears and how some of them were based on irrational beliefs.

She no longer worried about the possibility of Max being a government agent, trying to discover their secrets. If the government or military wanted, they would just raid Cesar's shop. She soon began to see Max as more of a competitor who could be trying to exploit her invention. In that case, he would have the same concerns about the military discovering it. Regardless, they would have to be careful if they decided to tell him anything.

Max spent a lot of time explaining how his grandfather tried to fill the gap that his father left in his life. The only moral direction he ever received came from his grandfather, but he failed to appreciate it until he got out of his teenage years.

The most difficult experience in his life came when he and his sister realized they could not enjoy each other's presence anymore. While growing up, she had been his closest friend, and sometimes he'd thought of himself as her twin. After an extended period of separation, due to their different school situations, she began to accuse him of self-centeredness, greed, and apathy toward the Earth and all of its inhabitants. She began working for the Council on Foreign Relations and became absorbed in all of their collectivist activities. She rarely talked to him anymore, and when they did meet, he always left with a guilty desire to never see her again.

He spent a lot of time trying to resolve her anger toward him. Some accusations hurt him more than the others. She accused him of focusing solely on making money and attaining his own business goals. He was giving nothing back to the society that put him in his lofty position.

For a while, he believed in the truth of her accusations and let them cause tremendous guilt. But when he began to look into her work, he failed to see any net benefit from all of her beloved social programs, especially for the alleged target population, the poor. He saw only government bureaucrats, megacorporations, and bankers benefiting from all the social spending. Beautiful public buildings and skyrocketing public debt were the only gifts to the masses.

In college, he was briefly exposed to the works of Ayn Rand and Murray Rothbard, but his professors scoffed at their ideas of individualism, so he gave that ideology no further consideration. One day he had decided to order an Ayn Rand book and give her ideas a second chance. He found her stories to be almost unbearably dull but fell in love with all of her non-fiction publications. He soon realized his sister's misplaced trust in authority and recognized the establishment's war on individualism. The rival ideology meant an end to the current power structure in society, and so they fought against it with their whole arsenal of physical and psychological weapons.

As a side effect, he began to feel better about his life and understand the flaw in his sister's judgment. He was repaying society for his good fortune. By creating jobs, he rewarded people for the effort they had put into their education and at the same time, advancing technology and global communication.

Although she agreed with what he said, Taylor had to press her lips together to keep from contradicting him. She read about his company and how a significant portion of their revenue came from the government, from stolen money. His company was part of the military-industrial complex.

—※—

"Okay. So you feel good about your life and what you're doing," Taylor said when he paused. She spoke in a tone of light teasing and kept a smile on her lips, but her eyes looked serious. "And you claim to believe that humans should be free, but what motivation can you really have to live in a society like the one Rothbard describes? What are you willing to sacrifice? Ten percent of your wealth? Twenty? Thirty?"

"What do you want to know exactly?" he asked and looked genuinely confused. "Do you want a dollar amount?"

"I want to know if you really believe in what you just told us," Taylor said after a moment of thought, "or if it's just a nice idea that makes you feel better. Are you willing to risk going broke? For what you believe?"

"That's a hard question," he said, and his smile disappeared. He faced forward and watched the trail for a few steps. After a moment of walking in silence, he turned to them. "I don't know."

"Don't worry," Taylor said, feeling surprised at his inability to answer. "I'm not asking for an investment, just testing you."

"Do you believe people can change, Miss Taylor?" he asked.

"Yes," she said without thinking, "but I haven't seen it happen often."

"And what causes us to change?"

She recognized his attempt to build camaraderie but experienced difficulty in including herself in any group that included him. The discussion could easily become a long philosophical debate, so she had to consider her response carefully. "I think people can only change when they choose to react differently to their experiences. Change is rare because people are conditioned to react the same way they always do."

"Well," he said and laughed. "I had a traumatic experience with my grandfather once, and I always remember it, but I don't think I had a choice in my reaction. I'll have to think about that."

"What happened?" asked Gerald and shot Taylor a warning glance.

"It probably won't impress you," he began. "After I turned thirteen, my grandfather took me to visit an old friend of his in prison. I'll always remember it, especially the smell, a mixture of sweat and despair, or something. I was also scared of the people there. They all looked so violent, but then again, I was only thirteen, and everyone looks bigger when you're a kid. I'll always remember what my grandfather told me.

"These men in here will live out the majority of their lives in this place, or another place like it. Every day is the same, living like animals, where the most violent and aggressive ones dominate. All hope for their future is dashed like a wave on a rocky shore.

"If this is the only life they get, what kind of life is that? You and I live on our luxury yachts, our mansions on the hill, going where we want, doing pretty much whatever we please. Our futures are bright.

"There are other people outside of prison, who have almost as bleak a future. To some degree, those people are paying for our lifestyle. There's not much you or I can do about it because there are too many people who keep it that way. That's just the way it is. It doesn't mean that we should give all our possessions away, but it does mean we owe something in return."

Max stopped on the trail and looked out at the Puget Sound that had been visible for the past eighty meters or so. He took a deep breath of the salty air. In the following moment of uncomfortable silence, Gerald looked at Taylor, and they waited for Max to continue.

"It may sound too cliché," he began at last, "but I have been looking for ways to do what my grandfather recommended, not to give to charity but to invest in something I believe in."

"And what do you believe about us?" Gerald asked. "What did Mark tell you about us? You said he told you nothing, but you claim to believe in what we're doing?"

"Okay," he said, and for the first time, Taylor thought he looked guilty. "Once I found out who you were, I confronted Mark and made him give me more information. He only told me you wanted his help developing life support systems. I filled in the rest of the blanks myself."

"And what do you think are in those blanks?" asked Taylor.

"You're obviously building a vessel to take into orbit," he said confidently. "Since I could find absolutely no significant resources at your disposal and you hid your website, I'm betting that you're hiding something that significant."

"Now don't be angry with Mark," he said to Gerald before either of them could respond. "He can't hide anything from me, but he did try."

"It's not your employee I'm mad at," Taylor said, furiously squinting at Gerald, who looked away.

"Like I said, mere words cannot prove my sincerity," Max said and stopped Taylor from saying anything further. "So I am willing to discuss TerraWatch's resources and how they might be of use to you."

Max stopped on the trail and pulled his backpack in front of him, then handed it to Gerald.

"What's this?" asked Gerald.

"Open it up," he said, "and you'll find two hundred thousand dollars."

Gerald opened the backpack and only glanced at the money, then quickly brought his eyes back up to meet Max. "This is not about money."

Taylor tried her best to appear as disinterested as Gerald, but her thoughts kept returning to how that money would pay off her mother's mortgage. She placed complete blame on Max's father and his banker friends for her mother's financial dilemma. After the subprime mortgage fiasco of the previous year, their home value plummeted and ruined her mother's plans to sell their house and buy a less expensive one.

She now owed more money on the house than it was worth and could not possibly sell it. The money brought her anger back to the front of her thoughts, but his next statement returned her to the present.

"My only stipulation," he said and looked at both of them together, "is to accept my invitation to meet with Mark and me at my grandfather's home in Boston. We can discuss a possible working relationship. No matter what decision is made there, you can keep the money, no strings attached."

"I think we can make that appointment," Gerald said before Taylor could stop him.

Taylor was shocked by Gerald's failure to consult her and could think of no way to protest, as the offer seemed so benign. She felt as though they had just bitten into a hook and were being drawn to the surface—to their death.

FOUR

Max

After standing motionless outside the car for a few seconds, Max Garner noticed the driver patiently waiting for him to move so he could shut the door and take the car to the garage. Max failed to recognize the man. His father had hired the new chauffeur since Max last visited his father's estate in Chicago, his primary residence.

"Oh, thank you," Max said politely, then removed his hand from the top of the door.

"No problem, sir," the man said.

Although Max last visited his father's estate in Chicago three or four years ago, he last saw his father at his grandfather's home in Boston earlier that year. He usually visited his father there or at some private club but never for the current reason, a private audience just for him and his sister Audrie.

As Max looked at the estate, at the last home he'd known as a child, he felt like a burdensome child again. He lived there until his father sent him to his first private boarding school experience where he spent the remainder of his childhood.

Before he entered the house and initiated the meeting with his father for the important announcement, he decided to take a stroll through the grounds. He wanted to overcome the emotions that accompanied the place. As a child there, he'd felt small and powerless. When he met with his father later, Max wanted to feel in control, to be the person he had become and not revert to the obedient child who feared to displease the man. Max had created a successful company and needed to remember that when he met his father.

At that point in his life, Max liked to face the future and forget his younger life even though pleasant memories had filled his childhood. Before going inside, he planned to surround himself with those pleasant memories.

While living there with his father, he and his older sister had little contact with other children. Whenever a child of a servant lived at the estate or visited, he and his sister would play games with them. Max liked the game of hide and seek the best, and Audrie usually acquiesced to her younger brother's requests. She had always made sure they had fun.

Their father, Henry Garner, liked to rotate the staff between his three estates on a bi-monthly basis. He told his children that he wanted to keep the servants lively and alert, but Max knew his father disliked his kids getting too close with any of the help. He intentionally chose nannies who exhibited indifference, so his children would not be tainted by anyone of lower station.

He started walking up the stone path toward the front door but then turned and followed an alternate route leading into one of the garden areas. He took a deep breath, enjoying the thick and heavily scented air. He walked past beautiful flowers and shrubs lining the walkway and then stopped at the pond, where large gold and white fish glided gracefully beneath the murky water.

For several minutes, he listened to the sound of the trickling water. As a child, he liked to see the statue in the middle of the pond, a woman holding a pitcher with water trickling out of it. He always imagined her frozen in deep thought, watching some invisible water nymph swimming around her. Sometimes he thought of the statue as his mother, the woman who left them shortly after his birth, the woman he never knew.

As he stared at the statue and inhaled the fresh air, he closed his eyes and focused on the good memories, which mostly involved the time spent with his older sister, his best and only friend throughout his childhood. He used to attach himself to her like a parasite, but she never complained about the inconvenience. They usually did what she wanted to do, but sometimes they would play with his LEGO sets together, or she would help him build his latest robot kit. After his father sent her away to boarding school, he withdrew into himself and fell into a month-long depression.

Fortunately, the regular visits with his grandfather continued and spared Max from complete loneliness. Their grandfather, Erik Garner, would take Max and Audrie to live with him at his home in Boston, usually for several weeks at a time. He would take them to amusement parks, the zoo, the theater, museums, and sometimes the movies, activities their father would never do. Sometimes they would just wander aimlessly downtown Boston until their legs surrendered and then stop at an ice cream shop. Max did not care where they went or what they did. He just liked being with his grandfather.

Max never knew his mother or grandmother, but at least he knew what happened to his grandmother. She died shortly after his birth. After his grandfather recovered from that tragedy, he always had another woman stay in his home with him but never for more than a year or two, and he never remarried. But all of Max's artificial grandmothers loved Max as their own. His grandfather knew nothing of their continued contact with Max, the only secret he kept from his grandfather.

—※—

After spending several minutes at the fountain, Max decided to go inside the house and initiate the meeting with his sister and father. As he entered the parlor, Max saw a strange man standing off to the side by the window, motionless. The man had dark brown hair combed to the side and cut so short that only hairspray could keep it flat to his head. He seemed out of place, not like one of the servants who usually stayed out of sight. He stood like a statue, but his eyes followed Max and reminded him of the lizard he used to keep in his room. The lizard used to stare at him like that, with eyes cold and devoid of emotion.

He gave Max the impression of a soldier standing guard, a soldier wearing a plain dark suit with a shimmering black tie. Max failed to notice the woman sitting to his immediate left on the opposite side of the room. After hearing the sound of a magazine being placed on a table, he turned and the woman started to speak.

"Hi, Max," said the familiar voice. "I'm glad you decided to make it."

"Audrie," he said through gritted teeth and a forced smile. "Sorry, I didn't see you there. I was just wondering who this man was."

For the sister who only saw him twice a year at the most, she never wasted an opportunity to intentionally annoy him. She looked at him with a polite but cold smile, her dark brown eyes floating in the paleness of her face. Her dark blond hair looked the same, cut just above her shoulders and pulled back with two plain hairpins. A pair of glasses sat next to an open journal on the table in front of her.

He knew what to expect when visiting his sister but always hoped to have a better experience than the usual sarcastic pretense of sibling affection. The former close relationship of their childhood vanished after their father sent her to school. Somehow being away at school, Audrie had become more like her father while he remained like his grandfather, and they had the same relationship as their father and grandfather, like a match and a spark.

"Oh, don't pay any attention to him," she said as she waved her hand in the direction of the stranger, one of her annoying habits when she wanted to dismiss something of insignificance. "How was your flight?"

"It was a flight," he said and then glanced back at the man who had turned to look out the window. Max disliked having unidentified people in his immediate vicinity, and his sister probably enjoyed keeping him in ignorance. For the moment, Max would accept his assumption of the man's identity and purpose, a government security agent assigned to his father.

"How's the IDA?" he asked, turning back to his sister.

Before answering, she looked at him as if searching for signs of an attack. He noticed her eyes change from suspicious to relaxed. "Things are progressing well," she said cautiously.

"That's good," he said, expecting her to respond with a query about his work.

She answered by grabbing the journal from the table and opening it randomly. For a moment, Max wondered if she intended just to read the journal and leave him in silence, so he took a seat across from her.

"We're working to pull the third world out of poverty, you know," she said casually, while her eyes scanned the journal.

Before responding, Max took a deep breath. The onslaught had begun. His sister intended the comment as bait for an argument, but he would let the hook dangle in front of his face for as long as possible.

She knew his disapproval of the World Bank and its affiliates. They had argued many times about the same topic in the past. He saw the World Bank as a beast used to enslave the third world, drain its resources, and prevent fair competition in the world market. He often wondered how his sister could be deluded by the organization's ridiculous claims. But accepting her challenge would lead nowhere.

"Well, I'm glad you're staying busy," he said as amicably as he could.

She looked up from her reading again.

"Oh come now, Max. Why don't you tell me what you really think."

"Wow, she's really trying," he said under his breath then he spoke loudly enough for her to hear. "You already know what I think, Audrie. I'm more interested in what Henry wants to tell us."

"Well, whatever it is," she said, her focus returning to the magazine. "I hope that you support him."

"You know what this is all about already. Don't you?" he asked as an accusation. "But let me guess, you're not going to tell me?"

"Why would you think I know?" she said in an innocent tone, an unnatural sound from his sister.

"Whatever it is, I can wait," Max said and smiled.

FIVE

Max

At five-fifteen, a young female servant came to announce that they would serve dinner soon. Before leaving the parlor, Audrie took a minute to write some notes in her journal. She had spent the majority of their time waiting, by writing in the journal and ignoring his existence. Max said he would meet her at dinner and left the room with a backward glance at the unknown man. They made brief eye contact.

He went to visit the room he used to occupy as a child and for the next few minutes, he sat on the bed and looked around at the familiar space. None of his former possessions remained, and the bed looked different even, but the room helped him recall many of the same memories he had in the garden.

After Max left his room for dinner, his sister met him at the entrance to the dining room. They nodded in silent acknowledgment and entered the room as if they had planned their combined entrance. Henry Garner sat at the head of the table and made eye contact with them the instant they entered. He stood and met them halfway to the long table.

Max stood almost eye to eye with his father. Henry Garner still had a full head of brown hair, streaked with gray. Henry liked to keep his hair cut shorter, just long enough to comb to one side. A white silk shirt covered his lean and muscular body, and a black tie hung just above his dark blue pants. He looked about ten years younger than his actual age of sixty years. Max hoped to look as good when he reached that age.

When Audrie saw her father, she hugged him with one arm.

"Hello, Father," she said warmly.

"Good to see you again," Max said as he shook his father's hand. He would have felt awkward to show his father more affection than his father ever showed him. The only hug he had ever received from family came from his grandparents.

"Good to see you too," said his father formally. "I'm glad you both could make it."

Henry spoke with a naturally deep voice, which usually turned the heads of everyone within hearing range. He often spoke on behalf of the bank he managed instead of their public relations employees. When Henry Garner spoke, people listened.

After the brief greetings, they all sat at the table, and two female servants began to set the first course before them, soup with parsley garnish. Max smiled at the young woman as she laid his meal before him, and she returned the gesture, but she glanced at his father to see if he noticed.

"I hear you were at the grove last week," Audrie said with some enthusiasm. "Was it an enjoyable visit?"

Audrie often asked her father about his visits to the Bohemian Grove in Monte Rio, California, where the elite went to relax and network, among other activities. Some of Audrie's male associates visited the place as well. From what Max could remember, almost every president of the United States had visited the grove along with many other prominent government and finance leaders.

Their father never gave many details, but Max attempted to refrain from curiosity about the place, especially considering all the rumors of homosexual and heterosexual orgies and ritual sacrifices. He would rather not imagine his father participating in some of the ancient pagan rituals where the grove acquired its name and reputation.

Diverse sexual encounters were probably just one of the services provided for the elite visitors who could afford anything the world had to offer. Many of the people in the upper echelons of society had everything they could ever want. Extravagant and expensive experiences inevitably became insufficient to satisfy normal human needs for variety and led to more extreme amusements. Max had some similar experiences.

In college, Max and his privileged friends occasionally employed the services of high-end escort agencies. After the initial thrill of satisfying all their sexual fantasies with one woman at a time, his friends soon found that the experience failed to satisfy their bloated sexual appetites. When his friends inevitably started experimenting with multiple partners, Max decided to travel down a different path. Other diversions seemed safer, emotionally. He feared that those kinds of activities might hurt any future romantic relationships.

Consequently, he distanced himself from those friends and began swimming in different social circles, but he liked to keep in contact with them for the benefits of networking. Some of those friends from school had become prominent members of society, as Max had. Just recently, one of his friends became a governor, and another became the dean of a prestigious business college.

"Yes, I visited the grove just last month," their father said in answer to Audrie's question. "It was very therapeutic."

"Well, if anyone deserves a break, it's you, Father." Audrie turned to Max across the table from her. "Doesn't he, Max?"

"Of course you do, Father," Max said, sipping a spoonful of soup and inhaling the salty aroma. He smiled at his sister's manipulative question. Did she expect him to elaborate or say something different? Maybe she just enjoyed making the implication that he disagreed.

"You're both probably wondering why I asked you to come for dinner."

Max looked at Audrie, expecting her to say something first. Being the oldest, she usually took the lead in the family, at least when the action involved their father. To his surprise, she was looking at him with a strange smile. Her dark brown eyes hung lazily open, waiting.

"Well, I for one, am curious," Max said with a return look to Audrie. "It must be important for you to ask us both for a personal announcement like this."

Henry paused before speaking and met both pairs of eyes looking at him.

"I didn't want you two to be confused when the media fiasco began. I wanted you to be prepared. I need you two with me on this."

Henry Garner stopped looking at Audrie and fixed both eyes on his son. Max felt a wave of anxiety ripple through his body. Their father never intimidated his sister. She idolized the man, while Max always felt a desire to prove him wrong. His father almost looked anxious.

During that brief moment of eye contact, Max attempted to recall the last time he saw his father more anxious about anything other than the return on his investments. His father led one of the largest banks in North America and confidently stood before the most influential people in the world, but now Max thought he saw a little trepidation in his father's eyes while he looked at his two children.

Henry Garner had seen his fair share of media attention, similar to the kind of attention that entertainment celebrities received. Henry experienced a more refined version, however, a spotlight without surprise or the unanticipated, thanks to his business collaboration with the major media outlets. But the limelight never extended to his children. In their privileged social circles, they had their own isolated form of glory. It simply failed to show on the evening news.

Max wondered if the media fiasco would involve him and Audrie this time. Would it involve his company? Did some of his father's investments fail, or did he make some mistake and become an outcast? The smirk on the corners of his sister's lips suggested a more favorable explanation.

"Go ahead, Father," said Audrie. "You can tell us."

"I am going to be the next Secretary of the Treasury," he said, smiling with a mixture of pride and anxiety.

"Secretary of the Treasury," Max said hesitantly. He had to consciously keep his jaw from dropping but managed to keep his expression contained. "Of the United States?"

SIX

Max

"**Y**es, Max," his father said as if speaking to a child. "The United States Secretary of the Treasury."

"Congratulations, Father," Audrie said quickly, with a brief look of displeasure in her brother's direction.

"What do you mean, you're going to be the Secretary?" Max asked as if coming out of a daze. He felt a little confused. "The Senate has to approve the appointment first, and the media hasn't even mentioned that you are being considered yet. What about Timothy Geithner? They're not replacing him because of the bailout scandal are they?"

"Oh, don't be so naive," said Audrie. "If Father says he's going to be the Secretary, then he will be."

Henry held up his hand, a sign for them to be silent.

"All that will come later, which is one of the reasons why I wanted to tell you beforehand so you wouldn't be confused, or angry that I failed to tell you about it. They're going to dig up some dirt on me, and I didn't want you to be surprised. But it's all just part of the process. They've got to make it look like they are being thorough, as if they have a choice in the matter."

"And the other reason you wanted to tell us beforehand?" asked

Max, sounding more concerned than he wanted to reveal.

"Things are going to change, and more for you, Max, than your sister," he said. "You need to start watching your comments and being more careful with whom and what you disagree with. I haven't been successful at influencing you, but the network might exert a more uncomfortable pressure."

Max sat back in his seat and shook his head. Was his father more concerned about his son, or himself? Perhaps his father should have said, "You had better not ruin this for me."

"Hear, hear," said Audrie. On the table in front of her, she tapped her fingers in quick succession while looking at Max. "In my opinion, you shouldn't talk to anyone in the media. I don't trust that you can control your tongue."

"I doubt the media will be directly communicating with him," said their father. "But if you do something too conspicuous, they'll have to cover it."

"I won't have to say anything," Max said with a hint of anger in his voice, directed more at his sister than his father. "The appointment of another ex-banker is such a blatant conflict of interest as Secretary of the Treasury that even Fox News won't be able to deny it."

"And why would they deny it in the first place?" Audrie asked calmly. "That's how the system works. It will only be mentioned once or twice in passing, scorned and then forgotten. Besides, who else can handle the nation's money better than Father?"

When he saw his sister getting pleasure from his reaction, Max decided to conceal his anger and frustration.

"This world's already bought and paid for," he said calmly. "I really don't feel the need to waste my breath saying anything else about the matter."

"Knowing you," Audrie said. "I wouldn't be surprised to see your face in the crowd at an *End the Fed* rally. Then Father and I wouldn't be able to show our faces at the council ever again without publicly denouncing you as an economic terrorist."

"Is that true, Max?" asked his father. "Are you involved with the

End the Fed movement?"

"I'm not a part of any movement," Max began while glaring at his sister. "But they're not as bad as it sounds. All they want is to–"

"We know what they want to do," said Audrie impatiently. "Those fools want to undermine all this society has accomplished in the last hundred years. You cannot deny the progress we've made, and it wouldn't have been possible without our monetary system."

"All they want," he continued, directing his words to his father, "is to allow people to use whatever form of money they want. It's freedom they want, and I cannot disagree with it, especially with inflation as it is."

Max turned to his sister.

"Our freedom, as limited as it is, is responsible for the progress, not the dollar. If people operated with true autonomy, we'd be far more advanced. Uncorrupted competition would eradicate stupid ideas and practices instead of being upheld by bureaucracy."

"Enough of this nonsense," said Henry, looking directly into his son's eyes. "If you align yourself with this subculture movement, you'll put a black mark on your own reputation. For your own good, listen to your sister and keep this talk to yourself. I cannot control your opinions, but I won't allow you to make this family into a joke."

"You won't have to worry about me, Father," Max said with faint sarcasm. "I'm not going to do anything to embarrass you, but you're right. I do believe in a different world than you two."

Silence followed his statement and a look from his sister, which she meant to convey as indifference as if his words meant nothing to her. Max wondered if his father would accept his response.

"I certainly hope I can trust you," Henry said to his son after relaxing the muscles around his eyes. "This is very important for me, and I cannot have any distractions from my family."

As usual, Max wondered if his father considered him a distraction, something that might get in his way. During his whole childhood, his father had made Max feel like an impediment. If not for his grandparents, Max would have believed the notion.

"Grow up and move on," Max told himself silently.

Although their father showed no similar disappointment with Audrie, he probably considered her a potential distraction too. Max wondered if their father's opinion mattered to Audrie or if she just cared about what she could gain from the man. Had his sister truly become like their father, someone whose only interest in humanity centered on its exploitation?

Then another question made him sad. If Audrie had nothing to gain, would she come to his aid? He hoped never to learn the answer.

SEVEN

Sadi

Sadi slept in the same room with Helen and Daryn for the first two nights after Helen returned home from her abduction. The anxiety of being unable to see her daughter would have made sleep impossible otherwise. She had to have Helen within eyesight at all times, and the new girl also refused to leave Helen's side.

Craig Swenson, the private investigator who had attempted to find Helen, had listened to Freddy's side of the story at Mr. Smith's house and then visited Sadi at her home. She dreaded his visit, expecting to feel the horrible experience all over again, but strangely, the big man provided comfort instead of more anxiety. Sharing her version of the events was cathartic.

He asked many questions about the old man who had held Helen, the one she'd kicked in the head. She'd failed to see him clearly in the dark room, especially since he cradled his head after she kicked him. The back of his head exploding had overshadowed most of her other memories. Her mind refused to recall most of the details of her encounter with that horrible man.

Craig offered advice about how to handle the reunion, how to recover psychologically. He said to leave town for at least a week, so Sadi decided to take Helen and their new resident, Daryn, to the Oregon coast. The thought of going back to work caused too much anxiety to consider. She needed to get away from her routine schedule. She invited Jen to accompany them, but Jen had college classes to attend instead.

Craig would inform the police that Helen had been found at her friend's house and Sadi would probably not have to do anything afterward. He planned to invent some story and felt confident the police would believe him, glad to remove a case from their list. He had more concern about the police investigation of Helen's recovery, the murders at the hotel.

"I'll be watching the police reports from last night and will keep you informed as to what they find, or at least what they report. I suspect the FBI will claim jurisdiction over the investigation."

"What is the likelihood that they will make the connection to Freddy and me?"

While waiting for him to answer, Sadi's heart pounded in anxious anticipation of his response. The possibility of a government investigation of her family filled Sadi with dread. They would certainly take Daryn away and put Sadi, Helen, and Freddy in another horrible situation. Sadi often felt sick to her stomach after thinking about what her daughter had experienced.

"From what Freddy and you have told me, I think it unlikely that they will make the connection." Craig spoke as if he had no concern, as he sipped the coffee Sadi had given him. "That Freddy is a smart kid. He took care not to leave much evidence, especially living adult witnesses. Let's just hope his old caseworker can keep the two other boys' story a secret. That's the greatest potential weakness in our case. I'm going to go see her next."

Craig paused and put one of his giant hands on her shoulder.

"Miss Jacobsen, your daughter is safe. Don't worry about her right now. If anyone gets suspicious, I should know it well beforehand and can help defuse the situation."

Sadi looked up at the large man and felt assured by his explanation, but then she began to worry more for Freddy. He'd shown himself capable of handling the dire situation, far more than she had ever imagined. Since the whole business with the alien, Sadi had considered his problems as above her realm of understanding. He had more than just government officials to concern him. Sadi wanted to share the information about the alien with Craig, but she knew Freddy had already decided to keep that information from him, probably for his own sanity and protection.

"I know you're getting paid to help me, but thanks all the same."

Sadi felt a sudden paranoia and wondered if Craig would ever report incriminating evidence to the authorities to clear his name of any complicity. She loathed how he held such evidence against her, but she had to trust logic. His professional reputation depended on keeping his client's activities confidential. One final realization provided additional comfort. Freddy would know if they could trust Craig.

Although she was fortunate to have Craig's services, she owed her daughter's safety to Freddy. Craig had obviously attempted to help, but he hadn't helped find Helen. Perhaps Craig would prove useful in handling the resulting police investigation.

"What are you going to do about Daryn?" Craig asked.

"Daryn's staying with me," Sadi responded abruptly. She refused to consider the option of returning the poor girl to the system that had betrayed her. "I don't know how, but I'm going to make sure she's okay. She and Helen have a bond that I don't have the heart to break. Helen will never forgive me if anything ever happened to her, and I would never forgive myself. What do you suggest I do?"

Craig looked at her for a few seconds in silence, possibly reconsidering his recommendation.

"Right now, I really don't know. Just go on your vacation, and I'll try to think of the best course of action. I'll check into the Oregon foster care system to see what I can find out about her."

"Thank you, Craig. We owe you."

"You're welcome," he said in a tone indicating disappointment. "But most of the thanks goes to Freddy."

EIGHT

Sadi

Although leaving Helen for a day caused her almost physical pain, Sadi wanted to make one normal appearance at work. She had claimed to need the three days off due to illness, an unprecedented occurrence for her. The usual definition of illness failed to come close to her state of mind and body, from Helen's abduction, so she felt no guilt for using that excuse, but she might need to put her coworkers' minds at ease, especially her best friend, Zoya.

Zoya had called Sadi several times and sent many messages via Facebook. Sadi had answered the phone once, inventing some excuse, but she could not remember what excuse she'd used. When she returned to work, Sadi expected difficulty diverting questions about her current life dilemmas.

As expected, Sadi's boss asked no questions when she requested the next two weeks off for personal time. He even seemed happy about the request.

"I was wondering how long you could go without taking a break from this place," he said. "Go. Have fun and come back ready to get back to your projects. I hope you're feeling better."

After the discussion with her boss, Sadi decided to spend only half of the day at work and needed to prepare Zoya to handle their lab projects in her absence. Before the inevitable and awkward encounter with Zoya, Sadi tried imagining how she would handle the situation. She felt an overwhelming desire to share what happened, but she could not trust that kind of information with anyone. She intended to focus on her desire to see Helen again and get out of town, away from everything.

"Where do you want to go to lunch?" asked Zoya when they met later. Her dark blue Persian eyes caused Sadi to feel uncomfortable. The woman acted as though she had absolutely no curiosity about Sadi's state of mind.

"I really don't have time today," she said, avoiding eye contact. "Sorry."

"Hmm," her friend said with a tone of innocent curiosity. She placed her right index finger on her chin. "You leave us for three days and come back just to take off again for a couple of weeks. And you think you're getting out of talking to me?"

"Zoya," Sadi said apologetically. "I'm really sorry, but we're leaving tonight, and I have a lot of work to do, so I'll be leaving early today. When I get back, I'll take you to lunch and satisfy every curiosity you have."

To her surprised relief, Zoya reluctantly agreed but only after looking into her eyes for several seconds. Sadi could see the frustration on her friend's face and felt sorry for disappointing her. She needed to convince her friend there would be no lasting secrets between them.

They spent the remainder of the morning reviewing the status of Sadi's two major projects. All her other work could be put on hold, and Sadi had confidence in her friend's ability to continue the testing and results analysis without her. Zoya looked forward to taking the lead in preparing the necessary DOEs and executing them. In any case, she would be too busy to worry about Sadi.

Sadi waited until noon to leave for the day and walked with Zoya to her car. On the walk, her friend's behavior seemed odd. She asked no further questions about Sadi's condition, apparently showing no interest in her friend's personal life.

When they arrived at her car, Zoya surprised Sadi by grabbing her car key and then opening the passenger door. She sat in the passenger seat and patiently waited, facing forward as if ready to drive away with her. Sadi tried looking angry but failed.

"Listen," Zoya said after Sadi sat in the driver's seat. "You can't have your keys back until I'm satisfied."

"Alright," Sadi said while sighing and trying to think of what to say. "My life's complicated at the moment, some of it I can't talk about."

In surprise, Sadi felt tears welling up in her eyes, and she knew there would be no stopping the subsequent flow of information. After wiping away her tears, she took a deep breath.

"Oh my dear," Zoya said, handing Sadi a tissue from her purse.

"Something horrible happened," Sadi began.

—※—

Zoya sat in silence and shock as Sadi told her all about the abduction and retrieval. She used no names and only referred to Freddy as her friend and excluded his extra senses and the crystal. Sadi felt like the screen during a horror movie with Zoya as the only audience member. She knew Zoya would have questions about how Freddy had found Helen, and how he had managed to accomplish the retrieval all by himself. In her weakened emotional state, Sadi pretended to act ignorant.

When Sadi started telling the part where Helen came running into the hallway, quietly calling for her mother, she had to stop and put her hand to her mouth. For the first time during the story, she saw tears appear in Zoya's eyes.

"That was the happiest moment in my entire life," Sadi said and smiled.

All the emotions from that horrible night returned to her again.

"I can imagine," Zoya said quietly while shaking her head in disbelief.

"It wasn't over though," Sadi continued and felt an incredible urge to relay the next part of her memory. "Helen said that her new friend was in trouble and needed my help. My instincts told me to grab my daughter and run, but that amazing little creature pulled me back toward that apartment. She could only think of others, and I had to be as brave as her. I've never been more proud of her. For a moment, I didn't care if we lived or died. We were going to go back into that apartment and save him."

When she began telling the part where she saw the man on top of Freddy, her heart began to race.

"It will sound harsh," Sadi began, then paused while trying to think of the appropriate way to explain. "But it felt amazing when I kicked that piece-of-shit's head in."

"I wish I could have seen it," Zoya said with a smile that helped validate Sadi's sadistic feelings.

At the end of the story, Sadi told how Daryn came home with them, and how she had no idea what to do with the girl.

"You actually took her home?"

"Helen said she wasn't going anywhere without her friend. When I heard that, I could not leave her. It would be like leaving Helen. She would never forgive me."

"I don't blame you," Zoya said. "I might be able to help with that girl. Let me think about it."

"Yeah, I don't know what to do. That's why I have to get away, but I feel like no matter where I go, it won't be far enough."

"Where are you going?"

"I don't know where," Sadi lied. Craig had said not to divulge the destination to anyone. "But far away. I just don't know anything anymore. My life's been turned upside down by this. I don't even feel like the same person anymore."

"Well, you can't have that girl forever," Zoya said with regret. "Eventually, you're going to have to turn her in, or have someone turn her in for you."

"I cannot think about that for now. If I send her to social services, will she end back up where she was? Being used as a sex slave? That is not an option. This world is not safe for the innocent."

"There's still a lot of good people in the world, Sadi, but maybe you're right. We can worry about that later."

"I really just need to get out of here," Sadi said and looked at her watch, a blatant reminder to Zoya that she wanted to leave. "If it weren't for my friend and his employer, I wouldn't know what to do. I would have gone to the police, and we never would have found Helen."

"The system is such a fraud," Zoya said, her anger suddenly rising. "The police who care are bogged down by too many laws and regulations. Their focus isn't protecting people. Sometimes they're good at catching a murderer, after the murder happened, but I'd rather pay for someone to prevent my murder. In a more free society, if a police company failed to keep us safe, we'd stop paying them and hire new ones."

"I'm sorry for going off on a tangent," Zoya said apologetically, taking a deep breath. "At least she's safe now. That's all that matters."

"But now that she's found," Sadi said, unintentionally continuing the conversation, "we're connected to five dead guys, and two of them are high profile scumbags."

"No, not a good position at all," Zoya agreed.

"I wouldn't be surprised to find that guy's death, in the paper or on the news, being explained by old age, followed by a beautiful tribute to his life and accomplishments. I want to see that bastard's head on the front page of the paper, with the hole I kicked in it. The headline should read: *Repulsive child rapist, slaughtered by the victim's enraged mother.*"

"Yeah," Zoya said with contempt. "I wouldn't expect the news to report anything close to the truth."

"Those rich bastards can get away with anything," Zoya continued, her anger rising again. "Even after they're dead. In my home country, the well-connected escape trial all the time. Innocent victims, awaiting justice, disappear and are never heard from again. No one asks the questions because they don't want it to happen to them."

"Although it's slightly different here, the result is the same in the United States," Sadi answered sadly. "The land of the *free*."

"That's the truth," Zoya replied with a huff. "Things will go back to normal for you at least. Helen's a tough kid, and you're an awesome mother."

"I really need to get away."

Zoya grasped Sadi's hand.

"Life will get back to normal, I promise."

Sadi smiled, but she experienced a sudden sense of foreboding. After her son had died, her life had never returned to normal. Her future seemed like a sleeping leviathan at the bottom of the ocean, waiting to make a destructive appearance in the world.

NINE

Audrie

Before ascending the stairs to the main entrance, Audrie Garner stopped to admire the beautiful five-story building looming above her, the Washington D.C. office of the Council on Foreign Relations, the CFR. Due to the pleasant memories associated with the place, she loved the building probably more than the White House. She appreciated the simplicity and quality of its design, both the exterior and interior. Nothing about the building came across as overindulgent or gaudy as might be expected from an organization with so much money and power.

Before graduate school, Audrie had spent time there as an intern at the CFR, making valuable connections with influential people who became lifelong friends and business associates. One of those friends became the CFR Senior Vice President, Director of Studies. After graduate school, he occasionally asked Audrie to act as a special assistant.

Audrie would do whatever she could to remain active in the organization and keep her connections strong. She felt indebted to the Council, but more importantly, she knew the value of nurturing career-advancing networks. Due to her full-time employment at the

World Bank, she had little time for regular CFR duties, so Audrie accepted special assignments like the one she came there to perform that day.

With this particular assignment, she would be coordinating a necessary business function for the CFR, a task she did not look forward to performing. She came to deliver a special letter from the board to Michael Flanagan, the director of the Center for Monetary Centralization. Although Audrie had not read the letter, she knew its contents, a sincere thanks for the man's services along with a pronouncement that he would no longer be performing them.

To receive anything other than a personal disclosure from an official CFR representative would be considered a tasteless insult to the man who had served for so long. Since no one on the board or any other officer wanted the inevitable unpleasant confrontation with the man, they gave the task to Audrie Garner. She possessed the intelligence, sagacity, and charm necessary to avoid an embarrassing encounter with the man who could potentially mar the CFR's image.

With a deep breath, she put her foot on the first stair leading to the front entry and continued to make her way to Michael Flanagan's office. The area leading to his closed office door reminded Audrie of her own time as an intern on a different floor of the same building. She loved the simplicity and orderliness of the Council on Foreign Relations building interior. She loved the dichotomy. The face of the organization failed to reflect its immense power, its impenetrable influence over multinational, government policy.

She walked to the receptionist desk where a young woman sat. Three other young people sat quietly at other desks, their backs to her. As she walked past them, she glanced at the papers strewn over the closest desk and noticed a summary report from her department at the United Nations.

"Good morning, Jane," she said to the young woman sitting behind the simple desk in the open office area. She had only met the new intern once, but Audrie always took the time to remember the names of those she would probably meet again. "I'm here to see Director Flanagan."

"Good morning, Miss Garner," the girl said, her smile unchanging. "He's in his office. I'll just tell him that you're here."

"Thanks, Jane."

Audrie attempted to smile warmly, and as usual, the action felt unnatural. She felt like a falcon diving toward her prey. Her father said she had the eyes of a falcon, close together and severe enough to cause a mental burn on the psyche of her target. When she focused on someone, they almost always looked away, even the dominant males who thought they knew their place in the world.

Sometimes she enjoyed her effect on people, but not when she wanted a sincere interaction. Audrie dealt with a world run mostly by men, and they were always attempting to impress her, especially the married ones. Women, on the other hand, seemed always to be comparing themselves to her and often experienced difficulty focusing on the topic of discussion. In her opinion, human emotions hindered more than they helped, so at least they could be manipulated.

Audrie Garner acquired her membership just four years earlier, a relatively new member of the CFR. She received her recommendation from her friend on the board of directors. Her father offered to recommend her, and his endorsement would have been enough to secure membership, but Audrie wanted to rely on her own connections, so she politely refused. She was not naive enough to think that her family relations had nothing to do with her elevated position in life. But despite her connections, she had earned her place near the top, above the other privileged people who had competed against her.

In her brief time in the organization, she had become well-respected. Several of her articles had been published in their bi-monthly journal, Foreign Affairs. Many of her ideas, she learned with satisfaction, became topics of debate with several high-level public officials including the United States Vice President. She even had met to discuss some of her ideas about the World Bank's role in third-world development.

Her involvement with the CFR eventually resulted in a referral to a position with the World Bank, as a managing director of the International Development Association, the IDA. A fellow CFR member worked for the International Monetary Fund and had the necessary connections to help Audrie attain her position. The department she headed provided much of the data the CFR and other organizations used in their investigations and decisions for international funding.

The Center for Monetary Centralization, headed by Flanagan, and the IDA worked closely together. She enjoyed her brief association with Michael Flanagan and felt a moment of regret to bring his position to an end. Over the years he had worked intelligently and had accomplished a lot for the CFR.

When she had explained her concerns about Michael Flanagan to the CFR board, she feigned shock and indignation at his most recent publication. The document clearly demonstrated his change of heart toward the CFR's mission and his unfavorable views of a recent IMF loan for a government project in Africa.

When she received the assignment to deliver the letter, she'd felt almost euphoric. Apparently, her performance had been convincing to the board.

Audrie had no difficulty suppressing the guilt at instigating Flanagan's demise. If she had ignored her observations and taken no action, someone else would have done it. Lions could not feel guilty for taking down the weak and elderly.

Their competitors would beat them to the valuable food source and leave them to starve. Besides, this experience would show her worth and dedication to the organization whose members held most of the power in the Western world.

She knocked on the door of Flanagan's office and waited a moment, not to ask for entry permission but as a warning of her imminent intrusion. As she twisted the door handle, she heard the director's muffled voice saying to enter.

The man sat at his desk with his head facing the laptop in front of him. As she shut the door, he looked up and then leaned back against his seat.

TEN

Audrie

"Good morning, Michael," she said as warmly as possible and then waited only a second before he responded.

"Miss Garner," he said in sudden recognition, putting his glasses higher on his nose. He motioned to one of the two chairs in front of his desk. "Please, come in and have a seat."

"Thank you."

She sat in a chair, crossed her legs, and folded her arms.

"This is a pleasant surprise." Even though he looked concerned, she felt his sincerity and the emotion caused another small twinge of regret.

"I hope you have the same sentiments when I leave," she said and brushed a few strands of blond hair back behind her ears.

"What are you doing in Washington?" He seemed to have noticed her ominous tone.

"Coming to visit you."

"You came all the way from New York just to visit me?"

"Yes," she said and smiled ruefully. "Well, I do have a couple other things to do here. I like to multitask."

"Well," he said. "I'm honored, but I won't flatter myself to think you're here just to say hi."

"I wouldn't flatter myself to presume that I can have a social visit with you at any arbitrary time." Audrie smiled and continued before she lost her nerve. "So how are things going here for you?"

She had already prepared her approach, but she was suddenly uncomfortable actually bringing up the topic tactfully with a man almost three times her age, and with an ocean of experience she would be lucky to have one day. She hoped he did not find her tone patronizing.

"Things are very busy lately," he said and relaxed a little. "I'm just finishing up a report for the Senate Finance Committee. I've got a meeting with Senator Hatch next Thursday."

"Is it as good as your last pamphlet?"

"Which one?" He looked confused.

"You know, the analysis of the river project in Mauritania." Audrie looked directly into his eyes, and she let her smile fade a bit. After a few seconds, she blinked and turned her attention to examine her fingers.

"Okay. What did *you* think of *our* analysis?"

"To be completely honest, it made me a little anxious." She turned her hand to inspect the palm, for some invisible irritation. "It made some others anxious as well."

"So why then would it glide through the review process? If it had something undesirable, it should have been stopped."

"You gave quite an unfavorable assessment of the fund allocation."

He laughed sarcastically then looked at her with piercing eyes.

"So you've found our analysis unfavorable? You cannot argue that it was a waste of public money. Now the people of Mauritania are in even more debt but with nothing to show for it. Do you disagree with that?"

His eyes challenged her to disagree and looked ready for a fight as if he wanted an argument. The challenge made her smile. She loved a challenge, but she would not challenge him the way he wanted. She felt another stab of guilt for not taking the bait.

"That's not what this is about. You're not looking long-term."

"So you think that we must sacrifice the present for the long term?" he asked again. "That kind of sentiment looks great on paper, but in people's lives, it can be a horrible thing."

"Sometimes, I'll give you that," she admitted. "But most people can't see two feet in front of them. Someone's got to be thinking long-term, for their sake."

He took a long breath and sighed then spoke while rubbing his eyes.

"I'm beginning to think that long-term means eternity, something that will never be realized. Do you know, Miss Garner, that the longer I've been around, the more I see the future being pushed further and further ahead. We need to put more weight on a venture's direct and immediate effects."

If she had not already considered that argument, it might have caught her off guard, and perhaps with his vast experience, he might have been able to derail her. Fortunately, she knew exactly where an argument with him would lead, so she could not indulge him. She had learned to avoid ideological debates and preferred pragmatic ones. She liked to stand behind numbers and authority, the only arguments she understood.

Besides, if she accepted his challenge, the argument would never end. She came to deliver a message, not to argue with him. Words would have had no power in their particular situation and to argue would be pointless. The decision had already been made.

"Unfortunately, I am not here to argue with you but to deliver a message." Audrie paused to take a deep breath and withdraw the letter out of her bag. "Believe me. It gives me no pleasure."

As the words left her lips, she felt like a student giving one of her professors his grade for the term. She felt no guilt anymore but embarrassment and a strange comfort. She felt as if relieving him of a great burden. Sooner or later, this would have happened.

"They sent you," he asked incredulously, his eyes becoming slits. "With a letter?"

His eyes pierced the letter almost like a sword. He paused and seemed to be reading the letter through the envelope. After a short moment, he laughed, and his smile looked genuine.

"I probably don't need to tell you about the contents of this letter." She handed it to him, and he put it on the table in front of him. He would not be opening it in front of her.

"I can guess, but why don't you just tell me?"

She wondered if he was enjoying her awkward situation. At the least, she could provide him with that small and insignificant revenge.

"The board has decided to put someone else in charge of the center," she said as confidently as she could while maintaining eye contact. "After your official resignation of course. They don't want you to feel like your talents are unappreciated. Only the board and I know about this letter."

"Why are they sending you to deliver this letter?" he asked as if he had become unexpectedly tired. "You wouldn't be my replacement. They would never appoint a high-level IDA executive such as you to be a member of a think-tank studying the strategy and effects of monetary centralization."

"No," Audrie said, and his words offered relief. He seemed satisfied with giving her just a small moment of social awkwardness. "I'm not your replacement. I'm not as experienced as you are, or as talented. If you didn't know, I'm a special assistant to the board. They needed someone to talk to you in person. They probably thought I would be one to do it nicely."

She wanted to say that the board sent her to do a job no one wanted, but she kept silent. No one wanted to get into a philosophical argument with Michael Flanagan. She hoped for one thing only, that her accomplishment of the task would solidify her tenacious reputation.

"So what do they expect me to do, just drop everything I've been working on? What about the report for the Senate Finance Committee?"

"Don't worry about your report. It will be finished by the new director. Senator Hatch can wait a little longer."

Michael stared at her directly for a few seconds and smiled again.

"There's two obvious reasons why they chose you to be the messenger. I cannot argue with you because you have no power to change their decision."

"That's true," she said, trying to smile reassuringly. "You are free to go talk to one of them directly, you know. And what's the second reason?"

"It's hard to be angry when a beautiful and intelligent woman, such as yourself, makes a visit."

"That's nice of you to say," Audrie said while straining to smile. *Did he intend that as a compliment or an insult?*

The compliment would have given anyone pleasure, anyone except Audrie. She hated the thought of her physical appearance having any primary significance to her position in life. She hated that thought more than the idea of affluence having any primary significance. They were just secondary factors, nothing more.

"To be honest, even though I'm still in shock at their methods, I really don't want to waste my energy with the board."

He looked at his computer screen for a few seconds then slowly closed his laptop. When he looked back at Audrie, his eyes looked tired.

"I'm glad you don't seem to be as upset by this as I expected."

"Can we speak confidentially, Miss Garner?" he asked.

Her dark brown eyes opened wide, and she sat back.

"Of course."

"You're not like your father, you know," he said, and his mouth softened into a relaxed smile as if for the first time she saw his true emotion. "You, or your brother Max."

She winced at the mention of her brother. *How does he know so much about my family?* In their brief encounters, Michael had never mentioned her father, a man about the same age as himself. She also never remembered her father referring to the man.

"How is that?" she asked.

"To be like your father, you need to be a cutthroat. I don't see that in you."

The conversation had turned down a road she never saw on the map. And to make the situation worse, she became the passenger rather than the driver. In the brief moment he gave her, she tried to decide if she wanted to divert the conversation or see where it led. She failed to hide the surprise in her eyes and cursed herself for being so transparent.

"When I look at you and your brother Max, I see more of your grandfather."

"I hardly think you know me that well, Mr. Flanagan," she said somewhat insulted at his presumption. "How do you know my grandfather?"

"I used to work for him."

—※—

For the next several minutes, he spoke about his connection to Audrie's family. As a young man, Michael had worked for her grandfather at his venture capital firm in Boston. Although her grandfather had been a strict boss, Michael spoke of him fondly. He remembered when Audrie and Max were born, how proud her grandfather had been, and how he let everyone know about his excitement.

In the short time of their conversation, she found herself becoming nostalgic and had to exert extra effort to maintain her emotional guard. She had to keep the situation professional and not let him transform it into a sentimental family reunion. Did he intend to gain something from purposely manipulating her emotions? Probably not. She failed to think of a possible motive unless maybe building an emotional connection. Considering what she had just delivered to him, what was the value of an emotional connection?

"You mentioned that I haven't been thinking long term," he said, bringing their conversation back to an earlier point in time. "In your honest opinion, what do you think of all our activities? Remember, this is just between us."

"Do you mean the Center for Monetary Centralization or the CFR as a whole?"

"The Council on Foreign Relations as an entire organization."

The vibrant tone of his voice suggested to Audrie that his energy and enthusiasm had been restored. She would rather not discuss her real opinions with him, but she felt obligated to at least tell him that much.

"We're helping the world move forward," she said bluntly. "Wouldn't you say?"

"To be more precise, we're shaping the human political and social environment. *Forward* is just an opinion."

Her eyes widened.

"Are you implying that you disagree with the direction?"

"It doesn't matter if I disagree or not." The look in his eyes turned dangerous, but Audrie met his gaze without blinking. "You can't argue that we're reverting into sort of a quasi-feudalistic society. Chronologically speaking, that's not forward but backward. The only good thing we can say about it is that living conditions have improved. That's the only thing keeping the masses from revolting, the only thing keeping them playing the game."

"You speak of living conditions as if they are a trivial matter." Audrie did not wait for a response. "All the poor dream about being rich because of their living condition."

"Ah yes," he said slowly. "The poor dream about being rich. But what do the rich dream of?"

Audrie smiled and laughed, surprising herself. "We have the same dreams. We dream about being richer, having more, never losing our possessions. What's your point?"

"Having more than the next guy, yes, and more than what we presently have even if it's sufficient. Does that sound healthy to you, Miss Garner? Sounds like a mental disease to me, some kind of neural virus. Have you ever noticed that the world is run by people who are inflicted by an advanced strain of that virus?"

"I don't know if we can think of it as a human frailty or disease. If human behavior was any different, what would drive progress, if not for the desire for personal advancement?"

Audrie felt as though the conversation had been put into a blender. She never expected a discussion about human psychology.

"People forget to consider the law of parsimony," he said and paused while glancing at the computer on his desk. As he spoke, he smiled, and she felt as though listening to her grandfather tell one of his stories. She listened with skepticism and interest, completely forgetting to hide her emotions.

"That's one of the problems, I think," he continued without showing any awareness of her reaction. He turned to her, and they locked eyes. "Mature adults, like you and I, over-analyze everything. We over-analyze things until we can't see the big picture anymore. My little grandchildren know what's most important in life and they didn't need college for that. I think the younger they are, the more they know it. Their understanding is the same thing that infuriates parents the most and leads to one of the most tragic events in a person's life, when they are convinced of the *proper* way to look at the world and how to live in it."

"I have to admit, Mr. Flanagan," Audrie said and felt like a child accidentally walking into a general relativity lecture. "I don't see where you're going with this."

He looked at her with a curious expression, as if deciding whether or not to proceed with his explanation. He seemed disturbed or frustrated but not angry as she imagined he should be. On the trip to see him, she had thought more about the honor of being sent by the board, more than any feelings of guilt about his reaction.

When he responded, she knew their conversation had ended.

"Audrie, one day I hope you will understand."

ELEVEN

Sadi

The morning after the experience at the hotel, Helen's new friend, Daryn, had acted overly polite and timid during breakfast, asking for small portions of food to eat, or a little water to drink, just a little. When Sadi told Daryn that she could take anything she wanted from the refrigerator and if she ever needed anything to eat, she did not even have to ask, the girl acted confused and afraid as though Sadi wanted to trick her. But when Sadi saw the little girl's disbelief transform into excitement, she had to turn her head away to hide her moist eyes. Jen noticed the look and took the girl to the refrigerator to show her the contents.

"Jen," Sadi said after the girls returned to the table. "Can you take Helen to her room for a while. I want to talk to Daryn alone."

"Sure, c'mon Helen."

"Where are your parents?" Sadi asked after Jen and Helen left the kitchen. "If you don't want to talk about it, that's fine. We can talk another time."

"I think they're dead," she said bluntly. "My mom's dead. I don't remember my dad."

"So you were living with your foster parents? Where do they live?"

Sadi suddenly imagined Freddy going to their house and killing them. "Do they have any other kids?"

During the following conversation, Sadi learned the basics of Daryn's living situation. Her foster parents, the Becerras had taken care of Daryn for the past two years, but before them, she'd lived in another horrible situation with another couple. The poor girl spoke of her life as if talking about a used toy at a second-hand thrift store. During the conversation, Sadi allowed her growing anger to replace the sadness of the story.

Later in the afternoon, after Helen showed Daryn everything in the house and their backyard, Sadi asked both girls how the abduction happened. Daryn looked at the ground and began silently and slowly shaking her head from side to side. Sadi placed her hand on the girl's shoulder, but she jerked away.

"It's okay, Daryn. You don't..." Sadi began to say, but Helen stepped between them.

"It wasn't her fault mom," Helen said defensively. "Mr. Becerra made her."

Daryn put both hands over her eyes and became still. Sadi looked into Helen's eyes and saw indignation, then she turned to Jen, who sat on the couch pretending not to listen.

After a short pause, Sadi made another attempt to comfort the girl. She extended her hand in an attempt to pull her close, but Daryn pulled free of Sadi's grasp and ran from the room. Without looking back, Helen followed her friend.

—✳—

In preparation for their trip to the coast, Jen helped Sadi pack for the two girls. She went to the store and bought food and other supplies, using her own money and refusing reimbursement, likely motivated by feelings of guilt about letting Helen escape at the mall. Sadi did not blame her. She knew how quickly her daughter could slip from sight while in public. Jen would never make that mistake again.

Jen bought several different kinds of treats for the car ride, most of them very unhealthy items the kids would like, but which Sadi would usually forbid. Sadi planned to concentrate solely on having a fun time and hoped to let the experiences of the past slip into a more distant memory.

Sadi planned to drive directly to Seaside, Oregon, and then intentionally let the rest of the plan remain blank. They would spend a little time in Seaside, but Sadi did not want to stay there. That place did *not* feel far enough away. Helen loved the entertainment there, however, especially the bumper cars. If Sadi ever attempted to just drive through without stopping, she would hear a multitude of complaints from her daughter.

Sadi loved the Northwest coast and expected to feel the familiar sense of isolation the ocean instilled. Whenever she stood on the shore and looked beyond the waves, she felt like an explorer staring into the unknown. She had the same impression while gazing at the stars.

Before leaving town, Sadi wondered if she should pay a short visit to Mr. Smith and Freddy. She felt the need to thank them again but wondered if seeing Freddy would force them all to recall the nightmare. After pulling out of the driveway and waving goodbye to Jen, she decided to make the visit. Both men deserved to know her gratitude and plans.

When she reached the gate of Mr. Smith's estate, she waited anxiously to see who would answer her call, Mr. Smith or Freddy. After a long minute of waiting, the gate finally opened, and the voice of an old man instructed them to meet him at the front door.

"Hi, Miss Jacobsen," Mr. Smith said after he opened the door. "Please come in. I'm glad to see you, but I'm afraid Freddy is not here at the moment. He's in class."

Sadi stepped over the threshold, and her two little girls followed.

"I would have called, but I didn't decide on coming until after we started driving. I just want to say thanks again."

"Glad to have you," he said. As the girls slid past him, he patted their heads and smiled. "Hi, girls, come in."

"Wow, the ceiling is so high," said Helen after Mr. Smith shut the front door. "Wow, look at the size of that staircase!"

"Helen and Daryn," Sadi said in a serious tone. "Do you remember Mr. Smith? He helped us find you."

Before he could say anything, Helen put both arms around him and held him tight for a few seconds.

"Thank you, Mr. Smith. Are you Freddy's dad?"

"No, I'm afraid not," said Mr. Smith with obvious delight. "He works for me. He takes care of this house and many of my affairs."

"You have affairs?" said Helen quizzically as she let go of him.

Mr. Smith laughed heartily.

"No affairs here, sorry to say. I meant that Freddy takes care of my things."

"Oh," said Helen with disappointment.

Daryn stood quietly behind Helen and looked wary of Mr. Smith. She looked up at him with a small, polite smile. For the next few minutes, he took them on a tour of the ground floor.

"Forgive me if I don't take you upstairs, but that trip I only like to do once a day. My bedroom is up there. Besides that, there's not much to see. While your mother and I talk," he said, placing a hand on the shoulder of each girl. "Would you girls like to go exploring?"

"You mean go anywhere we want?" Helen asked, looking at her mother with pleading in her eyes.

"Anywhere," Mr. Smith answered with a wide smile. "Upstairs is my room and many guest rooms and all downstairs is Freddy's. If you decide to go downstairs, be careful with his things and try not to pick anything up. I'm sure Freddy won't mind if you have a look around."

"Are you sure that's a good idea?" Sadi asked.

"That's what I'd want to do if I was that young again."

"All right," Sadi said and then turned to the girls. "Remember what Mr. Smith said."

With obvious pleasure in his eyes, Mr. Smith watched the girls walk up the stairs. They held hands and ascended slowly, their heads turning in unison to stare at the ornate white banister and then at the portraits on the wall. Sadi never expected their vacation to begin so early and she already felt a large emotional weight removed from her huge bag of concerns. After seeing the broad smile on Mr. Smith's face, she stopped worrying about intruding or interrupting his day.

"Come with me to the kitchen," Mr. Smith said. "Let's have a drink."

Sadi had no intention of disagreeing with him. He spoke with a command in his voice that shut any form of disagreement from her mind. Once in the kitchen, he poured Sadi a cup of cranberry juice and he had the same.

"This will help you relax," he said without asking if she wanted the sour red liquid.

He spoke like a grandfather advising his grandchildren about nutrition, and she felt happy to receive his concern. They took a seat at the large table in the middle of the room, away from the surrounding stainless steel kitchen appliances, which reflected the sunlight from the windows. Sadi rested her elbows on the unblemished marble table top and enjoyed the cool sensation. Her muscles began to relax as the cold cranberry juice slid down her throat, leaving a tingling sensation on her tongue.

"I love your kitchen," she said looking around at the impeccable condition. "Freddy takes good care of it."

"He does, he does. I like the kitchen. It gets a lot of sunlight. So were you on your way somewhere?"

"We're getting out of town for a couple weeks," she said after taking a sip of her drink. "Like I said, I wasn't planning to visit, but I just wanted to thank you for your help again."

"I think Freddy deserves all the credit. I hope you all can recover."

"Yes."

Sadi felt an uncomfortable moment of silence. She turned from his face to look at their surroundings in an attempt to think of how to continue the conversation. Mr. Smith filled the void first with a deep breath.

"Getting away is a good idea. I hope it helps you. Can I tell you a story, Miss Jacobsen?"

"Of course," Sadi said, glad for the reprieve.

"When I finished with school, I had my dream job at a meat processing plant," the old man began and shifted in his seat to get more comfortable. "Since I was a college graduate, they started me out as a low-level manager. See, in those days, having a college education meant something. Nowadays, you need a master's degree or doctorate to get anywhere, as you probably know."

"Well, where I worked, it was a large operation, and there were many opportunities for advancement. I planned on staying there for a long time, and that was important. People stayed at a job back then. Sorry, I don't mean to compare then to now, but it sure seemed better in many ways. I know it's easy to look back at things, only see the good and neglect the bad. I try not to do that. I do try to see the whole picture, blemishes and all."

"I can understand that."

"Not only was I comfortable in a financial sense, but I felt that I had the wherewithal to propose to the woman I was courting."

Sadi adjusted herself in the chair to prepare for a longer story than she anticipated. While she listened, all anxiety left her mind, and she began to feel more at peace.

"It seemed like my life was set," he continued. "At least, I thought that at the time. I'm sure you can tell where this is going. In everyone's life, there are periods where things seem to be going one way or another, and then your life takes a dramatic course adjustment, all on its own it seems. As it happened, the plant went out of business, leaving me out on my backside."

"So you lost your job?" Sadi said in confirmation, after hearing the pause in his story.

"At the time," he nodded and smiled. "That was the second worst thing to happen. The worst blow was when my new wife left me. We had only been married for a few months when my job vanished. When I told her we probably would have to move in with my parents, for a short while, that's when she told me she could not live with that condition."

"How horrible of her."

"That almost broke me," he admitted, shaking his head. "I spent the next four months looking for a job and trying to get her back. I really flipped my wig over her."

"Did she ever talk to you again?"

"She led me around like a stupid ass," he said while laughing sardonically at the memory. "She said she would come back when I made something of myself."

"Not very *for richer or poorer* of her," Sadi said. "At least you can laugh about it now."

"I finally realized that above all, she just wanted a life of ease and it didn't matter who with. I know that's not a horrible thing, but I deserved a woman who loved me. Don't you agree, Miss Jacobsen?"

"Of course," she said. "Did she ever realize the big blunder of letting you go?"

"I will never know," he said. "I finally got another job as an inspector with the Department of Agriculture. It paid much less than my dream job. That's when I realized that I could not get her back. I felt glad to have a job but devastated at the same time. I never saw her again."

"Good riddance," Sadi said, trying to attenuate her annoyance. "If she didn't love you enough to stick with you during that little setback, you were better off without her."

"You are very kind to an old man," said Mr. Smith while looking directly into her eyes. "I think the huge age difference between us gives me the prerogative to dispense advice, whether called for or not."

"You can give me your advice anytime," she said, eagerly waiting to hear what he had to say. Maybe he would say something to help her feel normal again.

"None of my experience can probably compare to yours, but my advice is don't try to get back to the life you knew. That usually leads to wasted resources and heartache. The past is always gone anyway. There's no need to try and get it back. Your future is brightest when you spend your time looking forward. The sun's never as bright as when you're looking straight at it."

"That's very good advice," Sadi said in an exaggerated tone of gratitude.

Although she loved the advice and needed the reminder, Sadi had hoped Mr. Smith would reveal a great secret only he knew, one that could restore her life to normal.

"Miss Jacobsen," he said, and the grandfatherly tone vanished. He spoke as a friend of the same age, someone with the same set of problems. "I want to ask you a different kind of question."

"Yes."

"What do you think of what's happening to Freddy?" he asked imploringly. "All that's happening with him is out of my experience. I feel like a child again, when everything in life was a mystery and slightly intimidating."

Sadi had spent much of her conscious time, recently, attempting to avoid the answer to his question. Those answers led to more frightening questions. She hoped to leave them behind as she drove to the coast.

"I don't understand any of it, but I don't know if I can complain. So far, it's helped me. That's a pretty good measuring stick."

"The timing of that probe thing and Freddy's new ability and the abduction is not a coincidence. That thing or alien or whatever you want to call it, I believe it caused all of this to happen. I don't know why, but I don't like it."

"I'm not going to complain," Sadi said quickly. "Because of Freddy's new ability, he could do what he did."

Did Mr. Smith hear the defensiveness in her voice? He quickly looked at her eyes with suspicion, then took a drink and looked away.

"At the barn, you had the same reaction as I did, but the experience seemed to excite your friend, the lawyer. Why is that?"

"I think he likes the idea of an alien," Sadi said, smiling at the memory of her conversation with Gerald after the barn incident. "He probably hopes it will help his friends."

"I don't believe in free help," he said cynically. "Everything comes with a price."

"I know," she said and wondered about the help he provided. She wanted to change the subject. "I just need to get away."

Mr. Smith turned from staring at the table to looking out the window. The sun caused his white skin to shine, but the deep wrinkles on the side of his eyes still held dark shadows. Before continuing, he turned to face Sadi. "I see net damage from this whole affair. Do you worry about Freddy? I fear for him. He seems to have lost his innocence."

"We all lose our innocence, at some time, but I'm afraid Freddy lost that a long time ago. He's been through a lot in his life, and I don't worry about him now, especially since he has you. My brother and I can help too."

"Maybe you already have. Maybe I should take my own advice and not wish for the past." He laughed and seemed to have a slightly improved mood. He waved his hand around at their surroundings, at the spotless kitchen, the polished stainless steel and shiny stone tiles covering the floor. "So you like my home?"

She answered with wide eyes and a nod.

"You make lots of friends when you hold powerful political positions, Miss Jacobsen. If you make the right people happy, you get rewarded for your cooperation, and by cooperation I mean by keeping the river of money flowing from somebody else's pockets."

"It took me a long time to realize it, but I sold out, Miss Jacobsen. I fell for the criminals who control the money and wrongly equated their money and influence with credibility. I would have been a lot happier and more content if I could have made my own way in this life without participating in the plunder of the world population."

"In a world with freedom for the individual as the supreme philosophy of the land, my life would have been impossible. You should be proud of yourself, Miss Jacobsen. Your chosen path in life took courage and determination. People like you should be the icons in our society, not me and all this."

Mr. Smith again waved his hand in a sweeping motion in front of him, referring to the lavish surroundings of his immaculate kitchen. She smiled again but failed to think of a response.

"You must forgive me, Miss Jacobsen," he said and gently slapped his hand on the table. "I'm just an old man haunted by memories of a long life."

"You rescued Freddy," Sadi said, relieved to think of an encouraging comment. "Not just at the barn but from the nightmare of his former life. You're better than I am. When I was younger, I could have helped him more than I did, but you took him into your home and saved his life, figuratively at least. That's redemption for anything you might have done."

Mr. Smith's eyes became moist. Sadi saw no tears, but she knew her words had resonated with the old man.

"That's nice of you to say," Mr. Smith said with a polite smile. "But it's kind of backwards. Freddy saved me."

TWELVE

Gerald

Before Taylor and Gerald left for Boston, they discussed the visit with everyone, what they felt comfortable revealing, and if they could trust Max. Gerald said they had no reason to distrust him. Doroteo had no opinion of Max but thought Gerald had made a foolish decision to reveal some of their intentions to someone so far removed from their influence. Cesar admired how Max showed deference to his grandfather and seemed to base his entire judgment on that one point. He had a great respect for Max's grandfather and said if he claimed they could trust his grandson, then Cesar would be satisfied.

Taylor said she would give Max a chance to prove himself in Boston but refused to provide any conditions where she would agree to share their secrets. She had to feel good about it. Even Gerald agreed they were taking a lot of risks, but he felt that the benefits made it worth exploring and they all agreed.

"What's your problem?" she asked with a frown when Gerald arrived at Cesar's house to drive them to the airport. Making eye contact with her had taken longer than usual, and she noticed.

"You look nice," he gulped. He could not recall a time when he saw her in a skirt. "I just wasn't expecting to see you out of your ordinary attire."

"Thanks," she said and walked past him to the car, shaking her head in annoyance.

He paused just a moment to watch Taylor walk away then hurried after her. Cesar returned to the house, and only Dominga watched them go. Gerald could almost feel her eyes on him and wondered if she knew his thoughts.

Taylor wore a white blouse with a pencil skirt and wedge heels. When he got in the car, he caught himself staring at the bottom of her skirt, a few centimeters above her knees. He had never seen her legs before and quickly turned his attention to his seat belt. Fortunately, she had failed to notice his pause.

At the airport, Gerald followed Taylor into the private jet and enjoyed seeing her expression of amazement. During takeoff, she sat forward in her seat, looking out the window. When they ascended above the dark clouds, bright sunlight flooded the cabin. Gerald felt his morale increase with their elevation. Taylor's smile helped too.

When Taylor finally relaxed enough to sit back in her seat, Gerald convinced her to have a drink, and they talked about what it must be like to have such luxuries at their disposal.

"It must be easy to forget about all the world's problems," said Taylor as she sipped at her daiquiri, "when you're sitting in luxury like this, with other people taking care of your every need. It's hard to remember or care that the government is controlling other aspects of your life."

"That's true," he said, smiling. "Right now, I've forgotten about all my problems. What are we doing here exactly?"

"Ha ha."

"You'll get to meet my friend Mark," said Gerald. "Saw him last time I went to D.C. He's an engineer, like you. You'll like him."

"I know," she said. "All engineers like each other and know each other, obviously." She smiled and then laughed without any hint of irritation. Maybe the alcohol helped her forget her grievances against him.

"You know what I mean," Gerald said and shook his head in mock irritation. "He's a good guy, and he wants to help us."

"And you said he knows nothing about us? Right?"

"He knows we want help with some life support systems, but no, he doesn't know about the fusion reactor and your NMG, or that we have anything secret."

"Tell me again, how you know we can trust him?" she asked. "Because he's your friend?"

"Because he said so," Gerald said after failing to think of a good reason.

"You're full of laughs today, Gerald."

"I know."

—※—

They landed in Boston at noon. Gerald noticed Max waiting for them at the bottom of the stairs from the plane.

"Good to see you, Miss Taylor," Max said as she descended the ladder. "And you, Gerald."

Max escorted them to a Lexus sedan, where their driver waited, the same man who had accompanied Max on the trail in Seattle. After he made brief eye contact with them, he sat forward and let Max get the door for Taylor. She and Gerald sat in the back seat while traveling to Erik Garner's estate in Brookline.

Before heading to his grandfather's home, they spent about twenty minutes driving through the central part of Boston, Max acting as the tour guide. With a hint of nostalgia in his voice, Max told them about the city where he'd spent some of his childhood. For the most part, Gerald did most of the responding and Taylor listened without comment. The driver never said a word.

After forty minutes of driving, Max pulled into the gated drive of his grandfather's house. The estate made Mr. Smith's home in Portland look like a beach house. On the drive from the gate to the covered archway, they passed a beautiful garden of flowers surrounding a small pond with a tall fountain in the middle. The main house had a smaller guest cottage on one side, connected by a covered path and a grove of trees on the other. Gerald thought he saw a building in the trees. Taylor remained silent, but her eyes revealed to Gerald her impression of the place.

After getting out of the car, Max bent down and talked with his driver. Gerald thought he heard Max ask if he wanted to stay but could not hear a response. At the end of the brief conversation, Max shut the door, and the man drove back down the drive out of sight. Without a word of explanation, Max led them into the house. An older woman with a stern expression shut the door softly behind them.

Max led them a short way through the house to a huge room with paintings on every wall and two large chandeliers hanging from the thirty-foot-tall ceiling. On the side of the room, facing a wall of windows, sat two men, a man about Gerald's age and an older man who appeared to be in his late seventies or early eighties.

When Gerald recognized his friend, Mark, the sight of him brought a flood of memories from his undergraduate days. Gerald noticed several streaks of gray in his short dark hair, and his receding hairline seemed to have crept slightly higher up his forehead. Gerald still had all of his dark hair with no trace of gray in it. When he found an appropriate opportunity, Gerald would tease his friend about it, or maybe just save it for an email. Mark was sitting next to the old man in an elegant recliner, talking with him. When Mark saw Gerald enter the room, he stood, smiled, and then waited for Gerald to approach.

"Help me to my feet, will you, Mark?" the older man asked politely.

"Gerald and Taylor," Max said. "This is my grandfather, Erik Garner."

"Gerald Foster," he said first, taking his hand and squeezing it hard. "It's a pleasure to meet you."

Max's grandfather reminded Gerald of the scarecrow from *The*

Wizard of Oz, a tall and skinny man who wore a severe expression. When he smiled, deep wrinkles appeared, filled with dark shadows.

"It's an honor, sir," Gerald said.

"I've read about you," Erik Garner said while still shaking hands. "Got implicated with the Federal Reserve break-in incident, eh," he said and laughed hard. He turned to his grandson, and his voice became more serious. "Don't let your father discover that you're meeting with someone like this."

Gerald smiled and felt slightly embarrassed. He had hoped the subject would not resurface. Max's grandfather turned to Taylor, the only female in the room.

"Taylor Evans," he said, and his smile widened. "The mechanical engineer who could take the car industry to the next level, that is if the oil guys ever get their slippery fingers off the politicians' puppet strings. It's a pleasure to make your acquaintance. I don't often get visits from such a lovely girl."

"Good to meet you too, sir," she said, blushing slightly. "I see you've done your homework."

"I like to know who's coming to my home," he said and put his hand on the shoulder of the man standing patiently at his side. "This is Mark Salmon, the brilliant man who keeps Max's company from falling into an endless government paperwork abyss."

"He gives me too much credit," Mark said, keeping his eyes on Taylor. He shook her hand vigorously. "Just call me Mark. Good to meet you."

"Good to meet you too," Taylor said.

After a polite smile at Taylor, Mark turned to Gerald who stepped forward and held out his hand. Mark grabbed it and then put his other arm around his friend.

"It's been too long," Gerald said without trying to hide his pleasure.

During the introductions, Gerald imagined an electric current flowing between them all and felt good about what would come of the day. Even Taylor looked excited and without even a hint of her usual cynicism.

Max's grandfather pointed to the two empty French-style chairs next to him and then the matching white leather couch. "Please sit wherever you like. I think we have some serious matters to discuss."

Almost a minute later, the same woman who met them at the door, entered the hall with a younger male servant. They silently placed several trays of food, pitchers of water and juice, coffee and tea on the cool marble surfaces of the two cocktail tables. They worked so silently and discreetly, Gerald thought they could have been ghosts. Before leaving the hallway, the woman made eye contact with the old man, and he nodded in appreciation.

While they talked, Gerald enjoyed the view through the wall of windows, of the pond and large oak trees surrounding the house. The scene helped give the illusion of being in the middle of a forest.

Gerald had a few major concerns for the afternoon discussion. How much intimidation would Taylor feel from their company and would her cynical disposition prevent her from recognizing an acceptable risk? Notwithstanding his confidence in her intelligence, she had little experience dealing with these kinds of people. Her underprivileged adolescence and general disposition could be a significant disadvantage. He was accustomed to dealing with clients who could let powerful people deceive and manipulate them, but he had little experience with people who had the opposite problem, like Taylor. Hopefully, he could persuade her to consult him before shooting down any suggestion he found perfectly reasonable.

Despite his concerns, he had confidence in her abilities. She had a strong will and seemed to thrive under pressure. If she could tame Doroteo, she could handle a rich old man and his grandson.

—※—

"Max thinks I can convince you to let him join your business venture. Is that correct?" Erik Garner asked after everyone had poured their drinks and filled a plate with food. He crossed his legs, rested both arms on the chair, and then shifted his gaze from Gerald to Taylor.

Gerald and Taylor made brief eye contact with each other, then in slow reptilian motion, she turned to meet the elderly man's gaze. "We're here at Max's request. I think he just wants to find out what we're up to."

"Curiosity killed the cat," Max interjected before taking a sip of his coffee.

"Apathetic cats die of starvation," Erik said and laughed again. "Max can smell a business opportunity from twenty miles away and I can probably guess what else ran through his mind when he first saw you."

Max forced a cough to bring attention to himself.

"Oh, come now," he said and laughed dismissively. "I made no such indication!"

Erik ignored his grandson and kept his eyes on Taylor.

"Forgive me, Miss Evans."

"Call me Taylor," she said politely.

"You'll need to let an old man indulge himself. In the uncertain time I have left in this life, I need to take advantage of every opportunity for enjoyment, and I particularly enjoy making my grandson squirm."

"I can appreciate that," she said.

"Now before I attempt to convince you of anything," he began, and the mirth in his voice almost disappeared. "Can either of you tell me any preliminary information? I failed to get anything substantial from these two gentlemen."

"We're working on sensitive material and don't want it stolen from us," Taylor said and briefly glanced at Max. "We're depending on Gerald's assessment of character, which doesn't happen to be one of my strong points, unfortunately."

"Our major problem is that we cannot rely on the courts to defend our exclusive property rights," explained Gerald for more clarification. "There are certain entities who would steal all our work and the government would not stand in their way."

"And who is the leader of this venture?" asked the old man.

"Gerald and I share that task," Taylor said quickly. "We both have to agree on any course of action, and I'm the more paranoid one."

"That can be a good character trait," said the old man.

"Taylor's the one who instigated this whole venture," Gerald said, paying her a sincere compliment. "If it weren't for her, we would not be here right now."

Although the old man seemed genuinely sincere in his praise of Taylor, Gerald wanted him to take her seriously. Gerald thought of himself as her assistant, but he felt honored to be called her partner. In his peripheral vision, Gerald saw the reflection of a maid in one of the windows. She appeared to be working somewhere else, out of earshot.

"I just want to say," began Max in a tone of apology for the interruption. "That I've only told my grandfather what I told you at our meeting in Seattle. He only knows you might be working on going into space. Mark hasn't told me anything else, and I haven't inquired further since we last met."

"I wanted to hear the difference between your explanation and what Max told me," said his grandfather. "You can learn a lot by listening to the same story from different angles. I'm also looking for consistency."

"Did we pass your test?" Taylor asked.

"Of course," he answered and shifted his weight in his chair. "Now, I'm very interested in hearing about your efforts. Tell me if I've come close to hitting the mark. You've found a way to travel into space without the use of governmental resources, and you have more in mind than just experiencing free fall.

"Considering the relationship between space travel and national security, I assume you have more concerns than just property rights. In this case, Taylor, I think your paranoia is justified, and you are likely already aware of the risk in associating with a company like TerraWatch due to their relationship with potentially interested military entities."

"And your son," Gerald interjected. "What about the risk in associating with him? He's a high profile figure."

"Ah yes, my son," said the old man. "Henry must be kept out of this for sure, but you should be more concerned with Max's sister."

"Grandfather," interrupted Max as if taken by surprise. "Audrie is too busy with her own life to concern herself with what I'm doing."

"All I'm saying, Max, is that you should take your sister into consideration when you get involved in any potentially tarnishing activities." The old man spoke of his granddaughter like a poisonous snake but with a tone of extreme pride. "Your sister is like the rest of us, very concerned about her own goals. She knows that any waves you generate can crash against her."

"It sounds like you're trying to convince us why we shouldn't let your grandson join our venture," said Taylor with a mixture of concern and amusement.

"I just don't want to paint an unrealistic picture of the situation," said the senior Mr. Garner. "Now, as for Max. He would never betray your trust. I trust him and stand by him. Unfortunately, I cannot say the same about my son or granddaughter."

Max breathed in deeply and looked toward the window. His grandfather's words seemed to trouble him, and Gerald thought he saw a small look of sorrow in his eyes.

"Another member of our group is an admirer of yours, Mr. Garner, but I'm afraid you wouldn't know him," Gerald said in the hopes of lifting the mood in the room. "He has full faith in your opinion, and I already have shown that I trust Mark and he trusts Max."

"Then let me try to put our situation in the proper perspective," the old man said, and the mirth in his voice returned. "We have two unique arrangements of, A equals B and B equals C, then logically C must equal A. Of course, we're not talking about equality but trust."

"I was feeling guilty, Gerald," Mark said after sitting forward and putting his cup of tea on the table. The sound of the ceramic hitting the marble surface seemed to emphasize his next words. "Guilty for letting Max catch me looking at your website and causing all this trouble, but maybe it will turn out to be a fortunate mistake. I apologize,

Taylor."

"Thank you," Taylor said. "I hope so."

"If it makes you feel any better," Max said with a laugh. "I threatened to fire him if he didn't tell me about your group, but he stuck his head on the line for you and called my bluff."

While looking out the window, Mark snickered and then silently shook his head.

THIRTEEN

Gerald

"Since Mark already knows a little about what we're doing, it should be okay to have him share the rest. We've just been extremely paranoid since we caught the FBI spying on us a while ago. It turns out," Taylor paused and shot Gerald a derisive glance, "they were only spying on Gerald, and we're pretty sure they didn't get anything on us, but it puts us in a very precarious situation."

"What happened?" asked Max, sitting forward in his seat. He looked more worried than when his grandfather mentioned his sister. "How do you know what the FBI learned or did not learn?"

For the first time, Taylor looked uncomfortable, and Gerald thought he might hear a different story than the one told by Cesar, how Doroteo had been closely monitoring the situation, claiming to find no evidence the FBI had any interest in the shop other than checking on Gerald.

"We have an experienced security expert working with us," Taylor said. "Nothing gets by him."

Before responding, Max exchanged eye contact with Mark.

"That's definitely a cause for concern."

"I'm afraid that the FBI has been trying to entrap me," said Gerald in explanation and felt more embarrassment. "After they failed to indict me with, well what happened."

"Well, I can assure you that my home is secure," said the senior Mr. Garner. "I have my own security staff, and they keep it that way for me."

"Okay," began Taylor, after making eye contact with Gerald. He gave a slight nod for her to continue and was relieved when she diverted the conversation away from him. "Why don't we have Mark tell you what he knows, and we'll go from there. I'd also like to hear what he thinks of it all."

At the mention of his name, Mark sat up straighter. In the natural light of the room, his black pupils contrasted distinctly with his light blue eyes. He cleared his throat before speaking.

"When Gerald asked me if I could keep something confidential, I had no idea what I was getting into."

"Neither did we," Gerald said and thought his friend sounded like a man speaking to an emotional support group. "Sorry, continue."

"As I understand it," Mark began. He mostly addressed Erik Garner but every few seconds looked at Max. "They are making a vessel to take them into space, a vessel with a new propulsion system. Gerald asked me if I might be able to help with some communication and life-support systems."

"Hold on," Taylor said, and Gerald heard a dangerous tone in her voice. "Gerald told you that we had a new propulsion system?"

For a moment, the angry look in Taylor's eyes erased Gerald's memory. To regain his concentration, he turned his attention to the window. He honestly could not recall saying anything about her invention or his discovery.

"I didn't say anything about a new propulsion system," he said, directing his comment to Mark and avoiding eye contact with Taylor.

"Maybe I just assumed," Mark said, acting confused. Gerald peered closely into his friend's eyes, looking for signs of subterfuge, an attempt to trick them into an inadvertent revelation, a familiar tactic to Gerald.

"Is it true?" asked Max, looking at Taylor.

"I would like to hear how Mark came up with that conclusion," interjected Gerald, a blatant attempt to dodge Max's question.

Max looked at Mark, waiting for his answer. Gerald saw the faintest trace of a smile on their faces. In that instant, he knew they intentionally planned the maneuver.

"Maybe," Mark said. "Maybe I just assumed that with your lack of resources and your desire for secrecy, you had developed a more efficient system, something the industry would try to steal from you."

Gerald turned to Taylor and forced himself not to flinch at the fierce anger in her eyes. But when she turned to Mark, the wrath in her expression quickly relaxed to slight amusement.

"Maybe you are correct about this turning into a fortunate situation," Taylor said. "But today, we are not prepared to reveal what we may or may not have developed. I would like to hear what else Gerald told you. Your version of the story is very enlightening."

"He said you want to travel into space because in space you are out of everyone's reach." He looked confused at that point. "That's all I remember about why. I've been trying to think of reasons. Maybe you want to start asteroid mining? I hear they've discovered a significant amount of gold on several asteroids. When I start thinking of all the other possibilities, I get sidetracked."

"I have no valid idea really," he continued. "Even with a new system, it would take a massive amount of money. If my original assumption is correct, you would want to develop a prototype and seek funding, but funding is not what Gerald asked for, so that's why I'm trying to get something more substantial out of you, and I'm failing."

"Right now, we're just working on R&D," Taylor said and laughed with him. "Of course we're interested in making a profit, but we also want to change the world without getting killed by those psychopaths who own the government."

"So what do you want to change?" asked Max.

Taylor turned to Gerald with a hint of a smile. Did Max suspect that Taylor had just insulted people like his father and grandfather?

As they waited for her answer, Gerald looked for evidence of offense and was relieved when he saw none.

Several more questions flashed through Gerald's mind. How could she answer their questions without revealing all her secrets? How would she explain their anarchist ideology without sounding like fanatical extremists? Would they have the typical reaction and let the artificially engineered social stigmas expunge all rational thought?

"Just for fun," Taylor said, "let's say we developed a far superior propulsion system, and we could easily go anywhere in the solar system. If we told the government of our plans to mine gold on asteroids, what do you think would happen?"

Gerald felt relief at discovering her tactic. Rather than directly revealing what motivated them, she attempted to lead them to her conclusions while at the same time including a diversion. While waiting for their response, he silently drew a deep breath and felt his tension relax a bit. He enjoyed watching Taylor in action.

"Well," Max said, slightly squinting his eyes in reflection. "They would consider it a security risk. There's a lot of permits you'd have to acquire."

"What do you think of that?" she asked. "Is that justified? We built it with our own intellect and resources. We should be able to use it how we want, not pay someone else for us to use it, as they allow."

"But with superior maneuverability, you could locate and damage military and commercial satellites."

"Then they can watch us closely and prosecute us for destroying property," Taylor said and Gerald noticed a slight irritation in her voice, hidden behind a smile. "That's the whole purpose of a judicial system. Right?"

"But you could be working for one of our enemies and escape prosecution here."

"Spoken like a true collectivist, using fear to justify the threat of violence," Taylor said, laughing, but she began to speak more forcefully. "It's not my responsibility to make them feel good about us. They can threaten to send a missile after us if we get too close to anything important."

Instead of acting offended, Max held up his left hand as if to block a physical punch.

"Hey, Taylor," he said and smiled. "I didn't say I agree with it. I just understand their position. They're using the laws as a shield because they can. That's how they protect their property, just like you use a lock and key to protect yours."

"I guess that's some consolation," Taylor said as if unaffected by his deflection, "to know I have a chance of reasoning with you, but let's continue with this hypothetical situation. Let's say we decided to jump through all the hoops to get the permits. Then what?"

"They, the Pentagon, would want to make sure you weren't carrying any weapons," Max answered and then paused to think. He looked at his grandfather, and they made a brief eye contact, then the old man turned to Taylor. The act reminded Gerald of the baton transfer in a relay race.

"They would not let you keep it," the old man finished for his grandson. "They would want it to remain a secret because it could be used to give us a military advantage against enemy states, countries like China and Russia."

"How long would they be able to keep it a secret?" she asked. "And would they really be that interested in a new military advantage?"

"That seems like an unreasonable question," Mark said. "Who wouldn't want an extra advantage against their enemies?"

"But it also brings uncertainty," the senior Mr. Garner said. "I think I see where Taylor's going with this. They would be able to keep it a secret for a short while, but it would eventually get out. Is that your conclusion, Taylor?"

She smiled with satisfaction.

"That's what Gerald and I concluded," she said. "So what's going to happen when the secret's out?"

"That depends on the specific attributes of your invention," he said, his eyes wide with an excitement Gerald could feel. "But after the cat is out of the bag, it could make a more level playing field, and that possibility would be unacceptable. At the moment, the Pentagon is the orca of the oceans, and it will kill any baby shark it thinks could possibly grow bigger than her."

"I like your analogy," Gerald said.

"Thank you," he answered and then returned his attention to Taylor. "You can't let anyone know about what you've made, can you?"

"That was our conclusion," she said.

"So how do you plan to move forward?" Max asked. "I'm starting to understand the magnitude of your trepidation to trust anyone."

Taylor turned to Gerald and took a deep breath. For the first time, Gerald began to doubt the wisdom of his decision to contact Mark. They might already know enough to cause them a lot of trouble.

Before she could respond, Mark cleared his throat for attention and sat forward.

"Let me interject an idea, and I'm not saying this to convince you to share specifics with us, but by even hinting at your claims, haven't you already put us in the same difficult position as you find yourselves? Hypothetically of course. Anyone who has dangerous information would be implicated, just for knowing about it."

"Actually," Max said before Mark could finish. "At this point, all we can say is that you might have developed something threatening to the system. If we went to the authorities with this information now, we could claim ignorance, and they would have little reason to worry about us."

"Don't even joke about that, Max," scolded the senior Mr. Garner and then turned to Gerald and Taylor. "Of course we're not going to do anything of the sort, and don't feel pressured to tell us anything right now."

"Nice try," Taylor said, smiling with sincere praise to Mark. "But you were the ones to make all the suggestions." She paused and turned to Gerald, her eyes wide. Gerald saw her request for his approval, so he nodded and smiled.

"We really don't know the best course of action," she continued after a sigh. "So we decided just to start making a vessel by ourselves.

I've always wanted to go into space, and maybe if we're ever discovered, we might be able to escape. Maybe, if we make it into space, they'll have a more difficult time to hide or eliminate what we've developed."

At her revelation, Max and Mark looked at each other with excitement. They seemed as though trying to decide who would answer, but the senior Mr. Garner spoke for them.

"We're not speaking hypothetically anymore are we?"

"I would like to make an invitation," Taylor said with a smile at the senior Mr. Garner. "Do you want to attend our takeoff in a few months?"

He laughed before responding.

"If I was only a few years younger, Miss Evans. If I can make it, I would love to, but I'm afraid I might pose too high of a security risk for you. I can probably, however, answer for our excited little puppies over here."

"How can we help?" asked Mark. "What do you need to expedite this demonstration?"

—※—

For the next few minutes, Mark and Max talked about all the assistance they could offer. Gerald sat back and enjoyed watching Taylor discuss the technical aspects. He noticed how she carefully avoided giving any details of their secrets and they stopped probing about it. They knew that all would be revealed in time.

Mr. Garner showed more interest in the political aspect and in their motivation. He understood the reason and sympathized with them while his grandson showed more interest in the scientific and technological aspects of their plans.

Through their company TerraWatch, they could covertly provide radiation shielding material, attitude control equipment, IR sensors, and sophisticated radar equipment to defend against possible military tracking. Taylor claimed they already had done much of the preliminary testing and only intended the first demonstration to be a short test flight.

Taylor agreed to Max's offer of having Mark visit Seattle to see what they were doing and offer technical advice. For the first time, Taylor agreed without first arguing with him.

"Although I would love to come with him," Max said sadly. "It's probably wise for me not to make more appearances until the official demonstration. It'll help you keep a lower profile."

Since TerraWatch had business dealings with the government, they had some knowledge of current military detection capabilities. Max had several concerns about how they were going to enter orbit undetected.

"So how does the military monitor the skies?" Gerald asked. He had spent so much time lately focusing on Sadi and her horrible predicament, that he left all other concerns to Taylor, Cesar, and Doroteo. He still needed to decide on a way to tell them about Freddy and the barn incident. "How can we do this undetected?"

Max looked at Mark who sat forward. "A lot of the military's efforts are on detecting ICBMs, intercontinental ballistic missiles. They use sensitive IR sensors on multiple satellites to look for the missile's heat trace signatures."

"That's fortunate," said Taylor. "Because we won't have anything like a rocket's typical heat trace."

"That is a definite benefit," Mark said, letting out his breath in relief but with a questioning look at Max. "Another fortunate circumstance is that the current set of satellites have nearly outlived their lives and the latest satellite known as DSP-23 mysteriously stopped working just a few months ago, just after being placed in its geosynchronous orbit. The military claims there is nothing suspicious about it, but some people suspect the Chinese had something to do with it."

"Is this related to the satellite the Chinese destroyed a few years ago?" Gerald asked, remembering that incident being in the news. "I think it made some people in the government pretty angry."

"I don't think it is related," Mark said and started chuckling. "But as we all know, the military just doesn't like it when other governments act without their permission. For several years now, however, Lockheed's been working on the next generation of satellites and should be putting the first one into orbit within a couple years. When these go up, it will be a lot more difficult to escape their notice. I wish we had access to their high altitude ones."

Gerald knew that infrared measured heat radiation and the realization gave him an idea. "What if we coincided our launch with July Fourth?" he asked. "You said the military uses infrared sensors to spot potential threats. With all the fireworks going on that night, it might provide some cover for our test flight."

Max, Mark, and Taylor all turned to look at him, and he noticed Taylor's lips curve into a surprised smile.

"Hmm, it might be something to think about," said Mark, scratching the stubble on his chin.

"Gerald may be on to something," said Taylor. "We were planning on our test at the end of June anyway. We really want to stick to our original timeline, but July Fourth seems fitting."

"Your own radar detectors will let you know if you're being tracked," Mark added confidently. "If you're detected, you'll probably have to come back down and get the hell out of there."

"That brings up another point we haven't discussed," interrupted Max. "Who is going to make this maiden voyage? You, Miss Evans?"

He said her name with just a hint of sarcasm.

"I was planning to go with another member from our group."

"Do either of you have flight experience in extreme conditions," he asked seriously, "under heavy acceleration? It could be dangerous. Some people lose consciousness."

Taylor looked prepared to argue with him but then acquiesced.

"Well," she said. "I definitely don't have any of that kind of experience, but the other guy is a pilot and may have. I'll have to ask him."

"Since I do have that kind of experience, I would like to offer to go with you." Max suggested with blatant hope in his voice. He looked around the room for any objections. "I'm not just saying this because

I want to go, which I obviously do, but because I'm a pretty good pilot and really want to help. I'd honestly hate for you to crash on your way back from a successful flight."

Gerald was impressed that Max would be willing to put his neck on the line like that. Gerald felt no such confidence or courage. "We'll definitely consider your offer," he said before Taylor could object. She sat in silence, in deep thought. She and Max held eye contact for a moment.

"I hope you decide to stay for dinner," Mr. Garner said to break the silence.

"Thanks," Gerald answered and looked at Taylor who seemed relaxed and satisfied. "We'd love to."

FOURTEEN

Helen

The two girls walked up the stairs hand in hand. They entered all the rooms on the upper floor, even the old man's bedroom. Only his room showed any sign of occupancy. Helen started ascending the stairs to the attic or next higher floor, but Daryn stopped her with a silent shake of the head.

"Okay," Helen answered with a shrug. "Let's go downstairs."

Helen heard her mother and the old man talking in the kitchen, so she led Daryn quietly past them to continue their exploration. If the adults heard either of them, the girls would lose the game of spy, as Helen referred to their prowling activity. She pressed her finger to her mouth as a silent shhhh to Daryn who also pressed her own finger to her lips.

The girls found a room on the ground floor with a few desks and many bookshelves full of books. While Helen guarded the door, Daryn searched through all the books for something interesting. She searched for several minutes, failing to find any books for children, so they decided to leave. In the dining room, each girl sat silently at opposite ends of the long table. A vase filled with flowers sat in between them, obscuring their view of each other.

"More wine, mister butler," said Helen, followed by a quiet giggle. She extended her hand, pretending to hold an empty glass.

"What's a butler?" Daryn asked.

"Someone who works in a rich house and brings people stuff."

After the dining room, Daryn wanted to go outside and see the garden and fountains, but Helen wanted to go downstairs to visit Freddy's rooms. She guessed there would be some cool things to see. Daryn capitulated grudgingly.

Downstairs, they first entered a room used for storage. Astronomy charts and different equipment filled the next room with two computers and at least ten different telescopes of different sizes. The screens scrolled through pictures of stars or galaxies, nebulae, and other celestial objects. The girls spent a long time in that room, inspecting and touching everything they could find. Daryn attempted to remind Helen of Mr. Smith's advice not to touch anything, but she eventually stopped after several failed attempts.

They tried logging into his computers but failed to discover the correct passwords. After each failed attempt, their giggling intensified and each girl took turns telling the other to be quiet. For passwords, they tried *panties*, *lollipops*, *Barbie,* and *poop*, but none of those worked.

"Do you think all this stuff is actually in the skies somewhere?" asked Daryn while looking at a picture of a galaxy.

"So maybe someone painted all of it?" Helen asked. "A trick?"

"Mr. Becerra used to draw stuff. He was good but not good enough to draw something to look so real. If it is real, how did it get there?"

Helen touched her chin, looking down at the computer screen.

"Jesus maybe."

"Jesus?" asked Daryn with confusion. "Is that an astronaut?"

"You don't know who Jesus is?" Helen asked incredulously and laughed. "He's kind of like Santa."

"Does he bring presents?"

Helen thought for a moment before answering.

"He brings presents, but they're not real."

"Sounds like Santa to me," Daryn said.

"Do you go on vacations a lot?" Daryn asked in a more serious tone.

"Not much," answered Helen. "Mom works too much, but me and Jen go places sometimes."

"Does your mom like me?"

"Yep," Helen said while typing another password attempt onto the login prompt. "I can tell. Don't worry. You're staying with us."

After becoming bored with the astronomy room, they visited the next room, which looked like a bedroom. Helen slowly opened the door, and they looked inside before entering. The room seemed different from the other ones. They walked into the dark room while leaving the door open. Only a few slivers of light entered the room from the windows.

"Is this Freddy's room?" asked Daryn.

"I guess so," said Helen. "It's huge. I want a room this big."

"You're lucky already, Helen."

For the first time since returning home, Daryn felt like an older sister to Helen. She liked the feeling of being a younger sibling, and then she felt guilty for sounding dissatisfied with something as trivial as the size of her room.

"I know," said Helen, and then noticed the crystal sitting on the table by the bed. The crystal looked familiar, but she could not remember previously seeing the object.

"What is that?" asked Daryn as she followed Helen's gaze to the table.

"I don't know," Helen answered, a feeling of excitement beginning to grow.

Both girls walked slowly to the table. Helen wanted to take the crystal from the table but found herself staring at the spider encased inside.

"It's creepy," Daryn said, afraid to touch the rectangular glass. "I hate spiders. They used to come into my room all the time, and I always had to get rid of them myself."

"I dare you to pick it up," Helen challenged.

Daryn slowly extended her hand and retrieved the crystal from the table. She held the object like a delicate flower, afraid to damage the petals. After several seconds of inspection, the spider's eyes began to glow with blue and orange lights. Neither girl possessed the power to look away from the light, and they became perfectly still. A moment later, Helen turned and silently shut the door.

FIFTEEN

Taylor

Two days after arriving home from Erik Garner's Boston residence, Gerald stopped by the shop. As planned, his friend Mark would be visiting for a few days to see everything, and Gerald wanted to tell Cesar and Taylor the news in person.

"Are you going to be here when he arrives?" Taylor asked. Over the previous two days, she had begun to feel better about including Max and Mark in the group. Once they knew all the dangerous information, it would implicate them with the same crime of scientific advancement.

"I wouldn't miss his face for the world," Gerald said. "When Mark sees my fusion reactor and your engine, he's going to faint."

Taylor smiled whenever Gerald referred to the fusion reactor as his own. She refrained from explaining how she and Cesar had done more work on it than he did and the original credit belonged to the two Mormons in Salt Lake City. *Let him have his fun*, she thought.

Mark arrived with Gerald at Cesar's house at three in the afternoon on Tuesday, May 26th, a beautiful day in the mid-sixties with semi-clear skies. Dominga met them at the door and spent a few minutes getting acquainted in the parlor. Later, Dominga told Taylor about

Mark's excitement and polite attempts to end the conversation so he could go to the shop.

Gerald could only stay at the shop for an hour before he had to leave, but he remained long enough to see Mark's reaction. Taylor had wanted to introduce the nuclear fusion reactor first, and after their guest recovered from that shock, she would show the NMG. Since Gerald had to leave, she had to deliver two knock-out punches in quick succession. Taylor and Cesar enjoyed seeing the reaction from both men, the thrill of discovery from Mark, and Gerald's excitement of watching him.

Gerald led Mark to the nuclear reactor in the middle of the shop and put his hand on it.

"This is our energy source."

"This is going to power your vehicle?" Mark said, laughing nervously. "What is it? A nuclear reactor?"

They answered him with silence. Gerald smiled. Taylor and Cesar waited calmly.

"What is it really?" he asked.

"A nuclear fusion reactor," said Gerald with a hint of pride. "To be more specific."

Mark turned to Taylor.

"What? Did you invent this?" He looked at her as he might look at an angel or a demon.

"No," she answered. "I did not invent it, but our bloodhound Gerald tracked down those who did. It's kind of a long story, and he can tell it best. With this, we'll have enough energy to go almost anywhere."

While Mark inspected the apparatus, Gerald told the condensed version of how he'd found the fusion reactor. He began the story by telling how he tracked down people who knew Eugene Mallove and how he eventually found himself in the place where it all began, Salt Lake City. He refused to give any names, explaining how the real inventors wanted to remain anonymous, for their own safety.

During the story, Mark kept quiet, but Taylor thought she imagined a million questions inflating his head like a balloon. She expected him to react to the idea of low-temperature fusion as the universities taught, with contempt and scorn. Maybe she would have an easy time when she explained her invention.

"What's the catalyst?" he asked. The amazement in his eyes and voice made Taylor smile. "Does it use heavy water for fuel? What's the power output? What levels of radiation are you getting?"

"We can get to all that," Taylor said, laughing and holding up her hand to stop the questions. "Since Gerald has to leave, I want to show you everything, then we can tackle all your questions."

"There's more?" he asked with shock replacing disbelief. "You have a nuclear fusion reactor and something else? I don't believe it. Please tell me it's not some kind of joke!"

Gerald laughed and grabbed Mark's shoulder.

"Calm down, my friend, take a deep breath. We don't want you to have a heart attack when you see what's next."

Taylor took a few steps away from the fusion reactor and stopped at the future engine for their prototype spacecraft. Almost a hundred different wires connected the engine to computers and sensor equipment and larger capacity wiring running back to the fusion reactor. A makeshift stand bolted to the concrete floor securely held the engine in place.

"This is our engine," Taylor said humbly. "It's driven by what I've named the NMG, or the Net Momentum Generator. It's going to take us into space, powered by the reactor of course."

"The NMG?" Mark asked.

"I like complicated things hiding behind simple names," she said and shrugged.

Mark closely inspected the jumble of wires and stainless steel as if looking for something specific. Several times he opened his mouth as if to ask a question, only to shut it again in silence. Finally, he spoke.

"This provides some sort of thrust?"

"Of course," Taylor said with a smug, yet sympathetic smile. "You'll probably need to see a more lively demonstration to understand. I'll go get our little prototype."

After returning from the office, she handed Mark the black box.

"Hold onto this with both hands," she instructed with a devious smile meant for Cesar and Gerald. She remembered Gerald's reaction when she showed it to him at Burgerville.

Taylor flipped the switch and stood back to watch Mark's reaction. His eyes instantly grew wide in amazement.

"What the hell?" he gasped when he felt the once-heavy box suddenly lose much of its weight and quickly become weightless. After a moment, he released the box, and when it started rising, he snatched it from the air in a panic and held it tightly with both hands again. He started feeling all around the surface for some invisible propellant.

"Mark," said Gerald questioningly, "are you still with us?"

"How in the world does it work?" he asked in a whisper, his eyes still on the box.

"It creates net momentum, which is to say, it propels itself without gaining or losing mass."

"But, that's impossible," said Mark, still in a whisper and more to himself than Taylor. "It defies the momentum conservation laws."

"It does just that," said Taylor as though speaking to a child. "And a good thing too. That's just what we need!"

Mark carefully pushed the black box toward Taylor as he would a sleeping cobra, afraid to awaken it. She took it and turned it off.

"No offense, Miss Evans, but this is impossible. I really need to know this isn't some joke."

"Here," Taylor said and pulled a stool away from one of the computers. "You're looking a little pale. Sit down while I try to explain."

"Yes, that's a good idea. I need to sit."

"According to Newton's Laws," Taylor began, suddenly feeling like a high school physics teacher. While facing him, she clenched both hands into fists and held them in the air. "If I hold two identical charged particles a fixed distance apart, the force between them will be exactly equal and opposite. If I let them go, they'll fly apart at exactly equal speeds, and the net momentum of the two particle system will remain unchanged. This is what you know as the conservation of momentum."

"I'm with you," he said, tentative acceptance in his voice.

"Now what happens," she continued, "if some collision moved one of these charged particles toward the other? This is where it gets a little hard to follow, so bear with me. Since the electric field shift, caused by the translated particle, travels at the speed of light, it takes a very short time for the other particle to feel the shifted local field. But the translated particle will experience an immediate increase in field strength from the stationary particle.

"During this brief period, the opposing forces will not be exactly equal. This establishes an imbalanced net force in a particular direction, and momentum conservation would be broken. As a side note, I'm beginning to wonder if the force originates from pushing against space itself, but I haven't figured that part out yet.

"Anyway, all the experiments that I know of, about electric field speed, are at relatively large distances and show that shifts in the electric field move at the speed of light, but I thought that maybe at shorter distances, like on the molecular scale, the speed might be slower. If I could disturb charged particles, such as atoms in a crystal lattice, at an appropriate frequency, I could extract this net momentum in a particular direction."

"Errr..." said Mark, struggling to comprehend the bathtub of logic Taylor had poured over his head. "That makes sense, I guess, but doesn't relativity theory predict the accelerated particle will gain a slightly larger mass, which would offset the force differential?"

"Wow, Mark," Taylor said, trying her best to suppress a sneer. "You're really grasping at straws here. According to relativity theory, both masses would increase by the same amount relative to each other because, at all times, they have the same relative velocity from their respective points of view."

"But one is being accelerated, and the other is not, which makes their reference frame different."

Taylor paused for a moment and took a deep breath, hoping to avoid replying with an angry tone. She would rather not yell at the man she was beginning to like. She forced her lips into an unnatural smile, but despite the effort, her frustration still showed.

"Mark, you're using the same tactic my university professors used against me, trying to unnecessarily complicate a proposition they disagree with, to make me capitulate. It's really very simple. Relativistic mass is based on velocity and only on velocity. Acceleration never enters into it, except to calculate the velocity. As an aside, relativistic mass increase is just one possible interpretation of experimental observations and can be explained with better logic, but I don't want to get into that now. Sorry, I don't mean to get angry."

During her tirade, Mark's eyes had grown wide in astonishment.

"Right now," he said defensively. "I'm still in shock, so I argue because my brain tells me you've got something wrong. I don't mean to doubt you."

"We understand your feelings," said Cesar with an almost imperceptible warning frown to Taylor. "I felt the same way."

"Sorry, but one more question. What about the conservation of energy?" he asked, in one last attempt to validate his former understanding of reality. "You're not saying that energy is being created out of nothing?"

"No, I'm not saying that," Taylor said with relief that he took no offense. "There's no reason why the energy cannot balance. All of my calculations depend on energy balance equations, and most of my models have been very accurate."

Mark made a weak attempt at a smile.

"Well, that's some comfort. I can accept that at least."

"I know why this is so hard to understand. Believe me. Why haven't we heard about any other scientists making this claim? Right?"

"I guess so, yeah."

"Because the conservation of momentum," Cesar interjected, "is such a fundamental building block of science and engineering, that no one ever thinks to question it, because it works. And there's another good reason—it's never been seen broken macroscopically! Statistical mechanics has shown time and time again how random varia-tion tends to average out. Taylor discovered a way to make it non-ran-dom."

"I had two major obstacles in my path," Taylor continued before Mark could generate another question. "First, how to create condi-tions where this kind of net momentum could be generated in signif-icant proportions, and second, how to create conditions to favor a specific direction."

Mark's mouth slowly widened into his first authentic smile during the discussion.

"Okay. So obviously, it works. How did you do it?"

"That's going to require a lot more time to explain," she said, taking a deep breath. "First, let's show you what we plan to put this engine into and what it can do."

—※—

They stayed in the shop until nine that night, answering Mark's ques-tions and explaining all their work and current status and how he could help them. Mark laughed hard after seeing the BMW and learn-ing of their plans to fly it into space.

Taylor found extreme satisfaction in showing the power output of the fusion reactor and how much thrust her engine could produce. Unfortunately, they proved unable to measure the full strength of the engine due to the weakness of the anchors in the cement floor. Taylor looked forward to the test flight when they could realize the full power of her engine. Mark wanted to stay longer in the shop that first day, but Dominga called and demanded they return home for dinner.

"You don't want Dominga angry at you," Taylor said with a smile. "At least not on your first day here."

After returning to Cesar's house, they met Doroteo at the door. He introduced himself and shook Mark's hand. Mark responded with a smile and looked surprised when the unshaven Mexican answered with a frown. Doroteo disappeared for the rest of the evening.

"So you plan on staying for two days?" asked Cesar at the dinner table.

"That's the plan," he said. "I am tempted to go back to the shop tonight and continue where we left off, but my body and mind would probably explode if I didn't get some sleep. It's going to take me all night for my brain to absorb all this. The world seemed normal this morning, but now, it's upside down."

As Cesar showed Mark to his room, Dominga turned to Taylor and spoke in a soft voice. "He seems very genuine, but do you fully trust him? I mean, so many people are becoming involved. I'm beginning to worry for you and Cesar."

Dominga's warning reminded Taylor of her own paranoia after they had kidnapped the FBI agent. When Doroteo promised to monitor any adverse repercussions, Taylor had forgotten her fears and turned her whole attention back to their work. The exhilaration of working with Cesar helped quarantine her unpleasant memories and anxieties.

—※—

In the end, Mark extended his stay by a week and a half, claiming a lack of willpower to let them have all the fun by themselves. Taylor knew his emotional immune system would be unable to withstand the highly contagious pioneering virus. His excitement and interest in their activities gave Taylor and Cesar an extra boost of energy.

To be ready for their July Fourth test flight date, they had to work twelve to eighteen hours a day. Taylor would often get out of bed before five a.m. with an overwhelming desire to visit the shop. She would sneak out of the house before Dominga noticed, skip breakfast then have an extra large lunch. Eventually, Dominga's complaints about their working schedule turned into a daily polite reminder of how their health would soon begin to deteriorate. Despite her extreme feeling of urgency, she had confidence in being ready for the July Fourth deadline.

She called home to her mother every three to four days and felt guilty for not calling more often. Her mother never complained, but Taylor could hear the worry in her voice. After the first few weeks, her mother quit trying to get any information about her daughter's activities. Taylor knew that eventually, her mother's patience would end and she would have to make a visit home or invite her mother to Seattle.

Overall, they were progressing as scheduled and with only a few minor delays. Their most significant setback occurred two days after Mark's arrival when the structural support system for the BMW fractured. They either miscalculated the strength of the NMG or overestimated the strength of the joints and they had to reconstruct their enhanced chassis.

They gutted most of the usual automotive systems in the BMW: the transmission, steering, cooling system, drivetrain, and the engine. Both Taylor and Cesar worked simultaneously on everything, but they each had their specialties. Taylor had more expertise in computer interfacing, so she worked on connecting all the components into the control system. Cesar prepared the power distribution network for all the different systems. Mark helped them incorporate many auxiliary systems such as life support, guidance, and a myriad of various sensors.

In the end, they needed the craft to retain its appearance as a car. When not flying in the sky, they wanted the spacecraft not to cause suspicion on the road. Taylor had only one major concern, the tinting of the windows. Mark explained the obvious reason, to block the intense sunlight, which would easily fry them. She had expected that explanation, but she had not felt prepared to hear the other reason.

"We also have to add this special fluorescent layer," Mark had said, "so you'll be able to see the stars. Without some attenuation, our eyes are not sensitive to their frequencies."

The shock of hearing such a statement reminded Taylor of how much she loved working with people like Mark and Cesar. They had many things to teach her.

That night, Taylor dreamed of their initial flight. In some dreams, she shot into the sky with Cesar, sometimes with Doroteo or Max, and once with her mother. In the dream with her mother, she gave Taylor flying directions from the back seat. They never made it all the way out of the atmosphere. After waking, she felt cheated.

Even in dreams, her father was still dead, and her dreams felt a little empty without him there. She attributed many of her accomplishments to his credit. More than anyone, her father would have enjoyed being with her on the trip.

SIXTEEN

Taylor

After a shorter-than-usual day at the shop, they went home for one of Dominga's more elaborate meals. Even though Taylor felt mentally exhausted, she liked to help in the kitchen whenever possible. Taylor found those times with Dominga to be very therapeutic, where her mind could take a break from engineering issues.

While a pot roast baked in the oven, Taylor stirred the pot of gravy as it boiled on the stove. She waited in anticipation for the liquid to transform into a highly viscous state and listened to Dominga talk about how her mother had taught her how to make gravy as a very little girl. The smell of chopped cilantro, parsley, and tomatoes mixed with the moist smell of gravy. The aroma started to make her very hungry. She turned around at one moment and put her hand to her mouth.

"Oh, my goodness," she began. "I forgot to tell you."

"What?"

When Dominga asked them to come home early for dinner that day, Taylor did not think to question her. For the past five to seven nights, they worked very late and came home to a cold meal. Both she and Cesar were expecting the demand.

"Mr. Foster is coming for dinner," Dominga said with a mock look of regret. "He said he had something important to discuss."

"Don't worry about it," Taylor smiled. "Did he give any specifics?"

Gerald had called that morning and told Dominga about his visit, but the call lasted only a few seconds, and she got distracted when she and Doroteo continued the argument of that morning.

Dominga relayed how he had accused Gerald and all citizens of the United States of being too impatient, but the complaints soon included stupidity, laziness, and spinelessness. As usual, Dominga had defended them. Taylor had witnessed some of the arguments and found them amusing.

Gerald arrived a few minutes before the food was ready. When Taylor and Dominga delivered the food to the dining room, Gerald turned from his conversation with Cesar and gave her a determined look, which meant official business. He did not look angry, just serious.

"Hi, Gerald," Taylor said with a smile. "I'm glad you can join us for dinner. What exciting news do you have for us?"

"I've actually got some stories to tell you," he said, looking at each of them in turn. "I'll tell you about it while we have dinner. And thanks for the invitation, Dominga. I haven't had a home-cooked meal for a long time, well, since the last time I visited."

"Oh, you poor thing," Dominga said. "You are always welcome here. You can even just drop in, anytime."

Before beginning his story, he took a couple of bites of pot roast then put his fork on his plate, sighing in contentment.

"I've been trying to decide how to tell you all for quite a while now. What I have to tell you will be a hard pill to swallow, so I'll just dump it on you all at once. Here it goes and hold your questions for when I'm done."

"Sadi Jacobsen has a friend named Freddy Carlson, a very special young man. He's maybe a little younger than you, Taylor, but very intelligent. I think he's got Asperger's syndrome or something. There's something else about him that you need to know."

During the pause, Doroteo interrupted him.

"So, you did not seek him out?"

"No," he answered. "Freddy went to Sadi and showed her something, and she thought it had to do with us, so she called me. This was back in April."

Taylor fought the urge to yell at him for keeping a secret from them, but then she remembered kidnapping Agent Pratt and how they kept it from Gerald. They decided to keep it to themselves to protect him, and she supposed he had done the same thing for them.

He first told them about an incident at a barn where he, Sadi, and the boy's employer had seen some alien probe. At the barn, the alien probe had placed him and the others in a trance and made them hallucinate, some test he assumed, to see their reactions. He claimed to have failed the test.

When pressed by Doroteo to give the details of the test, Gerald seemed to squirm in his seat.

"Leave him be," scolded Dominga with an angry glance at Doroteo. She placed her hand on Gerald's shoulder. "Don't listen to Doroteo. If it's personal, you don't have to tell us."

Taylor glanced at Doroteo, looking for any signs of a rebuttal. Fortunately, he decided to obey the woman. Taylor was relieved to escape the potentially long detour. She had a ton of questions and would rather not witness another power struggle between Doroteo and Dominga.

"Do you think it was an alien probe?" asked Cesar.

"I know it sounds crazy, but that's the only rational explanation. There's no technology that can do that, is there?"

His story felt too unbelievable to Taylor, but she decided to believe him for now, at least she would believe in Gerald's sincerity. He could be a victim of psychological manipulation. Usually, she felt confident in handling any situation, but in this case, she felt like a fish trying to swim in thick mud. She decided to ask her question with only a small attempt at tact.

"I don't mean to sound insulting Gerald, but I have to ask it. Could you have possibly been influenced by some drug?"

While finishing his mouthful of food, he shook his head. If Gerald was insulted, he hid it well.

"We considered that, but it cannot explain what happened. We were actually there. Like I said, we hallucinated some of the experience but not the space probe, not the bears, and definitely not the lights from that crystal thing."

"Why a spider?" asked Doroteo. "That could be a clue to understanding what we're dealing with."

"It has something to do with the kid. He has an infatuation with spiders."

"I can't believe that I'm asking this," Doroteo said incredulously, "but do you think the boy knows what the alien wants?"

"He claims not to know," Gerald said, then cleared his throat. He seemed uncomfortable with what he had to say next. "But he suspects the alien wants us to take him to something by the sun, or Mercury, I can't remember exactly. I'll let him come and talk to you himself, but that's what I think we should do next. I wanted to give you the story first."

"Holy shit, Gerald," Taylor said. "You think we should let him take our vehicle to Mercury?"

"No need to swear at me," Gerald said with genuine hurt and a hint of anger in his voice, the first time she heard him respond to her like that. "I've kept this all to myself for a long time, and it's really making my blood pressure skyrocket. There's more I've had to deal with too, so please keep your anger to yourself until after you hear the next bit, the worst part."

Taylor instantly regretted showing her anger but decided to save her apology until later. She had no idea Gerald could be angry at her.

Before continuing, the anxiety in his scowl disappeared and changed to a forced look of concentration. His next story about the kidnapping of the biologist's daughter brought chills to Taylor's spine. Shortly after describing what happened, Dominga set her fork loudly on her plate.

"That is horrible," Dominga said, covering her mouth with her hand. Cesar and Doroteo sat forward in their seats, their four intense black eyes attempting to suck the light from the room. Taylor could only suspect what kind of emotions the subject of kidnapping had on them, Cesar especially.

After a moment, Gerald continued. He told of how they had hired a very experienced private investigator to find the little girl. Doroteo silently nodded in approval and Taylor wondered if the man felt hurt that they failed to call him.

Cesar's eyes glistened with unfallen tears when Gerald explained how Freddy rescued the children. Taylor also felt relief for the safe return of the victims but more shock at Freddy's tactics and luck.

"After the barn incident, the alien gave the boy the ability to sense what others were feeling, and that helped him rescue the girls." Gerald explained the young man's abilities almost as an afterthought. "For the time being, the other little girl is staying with Sadi. We're trying to figure out how to deal with the situation."

After Gerald finished, each member of his audience sat in silent reflection.

"That was too much of a coincidence," said Doroteo, breaking the silence. "An alien contacts you and then the woman's daughter goes missing. I do not think this alien, or whatever it is, can be trusted."

"None of us got the impression of ill will from it," said Gerald, somewhat defensively.

"How are the mother and daughter now?" asked Cesar. "Yes, you are right. They must visit us immediately. How is their recovery going?"

"They seem to be doing okay, but of course she's still shaken up. I don't know how she'll be in the long run though."

"Of course, this poses a problem for the woman and for us," Doroteo interjected, bringing the subject back to his original intent. "It was a smart move to keep the girl, but what will Sadi do when someone notices that she has another daughter, and she will probably be on some missing persons list, and those boys are going to be found eventually."

"Doroteo," Gerald began and smiled deviously. "You underestimate me. Someone is working on identifying her. Once we have her background, it'll be easier to make something look legitimate."

Doroteo answered with a snort.

"The people this boy killed, their employers will be looking for him. It does not sound like a small operation. Dangerous people are involved, people who cannot stand the thought of losing control. It is naïve to expect that they will not follow the trail to its end."

His words appeared to stab Gerald in the heart, and his confident smile seemed shaken. His overly optimistic attitude might have gotten the best of him, but with Doroteo and Cesar able to help, Taylor felt they had a better chance of eluding the authorities.

"Freddy's employer has his private investigator following the case. They seem to have faith in him." Gerald addressed Doroteo. "If you want, I can put you in contact with them."

"Perhaps," Doroteo answered. "Who is this old man that employs the boy?"

"He's kind of famous. His name is Bill Smith. He was the..."

"The former Secretary of Agriculture?" Cesar said in shock. "Oh my God! First, you recruit the son of a big banker and now this ex-government official!"

"Like I said," Gerald said defensively. "They came to us. He's pretty sharp, and I don't think we need to worry about him. He knows about everything. I did not..."

"Thanks for telling us," Taylor said sarcastically before she could stop herself. She put her fork down loudly on the table, and the metallic tone caused everyone to look at her. All of the news had put her into a state of information overload. Aliens, kidnappings, and now another high-profile person knew about their group. She felt as though all of their work would soon come crashing down on their heads.

Gerald no longer appeared affected by her anger, as though he expected it.

"Taylor," he began calmly and looked at each of them in turn. "I know you can all appreciate the enormity of my news. Much of the events were out of my influence. I came to you when I could deliver the information into a package that made sense."

"Well," Dominga said loudly before Taylor could make another angry reply. "I think it's time to arrange a meeting with this woman and young man and his employer."

Taylor was frustrated at being interrupted but soon thankful for the diplomat in the group. She admitted reluctantly that in Gerald's position, she might have done the same thing.

—※—

The rest of the evening, they discussed the topic of a group meeting. They argued about the wisdom of inviting Franklin Harvey, their website administrator, but tentatively decided to include him. He thrived on the idea of space travel and alien contact. They all agreed on inviting Sadi, Freddy, and Mr. Smith. Gerald wanted to invite Mark and Max to the meeting, but Taylor did not like that option. She trusted Mark and Max's grandfather, just not Max. In her opinion, they did not need to know more at that time.

The possibility of extraterrestrial contact had completely changed the situation for all of them. How would Max and Mark react to alien contact? Would they feel the need to contact the authorities out of some sense of national security? Or, as she suspected, would Max consider it a way to enrich himself? Is that how he saw their group? Ultra-rich people like them often viewed life in terms of financial rather than emotional investments.

Gerald wanted to arrange the meeting for that Friday or Saturday, June 5th or 6th. After he left the house that night, they all sat up talking for a couple more hours. Cesar started the conversation by gently reminding Taylor about how they still had not told Gerald about the FBI agent abduction.

"I know," Taylor said with a sigh. "I did not mean to be so angry at him. I'll apologize later."

When they eventually told him about the abduction, it would be his turn to be angry at her. Maybe she would include that with her apology.

Initially, the idea of alien contact both excited and frightened Taylor. But as more time passed, fear began to replace the excitement. Judging from the others' reactions, she suspected the same from them.

She always thought alien contact would be one of the most exciting things to happen. Exploring the unknown always fascinated her, but the darkness of the unknown gave humans more fear and anxiety than probably anything else. In a futile attempt to rationally explain the situation, she almost wished that they would discover it to be a trick of the government. Unconsciously, however, she refused to accept that possibility. She could not imagine anyone affiliated with the government or military having that capability.

That night, terrifying aliens filled Taylor's dreams, beings who put people in suspended animation and transported them to their home worlds for display and experimentation. Taylor hung frozen in a museum with writhing, fearsome creatures staring at her and preparing to poke her with long, sticky fingers.

SEVENTEEN

Sadi

Sadi let the girls explore the estate for almost two hours. When she finally felt ready to leave and began looking for them, she searched the upper level, the ground floor then outside but could not find them. After calling down the stairs to the lower level and receiving no response, she felt a panic similar to when she learned of Helen's abduction. Before taking the first step to the lower level, she took a deep breath to calm herself.

"Helen, Daryn," she called again while descending the stairs. "Are you down here? It's time to go."

Again, she heard no response, so she walked to Freddy's room and heard the girls talking from inside. She felt instant relief at the sound of their voices but paused before opening the door. The situation reminded her of the first time she visited the house to help find Freddy when they had entered his room and then awoke in the car.

"Girls," she said after grasping the door handle. "It's time to go."

"Hi, Mom," Helen yelled through the door. "We're in here."

"Helen, why didn't you answer me when I called?" she asked once inside the room. She saw the girls on the other side of the room, their attention on a microscope sitting on a table.

"Sorry, Mom," said Helen after turning to face her mother, "we didn't hear you."

"Come on. It's time to go. Hurry and put back Freddy's things where you found them. I want each of you to thank Mr. Smith for letting you explore his home. If you're nice, I'm sure he'll have us over again. Would you like that?"

"Oh definitely, Mother," Helen said with a straight face, and then the girls silently followed Sadi back up the stairs. They met Mr. Smith at the front door.

"Come back and visit us when your vacation's over," Mr. Smith said. He patted each girl on the back. "Freddy would very much like to see you all again."

"Tell him we visited," Sadi said.

"I won't have to tell him anything," he said gravely. "Freddy will know."

On the remainder of their drive to the coast, Sadi's body and mind continued to relax. Before going to the beach, Sadi planned to take the girls on all the rides in downtown Seaside, Oregon, but both girls insisted on going to the beach first. Sadi was excited to witness Daryn's reaction to the ocean and watch her play in the sand. From the look on her daughter's face, Helen appeared just as excited for her new, older sister.

When they finally reached Seaside, Sadi found a space to park in the public parking lot off Oceanway Street, and then she walked with the girls down Broadway Street to the turnaround, the historic landmark for the end of the Lewis and Clark Trail. The girls did not even glance at the statue, but Daryn gasped while seeing the ocean for the first time. Sadi smiled wide, excited to see what the girl would do.

"Can we go touch it, Miss Jacobsen?" Daryn pleaded when they reached the top of the stairs leading from the road to the sand. As the ocean breeze blew the cold, salty air in their faces, the chill did not seem to affect the girls.

"Yes, just be careful. The water is really cold, and the waves can carry you out to sea if you go too far out."

After reaching the bottom of the cement stairs and touching the sand, Sadi said they could run ahead of her. When Daryn reached the water, she looked back at Sadi, seeking final permission. Sadi nodded, eyes wide.

"Come on," Helen said after grabbing her hand. "We'll go in together."

Sadi followed the girls into the water, wincing when the ice-cold wave engulfed her feet and ankles, draining all their warmth. The cold shock seemed to awaken all of her senses at once. After several seconds, her feet became numb to the cold, and she turned her attention from the beach to the horizon beyond the waves.

While the girls played in the water, Sadi imagined traveling across the ocean and finding a new home, somewhere other than Russia, China, or Australia. The endless expanse of water seemed like the doorway into a new life.

PART II

INNER SPACE

Enjoy that lofty place
Above the clouds
And then that final race

EIGHTEEN

Gerald

Gerald arrived at Cesar's home on Saturday, June 6th at two o'clock in the afternoon, thirty minutes before Franklin, Mr. Smith, Freddy, and Sadi arrived. Just in case someone followed them, Doroteo arranged for the Portland group to meet Franklin at his apartment first and then drive to Cesar's place together. Doroteo feared the possibility of the police or FBI connecting Sadi to the kidnapping fiasco. He wanted to be at Franklin's apartment when they arrived to watch for any evidence of police monitoring activity.

Before the meeting, Franklin told Gerald that he wanted to ask Freddy about the strange things happening to him. Gerald warned him to avoid talking about the kidnapping around Sadi. He did not want to risk opening any emotional wounds in the process of healing. Since they both had an interest in technology and science and were of similar age, Gerald thought Freddy and Franklin might become friends. Franklin had a pleasant personality and seemed to interact well with most people. With everyone focused on Freddy in the meeting, Franklin might even help him feel more at ease.

Ever since the kidnapping, Gerald realized and accepted the growing connection he felt to Sadi, even though the relationship was also dangerous. Could he be trusted to make rational decisions when other, less rational motivations fought for control? Would there come a time when he would feel compelled to show Sadi preference to the detriment of the group?

He had noticed the evident feelings Freddy had for her. Since the kid had the power to know other's feelings, Gerald had to guard his thoughts carefully when around them both. Would Freddy be jealous? Since he saved her daughter's life, did Sadi feel an obligation to return his affections? At present, he had no reason to consider the kid as dangerous, but he had the motive.

Sometimes he wondered about the wisdom of his decision to bring Sadi into the group. When he first met her, he felt an instant attraction but tried to ignore his emotional reaction and focus on her professional expertise. After starting the venture with Taylor, he wanted to gather a small team with members from different educational backgrounds.

Gerald had plenty of experience with physical attraction for beautiful women, but when out of their presence, he could easily resume his previous activities. The experience was completely different with Sadi. Whenever they parted, he had difficulty focusing on other things. Sadi refused to leave his mind.

When he and Taylor initially made their plans, they had slightly different visions. In his opinion, Taylor looked at the situation from too practical of a perspective. She wanted to start working on her engine and develop it for space travel. She saw the present task at hand in perfect clarity, but the end result of her actions was often more blurry. Gerald always tried to keep his focus on the big picture, gaining freedom for himself and his friends.

To his great surprise and delight, all the right ingredients had come together: propulsion, energy, money. Despite his optimistic attitude, he never expected to have such success, so early. Now with the possible alien involvement, Gerald began to wonder if they could travel to another world. The reality of that possibility scared him, more than it gave him excitement. On Earth, he knew the identity of his enemies and their motivations. What could motivate the alien, and how would they know for sure? He usually had confidence in his ability to weigh the risks of a venture. The alien had destroyed his confidence.

After Gerald had introduced Taylor to Cesar and his house guests, he invited another one of his close friends into the group, a German woman named Gerda Schreiber. She came to the United States after retiring from her position as a professor of botany at a German university. Gerald met her at a libertarian party function in Seattle. Her analytical personality instantly drew him to her.

At first glance, she seemed too severe and unapproachable, with bright blue eyes always half-shut as if peering intently at something. Her tight facial muscles and strict intensity reminded Gerald of the stereotypical nun in a Catholic school. She had blond hair streaked with gray, pulled back into a tight ponytail, and often used her small and pointed nose to indicate the direction for her listeners to focus their attention.

Gerda had arrived earlier that morning before Gerald arrived and introduced herself to Dominga and Cesar. When Gerald arrived, she was sharing her story about how she came to live in the United States.

"My daughter-in-law didn't like what they were teaching their kids in school," she said with a frown and heavy German accent. "She wanted to teach her own children rather than have them go to public school. If you didn't know, this is illegal in Germany."

Gerald and Taylor already knew Gerda's history, so they watched the others giving the older woman their full attention. As Gerald expected, the two non-native English speakers strained to understand the hard accent, especially Dominga. They sat forward in their seats.

"My son and his wife were very disturbed by this," she continued. "When they told me they were going to America, so they could have more freedom, I was in shock. Never in my life had I given freedom a second thought. I never questioned our wonderful German system, which protected us and kept us free. I thought only the poorer countries lacked real freedom."

"How did Gerald convince you to consider joining this group?"

asked Cesar.

As she answered his question, her eyes opened wider and the blue filled her face with color.

"Of course, I believe in what you're doing and what you want to accomplish," she began, "but when Gerald mentioned going into orbit and possibly spending significant time there, my mind became filled with all the experiments I could perform on plant growth in an environment of limited gravity and artificial atmosphere. As a botanist, this area of research has always interested me, and I wanted to be part of it."

"That possibility may be far in the future," said Taylor, shaking her head, "or never come at all."

"It is a slim chance, I'll admit," Gerda said, turning her attention to Taylor. "But like I said, I believe in the overall goal, freedom, for my son and me and his family. Even if there's a slim chance, I think it's worth the effort."

"You're right," said Taylor. "It's just easy to be skeptical."

"Yes, it is," Gerda agreed, "but I thought the goal was hopeless until Gerald told me about your plans."

"So did I," said Cesar. "Our amazing young woman here has given us something to work toward."

—※—

Before the other guests arrived, Gerda acted like a college professor and led the group discussion as though it was a lecture. She restricted the conversation to the implications of permanently incorporating the NMG and fusion reactor into society. Gerald congratulated himself again for adding the woman to the group.

When the Portland group arrived with Franklin, Gerald introduced them first to Dominga. Sadi entered first, followed by Mr. Smith holding onto her arm for support. Helen followed her mother with Daryn by her side. Instead of making eye contact with any of the adults, the young girls inspected their new surroundings like little explorers. Dominga immediately crouched down on their level and forced them to make eye contact with her.

"Oh my goodness," she said in an exaggerated accent, placing her hand on their shoulders. "What little angels! It is an honor!"

Freddy stepped into the home last, after the computer expert, Franklin, who quickly greeted Dominga with a shy smile and made room for Freddy to enter. When Freddy saw Dominga standing in the doorway to greet him, his smile almost vanished, and he appeared anxious.

"And this is Freddy Carlson," said Gerald.

"It is so good to meet you, Mr. Carlson," Dominga said, extending her hand. Gerald thought her movement caused some trepidation as if she expected Freddy to bite her hand. Gerald wondered if he should have told her about Freddy's telepathic abilities. But despite her apprehension, she acted as charming as ever. "We have heard very interesting things about you."

"It is good to meet you too," said Freddy, somewhat awkwardly.

Only Doroteo failed to make an appearance. Cesar told Gerald and Taylor that they could start without him.

"He's out there somewhere, making sure nothing suspicious is going on."

Knowing that Doroteo lurked outside, watching from the shadows, helped Gerald feel more at ease. He was more comfortable out of the man's presence anyway.

Before the group situated themselves in the parlor, Dominga convinced Sadi to let her take the two girls to a nearby room where they could watch a movie and play games. "We should be able to hear them," she said in reassurance. Reluctantly, Sadi let them go, and Gerald noticed her watching them leave.

The parlor accommodated the entire group with room to spare. After the introductions, they all sat in uncomfortable silence for a few seconds. Mr. Smith looked prepared to start the conversation, but Cesar beat the older man to it.

"Since this is my house, it's probably best for me to welcome everyone here," Cesar said and paused to look at each of his guests in turn. Gerald thought he looked extremely comfortable addressing many people in such an intimate setting and he found it easy to imagine the man as the mayor of a major Mexican city, at a press conference with hundreds of photographers facing him and the news cameras recording his every move. His eyes finally rested on Taylor, and he smiled. "I'm glad to host this event, but I don't want to take any credit for what we're all doing here. I think we should start with what you all probably want to do, listen to what Taylor has to say."

Taylor looked more stunning than usual with her dark red hair pulled back and a few wisps falling over her pale forehead. Her confidence seemed to outshine the beauty of her features. Gerald appreciated her appearance, but his heart beat faster whenever he looked at Sadi sitting next to him.

"Actually," Taylor said and paused to prepare the rest of her thoughts. "I thought that I should probably answer any questions that you have?"

"Can we all have a demonstration of the device you created?" asked Mr. Smith before anyone could speak. Gerald thought he heard a skeptical tone to his voice. Everyone else who had not seen it yet nodded, but they seemed more excited than doubtful.

"I knew someone would ask that," Taylor said with a smile.

"Don't get up, Taylor," said Cesar who stood and left the room. After a few seconds, he returned with the black box, their prototype. Gerald felt his lips stretch into an automatic smile.

When the box started levitating, everyone gasped in surprise. Even Mr. Smith's eyes grew wide, but he failed to smile like the rest of them. Gerda clasped her hands together and said something in German.

"Wow," said Sadi quietly at Gerald's side. He turned to her and nodded slightly.

"Anyone want to hold it for themselves to see that it's not a trick?" Taylor asked.

Most people in the circle turned to their neighbors, waiting politely for others to make the request. Mr. Smith raised his hand first. He started to rise, but Freddy jumped up from his seat and carefully took the box from Taylor. While the NMG prototype was still energized, Freddy carried it to his employer, a look of wonder in his eyes. Would it ever become a historical artifact, kept in a museum, Gerald wondered.

After handing the box to Mr. Smith and feeling it for himself, the old man finally smiled.

"This is unbelievable," he said with contradictory acceptance in his voice. "I am sorry for doubting you, Miss Taylor, but I had to see it for myself."

When the NMG device finally returned to its creator, she regained control of the conversation. "This is just a prototype," she said. "Cesar and I have been making a working model. And this is just half of it. Due to Gerald's investigative prowess, we now have an energy source powerful enough to take us into space, hopefully undetected by the military. When Cesar and I are done putting the craft all together, we can go anywhere in the solar system."

"If you don't mind my asking," said Mr. Smith in a friendly tone of curiosity. "Will you or someone clarify what you intend to accomplish with these advancements?"

"Gerald is the best one to make that explanation." Taylor changed her tone to one of mock disinterest. "I just like to make things."

"When Taylor came to me with her invention," Gerald said. "She wanted to share it with the world, and at the same time gain the financial rewards she deserves."

"That she earned," Gerda interjected.

"And you realized they would never let you have it," Mr. Smith said with a strange regret in his voice as if he felt partly responsible.

"Yes, that's right," Gerald said. "How do we get it out, without getting killed? That was the big question. If they caught us before we let the world know, it would be the end. We had to find a way to escape their grasp, and space is the only place they do not control, yet."

"Thanks for clarifying. I think it is a very noble aspiration." The old man's shaking voice seemed weak but filled with confidence. "But I hope you all can appreciate the danger of that goal! When the world has much easier access to energy and the ability to travel in space, local independence will result, and centralized control will be much more difficult to maintain. That is why those holding the power will stop at nothing to assure your failure."

When he finished speaking, he sat back in his seat, his eyes challenging anyone to disagree with him. The silence in the room felt like a living thing. For the first time, Gerald noticed the sound of a movie playing in the other room.

"As far as I see the situation," said Gerda, breaking the silence. "We are all willing to take that risk, for the overall goal of producing a free society, for ourselves and our children."

"Unfortunately," Gerald said and turned to Freddy. "The situation is no longer as simple. We need to discuss the reason why Freddy is involved with our group. He is the one that I did not seek out, but he found us. What's been happening to him and Sadi and how it affects us all is the reason why I called this meeting. What we've been talking about is the straightforward part, I'm afraid."

"I think it would be easier for everyone if they heard the story first from you," Freddy said. "Someone they know."

"You're probably right," Gerald said.

In the next moment, Doroteo appeared in the hallway. He slowly walked to the small gathering and waited. All eyes turned to the unshaven man standing over them like a dark shadow.

Gerald stood before Cesar could and introduced the newcomer to everyone. Doroteo nodded impassively at each of them, holding eye contact with Freddy longer than the rest. To Gerald's surprise, Freddy maintained eye contact until Doroteo turned and sat in a chair by Cesar, on the other side of Dominga. He leaned toward Cesar and whispered in his ear. Cesar nodded almost imperceptibly.

Before Gerald revealed the barn and kidnapping incidents, he told about Max and TerraWatch but without giving specific names. No one became angry at him, as Taylor had, for contacting his friend Mark and what happened afterward. They all showed concern, especially Mr. Smith.

Franklin spoke for the first time.

"Okay, so this CEO is the one who found out about us on his own?" he asked. "He's the one who hired a private detective to follow me?"

"Yes," Gerald answered and Franklin smiled with a look of self-importance. "We visited with him and his Grandfather, and even Taylor feels good about them."

"I trust your friend," Taylor said. "But they're both absent today because I don't completely trust his employer."

"So tell us about what happened to Freddy," Franklin said. He seemed oblivious to the concern in Taylor's voice. "I couldn't get him to tell me on the ride over here."

"Okay, Franklin, that requires some background." Gerald shifted his position to better face Sadi sitting next to him. "I wanted someone from different fields of study working with us and wanted an expert in human biology..."

"Biochemistry and immunology," Sadi corrected, and her polite smile caught him off guard.

"And so I asked some friends of mine, some libertarian friends, if they knew of anyone. I told them I needed a consultant for one of my clients. It turned out that I only needed to ask Gerda because her son knew of someone. He lives in Portland and has a mutual friend who works with Sadi. Anyway, Gerda put me in touch with her, and here we are."

"I'm very sorry, my dear," Gerda said sadly, nodding toward Sadi with her pointy nose. "Maybe I should have kept my mouth shut."

Sadi nodded briefly in appreciation for the comment, then turned back to Gerald.

"After communicating with her through email," Gerald said quickly before Sadi could become emotional. "I decided to introduce her to the group. After she decided to become involved, Freddy, an old friend of hers contacted her and delivered some unusual news."

Gerald briefly told them about Freddy's crystal and how lights came out of it, which put him in a trance. He explained how Freddy thought it somehow related to Sadi and how Sadi brought it to Gerald's attention, thinking it related to the group and not knowing what else to do with the information. At that point, Gerald turned to Freddy and all eyes focused on the young man who looked extremely uncomfortable in the spotlight.

"Freddy, did you bring the crystal?"

"Yes, should I show everyone?"

"Only if you think it's safe."

NINETEEN

Gerald

Freddy retrieved the crystal from his pocket and brought it into everyone's view. He held it vertically to show the flat spider inside.

"So lights came out of this thing?" Gerda asked. "Can I hold it?"

"Yes," Freddy said, handing it to Mr. Smith who passed it to Gerda. "Just do not look too closely at the eyes."

Before continuing, Gerald allowed time for Gerda and everyone else to hold the crystal. To his surprise, no one asked any further questions about it, not even Doroteo. After less than a minute, the crystal returned to Freddy's possession and he held it in his hands on his lap.

"That was just the start," Gerald continued as if uninterrupted.

Everyone listened to the story of the barn incident, confusion and uncertainty apparent in their expressions. While speaking, Gerald made the conscious effort to sound as if he was describing a real event, rather than a horror movie. When he told about how they ran from a light in the woods, he noticed Taylor and Dominga exchange concerned glances. After telling them about the probe hovering directly in front of his face, the memory caused Gerald to shiver.

"Oh my God," said Franklin, sitting up straighter in his seat and looking around at the others. "What do you think it was? An alien?

That is awesome!"

"That's the only logical explanation," said Mr. Smith in an analytical tone. "I wouldn't have believed it, but the three of us had the same experience. That contraption was not from Earth."

Mr. Smith's fragile voice left the room in silence. Sadi was nodding in agreement.

"So what is that thing you have, Freddy?" Gerda asked. "Did the alien make it? How did you get it? Can I see it again?"

Freddy reluctantly passed the crystal to the older woman and then told his story about how he had acquired it. He included his experiences of the crystal putting him into a trance-like state and briefly explained how the alien communicated with him in the form of a woman.

Gerald had a sudden doubt about Freddy's story. *What is he not telling us?* Immediately after he asked himself that question, Freddy paused in his explanation to look at Gerald.

Gerald gulped. *He knows what I'm thinking. And now he knows that I know he knows.*

To Gerald's relief, Freddy returned his attention to the group

"I do not know why she wanted me to find you," he said. "She told me nothing about her reasons. She thought it would be more fun that way."

"If I remember correctly," Gerda said, aiming her pointy nose at Freddy and then Sadi. "The alien told you to seek Sadi, and she chose to bring the information to Gerald?"

"You are correct," Freddy said.

"It was too much of a coincidence," Sadi said somewhat defensively. "Immediately after I received Gerald's invitation to join you, Freddy contacts me and tells me he needs to see me, and we haven't seen each other for several years. When I saw that crystal thing and his video of how it put him in a trance, I had to ask Gerald what he thought, then Freddy went missing, and we went to that barn and saw that thing."

"I understand your motivations," Gerda said in a softer tone. "I did not mean to accuse you."

"We are where we are," said Mr. Smith. "I believe Miss Jacobsen made a reasonable decision. This alien, or whatever it is, wanted us to find you all, for good or bad."

"Agreed," Gerald said quickly, an attempt to bring the conversation back under his control. "No one is accusing anyone of anything. We have to determine what it wants. And what it is. It had to come from somewhere that supports life, somewhere else."

"Not necessarily," Gerda said. "It would be a mistake to believe all life is organic, or something we can understand. It's also unwise to assume an origination point."

"That probe seemed to be testing us," said Mr. Smith. "I don't know what it showed Sadi or Gerald, but it wanted to see how I reacted in a very emotional and personal situation. I did not feel any danger from it, but that's not to say I trust it."

"Maybe it's just trying to learn more about us?" ventured Dominga.

"Has it shown any signs of hostility?" asked Doroteo. "We cannot let our feelings cloud our judgment."

"We know what it could have done," began Sadi. She had crossed her legs and held both hands on her right knee. "It could have easily killed us at the barn, or on our way to the barn. It also protected us from those government agents."

"Yes. It could have made us do anything," Freddy said and nodded in agreement.

"We would be stupid to trust it, no matter how much it seemed to help you." Doroteo looked directly at Freddy and then Sadi.

"I do not know its intentions," Freddy countered. "But there is not much we can do to oppose its will."

"That's a good point," Gerald began before Doroteo could respond. "So what are our options?"

He did not wait for someone to answer.

"Option A, assume the alien wishes to assist us, in which case we should continue with our plans and expect good things to happen, or option B, assume antagonistic motivations. If that's the case, I don't know how to proceed, unless we can think of a way to stop it."

"Freddy," Doroteo said, sounding less accusatory. "It's a bad idea to have that crystal while we are discussing things. Has that thing been with you during all of the anomalies?"

"Not all of them," he said with an embarrassed smile. "I was led to the barn without the crystal."

"That's right," Gerald said quickly, hoping to cover his thoughts with his spoken words. "We had it when I drove to the barn. Do you think it's listening to us now, Freddy?"

"I think," he said and paused for reflection, "that it can hear what I hear, maybe not at this moment, but it can access my memories when it wants. Maybe I should not be here."

Doroteo nodded his head in agreement, evidently impressed with Freddy's answer.

"That is a very good suggestion, but before you leave, we need to know everything you can tell us. What can we say of its actions? Did it decide to make us aware of its existence, or did it happen by chance?"

"Perhaps it discovered you all by accident," Freddy said. "but it sought me out on purpose."

Cesar sat forward in his seat.

"That's an interesting thought, Freddy. Maybe when Taylor had her inspiration, it gave her the idea to contact Gerald, because it knew he would seek my assistance. And then it somehow made Max aware through Gerald's friend Mark."

"What are you saying?" Taylor asked, her eyes narrow slits.

"I'm saying," Cesar answered with a smile that Gerald recognized as an attempt to placate her. "If it discovered you and the NMG, maybe it's responsible for giving you all the necessary resources to develop it."

"There is something else I have not told you," Freddy said, pausing as if he did not know how to proceed. While looking at the ground, he brushed white hair from his forehead. "I recently had another dream or vision with the alien. She showed me a structure on a planet or asteroid near the sun, where it wanted me to go."

"Mercury?" Gerda asked.

"Probably."

"Is that where this thing lives?" she asked.

"I do not think so," Freddy answered. "A kind of black hole came out of the structure and we flew into it."

"Interesting," Gerda said, staring at Freddy for a long time before continuing. "Have we encountered incorporeal life? Has it created an entrance to the intangible?"

No one responded and Gerald felt as though her words had cast a shadow on the room.

"You flew into a black hole?" he asked. "What did it feel like?"

Freddy was looking at the ground again, deep in thought. He answered without looking up.

"Not a black hole, as you understand the term, but more like a hole in space. After crashing through it, I felt heat and woke up extremely thirsty. It is hard to describe."

"I knew it," Franklin said excitedly. "It wants our water, like on that show *V*."

Although Franklin's eyes suddenly looked cold and severe, he seemed undisturbed by the idea.

"Are you sure they don't want your blood?" Taylor asked sarcastically.

"Hey," he said defensively. "We've got little evidence to base our judgment on, so it's something to consider."

Franklin stared at Taylor as if slightly offended. She returned the look with a smirk, almost playfully.

Doroteo ignored them both.

"And that's the last thing you remember?" he asked.

"Yes."

"How do you know it wants you to go? How did it tell you?"

"She did not tell me in words," Freddy answered, "but she does want me to go there."

"Does it just want you? If it only wants you, then why involve us? It cannot transport you there on its own?"

"I do not know," Freddy said.

"Can we talk to it through this crystal?" asked Doroteo.

That possibility scared Gerald but seemed just another option to Doroteo.

"You can try, but I think it will not answer you."

"Can I see the crystal, Ms. Schreiber?" Doroteo asked, and she reluctantly passed it to him.

"Is that a good idea, Doroteo?" asked Dominga.

He ignored her and everyone else as he turned it over in his hand. He inspected it thoroughly, but nothing special happened, except that Gerald thought he saw the man blink uncomfortably once or twice.

"Maybe it's like Star Trek, like the prime directive?" Franklin asked over the silence.

This time, Doroteo acknowledged Franklin's presence, albeit with suppressed annoyance. "Prime directive?" he asked.

"Yeah, you know, like how the alien can't interfere with our current state of technological advancement. That's why it's using Taylor and her propulsion system, so it doesn't have to show us how to do it."

He looked around the room in support of his hypothesis. Everyone answered his question with befuddled expressions, including Gerald. He remembered watching a couple of episodes of Star Trek as a kid but nothing about a *Prime Directive*.

"That is an interesting thought," said Mr. Smith. "And perhaps Miss Schreiber is correct, and this thing has completely different motivations than us. Maybe it thinks of us like ants in an anthill. Can a group of ants survive outside the collective? Can they handle the introduction of the NMG and nuclear fusion reactor? Maybe it is trying to determine that."

"Yes, that's the prime directive," Franklin said with a smug smile directed at Taylor.

"What do you think, Freddy?" Mr. Smith asked. "You're the one who has actually talked to it."

All eyes turned to Freddy again, and he finally looked up from the ground. He looked at Mr. Smith with regret in his eyes as though confessing an embarrassing secret.

"I only know of two things she wanted. She wants to change me and second, she wanted to connect me to this group. I think that she wants me to make decisions on my own, but I may not have the choice in the matter. I do not know the reasons."

"How is it changing you?" asked Doroteo with a hint of a threat, his eyes narrowing to black slits. "Should we be worried about you?"

Mr. Smith and Sadi jumped to Freddy's defense, sitting forward in their seats. Sadi beat the old man with her response.

"It hasn't changed who he is, just what he can do. I put my life in his hands before, and I'd do it again."

"And I will vouch for him," Mr. Smith said. "He's no threat to any of us."

"So what can you do now that you couldn't do before?" Doroteo seemed unaffected by the remarks in Freddy's defense.

"I know what others are feeling."

"And this helps you?"

Even without the power of Freddy's telepathy, Gerald saw the defensiveness in Freddy's posture. He met Doroteo's piercing black-eyed stare with regret and a sigh.

"You feel vulnerable in my presence but act suspicious and threatening. You hope to provoke me into saying more than I usually would."

For the first time in Gerald's memory, he saw the danger in the man's eyes deflate. Doroteo suddenly looked defenseless, but the impression lasted only a moment, and then he smiled. Freddy nodded to him then returned his attention to the floor.

Had Doroteo just sent a thought or feeling to Freddy? Maybe Gerald would ask later. If only Gerald possessed Freddy's abilities, he could be the most successful lawyer in the world. For a moment, he considered the option of hiring Freddy as a legal assistant, so he could be present when meeting with clients, the opposing counsel, or the judge. Those thoughts nearly made him salivate with anticipation, but a different thought stopped his speculation. The alien most likely intended an entirely different future for the kid.

Gerald inspected everyone in the circle as he would members of a jury, attempting to assess their emotional states. Sadi's body language seemed to indicate an expectation of sudden flight as if prepared to check on the girls at any change in their noise level. Gerda looked confused and a little overwhelmed. She sat back in her chair and shifted her gaze to different members of the circle as if trying to see inside their thoughts, like him.

"We can probably speculate all night about what the alien wants or what it's going to do." As Cesar continued, he directed his comment to Taylor. "I suggest we start discussing what we're going to do."

"Yes, I would be interested to learn of your next set of actions," Gerda said before Taylor could speak. "At least that's something I can probably understand."

"Well," said Taylor, smiling in return. "Cesar and I are finishing our prototype vehicle, and we plan to take it into space on July fourth. We want everyone to be there."

"Awesome," Franklin said.

—※—

At the mention of the upcoming space flight, the mood instantly changed to one of excitement and Gerald realized how talk of the alien had placed a damper on the group's morale. Almost everyone joined in the animated conversation, including Sadi. Only Freddy and Mr. Smith remained mostly silent. Freddy was likely overwhelmed at trying to separate each individual's words from their feelings. It must have been exhausting, Gerald thought.

By far, Franklin showed the most excitement. When Taylor told him of how the mysterious CEO and she would be the only ones going on the test flight he looked physically depressed.

"I call shotgun on the next trip," he said sarcastically.

"What's the plan after the July fourth flight?" asked Gerda. "If successful, what next?"

Cesar spoke to everyone but kept his black eyes fixed on Gerald.

"Well," he began. "On the flight, we'll be looking for ways to make improvements, but we have no definite plans beyond that. That's one reason to call this meeting."

"Before we talk about that," Gerald said. "We'll have to ask Freddy to leave, but I have a question for him first."

"Do we really need Freddy to leave?" Sadi asked. "He'll be able to know what we're talking about, from anywhere in the house."

"It's usually a good idea to take precautions," Mr. Smith said. "But in this case, I don't think we can keep our plans or discussions out of this thing's awareness. I propose we let Freddy stay."

Everyone turned to Doroteo, expecting him as the one most likely to object.

"As long as we all agree not to say anything too specific," Doroteo said, glaring at Gerald.

"Freddy," Gerald said tentatively. "How do you feel about doing what the alien wants you to do?"

"That is out of the question," said Mr. Smith emphatically.

"Why?" asked Gerald.

"For the time being," Mr. Smith answered. "I'm willing to assume the alien means us no harm. That doesn't mean we send Freddy to where it can have complete power over him."

Gerald was prepared for this argument.

"What if it anticipated our reaction and wanted another one of us to go? And that's the reason it led you to us?"

"This is a case where we need to trust our own instincts," said Cesar. "There's no way for us to know what this thing is thinking unless Freddy can discover it."

"I am trying," Freddy said.

"I think Mr. Smith is right though," Cesar continued. "About not sending Freddy out there like it claims to want. Let's just focus on the test flight and go from there."

"I agree," Taylor said and nodded. "We stick with the original plan. A lot can happen between now and then."

TWENTY

Taylor

Taylor and Cesar drove together to the designated launch site in the recently completed BMW, or as Taylor began referring to it, *The Convertible*. The engine and power system worked perfectly as their numerous tests had already shown. The vehicle's radiation shield windows were too dark to be legal, but neither of them worried about being pulled over for it. They could hardly see out of the reinforced gray glass anyway and had to rely on the multiple camera views to drive safely.

Gerald wanted to stagger the convoy, so the group drove in several vehicles and not all together. It would appear less suspicious and noticeable if they all pulled onto the side road separately. In the very slim chance the authorities stopped one of them, the others would be in a better position to help attempt a rescue. Doroteo insisted that one person in each car carry a gun with them. Taylor felt better just knowing about Cesar's gun, but she doubted their ability to rescue anyone from government agents or military personnel. She was more concerned about the flight and returning safely to Earth.

Gerald and Sadi drove right behind them, with Max and Mark separated by at least a kilometer. Mr. Smith, Freddy, and Franklin drove behind them by about ten kilometers. At the very back of the convoy, Gerda drove with Dominga. Doroteo had been around the location all day, scouting the place to make sure they had a good escape route.

One by one, they all turned down a little side road about sixty kilometers east of Seattle. The day had been a hot one with only a few clouds overhead. Taylor was grateful for the cloud cover but secretly wished for a clear sky. Reality became a mixture of what she wanted and needed. Providence, she thought.

When Doroteo appeared out of nowhere, he waved his hand and motioned for them to pull onto the side of the road to park under a clearing of trees. He waited to meet them as she and Cesar stepped out of the car.

"If we would have waited just three days, it would be the night of the full moon," Doroteo said, smiling. Taylor had never seen him look more animated. The smile on Doroteo's face could only be a good omen and made Taylor begin to feel more at ease.

"It'll be bright enough, my friend," Cesar said, patting him on the back.

As they waited for everyone to arrive, Taylor's anxiety levels began to rise again. While transforming the BMW, she had only felt excited about the test drive. She knew the risks they would be taking, but the risks seemed detached from any real-world, physical consequence and only as dangerous as an insignificant monetary investment. When Max arrived, her imagination started producing thoughts of losing all power and accelerating back toward Earth.

"A good night for a flight," Max said to Taylor after he and Mark exited their vehicle. "How are you feeling?"

"Never better," she said, acting unaffected by what they planned to attempt. She refused to give Max a view of her true mental condition.

"We can't wait to see the convertible in action," Mark said.

He stepped away from them to get a good look at the vehicle he had helped to build. Taylor could see the pride in his eyes, and she felt the same. While working with Mark, she had come to enjoy his company, and his presence helped curb the uncomfortable feeling Max seemed to give her.

The last rays of the sun disappeared right after Dominga and Gerda finally arrived, and they waited another forty minutes for it to get dark before Taylor and Max started to put on their suits. She had wanted to launch in darkness and when all the fireworks had begun. Even though Taylor could do it herself, she let Mark help to put on her specialized flight suit. He wanted to make sure they had everything correct. After clicking her helmet in place, he patted her on the shoulder.

"Feel good?" he asked loudly.

Taylor paused to take a breath and was relieved when her moist breath failed to fog her view. As she removed the helmet, an irritating thought crept into her mind.

"Oh my God," she said in frustration. "It's probably not going to make a difference, but..."

She walked to the back tire and started deflating it. Max took off his helmet as well and looked at her quizzically, but Gerald spoke first.

"Taylor," Gerald said with concern in his voice. "What's wrong?"

Smiling to herself, she shook her head.

"The tire air pressure differential might become too high in the vacuum. I don't want the tires to burst if we decide to leave the atmosphere. It's the little things that are going to get us killed."

Had she forgotten anything else?

"You only need to knock off fourteen psi," Max said. "Probably won't matter."

"Working on it," she said, trying to hide her irritation. *Does he really think I don't know what one atmosphere of pressure is in pounds per square inch?* After finishing with the first tire, she walked to the next one. "I've got this. Just finish getting your suit on."

When done with the tires, she put her helmet on the seat and patiently listened to Mark repeat how to connect their suits to the tank of air on the back of the seat, should they lose atmospheric pressure or normal oxygen levels in the car's interior. The tank could also be detached from the seat and attached to their suits instead.

At the end of the lesson, Max sat down in the driver's seat and started putting the safety buckles and straps over himself. He kept his door open while waiting for Taylor to do the same, but she stood motionless with her eyes on the car. After pausing a moment, she placed her hand on top of the opened passenger door.

"Wow," she said to herself and shook her head in amazement at what she planned to do.

The months and endless days of labor came crashing down on her all at once, and she had to hold onto the door for balance. She felt her eyes begin to well up with tears but somehow found the strength to keep them from sliding down her cheeks. She suddenly felt the need to say something. To help focus her thoughts, she looked up into the dark sky, at the stars in between the clouds and then the tall pine trees on all sides of them.

"One small step for mankind," she said, smiling wide, then looking from Dominga to Cesar and then the rest of them. "Just kidding."

"Go on," said Gerald, laughing lightly. "Stop stalling and get that thing off the ground. We're probably as excited to watch you take off as you are to fly."

"I know, I know," she replied defensively. "This is such a big moment. It seems deflating to leave without saying something significant. Oh, well."

Her mind attempted to contain a mix of conflicting emotions. She was anxious, an overwhelming fear that nothing would be the same again. She felt the excitement and something else she failed to accept consciously, the possibility of saying a real goodbye.

"You bring her back safe to us, Mr. Garner," said Dominga, holding up her finger like a teacher. Taylor saw her eyes glistening with reflected light from all the flashlights, her cue to get in the car before her tears started falling. She hated to see Dominga upset. The sight erased all of her other emotions.

"I will do my best, Miss Florez," Max said and then shut his door, encasing them both in silence. His failure to promise a safe return filled Taylor with a small twinge of foreboding.

Taylor felt the sharp contrast between the natural setting of trees and cool air and the artificial combination of sensors, electricity, and a controlled atmosphere. For the first time in her life, she felt at one with nature and technology.

While securing herself to the seat, she looked at the window separating herself from her friends. Only dots of light from the flashlights could be seen through the glass radiation shield. She put her hands on the controls, which moved the cameras on the side mirrors and switched from the left side to the right side, then switched to the cameras installed in the headlights. "We have visual control."

"Ready to move?" he asked, glancing briefly at all of her straps and clasps.

"Ready if you are."

When their eyes met, he smiled and she took a deep breath, her eyes wide. Their mutual excitement pulsated like an electrical current between them and for a moment, she forgot her usual reaction of distrust at seeing him.

They designed the controls to resemble those of a manual transmission automobile but with a stick shift for each hand to orient the direction of the primary and secondary NMG engines. In street mode, they set the primary NMG thrust for a single axis, forward and reverse, but in flight mode, they used two separate NMG engines with three-axis control of each. The steering wheel only controlled the wheels, which were useless in space, of course, and they decided not to give it a dual purpose. The accelerator pedal controlled the thrust of the primary NMG while the brake pedal controlled the secondary NMG.

In an emergency, if they experienced a malfunction of either NMG, the remaining one could be used to fly but with severely hampered mobility. Due to the size and complexity of the fusion reactor, however, they had no redundant power source other than a battery, which had enough capacity to sustain the engine for almost fifteen minutes. After that, they would have to hope the parachute would prevent their destruction. Taylor felt assured of the fusion generator's integrity due to its performance in testing, but it was her primary concern.

"Here we go," Max said while looking forward.

"Switching to video view," Taylor said, feeling silly to explain the obvious, but they already decided to communicate actions verbally. Since he needed all his attention on flying, she did not want to give him any surprises, no matter how small.

The four embedded computer screens came to life, the two on either side of the car and the two on the dashboard, each showing a view of the outside from the four different camera angles, from the headlights and tail lights, top and bottom. As they slowly rose into the air, they listened to the only sound, the quiet humming of the NMG engines. During low output power, the fusion reactor operated in complete silence.

"Pretty smooth," he said approvingly.

"Nice huh," she responded without trying to hide the pride in her voice. "We kept the convertible operating as high as our thrust sensor would allow, for about twenty hours and with less than half a percent fluctuation. It feels good to feel it for real."

Even the small acceleration of their slow ascension felt amazing, and she waited with intense anticipation for heavier thrust. As they watched the IR image of the ground get farther away, they could see the others standing with their faces turned to the sky and their hands waving. She could almost hear the cheering. Both Max and Taylor watched them until they became indistinguishable points of light in the trees.

"You've assembled some pretty amazing people," Max said. "I'm impressed."

As she watched them on the screen, she nodded.

"Yes, they are."

Will I ever see Dominga again? Or Mom?

She turned toward the front camera to watch the horizon and change the direction of her thoughts. As they gained more altitude, the light on the horizon grew brighter. Even through the camera lens, the scene became more beautiful than she had imagined it, but the view suddenly made her sad, and she spoke before she could stop herself.

"I wish my dad could be here, instead of you, no offense."

He looked over at her, not saying a word. But after a moment, he returned his attention to the screen and then replied.

"None taken."

She waited for him to say something else, like an inquiry for more information, but to her relief, he chose to remain silent. He was probably too absorbed in the experience of flight to discuss anything anyway. The situation felt too much like a dream. Had she imagined speaking?

At first, they ascended slowly enough for Taylor to feel only a slightly larger force than one G. As she opened her mouth to ask him why they traveled so slowly, he pushed harder on the accelerator, and she felt her body push against her seat.

"Giving her more acceleration," he said.

"Thanks for the warning," she said sarcastically, but her smile gave the impression of being grateful.

Taylor turned to the altimeter, and it showed them at almost a thousand meters. She could no longer distinguish the area where all the cars were parked. The people there were just tiny dots, quickly shrinking into one faint dot. Chills ran through her body.

TWENTY-ONE

Taylor

"I'm going to start flying laterally," he said conversationally. "So that we don't pin a bright target on our friends down there."

"What do you mean?"

"If our movement is detected," he explained like a flight instructor. "Directly below us will become interesting to any viewers. Our point of origin might be too easy to determine."

"Of course," she said, feeling slightly angry and not showing it. They had talked about this already, but in her excitement, she had forgotten. As their upward ascent stopped, she felt the force on her body lighten. The forest and the road slowly began to move below them like scrolling on an online map. He gently turned the car to face east, toward the dark horizon.

When he pushed on the accelerator, Taylor's head responded by hitting the back of her chair. "Hey, give some warning when you're going to accelerate like that."

"Sorry," he said, sounding sincerely apologetic but with a smile. "The response on this thing is amazing. I'm fighting the temptation to push it to maximum acceleration. You should be glad that I'm holding back."

He reminded her of a little boy who just got his first remote control car. The thought triggered a similar memory from her childhood. She got to control that car only once before her actions had destroyed it.

Even though it hurt her pride to let him fly her creation before she did, she was grateful for Max offering to act as the pilot. Her ideal choice, Doroteo, had refused the offer. He said they were crazy and he would not be taking anything into space. With Doroteo by her side, she would have felt more comfortable and found it easier to suppress her feelings of jealousy at being the passenger instead of the pilot. But while in the passenger seat, she could more easily focus on enjoying the experience. She would have her chance to fly the convertible, sometime.

"Before you play around more, let's go higher," she said. "If something goes wrong, we'll have more time to resolve the situation."

"And crash harder," he said gravely.

"If we're gonna crash and burn, let's make it a spectacular experience," she smiled then became more serious. "Besides, if we were higher, people won't be able to see us with their naked eyes. It would suck to be spotted by some campers who thought we were a UFO and reported it to the police."

Would the police take that kind of call seriously? Probably not.

"Fine by me," he said as he grabbed the second gear shift. He slowly tilted the car upward to a forty-five-degree angle.

The experience reminded Taylor of a roller coaster ride when it would start going up the ramp. She could feel the adrenaline entering her blood and the increase in her heart rate. She used her extra energy to focus on the video of the sky above and not the ground. Unconsciously, she held onto the reinforced grip on the door and the other side of her seat.

"Try to be gentle this time!"

When he pushed on the accelerator again, he used more restraint, and they started moving slowly upward. But as he steadily increased the thrust, the seat pushed harder and harder against her back. After a few seconds, she decided to stop fighting the pressure and let her head rest against the seat. She looked at the computer screen on the dashboard. Their acceleration would soon reach 2G.

They crashed through the clouds at eighteen meters per second. Max let gravity decelerate them for a bit and then maneuvered the vehicle so they became motionless, hovering just above the clouds. When her heart resumed a normal pace, she took a deep breath and released her grip on the chair armrests.

They could see nothing through the windows of the night sky, so they had to depend on the cameras. When Taylor looked at the bottom camera view again, she could see the top of the clouds. She watched them for a few seconds as if in a trance.

"That was awesome," she said and then clasped both gloved hands together to get the blood flowing again. "It almost doesn't seem real, like a simulation at an amusement park."

"I'm getting the hang of this," Max said, nodding his head. "I'm going to do some maneuvers to see what this thing can do. How well do you handle free fall conditions?"

"I can handle whatever you do," she said in mock indignation. "Just don't mind me if I puke."

"If you start to feel nauseated, just don't look in my direction."

She looked into his blue eyes, the first time she'd noticed their color and tried to determine if he caught her sarcastic tone.

"I do fine at amusement parks, so I'll be okay, but I'll let you know if I need you to stop."

He laughed.

"This won't be like any amusement park ride. I can tell you that."

For the next fifteen minutes, he practiced maneuvering. Several times during his *practice* she came very close to her threat of puking, and she had to use all her concentration to hold onto the armrests. During the intense acceleration, close to five-G at one point followed by the sudden absence of acceleration, her stomach almost felt like it might separate from her esophagus. Somehow she managed to keep her breakfast inside her body. Pride would not allow her to show Max the extent of her physiological distress.

While she struggled to appear calm, Taylor noticed how Max struggled to contain his pleasure at the experience. Without her beside him, she imagined him howling with excitement.

The fun came to a halt during a 2G dive toward the Earth when they heard the loud beeping begin. As Max pulled out of the dive, Taylor quickly discovered the cause of the alarm. As she feared, the signal came from their radar detector. In just a few seconds, Max brought them to a cruising speed at constant altitude in the clouds.

For a brief moment, they let the beeping continue and watched the video feed, which only showed a dark mist. When Taylor tapped on the screen, on the radar sensor icon, the program opened and showed the signal location. While listening, she decreased the alarm beeping volume so they could talk.

"The source is fifteen degrees above us, to the south where we're headed," she looked at the other screen with the navigation program, but Max already knew their direction.

"Probably a high altitude drone. Are we going to stick to the plan?"

"Do you have any other ideas?"

"Do you think this thing can do it? I do."

"Yes," she said confidently but felt a panic burgeoning inside her. Images of falling back to the Earth filled her head. "It'll be fine."

"Is there a specific direction you want to go?" he asked patiently, but she detected a tone of excitement.

"Up!" she said. "But let's get farther away from the signal source and stay in the clouds for a bit, and if at all possible, try to keep me conscious."

She tried to fight back the intense anxiety, the fear of all her plans being ruined.

Keep it together! This is what I wanted!

Without saying a word, he pushed on the accelerator, and they ripped the clouds apart in the opposite direction of the radar signal. After a minute of heavy acceleration in the clouds, he turned the car at nearly a forty-five-degree angle, upward. The video showed the night sky above them, filled with stars. She focused on the view, and it helped slow her heart rate.

During their travel upward, the sky slowly began turning darker, and alternatively filled with more and more stars. The beeping continued, but the sight put her in a small trance until Max's voice startled her.

"Get ready for some heavy acceleration," he said. "We've got another signal coming from the south, just a few thousand meters above us. I'm going to try something."

Suddenly, Max reversed their direction and dove back down to Earth again but without changing the vehicle orientation. Taylor felt the seat belts pull her downward. They seemed to dig into her skin.

"Goddamn it," Taylor yelled as she pulled on the armrests. Her lungs suddenly felt inoperable, and she had to hold her breath. After two seconds, the beeping of the radar alarm stopped, but she barely noticed, because Max abruptly stopped the dive and pulled up again.

Taylor felt her eyes rolling in her skull, and she realized with dread that the light in the car began to dim. The image of her mother materialized, replacing the darkness, and for a moment, she watched as her mother called for her like in *The Wizard of Oz* when Dorothy watched her Auntie Em in the crystal ball.

"Mom," she attempted to yell, but the words escaped only as a whisper. "I'm ten miles above Earth, in a BMW."

TWENTY-TWO

Taylor

Taylor heard a voice call to her from the darkness. It spoke once, then again, then silence. After a moment, she felt a hand on her shoulder gently shaking her, and then the voice again. After she moved her head, she remembered the intense acceleration and everything turning dark. For the first time that day, she remembered the significance of the date July 4—Independence Day.

Slowly, Taylor opened her eyes. As her senses returned to normal, she recognized a new feeling of weightlessness and the pleasant flow of tension from her muscles. She looked down and saw her hands floating a few centimeters above the armrests.

"Welcome back, Taylor," Max said excitedly and with relief. "Are you okay? I'm sorry about that."

Before responding, she took a moment to control her angry reaction and become accustomed to her new situation. Even with the dark radiation shielding on the windows, bright sunlight filled the interior of the vehicle from her right. They faced the Earth, with the North American continent clothed in night and the blue expanse of the Pacific in the beautiful light of the sun.

"How long was I out?" she asked, her gaze affixed to the Earth.

"About fifteen minutes," he said. "Long enough for us to escape that radar lock."

"Wow," she said, not trying to hide her amazement. She tore her eyes away from the Earth to look at the computer monitor in front of her. "Eight thousand kilometers. How's the pressure integrity?"

Her anger dissipated as she realized their elevation, a quarter of the way to geostationary orbit. She found the readout from the pressure compensator to see the pressurization measurement log. It held steady at one and a half standard cubic centimeters per minute, the variable they chose to monitor to keep their target pressure of one atmosphere.

"Yeah, I know," he said disappointingly, "we got a leak, but it's not bad. We've got several hours of oxygen left. I'm willing to spend the rest of it out here."

She was glad he chose to talk about something other than her blackout. She hated how he had successfully remained conscious while she failed.

"That was too close for comfort," he said, almost in response to her thoughts. "I almost lost it too!"

"You shouldn't take that kind of risk," she said absently, turning to look out the side window. "If both of us were unconscious, we might have died. I trust my autopilot backup program, but we really don't want to test it."

Why was she angry at him, she wondered.

"I hope we were just a blip on whoever's radar it was," he said, looking at her with a curious expression, a mixture of confusion and amusement.

"Any idea who was tracking us?"

"Probably an AWACS, one of the military Airborne Warning and Control System aircraft," he explained. "I didn't give them enough time to position any satellites to get a picture of us, I hope. They probably thought we were just a blip, but they'll be watching for us."

"Well," she said, "it's stupid to assume the best case scenario. We'll see, I suppose."

"Yeah," he agreed. "For now, I don't want to worry. This is enough to distract us, don't you think?" He extended his hand to the Earth displayed before them.

"It is amazing," she said. "Even though I had no conscious doubts, I'm still in shock. I really couldn't imagine actually escaping the planet."

"I've done lots of amazing things in my life," he said, turning to her. "But this definitely beats everything. How can we go back and ever be the same?"

She felt a sudden connection with Max from sharing the powerful experience. Reluctantly, she knew they had developed a bond. She wanted to break the connection but knew it could not be undone. The bond should have been made with a close friend or relative, not a man her instincts told her to loathe. She required extra time to break eye contact with him, and she hoped he did not sense her frustration.

While attempting to grasp onto anything other than her thoughts, she remembered her desire to see the moon from space. After turning her head, she saw the moon behind them, visible through the back and driver's windows. As if for the first time, she stared at Earth's largest natural satellite. It looked only a little bit larger than usual and not nearly as bright as the sun, but the light reflecting from its light gray surface seemed as bright as the noonday sun on Earth. It looked lonely and barren.

"We're only three days away until the full moon," she said, almost to herself. "We couldn't have asked for a better time to make the flight."

"At first, I had a hard time deciding how to orient the convertible. Face the moon or Earth? The moon is amazing, but it pales in comparison to Earth, don't you think? Too bad we don't have time to go to the moon."

"My dad would have died to see this," she said wistfully.

"So you and your dad were close?" he asked.

She paused and cursed herself for mentioning her father. She did not want to talk about him with Max. Discussion of such a personal subject would likely strengthen their emotional bond.

"We were pretty close," she agreed. "I love my mother, but we don't have much in common."

"So your mother doesn't know about any of this?" he asked, sounding surprised.

"We thought it would be safer for her to remain in ignorance." Taylor smiled and shook her head slightly. "Besides, it's much better this way. She'd worry too much. She'd lose sleep over it, and probably nag me more than she already does."

"Would you have told your father?" he asked.

"That's a tough question," she said and paused to think. "I would have wanted to, but if I had told him, I wouldn't have been able to keep him away. Everything would have happened differently. I would have loved working on it with him, but I think it was good to work with Gerald and Cesar, oh, and Mark too."

She paused to laugh at what would have happened if her father was still alive. Two small tears unexpectedly slid down her cheeks.

"If I didn't tell my dad, he would have been so mad at me when he did find out." She wiped her eyes with the back of her gloved hand. "Sorry."

She kept her gaze on the Earth, feeling embarrassed for showing emotion but not bothering to hide her tears. Max pretended not to notice.

"Is that where you got your interest in engineering?"

"My dad loved learning and creating," she said and failed to hide her pleasure at the memory. "He taught me never to fear breaking things or making mistakes. *Can't build it if you're afraid of it,* he used to say."

"I like that," he said, looking straight at her. "My father loves money. That's about all I got from him."

"Are you saying you broke the cycle?" she asked while still smiling and attempting to sound indifferent. Did he really break the cycle, or was it just talk to get Gerald and her to believe him?

"What cycle?" he asked sincerely.

"You know," she began in a sarcastic tone, "the baggage some parents pass down to their children. In your case, the power-hungry, world-government-psycho-virus from an international-banker-father."

"What do you think?" he asked with a sneer.

"I really don't know," she said, wondering if her words had offended him. "That's why I'm asking."

"Do you think I'm not sincerely trying to help you guys?"

This time, she heard the warning tone in his voice but failed to feel intimidated.

"Come on," she said as if lecturing a child. "Let's not change the subject, and I'm not doubting your intentions. Your focus in life can still be on money and you can be a good person."

He seemed to look at her without emotion in his eyes, but she could almost feel his tension building. After a moment, his face relaxed, if just a bit.

"Okay, fair enough," he said. "If it weren't for my grandfather, I might have turned into my father. He never focused on the money. If I would have spent as much time thinking about money and power, like my father, the cycle would have continued I guess. Maybe I don't deserve any of the credit."

She did not intend to let him end the argument so easily.

"That's probably true, but tell me this. What's the difference between how your father makes all his money and where you get all yours? As I see it, if it weren't for fat government projects, funded by fraud, your company would be out of business."

From the look in his eyes, she wondered if her words had struck too deep. But no matter how he reacted to her accusation, she felt prepared. He turned to stare back at the Earth. Unexpectedly, his lips curved into a slight smile as if recalling a bitter memory.

"Someone else already stabbed me with that one," he said. "All I can say is that I'm doing what I love, and it got me where I am, in space with you, and in style I might add."

—※—

His comment caught her completely off guard and left her without an immediate response, either her usual sarcastic retort or a counter-argument. She had expected him to worm his way out of her accusation or change the subject. He denied nothing and somehow had come to peace with himself.

His elation at being in space and specifically in her presence caused Taylor some anxiety. Did he have an interest in her? For his sake, she hoped not, but a dark and scheming voice in her head said she could use his feelings for her benefit. Consciously, she rejected the idea, but the thought lingered like an addictive song loop. She would rather not hurt him and doubted her ability to ensnare anyone with romantic charm.

The possibility of a romantic relationship with Max almost made her laugh. Even if possible, she would not allow herself to receive a life of privilege just handed to her on a platter. She had to earn that life by herself. She would not become the object of her ridicule.

"I almost expected to hear the excuse that if someone would be profiting from the government, it might as well be you."

"I've thought of that," he said and laughed, "but it's a weak argument. The same could be said of a murderer killing someone for money to beat the next murderer. Living things will do what they can to help themselves in nearly all cases, but in this case, it's not my fault the system lets it happen. Before you make any other accusations, TerraWatch doesn't make all its money from fat government contracts. We do a lot of work for many private businesses."

"But," she started to say, then the frustrated look in his eyes made her pause but only for a second. Momentum prevented an end to her tirade. "How many of those private clients of yours have fat government contracts as well? Your kind of logic justifies what Congress just did to everyone—rape the public and give all the money to the financiers, people like your father. The system let that happen."

He looked at her with hurt in his eyes, and she instantly regretted her angry and accusatory tone. She had not intended to get so heated, but for some reason, she wanted to catapult all her frustration on him, as if he had personally sent her brother to Iraq and made her mother go almost bankrupt and somehow caused all the other problems in the world. Just like everyone else, he had his demons, and throwing more food at them would not help him or the situation.

"You're right," he said and then several seconds passed in silence.

Taylor felt the tension between them intensify. To avoid the pain in his eyes, she turned her attention to the key still in the ignition. The key looked out of place, embedded in the driving wheel column with the rest of the chain levitating in the air.

"You know," she said, intending to redeem herself somehow. "For the moment at least, we're in the same position, two humans off their home world but not entirely out of her grasp. We're having the most amazing experience of our lives, together, and even after you knocked me out. Thanks for not getting us killed."

He smiled but remained silent. She hoped her comment had given him some kind of relief that she at least didn't hate him. When their eyes met, she smiled and then turned to look out the window.

"Maybe being away from Earth is doing us some good," he said, stretching his legs and pushing against the seat.

"I feel like we need to celebrate somehow," Taylor said. "Like a toast or chocolates. We should have brought something."

Max looked at her with amusement then held both hands out toward the Earth.

"Is that not enough for you?"

"To the Earth," she said, extending the palms of her hands toward the planet.

TWENTY-THREE

Taylor

For the flight, she kept most of her hair in a braid, tucked into her vacuum suit, but during the free fall of their orbital velocity, some wisps kept floating horizontally from her head and she kept pressing them back in place. She usually hated dealing with her hair, but not for concern about her appearance. She preferred to concentrate on more important matters. In the car, she almost laughed at the absurdity of the effort. Finally, she gave up and just let it float.

For several minutes, they took turns trying to locate state boundaries, country boundaries and major geological features, but the dark surface made the job difficult if not impossible. With every passing minute, they watched as the shadow swept over the Pacific Ocean. Taylor could feel the time slip away, like a weekend coming to a close. She knew they had to get back soon.

"Well it's been about ninety minutes," he said with a sigh. "We don't want to make them wait forever, worrying about us, but I hate to leave."

"They're not expecting to hear from us before midnight," she said, then looked at the time on the computer screen, which showed eleven-thirty, "so we've got a little time left."

"Are you ready for re-entry?"

Taylor looked out the front window again at the Earth. The breathtaking sight made her shudder. Part of her wanted to continue staring at it forever. Being so far away from her troubles helped diminish the significance of their plans, the reasons they spent so much time and effort preparing for the journey. Nothing seemed to matter as much anymore, and at the same time, it mattered more than ever.

"Let's do it," she said and smiled. Her thoughts kept returning to the idea of how the return trip symbolized death, the body returning to the Earth. The fusion generator had injected them with so much potential energy, she felt like a human atomic bomb. "It will be the final test for this contraption."

"I must admit," he said seriously. "I'm a little nervous about getting back."

She tried smiling, but the action felt weak. For the first time during the journey, she considered how it must have felt to be the pilot. Her previous feelings of guilt returned at how harshly she had accused him when he put his life on the line to help them.

"That makes two of us," she said. "Even if we survive, we might have someone waiting for us."

"I think it's unlikely they tracked us out here."

"I know, I know," she said, cutting him off. "We're a four meter object in the middle of a two billion square kilometer ocean, but we're also shining like the moon against a sky of darkness."

"We're just another star."

"The law of the jungle is, *always be on alert*," she answered. "That's how you stay alive. Let's just assume they'll be looking for us when we get back."

"Good point," he said.

"So, we head for the cascade range," she said after looking at the navigation program on the screen. Turning her attention to their current task would help ease her anxiety. "Between Mt. Rainier and Mt. Adams, then north at low altitude to the rendezvous point. We should be able to lose anyone tracking us in the mountains."

"I remember," he said and laughed, "but let's first focus on getting back without getting vaporized."

"Not getting vaporized would be nice," she said, mimicking his sarcastic tone.

Before bringing the NMG engines back to life, they sat for a few more seconds in silence just staring into space. Taylor glanced back at the moon and felt it silently stare back at her.

"Here we go," said Max after taking a deep breath. "We'll be gaining speed pretty fast but not feeling it. I'll stop when we hit our target velocity. Try to enjoy the ride. It'll make me feel better to see you smiling."

"I'll try."

—※—

When Max started decelerating the vehicle out of their orbital velocity, Taylor jolted in surprise. She had been expecting the sensation but felt unprepared for being pushed back in her seat. After her initial shock faded, she felt some comfort at the familiar sensation of force on her body.

For five minutes, he kept the thrust at a steady one-G, the weight they would usually feel on Earth, and Taylor felt as though her anxiety had increased along with their speed. At the end of the five minutes, when he stopped the thrust, she noticed the Earth slowly growing larger as they fell toward it. When she looked at their velocity relative to the Earth's surface, they were falling at fifty-eight hundred meters per second.

"Ready to hand our lives over to your re-entry program?" Max asked, keeping his full concentration on the approaching Earth. "Or do you want some more free fall time?"

"Let's just get back," she said after double-checking the real-time descent schedule. The longer they waited, the more deceleration they would have to endure, but she understood his hesitation to begin. After a moment, she decided to look at their altitude readout again, then to the detailed re-entry plan, trying to see if the program's thrust, velocity, and altitude predictions made sense. A simple error in the program code could equate to their vaporization.

"I'm ready," Max said, then waited for Taylor to indicate agreement.

After she nodded, he clicked on the icon, which would give the NMG engines' thrust and orientation control to the computers, then they turned their attention to the readouts of the flight systems' performance. Instantly, the engines started decelerating at a comfortable 0.6-G.

Taylor felt the sudden pull of the straps again as they prevented her from crashing into the dashboard. She felt as if she were trapped in a spider's web, but Max seemed either unconcerned or simply unaware of the pressure.

In some relief, she watched their velocity diminish, but at their horrific speed, the Earth seemed to be growing larger too quickly. For her sanity, she decided to trust the plan and ignore paranoia.

"I have a great idea," Taylor said with some sarcasm after enduring the discomfort of the straps for several minutes. The pain in her shoulders and breasts had become too distracting. "Why don't we re-orient the car so we're not being pulled toward the windshield? It's making me nervous."

"Oh, sure," he said as if coming out of a trance. "I was just enjoying the view."

As he reoriented the convertible, she felt dizzy and closed her eyes. When the maneuver stopped, the pressure moved from her chest to her back. The change brought a rush of blood to her head, but the dizziness soon passed.

Within less than a minute, Taylor began to recognize a strange sensation. The car had begun to shake a little bit, more than any time on their journey—not a good sign. She looked at the outside pressure readout, hoping to explain the shaking by the increased outside pressure. But unfortunately, they had not yet hit any significant atmosphere. The shaking had to be an internal problem.

"Do you feel that?" she asked.

Before he had time to respond, a huge jolt made Taylor's teeth slam together. A loud sound followed the jolt, like two heavy pieces of metal crashing into each other. The computer started beeping, and they entered free fall again as the engines shut off.

"Holy shit," she said in a panic, and they turned to the dashboard at the blinking red warning icon, an exclamation point surrounded by a triangle. She reached out and clicked it off. "What the hell was that?"

"Looks like we've lost the primary NMG," Max said quickly, without any sign of distress.

Taylor fought her initial reaction of panic and the added concern for a possibly chipped tooth. After some more thought, she realized exactly what had happened. The NMG suddenly lost all its accumulated internal momentum, similar to the water hammer effect. Hopefully, the shock did not damage the integrity of the chassis.

According to the previously planned deceleration schedule, just over seven minutes remained before they reached their next target speed of a kilometer per second. She found herself staring at the decreasing time. At around a hundred-fifty kilometers, they would start hitting significant atmosphere. If traveling too fast, they would begin to experience some dangerous ionization heating.

"Damn it," she said after noticing their speed. "We're still moving at over three and a half km per second and gaining."

"Good thing we've got a backup engine," Max said in a forced positive tone.

"It's okay, it's okay," Taylor said, taking a deep breath to calm herself. "We've still got just over two thousand km to slow down."

Taylor looked at the screen at the prompt asking when she wanted to resume the program under their new conditions. She remembered writing the alarm message in the program code. She reached out and prepared to click on the okay button. "Tell me when you're ready!"

"Go for it," Max said. This time he tried smiling, but the effort looked more forced.

In just a few seconds, the feeling of gravity returned and pushed them into their seats again. The feeling of resistance gave her some re-lief, but she still held tightly to the armrest.

"Well it's working, thank God." Taylor took a deep breath and tried concentrating on positive thoughts.

For several minutes they sat in silence and watched the NMG slowly eat away at their descent velocity. Taylor found it impossible to relax. She feared that at any moment, they would lose the second NMG, so she felt for any sign of vibration or suspicious noise. Despite the million other things that could go wrong, she could only focus on that one possibility. She needed something to distract her mind, but unfortunately, she could only stare at the velocity readout. Watching it get smaller gave her some relief.

Six minutes later, they were nearing their next target speed of one km per second, and the altitude readout showed just under one hun-dred fifty km. Taylor breathed a sigh of relief and relaxed her grip on the armrests. She had a small fear of the external atmospheric friction being too turbulent for the external sensors, tires, and cameras, but Max assured her that their continued deceleration would keep it from happening.

"Do you hear that?" asked Max after a few minutes.

Taylor listened carefully, afraid of hearing the same vibration sound. Fortunately, this sounded completely different.

"What is it?"

"It's air rushing past us," he said and smiled wide.

At first, she could barely hear the faint sound. Since leaving the at-mosphere, she had gotten used to the silence and forgot about the sounds always present on the Earth's surface. Now that she heard the faint sound of wind, it reminded her of being back on solid ground. She looked back to the video feed, and the screens showed a dark North American continent with light gray clouds.

They were aiming for the Cascade Range, between Mt. Rainier and Mt. Adams, and had to trust that their sensors had kept accurate track of their position and would deliver them to where they wanted to go. Once back near the surface, they would fly north at low altitude to the rendezvous point. If someone or a group managed to track them, they hoped to escape into the mountains and forests.

When they finally could see mountains, the general contour of the Earth, and then the individual trees, Taylor felt her tension start to dissipate but not completely. Would they find a military welcome party at the rendezvous point instead of their friends? Even if they managed to return unscathed, she would probably be sick once the anxiety completely left her.

During the last few seconds of the descent, Taylor kept waiting for him to level the car, but he seemed intent on crashing into the Earth. She unconsciously pushed against her seat as if she could prevent them from hitting the dark trees below.

"Do we have to fly so close to the ground?" Taylor asked after he leveled out. "If the last NMG goes out, we're dead!"

"We're dead anyway if that happens," he said almost as if the thought excited him, but then he attempted to look more serious. "Sorry, I didn't mean to scare you."

They flew close to the top of the trees, at about a hundred meters. Since the engine and NMG were almost noiseless and emitted no exhaust, the only noise they made sounded like a stick being slashed through the air. Anyone who happened to hear them on the ground would not be able to locate them. By the time they heard the noise, Taylor and Max would be out of sight.

To minimize distractions, Taylor avoided speaking. With only one NMG engine to maneuver and fight the aerodynamic resistance, Max had to put more effort into flying, but he seemed to enjoy the extra challenge. He had half the mobility than what he had on the ascension. Taylor spent her time just trying to enjoy the trip. She especially enjoyed flying past Mt. Rainier. In the dark, the mountain lost none of its beauty and looked almost mysterious.

The navigation program helped to guide them to the rendezvous location coordinates, located about fifty kilometers from the takeoff point, a third of the way from Seattle to Spokane. For safety, they chose a different location than the meeting point and refrained from any communication during the entire journey. Only Dominga had tried objecting, wanting to keep in constant contact. Taylor could only imagine her impatience and anxiety to hear from them.

When they finally arrived at the designated location, they hovered silently at over a hundred meters and scanned the trees below them, searching for signs of their friends.

"There they are," said Taylor after spotting several cars off the road. The brake lights from a few of the cars illuminated the scene in an eerie red glow. She pointed to the spot on the video screen indicating their landing site.

"Looks like it's only them," Max said in relief at finding no sign of army personnel or police officers. "Ready to go meet them?"

Taylor paused for a second to consider his suggestion. Initiating the final descent to the Earth gave her some anxiety.

"It's strange, but I feel almost happy to touch the Earth again like it missed me."

"Yes," he agreed, "almost like an addiction or a psychological need."

Taylor was excited to see everyone again and especially wanted to talk to Cesar, to tell him how the convertible had worked and the major failure. She felt a sudden regret that he missed the experience. Maybe she and Cesar could make a similar trip in the future. She would have to ask Gerald what he thought if he also felt bad for not getting to go.

As they slowly descended, Taylor watched for signs of anyone in the group noticing them. With their lights off, the car might not be seen until they reached the top of the trees. At just above eighty me-ters high, no one made the signal, but when they had descended to thirty-five meters, Taylor saw a single flashlight illuminate and begin searching the sky. After the beam flashed across her camera, several other lights began focusing on them.

One of the lights blinked three times slowly, the sign to continue descending. If they saw two quick pulses of light, they were supposed to get out of there. All the other flashlights bathed the bottom of the car in light and nearly saturated the pixels in the camera.

The group of people formed a circle where they intended Max to land, and the scene reminded Taylor of some strange Wiccan ritual, preparing for a possible sacrifice or appearance of a God.

When they came to a final stop, Taylor tried looking out the windows, but they were too dark to see anything except for the faint points of light from the flashlights. Taylor waited impatiently for the pressure inside the car to balance with the atmosphere outside. The distinct sharp break of the airtight seal made her heart jump in excitement. Dominga stood closest to the car on Taylor's side, prepared to help her step onto solid Earth.

"You're alive," Dominga almost yelled as they embraced.

"Whoa," Taylor said, smiling and wobbling a bit on her feet. "It feels like we've been flying for an entire day. My legs are dead."

After everyone had gotten their greeting out of the way, Cesar stepped forward. He had been holding back, and his patience suddenly expired.

"Did you experience any problems?" he asked.

"At the start of re-entry, we lost the primary NMG," she said in disappointment. "Other than that, everything else went better than expected."

"So you actually made it into orbit?" Gerald asked with excitement.

"We sure did," said Max, coming around the car to stand with Taylor.

"We made it to eight thousand kilometers," Taylor said proudly. "It was amazing and beautiful. I wish you all could have come."

"Eight thousand," Cesar said. "That's farther than you planned."

Max cleared his throat before answering.

"We were being tracked by radar, and when we escaped, I kind of just kept going."

"Yeah, since I was unconscious at the time," Taylor said, laughing, "you could do whatever you wanted. What else did you do?"

"You were unconscious?" asked Dominga with some concern.

"You were being tracked by radar?" Doroteo asked.

Max and Taylor relayed the story almost as a competition between them as if they were on opposing hockey teams fighting for the puck. At the end of the story and after they had answered everyone's questions, Doroteo said that they needed to get going. He wanted to leave the crime scene as soon as possible.

TWENTY-FOUR

Max

Instead of changing from their vacuum suits and driving separately, Taylor and Max decided to drive back to Cesar's house together. Taylor had insisted that she drive on the way home and Max did not even consider arguing with her. The look in her eyes said he would be losing any argument to the contrary. Max completely understood the unfairness of the situation but refused to feel any remorse. If she had piloted the convertible, as she liked to call their amazing creation, they probably would have crashed or gotten caught, or both. The situation probably caused considerable irritation to her, and he would have felt the same.

The whole experience still felt like a dream to him. Memories of their journey together swirled around in his head, and he wondered when the dream would end, when he would stop thinking about what they saw together and the experience of flying in space with such a beautiful and intelligent woman. While sitting in the passenger seat, he enjoyed watching her take control of the vehicle. He loved her confidence, eagerness, and especially her aggressive driving style.

Max had the feeling that people were following them, and he blamed it on his imagination, since he had no real evidence. They saw no military helicopters, police cars, people looking at them, or any other suspicious activity. If caught by any military or civilian authority, he would be taken away with them, and his father would be very unhappy about the situation. Max would be set free eventually, but his new friends would not. They had no political connections.

On the short drive, he tried sorting his conflicting emotions. He almost felt like an adult on a playground with a bunch of kids. He had respect for the intelligent members of his new group. They were definitely not children, but he felt accustomed to socializing with the owners and CEOs of major corporations, with military leaders and politicians, not with people who made under a million dollars a year, people who had no political power.

"I am so tempted to just take off into the sky," Taylor said when the lights of Seattle came into view. The sound of her voice broke his internal reflection. "It would be so easy."

"I know the feeling," he said without turning.

While they reminisced about their adventure, he failed at trying to ignore his physical attraction to her. He loved her curly red hair pulled into a ponytail, how her white skin looked almost the color of marble, and how her green eyes sparkled on her face. Max had several encounters with beautiful women in his life, but never had one made him forget to breathe when she looked at him. He kept remembering how stunning she looked in her vacuum suit and wished he could have taken a picture of them together.

Everyone in the group finally arrived back at Cesar's house at one-thirty in the morning. Before going to their beds, they had a short discussion at the dining room table. Dominga insisted on providing everyone with something to drink. Max chose water, but most chose tea or juice.

Cesar sat at the head of the table next to Taylor and Max at her side. Gerald sat on the opposite side of Max with Dominga between him and Cesar. Doroteo sat on the other end, silently sipping his coffee. Max couldn't remember the names of the rest, the elderly man and woman, the dark-haired woman, and the two young men. Everyone was talking quietly with their neighbor.

Max found the group dynamics interesting. Everyone seemed to feel comfortable sharing their opinion or views, but they all looked at Taylor and Gerald to make the final decisions. She and Gerald seemed to share the responsibility, but sometimes even she looked at Gerald to provide ultimate approval. Max had respect for anyone who could lead a group of volunteers in a non-profit venture with only ideological motivations. Max never knew such a group could be successful. Time would tell.

"I don't know about the rest of you," Gerald said to the entire gathering, interrupting the individual discussions around the table. All eyes turned to him. "But this is very exciting, and we need to talk about our next plans."

Max waited to see who would respond first. While glancing around the group, he noticed the young man across the table staring at him, the one with messy white hair. After making eye contact, the young man quickly looked down at his drink, and Max wondered what part he played in the group. There was something strange about him. His curiosity was soon broken by Doroteo, the dark man everyone seemed to fear, except for Cesar.

"We are lucky that the military is not at our doors this night." He turned to Gerald with his black eyes, and Max had to admit that the man intimidated him. He wondered how his chief of security would react to him. Several heads bobbed in agreement, including the old man across the table.

"So how do you suggest we proceed with our plans?" Gerald returned his stare without flinching.

"Your plans?" Doroteo asked.

"I think what Gerald wants to know," Cesar interrupted, "is that, as the security expert, what is your opinion?"

The two old Mexicans held each other's gaze for a moment, and a silent conversation seemed to take place between them. To Max's surprise, Doroteo turned back to Gerald and smiled. "We cannot possibly keep this a secret for much longer, under our current testing environment. I think we need to change your working environment."

"Can you be more specific on changing our working environment?" asked Taylor.

"I think what he means is that you cannot continue your work in Seattle," Dominga said with curiosity on her stately face. "Am I right?"

"More or less," Doroteo answered.

"Big picture everyone," said Gerald before anyone else could answer or start their own private conversations. "Before arguing the details, we need to discuss our next course of action."

"I agree with you, Gerald," said Taylor. "We will need a better vessel, one to accommodate more people. If we're going to show the world what we have and what it can do, we need to have something larger, something we can use to escape their grasp when they try to come after us."

Max mostly listened to the ensuing conversation. Everyone who spoke seemed to agree with the decision to build a larger spacecraft, even Doroteo. Max agreed as well. His company built devices for satellites and spacecraft and helped deliver them there all the time, but Taylor's idea filled him with more excitement and pleasure than his job usually gave him. At the moment, he wanted more than anything to fly back into space and the thought of another journey with Taylor was as exciting as seeing the Earth itself.

Despite the energy in the room, a nagging concern tainted his excitement, a concern supported only by intuition rather than any tangible evidence. Were they hiding some information from him and Mark?

Max wanted to appear completely trusting of the group and not change the dynamics by showing any suspicion. Rather than making an uncomfortable accusation, he made plans to talk with Mark about his suspicion later, to see if his friend felt the same or knew anything.

The possibility of Mark keeping something from him failed to make even a fleeting appearance in his mind.

When they started discussing the specifics of making a larger spacecraft, he forgot about his concerns. He and Mark had already discussed that option and had a tentative plan to propose, one that would even satisfy their security agent, Doroteo. Max waited for an opening in the conversation and Gerda gave it.

"I thought it was an excellent idea," the older woman said to no one in particular. "An excellent idea to convert the car into the vessel. It probably saved a ton of money. Is that what we're planning to do next but something bigger?"

"TerraWatch may be able to provide an adequate solution," Max said. All eyes turned to him. "Doroteo is correct with his concern. What you want to do cannot be done in secret here."

"When you say here," interjected Taylor. "What do you mean? Seattle? Washington? The Pacific Northwest?"

"No, I mean the United States."

"Okay, so where then?"

"We have a facility in Brazil," Mark said, sitting forward in his chair and putting his elbows on the table, "with a secure hangar that we can use to build the next vessel away from any curious federal agents. We just acquired a new company jet and were getting ready to sell the old one. We think it's the perfect size for what you want to do."

Gerald sat back and looked like a casual observer as if he knew what would happen. Max and Mark stared at each other for a moment, then looked around the table at everyone's reaction. Cesar and Doroteo looked concerned. Everyone else looked at Max and Mark then at Taylor and Gerald, then back. From the smile on Taylor's face, Max knew he would be able to convince them.

"Let's sleep on it," she said.

Max's announcement put an end to the conversation and gave everyone an excuse to go to bed. At Doroteo's insistence, they all planned to stay the night at Cesar's house. Dominga showed Max and Mark to their rooms on the second floor. Before retiring, Max asked

Mark to come into his room for a few minutes.

"What do you think?" Max asked.

"I think you're the luckiest guy alive," his friend said while smiling and rubbing his eyes. "You went into space and with that beautiful little genius no less. Isn't she amazing!"

Max suppressed a smile, almost.

"Yes, you're right. I am very lucky. But I meant, what do you think of their plans? Do you think anything strange is going on?"

"It all sounds perfectly normal to me," Mark said with his dry humor. "You just got to pilot a fusion-powered-magic-momentum-generator-spaceship, and now we're going to help them build a larger one. Perfectly normal."

"No, I know nothing we're doing is normal, but did you feel any-thing strange going on between them? Something they're not telling us?"

"Okay, you're serious," Mark said, pausing to think. He rubbed his eyes and ran his hand through his hair. "If they're keeping something from us, I cannot imagine what it could be. I mean, they've shared two of the most important secrets they could keep. I don't think they're keeping anything else from us."

Max turned away from his friend and looked at his bed. He imag-ined how good the sheets would feel and how much he wanted to wrap them around himself.

"I guess you're right," he said at last. "With all these dangerous se-crets we're holding, I'm probably just being paranoid."

"Even if they are hiding something from us. I don't care! There's only one thing I want out of all this."

"What's that?"

"I want to fly in that thing too, in space."

"I'm glad you feel that way," said Max, putting his hand on his friend's shoulder, "because you're moving to Brazil. I want you in charge of this little venture."

TWENTY-FIVE

Freddy

On the morning of July 5, the day after the test flight into space, Sadi, Mr. Smith, and Freddy drove back to Portland together, leaving Cesar's place around noon. Freddy drove while Mr. Smith sat in the passenger seat beside him. The old man tried giving his seat to Sadi, but she insisted on sitting in the back. On the way home, they talked mostly about the previous night's event and avoided discussion of the future.

"It's still too hard to believe," said Sadi. "I can't believe they actually went into space."

"This is too much for an old guy like me to take in," said Mr. Smith in agreement. "I still remember being in shock when we made it to the moon. That took thousands of people and billions of dollars to achieve, but Taylor and Mr. Sanchez can accomplish it for under a million dollars. Remarkable!"

Before leaving Cesar's house, Freddy wanted to say goodbye to his new friend, Franklin, but decided to let him sleep. In the short time they had spent together, Freddy had already begun to feel a strong connection with him. He liked how Franklin made no attempt to hide his emotions or real thoughts. They both loved computers and technology and felt socially awkward around unfamiliar people.

When they arrived at Sadi's home, Freddy could feel her relief at returning safely and seeing the girls again. During the entire trip, Freddy had sensed her disturbing feeling that something terrible might happen. He had tried to offer comfort by reminding her of his ability to detect anyone with belligerent intentions, but his attempt had failed to stop her concern. He understood how she felt and enjoyed her final emotions of safety.

When they drove away from Sadi's house, Mr. Smith asked Freddy what he thought of Sadi when they were younger. The old man suspected that Freddy had romantic feelings for her and to Freddy's surprise, he felt no shame about the possibility of telling his boss. He trusted Mr. Smith with the secret.

"Yes," he said. "I was in love with her."

Mr. Smith paused, feeling a longing for youth again.

"I don't blame you," he said finally. "She's a pretty lady."

—※—

Strange dreams filled Freddy's sleep that night, and when he woke the next morning, he could only recall one. Mr. Smith, Sadi, and his new friend Franklin had been walking far ahead of him in a thick black fog. At first, he could see only their outlines and the lights from their lanterns. He attempted to run so he could catch them, but he could only walk. They got farther and farther away until their lights became blurry flickering stars, which eventually died. When he could no longer see them, he stopped and wept.

Freddy spent the next day taking care of his responsibilities for Mr. Smith. With his school work and all the recent events in his life, he had spent insufficient time on his official job. Most of his time involved responding to letters and handling all Mr. Smith's financial affairs through his accountant. Freddy knew where every cent of his boss's accounts went, and made sure no one took advantage of him. He attempted to keep his boss up to date with the status of his affairs, but Freddy's new sense confirmed what he always suspected. Mr. Smith had only pretended to show interest.

When finished fulfilling his employment responsibilities, he devoted the rest of his time to preparing for his finals, which would be taking place in just a few weeks. He felt prepared for them, but the volatile nature of his recent life made the future seem too uncertain. He had to over-prepare for any other interruptions.

In the dark dungeon of his mind, he kept his greatest fear chained like a beast to a wall. But no matter how much he kept it secured, he feared the beast would get loose. He feared something would prevent him from finishing school in the fall, a goal that had come to define his future. After the current semester, he only had two more classes to graduate with his BS degree. Freddy had begun to equate the achievement of graduation with finally conquering his past. Graduation felt so close, and yet seemed too easy to lose at the last moment.

Every day after the test flight, Freddy had checked the website. He was extremely curious about Taylor's progress on the project in Brazil but always came away disappointed to find that Gerald had posted nothing new. Although all members could give updates to the site, only Gerald and Franklin ever sent them. Freddy understood the fear of posting incriminating information, even with the site's security encryption.

Franklin, their website administrator, would occasionally post an update about a new security feature. But after the test flight, he started posting fake confessions about drug use to promote the public purpose of the site, an online addiction support group. He also created a couple of extra fake users to enhance the illusion.

A few nights after the test flight, at nearly two-thirty in the morning, a beeping from one of Freddy's computers woke him from a light sleep. He kept the computers in his room operating all the time, and whenever he got a message on the website or an important email, a beep would notify him. Due to his increased anxiety levels, the soft beep could easily wake him.

Freddy wiped sleep from his eyes and shuffled over to the computer three meters from the bed. The LEDs from his computers and electronic equipment were filling his room with dim, slowly pulsating red light. The lights gave an impression of being in a dark spaceship command room but decorated with Christmas lights.

Franklin used the website chat feature to communicate.

Franklin: *Hey Freddy! Did you try those tricks I told you about?*

Freddy: *Yes, the computer code worked as you promised. Thank you.*

Freddy had always preferred communication through email to speaking with others face to face. He could put his entire focus on words and did not have to interpret body language or tone. Words alone seemed to put him on the same plane with others. With his new ability to sense feelings, he finally felt as though he understood people and could almost interact with them as a normal person. His unfair advantage seemed like payback for a lifetime of confusion.

Now through the website, his ability to read Franklin's thoughts and feelings was hidden from him again. Nevertheless, he enjoyed waiting for the text replies rather than knowing them in advance. As he had discovered at the hotel, when rescuing Helen and Daryn, he could only sense the feelings of others when they were within the immediate vicinity.

Franklin: *Are you always up this late?*

Freddy: *I was asleep, but this is fine. You can message me anytime.*

Franklin: *Okay man, I've been meaning to ask you about this, but tell me if you don't want to talk about it. You've seen this thing. What does it look like?*

Freddy: *When it communicates with me, it appears as a human. We did not see any sign of biological life when the probe visited us.*

Franklin: *Yeah, Gerald told us about that. It scared the shit out of him. Wish I could have seen that. Ha ha ha.*

Freddy smiled at Franklin's written laughter.

Freddy: *What news of Taylor? Is she in Brazil yet?*

Franklin: *She flew out just yesterday, on a private jet no less. She's really excited to get started and did not want to delay. It's awesome!*

Freddy: *What about Cesar and his friends, Doroteo and Dominga?*

Franklin: *Cesar wants to make some improvements to the BMW. I don't think they are planning to move to Brazil. You're gonna go on a test drive right?*

His replies appeared almost instantly. Freddy was impressed.

Freddy: *You type very fast!*

Franklin: *It's a matter of necessity. Keyboard's on fire. Can't keep my fingers there for long. Are you changing the subject???? Your boss was not overjoyed at the thought of sending you into space to meet that thing.*

Freddy: *Yes, I will go on a test drive first, then I can go where she wants me to go. I should be excited to make the journey, but it does frighten me.*

Franklin: *So you're planning to go?*

Freddy: *I think that I should.*

Franklin: *Why?*

Freddy: *I do not have a choice. She can make me do it, I am sure, like what happened with Helen.*

Franklin: *I see your point. Want some company?*

Before responding, Freddy paused to fully understand the question. Was Franklin willing to go with him? Did he realize the significant probability of never returning?

Freddy: *You would go with me?*

Franklin: *Hmmm, hold off on that thought. Now I know your hesitation. It is a little intimidating. Any more communications from u-know-who?*

When Freddy imagined the experience of traveling to Mercury and meeting the creature from his dream, a cold sensation made him shiver. During his experiences with the alien dream creature, he could not remember being afraid of her, or it. Why did the possibility of meeting it fill him with so much anxiety? Did he fear just the possibility of being lost in space and dying in a cold void? For some reason, his fear seemed to originate from another source, one that his mind was refusing to acknowledge.

He left Franklin on hold for more than a minute. If they were talking on the phone, Franklin would have already cut the connection.

Freddy: *No, I have not had any more communications with it. Still there?*

Franklin: *No worries, still here. Working on other stuff while we com. Have you tried contacting it again?*

Freddy: *Not emotionally ready yet. I am busy with school.*

While Freddy waited for Franklin's reply, he composed a message for Cesar, a message he had postponed for several days. But instead of hitting send, he just looked at the words as if they could sting him. *Is the BMW ready for another flight?*

The next message from Franklin drew his attention to the other screen.

Franklin: *When you finally do get a hold of the thing, let me know if it will allow you to take a guest with you. I took some time to think more about it and put the two options on the scale. The 'exciting adventure' alternative outweighed the 'being used as food by hungry alien monsters' option.*

Freddy laughed quietly, and the sound filled the room. The possibility of the alien luring him away to be eaten had never crossed his mind. If the alien just wanted food, a cow would provide more meat than any human, and the alien would not have to work so hard to get the cow. The comical thought helped lighten his mood, and he decided to hit send on the message to Cesar.

While waiting for Cesar to reply, he turned to the screen of the conversation with Franklin.

Freddy: *That is very nice of you to offer, but if something does happen and we do not return, Gerald probably would not want to lose his computer expert.*

Franklin: *Screw Gerald. He can't stop me from going, and the site is up and running anyway.*

Freddy: *Cesar and Taylor can stop you. It is their spacecraft.*

Franklin: *So you don't want me to come with you?*

Freddy suddenly wondered if he had offended Franklin and wished for his telepathic ability to travel through the fiber optic lines.

Freddy: *I want your company, yes. I hope it works out that way.*

Franklin: *I can be a stowaway then. You wouldn't tell them, right? Pay no attention to the lump in the back seat! ha ha.*

I do not think that will work, Freddy typed then deleted the words instead of hitting enter. After looking at Franklin's written laughter, he realized the joke, that his friend did not really intend to become a stowaway.

Freddy: *Yes, I will say those exact words. Ha ha.*

In real life, his attempt at sarcasm would have fallen flat, and he would not have been able to delete his words. He did indeed prefer electronic communication to verbal.

Franklin: *Whenever you're awake in the middle of the night, send me a text. We should do this more often. Chatting in between programming is actually making me work faster.*

Freddy: *Yes, good idea. I just sent a message to Cesar, about letting me know when the BMW will be ready. For a longer trip, we will need to take care of digestion issues.*

Franklin: *I hadn't thought about that...*

Freddy chose not to elaborate. The next day, Cesar replied via the website.

Cesar: *It is very good to hear from you. The vehicle will be ready for another trip in a few weeks. Have you decided what you want to do??? I will not try to push you. Just know that it will be ready for you when you are ready.*

TWENTY-SIX

Sadi

A week after the July 4 test flight, Craig Swenson made a surprise visit to Sadi's house. She attempted to hide her anxiety at seeing him, afraid of the information he had to share. His smile helped her to feel a little better.

"Come in, Craig," Sadi said, returning the smile.

Neither Helen nor Daryn greeted the huge man and Jen only nodded at him. Helen kept one eye in his direction and the other on her mom. She looked ready to ask a million questions but kept silent. Before her kidnapping, she would have run to him and asked random questions with probably a comment or two about being slightly overweight.

The change in her daughter made Sadi sad. She hoped Helen would eventually return to her old, slightly neurotic self. Sadi noticed the big man's pleasure at seeing the two girls. He probably understood the association he caused in their little minds and so did not become offended that they failed to show excitement at seeing him.

The big man and Sadi went into the kitchen and sat on opposite sides of the counter. Sadi made Daryn and Helen go downstairs. She asked Jen to keep them away while Mr. Swenson visited.

"Do you have any children?" she asked.

He turned from watching the girls go.

"Just one daughter. She's in college now, but I'm hoping for a couple grand kids in a few years, no sooner though."

Sadi tried to think of other small talk, but she really wanted to hear what he had to say. Sitting with him reminded her of when she first met him at Mr. Smith's mansion. She remembered having difficulty keeping the smile on her face.

"So what is going on?"

His answer had the power to alter the course of her life, for better or worse.

"Have you seen anything in the news about the incident?"

Immediately following Helen's rescue, Sadi had closely followed the news in hopes of hearing something related to the incident in Salem. The fear of finding a related news story had lingered for several weeks and prevented her from having many peaceful moments.

Nightmares had stalked almost every moment of sleep, visions of Helen or Daryn on the TV screen as potential suspects in the case instead of the victims. Other nightmares had taken place in the hotel where she'd gone back in time and found empty rooms instead of her daughter. The dreams, however, were much better than when she would dream of her dead son.

"No, I haven't seen anything," she said, "but I have been watching."

"So, I've been keeping informed of all the news reports about the incident," he said, "and in none of the actual incident updates did the names of the victims get revealed, just as I thought. The media is being paid to protect people with money. The reports didn't even mention the involvement of a child sex ouperation, at least not in the public news media. I did manage to see some of the police reports and they, of course, were more informative. But sometimes, what is not included is more revealing than what is."

"How close are they getting to figuring out what happened?"

Sadi stared intently at him while waiting for his answer. His use of the word *victim* made her angry. In the police reports, the scum that Freddy had killed would be the victims. The real victims were Helen, Daryn, Freddy, and Sadi. She made a pitiful attempt to hide her annoyance, but he did not show any recognition.

"They're still working on it," he continued. "You can be sure about that, but they are stuck for now. Your friend did a very good job of removing the evidence of your presence in that hotel."

Sadi breathed a sigh of relief and made a mental note to relay the compliment to Freddy.

"So do you think we're in the clear now?"

"I don't want to make you overconfident, because the front desk girl remembers your friend, and she thinks that a woman was with him, but her memory of your appearance is fuzzy, and the investigators are not even sure if it is relevant."

"Is that the best lead they have right now? A man and a woman could be anyone."

"It is for now," he said with a serious smile, "but I can see that the key to solving this case lies with Helen's abductors, the Becerras. Fortunately, I don't think the police have any idea that there is such a couple, but the pornography organization is probably checking up on it. For the moment, they think the motive might lie with a rival child pornography organization."

"I'm trying to locate that couple," he continued. "From what Helen told us, I think they fled the country. They probably don't even know about what happened. If I can find them, I hope to help keep them that way."

"I'm worried about those boys that we helped escape," Sadi said after taking a moment to comprehend his words fully. "They could probably lead the police back to us."

Craig paused and looked down at the glass of water that Sadi had gotten him.

"That is indeed a danger. If they haven't located them now, they probably never will. I checked on the social worker you took them to. She has a good record and should know how to handle the situation."

"So you're still working on this?"

"I'm just following up," he said. "Sometimes it's hard to stop an investigation completely. But don't worry. You don't owe me anything. I'm actually glad to help on this one."

Sadi began to wonder about a hidden purpose of Craig's visit, if he told her everything or had more information. Seeing him made her feel nervous.

"Is this nightmare ever going to end?" she asked, trying to look superficially exasperated.

Craig put his massive hand over hers.

"Try not to worry too much. I'll do my best to keep them off your back."

Seeing his sincerity gave Sadi the strength to smile.

"I know."

"As far as our legal system goes," he said, returning to a business tone of voice. "You have little to worry about. No jury is going to convict you of anything. If it ever comes to that, your friend Freddy will take the blame, but he's got a pretty good self-defense plea."

"There is no way I can let him take the blame."

"Yes, I know," Craig said as if she interrupted his flow. "On the other hand, your greatest danger is from the criminal organization. They're the ones to worry about."

"Do you have any access to what they know?"

"No, but I know that top people in law enforcement protect this child sex ring, help to keep it operating behind the law. There's no way they could perform their operation in secret."

"Freddy said something about that."

Craig's intensity changed when Sadi said that. His eyes narrowed.

"That's something I want you to tell me. How did Freddy know so much?"

Sadi gulped as discreetly as she could. She was intimidated but wanted him to think otherwise.

"He's special."

"I can tell, but how and why? He could not have known where to find your daughter unless he had some sort of connections. People with those kinds of connections can be dangerous."

"I have no idea, really," she said defensively. "I know he's not dangerous, at least to good people."

For several seconds, he looked at her suspiciously as though his intense gaze could pull words out of her mouth. She was uncomfortable but refused to reply, and after a moment, his look softened.

"I could not get anything out of him either," Craig said, laughing. "Don't worry, I won't hold it against you, but will you promise me one thing?"

"Maybe," she said.

"You'll tell me one day?"

Sadi thought about it for a second. She tried thinking of a future condition where she could let Craig know of her confidential information, about the alien and the spacecraft.

"I will, one day."

For the last few minutes of his visit, their conversation transformed into small talk. At the end of the visit, Sadi felt a little better. At least she did not feel any worse and had a more up-to-date status of the investigation.

TWENTY-SEVEN

Taylor

A few days after her journey into orbit, Taylor left Cesar's house and traveled to Brazil with Mark Salmon. Never before in her life had she endured such a long and miserable plane ride. The comfort of the luxury private jet wore off after the first refueling. Early in the flight, Mark offered her a sleeping pill so that she could sleep through a good portion of the journey, but she did not like taking drugs except for the occasional painkiller.

Although Mark was excited flying with her and taking charge of the new project in Brazil, Taylor knew he went with her as an unwilling participant. From the way he talked about his wife and two young sons, Taylor knew how much he would miss them. He would rather be with them than with her, and she understood.

Early on the flight, Taylor and Mark had exhausted their topics of conversation. She had asked if he ever visited Brazil. He had. Did he like it? Yes, but he did not want to live there. Why did they need to convert a jet into a spacecraft in Brazil? Couldn't they do it closer to home, in the United States? TerraWatch partnered with a Brazilian company for cheap labor to build some of their components. They owned a hangar, a warehouse, and a small production facility. At the moment, it employed only a couple of people, mostly to keep track of inventory.

Taylor tried focusing on future tasks rather than her irrational feelings of abandonment and loneliness. She missed her mother, but most of all she missed her friends from Mexico: Dominga, Cesar, and even Doroteo. Dominga had taught her how to appreciate the feminine things in life, a stark contrast to her mother. Taylor's mother had always been more of a tomboy. They had nothing pink or with lace in their home. Taylor had only ever seen her mother in pants and shorts rather than dresses or skirts. Taylor had acquired an unconscious distaste for purely feminine things. But that kind of attitude had been almost impossible while living with Dominga.

After the long flight, Mark and Taylor landed finally in the Luis E. Magalhaes International Airport in Salvador, Brazil. When Taylor exited the plane, the warm and muggy air wrapped around her in a moist embrace. Almost as soon as they stepped onto the tarmac, the private jet left their sight in preparation to fly somewhere else. After the jet departed, Taylor felt as though their last tie to her home had been broken. Their first task would be to find their contact, and then he would take them to the private airport where they would see the plane, their next spacecraft, a wild beast ready to be tamed.

"So have you met the man we're meeting?" asked Taylor as they walked through the crowded airport. Perspiration covered her whole body from the humidity. She would need a few weeks to grow accustomed to her new climate.

"It's been a few years since I've seen him," Mark replied. "He's a technician turned engineer, very sharp. He runs this place now, named Yuri Burkov."

"Sounds like a native Brazilian to me," said Taylor sarcastically. "Where's he from?"

"He's a local guy, believe it or not, but I believe his parents were from Russia."

Shortly after their conversation, a man hailed them in broken English from behind. He called for Mark and her first name. After turning to see who called her, she saw a man just under her height waving to them. He reminded her of a rhinoceros, solid and heavy. He wore a black baseball cap with Portuguese words on the front. His long brown hair seemed to flow out from under the cap like a river. She imagined running into him at full speed and being knocked unconscious in the process.

"Nice to see you again, Mr. Salmon."

He spoke with a strong Portuguese accent and seemed to have difficulty saying Mark's last name. He shook Mark's hand and then turned to Taylor. While shaking her hand, his eyes performed a quick, full-body scan. Taylor bit her lip to prevent herself from speaking her thoughts. *Want me to turn around for you?*

"Please call me Mark," he said with a smile. "And this is Taylor Evans, our aeronautical engineer."

"The pleasure is mine," he said while shaking her hand. She noticed that her fingers failed to make contact with each other on the back of his thick hands.

Taylor hoped Yuri would be ignorant of aeronautical engineering. Otherwise, she might have to become familiar with some of the jargon. She needed to sound authentic but only had limited knowledge of aerospace engineering science, enough to fool the general population, but insufficient to fool an expert. Mark assured her that the concern would not materialize.

"What do you want to do first, Mr. Salmon?" asked Yuri. "Go to your apartments or to the shop or to the hangar?"

"I'd like to see the jet first if you don't mind."

"No problem," he said and took one of Taylor's bags. "So you're doing some aircraft modifications for high altitude flights eh! At least, that's what the email said about your visit. How long will it take?"

"I suspect it will take a few months," Mark said with a hopeful smile. He turned to Taylor for confirmation, and his eyes seemed to say that he felt confident in his assessment and that Yuri would have no reason to be suspicious of their deceit.

"Hopefully no longer than that," said Taylor in agreement.

While they drove away from the airport, Taylor sat in the front with Yuri and Mark sat in the back. Yuri kept turning around to address most of his comments to Mark with the occasional glance at Taylor. As he weaved through the crazy Brazilian traffic, she wished he would keep his eyes focused on the road. She kept her hand gripped tightly on the seat.

They required nearly sixty minutes to get through the heavy traffic in the city. Everything about her new surroundings felt foreign to Taylor and it almost overwhelmed her senses and emotions. The view of the bay, the buildings, and all the dark-skinned Brazilians filled her with the wonder of a new land to explore. So far, she enjoyed the experience.

Yuri drove them far outside the city and into the country, to a small airport with five hangars and theirs at the far north side. When Taylor first saw the jet, the enormity of their task was almost overwhelming, not a simple road vehicle. Mark gave her a tour of the craft, a Hawker Beechcraft 400 series. He spoke of it with fondness as though it recalled pleasant memories. Despite its worn and disused appearance, the jet was a very impressive aircraft.

After inspecting the jet more closely, she began making a mental list of tasks to perform. She would be replacing the twin engines with scaled-up versions of her NMG, a design Cesar helped create. Exciting thoughts of transforming the jet into a spacecraft quickly replaced her anxiety about the required work.

"I give Cesar less than a month before he comes down for a visit," said Taylor, her lips curved into a smile. She wiped the sweat away from her forehead. "Doroteo talked him out of coming with us, but he can't be kept away for long."

TWENTY-EIGHT

Taylor

Taylor spent her first few days in Brazil almost entirely with Mark. They lived in an apartment building, just a few kilometers away from both the hangar and the small production facility that Yuri managed. Taylor stayed in an apartment right across the hall from Mark. She had two separate bedrooms, a bathroom, and a small kitchen area. For the first few days, she felt guilty for having so much space to herself. TerraWatch would pay the rent, and Yuri had chosen the site, so she had no reason to complain.

Her accommodations paled in comparison to Cesar's house, but despite the smaller space, she loved the feeling of living alone. She had nearly always lived with her mother, even during college. She lacked only one item to feel completely self-sufficient, a bike. So, on their first day, she convinced Mark to purchase a bike with her.

"Since we're living so close, it'll do us good to ride."

From their apartment's location, they could ride their bikes to the shop or the hangar in fifteen minutes. Although Yuri provided them with a car, Taylor chose to use a bicycle whenever possible. She loved the feeling of using her own energy for travel. It helped keep her head clear. Traveling by bicycle would also help her appreciate the local landscape.

On the second day, they visited the small production facility, and Taylor found the shop equipped with many nice machining tools. Yuri enjoyed showing the machinery to someone who appreciated them as he did. By the end of the tour, she could listen to his speech without getting distracted by his accent.

Other than Yuri, TerraWatch employed only two people at the facility. When needed, Yuri hired out for more help. Taylor instantly disliked the two regular employees. They spoke no English and showed no interest in becoming acquainted with her. Yuri explained to them how Taylor had full access and full priority for any tool she needed. They were also to do whatever she wanted. Over time, they came to avoid her as they would a disease. At first, she took it personally, but she quickly realized the real reason. They did not like to work, and she always had work for them. But when they did a job, they performed to her satisfaction.

"I'm not complaining," she said to Mark on their third morning. "But how am I supposed to work with them?"

Before responding, Mark laughed. "I don't think a little language barrier is going to stop you. I have faith that you'll figure out a way. Engineering is its own language right?"

"Well, I'm not going to waste my time learning Portuguese," she said in irritation. "If I can't get through to them, then Yuri will have to do it for me."

"I'm sure you'll do just fine."

For that first week, they mostly kept out of contact with everyone. Taylor used the website's discussion board to give a couple of cryptic status updates and only once talked to her mother and Dominga on the phone. Mark would occasionally relay a message from Max, but for a reason Taylor could not understand, thoughts of Max resulted in irritation and mysterious anxiety.

At first, she attempted to ignore her reaction, but the feelings remained, and she could no longer deny them. After some conscious effort, she succeeded in understanding at least part of the issue. Her emotions had two different components. She was excited to hear news from Max, and she was irrationally afraid of hearing his voice or talking to him directly.

She had suffered the natural consequence of sharing an amazing experience with another person, specifically going into space with Max. Her brain had made a new association, pleasant memories and Max, and she still felt an innate dislike for who he represented. Her reaction had nothing to do with any personal feelings for him, she concluded with relief.

While working on making the aircraft airtight and designing how the NMG and fusion reactor would be incorporated, she realized how much fun they were having. All her physical needs were filled, and she spent all her time doing what she loved. She often had difficulty remembering all the horrible things she despised in the world. So, every once in a while, she would consciously remind herself of some injustice and how the state-approved threat of violence had produced it. Strangely, the resulting anger and indignation helped her feel better and work harder.

Mark and Taylor spent most of their time together talking about work. On rare occasions, they talked about personal subjects. He shared a love of science with her, and she had come to really like him. After working long days, they often ate dinner together and talked late into the evening. He enjoyed their work and believed in their mission. He had only one regret, being away from his wife and two young boys.

At the end of July, Taylor was frustrated at their slow progress. She had wanted to start working on assembling the larger NMG engines, but making the jet airtight began to feel like a never-ending task. She and Mark spent a lot of time pressurizing the plane, then leak checking, and finally patching just to find that they had to start all over again when they found a new leak. She had never done so much welding in her life.

Fortunately, back in Seattle, Cesar helped to make the parts they needed for the NMG engines and fusion reactors. Those parts were too complicated and sensitive to trust with Taylor's pair of local helpers. At first, she would often raise her voice at them for their laziness and poor attention to detail, but when her anger failed to motivate them properly, she decided to show more patience. Over time, their working relationship began to improve. She even learned a few Portuguese words—mostly insults directed at her. Eventually, their relationship achieved a comfortable equilibrium.

After the first few weeks, their hatred of her had shrunk to a moderate dislike, which she could manage. She gave their feelings little consideration, however, and cared only about the quality of their work. She let Yuri worry about their emotional health. He seemed a little frustrated but never said anything about the situation.

—※—

During the afternoon of Friday, July 31, Taylor was welding in the gutted cabin while a podcast played in the background. Living far from native English speakers, she had come to enjoy listening to anything in English, the topic of discussion a secondary concern. She often took a break from welding to let her fan dry the sweat from her face. During one of these breaks, the fan's noise muffled the voice of someone calling her name. When she turned to face the unknown person, Max Garner ducked to avoid getting hit in the face by her welding gun.

"My God," he said in surprise but with a smile. "I just got here and you're already trying to kill me."

"Max?" Taylor asked, setting the gun on the table.

"Hi, Taylor," he said pleasantly. "I was enjoying watching you work."

While trying to absorb the situation, Taylor forced herself to smile. She did not like the thought of him watching her.

"Even with all this sweat?"

"Even better," he said, grinning as he glanced around the cabin. "Looks like you've been busy."

"How long have you been standing there?" she asked. "When did you arrive?"

"Just got here. The company jet is out on the runway."

Taylor put down her wire feed welding gun and cut the power and gas flow. Her surprise at seeing him transformed into a slight annoyance. The situation seemed like a relative had just shown up on her doorstep and announced his intention to stay indefinitely.

"Thanks for giving me some warning about your visit," she said. "Did Mark know you were coming and forgot to tell me? Or, did you tell him not to tell me?"

As if to avoid her angry eyes, he turned his attention to the wires hanging from the ceiling and then to the gutted cockpit to his left.

"Uh, sorry about that. No, I didn't tell Mark, but he's used to me popping in on him."

"So, why are you here? To check up on our progress?"

"Yes," he said with a bit of relief in his voice. He placed his hand on the wall and seemed to enjoy the sensation. "I did want to see how things were coming. It's one thing to get a progress report from Mark but quite another to see it for myself. Looks like you're doing a great job destroying our old company jet. You probably know more about this old bird than I do. Lots of memories here."

"I'm giving her a makeover," she said with a mock-angry frown. "You're not supposed to see before we're done."

For the next thirty minutes, they talked about their progress, and she felt impressed by all of his detailed questions. Taylor took him to see the outside of the plane at the empty holes where the engines had been. She explained all of their plans, frustration at the slow progress of the leak-proofing, and how many of the engine parts were waiting for installation.

"Where's Mark?" he asked after they had returned to the inside of the jet. They sat across the aisle from each other in the back row, the only seats still fit for use.

"He's been working on engine parts at the shop. I don't expect to see him until I go home this evening. Some days, it's just like that. If we don't plan on crossing paths, we will usually touch base with each other in the evening."

"So," she said. "You said there was another reason for your visit?"

"I came to see you actually," he said, then quickly turned to look out the window.

"Well, now we're getting somewhere," she said with wet sarcasm. "Mission accomplished! You're looking at me. Now you can go back."

"Since it's the weekend," he said tentatively, "I thought you might want to take a break and go somewhere? I wanted to talk to you anyway."

For a brief moment, her confusion and anxiety felt exposed. Did he mean *you* plural, meaning she and Mark, or *you* singular? Was it a date?

"Weekend?" she said with authentic surprise in her voice then looked at her watch and laughed. "Hmm, Friday. That's weird. Mark and I haven't taken a whole day off since we got here."

He spoke with mock audacity.

"Let me guess. You want overtime pay?"

Taylor felt her muscles tense. Other than providing their living expenses and other needs, she never gave a second thought to TerraWatch actually paying her. She spoke without thinking.

"Last time I checked, I wasn't working for you."

He looked at her with a mixture of confusion and amusement.

"Well, I plan on paying you eventually. You deserve some kind of recompense for your work."

Taylor had to pause and think about the new information. For her reason to enter the country, they had given the excuse of work, but she did not give the claim serious consideration.

"Am I on your company records, as an employee?"

"To make it look official, we did have to make you an employee of TerraWatch. I'm sorry, Mark didn't explain that to you?"

"Well," she said and laughed, "if you're expecting me to refer to you as boss or sir, you're going to be disappointed."

Since graduating from college, she had spent no time looking for her first real job but instead spent her time developing the NMG. Being suddenly employed felt like jumping into cold water.

"No, I'm not your boss," Max laughed. "Technically, that would be Mark."

"That's better, I suppose," she said with a forced smile. "Then I'll have to ask him about my salary."

With Max sitting right next to her, she wondered for at least the twentieth time, if letting him know about the group had been an acceptable risk. All the successful people she knew had taken a big risk to get what they wanted, so she should as well, but had the temptation of his company's resources unwisely influenced her decision and clouded her judgment? The opportunity seemed to come at just the right time too. Taylor did not believe in coincidences, at least not as many as they seemed to have. Whenever she thought of their precarious situation, she felt tempted to run away and hide.

"So where do you want to go?" he asked, interrupting her thoughts. "We've got the jet waiting. The whole world is open to us."

"I have no idea," she said, suddenly feeling at a loss for words. She'd never had the option of going anywhere in the world, and he seemed to intimate that they should go somewhere far away. The thought of a long flight felt exhausting, and somehow, the idea felt wrong. During her brief stay in Brazil, she had not yet done any exploring of her immediate surroundings.

"Although that sounds fun, I haven't been anywhere local yet. I'd rather see what this city has to offer us. Maybe Mark has somewhere he'd like to see."

"I guess that would be alright," he said slowly as if trying to convince himself of an unfavorable option, "but for this afternoon, I just wanted to go with you alone. We could reminisce about old times, like when we went hiking or that one time when we went into space."

"That's all we've done together," she said with fake exasperation. At the same time, she attempted to hide her feelings of confusion and annoyance. She hated when people caused distractions.

So far, the afternoon seemed like a boxing match, and her opponent had just delivered his second knockout punch. She wanted more time to think about the current situation and discover if his motivations were personal or professional. If romantic interest played any role in his decision to visit, she needed to find a way to diffuse that potential bomb. At this point in her life, she could only focus on one thing.

Normal females would desperately hope for romantic interest from a wealthy and attractive man like Max, if not openly, definitely on a subconscious level. After a brief moment of thought, Taylor could honestly deny any such hope. She also realized the improbability of romantic intentions. There were plenty of other girls more feminine and more stable, girls willing to sacrifice anything else they wanted for the first rich and charming bachelor to come along. She was out of his social circle anyway.

"Actually," he said, "staying in Salvador might be enjoyable. The thought never even crossed my mind. We can rent a car and go check it out. What do you think?"

She thought about the proposal for a moment but then found a plan more appealing to her need for physical exercise. After welding for so long, her legs and back felt stiff.

"I've got a better idea. Let's go on a bike ride. Mark and I have had fun riding to work."

Max looked hesitant, so she persisted.

"Come on, Max. You're not worried about being away from your precious bodyguard are you?"

"No, but yes, I guess," he said in brief, personal confusion. "It's been instilled in me, to always have someone providing cover. People like my father have to, I mean, feel the need to protect themselves."

"Who knows that you're in *Salvador*?" Taylor asked with a thick accent.

"Let's go on a bike ride," he said, not answering her question. "I just don't have a bike."

TWENTY-NINE

Freddy

The discussion with Franklin, another human his own age, was like a light in the dark hallways of Freddy's mind. The conversation helped get him back on track with school the next day. He would not let anything interfere with his goal of a college degree, the next significant milestone in his life. A degree would be an accomplishment he could hold in front of the world wherever he went. He could hold it in front of his sister's and mother's faces, and it would finally break their grasp on him.

His nights were often filled with nightmares of failing to graduate. In some dreams, he finished almost all his requirements, then forgot to take the final test. In other dreams, he went up to get his diploma at the graduation ceremony, but they told him he forgot to take a class in his sophomore year. His teachers laughed at him and kicked him off the stage and he would see his mother and sister laughing at him. Many times, he would awaken and require several minutes to distinguish reality from the dream.

For the most part, he enjoyed school and the learning experience, but most of his classes felt like such a waste of time. He wished more class time could be used to answer specific homework questions rather than lecturing. He was most prepared to learn after attempting to solve homework problems on his own when his brain had created its own questions. Only at that point did he feel prepared to learn. Education professionals admitted that most kids who sat through a lecture only retained up to ten percent of the material. Freddy hated the idea of wasting ninety percent of his time.

Along with the brief communication with his professors, his labs seemed to be the only real beneficial experiences. Occasionally, he got lucky and found a compatible partner who gave more than he or she took. More often, however, his lab partners would quickly drain his short social energy supply. Many of them were too slow or lazy, and he would ultimately perform most of the work.

In college, he had only one extremely unpleasant experience that reminded him of his childhood. One of his partners thought Freddy was mentally disabled and demanded to do everything himself even when he failed to follow the directions correctly. At the end of those labs, Freddy went home and lay on his bed in the dark, breathing deeply in the hopes of restoring his self-esteem.

Freddy left the crystal on his dresser so he could see it whenever he came into his room. He felt better knowing its location, but he never looked at the crystal for longer than a glance and fought the temptation to put it in his drawer, out of sight. He experienced a strange attraction to the object as if the crystal wanted him to touch it so that she could talk to him again and he could start the next phase of the journey, which he did not want to start. Eventually, he used a piece of cloth to cover the crystal and the beautiful spider embedded inside.

He managed to avoid it for the next two weeks when the first summer session ended. The night after finishing his final exams, during dinner, Freddy sensed Mr. Smith's curiosity about the group.

"So you did good on your exams?" Mr. Smith asked. "Of course, you did. Ready to start your last term?"

"Yes, I feel like I did good, and I am excited."

"What about the group? Anything new?"

Mr. Smith really wanted to know if Freddy had any further communication with the alien, but he felt anxious to say the words out loud. He had already checked the website and had the same information Freddy had. He waited anxiously for Freddy's answer.

"Gerald gave an update yesterday on the website. He says things are going well in Brazil. Taylor and Mark from TerraWatch are working on the new craft. It is coming along fine."

"Anything else?"

"I have no other updates."

Mr. Smith looked at him for a few seconds then looked back to his plate, relief in his eyes. He believed Freddy, and he knew Freddy knew.

After dinner that night he hurried downstairs to work on a computer program he had started. He did not plan to look at the crystal, but when he opened the door, he noticed a light coming from under the cloth. He intended to close the door and go back upstairs, but he took a step toward the dresser instead and shut the door behind him.

With his heart pounding hard in his chest, he took the last two steps toward the glowing cloth and picked it up. He stood for several seconds, holding the wrapped crystal in his hand and fighting the temptation to look inside at the beautiful light. His instinct to reveal the crystal was like a powerful thirst. To his surprise, he found the strength to place the crystal in his pocket, still wrapped in the cloth.

THIRTY

Freddy

"**I** need to meet with one of my lab partners to go over a problem with our final project," Freddy said on his way out of the house that evening. Mr. Smith looked up from his laptop. He almost did not believe Freddy.

"When can I expect your return?" he asked.

"After dark, maybe ten," Freddy said.

He felt guilty for lying to Mr. Smith, but Freddy wanted to prevent him from worrying. Since the barn and kidnapping incidents, a heightened sense of paranoia had crept into his boss's thoughts and simple things began to worry him, especially anything related to the alien. If he had some kind of episode with the crystal at the house, Mr. Smith might find out. Freddy planned to confess the truth sometime in the future.

As he left the house, he wondered how his sense of right and wrong had evolved. His mother and sister had certainly made no impression on his values, or anyone else from his early life. Neither could he give credit to his recent friends or even Mr. Smith, since his values predated them. Perhaps the experiences he had suffered had beaten his sense of morality into him.

After Mr. Smith had hired him, Freddy spent a lot of time trying to define his sense of the world and trying to catch up with what he had possibly missed. Among others, he'd read many of the non-fiction works of C. S. Lewis, the famous Christian writer. He believed the philosophical part of what he read and even found the religious stories to be interesting. Suffering did help to establish many good character traits, but believing that had failed to make him feel better about his past.

The humid and warm evening air soaked his dry skin and clothes. He liked the feeling of the fresh air, a stark change to the air-conditioned and filtered house air. He started driving with the windows down, the spider crystal in the passenger seat covered by the cloth. He concentrated on traffic and only glanced a few times at the cloth bundle. Eventually, he entered downtown Portland and passed a movie theater near his school.

When he noticed the *Harry Potter and the Half-Blood Prince* movie advertisement he remembered seeing the first Harry Potter movie with his sister. His mother had scheduled to visit with him that day but convinced his sister to take him to the movies instead. Despite being with his sister and her rude friends, he liked the first Harry Potter movie and longed to see the others. For months afterward, he dreamed of being Harry Potter and having magical powers and friends, but deep down he knew that he would still be the one who had no friends. He would have no special powers, and even the nice kids like Harry and Ron would shun him.

He never saw any of the other movies and forgot about them until he drove past the movie theater that evening. Did the alien lead him to the theater and make him notice the advertisement? After driving past the theater, he decided to go in by himself and watch the movie. Watching a movie in a cool dark theater might help make him feel normal or at least forget about his anxiety for a couple of hours. After finding the seat in the precise center of the theater, he kept glancing at his pocket to check for lights through the fabric. By some piece of luck, the crystal let him enjoy the movie in peace.

After the movie, he went directly home and called up the stairs to inform Mr. Smith of his return. Without waiting for any acknowledgment, he ran to his room, lay on the bed, and stared at the spider in the crystal. As usual, when he tried focusing on the spider's eyes, his vision blurred, but he felt no different. At the end of each minute, he checked his watch to see if any time passed without his noticing. With a mixture of relief and disappointment, he could account for each minute—no trance.

At ten o'clock, he fell asleep with visions of the Harry Potter movie filling his head. He made no response when Mr. Smith called on his phone around ten-thirty. His phone blinked once, twice, and then went silent.

At midnight, a noise woke Freddy from a deep sleep. He sat up in bed and looked around at the dark room and waited to hear the sound again. While he listened, the blinking LED lights from his computers cast silent shadows on the walls. When he failed to hear anything other than the sound of his breathing, he decided to stop breathing and see if he could hear his heartbeat.

His eyes slowly adjusted to the dark and he could see everything clearly, except for a shadow in the corner of the room. After focusing on the dark corner, he noticed a human form suddenly materialize and his heart froze when he realized someone stood in the room with him. Seeing the stranger brought an unpleasant rush of adrenaline, but what really frightened him was what he *failed to sense.*

He could discern nothing from this person in the shadows. It seemed devoid of feelings and emotions, a sensation Freddy had failed to experience for many months. He could still feel Mr. Smith's presence upstairs, so he knew his senses had not been taken away from him. The being in his room felt like an empty shell, and his mind immediately imagined a ghost standing before him, some malevolent apparition. Rational thought failed to comfort him.

For several seconds, he sat motionless in bed and stared at the person in the shadow. Freddy glanced down at the crystal lying at his feet on top of the covers only to see a reflection of the blinking LED lights from the computers. When he looked back to the shadow, the person had moved out of the shadow to stand closer to him. The blinking lights illuminated the slender form of a human female, skin as smooth as a snake.

He felt the urge to scoot farther up the bed, away from her, but waited in a panic for the woman's next move. Freddy blinked then rubbed his eyes, thinking it might be a trick of his imagination—until she took another step toward him.

Slowly, the woman moved closer. For the first time since he'd rescued Sadi's child from the kidnappers, he felt real fear.

"Who are you?" he said. "What are you doing here?"

She made no response but just kept moving slowly toward him. In a few seconds, she would be directly opposite him against the wall.

"Do not come any closer."

When she came within a meter of his bed, she stopped and turned her head slightly as if attempting to recognize him. She spent several seconds staring at him, everywhere but his eyes. During those few seconds, Freddy realized with shock at what stood an arm's length away. All of her physical attributes were human, but she was not. His previous visions with the alien were obviously dreams, because this felt real. He looked around his room, and everything seemed normal and solid, no flat plane extending to infinity.

The creature had dark blond hair, cut short and falling straight just above her shoulders. The whites of her eyes reflected the blinking LED lights as if the light originated from her eyes. She stood almost eye to eye with him. Without saying a word or making any noise, she turned away and stepped toward the door. Before entering the hallway, she glanced back at him and smiled.

As she walked away, he watched her hair swing back and forth. In that instant, his fear evaporated like a drop of water in a hot frying pan. His attraction to her quickly replaced his fear, driving all fatigue from his muscles. He jumped off the bed and followed her into the dark hallway. She walked ahead of him slowly toward the stairs.

His instincts pulled him along behind her like a strong river current. Watching her move helped erase his concern about her identity and almost forget about the possibility of her non-existence. He forgot about Sadi and his juvenile infatuation with her. Who was Sadi, compared to this creature? He wanted nothing more than to follow the female in front of him.

She walked up the stairs, wound through the hallways, and went to the front door. Silently, he followed her outside and closed the door softly behind him. In his semi-conscious state, he followed her beyond the gate and onto the sidewalk. The bright streetlights and half-moon in the sky provided plenty of light to fully illuminate the human female body.

He maintained his distance at two meters behind her, enjoying the experience of seeing the movement of her hips and her hair gently swaying as if suspended in an ocean current. A small voice in the back of his head told him to look around and try to see their destination, but his other thoughts were a complete distraction.

They passed a couple of their neighbors' houses then exited the sidewalk and entered a trail, which led into the dark interior of a small group of trees, away from the streetlights. He had been on this short trail several times. The trail followed a stream to a small clearing with a public bench. As they approached the end of the trail, he was excited to see her face in the light.

What would he see in her eyes? Any trace of humanity? She stopped and looked into the sky, at the moon.

—※—

"It's a beautiful night, isn't it Freddy?"

Her words helped return his senses to him. The sound of her voice felt like cold water splashing on his face. When she turned to him, he had to catch his breath. Her eyes looked like black marbles surrounded by brilliant white snow.

"I know who you are," he said after swallowing the lump in his throat.

"Your speech is so formal, even for humans. Why is that?"

He hesitated before responding.

"I like people to understand what I am saying."

"Why are you so worried about other people?" She cocked her head to one side and shifted her hip to the other. Her breasts shifted enough for Freddy to notice. "A search for personal perfection. Is that it?"

"I suppose." Freddy stood still, but inwardly he fought an urge to step toward her. High over their heads, branches responded to the breeze and cast shadows of the moonlight.

While looking at the creature, he realized what he saw. The alien had enhanced her features, but the creature before him represented a real human woman, someone that he would meet.

"I want to show you something, Freddy," she said at the exact moment he completed his thoughts. She looked at the sky and pointed. Freddy tore his gaze away to follow her index finger.

At first, he saw nothing other than the stars above the branches, but he kept watching until he noticed one star growing brighter than the rest. After a few seconds, light from the bright star began to intensify around her feet like a spotlight. It illuminated her hair and shoulders, and the tip of her nose.

The source of the approaching light above the woman transformed into the probe he saw at the barn. The probe slowly reached within touching distance of the woman, and she extended her finger to touch the sharp, polished chrome tip. After her finger made contact, the probe stopped motionless in the air, and she reached her other hand out to Freddy.

"Take my hand, Freddy Carlson," she said.

While stepping toward her, he reached in anxious anticipation of grasping her slender fingers. But just before their fingers touched, he noticed a strange light coming from her skin. With a mixture of disappointment and wonder, he realized the light source, the sparkling water in the stream behind her. He was beginning to see through her.

He was immediately disappointed by the thought of being unable to touch her. When their fingers did make contact, however, an electric shock shot through his hand, up his arm, and into his heart. Her hand had substance and was like the live end of a car battery but without the pain. His gaze shifted from her sparkling eyes to the probe above her.

"Are you ready to come home?" she asked, looking at him with a blank expression.

"This is my home," he responded.

Her expression did not change. As they continued staring at each other, he saw the absence of humanity in her eyes, no warmth, no understanding, no empathy. His physical attraction to her evaporated, the lust that had drawn him into the dark night disappeared but was not forgotten.

Even without the attraction, he felt no fear and his emotion transformed into an intense curiosity. What kind of being looked at him from behind those eyes? Could the entity possibly understand Freddy, his motivations and fears? In those few seconds of contact, he had the impression that it knew him, more than he knew himself. He imagined looking through her eyes and into his own, into him.

In the next instant, the woman transformed into a cord of blue and orange light strings, connecting his hand to the probe like an electric rope. Hot energy flowed into his body from the probe, filling him like liquid into a dry sponge. After a few seconds, he had to close his eyes or the energy would explode out of his eye sockets. His mind filled with an intense light.

After slowly opening his eyes, different objects began to materialize in the light. He noticed the sun first and its intense radiation filled the vacuum of the entire solar system. He could see all the planets and their satellites, large asteroids, and a few comets with their glowing plasma tails.

Due to its increasing size, one spherical body caught his attention. The gray rock reminded him of the moon, but he soon realized its identity due to its proximity to the sun—Mercury. Its growth rate indicated a fast approach. In just a few seconds, the sphere of rock doubled in size, filling a quarter of his view.

The planet continued to grow, quickly consuming his view of everything else. As the surface rushed to meet him, he realized in horror that he was going to crash. But before impact, he noticed the structure on the ground and the bright light shooting out of it.

The light brought cold instead of warmth, draining instead of giving. When he crashed into the new light, it sucked all the energy from him. The traumatic experience lasted only a brief moment. After passing through the cold void, a more vibrant energy embraced him—the warm glow from a new planet.

When the sensation of his corporeal form returned, he felt the ground under his feet again. He opened his eyes and found himself standing alone in the clearing. The probe was gone, and only the moon illuminated the scene. He could smell the pine trees, hear the stream, and feel the cool air on his face, but in his mind, he could still see a new light of blue and white.

THIRTY-ONE

Taylor

While Taylor finished putting away her tools and getting ready to leave for the afternoon, Max visited his pilot to tell him of their plans. When they arrived back at her apartment, she found Mark there, and he seemed only slightly surprised to see his boss. As she watched Mark's reaction, she failed to see signs that he already knew about Max's visit. He borrowed Mark's bicycle, and due to Taylor's insistence, he reluctantly borrowed a helmet.

"If you fall," Mark said, "try not to damage my bike or helmet."

"Thanks for the concern," Max replied seriously.

Taylor had gotten accustomed to her coworker's dry humor, but she sometimes had to wonder if he spoke in jest or earnest. After adjusting their helmets, they said goodbye and rode away. When she looked back, she noticed Mark watching them.

Taylor felt surprised and a little disappointed when Max showed no problems riding a bicycle. She had unconsciously anticipated enjoying a poor performance and inserting a playful insult or two.

"I haven't ridden since before college," he admitted with some shame, "but it's true what they say. Once you learn, you never forget. Do you have anywhere specific in mind?"

At the four-way stop, Taylor looked in each direction, deciding finally to head south.

"Since we only have about four more hours of daylight, we shouldn't ride for more than two hours in any direction. The nearest town's called Simões Filho. It's the way we're headed."

A few weeks back, Yuri drove them into Simões Filho for some supplies, the first time Taylor had left the vicinity of the airport, her apartment, or the shop. As she had expected, riding a bike transformed the same route into an entirely different experience. In a car, ninety percent of the sites and experiences were lost in the blur of speed. On a bike, she could more fully appreciate the experience. Taylor loved seeing the sights, the dirt on the side of the road, the houses and farms, the wind on her face, and the smell of fresh air. No one could claim to have visited a place if they'd only driven through it.

Clumpy clouds dotted the sky that afternoon, shielding the sun most of the time. Occasionally, they rode through patches of sunlight. At twenty-eight degrees Celsius, the air felt warm even for the evening, and despite the high humidity, the wind had no problem carrying their sweat away. Taylor found it pleasant.

Taylor led the way for the first few minutes. For most of that time, she had the distinct impression that Max was watching her more than the road. But after a while, he caught up to ride alongside her.

"Did you do a lot of biking back home?" he asked.

"Not as much as I would like," she replied, "especially after graduating. Back in college, I used to ride to school and between classes. It really helped relieve stress."

"And helped keep your mind clear I'm sure."

"It's ironic how easy it is to exercise when all your time is filled with school work and your job. Of course, you wouldn't know anything about working a job and going to school."

"I hope that's not meant as an insult?"

"Sorry," she said, silently reprimanding herself. "I'm working through my anger issues. My therapist says not to keep it inside."

He laughed and sounded sincere, not just polite.

"For some reason, I can't picture you sitting down with a therapist and telling him all your problems. What kind of jobs did you have in school?"

"Ya know," she said with thick sarcasm. "Jobs that really tested my mental abilities, like grocery stores, call centers, a teller in a bank. Actually, I spent a lot of time helping my father in his shop, but since he couldn't pay well, I had to get employment elsewhere. For the last two years, I worked in one of my professor's labs, and he helped pay my tuition."

"So you were a banker too," he said seriously. "I know a guy who can get you into a good position."

"I hope that's not meant as an insult," she said, talking loudly to be heard over a passing truck. She pushed the bike forward at a strong pace but not at full speed. She wanted to appear casual.

"No offense intended," he said, and he seemed sincerely concerned about upsetting her.

"I'm just kidding," she said, deciding to stop her sardonic tone and look him in the eyes with a smile. "I like science and engineering, learning about natural laws, not artificial rules and regulations of business. If I remember right, you went to business school?"

"After I got my BS in physics at MIT, I went for my MBA at Yale."

Taylor bit her tongue to prevent a snide remark about how he emphasized his Ivy League record. She had no justification to blame him for the decisions he made, or for all the injustices in the world at the hands of his schoolmates. But the temptation to treat him as a scapegoat felt almost unbearable.

"So what do you like more?" she asked. "Science or business?"

"Science," he said without hesitation. "If I hadn't gotten my MBA, there would have been hell to pay from my father."

"Did he want you to go into banking?"

She wanted to ask, *Did he want you to be a bankster?*

"Once he saw how I enjoyed taking things apart rather than accumulating money, he turned his focus to my sister. I showed little interest in investing or business trends, but he made his requirements very clear. I needed training in some sort of business at a respectable institution.

"There are two main reasons people study business at the top schools, and the less important of the two is to learn how to do business. That's where we make all our business connections, in the clubs and social circles. It's a strange experience, one that I got caught up in, for a while at least."

She imagined his father dangling a ton of cash in front of his young son and making it clear what Max needed to do to bite the hook. Taylor decided to change the subject.

"So your sister is your only sibling?"

"Yes," he said and laughed sarcastically. "I don't think I could have handled any other siblings. She's my father's shining star."

"So you don't get along?" she asked. Back in Seattle, Taylor remembered him speaking of his sister and was curious to learn more about her. But when working with Mark, she would always forget to initiate the subject.

"As kids, we used to be good friends," he said after a pause, "but now when we see each other, it's not that pleasant. She knows I don't agree with her work, and she won't forgive me for it."

The wind in her ears made it difficult to hear his tone. Taylor thought she heard pain in his voice and considered changing the subject, but conversational momentum and her natural curiosity kept the questions flowing.

"What does she do anyway?"

Max looked at her strangely, then shook his head as if with some private regret.

"I'm not sure that telling you would improve our conversation."

"Now you have to tell me, or I'm going to have to run you off the road."

She smiled at him and realized the absurdity of her threat. She rode close to the edge with him shielding her from traffic. He had a better chance of running her off the road.

"She works for the Council on Foreign Relations."

Several sarcastic remarks fought to escape her lips, and Taylor only had the strength to choose the mildest one.

"This just keeps getting better," she said, laughing in capitulation. "We jumped into a croc pond when we met you. Your father funds all the financial sharks, and your sister writes their foreign and domestic policy. Does she know what really goes on there, or is she another lackey who thinks it's just a prestigious résumé-polishing club?"

Taylor was surprised at her words. They came almost without bidding or thought. He looked at her through half-closed eyes, appearing both offended and surprised.

"She knows what's going on there. She's no lackey. In some ways, she reminds me of you."

"I remind you of her in a good way?"

"Of course," he said with a playful smile.

While pedaling, Taylor focused on all she knew about the CFR. She understood the basics, how it helped to connect the government with the financial leeches at the top of the money chain, but she never spent much time doing a thorough investigation. She knew enough, however, to seriously doubt its integrity and credibility.

The CFR claimed to be an open organization, an innocuous think-tank providing unbiased information for policymakers. But their claims were meaningless to Taylor. She usually ignored public declarations and preferred to assess an entity's true objectives by the results they achieved. Policies endorsed by the CFR ultimately transferred control of resources from individuals to governments, exactly what men like Max's father wanted. They used governments and other puppet organizations like the United Nations and the World Bank for their own enrichment.

Taylor had to be careful in her choice of words. Discussions about the connection between the CFR and banking cartels usually made people anxious. Would Max retreat into the warm and comfortable world where the worst criminals were behind bars and not sitting in corporate offices, government buildings, and pleasant palaces?

"What do you think about the Council on Foreign Relations or her work there?" she asked as neutrally as possible. "Does she really believe in what they're doing, or is she just trying to grab a piece of the pie?"

"We don't talk about it, anymore at least. I don't know."

"Then what do you think? You know who she really is, on the inside, don't you?"

Max looked ahead, pedaled fast, and then let the bike glide. Taylor did the same.

"I really don't know what to think. It's just sad that we don't talk anymore."

Taylor finally heeded the quiet voice of her female intuition and stopped pressing him on the subject. She gave Dominga credit for helping revitalize her feminine instincts.

"I'm sorry about that."

She could hear a car approaching from behind them, so she pushed on her brakes slightly and fell behind Max until the car passed. In the bed of the passing pickup truck, a dog stood with its head extending over the edge and its mouth wide open. Taylor made brief eye contact with the dog and smiled.

—※—

They began passing more houses than farmland and soon entered the more densely populated area of Simões Filho. As they maneuvered through the narrow city streets, they mostly rode side by side, but once in a while, they would have to go single file. She concentrated mostly on the pleasant experience of seeing the city.

The narrow roads, small shops, old houses, and apartment complexes united to form a chaotic scene totally unfamiliar to Taylor. She felt more accustomed to wide streets and stricter zoning laws. While enjoying the foreign aspect of the place, she wondered if Max felt the same. Would he rather be in a more affluent location? She watched him for a minute and was relieved to see no sign of annoyance. He seemed to be having fun.

"It's nice to travel by our own power, isn't it?" she asked more to herself than Max. "Gives a feeling of independence and freedom, I think."

"This is a different experience for me," said Max as he scanned the houses and homemade shops around him. He spoke as if he heard her thoughts. "I feel like an explorer."

Despite herself, Taylor smiled at his reaction. He sounded like a kid.

"Are you hungry too?" she asked, pointing ahead of them to a restaurant on the side of the road. "What about there?"

When she first looked at the entrance, she had difficulty recognizing the establishment as a restaurant. The door was set in the wall that looked like the bricks had been broken out with a sledgehammer. As a strange contrast to the shoddy external construction, a nice restaurant sign hung above it.

Whether she would enjoy or dislike the food did not concern Taylor. Either way, she thought the experience would be memorable. Before responding, Max paused and looked suspiciously at the entrance. She remembered Gerald at Burgerville and his questioning look at the hamburger. The memory made her smile. Would she have a similar experience with Max?

"I can see you're not impressed," she said with a laugh. "I'm sure we can find a better place."

They rode casually through the city for a short while longer, looking at the sights and not talking about anything serious. The hours of welding that morning and the long bike ride gave Taylor a good appetite, but the thought of food seemed to drain her energy even further. Finally, she found an acceptable location just before collapsing from hunger. The restaurant had bamboo doors and walls on the outside with a sign above that read, Bamboo Chalé.

"I'm voting for this place," she said, stopping to the right of the entrance. Max wiped the sweat from his forehead and nodded in agreement. They locked their bikes to a nearby signpost, next to another bike. Max followed her inside like a child following his mother. *Well, at least he's not frowning*, she thought. "It's definitely not in the top twenty restaurants in Brazil, but at least we're mingling with the locals."

"I'm sure this place'll be fine," he said while inspecting the interior.

To her relief, they found a buffet inside. Taylor preferred to handle her own food and control the serving size. The first server to approach them did not speak English. After trying to communicate with them for a moment, the young woman left and came back with a man who looked as if he could be the restaurant owner. He wore a white dress shirt with a tie and beige-colored slacks.

"Welcome," he said with good English pronunciation. "Won't you start with a drink?"

He took their drink orders and motioned with his hand in the direction of the buffet tables then left to get their drinks while they got their food. To Taylor's surprise, she recognized many of the vegetables—lettuce, carrots, tomatoes, and cucumbers—but none of the fruits. Out of curiosity, she sampled each one. All the meat choices looked delicious, and the smell of salty fat brought a fresh wave of saliva to her tongue.

"Well, it looks good," he said before eating and in a tone of sincerity. "The bike ride helped build my appetite."

About twenty dark-skinned natives filled the open dining area with several tables still unoccupied. She and Max were the only two pale people in the restaurant, and Taylor felt more like an animal on display than a restaurant patron. She noticed several curious glances from their immediate neighbors but felt no indication of suspicion or animosity from the people. She enjoyed hearing the hum of Portuguese conversation and felt free to talk openly about anything.

"Do you think your two helpers at the shop have any idea what you're doing?" Max asked after he placed a piece of pork in his mouth. Some kind of brown bean sauce covered the meat.

"Carlos and Marcelo seem to be living in their own worlds," Taylor began, speaking of the two Brazilians at the shop with Yuri. "Most of the time, they do a pretty good job, but I've noticed that while working, they don't seem to be concentrating on their work but personal stuff. That's just the impression I get."

"Well that's a good thing, I guess, as long as they do the job satisfactorily."

Taylor laughed out loud.

"It took about a week to whip them into shape, to get them to my way of thinking. Now it's fine, although I know they don't like me much."

To her surprise, Max laughed too. She expected a slight reprimand for treating co-workers poorly. If he knew how much she had yelled at them, would he have had the same reaction? She decided to keep that part of the story a secret.

"I wouldn't want you as my boss," he said with a smile, then took a drink of his Cerveja, the local beer he ordered. As the cool liquid slid down his throat, he winced. "Now I remember why I don't like beer."

Taylor smiled but ignored the comment.

"No one's going to notice what we're doing, right?"

"We're much safer here than in the United States," he said. "The Brazilian government doesn't watch everything as closely as our own government back home."

"We probably have more to fear from the damned CIA here. Don't you think?" She waited for a reply, but he just shrugged, so she continued. "I wouldn't be surprised to find more people working for our own shitty government than natives working for Brazilian security agencies."

"You mean that here in Brazil, we have more to fear from the CIA, than from local security agents?"

"Yes, that's what I was trying to say."

"I'll have to ask Simon," he said apathetically, then his tone turned to one of concern. "Do I detect a bit of bitterness in your voice? Is there some personal reason, something you haven't told me?"

Without thinking, she told Max about her brother's rage at the September 11 World Trade Center collapse and how the event prompted him to join the army to fight the evil terrorists. As she told him of her brother's suicide, she could feel the tension in her muscles growing.

When people asked her about how he died, she just said he died in Iraq. No one questioned her for more details. Max let her talk without interruption.

"At that time," she said, then paused for a moment to wash down her food with a gulp of mango juice. "I had no idea what to think about the terrorist attack, but I knew the government story was complete bullshit and that starting a war, a very profitable war with another country, would only end up hurting people. I tried to tell my brother that, but he wouldn't listen to me."

She shook her head at the memory. Over the years since the incident, her anger had grown into a much larger beast, an uncontrollable entity with rage directed more at the government and those who profited from the war than at her brother. When she told the story to Dominga, they cried. But while talking to Max, not a tear was shed.

"I'm sorry to hear about your brother," he said sincerely, "and I understand about the rest, really I do."

"It makes me so angry, so I try not to think about it," she said.

"Well, at least you're not angry at me."

"Maybe just a little," she said, making a space between her index finger and thumb. "So tell me. What do you think of the plan? Will it work?"

"I don't know really, but I think that circumventing the established procedures is the right direction. It's genius. I probably would have spent millions going through the proper channels, filing for patent protection and manufacturing rights and in the end, the military would have classified it as a national security risk and put a cork in it."

"I'm glad you think so too," she said. "The credit goes to Gerald."

"Why do I get the impression that he's hoping for a dramatic game change?" Max asked his question casually, but Taylor thought he seemed a little too anxious for the answer.

"What?" she asked.

Did he come to Brazil not just to see her but to ask this question? She never felt any guilt from concealing their secret of the alien even at the meeting or on their journey into space. The option of revealing the alien seemed too dangerous of a card to play. His lack of that information was probably the only power she had over him.

After arriving in Brazil, she had a lot of time to think about the addition of Freddy to the team, the alien, and their implications. At first, she was angry that Gerald would keep the information from her, then her anger transformed into fear and anxiety. Even with Gerald's contagious optimistic attitude, Taylor could not discard her dark feelings about the alien. Whenever she thought of it, she would think about Sadi's horrible experience.

"I don't know," he said. "Like nothing concerns him and there's got to be a reason for his optimism."

"Gerald has always been a very optimistic guy," she said, smiling at the memory of her friend. She suddenly realized how much she missed him.

"Is he religious?"

All of a sudden, Taylor imagined Gerald praying, and she laughed out loud.

"That's a good one, but no. Gerald hates religion. I'm not sure why. Now, this is just my opinion, but he seems to think a small group of smart people can overcome anything. I'm not that optimistic, but we've been successful so far, don't you think?"

"Yes," he said in agreement. Her words seemed to placate his suspicion. "This is very exciting. I'm just glad to be a part of it."

"Come on, Max," she said in a challenging tone and then lowered her voice. "We're either going to make history, or we're gonna to die, and you're telling me you're just glad to be a part of it? What do you want at the end of everything?"

"I hope you're not doubting my motives," he said and seemed almost hurt. "Sure, I think we can make some money, but I really want to see these things introduced to the world too. Although, our experience in space might even be enough for me."

The memory of their experience together stretched her lips into a smile. She almost felt the same as Max, but she wanted her NMG made available even more than visiting space again.

For that moment at least, his answer satisfied her.
"Yeah. That was nice."

THIRTY-TWO

Taylor

After finishing most of their food, Taylor and Max sipped their drinks and talked for over an hour longer. Taylor usually kept good track of time, but the afternoon slipped quietly past her, and she didn't notice when the sunlight faded from the dining area. When a crying child drew her attention away from the conversation, she glanced out the window.

"Oh my God," Taylor said. "We should get going. I don't want to ride back in the dark."

The thought of riding on the dark and foreign roads seemed too dangerous of an option. Back home in the Pacific Northwest, that would not have been a concern, but being in a foreign country made her a little nervous, especially since there were very few street lights on the way back, and the natives drove like crazy people.

Max looked out the window.

"Should we call a cab?"

"That's no fun," she said before taking the time to consider his suggestion. "Besides, it's cheating. We rode in, so we should ride out."

"Fine by me. Let's go."

On their return journey, they continued with their conversation as if they still sat at the restaurant. During the last half, the quarter moon lit their way. Max seemed undisturbed by riding in the dark, but every time they heard a car, Taylor listened intently until the vehicle passed.

She was relieved when their apartment complex finally came into sight. After locking their bikes in the stairwell, they walked up the stairs to Mark's apartment. But before Taylor could knock, the door opened and revealed the man she remembered from Boston and the trail in Seattle when she met Max.

His personal assistant and pilot, Simon, blocked the doorway. The man's taller and more muscular build made Max and Mark look skinny and short in comparison. He had short blond hair and gave Taylor the impression of an off-duty soldier. For a moment, she thought of her brother when he came back from Iraq.

"Hi, Simon. Gonna let us in?" Max asked.

The imposing man looked down at Taylor as if deciding what to think of her.

"I guess," he returned. "Apparently, you're going to do whatever the hell you want anyway. Where have you been? I thought you were just going on a bike ride."

Simon moved aside to let them enter. As if protecting her from the taller man's wrath, Max held out his hand as a gesture for Taylor to go ahead of him. She could see Mark in the living room sitting on a couch with some papers in his hands. He watched them with a curious smile.

"We went into town for some dinner," Max said in slight irritation. "By the way, you remember Taylor, don't you? I don't think you were ever properly introduced."

"I remember," he said in irritation.

"Good to see you again, Simon," she said with a fake smile.

Since he failed to greet her properly, she decided to ignore him as punishment. She sat down by Mark and looked at the papers in his hands, a collection of drawings for the engines.

"Have you been working on this all night?"

"No, just for the last hour or so," Mark said. "We had dinner and have just been talking." He leaned in closer to Taylor and whispered to her. "He's not mad at you but at Max. He's used to knowing Max's location. He's a decent fellow, deep down, somewhere."

When Max and his companion joined them in the living room, Max sat on the couch next to Taylor, but Simon stepped in front of her and extended his hand.

"I didn't mean to be rude back there."

Taylor thought the gesture originated from a desire to obey social propriety rather than atone for rude behavior.

For a microsecond, she let his hand hang awkwardly in the air but then quickly grabbed it and smiled.

"You can blame me for taking him out of bounds. I didn't realize he wore such a short leash."

Simon grunted a polite laugh then sat down on a loveseat across from them. After pulling out a smartphone, he focused his eyes on the screen and seemed intent on excluding himself from any further interaction.

Taylor recognized the new iPhone 3GS. Earlier that week she discussed with Mark an article she read about it. She wanted one but considered the new GPS capability too much of a security risk.

"I'm never getting one," Mark had said emphatically. "Apple's going to use their iPhone to turn humans into mindless consumer-zombies!"

"Totally!" she answered him with thick sarcasm.

Taylor found herself staring at Simon's phone. His attempt at isolation was a challenge to engage him in conversation.

"So, you're the pilot," she said with a dramatic smile only Mark recognized as insincere. "You were also the one who came with Max to Seattle?"

"Yeah, that was me," he said without emotion. "I go where Max goes, except for today apparently."

"This is Simon's way of showing me that he cares," said Max with a smile, seeming unconcerned about the other man's mood. "But you're right. I should have brought my phone, so you could at least see my location. But it felt good to be off the grid. Too good!"

"All right, all right," Simon said in annoyance.

"That was quite the adventure," Taylor continued. Simon's obvious desire to end the conversation made her want to laugh and prompted her to continue. "I'm glad you didn't have your iPhone on you. Those two muggers would have seen it and probably killed us to get it."

Simon looked up from his phone, his eyes wide.

"What happened?"

"Nice try, Taylor," said Mark with a nervous smile. "You're joking, right?"

Taylor turned to Max and attempted to look serious.

"Max will back me up. Tell them what happened, Max."

Max shifted his gaze between Simon and Taylor as if trying to decide which person he wanted to betray. He held up both hands.

"I think I would have remembered muggers."

"You sure know how to ruin my fun," Taylor said, acting angry.

For the next twenty minutes, they sat and talked, and Simon hardly said anything. Although Max had ruined her joke, Simon reacted as Taylor had hoped. He seemed more annoyed to be there. Maybe he would be more careful around her.

At ten minutes after nine, they heard a knock on the door. Mark opened it to find Yuri standing on his doorstep. He asked to see Max outside. Simon followed the two men into the hall and shut the door.

"What's that all about?" asked Taylor.

"Don't know," Mark said, acting as curious as she felt. "I wasn't expecting Yuri tonight."

When Max and Simon returned to the apartment, Yuri did not reappear. Both men resumed their previous positions as if nothing had happened. Taylor considered asking about the reasons for the encounter but decided to ask later if she remembered. Max had many other responsibilities than just this pet project to handle. Yuri was just another employee he had to manage.

For the rest of the evening, they talked about the current project of the jet retrofit. Max and Mark made sure to exclude any information about what technological advancements they had developed and kept the narrative about design innovations. Simon appeared to give their conversation little attention, but Taylor assumed he was listening.

The curious or casual observer would probably think they intended to make the aircraft capable of high-altitude flight. There should be no reason for Simon, Yuri, or her two helpers to be suspicious of their real intent, yet. Even after installing the engines, only an expert would find reason for suspicion. When they started installing the fusion reactor, they would have to take security more seriously.

At eleven, Max and Simon stood from their seats and planned to return to their jet, where they would sleep that night. In the morning, they would meet Taylor and Mark again. Before leaving the apartment, Simon shook Taylor's hand and smiled sincerely.

"It was a pleasure to see you again," he said, and Taylor thought he seemed genuine.

She responded with a polite smile.

THIRTY-THREE

Taylor

"Okay. What was Max's visit all about?" asked Taylor after their guests departed.

"I think Max was hungry and wanted something to eat. You were dying to go with him, so it seemed like a pretty good match."

"So, he flew all the way down to Brazil because he wanted dinner?" she asked, ignoring the dry sarcasm. "Come on, Mark. Why did he want to go with me alone? We didn't talk about anything out of the ordinary, and I'm sure he's gotten all the information about our progress from you."

Mark stood from the couch and returned all the empty glasses to the kitchen.

"Okay, Taylor," he said from the kitchen, and his tone had changed from sarcastic to serious. "I'm assuming part of his intentions were to get your take on our progress. He's very interested in what we're doing, and mostly for personal reasons, I believe."

"Wait a second, part of his intentions? What were his other intentions?"

Mark turned away from her.

"I think he might find you interesting."

"Do you mean he finds me romantically interesting?"

When Mark talked without sarcasm, he had a bad habit of being a little ambiguous. She liked when people got to the point. She hoped her tone conveyed hope for a negative answer rather than a positive one.

"Perhaps," he said with a little irritation in his voice at being interrogated. "Taylor, all I can say is what I see, but I haven't seen him act like this with anyone else while in business mode."

"Act like what?"

"Like he's not in charge or something. He's my boss, so I am always listening for instructions or feedback on work. Tonight, he talked with you like you were his business partner or something, and not an employee."

"Oh my God," she said in frustration. "I had this same conversation with him. I am not his employee, well, at least I never consciously chose to be his employee. I did just find out that I will be getting a paycheck. Thanks for keeping that one from me!"

"I never told you, did I? Sorry about that."

She thought he seemed the opposite of sorry.

"I just thought you knew," he continued, "but I suppose the situation is unique, considering we're talking about very dangerous developments. Maybe that distracted me."

"So your answer is no?" she asked. "He has no romantic interest in me?"

He smiled.

"I can see that he definitely enjoys your company, and you don't seem to mind his."

She responded with a long exhale and then looked out the window. Maybe she needed to show less enthusiasm around Max.

"I don't want any distractions."

—※—

The next morning, Mark and Taylor went to the hangar to see Max, and he asked if they wanted to fly anywhere for the day. Taylor felt tempted to accept the offer, but the urgency she felt to finish the jet changed her mind. Work felt like a drug, and as an addict, she needed another hit.

"We have a lot to do, sorry," Taylor said.

"I understand," Max replied, and Taylor thought he looked disappointed. She felt a twinge of regret.

After Max and Simon boarded the jet and closed the door, Taylor realized that she had been staring at them. She turned and noticed Mark looking at her with a curious expression. For a very brief moment, she felt embarrassment, an emotion she rarely felt.

"What?" she asked abruptly and then walked away.

Even without seeing him, she could feel Mark's smile.

THIRTY-FOUR

Max

Max's best friend and bodyguard, Simon, piloted the jet as Max looked out the window at Mark and Taylor fading into the distance. When he could no longer see them, he sat back in his seat.

"Can't say I'm surprised they wanted to stay," he said. "It's pretty exciting, what they're doing."

Simon concentrated on getting to cruising altitude where he would engage the autopilot. He took a deep breath before responding.

"I still don't buy your story, by the way," he said with a small, almost imperceptible smile. Only those who knew him would be able to see the uncommon expression.

"I know," Max said, laughing. "I never expected you to believe it, but it's top secret company business and cannot be shared." Max stressed the sarcasm in the term, *top secret,* with the hope of trivializing the topic.

"So top secret that only you, Mark, and that girl know about it?"

"Her name is Taylor, and yes, only the three of us."

"Sounds like another one of your pet projects to me, but whatever. I don't really care. What if the board discovers your activities?"

"They have no reason to be suspicious about what goes on down in

Brazil." Max laughed contemptuously. "Besides, the money is coming from an account they don't know exists. Yuri's shop actually makes a profit, but they think it's only a liability. Mark makes sure to divert all of their profits into a secret account only we know about."

"Does the girl know anything about that?"

"No," Max said and wished his friend would use her name. "What's your problem with *the girl*?"

"I can tell that you like her, or want her. If there's a difference, it probably doesn't matter."

Max smiled to conceal his feeling of failure.

"Was it that obvious?"

For the first time, Simon turned to face his friend.

"Yes, obvious to me, Mark, and the girl herself. I have no doubt about that."

Max laughed.

"Okay, okay, so why don't you like her?"

"I never said I didn't like her."

"Come on, Simon," he said accusingly. "You're at least polite to people when you first meet them. You instantly didn't like her, and you let her know it."

Simon turned to face the front of the plane.

"You really pissed me off, to start with, and I especially don't like when I see someone leading you along like a jackass on a rope."

"Did you just call me a jackass?" Max asked in mock offense. "Do you really think I'd let Taylor lead me along?"

"You've got to look after your image," Simon said in a tone of concern. "You can't lose your head over a girl. Who is she anyway? What are her credentials? Who are her parents? She's beautiful and seems intelligent. I'll give you that. She even had me going with that gag she pulled, about running into thugs."

Max smiled at the memory. He could not deny falling for the girl and took a moment to articulate his emotions.

"She emits some kind of intense gravity. I don't know. Maybe it's just her intelligence."

"How is she so intelligent?" Simon asked, curiosity replacing his sarcasm.

Max smiled again.

"That's top secret."

"Fine, don't tell me," Simon said. "How much of your interest involves the girl and how much involves business?"

"I don't know," Max said honestly, then shook his head. Until that point, the question had failed to cross his mind. He had only considered interaction with Taylor as an added bonus. His motivation originated from profit and the human need for exploration.

"Then what was that secret transaction between you and Yuri?"

For a few microseconds, Max considered lying to Simon. In the end, he decided to take the easier path of the truth or at least part of it.

"Yuri gave me detailed photos of their activities. I need to keep tabs on them."

Simon considered the comment with apparent confusion in his eyes. "So, you don't have access to all their information, or you think they're keeping secrets from you?"

"Due to some proprietary considerations," Max began. He hoped the word *proprietary* would excuse him from answering any further questions, but in return, he would be giving his friend more cause for suspicion. "I can't answer that. Let's just say that Taylor likes things under her control. She doesn't fully trust me."

"It seems she's also a good judge of character!"

THIRTY-FIVE

Freddy

For the next two weeks, Freddy's experience with the alien drifted in and out of his thoughts. The second experience of traveling to Mars replayed in his dreams every night, and he often went to bed early, hoping to see the new alien woman again. Was she a real person or some creation of the alien creature? His brain told him that she existed, but he wanted concrete evidence. Her reality would justify his dreams.

At the end of the first week in August, Freddy sent another message to Gerald, asking when he could test the BMW. Gerald replied the next day, with the news that Cesar would travel down to Portland whenever Freddy felt ready. Before he could do a test flight, Cesar would show Freddy how to operate the BMW.

Freddy knew his boss disapproved of following the wishes of the alien and Freddy also understood the objections. Mr. Smith had valid concerns, to be sure. Freddy could die or be used for some horrible and inconceivable end. The safest path would be to just continue with his life, but his desire for discovery and exploration pulled harder than the desire for comfort and stability.

The idea of keeping Mr. Smith unaware of his plan to proceed felt wrong to Freddy and he could not even consider the possibility, although the thought momentarily flashed across his mind. Freddy had to tell him before Cesar appeared at their front gate, so a few days before Cesar's visit, Freddy decided to tell Mr. Smith about the plan during breakfast. They usually ate breakfast together when Freddy had no early morning classes. Mr. Smith seemed to be in his best moods then.

"Cesar will visit us this weekend," Freddy said after talking about his last class of the summer and what he planned to do before classes started again.

"Why?"

Mr. Smith looked up from his food, making eye contact with him. The old man's suspicion tasted sour. Although Freddy pretended to participate in the conversation like a normal human, he knew Mr. Smith had not forgotten about his extrasensory perception. Nevertheless, he still acted as usual, pretending ignorance of his boss's reaction and giving the illusion of a normal conversation. Freddy knew how humans often had difficulty remembering reality in an artificial environment.

"He will teach me how to operate the BMW," Freddy said. He chose to use the word *operate* instead of *fly*, but the small consideration made no difference to Mr. Smith.

"So you're planning on going into space to meet this thing?"

"I have not made that decision yet," Freddy began. "For now, I would like to test drive it."

Mr. Smith put his fork down gently, but Freddy knew how much he hid his frustration.

"Of course, you know that if something goes wrong, no one can come to help you."

"We could wait for the new ship to be completed," he said sincerely. "At least then, if something goes wrong you all will have a way to make a rescue attempt."

"Well, I can't do anything of the sort. I'm eighty-five years old." Mr. Smith stopped trying to hide his irritation. "I just can't understand how you can put your life in this creature's hands."

"May I tell you why I want to do this, why I feel compelled to do this?"

"Of course, you can tell me anything, Freddy," he said with irritation at having to be patient. "You know that."

Before responding, Freddy swallowed.

"I am not saying this to convince you of anything, but this feels right to me. It feels like I am supposed to be doing this."

"You should not always trust your feelings, Freddy," Mr. Smith said, interrupting him. "Feelings get a lot of people in trouble. Let your mind determine your path. What does your common sense tell you to do?"

Freddy paused as if taking time to consider Mr. Smith's comments.

"My feelings are telling me that this cannot be happening, that there is no alien, and that it is just a part of my imagination or the government. Fear is telling me that I am going crazy. That is what my emotions are telling me.

"Logically, I have no reason to distrust this creature. All evidence is consistent with the hypothesis that it wants to help me, to help us. I am choosing to put my trust in the evidence in front of me, in spite of my feelings."

"You should consider this very carefully," Mr. Smith said after a long pause.

"I have," Freddy said, looking away. He did not want to give the situation a negative aspect, but Mr. Smith needed the whole answer. "I am also thinking about what happened to Sadi and Helen. Something else might happen if I do not go."

THIRTY-SIX

Cesar

As Cesar watched Taylor get into the TerraWatch company jet for her new home in Brazil, tears appeared in his eyes. When he thought about going back home without her, his heart hurt. Up until that moment, he had failed to realize how much he loved the girl. Perhaps he just missed his daughter, and Taylor had become a balm on the open wound. While watching the jet take off, he made a promise to himself to call his daughter and convince her to visit him.

Dominga came to the airport with him, and Doroteo stayed at the shop. Dominga stood by his side, and their hands dangled dangerously close to each other. He often felt tempted to take her hand in his, and now the temptation felt almost too strong to resist, so he turned around and made preparations to leave the airport. He imagined his daughter with a disapproving look in her eyes.

Dominga and Cesar's wife had been lifelong friends, and he often wondered if his wife made Dominga promise to take care of him if something happened to her. He never asked and feared to know the truth. If his wife had made that promise, he would feel compelled to take Dominga as his wife, but that thought initiated an anxiety he could not describe. With Taylor in the house and all the excitement of their present circumstances, Cesar had been too preoccupied to worry about the situation with Dominga. With Taylor gone, he might have to make a decision.

When he looked back at Dominga, he noticed her wiping away her tears with her handkerchief again. Cesar had to smile at the sight of the beautiful woman.

"We'll see her again," he said with as much confidence as he could generate. "Probably by the end of next month."

"I cannot believe how fortunate we were to have her," Dominga said, then blew her nose.

She kept her eyes on the departing jet through the window. Cesar waited for the woman to follow him and leave the airport. Cesar had come to hate airports. They often meant goodbye, and the new security protocols also made him feel nervous, as though electronic eyes were watching his every move.

"Yes," said Cesar. "Very fortunate."

"That Doroteo," Dominga said while still looking out the window. "He hardly gave any kind of respectable goodbye to Taylor, like he hardly knew of her leaving. He should have come to the airport with us."

"Doroteo did care," Cesar said with a smile. "Taylor knows it too. For the past week, she's been reminding him with the hope that he'll show how much he does care, which is probably even more than Doroteo can admit. Not coming to the airport is his way of saying that he can't handle saying goodbye. That man will never shed a tear in front of us."

"Well, then I'll write a letter and tell her how much Doroteo cried when we got home from the airport. She'll find that amusing."

Dominga started to laugh, and the release of emotion initiated another flood of tears. Cesar patted her on the back and put his hand on her shoulder. The gesture came as close to an embrace as he could give, and she let him pull her away from the window. They walked side by side out of the airport.

—※—

During the next few weeks, Cesar returned to work on the BMW but kept his shop closed for regular business. He could allow no one outside the group to see the shop with all the clandestine equipment present. He still felt excited about their project but also very lonely there without Taylor.

When Gerald contacted him about the request from Freddy, he felt a mixture of excitement and foreboding. The kid claimed just to want driving lessons, but Cesar knew the request meant he also wanted to follow the alien's instructions to visit Mercury. Although Doroteo said nothing in protest, Cesar could see his friend's disapproval.

Doroteo warned about the possibility of being pulled over by police. A cop might try to confiscate the vehicle if he saw the inside, and then they would be forced to flee and hope they could get away from the police without being noticed. Cesar said he would be able to talk his way out of any suspicious requests.

On August 15, the Saturday he arranged with Freddy for the test drive, Cesar awoke from a nightmare just after midnight and found himself drenched in sweat. In his dream, soldiers surrounded his home and then kidnapped them all: Taylor, Gerald, Doroteo, and Dominga. The army confiscated the car and the other devices they made, then the soldiers took them all to a secret military prison where they had to wait alone in cold and dirty cells. Cesar woke up right as they were taking Dominga away.

Cesar had other nightmares of the same theme, but none so terrifying. Those kinds of dreams reminded him of the dangerous game they were playing. After getting a drink, he returned to bed and slept fitfully for the rest of the night but without nightmares. He woke up an hour before he planned for the drive to Portland. Dominga and Doroteo were still asleep, so he left a note. Before driving away, Doroteo came out of the house to say goodbye.

"Come back in one piece," he said with a devious smile. "Or don't come back at all."

"I think those are the only two options available," Cesar said.

—✳—

On the drive, he glanced every few minutes through the rearview camera, afraid of seeing flashing lights behind him. But even with his paranoia, he still had fun driving the enhanced BMW on the roads. With so much power at his disposal, he had to constantly fight his urge to stay in line with the other cars and not fly past them. He required even more restraint to stay connected to the earth.

When he arrived at the estate, Cesar thought the place made his home look like a cottage. Cesar felt no jealousy, though. He was satisfied by his own good fortune and secure in his accomplishments and status. Before Freddy joined Cesar in the BMW, Mr. Smith acted cordially and did most of the talking. Cesar got the impression that there had been a lengthy discussion between Freddy and his boss about the driving lessons.

"Try not to worry, Mr. Smith," Cesar said after Freddy sat in the passenger seat and closed his door. "We'll take it slowly, and we won't be leaving Earth."

Acquiring Freddy reminded Cesar of being a child when he would visit his friend and ask to play. Instead of watching them drive away, Mr. Smith went into his house without looking back. Cesar hoped the old man felt no anger toward him.

Cesar remembered how Freddy had an extrasensory perception that enabled him to find Sadi's child. When they found an acceptable place to trade places, he planned on testing him. He wanted to get the mind reading out in the open.

"I can sense what you are feeling rather than the words flowing through your mind," Freddy said in answer to the unspoken thoughts.

"It seems to be working," Cesar replied with a smile and surprise that the ability inspired no fear or distrust. With access to Cesar's most valuable secrets, Freddy could exercise great power over him, but Freddy seemed to be without guile. "So this alien gave you this ability?"

"Yes," he answered quickly. Before Cesar could ask the follow-up question, Freddy answered it for him. "But I do not know why."

"Do you have any idea how it works?" Cesar had not planned on asking this question. The answer felt important.

Freddy paused several seconds before answering.

"I have also been wondering this," he said, taking a deep breath. "At first, I thought that maybe humans emit some kind of signal related to our emotions, and she gave me the ability to detect it. But what if my interactions with her are responsible? I always meet the creature in some kind of dream dimension. My new ability might be a natural result of this interaction."

"Wait a minute," Cesar said, confused. "Is the creature giving you dreams, like how a television receives a signal and converts it to images and sounds?"

"I do not think so. I am meeting her, not getting a signal from her. I probably cannot explain it well."

"Well," Cesar began after failing to think of a good follow-up question. "You've given a lot more thought about this than me. I'll have to give your premise some thought. The creature's intentions are of more importance. What does it want?"

"I feel no malice from it. I think it wants to help us."

"Help us do what, and what does it want in return? There's no such thing as charity." Cesar paused and smiled. "If I'm wrong, then it is truly alien."

"It is willing to help us, I think," he said. "And I think it wants me."

"You, huh," Cesar said and turned away in thought. "So, if something goes wrong on your journey, it will take care of you?"

"I hope so."

They drove on the Sunset Highway toward the coast and had a long time to talk. Cesar thought he sensed some anxiety from the kid, so he told Freddy about his life in Mexico, how he had come to the United States, and why. The boy listened attentively.

When almost halfway to the coast, Cesar found a side road. His GPS unit showed the road winding aimlessly for many kilometers, a road to nowhere, a good place to let Freddy practice driving. The road looked like it had very little traffic.

At first, Freddy drove under the speed limit and very cautiously. He seemed as though he would require much more time than Cesar had expected. In about thirty minutes, however, Cesar felt like the boy had mastered the two-dimensional control of the vehicle. The pleasure in his eyes helped Cesar feel satisfied as a teacher.

"So you've mastered the control on the ground," Cesar said. "Are you ready to do three dimensions?"

"I think so."

For the next few hours, Freddy practiced driving at a constant height above the road. For the first fifteen minutes, they drove slowly, bumping up and down on the road like a bouncy ball. When Freddy gained the ability to appear connected to the road while hovering a few centimeters above it, they could proceed to the next stage. Eventually, Freddy became adept at the controls. Time went by fast.

"Well, I really thought it would take longer to master this vehicle," Cesar said and then clapped the boy on the shoulder. "It's not dark enough yet, so let's get to Seaside, and we'll try some higher altitude when it gets dark, over the water. No one's going to see us out there, especially if we stay low enough."

"You have a lot of trust in this vehicle," Freddy said with a complimentary tone in his voice, but Cesar wondered if he had doubts.

"Thank you. We spent a lot of time testing it, and don't worry. The engines won't have the same problem as last time. I've taken care of that."

Freddy talked more on the rest of the way to the coast. He briefly summarized his life and how his mother had placed him into foster care, and then how he came to live with Mr. Smith. When he started talking about Mr. Smith, his tone changed completely from sadness to relief. At the end of the story, Cesar felt glad that things were finally going well for the boy. He tried his best to keep his feelings to a minimum. Thankfully, Freddy said nothing about them.

They made it to Seaside at five in the afternoon. As the ocean came into view, Cesar thought of Mexico and the difference between the colder Northwest climate and his homeland. The frigid water kept many people away and gave a more remote feeling than the crowded beaches of Mexico. He enjoyed visiting the coast, but it usually made him homesick.

Before starting the next part of their practice, they needed to eat. Neither of them had taken time to eat anything since breakfast. They decided to have dinner in a restaurant with a view of the ocean, and Cesar insisted on paying. He made sure to have the BMW in view.

"Want to go for a walk?" Freddy asked immediately after they had finished eating, just before Cesar suggested the same thing. After all the driving and then sitting at the restaurant, he needed to stretch his legs. They walked on the beach until a few minutes past seven, then decided to go back to the BMW.

For the next thirty minutes, they drove south on Highway 101 in search of a more secluded location where they could quietly watch the sun settle into the ocean. On the drive, they continued talking about the group and the dangers of being caught. Cesar was surprised at how little Freddy worried about the possibility of the government catching them. Freddy claimed that no one would be able to surprise him, but the boy's confidence failed to comfort Cesar.

"It's dark enough, I think," Cesar said. "We should start soon if we don't want to be out all night."

Freddy looked down the cliff with wide eyes. He turned to Cesar with an expression of anxiety instead of the excitement that Cesar felt. He did not need any extra sense to know Freddy's emotions.

"What if we fall into the water?"

Cesar laughed, then put his hand on Freddy's shoulder and squeezed reassuringly. "This thing's air-tight, Freddy. It can survive taking a little swim."

"I will try to keep it in the air if it is all the same to you," said Freddy in a weak attempt at humor. "You designed it to be airtight, but the environment under the water is completely different. Instead of fluid wanting to get out, like in space, under the water, fluid wants to get in."

They had to wait about two minutes before they could launch into the air without being seen by any other people. They hovered for a few seconds and then started slowly drifting out over the cliff. Cesar found himself holding his breath with an irrational fear of falling to the rocks forty meters below them.

"Now nice and easy, west."

For extra emphasis, he pointed over the crashing waves.

When they failed to fall and remained steadily floating in the air, Cesar's anxiety turned to excitement and anticipation of flying over the water. Putting themselves at the complete mercy of his creation got his adrenaline flowing, and by taking away the safety of the road, he felt completely dependent on Freddy's performance. After taking a breath, Freddy tilted the car at a slight incline and started accelerating.

"Here we go," he said.

They soon moved beyond the beach and then over the water. For the first few minutes, they slowly picked up speed and watched the shoreline fade away in the darkness. The quarter moon cast enough light to see the water below them. Freddy kept the vehicle at only a few meters above the water and stopped accelerating when they reached a constant speed of a hundred kilometers per hour.

While Freddy controlled the car, Cesar watched the radar, the nuclear fusion reactor output, and the other parameters used for monitoring the vehicle's performance. As he hoped, all the control systems worked flawlessly. While keeping watch for any approaching ships, Cesar tried to focus on enjoying the journey. If he never got the opportunity to go into space, then maybe he could be satisfied by the experience of flying with nothing but water in every direction.

"We'll soon be in international waters, a little safer than so close to the mainland. Let's go higher and put this thing to the test. It's best to get all the experience you can at the planet's surface, where it's safest.

Let's gain some speed."

"How fast do you want me to go?"

Cesar looked at his companion and smiled, no response necessary.

Freddy took the vehicle to three hundred kilometers per hour and kept it steady for a few seconds, still heading west. Cesar thought he understood the boy's trepidation. He probably had a fear of running into a boat or offshore oil rig or something.

"How strong is your stomach?" Cesar asked.

"You mean, how easy do I throw up?"

"Yes," he said, suppressing a smile and attempting to hide his amused emotions.

"I should be able to keep everything inside my body."

"Then let's go up for a while."

"Okay," Freddy answered and then changed their pitch to a forty-five-degree incline.

While steadily gaining altitude, Cesar focused on the altimeter reading. Every thousand meters of altitude increase, Freddy turned to Cesar, giving the impression that he wanted to say something, but he remained silent. When they hit six kilometers, he finally spoke.

"Is this a good height?" Freddy asked and smiled weakly.

"I suppose so," Cesar answered. "Can I take control for a moment?"

Cesar reached over, and Freddy relinquished the control to him. He immediately flipped the car upside down and then cut the power to the NMG. After disengaging the engines, the feeling of acceleration vanished, and the sudden sensation of free fall resulted in a momentary fear of ejecting his dinner. He required only a moment for his disorientation and panic to transform into a pleasurable endorphin rush.

"We might as well be in space," he said.

"Can I take the controls again?" Freddy asked with forced patience.

"Not yet."

While falling, they watched the altimeter readout become smaller and smaller, and Cesar could almost feel the boy's tension levels rise at the same rate. He fought the temptation to return the controls until the warning from the computer.

"Impact with Earth in sixty seconds," said the mechanical female voice.

Freddy put his hand on the accelerator, but Cesar reached over and shook his head. Together, they stared at the computer screen at the continued countdown. Cesar smiled and forced himself to feel calm, although his heart rattled in his chest like a broken piston.

"Not yet," he said when the countdown hit forty seconds.

The next ten seconds felt like twenty minutes. With every passing second, Cesar felt more and more impressed with the boy's stamina. When the computer voice said, "Thirty seconds to impact," Cesar let go of Freddy's arm. He restarted the engines and immediately began deceleration.

—※—

While in the passenger seat, Cesar had more fun than he ever had flying on his own. He loved the feeling of acceleration and how hard the seat belts had to work just to keep him stationary relative to the vehicle.

At their most extreme, they experienced almost 3.5G when he told Freddy to save them from crashing into the ocean. After they safely pulled out of the dive, Cesar felt a little guilty for scaring him, but he knew they had plenty of time to avoid death.

They never completely left the atmosphere and reached a maximum altitude of seventy-five kilometers. If any hostile entity had spotted or hailed them, Cesar assumed they could disappear from tracking by going into space, and he secretly hoped for a scenario like that to happen. After practicing different maneuvers for over an hour, Freddy was suddenly worried.

"I think we should get back," Freddy said after bringing the vehicle to a stop just a few meters above the water. Although Cesar would have happily practiced more, he trusted the boy's instincts and also began to feel a little anxious about all their higher-altitude flying.

"Okay," he answered. "I think you've got the hang of it."

Freddy had exceeded Cesar's expectations in almost every way, except he needed a little more confidence, which should come from more practice. Cesar was confident in the boy's ability to fly the BMW, but in the case of a major system failure in space, no one in the group could help him unless he waited for the new spacecraft to be ready. Freddy seemed to have confidence in the alien's ability and desire to ensure a successful trip. Cesar believed it too. Would the alien go to all the trouble to help this kid and let him die in space? That possibility seemed unlikely.

On the entire return journey, Cesar worried about the Coast Guard tracking them, but his rational mind reassured him about their ability to escape capture. Even if the Coast Guard used helicopters and missiles, Freddy had the resources to escape. If they were caught in a helicopter chase, they could even go into the water. The experience would be good practice for Freddy, but even if they managed to escape, he would not escape the wrath of Dominga or Doroteo.

On their way back to land, they traveled southeast for the first half of the journey, then northeast for the last half. Their sensors detected no radar locks, but Cesar only stopped worrying after driving on the road for several minutes without notice. Freddy drove the whole way back to Portland. To help pass the time, Cesar tested him on everything about the car, and Freddy answered all the questions to his satisfaction.

They returned to Freddy's home at three in the morning and found the house quiet.

"Let me show you one of the guest rooms," Freddy said.

He escorted Cesar to the room and turned to leave. Before shutting the door, he called Freddy back to the room.

"Do you want to schedule another practice session? I'm willing to come back as many times as necessary."

"No, Mr. Sanchez," he said politely. "I feel quite ready. Thank you."

THIRTY-SEVEN

Freddy

Freddy escaped his dream at two in the morning, right before crashing into the bright light on Mercury. Sweat covered his pillow and beaded up on the side of his head. He opened his eyes with the vision of the light and the woman fresh in his mind's eye. He felt a sudden urgency to get out of bed and go to the internet.

Without thinking, he opened up a web browser and entered the address of his favorite orrery site, a live view of all the planets in their current positions. He zoomed into the inner planets and saw the location of Mercury in relation to Earth, an action he had been planning but not yet attempted. Mercury had floated within the closest distance to Earth in its orbit cycle, currently at about a hundred million kilometers away.

He spent a few minutes calculating the length of the journey. If he traveled the first half at 2G then decelerated at the same rate, it would take him two and a half days. *Can my body handle the constant acceleration for that long?* 2G seemed uncomfortable but not unreasonable.

After his next moment of reflection, another complication presented itself, basic human digestion requirements. Handling liquid human waste certainly seemed feasible, but solid waste would be more difficult, and he felt sure that Cesar had not prepared the solution to that dilemma. He was confident in the ability to time his bodily needs for a two-day trip, but he could make no such guarantee. Could he overcome his feeling of embarrassment to broach the subject with Cesar? After a moment of gathering his courage, he sent an email to Cesar.

After sending the email, he felt an almost overwhelming realization of what he planned to attempt. Until that point, the idea existed only as a possibility, something fun to consider and talk about with friends, but sending the email felt as though he was unlocking the door and opening it.

The more he thought about the plan, the higher his anxiety levels rose. He needed to talk to someone, or else he might have a panic attack. He immediately dismissed the option of talking to Mr. Smith. His boss already hated the idea and would attempt to dissuade him. Freddy needed someone else from the group, and there seemed to be only one option, Franklin.

Freddy typed a message to his new friend and then hit the *enter* key. Franklin replied just a few seconds later.

Freddy: *You awake?*

Franklin: *it's before 3am right. Wazzup???*

Freddy: *I made the decision. I am going!*

Franklin: *2 u-know-where?*

Freddy: *Yes!*

Franklin: *hmmmmmmmm...and you want me to go w/u? I said I would...didn't I?*

Freddy: *No, I need to go alone.*

Franklin: *whewwww....tooooo bad, I was totally ready to go with you, ha ha ha, can I catch the next flight?*

Freddy: *If there is a next flight.*

The light banter with his new friend had already helped Freddy feel better. He then spent the next twenty seconds trying to determine how to broach the topics he wanted to discuss.

Freddy: *It seems like a trite science fiction novel, traveling through some door to another place. What do you think?*

Franklin: *sounds awesome to me!!!*

Freddy: *Okay, good.*

Franklin: *traveling through thousands of lightyears of space seems more ridiculous, doesn't it?*

Freddy: *Why?*

Franklin: *idk, just seems unreasonable, seems like you'd run into something, toooo risky, if an alien did make it to Earth, seems like they would find another way less 'trite' as traveling through space, that's lame.*

Freddy: *If I have the chance, I will ask her and let you know.*

Franklin: *so it's a girl, hmmm INTERESTING, there's always a girl, I bet she's out of this world! seriously though, is she cute? tell me she appeared to you naked, please, please tell me she was naked!!!*

Freddy laughed out loud and was immediately embarrassed, and then he felt stupid for being embarrassed by himself when no one could hear him laugh.

Freddy: *No, she was not naked.*

Franklin: *ok then, would you want to see her naked? my love life's dead, so I need you to help me, make something up if you have to, I need to know if she was at least attractive!*

Freddy: *Yes, she was attractive.*

Franklin: *ok, that's a start, I'm jealous, where were we?....I kinda got distracted.*

Freddy: *Why Mercury? I mean, why not on the other side of the moon that no one can see?*

Franklin: *well, it's a lot hotter there??? IDK, you're the scientist, what do you think?*

Freddy: *NASA says that Venus is hotter, but I do not know. Maybe it needs lots of energy to do what it has to do, and Mercury probably has the most seclusion where few people will be looking. Also, maybe it can get the energy from the sun. Its intensity will be much stronger there. That is my guess.*

Franklin: *sounds good to me, but won't you fry out there in space, flying so close to the sun?*

Freddy: *The BMW has a reflective coating. They say it will not heat too much.*

Franklin: *I guess they would have thought of that. Gerald has a lot of faith in Taylor. She's a genius I guess...but really and I'm not just saying that to make you feel better...okay, it's my turn to ask a question, RU scared?*

Freddy: *I am not afraid in the usual sense.*

Franklin: *you're afraid in an alien sense?*

Freddy: *I am not frightened of dying, and that scares me! I do not know myself anymore.*

Franklin: *maybe you'll find yourself, sorry, that's cheesy.*

Freddy: *Maybe you are right.*

Freddy stared at the screen, contemplating the cause of his anxiety. Did he want to find himself? He did not know what that phrase meant. The opportunity to fly in space suddenly seemed like a worm on a hook.

Freddy: *I need to go back to sleep. Thank you for texting with me. I feel better.*

Franklin: *no problem, sigh...I probably should get some sleep too. good night and don't leave w/o saying anything!*

Freddy: *Good night.*

Freddy sat back in his chair and sighed. Franklin probably wanted to keep the conversation going, but Freddy's social energy had drained faster than usual.

After switching back to the orrery website, he stared at the depiction of Mercury and then increased the flow of time so that the planet spun around the sun every second. Watching the orbits with increased speed helped him feel even more urgency to start his journey.

"Who are you?" he typed on a Notepad program window and then stared at the words. Until the conversation with Franklin, he'd felt a nebulous, indefinable fear. Now, he felt as though he had been digging a hole and finally uncovered a locked chest in the dirt. Would he find the key on Mercury? When he opened the chest, would he find someone sleeping inside?

After a few minutes, he deleted the words and lay down in a futile attempt at sleep. For the next hour, he lay on his back with his eyes closed and tried imagining the flight into space. In just a short time, excitement began to replace his apprehension.

Later that morning, Cesar replied to his email. He wrote that whenever Freddy wanted to leave, Cesar would drive down to meet him. He also wrote that they had a method to handle any human digestive need, so he did not have to worry about that. Freddy felt better, but he still planned to have a liquid diet to decrease the probability of having that specific issue. For breakfast, he had orange juice and nothing else.

If he left the next night, Thursday, he might return by the middle of the following week for school. After considering that possibility, he laughed quietly to himself. It was such a ridiculous concern as if he were planning a simple trip to a resort rather than a journey through space to visit an alien facility on Mercury. The enormity of the situation almost made his head hurt.

A new concern suddenly materialized in his mind. What if the alien had no intention of letting him return? *Would that stop me?* After just a moment, Freddy decided to stop thinking more about it. He definitely would not mention that concern to Mr. Smith.

Now that his plan seemed to be set, he would have to tell his boss as soon as possible. In anticipation of the encounter, Freddy's heart started pounding. He found his boss typing on his desktop computer in his study.

"I have something to discuss with you," Freddy said, and his tone caused Mr. Smith to turn from the computer. When they made eye contact, Freddy knew that Mr. Smith knew.

—※—

The following evening, Freddy and Mr. Smith drove to the same location on the coast where he and Cesar had launched for his test flight. While waiting for Cesar to arrive, they sat in his Lexus sedan and watched the sun slowly dip into the ocean. Clouds between the sun and water floated like a fluffy blanket with beautiful streaks of blue, orange, and pink.

At any minute, Cesar would be arriving in the BMW with his intimidating friend Doroteo. Freddy dreaded the moment of their arrival almost as much as he yearned for it.

He felt as if he were sitting at the apex of his life, gazing down at a new and mysterious land. The kidnapping, the visions, and his new friends all seemed to have prepared him for this journey, and he felt ready to leave. Once he shot through the atmosphere, his old life would end, and even if he returned to Earth, nothing would ever be the same.

Mr. Smith was experiencing something similar. Their two sets of emotions swirled together in Freddy's mind so that he could not distinguish one from the other.

"They are here," Freddy said a minute before the two Mexicans arrived. When the two cars pulled up on either side of them, Freddy kept his eyes on the sun. Cold anxiety filled his core, and the sadness emanating from Mr. Smith made his feelings worse. After a moment, Freddy opened the car door and said hi to Cesar and Doroteo with a forced smile.

"I'll never forget this spot," said Cesar as he shook Freddy's hand.

The cool breeze from the ocean moved the dark hair on the top of their heads like the waves below the cliff. A broad grin spread across Cesar's face, and Doroteo looked solemn as usual. Freddy wondered if he would ever hear the sound of the surf again.

They used the time before sunset, reviewing the use of the suit and all the safety precautions they had already discussed when Cesar visited the previous week. If Freddy became unresponsive, the autopilot program would control the vehicle, so he did not need to worry about that. If the vehicle sensors detected a non-orbiting free fall to a gravity source, the engines would counteract the acceleration and keep him from crashing into any massive astronomical body.

Freddy waited only a few minutes after the sun had sunk into the Pacific Ocean before deciding to leave. He could not bear the tension he felt. Cesar gave him a crushing-hug goodbye, and Doroteo squeezed all of the blood from his hand again.

"Use your head," said Mr. Smith as they embraced for the final time, tears appearing in the old man's eyes.

"I will see you all in a few days," Freddy said, wiping the tears from his own eyes.

Cesar smiled, and Freddy felt his excitement to watch the BMW fly into the sunset.

"We'll start to worry if we haven't heard back from you by next Wednesday evening."

"Please try to come back," Mr. Smith said.

THIRTY-EIGHT

Freddy

While cars drove past the viewpoint on Highway 101, they waited for a good opportunity for Freddy's departure. He kept the BMW hovering a few centimeters above the pavement, waiting patiently for the signal from Cesar to safely launch without being noticed. Mr. Smith waited in the vehicle with Cesar and Doroteo. The windows were so dark that Freddy could hardly see them, but he knew they were talking about the possibility of another world and trying to comfort Mr. Smith.

After about fifteen minutes, a knock on Freddy's window brought him out of a trance. He had been thinking about the journey ahead and was unaware of Cesar standing just outside. After glancing up and down the highway, he made eye contact with Freddy and pointed toward the Pacific. Freddy held up his thumb, and Cesar stepped back.

Freddy shifted the front of the car a little higher into the air and then shot out over the beach. The acceleration pushed his head back against the headrest, and after only a few seconds, he could no longer see the land from the rear camera. He wondered what Mr. Smith thought about his quick takeoff.

With no one else present, Freddy did not feel the need to proceed with caution. He quickly accelerated the car to 3G and arced upward. In just a few minutes, he had placed two hundred kilometers between him and the continental United States. After reaching a completely vertical ascent, he stopped worrying about being discovered and enjoyed the slow transition between the atmosphere and the vacuum of space. The sound of wind eventually faded to nothing, leaving the car in an eerie silence, and he finally experienced what he had always dreamed of doing, leaving Earth and entering space.

The west-facing camera view suddenly filled the car interior with bright sunlight, nearly blinding him. Using his hand to shield the light, he scrambled to close that part of the view screen. As he waited for his eyes to recover, he was reminded of the late hour, which seemed ideal. If he could sleep for the next ten hours, the trip would feel that much faster. After setting his course, he took a deep breath and tried to relax, hoping to resume the sleep cycle.

Freddy spent several minutes watching the stars become brighter through the windshield until their combined light illuminated the interior in a soft glow. When he turned his attention to the receding Earth on the computer screen, the scene felt disconnected from reality, but the pressure from his seat reminded Freddy of his increasing speed.

Before Freddy transferred complete control to the autopilot, he decided to make a small detour. Since he needed to travel in the moon's general direction anyway, he wanted to get a closer look. With its present orientation between him and the sun, he could distinguish the moon by how it blocked the light of the stars. So, he did not need the navigation program to indicate its location. He redirected some thrust toward the moon, and over the next twenty-two minutes, he watched as it slowly grew in size. The surface illumination from the sun grew from zero to one hundred percent, essentially the moon phases transforming fast forward.

He felt a strong temptation to make a moon landing but decided to use its gravity and slingshot around it instead, as he remembered seeing in so many science fiction movies. The NMG engines and fusion reactor were powerful enough and did not need to slingshot, but Freddy thought it would be fun. Staying near the moon for long, however, seemed like too much of a security risk. Many people watched the moon, including the scientific community. He could not let his selfish desires jeopardize the other members of the group.

He never memorized the names of the moon features and really only knew one, the Sea of Tranquility, but after getting close, he could not with certainty find its location. He laughed at his brief disappointment at not finding it. Among all the other amazing features of the moon, he could barely see enough of one before another came into view. He could have spent days there. Eventually, he swung around it and shot away when the Earth came back into view.

Freddy only glanced at the Earth before orienting himself to face the general direction of his destination, Mercury. He was too excited to get on his way. He had spent his whole life on Earth and would be seeing it again in just a few days, so he fought the temptation of turning back to admire the amazing view.

He aligned the top of the car to Polaris, the North Star, with the sun at his right and out of sight. According to his computer navigation program, Mercury was straight ahead.

Just before initiating the autopilot program, he stared at the video feed of the Earth again on the view screen. Something about Earth seemed wrong. Cloud cover had obscured most of the surface, but for some reason, Earth looked much larger than he imagined. Either that or the continents seemed smaller. *Hmm*, he thought with some confusion. A moment later, he decided to ignore his bewilderment and proceed with the plan. He would have more opportunities for observation when he returned.

When he finally engaged the autopilot program, Freddy felt an immediate shift in direction until the program aligned the vehicle to the exact pre-programmed velocity vector. The BMW accelerated until reaching a solid and slightly uncomfortable 2G. After a few minutes, his body became accustomed to the sensation again. He hoped to remain that way.

For the first two hours of autopilot control, he felt fully awake, content to just watch the stars. He used the cameras whenever he wanted to look more closely at a particular star cluster or planet and had more fun than he ever had stargazing from home. When the time passed one in the morning, his eyes finally began to feel heavy. Surprisingly, the acceleration helped him relax, feeling almost like a heavy blanket. After deciding to abandon the amazing view and close his eyes, he fell into a deep sleep.

—※—

When Freddy became aware of his surroundings again, he felt as though only a few minutes had passed. With his eyes still closed, he experienced an irrational fear of finding himself in his bed at home. For a few seconds, he lay still in his seat and concentrated on the comforting sensation of being pressed against it. The magnitude of the acceleration was definitely greater than Earth's gravity.

"Not a dream," he told himself with a smile.

The sound of his voice seemed odd, like an echo from far away, and the sensation kept him from wanting to open his eyes. When the echo faded to nothing, he recognized the presence of another creature, its raw emotions coming from the back seat.

In a panic, Freddy tried recalling when he had entered the BMW. Had he felt anything strange then? Had the excitement of the launch distracted him? No. The creature must have been able to shield itself from him. Perhaps the alien had placed the creature there, but for what reason? A companion? That felt wrong. The emotions were not pleasant. While Freddy gathered the courage to look in the back seat, the creature began to cry, sounding like a young child.

Behind the physical sound, however, Freddy sensed an emotion similar to humor. The crying sounded like it originated from a bad actor. The creature in the back seat wanted Freddy to submit to his curiosity and open his eyes. For almost a minute, Freddy listened to the awful noise and hoped it would stop.

This is irrational, Freddy thought. With all the courage he could muster, Freddy opened his eyes and looked through the front windshield at all the stars. The sight gave him some comfort, but the sound of crying continued. To look in the back seat meant to give in to his fear. He should keep his eyes forward, and the sound would stop when he came to his senses. Nothing could have entered the vehicle without his awareness. He was traveling alone in space and had brought nothing with him.

He eventually decided to look. Almost casually, he turned to the back seat and saw a child hugging his knees and his head bowed. When he saw the child, his blood froze in his veins. He recognized the boy, a five-year-old version of himself, his age when his father had disappeared.

The boy slowly tilted his head upward to face Freddy, and his lips spread wide in a demonic grin. The whimpering transformed into laughter. Its mouth opened wide, showing glistening white teeth, sharp as razors.

Freddy jolted awake and opened his eyes. His racing heart contrasted sharply with the peaceful silence. The emotional signature of another creature was gone, so he did not look in the back seat for visual confirmation.

The view through the windows appeared the same as before he fell asleep. When he noticed the receding Earth through the rear camera, it was only a blue dot the size of a BB at arm's length. The time on the computer screen showed eight-thirty in the morning.

The memory of the dream faded as he reviewed the major control parameters for the vehicle—pressure, leak rate, oxygen levels, temperature, and engine power, which all seemed to be normal.

He kept his head against the headrest as much as possible to keep his neck from getting sore. His legs and back felt tired, probably from fighting the higher force levels. To provide some relief, he considered cutting the power and coasting for a while, but he disliked the thought of lengthening his journey. He might have to take a break sometime, but for the moment, he could handle the extra pressure.

The next few hours of wakefulness were enjoyable and passed quickly. Seeing the stars and other celestial objects from the blackness of space seemed to make them more real. Space was brighter and more full of light than he ever imagined. Could he ever become bored with the experience? He could not imagine it.

Even though Taylor, Cesar, and Mark had installed a high voltage antenna to deflect charged particles from space, he could not completely ignore the thought of gamma rays and high energy particles ripping through his body and damaging his DNA. Those thoughts reminded him of the natural protection on Earth, which he had abandoned. His journey needed to be as short as possible. Otherwise, the cumulative effect of the radiation could overcome his body's ability to repair the damage.

Sometime that afternoon, Freddy found himself drifting in and out of consciousness. The constant light level was probably to blame, he assumed. Thoughts and reflection began to mix with daydreams and reality. For a long while, he imagined himself as an asteroid floating through space for all eternity, the view of the surrounding stars, galaxies, and nebulae remaining constant.

For some strange reason, he wanted to see something fly past the vehicle, any other object moving in relation to him. Acceleration was the only evidence of his condition—negative velocity in relation to his destination. But over time, the NMG engines' thrust had come to feel like normal gravity. Freddy wanted to feel like he was moving.

At that time, Freddy found little need for concern for his present state. He was even enjoying the surreal experience, but if he were to encounter a problem, he would need to remain fully alert. He should have brought some music, movies, or even a video game. Any of them would have helped the time pass quickly.

The thought of playing the latest version of *Diablo* on his way to Mercury made him laugh out loud. The sound of his laughter triggered a more intense laughter than he ever had experienced and almost brought tears to his eyes. He stopped when the sound transformed into something he might hear in an insane asylum.

"What do I need?" he asked himself.

While thinking of all the possible options, *Twinkle, Twinkle, Little Star* began playing in his head—the only song he remembered from childhood. After whispering the first few lines, he unconsciously started humming along, and the vibrations deep in his chest helped comfort him. He looked through the window, and after finding a particularly bright star, he sang the words softly.

Up above the world so high
Like a diamond in the sky

—※—

After spending some time considering his options, he decided to increase the acceleration for a few minutes and then bring it back to 2G. That might physically remind him of the vehicle movement and hopefully re-establish his senses in reality. As he prepared to disengage the autopilot program and take manual control, a beeping from the computer returned his attention to the computer monitor. While inspecting the screen, he noticed the time, four in the afternoon, and then a pop-up box appeared with a message.

Good afternoon, Freddy! We hope to find you alive and well.

The following is a link to some video messages we prepared for you.

His lips stretched into a wide smile. He could not think of a more welcome surprise. As he opened the folder and looked at the icons, he held his breath. There were three messages: one from Taylor, one from Gerald, and one from Sadi. He decided to watch the one from Gerald first so that he could concentrate on the messages from the women. Even though he liked Gerald, he was more excited to see the two beautiful females.

Gerald spent about five minutes on his video. He talked about how exciting it must have been for Freddy to be on his way through space and then expressed his wish to have made the journey with him. Before watching the message from Sadi, Freddy viewed Taylor's video twice. When he first met Taylor, her physical appearance immediately impressed him, but her confidence and fearless honesty outshone the rest. One day, he hoped to gain the same qualities.

"Hi, Freddy," she said smiling, her red hair pulled back in a pony-tail. "We thought it might be a bit lonely on your journey, so we wanted to make a video message for you."

She spoke for only a couple of minutes, giving a brief update on the progress of the new spacecraft. She spent most of her time talking about her experience of living in Brazil and how he needed to visit them after his return. In the end, she gave a warning, and her tone confused him. Without his new ability to sense her emotions, he had difficulty characterizing his impression.

"Try not to die or anything, and I want my convertible back!"

As the video ended, she waved goodbye and smiled. By her pleasant look, he guessed that she was not too angry with him for taking her spacecraft, but he would have to apologize to her after returning. Having to speculate about her feelings while she spoke reminded him of how much he had grown dependent on his new extrasensory per-ception.

Before clicking on Sadi's video icon, he wondered if watching her would make him depressed. Sometimes, a strange solace accompanied his memory of her. The emotional stew was a mix of pleasant memo-ries of his time with her but also the realization that she would never love him as he had loved her. With a sigh, he opened her video and clicked on the triangular play icon.

"Hello, Freddy," she said slowly, almost as if intentionally giving him time to recognize her. "I hope your journey is going well. When Gerald told me that you were going, I wanted to come over to see you, but it all happened so fast. I didn't have time."

In the video, Sadi sat at her kitchen table, and the camera appeared to be on the other end, tilted so that he looked up at her, the top of her head touching the top of the frame. After her greeting, a pair of famil-iar faces appeared by Sadi's side: her daughter and Daryn, the other girl he had helped rescue.

"Hi, Freddy," they said in unison, looking straight at the camera. Daryn showed a polite and forced smile, then remained silent for the rest of the video. Helen turned to her mother.

"Mom, why won't you tell me where he is?" Her frustrated tone made Freddy smile. He understood children and loved how they wore emotions like hats.

Sadi spoke with a small laugh and pointed to the camera.

"Helen, don't talk to me. This is a message for Freddy."

"When you get back, you need to tell me where you are." She seemed to be growing angrier. After a moment, the two little girls disappeared from the frame.

"I don't have much time because Cesar is coming to pick this up soon. I hope you find what you're looking for. This whole affair is so confusing. I don't understand any of it, but it kind of makes sense in a weird way. I know you've always wanted to go into space, I mean, who hasn't, right?"

She spoke for just a few more minutes, talking mostly about how much she owed him for his help and how much she enjoyed having Daryn. She felt fortunate to have known him and glad he had come back into her life. While watching the video, his present concerns and anxiety faded away, and he realized a significant change in his attitude toward Sadi. Seeing her seemed as though she was reuniting with a dear friend, a purely platonic friend. The sting of unrequited love had vanished. Her final words returned Freddy to reality.

"Please don't let this alien prevent you from coming back to us. Have a good journey, and we'll see you when you get back."

After waving, she stood up and exited the frame, and a moment later, the video stopped. Freddy watched the videos again, then sat back in his seat and closed his eyes. The increased gravity in the car felt normal now. Pulling his head away from the back of his seat required less conscious effort to accomplish, but his neck muscles still ached.

Freddy returned his attention to the stars and other celestial objects. At six in the evening, he looked through the rear camera and could no longer locate Earth. He expected Earth's absence to make him feel lonely, but instead, he felt empowered. If he wanted to return to Earth, he could. If he wanted to go to Venus, he could change direction and do that. Freddy felt as though he had total control of his life.

Venus held more interest to Freddy than Mercury, at least it did before all the recent events. That planet was purported to have a beautiful atmosphere with more interesting features. A sightseeing visit to Venus would add several days to the journey, time he did not have. For just a moment, he mused about going there when done with whatever the alien had planned.

While beginning to consider the other possibilities, a frightening thought crashed into his mind. With such great distances in the solar system, he could easily become lost and have difficulty finding Earth again if the navigation program crashed. He needed to focus on the plan.

About eight hours remained before he would start deceleration, so he decided to take one of his sleeping pills. If he could sleep until the autopilot initiated the change—the shift in acceleration would most certainly wake him—then he would be rested enough for whatever happened at the end of his journey. And with the sleeping pill, he might have less disturbing nightmares.

After swallowing the pill with some juice, he decided to relieve himself of one bodily need, a task he had been dreading. He urinated into the tube that Cesar provided, which emptied into a container under the seat. Fortunately, he had successfully escaped the necessity of emptying his bowels so far.

Freddy wanted to know how long the pill would need to take effect. On the control panel, he clicked on the clock and initiated the timer function. While watching the seconds pass, he kept his eyes open, but he failed to remember closing them.

—※—

Freddy opened his eyes to the familiar and comforting view of the stars. He took a deep breath, which transformed into a yawn. After unbuckling himself, he flexed his stiff arms and legs, stretching almost until his calf muscles tightened into knots. He could not remember feeling so rested. After the rush of endorphins and the return of his vision, he looked at the computer screen and noticed the time. It was eight a.m. the next morning. He had slept for fourteen hours!

"What?" he said, sitting forward in panic. After taking a deep breath, he verified the time and became angry at his careless failure to set an alarm. The possibility of sleeping so long never occurred to him. He never overslept, but he never took sleeping pills either.

For the next thirty seconds, he inspected all the other critical monitor items. After noticing the velocity vector and acceleration, he started to panic even more. According to the navigation program, the autopilot had failed to initiate deceleration at the halfway point to Mercury. He had slept through that crucial turning point like a mindless baby. The change in velocity for his journey should have been automatic. At his current speed, the thrust needed to decelerate in time would be too much for him to bear. What if he made a mistake on the updated navigation route? He could be lost in space.

"Okay, breathe," he told himself. "Breathing is what I can do right now."

After several deep breaths, his panic subsided enough for him to begin thinking more clearly. He would start deceleration at the planned rate and then overshoot his target a bit, only a delay of less than a day.

He rechecked the navigation program and saw the representation of Mercury situated in his present trajectory. At the present distance, he should be able to see the planet, and that exciting thought temporarily replaced his feeling of panic. When he looked at the camera facing the direction of Mercury, he noticed a single star brighter than the rest.

Although he knew his speed in relation to Mercury would be tremendous, the number on the navigation window still shocked him: just over twelve hundred kilometers per second. At the present speed, the ETA should be just under ten hours. After another moment's thought, he decided to stop acceleration altogether for just a few minutes before initiating the slow-down phase of his journey. With excited anticipation, he recalled the absence of force on his body.

After cutting power to the engine, he experienced weightlessness again. The sensation felt wonderful, and for a moment, he almost lost consciousness due to the rush of hormones and other chemicals into his blood. All of his muscles slowly began to relax.

"Good thing my stomach is empty," he whispered.

The feeling of elation faded after a few minutes, and he began to feel a sense of urgency to discover why the autopilot program had failed to initiate the deceleration phase. With every passing second, he came twelve hundred kilometers closer to his destination.

He remembered Cesar showing him the navigation log files, but he did not remember their location. For the next few minutes, Freddy searched the computer for a history of the engine activity in the hopes of finding some problem that might have stopped the autopilot. According to his understanding, the action should have been automatic. In the navigation program, he found what were called *Journey Log* files, but they showed nothing interesting after leaving the moon—when he engaged the autopilot.

For thirty minutes, he searched in vain through all the log files for the cause of the problem. With every passing second, his sense of urgency to initiate the deceleration became more intense until he paused the investigation. He needed to reverse thrust and reorient the vehicle so that he could be pushed against the back of his seat on the second half of his journey.

As he moved the mouse pointer to open the navigation control window, a bright flash from outside the window illuminated the inside of the vehicle. Before turning to see the light source, Freddy squinted and used his hand to shield a possible glimpse of the sun. Had the vehicle spun around to allow sunlight through the windows? If so, he could not expose his eyes to its intense radiation, even despite the window shielding. But after failing to feel any heat from the light, he knew it had to be something else.

With his hand between him and the light source, he slowly opened his eyes wider. Before he could move his hand out of the way, the light disappeared. When he looked out the window, he saw the same view of space he had seen for the past day and a half. When the source of the light reappeared a few seconds later, he recognized it—the probe from the barn. Bright sunlight reflected off its mirrored surface, but it did not hurt his eyes this time.

In the probe's mirrored surface, Freddy saw a reflection of the vehicle and a dark outline of himself staring back.

"Have you been following me this whole way?" Freddy asked softly, almost expecting a reply. The mirrored surface of the probe answered with silence.

The nose, or front of the probe, looked the same, as sharp as a needle. Extending from the back of the probe, strands of light floated as if suspended in some fluid. The lights behind the probe looked so beautiful, he could have watched them for hours.

When he heard a voice from the speakers inside the car, he jolted. *Am I dreaming?* No, definitely not a dream. The woman who had visited him in his room was speaking to him.

"Did you enjoy your sleep?" the voice asked. Freddy looked at the shiny probe surface for signs of life, then at his computer screen. He almost expected to see a picture appear with the sound.

"Are you in the probe?" he asked.

"No."

"Did you stop this vehicle from engaging the autopilot program?"

"No," the voice said, followed by a long pause. "You did."

Freddy forgot his amazement at the situation and felt immediate anger.

"This is the second time where you made me do something against my will. How do you justify that? Do you consider me of lower intelligence, and that makes it acceptable?"

"It was not against your will," said the voice with some amusement.

Freddy realized his mistake.

"Yes, but you forced me to do it while I was not conscious."

Every second that passed added to his anxiety. At that lethal speed, he imagined his life ending in a burst of light on the surface of Mercury. An instant and painless cremation would not be a bad way to stop existing, he thought absently.

"Have I ever used violence or threatened violence when dealing with you?" the calm female voice continued. "Do you feel misled?"

He imagined lying on a couch while a psychiatrist asked him personal questions.

"Not that I remember," Freddy said and paused, wondering what tools of persuasion the alien had used against him during the forgotten experiences. "So if I turned around and went back to Earth, you would not stop me?"

Although he could not sense any emotion from the alien, if it had any, he knew his bluff had not fooled it. The alien knew he still wanted to continue with the plan.

"You own your life," said the female voice as if he had asked a silly question. "I will not steal it from you."

"So why did you stop me from decelerating?"

"For the expansion, you require a certain speed."

"What expansion?" he asked. His curiosity began to replace his frustration. "Is that the path to the other planet?"

"You have plenty of time to discover that on your own," the voice said in the same chiding tone. "Telling you the answer would be highly unsatisfying to both of us."

The million other questions filling his head would have to be asked later.

"So what should I do now?"

"Your course is set. You have just a few more hours."

Freddy opened his mouth for another question, but the probe shot away from view. He leaned forward in a failed attempt to find it again.

"So, I just coast the rest of the way?"

"Try to enjoy the break and relax because your body will need the rest. I will see you soon."

Although he continued searching for it, Freddy heard nothing more from the probe, or more specifically, from the speakers. He decided to take the alien's advice and try to relax.

During the final hours of his journey, his body began recovering from the extended period of extra pressure. He started to feel better physically and mentally. While relaxing, he focused on the excitement of discovery, but he also felt as if he was waiting at the dentist's office for a root canal. Many of the events from his recent metaphysical experiences felt like they were about to materialize.

While Mercury grew larger and larger, Freddy could hardly take his eyes off it. He spent several minutes looking through the camera and enlarging the image but decided finally to restrict his view through the window. The crescent of light looked like a small version of the moon. For just a moment, he had a strange sensation. Instead of Mercury getting larger, he felt as though he was shrinking.

"I should be afraid for my life," he told himself. "If the alien is lying, I will be dead in five minutes."

Suddenly, a forgotten dream came to life in his mind, another dream where he visited Mercury. He had seen the alien structure and could now recall the details. A round structure with a spire in the middle would be coming into view. But at his present speed, when he was close enough to see it, *whatever the expansion was* would have already begun. He could have used the camera for a closer look, but he could not take his eyes from the view through the window.

The next events happened too quickly for him to follow or comprehend entirely.

When Mercury became large enough for Freddy to notice craters, hundreds of tiny black discs began shooting toward him, originating from a single point on the surface. While approaching, they grew in size, and he noticed the circumference of each disc crackled with blue plasma filaments. The absence of sound made Freddy feel as if he were deaf. Nothing like what he was seeing could be silent. His ears hurt from the silence.

As the discs approached the vehicle, the blue plasma light surrounding each one exploded outward, and the black core of each disc coalesced with the others. Darkness expanded in the vehicle's path, forming a hole in space and eliminating all light from Mercury's surface below it. The only light remaining came from the blue plasma filaments surrounding the dark, which was quickly intensifying.

"Cover your eyes," commanded the female voice through the speakers, obliterating the bizarre silence. Freddy failed to respond quickly enough, so the voice returned louder, like an explosion.

"Now!"

THIRTY-NINE

Freddy

A hundred milliseconds later, a burst of blue light penetrated his closed fingers and eyelids. After the light faded, he removed his hands to view the scene, excited to see what had happened. Everything outside the BMW had disappeared.

The glass had lost its transparency, resembling obsidian. It felt as if he had been ejected from the physical universe. Only the BMW and its contents existed. Time might have even come to a stop. He could not tell. There was no sound and no other sensation to indicate movement.

He felt weightless, but the safety straps holding him tightly to the seat gave the illusion of gravity. As a test, he removed the small pad of paper from its pouch on the side of the passenger seat. He released it and watched it hover in the air in front of him. The BMW was no longer accelerating. The velocity vector readout showed the same speed as before the light burst. Logic dictated an imminent collision with Mercury, but the stillness and silence suggested he was safe.

"I would have crashed by now," he said, attempting to console himself.

To help erase the eerie silence, he began playing the video from

Sadi, but the activity felt strange and failed to keep his attention. He paused every few seconds to look through the windows, hoping to see something, anything.

The video of Sadi felt like a movie from another era where the actors no longer existed as living creatures but as rotting corpses under the ground. Before the video ended, he stopped it to avoid thinking of Sadi and her two girls as dead and gone.

After turning to the windows again, dark thoughts crept into his mind. *Do I want to see what is out there?* If he looked too long, he might see demonic eyes staring back at him. The possibility of finding something unpleasant eventually stopped Freddy from even glancing at the dark glass.

After an hour, all of his emotions and fears grew too intense to bear, so he closed his eyes, folded his hands across his chest, and focused on breathing. Eventually, the darkness seeped through his eyelids, extinguishing all conscious thought.

—※—

Freddy woke to a brilliant light filling the interior of the BMW. After opening his eyes a bit, he had to wait before they adjusted to the intensity. An immense planet filled the view before him, blue with swirls of white. Another object blocked part of the new planet, a large satellite covered with what looked like ice. The amazing scene banished Freddy's emptiness and isolation.

The vehicle was oriented such that the planet filled the entire view through the windshield. The blackness of space showed only in a portion of the side windows. For several minutes, he could only stare at the sight, mesmerized by what his brain was telling him—he had successfully arrived at his destination. For the present, he lost all interest in discovering how he had arrived. That answer did not matter. Freddy only wanted to explore.

After glancing at the computer, he noticed the time, just over an hour since the alien voice had told him to shut his eyes. He ignored the urge to find his position and speed relative to the planet and returned his attention to the amazing features.

At first, he saw mostly clouds with patches of blue oceans, but upon closer inspection, he had glimpses of multicolored terrains and even some white-capped mountain ranges. The planet looked very similar to Earth, except there were smaller and more numerous land masses. He saw one immense region, possibly one of the poles. The large area had fewer clouds and a lighter surface.

After several minutes of inspecting the beautiful scene, two massive walls began coming together in front of him, slowly eliminating his view of the planet. He suddenly felt like a captured animal but was still too much in shock to be afraid. The walls seemed to be composed of the same material as the probe, polished metal. On its shiny surface, the reflection of the BMW was visible. In less than a minute, the walls sealed together.

Freddy switched to the camera view below the car. A flat surface was approaching, and the BMW came to a gentle rest on it. The next change happened too slowly for him to notice, but eventually, he felt the familiar pull of gravity as the seat began to push against him.

He looked at his new environment and noticed the smooth floor. Different colors swirled together, resembling multicolored marble. A soft light came from above and cast a shadow of the car on the ground. The low light reminded him of early morning, just before sunrise. His new environment looked comfortable.

Walls surrounded the vehicle in all directions, about seven or eight meters away. Two strange objects rested on the ground at the edge of the walls, the only other objects in the room with him. They appeared to be made of metal and glass, shaped somewhat like large boxes. A single passageway ended in darkness.

"Hello," he said, then waited in vain for some response. "Are you listening?"

After the sound of his voice, the silence felt more absolute. Freddy waited for several seconds until a sudden fear interrupted his curiosity. If the alien appeared in its true form, would his mind go into shock or denial? Perhaps the human mind could not comprehend such a situation.

A glance at the external sensors confirmed the safe outside environment. The air was at normal atmospheric pressure, composed of the right proportion of oxygen to nitrogen, and at a comfortable twenty-two degrees Celsius. Before opening the door, Freddy paused to subdue his irrational fears and assure himself of the situation—the alien did not intend to trick or hurt him.

Upon opening the door, Freddy first noticed the smell and inhaled the fresh air as if he had been holding his breath. During his journey, he had been oblivious to the stale smell of the recycled air in the BMW. The atmosphere in his new environment smelled like the beginning of a thunderstorm. The cool air flowed refreshingly into his lungs.

While looking around at his new surroundings, he stretched his muscles and continued breathing deeply. After two and a half days of traveling in the car, his muscles felt as if poison flowed through them.

"Oh wow," he said as endorphins flooded through his system.

His present situation reminded him of a video game from his childhood, a role-playing game that put him in a series of different rooms, and he had to figure out what to do. He looked up to see the source of the light and noticed several glowing glass rings on the ceiling. A multi-colored plasma filled them. For several seconds, he enjoyed watching the light inside the rings shift and swirl.

He turned his attention to the only other objects in the room, the boxes near the wall to his right. After slowly walking to them, he bent down and touched one. The mixture of metal and glass felt cool and appeared to be a machine of some sort. He spent several seconds looking at the mix of tubes, rings, rods, and small compartments surrounded by glass of red, blue, and yellow.

He would have continued inspecting the boxes, but he felt a sudden urge to enter the hallway that led out of the room. When he got to the beginning of the hallway, he stared at where it turned sharply into darkness.

Before entering, he heard a noise behind him. The sound caused a momentary panic, and he realized his growing tension. He froze and felt his blood run cold. His instincts urged him to run to the BMW and lock himself inside, but he took a deep breath and turned around to see the source of the noise.

His eyes were instantly drawn to the boxes on the ground. After about twenty seconds, they had unfolded into some sort of mechanical creatures, like robots with multiple legs and arms. Once their transformation was complete, they began moving toward the BMW. Their intentions seemed benign and were focused on the vehicle.

"Hello," said Freddy tentatively, but the robots continued on their path and gave no response. When they reached the vehicle, they stopped with their appendages extended. At first, nothing seemed to be happening.

"What are you doing?" he asked.

A compartment with a yellow glass window rotated, stopping abruptly. He felt as though he was looking at a blank, mechanical face. He heard a voice that seemed to originate inside his mind. The words had no physical manifestation and seemed to enter his mind as an abnormally clear thought.

Your vehicle will not be harmed.

The compartment with the yellow window rotated to face the car again.

"Who are you?" he asked but felt as though he had spoken only to himself. He received no other response.

Part of him wanted to stay and see what the robots would do, but the urge to enter the hallway kept pulling at his thoughts. Even if the robots intended to destroy the BMW, what could he do? Nothing probably. The alien had no reason to damage it, no reason Freddy could imagine.

Before stepping into the hallway, he looked up at the five-meter-tall ceiling and felt very small. The pathway was three meters wide and seemed intended for creatures much larger than humans.

While walking through the hallway, his anxiety began to fade, excitement taking its place. The experience reminded him of when he went to college and started learning about how the world worked. Every class opened his mind even more. Learning about physics, biology, astronomy, and chemistry made him feel as though he had power. As he proceeded through the hallway, he felt ready to step into the next stage of knowledge.

In about ten meters, he came to a three-way intersection, with each direction looking the same. Without hesitation, he chose the right. It seemed correct. After about twenty more meters, he entered a large open area with even higher ceilings. The lights above him were so high the circles of plasma looked almost like large dots.

The place reminded Freddy of a huge showroom in a museum. In every direction, enormous cylindrical glass containers stood on marble stands. At the base of each one, strange symbols were carved into the stone in what looked like cursive writing. Behind each one stood another and then another farther back. Freddy could see no end of them. But when he saw what the displays contained, he had to fight his first instinct to run back to the BMW. Curiosity kept his feet firmly planted.

A single alien creature occupied each giant container, suspended in a murky silver fluid like translucent mercury. The size of the creatures ranged from shorter than humans to several meters taller than a giraffe. Most of the light in the area came from the illuminated crystal walls of the displays.

After his pulse returned to normal and he realized the creatures showed no signs of consciousness, he tentatively walked to the first column and put his hand on it. He expected the crystal to feel cold, but it was warm.

The creature inside was at least twice Freddy's height and resembled what he imagined a black abominable snowman might look like. The liquid obscured most of the creature, but Freddy could see enough of it to recognize its features. Short black hair covered its huge body, which must have weighed at least a thousand pounds. The huge face seemed to have the capacity for human-level intelligence, maybe more. Being suspended in the liquid gave the creature the perception of weightlessness.

Fortunately, its immense eyes were closed, and it appeared to be in suspended animation. He could not think of the creature as dead or artificial. The black fur had a healthy shine, and the black skin around the eyes seemed just as vibrant. Freddy looked at the face in fascination, but not for too long. He feared it would come to life, and he felt unprepared for that experience. His survival instincts said to consider something that big as a threat.

After his first encounter with the dream alien, he had spent little time speculating on how it would appear physically. The alien had only appeared to him in the form of a woman, and he assumed it would be his relative size or smaller. Never once did the possibility of a colossal being cross his mind. Did the alien choose to let him wander about the place so that he could become accustomed to a large creature before revealing itself to him?

He went to the next column and the next. Each one held a different creature. Most were huge, but some were his size, and a few even smaller. From what he could tell, most looked like land-based animals, except for two flying creatures with wings and a single sea creature with flippers. After moving through the silent museum of strange animals, he wondered what it all meant and why no living being had greeted him, only the robots, and they had seemed only interested in the BMW.

After inspecting several of the creatures, a new and frightening thought occurred to him. Did the alien plan to put him on display? His mind instantly rejected that idea. These creatures were beautiful and seemed to be the prime example of their species. If the alien wanted a human for display, it would have chosen a better specimen than Freddy Carlson. The realization made him smile in amusement.

But the thought did cause significant alarm and made the contents of the dark room seem more menacing. Freddy did not like the idea of the alien putting all these creatures on display by either killing them or putting them in suspended animation, especially since they all appeared intelligent. He already had a negative impression of the alien's nature due to its treatment of Sadi.

Eventually, Freddy reached a wall with another immense passageway leading out of the display room. A brighter light came from the passage, and he longed to escape. Freddy paused before entering the lighter room, but he had no other choice, and the light seemed to lighten his mood.

"Go to the light," Freddy told himself, but he felt like a moth entering a fire.

When he arrived at the source of the light, it wiped all dread from his mind.

—❋—

The much smaller room reminded Freddy of a planetarium. The ceiling caught his attention first. Stars could be seen through it, almost as if nothing separated him from the vacuum of space.

The stars cast a soft glow from above, but most of the light entered through a huge transparent circle in the floor with a view of the planet in full daylight. When he saw the scene, a rush of endorphins flooded his bloodstream and sent a tingling sensation through every cell. As he stepped to the edge of the circle, the light eliminated all shadow from his thoughts.

For the next few minutes, he stared in wonder at the new planet visible through the floor and failed to notice the rest of the objects in the room. When he finally tore his eyes away, he found the room surrounded by columns of different diameters and heights. They appeared to be made of black stone with swirling metal in random patterns, possibly the same shiny metal as the probe. Some of the columns were short enough for him to see the tops. Each column had a cap of multi-faceted crystal and refracted a rainbow of colors in all directions.

He also found the columns beautiful, but after just a few seconds of inspection, his gaze returned to the view of the planet. This time, he found the courage to step onto the transparent medium. When his foot touched the surface, the light rippled and caused a wave to spread across the whole glass, like when a pebble hit a smooth liquid surface.

After stepping back onto the opaque part of the floor, he leaned closer to see a particularly dark feature of the planet and then almost fell when the image zoomed into what he was trying to see. The rapid change in perspective gave him the sensation of falling.

His smile and eyes widened as he used the focusing feature to inspect the planet. For being an alien world, it did not seem that unfamiliar to him. On the surface, he saw mountains, rivers, vast deserts, beaches, jungles, forests, a polar ice cap, and oceans, and he even saw animals when he looked close enough. The activity soon absorbed all of his conscious thoughts, and he forgot about his current situation.

While searching over the surface of the planet, a question gently entered his mind, and he required a moment to recognize the individual words.

"Are you enjoying this experience?"

Before responding, he looked around the room but saw nothing new or any sign of life.

"I am enjoying it," Freddy whispered. The sound of his voice felt alien to his ears. "Are you going to show yourself?"

While waiting for some kind of response, he failed to notice the sensation filling his mind and body. He no longer felt alone in the room as though an entity had silently appeared behind him. Freddy felt like a kid again, waking up in the dark and imagining a monster or ghost under the bed.

While attempting to gather sufficient courage to turn and see what stood behind him, he kept his focus on the planet and breathing calmly.

"Why did you bring me here?" he asked without turning.

"Be patient," came the gentle voice in his head again. "There is plenty of time for your questions."

After drawing a deep breath, he turned to face his fear, but he found nothing behind him. He still felt the presence of another entity in the room with him, so he spent some time inspecting every visible space until he finally quit.

"Where are you?"

"We are going to use a different interface, something less distracting. You really do not want to perceive me yet. You are not yet ready for a true form."

When the word *interface* entered his mind, he thought of a computer program, but then he understood what the entity probably intended. It wanted him to return to the room with all the displays and choose one of the creatures.

Its next words arrived in his head with a sense of finality, and he knew it would not communicate anything else until after he complied with its wishes.

"It is your choice."

Before actually leaving the viewing room, Freddy mentally walked back through the creature display room and remembered the one he found the least intimidating. He had seen no human forms, but he had found something like a monkey just below his height. He remembered seeing a gentleness in its face, almost like a creature from a Dr. Seuss book. After making his decision, he wondered if the alien already knew the one he would pick.

"Do you know the one I've chosen?" asked Freddy. "Or do I need to tell you?"

No response.

Before Freddy turned to leave, he glanced back at the image of the planet and hoped to return to the room and see it again. As he walked through the display room, Freddy attempted to ignore the disturbing thought of being led by a prison guard to his cell.

He spent several minutes searching through the immense room, but Freddy finally found the creature and then stood in front of its crystal container. Like all the others, the creature was suspended inside the silvery liquid, motionless. It had short, silvery white fur with small spots of gray and green.

He peered through the crystal at the lifeless face, partially visible through the translucent liquid. Long white lashes extended from its closed eyelids.

When the white eyes opened, Freddy jumped in shock.

PART III

ROLLER-COASTER

Up and down the track we go

To where?

We don't know

FORTY

Sadi

On the morning of Thursday, August 20, Sadi woke to the sound of the phone ringing. She hurried to answer it so the noise would not wake the girls. When Gerald spoke, she instantly recognized his voice.

"Good morning," he said cheerfully, and his tone helped erase her panic of an early morning phone call. *Is Gerald always in such a good mood at five-thirty in the morning?* Even after two months, she still felt horror from any unexpected phone call.

She responded groggily.

"Uh, good morning. What's going on?"

"Your friend is leaving tonight," he said, then paused for her response.

As his meaning became clear, her fatigue fled. She was suddenly cold and tried thinking of a response, but he relieved her of the burden.

"Can you make a quick video message for him?" he asked. "So he doesn't get lonely on his trip?"

They discussed the details of when and how to upload the video message as if they were speaking about a simple two-day journey. At the end, she said goodbye and cut the connection. For the next several minutes, Sadi attempted to let her brain accept the information. She understood the meaning but not the significance.

Freddy would be traveling to another planet that night, to Mercury, then possibly somewhere else. The news seemed like a movie rather than real life. Talking about the possibility at the meeting had failed to prepare her for the actual news.

Ever since Helen's rescue, Sadi's feelings about Freddy had been conflicted. She'd always had the uncomfortable feeling that he liked her in a romantic way, and she was sorry for not being able to return the feelings, but now that she owed him more than she could ever repay, the situation had transformed into an entirely different beast.

Her debt to Freddy meant infinitely more than her mortgage. She could stop paying her mortgage, and the only consequence would be losing her house. She would never be out of Freddy's debt. Was saving his life sufficient repayment? Probably not.

If he still loved her, did she have an obligation to return it? When she thought about the possibility, it almost made her physically sick, and that feeling increased her guilt. He had nothing major wrong with him and had many good qualities. But the emotions felt as though she was attempting to become physically attracted to her brother. She felt confused, an emotional bomb with a lit fuse. How long was the fuse?

Other than making a video for Freddy, possibly a farewell video, her day passed like many others before it. Her life had become a new normal with her confiscated daughter. The summer vacation meant that Sadi could have a small break from worrying about what to do with the girl.

The first two weeks with Daryn were spent in various cities along the Oregon and Washington coasts, Sadi's favorite places. But she felt so paranoid that the time hardly seemed like a vacation. They would stay at a hotel for a couple of nights, but then Sadi feared the entire time that they were being watched, so she would change hotels. Toward the end, Sadi started to feel less paranoid. Watching the girls have fun kept her sane.

Fortunately, there had been only a few weeks of school left for Helen. While she was at school, Jen and Sadi's brother Brian took turns watching Daryn and assessing what she lacked educationally. Sadi knew Brian lacked the qualifications and aptitude for the assessment, but he did the best he could. He made a significant sacrifice by missing several days of work. His enthusiasm surprised Sadi. He also stopped drinking as much while helping. Daryn had a more positive influence on him than he had on her, Sadi thought.

That night, after Freddy had departed on his journey, Sadi dreamed of traveling in space with him. The dream felt so real that she woke up at one-thirty and spent a moment trying to separate imagination from reality. She vividly remembered the image of Freddy's face, illuminated by the sun, and his skin beginning to crackle and burn.

She lay back down and closed her eyes, hoping to go back to the dream, curious to see how it ended. Did her dream mean that Freddy had run into trouble? She hoped not. As she slowly fell back to sleep, the dream failed to return.

When she woke up in the morning, she remembered nothing else of her dreams, just Freddy's face burning in the sun. The memory left her with an unsettling feeling the whole day. Possible news of Freddy's status would not be available until the middle of next week, and the time seemed like an eternity. Freddy's well-being had become a requirement for Sadi's healthy emotional state.

After Sadi returned home from work that night, she went straight to the computer to check the group website for any news of Freddy's journey. As expected, she found nothing new, although Gerald said he would post a notice about it every day, about what they knew and did not know.

At seven-thirty that evening, Jen rushed into Sadi's room. When Sadi looked up from her laptop, she could see the panic in Jen's eyes.

"A police detective is at the door," she said and paused to catch her breath. "She wants to see you."

Sadi's heart stopped.

"Did you let her in?" Sadi asked. "Are the girls in their rooms?"

They had prepared for this moment at least a dozen times, and Jen had followed the planned procedure perfectly. She answered the door and then left the detective waiting outside while she fetched Sadi. After getting Sadi, she quietly put Daryn and Helen in their rooms, Daryn with her light off and door locked and Helen with her door open and light on. Both girls pretended to sleep.

"It's just one woman," Jen said as they walked to the door. "She looks nice."

Sadi's heart beat wildly in her chest, but she stood as calmly as possible and focused on breathing. After opening the door, she found a short and stocky woman patiently waiting on the doorstep.

The woman's light brown hair seemed too short for the tight ponytail it was pulled into, stretching her forehead and highlighting her pasty complexion. The sincere smile, however, brightened her entire appearance, making Sadi feel a little more at ease. She looked to be in her mid-forties.

"Hi, Miss Jacobsen," she said. "I am Detective Zimmerman with the Portland Police Department. May I come in? I have some questions for you."

"Sure," Sadi said, but her brain screamed at her to slam the door in the woman's face. They went to the living room and sat on the couch. Jen had disappeared before Sadi opened the door.

"I just have a few questions about your missing persons claim," she said. Sadi thought her voice sounded mechanical as if she had spoken those exact words thousands of times.

"I've already talked to the police about this," Sadi answered and tried sounding as calm as possible. Inside, she felt a raging fire, a hot panic. "Why again, after so many weeks?"

Detective Zimmerman sat forward in her seat.

"I'm investigating a possible connection between a kidnapping and another crime that happened around the same time."

"What kind of crime?" Sadi asked innocently. She tried acting as curious as possible without being too concerned. She wished Freddy had been there. He would have known the woman's intentions.

"That information is not at my leisure to divulge, but don't worry, Miss Jacobsen." The woman paused and sounded sorry to have brought Sadi discomfort. "You're not being accused of any crime. We just think there may be a connection between a kidnapping and this other crime since the timing is so coincidental. You are on my list of missing person reports that I'm checking up on."

"Do you need me to go over what happened again?" she asked as if the possibility exhausted her. "I really don't want to be reminded of it."

Sadi did not want to retell the story Craig invented for the police. If she said something inconsistent with the original story, the detective might get suspicious.

Gerald said that people should never talk to the police when involved in an investigation, at least without a lawyer present. Even when innocent of any crime, people incriminated themselves all the time. She could refuse to talk with the investigator without a lawyer present, but that would cause suspicion. The delicate situation required her to walk in a straight line when she felt most out of balance.

"I have the report," the detective said. "So I don't need to hear it again. Not unless there's something you want to add or change from your original statement." The woman's tone held a hint of encouragement as if she expected Sadi to offer new information.

"No," Sadi said quickly. "There's nothing to add."

Before continuing, Zimmerman looked at Sadi for a moment as though checking for any suspicious behavior.

"Like I said, the incident involving your daughter, Helen, and this other crime is just one of several I'm investigating. Although, I have to say that your case timeline matches up the best with the other timeline."

"Okay," she began slowly. Sadi felt unable to hide her frustration. "So what do you want from me? Places, dates, corroboration? I thought I was not being accused of anything."

"Please don't misunderstand me, Miss Jacobsen. I just wanted to introduce myself and give you my contact information. I understand the difficult situation you went through and certainly don't want to add any more stress. I have a pair of sons myself. They're older now, but if either one of them ever went missing, I would have lost my mind."

"And why exactly would I need to contact you?" Sadi asked this politely, even though it sounded a bit harsh. The woman's mention of her sons made Sadi feel slightly empathetic.

"I'm just casting my nets into the water, Miss Jacobsen. I understand that many people are wary to trust law enforcement to handle their safety. I just want to let you know that if you feel threatened at all, I can offer protection. You don't have to answer me now. Just take my card and hold onto it if you need anything."

Detective Zimmerman handed her business card to Sadi.

Sadi took the card and took longer than necessary to inspect it. She felt relief from not having to meet the woman's eyes. At the moment, she did not know what to think.

"Alright, thanks."

Detective Zimmerman's business attitude soon changed to something more human and inviting, as if she could now act like a new neighbor coming to introduce herself. After complimenting Sadi on her home and the neighborhood, she noticed the pictures of Helen and her son on the entertainment center and asked about them.

As relaxed as she could, Sadi gave a standard statement about how much fun she had with her daughter and then explained how her son died the previous year.

"I'm sorry to hear it," Zimmerman said with sincere sympathy in her voice.

Without intending it, mentioning her son's death had caused the woman to feel more empathy, and it might persuade her to give Sadi a break. They talked for a few more minutes, and then she left. At the end of the conversation, Sadi had come to like the woman on a personal level. She had felt a small temptation to confess everything but stopped herself.

After the detective drove away, Jen reappeared with a concerned look in her eyes.

"What was that about?"

For a moment, she stared at Jen and said nothing. Terrible and irrational thoughts filled her mind. She imagined the police breaking down the door and taking the two girls, a worse possibility than going to jail herself.

"I think the police suspect that we're somehow related to what happened at the hotel."

"What are we going to do? Can I do anything to help?" Jen grabbed Sadi's shoulder. The sympathetic look in her eyes brought Sadi some comfort.

"I don't know. I need to talk to Gerald. He might know what I should do."

"Is it even an option to tell that investigator what happened? I was listening, and she sounded nice."

"I don't know, Jen," Sadi said out of frustration and a bit harshly. Before apologizing, something caught her attention, and she looked at the stairs. Out of the corner of her eye, Sadi recognized Helen's bare feet at the top.

"Is it okay to come down?" Helen asked with noticeable concern in her voice.

Sadi held out her left hand.

"Come on down, dear."

Helen ran down the stairs and hugged her mother. With one hand, Sadi held her daughter tightly against her hip.

"Don't worry, Helen. Everything's alright."

Her words seemed to calm the girl.

"Was that the police?" she asked.

"Not the normal police," she said as calmly as possible. "She was a detective, a very nice lady who only wants to help people."

She sent Helen off to bed and apologized to Jen for being abrupt with her. Fortunately, Jen had taken no offense. Sadi could become hot-tempered but usually calmed down just as quickly.

Seeing Helen and being able to comfort her somehow made Sadi feel better like everything would turn out for the best. After her nerves calmed some more, she planned to talk with Gerald on the website. She loved having a lawyer as a friend, if only for legal advice. But calling him seemed too dangerous. If the police were going to pull her phone record later to see who she contacted, they might be suspicious if she directly called a lawyer.

Later that night, after the little girls were asleep and Jen went to her room, Sadi opened up her laptop computer and logged into the group's site. She sent a short note to Gerald.

Sadi: *Got a visit from the police tonight. Write back when you get this.*

She had to wait less than twenty minutes before Gerald responded. When he responded, their conversation began in real time. She told him what happened and how they might suspect a connection to the deaths at the hotel.

Gerald re-emphasized his previous advice about not talking to the police and always referring to her previously recorded statement. If the police returned and asked her to come with them to the station for questioning, she should not go but set up a time when he could be present. Gerald attempted to assure her that it would not make her look more suspicious.

Gerald: *Make sure they don't find Daryn with you. Hiding her in a room would not prevent the police from finding her if they got a warrant. If you suspect they might do that, send her to your brother's for a few days.*

Her conversation with Gerald failed to bring any comfort. She had trouble sleeping that night, more so than usual. Not until midnight did she start drifting in and out of consciousness. For a long time, she lay in a half-dream state, with images of people dressed in uniforms in her house, looking for Daryn.

FORTY-ONE

Sadi

"Is life ever going to get back to normal?" she asked herself while standing in front of her bathroom mirror the next morning.

At least she had Helen back safe and Daryn rescued from the claws of those monsters. Unless Sadi made a mistake, Daryn would belong to her now, and no one would be taking her away again. She had to be smart and diligent. Those thoughts reminded her of all those movies and books where the protagonist made empty promises. The words ran through her mind, full of sarcasm.

I promise that I won't let that happen to you!

I promise to protect you!

I promise that you're going to get out of here alive!

Sadi could make no such vows and could only promise to do everything in her power to protect the girls. Many things were out of her control, and she would not be promising certainty when it did not exist.

She felt a momentary temptation to beg God for guidance, an instinct embedded in her brain from childhood, but she could not bring herself to do it. The thought made her sick inside. The act of requesting supernatural assistance reminded Sadi of her dead son and the experience with the alien probe in the barn when she went with Helen into that horrible tunnel.

Surrendering to such desperation would steal her limited resources. Instead of devising a solution, she would be wasting time by hoping for an answer to magically appear. If an incredibly intelligent creature watched over her and cared about her, why would it require a formal request before giving assistance? According to that insane logic, Sadi had caused her son's death and daughter's abduction when she neglected to offer a formal request to keep them safe.

While Sadi watched her own eyes looking back at her in the mirror, she felt a sudden and unexpected urge. She needed to get Daryn out of the house before anyone found her there. Before the feeling turned into a panic, she calmly told herself that it could wait until after breakfast.

Sadi walked down the stairs in the low light of the early Saturday morning, entered the kitchen, and turned on the light. Before she poured some oats into her yogurt, the feeling came again.

Put down the yogurt. Get the girls out!

Sadi set her breakfast down on the table and ran to the window.

"This is crazy," she said quietly. "I'm being paranoid."

She made a thin opening in the curtains to view the street in front of her house. At five forty-five in the morning, it was getting lighter outside, with the street visible. On the other side of the road, in front of Ms. Holland's house, she saw a Ford Taurus with two men in the front seats. The one in the passenger seat was looking in her direction. Before making eye contact with him, she let the curtain fall back in place and ran upstairs to Jen's room. Her eyes opened instantly, and she sat up in bed.

"Jen, you need to get the girls in the car now. Hurry."

Jen stared at Sadi as if she could not understand English. A moment later, when the realization hit her, she jumped out of bed, and in less than a minute, she had the two girls shuffled through the garage door and into her car, Helen in the front passenger seat and Daryn in the back.

Jen still wore her pajama shorts and a regular shirt, so she looked dressed and ready for the day. As they had gotten ready, Sadi told her about the two men watching the house, and she had a feeling that the girls needed to flee.

"Where do I go? Your brother's house?" she asked, breathing deeply after sitting in the driver's seat.

"Mom, what's going on? Why do we have to leave?" Helen glanced at Daryn in the back seat. Sadi had no time to make up a story.

"I don't know. I don't know," she said, ignoring Helen's question. "It can't be where someone would look if they knew us. You need to take them to someone that no one knows we're connected with."

Sadi desperately tried to think of a good place to take the girls, but nothing came to her panicked mind. She ran to the kitchen cupboard and grabbed the money she had hidden in the bottom of her ugliest mug. She shoved the wad of twenty dollar bills into Jen's shaking hands.

"Take this and go somewhere safe. If you take them to a hotel, pretend that you don't have a credit card or your identification."

Jen started the car, and Sadi crouched down to Helen's level.

"Fasten your seat belts, girls," she said and glanced back at Daryn.

"Is this because of me, Miss Jacobsen?" Daryn asked.

When Sadi looked into her eyes, she saw raw fear. Her instinct told her to put Daryn in the trunk, but she could not bring herself to do that.

"Nothing is your fault, Daryn. You're going to have fun with Jen today. Will you do one thing for me?"

"What?"

"Lay down in the back seat until Jen says it's okay to get up?"

"How am I going to lie down with my seat belt on?"

"You can put your seat belt on later. For now, just remember to lie down."

From the driver's seat, Jen turned to face Sadi.

"When can I try to contact you?"

A sudden idea came to her mind, so she shut the passenger doors and walked around to the other side of the car. She told Jen the address of Mr. Smith and a brief explanation of how to get there.

"Can you remember that, or do I need to write it down?"

"I remember where he lives, Mom," said Helen from the passenger seat. Helen turned to Daryn in the back seat with excitement in her eyes. "Did you hear that, Daryn? We're going to that old rich guy's house."

Sadi had no time to be proud of her daughter's memory. She bent down and spoke quietly in Jen's ear.

"Tell Mr. Smith that I'm sorry to ask him to take Daryn, but it will only be for a couple days. If he lets her stay, take Helen to Brian's and wait for me to contact you. Just pretend that nothing strange is going on. Does that make sense?"

"Yes, but what's going to happen to you?" Jen's breathing had calmed a little, but she still had a wild look in her bloodshot eyes.

"If you don't hear back from me, try to get a hold of Gerald Foster. You can probably find his number on Mr. Smith's caller ID."

Sadi looked back at the garage door to the house and wondered how much time she had left. "When you leave, drive away from the car parked across the street. If someone tries to stop you, pretend that you don't see them. Drive until you are sure you're not being followed, then go to Mr. Smith's house. Please take care of them. They're all I've got. I trust you, Jen. When I open the garage door, you go. Okay?"

"Okay, Sadi. Everything's going to be fine. I'll see you later."

"Do what Jen says, okay girls?" Jen's words made her feel better. "Have fun, and I'll see you later. Everything's gonna be fine!"

After opening the garage door, Sadi ran back into the house and peeked outside at the car across the street. While watching them, the men turned on their lights and looked ready to follow Jen. Sadi held her breath and started to move toward the door, preparing to run outside as a decoy, but curiosity kept her feet from moving.

Jen backed out of the driveway and stopped a car length away from the other car while changing gears to move forward.

"Please don't follow them," she whispered to herself. "Please don't follow them!"

The Ford Taurus slowly rolled forward a few meters in Jen's direction but then came to a stop. With relief, Sadi watched Jen drive down the street without the Taurus following them. Once they left her sight, Sadi felt as if nothing else mattered. The men could get out of their car with machine guns in their hands and start running to her door, and she would still feel relief.

The men in the car pulled back to the curb and turned off the headlights, then made movements indicating a plan to exit the vehicle. A moment later, the two men stepped out of the car, and she immediately noticed their dark suits. Sadi quickly dialed Gerald's phone, and he answered during the first ring.

"I think the police or FBI are at my house."

FORTY-TWO

Taylor

On the morning of August twenty-first, Taylor received a message from Gerald on the website, also addressed to Sadi. After reading the message, Taylor sat back in her seat in shock and stared blankly at the screen. She felt a mixture of anger and excitement.

"What the hell?"

Gerald wanted them to make a short video message for Freddy, the young man who saved Sadi's little girl from the child sex traffickers. He planned to begin the journey to Mercury that night. The news seemed too sudden and unexpected. She only remembered talking about the possibility and thought her permission would have been requested before they made the final decision.

Taylor found it difficult to keep herself from experiencing a mental breakdown due to all the impossibilities in her life recently. She had a hard enough time accepting that someone in the group communicated with an alien. Now, she needed to make a video message for him on his journey to visit it.

At first, she was angry at Gerald for another decision he'd made without consulting her, but then she realized what had probably happened. The kid had some experience and contacted Cesar about making the journey, and then Cesar made the call. She attempted to feel indignation about taking the convertible without her permission, but she could only feel excited about what the kid planned. Besides, Cesar had just as much, if not more, right to make the offer.

"What am I supposed to say?" she asked herself, sitting alone on her couch and shaking her head. "Say hi to the alien for me. Oh, and I hope it doesn't eat your heart out." She snickered at her joke but stopped when she thought there might be some truth to it.

When she had met Freddy at Cesar's home, she'd instantly liked him and felt glad that life had improved for him since his younger days. Gerald told her about his horrible childhood and how that old man had rescued him like an abandoned kitten. After a few seconds of thought, she decided to try her best to make a good message for him. She imagined being all alone in space and how much she would appreciate a message from another human. For the next few minutes, she found herself daydreaming about what he might experience. The feeling of isolation seemed almost too much to bear.

The whole idea of a real alien was too immense. Up until that point, Taylor had kept the story of the alien hidden from Mark. Over the several weeks they had worked together, she had grown very fond of his company. Being her only confidant in Brazil had helped strengthen their emotional bond, and not being able to discuss the matter with him wore on her conscience.

Her relationship with Mark seemed similar to her relationship with Cesar. While she considered Cesar as a father figure, Mark had become more of an older brother, a partial replacement for her dead brother. Several times, Taylor had found herself on the verge of telling Mark about the alien and had stopped herself. But due to the recent development, she felt that Mark needed to know, and she could trust him to keep the secret.

In the video, she made sure to be vague and make the story sound like Freddy had gone on a simple trip somewhere on Earth. Taylor felt a bit awkward during the recording. She barely knew him, but their shared knowledge helped to compensate for the lack of a personal connection. At the end of the video, she sincerely wished him the best and admitted to her jealousy, hoping he would understand that she felt no rancor about him taking her vehicle.

After she finished the video, she uploaded it to the site and spent a few minutes sitting and thinking. She could not wait to hear about what happened and hoped that nothing bad happened to him.

All the next day, while she worked on assembling the engines, she imagined herself telling Mark about what happened to Freddy, Gerald, Sadi, and Mr. Smith and what they planned. The next day, she decided to make the shocking revelation that Freddy was on his journey to Mercury and the reason for the trip.

After working from sunrise to sundown the following day, they ate dinner in Mark's apartment. They usually dined together and would alternate locations, Taylor cooking one night and Mark the next. She liked the routine and felt as though it helped keep her sane. After dinner, they sat at the table and talked. Since she had not heard otherwise, she assumed the plan had gone as scheduled, and Freddy was flying through space.

"Mark," she began tentatively, her heartbeat slightly elevated. "I need to tell you something, but you need to promise me something first."

"Sure," he said without hesitation. "What is it?"

"I need you to promise that what I tell you remains strictly confidential."

He laughed.

"What's not confidential?"

"I don't want Max to know, not yet."

"Okay, you have my attention now."

"I need your promise!" Taylor attempted to look more serious than usual.

He hesitated for a moment.

"Does it have to do with you and him?"

"Nothing like that," she said. "Give me your word."

"Okay, but you know he's going to find out eventually. If he kills me for keeping it from him, I'm holding you responsible."

"Give me your word, please. I want to tell you because you would want to know."

"You have my word," he said after exhaling.

"Do you remember Freddy from the test flight? The kid that came with the old man?"

"Yes."

"He took the convertible last night and is on his way to Mercury."

"What?" he asked, smiling as though he'd heard a joke. When he put his fork down on the plate, it gave a loud metallic clank. His smile disappeared when he realized her sincerity. "You're serious. Why?"

"He's going because the alien wanted him to go there."

The absurdity of what escaped her mouth helped curb the temptation to laugh, but she failed to keep the shy smile from her lips.

"I'm not getting the joke."

Taylor shook her head and wiped the smile away.

"Sorry, but I'm dead serious. He's gone to Mercury to see the...the alien."

Mark required a full fifteen minutes of explanation to be convinced of the extraterrestrial claims. Gerald had successfully convinced her of what he had experienced and how it could not be of human origin. Mark recognized her sincerity but needed several minutes to accept it.

"Did Freddy leave of his own free will, or was he under the influence of this being?" During their conversation, Mark refused to use the term *alien*, and she found it slightly amusing.

She shook her head.

"Apparently, a few days ago, Cesar took him on a test drive, and Gerald said the kid was in total control of himself. I trust Cesar's judgment about it."

Mark looked down at his plate for a few seconds.

"Why don't you want Max to know about this?"

"I don't trust him," she said without any hesitation. "He's a nice guy, and I know you trust him, but who knows what he'll do if he found out. Maybe he'll think it's a national security issue and feel obligated to report it."

"You've had a lot of time to think about this," he admitted. "I will need some time to comprehend the information fully if I ever do. Don't worry, I will keep this a secret, but we can't keep it forever."

"What do you mean, I don't have to worry? You already gave me your word. Now you're giving it to me again!"

He looked at her in shock.

"Taylor, I'm not going to tell him. Okay?"

"Sorry. It just freaks me out. Aliens were not in my plans. I know you'll keep quiet about it."

Mark looked up from the table into her eyes.

"Do you think the alien is using us just to get Freddy?"

"I wondered that too," Taylor said, "but the evidence indicates other motives. Gerald, Sadi, and Mr. Smith all said it probed them. Gerald thought it was some kind of test. I have the impression it wants to help us somehow. A greater intelligence than ours? If it wants anything to do with us, its intentions are probably benign."

"I know there are stupid movies about alien invasions," Mark said more to himself than her, "but they could want to take our world for themselves. Maybe they are planning some kind of invasion?"

"You're being paranoid, I think," Taylor said. "They didn't say so, but the alien must have helped Freddy rescue Sadi's daughter. There's no way a kid like Freddy could have done that by himself."

"Hmm, okay. When do you expect his return?"

"Next week, he's supposed to be back."

"When will we know if he's not coming back?" Mark asked.

"I don't know."

"Did you have any other secret meetings without Max and me?"

"I feel bad about excluding you," she said with a sympathetic smile, "but we could not completely trust Max. It had nothing to do with you."

Mark seemed to accept the answer and did not appear insulted.

FORTY-THREE

Mark

During his conversation with Taylor about the alien, Mark had attempted to show as little shock as possible, but the new information scared him. Later that night, he had trouble sleeping. His dreams were composed of strange alien faces mixed with those of his wife and two little boys.

Did Taylor feel the same way when she first heard the news? He could not imagine what Gerald, Sadi, Freddy, and the old man felt about having their more intimate experience with the extraterrestrial. They'd already had their experiences when he met them and more time to accept the truth of it. He thought they looked like ordinary people, not psychologically altered or controlled by a malevolent being.

"I'll just accept what Taylor said," he said to himself the next morning, "until I can talk to Gerald."

He smiled at the thought of Gerald wanting to tell him the story and Taylor forbidding it. Her method of handling conflict caused him great amusement. She had little concern for how her words and actions affected others. On the first of their visit to Brazil, he found her yelling at the two shop helpers who build parts for them. If he planned to disagree with her about anything, he needed to seriously consider his arguments and have his reasoning backed with concrete evidence. Whenever he failed to sufficiently prepare for a disagreement, she shoved it in his face. But he was never offended and appreciated her intelligence and spirit.

Mark felt some guilt for how he had described Taylor to his wife. If she ever met Taylor in person, she would be highly suspicious about how he had described Taylor as an unattractive, slightly overweight college geek. He was walking a thin line. If either woman learned the truth, Mark would be in trouble, but he felt safe for the moment.

He rarely spent so much time away from his family, and his wife never complained, but lately, she kept asking when he would return. Almost every evening, he used Skype for video conferencing with them, and that helped relieve the sting of separation, but video conferencing could not replace physical contact with them. Whenever he saw his boys, he wanted to hold them more than he wanted to see his wife.

Being away from his wife and children was difficult, especially at night and when he had idle time. His only consolation, or way to deal with it, came from their work. It was like a drug to both of them, working on a jet they hoped to take into space.

Never in his dreams did he ever imagine his present situation, working with a nuclear fusion reactor and helping the inventor of the NMG with a spacecraft. No matter what happened, good or bad, they would be included in the history books somewhere. Unfortunately, one of those books might end up being locked in some secret government agency log file, along with the mere memory of his name.

After learning that he would be transforming their old company jet into a spacecraft, he thought it was too big a task for just the two of them. Part of this assumption came from his experience with power and control systems. A vessel the size and weight of a jet required a massive energy source to move it. Fortunately, their enhanced fusion reactors supplied the necessary amount of energy.

At first, Mark assumed they would make two large NMG engines, one for each of the wings, but Taylor had other plans. She liked the concept of redundancy, of building sixteen to twenty smaller NMG engines, where any four of them could move the aircraft to any altitude. The others would be used for extra thrust and maneuverability, and most importantly, backup.

Mark had expected, correctly, it turned out, that life support, metrology, and system interaction would demand most of their time and attention. Of course, they needed the engines and power supplies to work without issue, but they especially needed the carbon dioxide partial pressure to remain steady and the manual overrides to function in case they encountered insolvable software bugs. Since Taylor and Cesar already worked out much of that on the BMW, it would save them a lot of time. Mark had less concern about software issues than Taylor. TerraWatch had their own software packages they were incorporating.

While away from family, he could accomplish three times as much as usual, and that realization reminded him of how much he enjoyed being a regular engineer. He preferred that to his regular position, a project manager. Since Mark could completely focus on his objectives, all the components of the two fusion reactors were fabricated or purchased in about forty days. Mark estimated that it would take another forty days before they could begin testing it.

Since Cesar and Taylor already designed the smaller version for the BMW, he only needed to scale it for the larger aircraft. For the most part, he was learning from their designs, but he could see several areas for improvement.

After learning about the alien, Mark had more difficulty concentrating on his work. The alien presented a million different possibilities to his active imagination. But his thoughts were based more on emotion than logic. Fear, excitement, anxiety, and a small amount of hope constantly fought for control of his overworked mind. With every possibility he imagined, new unanswered questions arose. He would have to wait, but for the present, it seemed okay. Mark was a patient man.

FORTY-FOUR

Sadi

Every passing second meant that Jen and her two girls had moved farther away from her, away from the danger approaching her doorstep. Sadi admitted to her fright, but somehow she remained calm. Daryn and Helen needed her to think clearly.

Sadi only spoke with Gerald for a few seconds. He reminded her not to talk to them and to call him when they were gone. Then she cut the connection.

Soon, the two men had crossed the street and arrived at her doorstep. They knocked too loudly for so early in the morning, lacking the customary consideration when someone might be still sleeping. Their action helped transform her emotion from fear to anger, just what she needed. Anger was superior to fear.

For a moment, she considered not answering the door, pretending to be asleep or gone from home, or taking a long time after telling them she would be right there. She was pretty confident that they did not see her at the window.

With her heart pounding stronger than usual, she answered their knocking with a question instead of opening the door.

"Who is it?"

She put as much confidence in her voice as she could. Ordinarily, she would not just open the door to strangers who appeared before six in the morning.

"Open the door, Miss Jacobsen," one of them said. "We're from the Portland Police Department."

"May I see some identification?" she asked after opening the door a crack, keeping the chain latched. The closest man to the door held up his badge. It looked legitimate, but then again, Sadi would not have recognized a fake one.

When she disconnected the latch and opened the door, they just stood on the doorstep. She expected them to say something. Both had dark hair, cut short. The one who held up his badge had light eyes, and the other had dark. Those seemed to be their only distinguishing features. They could have been brothers.

"May we come in?" the light eyes one said after a few seconds, the man who showed his badge

She stood her ground and remained motionless.

"What is this about?"

"We need to talk to you. May we come in?"

"I'd rather not. It's very early."

"Are you refusing to allow us entry?" he asked threateningly. "We just want to ask you some questions."

"I already talked to Detective Zimmerman last night. I need to have my lawyer present before I talk to anyone else."

"Yes, we know about Detective Zimmerman's visit," he said. The man with dark eyes just stood there like a statue. "We have some follow-up questions we need to ask you. We can go over them either here or at the station."

"I'm sorry, but I don't consent to an interrogation." She spoke as though confidently defending her rights, but inside, her will began to tremble. "I need my lawyer present."

"Do you have something to hide, Miss Jacobsen?" he said. "Why did your nanny take your daughter away so early just now?"

"She was going," Sadi began, then realized that she did not have to make up a story for the two men to explain where Jen had gone. "Like I said, I want my lawyer present before I say anything else. I have that right."

"You don't have the right to withhold crucial evidence of a crime. That's obstruction of justice."

"She was going where?" the other man asked, speaking for the first time. "Where did your daughter and her nanny go? Why was it important that they leave so early?"

"Like I said, I have the right to legal representation since you seem to be accusing me of something." Sadi imagined Gerald nodding in approval at her refusal to comply. "I will contact my lawyer, and we can schedule a time to talk to you."

"That's not how it's going to work," said the other detective finally. "You're coming to the station with us, and we're going to have a nice conversation."

"Am I under arrest?" she asked. To hide her shaking hands, Sadi held tightly onto the door. "What is the charge?"

"We can do it that way if you want?" the light-eyed one asked with the beginning of a smile. He seemed to want that option. "Do you want to be escorted out of here in handcuffs?"

Sadi looked at them in disbelief.

"Okay, fine, I'll go make a call to my lawyer, and we can talk today." When the words left her mouth, she recognized the mistake. She should have refrained from telling them her plans. After turning from them and starting to walk away, she felt a hand on her shoulder.

"What!" she said, startled.

"Are we going to tell the judge that you were resisting arrest?" he asked her.

While speaking, he reached down and pulled a pair of handcuffs from his pocket.

"Fine, we can do it this way."

He forcefully pulled both of her hands behind her back and then cuffed her wrists together. His grip felt like hard steel. If she had tried to resist, the metal from the handcuffs would have hurt her wrist. She felt a mixture of emotions—fear, anger, and surprise. The possibility of being arrested so improperly had never entered her mind.

"What are you doing? You have no reason to arrest me. I did nothing wrong. I was just going to make a call."

"You can make a call from the station," he said.

With the handcuffs on her wrists, she felt a loss of freedom that she had never before experienced. The two men had total control over her. She could not even hope for an opportunity to resist. The feeling of powerlessness made her empty stomach feel like an abyss.

They refused to let her take anything with her from home, no cell phone, no purse. The only thing they did for her was to lock the door after removing her from the house. They escorted her directly to their car.

On the way across the street, she felt an immense embarrassment at being escorted like a convicted criminal, and the emotion added to her fear of not seeing Helen or Daryn again. She tried telling herself that Gerald would get her out of the situation, but the distance between them seemed infinite. Hopefully, she could avoid being intimidated into speaking until Gerald arrived.

She noticed no bars between the back seat and the front, as she had expected. On the drive, they rode mostly in silence. Both men became strangely silent, as if their desire for her to talk had died when they entered the car. They had only wanted to get her in the car, away from her familiar surroundings.

"Why am I under arrest?" Sadi asked slowly and firmly once they had started driving. She regained some of her courage, and her frustration began turning into irritation, but the man in the passenger seat spoke to the driver and laughed.

"Now she wants to talk," the man said, and they both chuckled. He turned around to look her in the eyes. "You'll get all the talking you want, don't worry."

While looking into his cold eyes, she failed to think of any useful response. Sadi was so angry she had difficulty thinking coherently. Words felt empty, and she could not uncuff her hands to punch him in the face. When they passed the turn for the Hillsboro police station, she guessed their true destination to be Portland. In just a few more minutes, they arrived in the crowded and busy downtown streets.

—※—

At the police station, she walked in her slippers through the lobby and went straight to an interrogation room below ground. She expected them to make her sign papers, take her mugshot, or present her to someone, but they bypassed any processing or involvement with any other police officer or clerk. Quite a few people looked in her direction, but she was still too shocked at being taken into custody to feel more embarrassed.

The interrogation room seemed typical of those she had seen in the movies. A large mirror stood on one side, with a metal table in the center. They left her handcuffed and sitting on one side of the table with the officer, who initially showed his badge, opposite her. His companion stood at the back of the room by the door.

"Aren't you supposed to take a mugshot of me or something? When do I get my phone call?" Sadi stared at the man across the table from her and concentrated on her clenched fists. She needed an outlet for her anger. He stared back as if he had been in that situation a thousand times.

"All in good time, Miss Jacobsen. All in good time. Can I get you something to drink? We're going to be here a long time." The man smiled for the first time as if suddenly transforming into a polite host. His change in attitude made her stomach sick.

"I don't want anything to drink. I want to talk to my damn lawyer. You're not getting any information out of me until that happens."

He became quiet for a moment, and his smile remained.

"On the seventh of May, you reported that your daughter was kidnapped." He waited patiently for Sadi to confirm his statement.

"How many times do I have to tell you? I'm not answering any questions until my lawyer is present."

How dare they treat her as a criminal when she was the victim. Sadi clasped her hands together so tightly that her knuckles had turned white. She could not let her anger control her words. As it had in the past, anger could cause trouble for her. Since they probably recorded the whole conversation, she needed to appear calm and reasonable.

During the following silence, she thought of another possible reason for her abduction. Up until that point, she had only considered their interest to be primarily concerned with her daughter and what happened at the hotel, but they could be investigating her involvement with Gerald's group. She could not completely exclude that possibility.

Would they attempt to use her daughter to scare her into making a revelation about Gerald and his friends? She secretly hoped for that possibility. It might put her family at less risk. Would she reveal all of Gerald's secrets to save her two girls? Unfortunately, the man sitting across from her gave no more time for further consideration.

"Do you deny that your daughter was abducted?"

Sadi answered his question with silence, her first attempt at responding with silence.

"Okay, I get it," he said with that same irritating politeness. "If I was in your situation, I'd probably do the same thing."

He almost sounded like a normal human being, someone who could empathize with his fellow creatures. The man presented this version of his face when working with the public when he wanted them to trust him. But if she had not seen him until then, she might have been fooled. The next question completely shattered her hope that, deep down, he was a caring human being.

"We'll just have to bring your daughter in for questioning," he said and paused, waiting for the statement to have an effect. She could not hide her emotional reaction, although she still said nothing. Her face communicated what they wanted to know. A thin smile spread across his lips.

"Where did your nanny take her? Helen, right?"

Hearing her daughter's name from this man pushed her over the edge of calmness, and she could not remain silent.

"You can't interrogate a child without the parent's consent," Sadi said with confidence, but she felt unsure about the accuracy of her statement.

"Agent Farley here wanted to stop them, but I didn't think that would be necessary." He looked over his shoulder at his partner, who shrugged his shoulders. "Looks like I might have been wrong. Was I wrong, Miss Jacobsen?"

She opened her mouth to answer but could not think of what the answer should be. She felt as though she was trying to drive a car with the inside of the dash covered by a film of mud.

"I'm sorry. I didn't hear you. Are you ready to talk now?" His smile vanished, and his eyes narrowed.

She held her lips together and tried to keep them from trembling.

The man got up from his chair and walked to the door, and his partner opened it for him. Before exiting the room, he turned back to her. "We're just going to leave you here for a while to mull things over."

"Do I get to make my phone call now?" she asked without expecting to hear a positive response.

"The law says you get to make a call," he said. "But I say when."

Both men left the room, and the door shut solidly behind them. Sadi heard the lock latch, and the harsh sound filled the quiet room.

She felt like a piece of meat being prepared for a barbecue. First, they removed her from familiar surroundings, threatened her family and friends, and then let her thoughts, fears, and anxieties tenderize her. For the first five minutes, she could only think of Helen alone in the same room with two grown men who could get her to say anything they wanted.

Sadi had already talked to Helen and Daryn about what to do if ever interrogated by the police or anyone else concerning the kidnapping. They were to say that she forbade them to talk about it without her present. Knowing Helen, adults could easily break her will. She would hold her ground at first, but she would break eventually. Children were easily manipulated.

As Sadi sat there, she considered making up some story, pretending to be effectively intimidated by their threats. Maybe she should do the opposite of what they hoped she would by turning off her thoughts or thinking about something else. In her present state of mind, thinking seemed dangerous.

Suddenly, disturbing questions crept into her mind. Were these men helping provide cover for the child sex racket that had abused Daryn? They seemed to be working outside of standard police procedures. She could not reasonably expect justice from their system. These thoughts chipped away at the anger she had generated.

Before more thoughts could work her into a panic, she decided to stand and stretch her muscles. After sitting down for almost an hour, she stood and extended both hands forward to get her blood flowing again. She walked over to the mirror and could only see her reflection, but she imagined the two men standing on the other side.

"Is there anyone in there?" she asked loudly. "When do I get my phone call?"

She waited for a response or any sign of life, but nothing. The sound of her voice felt good and helped dispel her dark thoughts.

For the next thirty minutes, she paced around the room. Sitting still would have been more difficult. When she heard the door latch, her pulse quickly accelerated as she watched a short and stocky woman appear in the open door: Detective Zimmerman, the lady who had visited her the previous evening. Sadi stared at her in shock and waited for her to say something. Was she part of her nightmare? Sadi felt hope and betrayal at the same time.

"Please have a seat, Miss Jacobsen," she said mechanically. Her tone had changed since the first time Sadi had talked to the detective, transforming into a business tone without cordiality.

Sadi remained standing in defiance.

"So far, I haven't been arrested or charged with anything."

Sadi felt her anger return and was a little less intimidated by a woman of shorter stature. She could show her anger more easily to a single female than to a pair of physically imposing men.

"We can't make any progress until you take a seat, Miss Jacobsen." Her tone softened but still sounded harsh.

Sadi paused a moment before taking a seat. She did not want to relinquish the only playing card in her possession, a refusal to immediately obey and sit. The detective patiently waited for Sadi to sit down. Sadi surrendered after just a moment and sat when she recognized a slight look of sympathy in the detective's eyes.

"I don't appreciate you withholding information from me last night," began Detective Zimmerman after Sadi took a seat. "Failure to divulge information pertaining to a criminal investigation is in itself a criminal offense."

Sadi still felt determined to refrain from divulging information, but maybe she could get this woman to do the talking.

"And what exactly am I withholding?" After Sadi asked the question, she feared the answer. The truth could be dangerous and painful.

Before responding, the detective looked directly into Sadi's eyes and paused.

"About what really happened to your daughter."

"Like I told the other officers, I'm not saying anything until my lawyer is present."

In the back of her mind, Sadi had the impression of living in a dream, and at any moment, something more out of the ordinary would happen, then she'd open her eyes and find herself in bed. She ignored the temptation to close her eyes, just to check. Maybe still wearing her pajamas helped her feel that way.

In an unexpected move, Detective Zimmerman put her right hand over Sadi's clasped hands. Instinctively, she attempted to pull her hands away, but the detective held her hand against the table. If she really wanted, Sadi could have pulled her hands away, but she felt something strange under the woman's hand. It felt like a small, folded piece of paper.

"Several people are dead, and you're protecting someone who knows about it, maybe even the person who did it." As the detective spoke, Sadi recognized a look of warning on her face. "You went above the law, Miss Jacobsen, and we want to know who else is involved. If you tell us, it will be to your benefit. Despite what you think, I am here to help you."

The woman raised her voice significantly. Her eyebrows went up, and she glanced almost imperceptibly at her hands. Before pulling her hand off Sadi's, she pushed the paper between Sadi's fingers. She raised her eyebrows in a warning gesture.

"Look at those handcuffs," Detective Zimmerman continued, then paused for emphasis. "This just might be your future. Is this what you really want?"

Sadi followed the suggestion and looked down at her handcuffs, then at her left hand, the one with the stuffed piece of paper in it. While carefully opening her hand to reveal the paper, she pretended to contemplate her situation. The paper looked like it came from a fortune cookie but had no printed words, only one simple sentence.

Say you have to use the bathroom!

FORTY-FIVE

Sadi

After reading the note, Sadi's mind went into autopilot mode. Until that point, she only guessed at what to do but had no confidence in the consequences of her actions. The note brought immediate hope, and she realized the meaning of Detective Zimmerman's peculiar body language.

Sadi crumpled the note in her hand and continued staring at her handcuffs.

"You're not scaring me," Sadi said, keeping her head down. "I have rights."

"Miss Jacobsen," she said as if trying a different tactic. "Who do you want to cooperate with? Me, or the other guys?"

"I get it now," Sadi said. She put her hands in her lap and squeezed the paper until it became a very tiny ball. She wanted to put it in her pocket but worried that it would be noticeable. "It's the good cop, bad cop game. I'll just wait for my lawyer."

The detective looked at Sadi with narrowed eyes.

"I think you need to think about this a little more. We'll be back later."

Sadi waited until the detective stood and turned to the door.

"Detective, there's one thing I really need to do right now."

Zimmerman turned around, and Sadi saw life in her eyes for the first time since her arrival.

"What is that?"

"I really need to use the restroom. Your two hitmen didn't give me any consideration."

The older woman looked at Sadi for just a moment as if contemplating whether or not to grant her request.

"Of course," she said without any emotion, even though her eyes looked relieved. She opened the unlocked door and held it open for Sadi.

Outside in the hallway, the brighter light caused a momentary pain. After her eyes readjusted to the new light source, Sadi felt a small weight lifted off her shoulders. At the very least, the note signified physical relief since she did have to use the bathroom.

Sadi appreciated any help Detective Zimmerman wanted to offer. The detective might just want to talk to her privately and not look suspicious at the same time. Sadi hoped the woman intended to let her make a phone call. The first two agents were intent on keeping Sadi from contact with the outside world, and she considered it an effective form of mental intimidation.

Before continuing down the hallway, Detective Zimmerman opened a door next to the interrogation room, revealing more darkness inside. She poked her head inside, and Sadi heard her quietly say they would be back in a few minutes, and then she shut the door again.

Once they reached a few doors away from the interrogation room, the detective increased her pace to walk at full speed toward the elevator. While walking, Detective Zimmerman kept her hand on Sadi's shoulder. They encountered no one on their walk to the elevator.

"Don't make eye contact with anyone," she said while they waited for the elevator door to open.

Her arms were tired, and Sadi let them hang in front of her. She felt very conspicuous and would have avoided eye contact with anyone even if not instructed to do so. When the elevator opened, two police-men in police uniforms exited.

"Morning, Detective," one of them said. Sadi felt both of the men look at her, but she kept her eyes down.

Zimmerman nodded.

"Good morning," she said mechanically. The two men walked down the hallway and disappeared from view when Sadi entered the elevator compartment. Before entering, Detective Zimmerman looked both ways and then at her watch. After the other police officers departed, she began to look very nervous.

"Are you going to let me call my lawyer?" Sadi asked after the door closed.

"Just follow me," said the detective, "and try to look like you belong in handcuffs. You'll blend in better." She said nothing else until the elevator door opened.

Sadi wondered how to follow those directions.

When the doors opened, the sound of muffled conversation erased the stillness of the elevator car. Zimmerman nudged Sadi out of the elevator and then followed slightly behind her. They walked down the hallway, passing men and women in uniforms and suits, as the one Zimmerman wore.

The hallway ended in a large open area filled with desks and people occupying about half of them. The room instantly made Sadi think of a beehive with everyone doing their job in chaotic harmony, and she wondered why she had failed to notice it all on her way to the interrogation room. While keeping her eyes down, she noticed no one else in handcuffs, but a few rough-looking men sat at desks while officers in uniform questioned them. As they walked, Sadi saw no one look at her.

No one stopped them, but a few people had to get out of their way. She saw a women's restroom to their right, and when the detective led her past it, she felt a sudden hope that they were heading to a phone instead, perhaps at Zimmerman's desk. From their position, Sadi could see the front entrance, where the only source of natural light began to blend with the artificial lights of the office.

"Hey, Zimmerman," came a voice from behind them.

The detective's hand stopped Sadi in mid-stride, and they turned to find a tall, skinny officer in a neatly pressed uniform. Zimmerman looked at the officer, then to the room around him.

"What do you want, Brown?"

"I can't believe Anderson's back," the officer said with excitement. "Haven't seen him in a year."

The man's eyes switched from Zimmerman to Sadi and then back. She had difficulty keeping her eyes on the ground rather than looking back at him. Instinctively, she would have returned attention when meeting someone new. He seemed excited, like a dog wagging his tail when his owner came home. He looked back at Sadi, and his face showed curiosity.

"They came in with her. Where are you taking her?"

"Don't you have something to do, Brown?" asked Zimmerman impatiently. "I don't have time to talk. They're working with me on this case."

"Since when did you and Anderson start working together?"

"Brown, what's your problem?" she asked, nodding her head in Sadi's direction.

"Oh, yeah," he said and gave almost a wink of acknowledgment. He leaned in to talk discreetly, but Sadi heard every word. "You're not thinking of leaving the department with him?"

"Brown, we can talk later about this," Zimmerman said with one final look up into his eyes. "Bye."

She waited for him to walk away, which he did a few seconds later, and he walked out of sight. Without another word, Detective Zimmerman turned and almost pushed Sadi forward toward the front door.

"Hey, Zimmerman," said a different voice behind them just before they got to the main entrance. The detective ignored the one addressing her and pushed the door open for Sadi. Without looking back, she gently nudged Sadi outside into the light.

They rushed to the agent's car, and Zimmerman pushed Sadi into the back seat. While trying to pull her seat belt over herself with handcuffs, Detective Zimmerman pulled out of the parking lot and into the Portland traffic. She drove as fast as possible without making her tires squeal. Over the back of the detective's chair, Sadi could see sweat on the side of Detective Zimmerman's temples. As the station disappeared from their view, Sadi's anxiety at being a prisoner transformed into a fear of pursuit.

"Where are we going?"

For about ten seconds, Detective Zimmerman concentrated on driving and acted as if she did not hear the question. She kept glancing in the rearview mirror but then cleared her throat before speaking.

"I feel like a doctor about to tell a patient she's going to die," she said, then extended her right hand to Sadi with a set of keys in her palm. "Here's the key to your handcuffs."

Sadi hesitated before grabbing the keys. Would the detective pull her hand away at the last moment and laugh at her? When Sadi felt the cold metal keys in her palm, she experienced the exhilaration of being given the keys to her freedom, and the sensation temporarily overpowered all other negative emotions. After removing the handcuffs, she remembered the detective's words.

"What's going on?" Sadi asked while stretching her arms and rubbing her wrists. "What did you mean about dying?"

"I don't quite know how to tell you this," the woman said tentatively and shook her head. "Wish I didn't have to."

She looked in the back seat and made brief eye contact with Sadi, then glanced through the rear window. Her look reminded Sadi about the memory of her paranoid reaction to cocaine. The detective had that same panic in her eyes.

"Tell me what?"

"The life you knew is over. You need to get to your daughter and figure things out."

"My life is over?" Sadi asked in confusion. Did she hear her correctly? What did that mean? Her old life, before the kidnapping and before meeting Gerald, had already vanished.

"Those two detectives were not police," she said, interrupting Sadi's thoughts. "They're DHS, Homeland Security agents working out of Salem."

The speed of the car suddenly felt unstable and dangerous.

"Then what am I doing with you, and what do you mean my life is over?"

Sadi hoped to resurrect her anger by concentrating on her unjust treatment that morning. Anger might help her cope with the paranoia that emanated from the detective like the stink from a dead fish.

"You weren't going to get a phone call," Detective Zimmerman said and then paused to let Sadi understand the implication. "You're lucky they brought you to the station. I think they were holding you there until they figured out how to get your daughter. That was a very smart move to send your daughter away. We need to find your daughter and take you somewhere safe. Is there anywhere you can go where no one would know where to find you?"

"What do you mean somewhere safe?"

All the words exchanged between them since leaving the station floated in Sadi's thoughts in random and unintelligible order. Only Helen's name took a sure footing.

"Take Helen in for questioning?" Sadi asked herself in a panic. "I need to get a hold of Jen and warn her. Can I use your phone?"

Detective Zimmerman handed her phone over her shoulder. Sadi took it and dialed Jen's number. It rang three times before she picked up and answered tentatively, "Hello?"

"Jen, where are you?"

"I went back to the house, but I left Helen and where you told me. Where did you go? You left your purse, your phone, your..."

Sadi spoke before Jen could continue.

"Those men were the police or working with them. They arrested me and took me to the police station. You need to leave the house!"

"Oh my God," Jen said in a raised voice. "Is that where you are now?"

"No, I'm not at the station anymore, but it's too complicated to explain right now. I want you to get Helen and..." Sadi stopped midsentence when a new fear exploded in her mind. She remembered the other officer's question to Zimmerman about working with the two men who took her. Was she working with them to find Helen?

From the front seat, the detective's voice sent chills all over Sadi's skin. It seemed so friendly and innocent, but Sadi feared something sinister beneath.

"Where is she?" Zimmerman asked. "I can take you to her."

Detective Zimmerman sounded as though she sincerely wanted to help, but could Sadi trust her? Maybe she just pretended to help and really wanted Sadi to lead her to Helen.

"Sadi, are you there?" Jen kept asking. "Sadi?"

"I'm here, Jen. Listen to me." Sadi took a deep breath and told herself to relax. She had to act smart and fast, for Helen and Daryn's sake. "Remember those backpacks I put together for us? Take those, then go to an ATM and use my debit card to withdraw as much as it will let you. My PIN is 3328. Can you remember that? Then take Helen to a safe place. Do you understand?"

"A safe place?" asked Jen with obvious confusion. "Do you mean..."

"Yes, the same place we talked about this morning. Remember?"

"Okay, I got it. I'll leave right now."

"I'll call you later when I can," she said, then breathed a sigh of relief. After cutting the connection, Sadi turned back to the detective.

"Why did they let you take me?" Sadi asked and focused the small amount of anger she had gathered into her words. "What do you suspect of me? Don't lie to me."

"Listen to me, Sadi," the woman said slowly and succinctly. "I found out about what happened to Helen, and it's my fault that you're in the trouble you're in now. But they would have found out eventually anyway. They were close."

They stopped at a red light, and the detective turned around to look at Sadi.

"Someone at the station must have been tracking my investigation and gave those two men the list of potential suspects I was tracking. They must have more information than I do because it only took them a few hours to focus on you since last night. I think they're protecting the people who run that horrible business in Salem. You and Helen and whoever helped you might know too much."

Sadi opened her mouth to respond but realized that her words would be futile outbursts of multilateral rage. Complaints about injustices would do her no good. She could indulge in indignation later. Rather than lament, she had to act, but she wanted to scream!

"So what?" she asked after taking a breath. "Are you trying to get a confession out of me now?"

If Sadi had been able to think more rationally, she would have kept silent about her suspicions, but anger overshadowed the warning in her head.

"Miss Jacobsen," the detective continued in the same slow and calm manner. "I am trying to help you, but I understand your mistrust. Where do you want me to take you?"

Sadi desperately wanted to believe the detective, and the woman sounded sincere, but when the lives of two little girls hung in the balance, she could not afford the luxury. The woman could not be trusted to take Sadi directly to either of her two little girls. She had to contact someone who could help her and do it without putting that person in danger.

"I've got to make another call," she said and changed her tone to a more agreeable one. "I'm sorry to be angry, and I appreciate your help. I'm just trying to think."

"I understand," the detective said in resignation.

Sadi wanted to call Gerald or Craig but did not have their phone numbers memorized. She usually had her phone with her and used it as an external memory. After silently cursing technology for her poor memory recall, she paused to think.

She could probably remember Mr. Smith's number. If she called him, then his phone number would be on Detective Zimmerman's phone and might ruin a potentially safe location to hide. Should she call her brother? For now, he had Helen, and the police would surely check up on him eventually. Finally, she decided to call her brother and have him take Helen somewhere safe and then meet her.

The phone rang five times before clicking over to her brother's voicemail, and she remembered how he only answered the phone when he knew the caller. In frustration, she left a message.

"Brian! Please pick up your phone when I call again from this number."

After waiting ten seconds, she called again and left another message on his voicemail.

"Damn it," Sadi cursed quietly, "he's not answering."

"I'm just going to keep driving until you figure things out. By now, Anderson's realized that we're not coming back."

She would wait three more minutes and then call one more time. If he still failed to answer the phone, she might need to call Zoya, but she wanted to keep Zoya's friendship a secret for as long as possible, just in case she needed her. Sadi only had a few good playing cards in her hand.

"So what happens to me now? I go into hiding?" After the words escaped her mouth, they seemed inconceivable. Bank robbers and murderers ran and hid from the police, not mothers who had their child kidnapped by sexual predators.

"Anderson and his partner were going to use the material witness statute against you," the detective said while driving. "That basically means that they can indefinitely detain you because your testimony will help with an active terrorist investigation."

"But I don't have anything to do with any terrorists!"

"I know," she answered, and Sadi heard anger in her voice, "but all they have to do is claim that your testimony is related. That's kind of how they're covering this sex trade activity in Salem."

"Let me explain how our screwed-up world works. Basically, criminal organizations are kept under perpetual surveillance or investigation. Whenever local law enforcement suspects something and starts to investigate, the local investigation is stopped because it will interfere with a federal investigation. Of course, the federal investigation goes on and on and on and never ends. They always claim to be building a case."

"Occasionally, there will be some indictments to give the appearance of legitimacy, but only low-level participants will be sacrificed or competitors eliminated. It's just like any business. All that matters is that the customers get what they want. The federal agents take their share. It's just a business expense. As long as the business keeps operating and the federal agents get a cut, it can go on forever."

"How can you work in an environment like that? Knowing that those things go on and you can't do anything about it?"

Sadi had no difficulty believing the detective's explanation, but she did not commit to the idea that the woman sincerely wanted to help her. On a subconscious level, a small bond had begun to form: empathy for the woman's similar experience of injustice and helplessness.

"I'm not completely powerless," she said with some hope in her voice. "This is a game the local law enforcement has been playing for years and years. Sometimes, we make a dent. Sometimes we don't. I was hoping to bring this investigation into the light."

"Not that it makes you feel any better," she continued, "but I put my neck on the line for this. Hopefully, I won't lose my job. I'm taking advantage of the fact that these guys really don't want to bring much attention to themselves, and they definitely don't want the extra work it would take to punish me, so maybe they'll forget about my interruption in their pursuit of you. Lucky for you, those two are idiots, but they are determined."

"If you really are helping me, I hope you don't lose your job," Sadi said with more empathy than she intended. "What am I supposed to do?"

"I am very sorry about your situation, Miss Jacobsen. Like I said, we're lucky you got out of there. You will need to disappear for a while. If they catch up to you, they will take you in again, and they will threaten to put your daughter in foster care if you don't cooperate."

Sadi dialed her brother's number, "Come on, Brian, please pick up. Please pick up!"

Before the end of the first ring, Brian's voice answered on the other end. "Sadi, is that you? Are you still with the police?"

Unexpectedly, tears came to Sadi's eyes, and she gulped down the saliva that filled her throat. She required a moment to answer in an intelligible manner.

"Oh my God, Brian, it's so good to hear your voice. How's Helen? Have you heard anything from them?"

"Yes, Jen just left with her. She said you were taken by some police or something, and now you're driving around with them? Tell me that I got it wrong. That can't be right."

"It's worse than you can imagine. I need you to come and get me. Please hurry."

"Of course," he said. "Where?"

"Come alone," Sadi said. She looked around at their location. They were going east on Burnside and just passed through Thirty-Ninth Street. Sadi's mind clung to the first idea that materialized. "Remember where we used to play when you cut your ankle?"

"That playground near Rosa Parks?"

"Park on the street, and we'll find you. Please don't tell anyone where you're going. Please, and thank you so much."

"Anything you need, Sadi? I'm leaving right now. Do you need me to bring anything?"

"No, just hurry. Thank you, Brian."

After cutting the connection, she handed the phone back to Detective Zimmerman.

"Where do you want me to take you?"

"Turn left at the next light," she answered and waited until they could see the intersection of Glisan. Just in case people were listening to their conversation, Sadi did not want to reveal their final destination.

"Turn left on Glisan."

While Sadi gave directions from the back seat, Detective Zimmerman acted like a silent chauffeur and just stared ahead at the road. They wound their way to the entrance to I-84 West, and Sadi looked for signs of being followed. To her relief, she saw no suspicious vehicles behind them. Apart from the CB radio, Sadi noticed no other indication of being in a police detective's car.

"After I drop you off at your location," she said after they merged onto I-84 westbound, "Feel free to contact me anytime, for any reason. Here's my card, just in case you lost my other one. What exit do I take?"

"It's in a little bit," Sadi said quietly, then turned to look behind her again for evidence of any cars following them. They traveled on the freeway until Sadi saw the sign for I-5 northbound. When she saw the sign for Rosa Parks Way, her heart began to beat in hopeful expectation of seeing her brother, a friendly face.

"Take the next exit and turn right," she said. "I'll tell you where to go from there."

"Before we go our separate ways," the detective said as they came to a stop. "It might help your case if you told me how you got her back. Did you hire a professional of some sort? I can't believe that you killed all those men."

"I got her back, isn't that all that matters?"

"I want to know," she said while turning right, "more for personal reasons than anything. I want to know how it felt to kill those bastards."

Despite herself, Sadi felt the smile spreading wide across her lips. The memory gave her a small adrenaline boost, and she made a mental note to evoke the memory whenever she needed some extra confidence. Her current predicament seemed like partial payment for the sweet memory of kicking that old man in the head. Sadi saw Detective Zimmerman looking at her through the rearview mirror.

In the brief moment of eye contact with the detective, Sadi recognized the look in her eyes. Detective Zimmerman knew that the memory brought Sadi pleasure.

"I don't know what you're talking about," Sadi said and looked away.

In just a few blocks, Sadi recognized the park where she and her brother had played as children. The sight brought a mixture of pleasant and painful memories, and despite her current circumstances, she felt relieved to be done with her childhood.

While they drove around the park, Sadi looked for Brian's car. As expected, she saw him parked on the street, right next to the playground, with several children on the play equipment and a few parents standing around them. When she saw her brother's car, she said nothing and let the detective drive past to ensure that Brian was alone. While looking suspiciously at every car, they drove around the park one more time.

"Pull over here," Sadi said, directing Zimmerman to a parking spot just a few cars in front of her brother.

While Zimmerman parked her car, Sadi scanned the area around them for one final check to see if any suspicious characters were watching from their vehicles. She paused a few seconds to admire the large open area in the park with the thousands of rose bushes surrounding a large water fountain. The sight brought many pleasant memories.

When satisfied with their security, she sat back and took a deep breath, preparing to exit. Concern for being seen in her pajamas lasted less than a second. She would definitely not be the only strangely dressed woman in the park. After putting her hand on the door handle, the ringing of the detective's phone broke the silence and stopped her. Zimmerman looked down at her phone to see the number.

"It's Anderson," she said absently, then nodded in front of them to the approaching dark-haired young man.

"Is that your brother?"

"Yes," she said, looking at her brother but concentrating on the ringing of the phone. "What are you going to say to Anderson?"

"Well, I'm not answering it," she said with a short and sarcastic laugh. "When he catches up to me, I'll tell him that he had no warrant for your arrest, so I took you where you wanted to go. If he takes it up with my boss, then I'll just tell the truth, that I brought you here and left you. That's about all I can do. I'm sorry."

Sadi looked at the woman and prepared to thank her, but Brian opened the door. For a moment, Sadi forgot all about her troubles. He helped her to stand, put his arms around her, and pulled her close.

"Are you okay?" he asked. The look of concern helped start a flood of tears down her cheeks. She was looking at a face she could trust, someone who loved her, the first friendly face since before Jen took the girls to safety.

As she wiped away the tears and composed herself, she claimed to be okay and that they had to leave. During the brief exchange, Detective Zimmerman had gotten out of the car and came to stand by their side. She kept glancing from them to the people around the park. The detective waited a moment, then grabbed Sadi's shoulder.

"I'll try to figure out a better way to help you," said Detective Zimmerman, "but for now, you need to get far away from here. Stay away from people and places where we would expect to see you. Don't directly contact your friends or family. Find a way to communicate covertly with your brother and try to let as few people as possible know your location. You're an intelligent woman, so I know you understand what I'm telling you."

"Thank you, Detective," said Sadi. "Sorry, I doubted you."

Brian looked at the detective with obvious suspicion in his eyes. He had more distrust of law enforcement than Sadi ever would, and he began pulling Sadi away while she said her thanks. As she walked away with her brother, she felt Zimmerman watching her back.

FORTY-SIX

Sadi

“Tell me what is going on, Sadi?” asked Brian after he pulled into traffic.

"I will," she began, "but you need to tell me about the girls first."

"Jen did what you said and left Daryn at Freddy's house. Then, before I left to meet you, she took Helen there as well. As far as I know, all three of them are there now. Jen probably shouldn't have told me where she was going."

"It all happened so fast, I don't expect her to have thought about that," Sadi answered and felt an intense relief flood through her. She knew her brother would keep their location a secret, even if the police threatened to take him to prison.

She took a deep breath before beginning her promised explanation.

"The police found out about what happened to Helen and the whole incident with the kidnapping. Then, some other Homeland Security agents found out about it. They were staking out my house this morning, and they took me to the station. Those assholes are covering for the kidnappers!"

Sadi had difficulty containing her anger. Indignation destroyed her former, more controlled state of mind. As she related the whole experience, Brian listened without many opportunities to ask questions. Sadi included every detail, and she found great satisfaction in watching her brother become as angry as she felt.

"So, where do you want me to take you?"

"Can we just drive around for a little bit before calling Jen?" she asked. "I just want to make sure that we're not being followed. I don't want to lead anyone to where the girls are staying."

"Sure thing," he said. "Sounds like a good plan. You were always the smart one."

"Smart's not going to get me out of this," she said with her anger building again.

Brian put a hand on her shoulder in an attempt at comfort. His firm grip felt good.

"Those fucking bastards," he swore in a low tone, squinting in the process. "How dare they do this to you. You're the victim. You should get in touch with that lawyer friend of yours. He seems pretty smart. He might know a way out of this. There's got to be some legal way to protect yourself from these assholes."

"From what that detective told me," she said, "they can lock me up and keep me from any legal help. It's part of some law to fight terrorism."

"Some country we live in," Brian snorted. "Land of the free, my ass!"

Sadi wiped her eyes and smiled at his outburst. She could almost smell his anger in the car and wanted to inhale it deeply into her lungs.

"I wanted to call Gerald, my lawyer friend, but his number is on my cell phone, and Jen has it."

Once Sadi and Brian felt confident that they were not being followed, they started driving toward Mr. Smith's house. Brian drove on the side streets, and the time required to arrive felt like an eternity. Finally, they pulled up to the gate and were about to press the call button, but the gate opened before Brian's finger touched the button.

As they entered the garage, Jen stood waiting for them with Mr. Smith behind her. The huge garage held three other cars, nice cars, but Sadi spent no time identifying them.

"Oh my God, Sadi," said Jen as they embraced. "I was so worried."

"I'm okay," said Sadi, but inside, she was amazed at how she'd escaped, which suddenly seemed impossible. If not for Zimmerman, she would still be sitting in that interrogation room. Sadi shuddered at the thought. "I'm away from them for now, and that's all that matters. How are the girls?"

"They're inside the house, playing."

As Sadi and Jen released each other, Mr. Smith stepped closer. Sadi was suddenly afraid of facing him, of showing the need for his help. A long time ago, she promised herself that she would never depend on anyone ever again. After being released from Jen's embrace and looking at the old man, the concern in his eyes melted all of her doubts. The deep wrinkles on his face filled with shadows in the poorly lit garage.

"I am very glad you are here, Miss Jacobsen." He spoke his words with care. "It is good to see you again, but sorry for the poor circumstances."

"Thanks for letting us stay here for the night. I should be able to figure something out tomorrow after I call my lawyer. Hopefully, he can help."

"Don't be absurd, Miss Jacobsen," Mr. Smith said with a poor attempt at showing frustration. Behind the act, Sadi heard the worry in his weak voice. "You will stay here until this whole mess is settled. Besides, with Freddy gone, I need some company. Sorry to sound happy about your circumstances, but your visit is just what I needed."

"Well, thank you for this hospitality. I don't want you to get into trouble because of me."

"Let's worry about everything later. Tonight, you need a good meal and rest with your daughters."

When the two girls saw Sadi, they ran to her and attached themselves like barnacles. Sadi held them for over a minute, her tears flowing freely.

The two girls thought of their visit as just a big slumber party at their new grandfather's house, and Sadi had no intention of destroying that perception. Hopefully, they could maintain the illusion for the entire time. The girls had been through too much trauma recently. She wanted to keep the truth from them as long as possible, that their former captors were still pursuing them.

Building up the illusion for the girls helped Sadi feel better and would give her a purpose until she came up with a final solution. *What a selfish thing of me to do*, she thought and laughed. *Ayn Rand would be proud.*

Mr. Smith, Sadi, and her brother made dinner that first night. Mr. Smith allowed her assistance only after she explained that making dinner would be therapeutic for her. While they all sat at the dining table, no one said anything about the police or the abduction, and neither Helen nor Daryn asked about what happened that day.

After dinner, Jen took the girls to bed, which left Brian, Sadi, and Mr. Smith alone. They concluded that Brian should stay for the night. The police or other law enforcement division might be surveying his place.

"I would love to stay," he said, "but I have a friend I can stay with, and he'll vouch for any alibi I come up with. Besides, I want to have him check out my place to see if anyone is there."

Since Brian acquired all of his money lately from playing in his band, he had a very open lifestyle. He could think of many ways to avoid the police or whoever might be following him. Sadi felt good about his plans. When Jen returned from taking the girls to bed, she offered to stay with Sadi and help for as long as she wanted.

"That is out of the question," said Sadi. "It's my problem and my life they've wrecked. I appreciate the help, but you have a bright future, and I don't want it on my conscience if that is ruined too."

"But this whole thing is all my fault," she said and burst into tears. "If I would have watched her more closely, they never would have..."

"It's not your fault, Jen," Sadi said, tempted to explain the reason Freddy suggested to her about the alien's interference. "We're all the victims."

Jen looked up at Sadi, her green eyes opened wide. The comment about her life being ruined probably scared her. *Does she think a simple phone call to a lawyer will solve the problem?*

"So, what should I tell people?" Jen asked and wiped her eyes. "I'll tell them anything you want me to."

Sadi thought about the question, but her mind produced no answer.

Brian filled the silence, directing his words to Jen.

"Yeah, we'll have to get our story straight. Of course, we'll say that Sadi didn't tell us where they went. They're going to assume Sadi was too smart to tell anyone where she was going. Simple enough."

"But they're going to ask us where we think she would have gone." Jen turned from Brian to Sadi.

"Just tell them I went to Canada," she told them. "That I have friends there."

"Pretend to cooperate and act ignorant," said Mr. Smith, and his answer seemed to satisfy them.

Before going to bed, Sadi logged onto the group website. With Mr. Smith's permission, she used his login instead of her own. Even if the police could hack into the website, they would not be able to distinguish between their login attempts and his unless she communicated like herself. She left a vague and brief message and hoped Gerald would understand. He responded within five minutes.

Gerald: *Give me some time to think about it.*

Sadi felt comfort just knowing that Gerald understood the message. A few minutes later, he wrote again and in vague terms, admitted to being unsure of what actions to take. He wanted the night to decide on an acceptable plan. He needed more information, and she assumed he was referring to the invostigation by the federal agents.

Sadi had no choice other than to accept his answer and wait.

She used a sleeping pill that night. As expected, she slept long into the next morning. Sadi preferred natural sleep instead of the drug-induced kind, but her upside-down world erased her concern about altered body chemistry. She knew enough about microbiology to appreciate the dangers of disrupting the delicate equilibrium of organic life. The risk seemed like payment for sleeping without disturbing dreams or the memory of them.

FORTY-SEVEN

Audrie

Audrie opened the door to her New York apartment after returning from a United Nations fundraiser for the victims of the recent typhoon in Taiwan. As usual, all the social requirements of her job were exhausting. She just wanted to relax in front of a fire and read the latest CFR bulletin until sleep won the battle for her eyelids. The reading activity taxed her mental capacity almost as much as her work, but she needed it.

She had become addicted to information. The world kept spinning and would not slow down for her to rest. After reading all the latest news updates from her elite publication, she wanted to see what the major media outlets were disseminating to the public. She usually visited Forbes, The Drudge Report, Time, The Huffington Post, and a few of the major newspapers like The New York Times and The Los Angeles Times.

Her department employed several analysts to summarize current events and significant financial transactions, but she liked to know as much as possible before reviewing their reports. Absorbing the same information multiple times and from different angles meant she would have the advantage over people who had only seen the information once.

At the end of her data feast, Audrie perused through some of the new movies playing in the theaters and those soon to be released. Two films with the most obvious political slant caught her attention: *District 9* and *Avatar*. The *District 9* film dealt with how governments treated their growing refugee population. She watched the preview and expected to see an allegory to apartheid, but she had difficulty determining the overall message. That film would not be one of the few she watched that year.

Her father never let her or Max watch any of the films in the theaters and only rarely let them see any at home. He often reminded them that he wanted to minimize their exposure to portrayals of activities in direct contradiction with reality. The world of fantasy left less room for rational thought. Later in her life, she concluded that her father also wanted to prevent his children from mingling with the general public.

"Live in the real world," he often said.

What effect did all the alien and monster movies have on the general population, especially the youth? Aliens, zombies, wizards, and demons could confuse and damage people's ability to react appropriately to real-world situations. Maybe it explained why the majority showed little to no interest in how the world really worked. Audrie found the real world much more interesting than fantasy.

The film *Avatar* intrigued her. It seemed like an allegory to the plight of the Native Americans and a brilliant method of connecting public empathy for them with the need for more environmental protection.

The film presented the usual, if ironic, method of protecting the environment and always made Audrie laugh to herself. In the real world, the corporate elite controlled the government, and the media convinced the population to allow the same government to take more control of natural resources. By that corrupted logic, the public believed that the corporate elite would then be unable to harm the environment. Although the manipulation seemed unethical, Audrie thought the corporate world took better care of the environment than the public. The ends justified the means.

After watching the *Avatar* film preview, she sat in her chair and mentally prepared to get ready for bed. A few seconds later, someone rang from the lobby. With a groan of discomfort, she arose and walked to the door.

"Hello?" she said, attempting to keep the displeasure from her voice.

"There is a woman here to see you, Miss Garner," said the doorman in the lobby. "She says her name is Yi-Min, and she won't give me a last name. She says—"

"Yes, I know who she is," Audrie said, cutting the man off in mid-sentence. She did not intend to sound rude. "Send her up. Thank you, Mr. Perry."

While Audrie waited for the woman to arrive at her apartment, her feeling of exhaustion transformed into dread. Whatever her friend from college had to say, intuition told her to expect disturbing news. From an early age, Audrie learned to trust in her ability to foresee important news, both disturbing and fortunate.

She considered her ability a great asset. When confronted with unwelcome and surprising information, most people lost valuable opportunities due to shock. Their emotional reaction of surprise stole mental energy away from their ability to make useful decisions, if only for a moment, which often gave Audrie an advantage. She dreaded the news but felt ready to receive it.

"Hi, Audrie," said the Chinese woman standing in her doorway.

"Hello, Yi-Min!" Audrie said and stepped aside to give the woman enough room to enter.

The shorter woman smiled and wiped raven-black hair from her eyes. As she walked over the threshold, Audrie glanced with suspicion at the empty hallway. She was suddenly paranoid, and she almost expected to see someone else accompanying her.

Yi-Min was only a few centimeters shorter than Audrie. She possessed a slender female figure and moved with confidence and elegance. Most people probably thought of her as attractive but not beautiful or particularly pretty.

Yi-Min came to the United States for her education and attended Harvard with Audrie. They had many things in common. Yi-Min came from a wealthy family in China, the daughter of a high-level communist leader. In their first class together, they were assigned to the same group and fought for dominance. At first, they hated each other due to their aggressive and confrontational natures. But over the length of the class, their mutual respect grew and blossomed into a very close friendship. During their entire career as students, they mingled in the same social circles.

Yi-Min claimed to detest the Chinese Communist government, but Audrie wondered if Yi-Min really just wanted to earn acceptance and trust from her peers. Political opinions never really mattered much to Audrie. She only cared about people's actions and if those actions improved their situation. Arguments over politics only served itself.

After graduation, Yi-Min stayed in the country. Even though she accepted an excellent position as an asset manager at a major hedge fund firm, the CIA also recruited her to help them monitor the activity of Chinese financial interests and possible money laundering operations. Eventually, she joined a small group of financial advisors, all of whom also worked as covert agents for the CIA.

"Here, let me get your jacket." Audrie took the woman's leather jacket with one hand and put her arm around her with the other. "Good to see you. This is not a usual social visit, is it?"

They walked into the living room, where the gas fire cast a fluctuating glow on the walls and couches next to it. After sitting down in the chair next to Audrie, the visitor exhaled dramatically as if exhausted from a long journey. Audrie put her hand on the woman's leg, and Yi-Min placed her hand on top of Audrie's.

"If you're still the impatient tiger I remember," Yi-Min said in her fake accent, "you do want to have bad news without the customary foreplay. Am I right?"

"Yes, of course! Tell me what my personal spy has discovered."

Hopefully, the bad news would not impede her projects at work or the CFR. Audrie focused on her old friend's black eyes. Audrie kept in contact with more business contacts from school than friends. While many of her other friends faded into memory, Yi-Min became one of the few who actually kept in contact. Visits by Yi-Min were always accompanied by pleasant memories of school, spending time together, and relieving stress. If she could return to the simple life of school, she would have more faith in the future and concentrate more on enjoying the experience.

"There is no nice way of telling this," her friend began, and her smile disappeared. She brought her eyes up slowly from their joined hands and into locked eye contact. "The FBI is investigating your brother. You asked I keep my eye on him, and well..."

Audrie's eyes turned from warm to cold.

"And why are they interested in him?"

"They think your brother started having a business dealing with a person of interest, a man named Gerald Foster. Do you know of him?"

In an attempt to place her mind into memory mode, Audrie looked above Yi-Min's head, slightly to the right.

"The name's not familiar. What kind of business dealing?"

"They don't know, or at least they claim not to know. Anyway, they're watching this Foster, and now your brother's business dealings are being watched too."

Audrie waited for her to add other information, but Yi-Min remained silent and looked into the fire.

"Okay," Audrie said and looked at the same spot in the fire. "So tell me what you know about Mr. Foster and why they're interested in him."

Yi-Min seemed to come out of a trance. While listening, Audrie watched for signs of emotional distress. Yi-Min looked as emotionally drained as Audrie felt physically.

When finished giving a brief history of Gerald Foster, Yi-Min looked into her eyes as if searching for a specific response. For a brief moment, Audrie wondered if Yi-Min had told her everything she knew or if she was hiding anything. After finding and feeling nothing suspicious from her body language, Audrie quickly decided to trust her friend. What reason could she possibly have for withholding information?

"From your description, Gerald Foster just seems like a past nuisance, a smoldering fire at worst. Has he done anything recently to catch anyone's interest?"

"Nothing I could find," Yi-Min said and looked into the fire again. "I was hoping you could answer a similar question for me. Why is your brother so interesting lately? I've even heard your name mentioned. What is changed?"

"My name, huh?" Audrie grunted and shook her head. She remembered explicitly telling her brother to avoid any entanglement with political dissidents. Their father depended on Audrie to keep Max out of trouble and to keep their name clean until his appointment. Audrie considered telling Yi-Min about the news of her father but decided against it.

"I can't go into all the details," Audrie said after a moment, "but my family cannot have this kind of publicity at this time. I was supposed to keep my brother out of trouble, and it looks like I've failed."

"Why cannot your family have this? What is coming? Is it concerning your father?"

Audrie knew Yi-Min would not quit trying to discover her secret, but for the present, Audrie had to disappoint her friend.

"If I could tell you, I would, Yi-Min," she said with real regret, "but I promised my father. Max is like a child we always have to remind not to play in the street."

"I understand. So what are you going to do about this?"

Audrie sat back and rubbed her eyes.

"Looks like I've got to make my own investigation. Like I'm not already busy enough."

"I could help," Yi-Min added, squeezing Audrie's hand.

Audrie sat back in the chair but kept hold of her hand.

"A good place to start would be to determine who Mr. Foster's associates are. Will you get me a list?"

Yi-Min made a great sigh as though her hopes were dashed.

"I've already started the list, and that's where the situation gets more interesting, but it leaves more questions."

"Do I want to hear this? It's worse than you first suggested?"

"Well, I already know of one of his associates," Yi-Min said with the sound of regret. "A former mayor of Ciudad Juárez, in Mexico."

"Yes, I know the city," Audrie said impatiently. "Just across the border from El Paso. It wouldn't happen to be Cesar Sanchez, would it? The one who now lives in Seattle?"

"That's the one," Yi-Min said and sounded impressed.

Audrie felt no need to impress her friend or pride herself on knowing some specifics of recent history.

"So, who else?"

"The military is involved," Yi-Min said and winced slightly in anticipation of shock, "but I don't know why."

Audrie sat forward in her seat, and her eyes blazed with the reflected firelight. Yi-Min sat back in surprise.

"The military? What the hell is my brother doing?"

She stood and walked around the couch and then back to her position before the fire, speaking as she walked.

"It must have something to do with his company, but even Max can't be stupid enough to risk making the military suspicious of anything."

"His company manages classified military secrets," Yi-Min said in an analytical tone. "They don't want the location of military satellites given to the Chinese or the Russians."

"Do they suspect him of leaking classified information?" Audrie spoke more to herself than Yi-Min.

"I'm sorry to be the messenger of this evil news," Yi-Min said. She stood and joined Audrie in front of the fire. "At least it gave me the chance to see you and offer my assistance."

Out of politeness, Audrie met her friend's eyes, but the action broke her contemplation.

"Yes, to have heard this from someone else or be surprised by the board would have been far less tolerable. The board has not spoken to me about any problems, and that's probably a good sign. I will need to take immediate measures to handle this. I'm going to make some tea. Do you want some?"

"I would like that," Yi-Min said, and the expectation of caffeine seemed to bring some life to her almond eyes.

Yi-Min stayed for another fifty minutes, and they talked about what needed to be done. She would compile a complete list of Gerald's associates with a background check on each, and Audrie would attempt to discover the reason for the military's interest. Audrie had many contacts in the Department of Defense who could get access to the desired information.

Before Yi-Min left, they made arrangements to meet in a few weeks or sooner, depending on the status of their investigation. They hugged for several seconds, and then Yi-Min departed. Audrie felt guilty for withholding the news of her father's upcoming appointment. Would it really matter if she discovered their family secret? Even if Yi-Min leaked the information elsewhere, nothing would come of it. Her father's nomination for the Secretary of the Treasury would come as no surprise to anyone. There were probably rumors already.

Audrie and her father had only cared about the appointment for one reason: the great honor of being appointed, especially at this time when several more major bailouts were planned across the Earth. As usual, the board and all the other interested parties needed a man they could trust to control the financial resources of the Western world.

Her father's elevation in the world would translate into an elevation of her status as well. Why did Max always have to detract from her excitement? His disinterest and apparent disdain for the situation filled Audrie with intense irritation. More than ever, he seemed like a mosquito feasting on her blood. Squashing her brother would bring some cognitive dissonance, but she would assist in his destruction for the good of the majority. It would be all too easy, especially with his new friends and his abandonment of hers.

FORTY-EIGHT

Audrie

While waiting for Yi-Min to deliver more information, Audrie spent the days considering all the possible reasons for the government's interest in her brother and his new friends. The answer likely involved his company. The military paid close attention to companies making craft capable of invading their territory—the skies. Audrie did not doubt Max's intelligence, but his hatred of government interference might encourage him to disobey the rules. Audrie could live with that possibility. They'd slap his wrist with a fine, take away special privileges, or revoke contracts. Her brother would listen to that. If necessary, she would not hesitate to hasten that process.

Audrie's other theories were more dangerous but seemed less likely. She already warned him about associating with non-conformist groups. His association might be interpreted as potential financial assistance for their subversive goals. Those groups usually lacked significant financial resources and were, therefore, never a threat to the system.

Although he openly agreed to discretion, she doubted Max's sincerity. Yi-Min's list of her brother's associates would help determine that. Many other tasks demanded her time, so concern for her younger brother could be put on the top of the waiting list.

Two days later, Yi-Min hand-delivered the list of Gerald Foster's associates. She had compiled names, birth information, and pertinent family history, along with their financial or legal history. After Audrie examined the document, Cesar Sanchez's friend Doroteo concerned her the most. He seemed dangerous and able to thwart possible surveillance efforts. The list also included the names of all his legal clients, and some of them were also on the FBI *persons of interest* list.

The list of names helped Audrie feel better prepared and out of the dark, but she had little time of her own to investigate further, so she hired a private investigator. She had hired him for a past investigation and found him acceptable. Yi-Min had more resources with the CIA, but she also had her own job to do, and Audrie had already asked enough of her.

While the private investigator worked on the case, Audrie returned to her own employment and made preparations for a possible vacation, just in case the PI came too close to sensitive information, and she had to finish the rest of the investigation.

Initial reports from the PI revealed a sudden trip to Seattle and several pictures of Max with the people from Yi-Min's list. The pictures showed nothing suspicious. The PI then visited TerraWatch, Max's company. After two days of silence, she received a notification of a preliminary report he wanted to present in person.

"You might want to follow up on this one," he said during their brief phone call.

The next day, she met with him in her apartment. Only a few people were allowed into her primary living space, but not due to any reclusive tendencies. She just liked the idea of having the inside of her living quarters as a sacred place like Stonehenge, Cenote Sagrado, or Mecca.

With the private investigator sitting opposite her in her living room, she politely participated in a trivial conversation about how much he liked her apartment and her small collection of historical artifacts. While listening, she noticed how his blond hair had begun to gray, and his eyebrows had become bushier in the few years that had passed between this and their previous encounters. Despite his physical degradation, his cold gray eyes still shined with intelligence and vitality.

"Thank you," Audrie said after she concluded that enough pleasantries had passed. "I do like living here. It's so close to my work that I can walk most days at least. So, what have you discovered?"

"Your brother has started a secret project down in Brazil with a contact from the Seattle area, a project not on the company's records."

"Okay," she said. "What are they doing, and who is this contact?"

"So far, I was unable to discover any information about the project, except that only two employees flew to Brazil in early July, one of his managing directors and a new engineer. Their names are in my report."

With his right hand, he patted a folder in his lap.

"What is my brother's relationship with this new engineer and the managing director?"

"Max and the managing director are old friends from school, but I don't know his relationship with the new engineer, a young lady, pretty and smart."

"I'm assuming you have the information on her in your report?"

Audrie had a lot of respect for the man, but she became annoyed at having to ask so many questions when he should have anticipated what she wanted to know. He also had difficulty giving his opinion if he lacked sufficient information.

"Yes, I have some information about her, but they are mostly items anyone could get on the internet. She has no connections or resources. She is friends with one of the men on that list you gave me, the lawyer Gerald Foster. My guess, and mind you, this is only a guess, is that the lawyer referred her to the managing director. They're also friends."

"Just friends?" Audrie said with some impatience. "Or have they done business in the past?"

"I could find no other relationship, only personal, just a friend from school."

"What is significant about this new engineer?"

"She went to a public school for her bachelor's degree in mechanical engineering, and this is her first job out of college. She stood out in college and won some engineering competitions. Her father died a few years back, and then her brother died from suicide after returning from a tour of duty. It's been just her and her mother since then."

"A girl with a possible gripe with the government," Audrie said and looked at the report in his lap. That might explain her relationship with Gerald Foster. "Has she ever been in trouble with the law?"

"Her record is clean."

Audrie sat back and thought about all he told her. She knew what she had to do, go to the source.

"Do you know where in Brazil their new project is?"

"I am fairly certain about the place," he said, smiling proudly. "I should not have any trouble finding it."

She took the manila folder from him and opened it. While looking through it, she answered him.

"That won't be necessary. You have done well. I can take it from here."

FORTY-NINE

Sadi

The next morning, Sadi began considering all the implications of her new life. She could not visit work or contact her boss or co-workers. Would the police notify her employer, accusing her of some crime, and then order them to divulge her location? Somehow, she had to contact Zoya and discover what was happening. Could Jen or Brian safely send a message to her? The possibility felt dangerous. She would wait for a few days before making the attempt.

Her own life and future also affected her two girls. They would eventually need to find another school and home, maybe even change their names. Could she enter a witness protection program? They could all get a new identity and past. That possibility filled her with anxiety and a little bit of excitement. The idea of starting life again was empowering. Could she escape the people who wanted her locked up? *Can I invent another educational background? Probably not.*

Sadi eventually got her emotional state of shock under some control by concentrating on Helen and Daryn. She had to be strong for them. She had to show them what it meant never to quit or lose their optimism or confidence.

"If it weren't for them," she said to herself, "I probably would give up."

The irony of that thought brought a quiet and cynical laugh.

After Sadi convinced herself that life would find a happy balance again, she decided to focus on planning for the immediate future. Although she felt relatively safe at the moment, she was still in danger of being apprehended again, and she doubted that Detective Zimmerman could help her the next time. Sadi would always be in debt to that woman, similar to how she was in debt to Freddy. She would have felt guilty for not acting grateful enough, but she felt too numb for any more emotions.

Brian left the night before but said he would return the next day and take Jen to her father's house in Portland. After he left them the previous night, he borrowed his friend's car and drove through Sadi's neighborhood, careful not to pass her house. He had worn a baseball cap and sunglasses and had not seen anything suspicious.

Brian returned to Mr. Smith's house just before noon. When the time came for them to leave, Sadi gave Jen a long hug. After several seconds, she tried letting go, but Jen held on tight.

"When will I see you and the girls again?" she asked.

"I don't know," Sadi said, tears forming in her eyes. She had not thought about when they would meet again. Arranging a safe meeting might be difficult. "But of course, we'll see you again."

Jen wiped the tears from her face, then bent down and picked each girl off her feet. She talked to them as though they were going on vacation.

"See ya later, Helen. Be good for your momma until I see you again, okay? You too, Daryn."

"We will."

"Here," Sadi said and held out a small piece of paper. "This is my friend's address. You remember Zoya, right?"

"Yes."

"I might want you to contact her and ask about what is happening at work, but wait until I say it's safe."

"Okay."

When Jen left with Brian, Sadi thought they looked cute together, and it felt like her first normal thought since the first time Detective Zimmerman had appeared. The idea felt bittersweet. These traumatic experiences brought them closer together. She had a twinge of jealousy, but the emotion soon passed.

—※—

Later that afternoon, she checked the website and found several messages from Gerald. He thought they needed to wait before they could meet in person. He might have extra surveillance on him due to his association with her and his already blemished record. He avoided revealing his true thoughts directly, but in essence, he made the same conclusion. If they apprehend her again, she would probably fail to escape.

Gerald: *Wait for Freddy to return. It might change the game.*

Freddy should return in a few more days, and then she would have to deal with whatever had happened or whatever he brought back with him if he ever returned. When she let her imagination get out of control, disturbing thoughts filled her mind. Gerald believed there would be no problem, and Sadi wished she could share his confidence and optimism.

A part of her hoped for Freddy to return, but part of her hoped he would not, and she felt guilty for thinking that. With Freddy out of the situation, he could not complicate any potential romantic relationships she might want. That disturbing thought helped her to realize how frantic her mind had become.

"Of course, I want him back," she scolded herself.

After she recovered from the loss of her brother and nanny, and while the little girls explored the house, Sadi approached Mr. Smith in his library. The setting would have usually put Sadi in a good mood, being in a quiet room filled with books. But at that moment, the peace of the room had little influence on the gloom she seemed to be inhaling like smog.

"Mr. Smith," she said. The old man sat at the large oval desk with his back to her. He sat at the same table they used when she first had come to see Mr. Smith with his private investigator, Craig Swenson, to discuss the abduction. "I want to talk to you about something."

While waiting for him to respond, the horrible memory of that meeting intruded across her mind like a shooting star.

"Of course," he said without surprise at hearing her voice. He turned to her and smiled. "What did Mr. Foster have to say?"

Sadi pulled out a chair opposite the old man, making sure not to choose the same spot where Craig Swenson had interrogated her.

"He said we should wait for Freddy to get back."

Ever since her arrival at his residence, he had only referred to Freddy but not talked with her about him. Not until this moment did she realize the potential pain it might cause him. He took a deep breath and looked down at the table at the open book he had been reading.

"Do you think he's coming back?" he asked, but the question sounded more like a plea.

"I can't predict the future, but my feeling is that he will. I honestly think that."

"I hope you're right," he said, closing his book. He seemed ready to start their conversation. When he looked at her, she thought he seemed happier, as though her words had delivered a small dose of Oxycontin. "What do you think of it?" he asked. "I mean about his trip?"

Before responding, Sadi took a deep breath, trying to let the quiet of the room seep into her. The two girls' voices could be heard upstairs, a distant and pleasant sound like a small breeze in a hot desert. Mr. Smith probably could not hear them.

"If we didn't see that probe," she began, "I would have been more concerned. I did not feel threatened by it."

"Me either," he said and then sat back in his chair and stretched his arms above his head. "What if he finds another place to live? Would you take your daughters there? It's almost as if you're being pushed in that direction."

That question had been hiding behind her awareness ever since the kidnapping. Every time the thought had intruded on her mind, she quickly told it to go away. She tried answering in a tone of superficial curiosity.

"I think that's what Gerald and some of his friends want. The concept is appealing to me, to live in another world, a free world, but can I make that decision for my daughter and now for Daryn? What if we all get killed? What if they get a shitty childhood?"

Mr. Smith thought about it for a moment and smiled at her profanity.

"Don't parents do that to their children all the time, move to someplace new? I never asked for my son's permission to move." He reached across the table and put his cold, bony hand on hers. "I'm not trying to convince you of anything."

"I suppose," she said, failing to think of a counter-argument.

"In the end, Miss Jacobsen," he began, "all this life can offer you are your memories of experiences and the ones you love. I cannot even imagine what kind of memories you'll have if you find another home. All this material comfort becomes pretty empty after a while." He waved his hand absently around the room.

She looked around the study at all the book spines facing her. She imagined them as living creatures, lazily napping without care. The conversation began to feed a small kind of anxiety, so she brought the conversation back to Freddy.

"Knowing Freddy, he should be in his element right now, flying around in space, visiting with aliens."

Sadi's psyche had a hard time accepting the words escaping her mouth. She suddenly felt like a character inside a science fiction book. Would she like what the writer had prepared for her?

"Yes, I imagine he will have the time of his life," said Mr. Smith. "How will he return, do you think?"

"What do you mean, how?"

"Intense anxiety always changes a person," he said as if lecturing her. "It's not always bad, but it always happens. I hope he made the right decision."

Sadi could see the pain in his old eyes.

"You've gotten quite fond of him, haven't you?"

"You know, I never had a cat, Sadi, but now I can imagine what it's like to rescue an abandoned, abused cat and nurse it back to health. What do you think? If we don't see him again, should I get a cat?"

In that instant, his sadness vanished, and he smiled.

FIFTY

Sadi

The next day passed, then the next. With each passing day, the girls became more impatient to go outside and play, eventually begging her for it. In Sadi's opinion, the girls should not have become bored with the huge house yet. But they craved the open air, and Sadi also found herself feeling the beginning symptoms of cabin fever. The idea of sending them outside sent a spike of fear through her heart. Every time the girls asked to go outside, Sadi would have to calm her nerves before responding. Her instinct to yell at them became too strong a few times.

Her paranoia levels seemed to increase as the days passed. She spent a lot of her time reading, and she found plenty of material in the house to keep her mind occupied. Although her many worries seemed valid, she wondered if she was thinking too irrationally. Would her internet searches be suspicious for an old man, if they were being monitored? She had to remind the girls repeatedly to stay away from the windows, and she peeked out of them every few hours, looking for suspicious people.

Mr. Smith caught her a few times and did his best to comfort her.

"There's no reason why anyone would suspect you of being here with me. I wish you could relax."

"We're waiting for Freddy to come back," Sadi said, "and we've made that the decision point. I was supposed to relax until that point, but all I can do is dread it. If he never comes back, then it seems like my misery will go on forever. Don't get me wrong. I want him to come back."

"He's supposed to return tomorrow," Mr. Smith said comfortingly. "Let's just be positive and plan for that. How can I help you?"

"I'm sorry, Mr. Smith," Sadi said, attempting to sound sincere. Her frustration burned like an acetylene flame, and it kept scorching the unfortunate souls who happened to be in her path. She needed to change the subject.

"You've done more to help me than you can imagine. There's nothing to be done right now. So what's the plan for meeting Freddy tomorrow?"

Mr. Smith paused to look at her as though deciding which topic to continue.

"Since we don't know the exact time, we can't meet him anywhere unless we want to camp out somewhere, but that might attract attention."

"So there's no plan to meet him somewhere? He took off from the coast. We can't go there and wait?"

The idea of going to the coast felt good to her. She felt safer there.

"There was no plan since he could not know when he might be done and I won't be surprised if it doesn't happen tomorrow. Knowing Freddy though, he'll do his best to return when we expect him. You know," he paused and looked at the window, at the bright light spilling through the spaces in the curtains. "I've been thinking about it. Since that thing wants Freddy to make the trip, call it an alien if you want, don't you think it unlikely that it would let him die on the journey?"

"That's a good point," Sadi said with a smile, but she thought it also might make sense for the alien not to want Freddy to return. "You're probably right."

Would she ever share the old man's optimistic attitude again? Maybe he was just doing the same thing she was, speaking as if he had hope. Maybe she needed to go outside and feel the fresh air.

When Sadi awoke the next morning, her first thought was Freddy's promise to return that day. Her fear of his return, she realized, had transformed overnight into curiosity and hope. She spent much of the day fantasizing about Freddy flying through space and exploring ancient alien tunnels inside Mercury. She also spent time thinking about her experience at the barn with the alien probe, but the memories of her panic and fear were not as potent anymore. The memory was now full of excitement, wonder, and a sense of alien benevolence.

When the last light of the sun disappeared, she and Mr. Smith were sitting around the fireplace watching the natural gas flames flickering in the waning light. Sadi had put the girls to bed in their shared room just a few minutes earlier. She usually let them stay up as long as they wanted and enjoyed watching them succumb to exhaustion, but she needed a break.

As the minutes passed without Freddy's expected return, the excitement of the day began to ebb. Every few minutes, Sadi would glance at the door or windows, then to Mr. Smith. On a few occasions, their eyes met, and each quickly looked back at their books. Did she see a hidden sadness in those old eyes? For the first time since arriving, she felt like the comforter.

"If not tonight, he'll be back tomorrow," she said.

"Or the next day," Mr. Smith answered and smiled. "When you get to be my age, three days will feel like one. At this time, that works in my favor."

The next day passed without Freddy, and so did the next day, and the next. Sadi could almost see the growing tension in the old man, and she also began to feel it herself. She attempted to keep Freddy and the alien out of her conversations and talked about the group activities. Mr. Smith and Sadi read every update that anyone gave. Most came from Gerald and were concerned with the progress of the airplane in Brazil. Gerald referred to it as the bird in the veterinary clinic and said the bird was getting almost strong enough to fly again but still needed more rest.

The fifth day passed as all the others. After putting the kids to bed, Sadi started walking down the staircase and noticed an intense light through the curtains. With her heart pumping wildly, she ran to the front door and looked outside just in time to see the BMW drive up to the front gate.

FIFTY-ONE

Gerald

Several days after Freddy disappeared into space on his journey to Mercury, Gerald started to feel uneasy. At first, he fantasized about all the excitement Freddy might be having, but his thoughts eventually transformed into more foreboding. He failed to think of any valid reason for his anxiety, so he tried ignoring it. *What if something happens to him? What if he never comes back? Would I be to blame?*

The anxiety and general feeling of foreboding never dissipated, so Gerald decided to visit Salt Lake City to see the two men who gave them the nuclear fusion reactor. He'd been thinking of making the trip for quite a while. They needed to know about the current events, told directly and not through some kind of cryptic email. Maybe they could take extra precautions for their own safety.

Gerald and Cesar kept in contact with the Mormons at Cerametrics through old-fashioned letters. Using an electronic form of communication was traceable and too dangerous. Even though Franklin designed the website to encrypt their electronic communications, the government stored their encrypted data somewhere in a database. Gerald would not allow himself the luxury of thinking his precautions were impenetrable.

Although he wanted to visit Utah directly, he hoped to divert the attention of any possible government agents following him. To give the impression of traveling to a different destination, Gerald chose a flight to Casper, Wyoming with a long layover in Salt Lake City. He had a client in Casper who would not be annoyed by a surprise visit.

His plane trip occurred without anything suspicious happening. On his drive to Cerametrics, Gerald felt confident no one was following. He called Ammon from the lobby and recognized the same secretary he had encountered on his first visit. On this visit, Ammon met him with a smile. Gerald remembered being greeted with suspicion when they first met.

Ammon looked the same as Gerald remembered, a short, pudgy man who reminded him of George from the TV show *Seinfeld*, the only show he used to watch. But beneath his polite smile, Ammon still looked paranoid and Gerald felt sorry for him. He looked like he was expecting federal agents to kick his door down and take them to some detention facility, never to be seen again. Gerald knew how he felt but decided to be more positive. Worrying was a bad move in the game of mind control.

He took Gerald through their facility to an empty lab room and then sat on a stool in front of a fume hood. His boss, Tom, leaned against the hood, waiting for them. Several beakers of white powder sat on the surface inside it.

"I wanted to talk to you about what we're doing with your fusion generator," Gerald said over the low hum of the fume hood exhaust fan. "If you want to know, that is."

Tom and Ammon looked at each other.

"Won't that incriminate us?" Tom asked.

"I've thought about that," Gerald began. "You already incriminated yourselves when you invented a nearly limitless energy source. That's the crime of the century. As I see it, we both have a mutually beneficial motivation to keep each other's secrets."

"Okay, just tell us," Tom said, exhaling in resignation. "If we're caught, we're dead men no matter what."

Gerald liked Tom a little more than Ammon, even though his overbearing and aggressive nature was intimidating. Gerald would never forget meeting the man, and how he thought Tom planned to kill him.

Gerald briefly told them about his friends, their prototype spacecraft, the current work on the plane, and their overall plan. Without revealing any names, Gerald included only the highlights and excluded the specifics of Taylor's invention. When he told them about the probe and how Freddy went to visit the alien and possibly an alien world, they looked at him with disbelief and suspicion.

"This kid went to visit the alien on its planet?" asked Ammon. "How do you expect us to believe that? How can you believe it?"

"Technically, he only went to Mercury, but we'll only know when he gets back."

Gerald shared his personal encounter with the alien probe and how two of his friends had similar experiences with him. At the end of the conversation, Gerald had successfully convinced them of his sincerity, just not his claim. They wanted more than just his testimony, something they could see with their own eyes.

He could not blame the two men for wanting something more substantial than his word but found their reaction incredibly ironic. They believed everything their adored prophet, Joseph Smith, wrote, despite all the evidence of him being a charlatan and megalomaniac. Of course, Gerald kept that opinion to himself.

"I know this is a lot to absorb," he said finally, "but let's speak hypothetically, as though there was a place to escape to. When we try to take this public, things could go wrong, and we may need to escape to this other place for a while. Would you come with us? They can't reach you there."

While looking at each other, they seemed to have a telepathic conversation. Could Mormons do that? What if they decided to come with him and his friends? Gerald had strong reservations about that possibility. Since he might be putting them in more danger, Gerald owed them the invitation, but he hated the thought of tainting a new world with religion.

"We'd have to think about it," said Tom, pulling Gerald out of his thoughts. "We have families. It's a lot to consider."

"Of course," Gerald said.

Ammon turned to Gerald and sighed.

"Gerald, don't take this the wrong way, but we've got a different perspective on this. We have faith that things will work out for the best here on Earth. God made Earth for us and not the other way around. In the overall scheme of things, our time here is insignificant. It's just one of our trials. God's taken care of us this far, hasn't he?"

"And what about all the people that he hasn't taken care of?" After Gerald asked the question, he saw where the conversation would ultimately lead, but he continued with his reasoning anyway. "You could be the next ones."

"Well, then in the next life, we'll know that we did our best. We can't be blamed for that."

"What if this is the only life you've got?" Gerald asked, suppressing a huff. "If God did exist, wouldn't he or she want you to do everything in your power to keep your families out of harm? The instinct for self-preservation is necessary for survival."

"When Jesus comes back, he'll fix all the problems. We need to stay and do our best with what we've got."

Tom remained silent but looked ready to interrupt.

"Are you saying that Christians aren't supposed to leave Earth?" Gerald asked. The idea seemed more ridiculous than anything else he understood of Christian theology.

"Well," Ammon said and paused to consider his next words.

In the silence, Gerald made a sudden realization. The Christian myth had become the main motivation for this man's entire existence. Arguing with them was futile.

"It's not official church doctrine," he continued, "but leaving the Earth would be a lack of faith. It would be showing that we don't think God can protect us or that our physical existence is more important than his plan for us."

"My gut instinct is that I shouldn't leave," said Tom. "Not just because it's too much to ask of my wife and kids, but because I think Ammon's right. We can only do so much, and then Jesus will take care of the rest when he comes again. I'm sure you don't understand, and I don't blame you."

Gerald bit his tongue to prevent further argument. They had complete faith in their religion and therefore refused to consider alternate possibilities, no matter how severe the impact on their lives. Humans rarely chose to consider ideas contrary to their beliefs, including himself sometimes, he admitted.

FIFTY-TWO

Freddy

Every kilometer of road Freddy traveled after returning to Earth reminded him of a former life he would never get back. He remembered a similar feeling after coming to live with Mr. Smith, except now it felt a hundred times more intense. The experience of being back on Earth felt like a tour of an ancient site.

Although he had not yet gotten out of the vehicle, holding the steering wheel seemed to have restored his connection to the Earth. In space, he'd had nearly total control, but back on Earth, he depended on the elements, gravity, and people. Although he missed the total isolation in space, feeling the emotions of other people again gave him some comfort.

Driving within an acceptable speed limit required all of his willpower. More than anything, he wanted to see Mr. Smith again, and the home that somehow had stopped being his home anymore. He knew Mr. Smith would be experiencing turmoil at his failure to return on time, and he needed relief. Freddy would tell him most of what had happened on his journey but would put extra emphasis on how still felt the same toward his employer.

Although he drove on the road like a normal human, he controlled an advanced interplanetary vehicle. The robotic mechanics on the alien's orbiting observatory had perfected the car's design, transforming it into a machine that would not malfunction unless damaged by external stress. It looked the same from the outside, but everything on the inside had been reconditioned with new materials. The engine and fusion reactor designs were mostly the same, with only small modifications for efficiency. He could not let it be captured and felt an urgency to return the vehicle to Taylor and Cesar. He would enjoy experiencing their excitement and wonder at the enhancements.

Not only was the BMW significantly enhanced, but Freddy also became similarly reconditioned. The robotic mechanics had refined his ability to feel the emotions of other creatures and not only humans. Instead of just feeling what they did, he could now understand why. He could also pause his ability, something he could not do before his journey through the void.

During his final ride home on the Sunset Highway, he practiced feeling the emotions of his fellow travelers. At one point, he drove behind a woman transporting her three children and felt the love she had for each of them. He wanted to feel that one day. It even brought tears to his eyes. Why did his mother not feel that for him? The question seemed to affect him less than he remembered.

When he pulled into his neighborhood, he felt a range of typical emotions from the people who lived near them. One man in particular interested Freddy more than any of the others. A few houses away, in a foreclosed house, a single man was listening to loud music on his headphones and watching Freddy's home. The man had been watching the house for several days, waiting for him to return.

Freddy knew the man would require his attention, but when he sensed the presence of Sadi and her two girls at his home, all other considerations became secondary. Her natural-born daughter and the adopted girl he had helped rescue had made a strong emotional connection with him. He thought of Daryn, in particular, as a daughter and couldn't imagine being any more attached to biological offspring he might have one day.

After stopping at the front gate, he pushed the call button to give them some warning of his arrival. Almost instantly, he felt Mr. Smith's and Sadi's heightened anxiety and awareness of his presence. The gate opened without any word in response.

As he entered the garage, he ignored all of his own emotions and focused on Sadi and Mr. Smith. She felt intense anger and frustration at her reason for being there, something that had happened after he left. Feeling her despair filled Freddy with both anger and curiosity at the cause.

The man watching the house knew of Freddy's arrival, but so far had not done anything about it. He continued to watch for further activity. Freddy would need to remain aware of his actions and prepare himself to deal with the watcher later. After everything that happened to him on his journey, he felt confident in his ability to handle the problem. He even felt a desire for the action to start sooner rather than later.

He found Sadi and Mr. Smith waiting for him in the garage.

"My dear Freddy," Mr. Smith said with tears in his eyes. He extended his hand to help Freddy out of the car. Before Freddy could get his balance, the old man's bony grip tightened around his left hand.

"It is good to see you too," Freddy said with a smile. He looked at Sadi standing a few meters behind his employer. She felt awkward at seeing him and being at his house. He held out his hand, but she embraced him and held him tight.

"We're so glad you're back safe," she said then let go and took a small step away.

"There is much to tell you," he said after standing back and facing them both, "but I really need to use the bathroom first. It has been a hundred million kilometers since my last stop."

When Sadi chuckled at his comment, he smiled. While he took care of his physical needs, Mr. Smith and Sadi went to the front parlor to wait for him. He sensed the two little girls asleep in a room upstairs and even had a glimpse inside their dreams.

"I know you want to hear about my journey," began Freddy once he returned from the bathroom, "but first, I want to know what happened for Sadi to be here. I know you have found refuge with Mr. Smith. I am glad of that."

After they took turns relating the story, Freddy decided not to tell them about the man watching their house. At the moment, Sadi did not need any more stress in her life. Now that Freddy knew the truth of the matter, he had no problem deducing the watching man's purpose.

He would do whatever was required to save Sadi from her current predicament, one way or another. She was disturbingly anxious about not being able to return to work or her normal life. Freddy had to swallow those horrible emotions before continuing.

"And other than these two men," Freddy began and fixed them both with a penetrating stare. "Does anyone else suspect our role with the kidnapping? What about the detective who saved you?"

Sadi required a few seconds to compose herself and did not immediately respond. She pulled her arms tighter around her waist, in an attempt to keep him from noticing the chills rippling all over her body.

"If it weren't for her, I would be in prison somewhere. She suspects something but knows nothing."

Freddy shuddered at what she felt.

Mr. Smith put his arm around her.

"I'm glad you came here, Sadi. Freddy and I will get your life back."

"If you want your life back, that is," said Freddy just loud enough for her to hear.

"Let's talk about that later," said Mr. Smith with concern. "It's your turn, Freddy."

Freddy had four curious and eager eyes immediately focused on him. At that moment, both of them found more interest in hearing about his journey, and he knew they would forget their troubles during the story. While he would satisfy their curiosity, he did not plan to tell them everything, at least yet. The entire truth would overwhelm them with emotional turbulence.

"You are probably most curious about my destination," he began, and he could feel their anticipation of the answer. "The alien moved me to another planet, a place capable of supporting organic life like us."

"Another planet?" Mr. Smith said, not intending to say the words out loud.

"How did you get there?" Sadi asked. Freddy could feel her scientific mind creating space for the answer. He was glad for the chance to tell them.

"There is an apparatus at Mercury that can transport objects through space, or to be precise, transport through the void in space. As you know, Mr. Smith, I never agreed with part of standard cosmological theory, which contains only pieces of the truth. With enough energy, space can be parted, and objects can slide through the opening. I do not yet understand how it works."

"What did you discover about the alien?" asked Mr. Smith. "Does it want you to move to this other planet?"

This is what he fears the most, Freddy thought. He disliked referring to the entity as an *alien*, but the truth would incapacitate them, so he would use language they could understand. The word was just a pronoun for a mysterious being. Humans felt better when disguising their anxieties in word form.

"The best way to think of the *alien* is as an influencer rather than a manipulator. In some ways, the alien likes us. At least, that was my impression."

"Well that's comforting," said Sadi with a hint of sarcasm. "So it wants to help us?"

"Think of the alien as a resource. If we want to go to this other planet, it will provide the way, like it did for me. I don't fully understand its motivations."

Their hopes and fears mixed in Freddy's mind like water and oil, and he had to wait a moment for them to separate.

"You keep referring to the alien as an it," added Sadi. "So it's not male or female?"

Freddy paused again to think.

"Before my visit, it always appeared to me as a woman, but I have difficulty referring to it as a female."

He needed to leave out some information about the alien. The truth would be too disturbing to them as it had been for him.

"What does this alien look like?" asked Sadi.

"I cannot describe the alien accurately for you to understand. Just know that it is a life unlike ours." Freddy attempted to refrain from shuddering at the memory, but Mr. Smith knew the memory caused anxiety. For the present, Freddy planned to keep the entire experience to himself. He might tell the whole story to his boss but not Sadi.

Sadi felt unsatisfied with his answer and prepared to ask other questions. Freddy decided to change the subject before she could continue.

"Do not ask me to describe the alien," Freddy continued. "I will tell you another time. Just know, that I do not believe it will attempt to harm us. I get the impression that the alien does not like the idea of using force to achieve its goals. That method would probably bore it."

"A libertarian alien," Sadi said, laughing to release some of her tension.

"So are there any others," Mr. Smith said. "I mean aliens?"

Freddy smiled at all of their questions standing in a line, waiting to be spoken. He expected Sadi to show more interest in the other world than the alien. Freddy liked talking to people who had an interest in things other than their petty lives. Both Sadi and Mr. Smith showed almost as much curiosity as he felt.

"I only met with one creature," he said, hating the way he was distorting the truth to help prevent their anxiety. "I think it finds interest in intelligence."

"In intelligence?" Sadi asked. "Like us?"

Freddy leaned forward and held one hand close to the ground but not touching.

"If this is the intelligence or mental capacity of a hummingbird," he said then raised his hand a meter above his first hand, "then humans will probably be here."

He then moved the hummingbird hand high above the human hand, as high as he could put it without standing.

"And this is the being I encountered."

He paused to let them more fully comprehend his visual example. By their emotional reaction, he had successfully relayed the intelligence level of the *alien*.

"Okay, is this other world her home?" Mr. Smith asked, wanting to discuss something he could understand. "Is there other intelligent life in this world?"

"Nothing quite as intelligent as humans live there," Freddy said and paused while memories of his visit filled his mind. "At least not anymore."

Both Mr. Smith and Sadi instantly became more curious, and hundreds of new questions materialized in their busy minds. Maybe he could divert their thoughts to less dangerous aspects of his journey.

"The alien being does not originate from that world."

Mr. Smith sat forward.

"What happened to the ones that lived there before?"

"They moved on," he answered. "That is another story for another time."

He was disappointed that he could not satisfy their curiosity and had to redirect their thoughts. A question standing behind other questions suddenly pushed its way to the front of Sadi's mind.

"Did the alien help Taylor invent the NMG?" she asked. "And did it lead Gerald to the fusion reactor?"

"Yes and no," he said regretfully. "But do not tell them. They deserve the credit."

Sadi unconsciously repressed the obvious follow-up question. *And Helen's abduction?* She feared that answer. It brought too many implications, too frightening for her conscious mind. Mr. Smith wanted to ask it as well but kept the question to himself.

"Why haven't these inventions happened before now," she asked instead. "Was it all just a coincidence? Taylor inventing the NMG and then Gerald finding the fusion reactor?"

"Like most chemical reactions, at least two reactants need to be present, and under the right circumstances."

"Okay, I'll give you that," Sadi said, "but that goes back to the same question. Why hasn't it happened before?"

"Well, in my opinion, the major stakeholders in the world are actively preventing the reaction from taking place. Here is an example. Do you know one of the most effective pest control methods?"

"Yes, I think so at least," Sadi answered and smiled at knowing the answer. "My company makes some of them. I've read the documentation."

"Then you will know that all they have to do is prevent a male from finding a female. Two insects in a field who fail to find each other can do only insignificant damage. When the right people get together, like Gerald and Taylor, they can do great things."

"That's interesting," Mr. Smith said, excited at learning something new. "They flood the fields with female pheromones so that the males don't know where to go."

"From what I understand, the world of humans is very similar. Flood the world with disinformation, such as false information about aliens, mind control, liberals versus conservatives, climate change, religion, science, patriotism, terrorism..."

He paused to take a breath.

"It all causes distraction and confusion and discourages the right people from joining together to find solutions."

"But Taylor didn't need the alien to tell her to call Gerald," Sadi said, squinting in confusion.

"That is true," Freddy answered with a smile. "But all of Taylor's education told her the idea would not work. I think the alien interfered somehow, and encouraged her to try anyway."

"And then Taylor called Gerald," Sadi said, shaking her head in sudden understanding.

FIFTY-THREE

Sadi

The night Freddy returned, Sadi went to bed with her head swimming in all the possibilities his journey presented. Did the alien offer an escape from all her present problems? Could she take her girls to a place where they would be safe? Did such a place exist? Although she trusted Freddy, her mind refused to accept that possibility. She would be trading one set of problems for a new set. *If he offers to take us there, would we even go?* At least those pursuing her would be unable to follow.

Freddy's simple statement rang in her ears, louder than anything else he said.

If you want your life back...

Sadi wondered if she could even answer that question. *What other alternative do I have?* She fell asleep while thinking about it. Sadi spent years in school preparing for her life, years of struggle. And for what? To help find the answers, she began to compartmentalize her life. If greater than half of her life's components were negative, would she consider leaving her home world?

Did she love her job? Yes and no. She used skills acquired in her formal education, a thing she always wanted to do. But given the choice, would she choose her specific assignments? Probably not. For her ideal job, she would develop cures for human affliction, but her current company developed substances to counteract symptoms. She found more interest in studying the causes of disease, because only after finding the cause could a cure be developed.

Unfortunately, the *alleviating symptoms* side of the business made more profits, giving companies little motivation to find cures when they could milk their customers for the rest of their lives. Sadi felt a twinge of guilt for being a part of it.

Other than her coveted position in the company and the accompanying pride, she would not be missing her job duties nearly as much as her coworkers. She longed to see Zoya again and imagined her worried to the point of illness. Every day, Sadi fought the temptation to text her. Anyone in authority, or anyone with access to those in authority, could retrieve every phone call record, every email, every electronic purchase, every bank transaction.

Early the next morning, while still dark outside, she awoke to thoughts of all the people in her life—Helen and Daryn, her brother, her other friends, her father, Helen's amazing school teachers. She could not leave them. No matter how much the possibility of escaping her problems tempted her, dread of the unknown loomed over her like a dark rain cloud ready to pour down its vengeance. She could not make that choice for her daughter. On the other hand, parents always made life-altering decisions for their children. How was this different?

Sadi fell back asleep and continued her dream of aliens watching from the bushes.

—※—

Sadi awoke to the sensation of someone silently shaking her arm. With dreary eyes, she looked up into Mr. Smith's face hovering over her. Instinctively, she scooted farther back in her bed, but after a moment, she sat up.

"What's going on?"

Instead of answering, he turned around and pointed to her door. Sadi cocked her head and listened to the sound of someone pounding on a door downstairs.

"They're at the front door," he said and offered his hand to help her get out of bed. "Go to the girls' room and stay there. I will try to prevent them from searching the house."

She jumped out of bed but stood too fast and her vision almost went completely black. Mr. Smith held her steady until her blood oxygen levels and vision returned to normal. They nearly fell over together, and Sadi eventually steadied them both.

He turned away from her.

"I need to get the door before they break it down."

"Where's Freddy?" she asked.

"He wasn't in his room, or anywhere else downstairs," he said with disguised panic, "but don't worry. He hasn't abandoned us. I called Craig Swenson, so someone else knows what's happening here."

Without another word, he disappeared into the hallway, moving faster than she thought possible. She imagined him falling down the stairs and unconsciously listened to the sound of his movement.

She put on her pants from the previous day and ran to her desk drawer to get the gun she had found in one of the closets. Before leaving the room, she had to consciously rip her eyes away from the gun, stuff it down the front of her pants, and then cover it with her nightshirt. She felt as though she was staring at a cobra just centimeters from her face. The cold metal on her skin ripped the residual sleep from her eyes.

"Helen, Daryn, wake up," Sadi said as she entered their room. She tried her best to move quietly to their beds.

"Is it time to get up?" they asked in unison.

Helen instantly recognized the worry in her mother's eyes, while Daryn rubbed the sleep from hers.

"You've both got to be very quiet," Sadi said and put her fingers to her lips. "Some bad men are downstairs, but there's no need to worry.

Mr. Smith and Freddy will handle it."

Daryn grabbed frantically onto Sadi's arm.

"Is it the Becerras?" she asked in a panic, tears beginning to form. "Please don't let them take me!"

The look on Daryn's face transformed the fear in Sadi's heart to extreme anger and hatred of the men downstairs, whatever their identities.

"No, it's not the Becerras." Sadi spoke through clenched teeth and hugged Daryn close. "You're not going back to them or anyone like them, ever. Okay? Just please keep quiet. While I listen at the door, I want you to go into the closet and keep quiet. If anyone comes into the room, just stay still as statues."

"Freddy is back," Helen said excitedly, turning to Daryn and putting her arm around the frightened girl to provide comfort. "I bet he brought us presents."

"I think he did," Sadi said and felt glad for the diversion. "When this is over, we'll ask him."

She heard Mr. Smith's voice in the distance and then walked to the door to listen. As she put her left ear to the door, she turned back to the girls and pointed to the walk-in closet. Both girls crept into it and shut the door.

She heard the front door open downstairs and Mr. Smith start talking.

"How did you get through the gates?" he asked. "Do you have a search warrant?"

"We know you're hiding the woman," one of them said, and Sadi recognized the voice of the man who'd put her in handcuffs. His face filled her mind. The target of her anger now had a name.

"It's called harboring a fugitive, and is a criminal offense," the other said.

"You still have not shown me any warrant documentation," Mr. Smith said with confidence in his trembling voice. "I do not consent to you coming into my home."

"Move aside, old man."

Sadi heard the door shut.

"Get your hands off me."

"Go find Miss Jacobsen, Farley. If she gives you any trouble, you know what to do." He paused, and Sadi heard one of the men walking around downstairs, opening and closing doors rather loudly.

"Go in there and sit down," the first man said, "and hold your breath about denying the woman is here. We know she's here."

As Sadi listened to the commotion, she walked back to the closet.

"Even if I leave the room," she whispered with her lips to the door, "stay in there and keep quiet."

"We want to stay with you, Mom," Helen said, opening the door to the closet a bit as if intending to exit. "They won't find you if you hide with us."

"Do as I tell you and keep the door shut. I might need to go help Mr. Smith."

Sadi spoke with as little panic as possible. A small sliver of hope existed that Freddy would take care of the problem. While clinging to that thought, she assessed the situation. The man was going to find her if she stayed there. She could be reactive and wait for it or be proactive. She would rather control the time they found her, not the other way around. Perhaps the girls would be safer that way.

As quietly as possible, she opened the door, stepped into the hall, then quietly shut the door again. Before moving toward the stairs, she paused to listen. The sound of opening and closing doors was much fainter, so she assumed the man had begun his search of the basement.

If she could get down the stairs without being seen, perhaps they would think she came from the ground floor and not go upstairs. She contemplated holding the gun in her hand but decided to reveal it as a last resort. The men searching for her had plenty of training with firearms in compromising situations, whereas Sadi had none, and they probably looked forward to any opportunity to play.

When she reached the stairs, she peeked down them and saw no one. Silently, she descended the first few steps, and when she heard nothing, she walked with more confidence and speed. At the bottom, she heard footsteps from the hallway behind her.

—※—

"Show me your hands," said the voice of the man sent to find her, Agent Farley.

"I'm unarmed," Sadi said as she slowly turned to face him. With her heart pumping wildly, she held up her hands. Her shirt lifted a bit to display some of her skin, but the gun remained safely out of his view. When she saw the gun pointed at her, she held her breath and could only stare at the muzzle. No one had ever pointed a loaded gun at her. She finished speaking without any oxygen in her blood. "I'm not going to give you any trouble."

"I found her," Agent Farley yelled.

"We're in the old man's study."

"Move it," Farley said, shaking the gun at her.

Sadi gulped and walked through the hall to join Mr. Smith in his study. He sat at the head of the table, visibly shaking. She ran to him and grabbed his shoulder.

"Are you okay? Did he hurt you?"

"I'm fine," he said, but Sadi could see his rapid breathing as if he'd just climbed several flights of stairs.

"What did you do to him?" she growled, turning to the man who gave the orders. Anger reminded her of his name, Agent Anderson.

"Have a seat, Miss Jacobsen," he said. "The old man is fine. Now, tell me. Did you really think you could hide from us? The only thing that Zimmerman managed to accomplish was to really piss me off. Now sit down."

"You don't have to go with them, Sadi," Mr. Smith said as she sat next to him. "My lawyer is preparing your case."

Agent Anderson shot a worried glance at Mr. Smith as he considered the old man's threat. But in less than a second, all evidence of the emotion disappeared, and he turned back to Sadi, his lips curved into a derisive smile. The man in the dark suit pulled out a small case from his sleeve, a narrow black tube.

When Sadi saw the tube, she sat back in her chair, away from him. In horror, she watched as he opened one end and removed a syringe full of a colorless liquid. He held it up to the light.

"Now this is where you're wrong old man," he said. "It makes no matter. Once we're gone, the best bloodhound in the world won't even be able to get a whiff of her. Sadi's not going to be any trouble this time."

She slowly pushed herself away from the table in real fear of the syringe, but also as an excuse to put her right hand under the table, on her lap. Only her shirt prevented her from grabbing the gun. As if getting ready to stand, she put her left hand on the edge of the table, and then with her last bit of energy, she turned her panic into anger.

"You're no better than those child rapists who were killed," she said, looking from the syringe to Agent Anderson's face. "What happened to them is one day going to happen to you."

"Did you hear that, Agent Farley?" he said, glancing at his stone-faced companion. "Sounds like a confession to me, and a threat, a two-for-one deal!"

Agent Farley spoke as if reading a list of offenses to a judge. He stood at the entrance to the study and leaned on the doorway, effectively blocking the exit. He still had the gun in his hand, now hanging at his side and pointing to the ground.

"No lawyer's going to get you out of this. It won't even go to trial," Agent Anderson said, putting his gun on the table, in an ostentatious display of confidence. Sadi took a brief look at it, then brought her eyes back up to meet his. "You are now a state secret, and no judge can touch you."

Sadi had to stall, in the hopes that Freddy waited in the shadows somewhere. He would be able to effectively hide from the men since he could feel their thoughts. She never once considered the possibility that he left her and Mr. Smith in such a dangerous circumstance.

Even with the gun in her possession, she could not imagine using it to escape successfully from their situation. She would have to shoot

Agent Farley first, then Anderson. Due to her inexperience with guns, she would probably miss them both, and the bullet would go through the wall to hit Freddy in his hiding place. She might even get shot in the process, or Mr. Smith, and where would that leave Helen and Daryn? She cursed herself for not preparing herself to use a gun.

"Why can't you just leave me alone?" she asked. "I am no threat to you or them."

"You're an unacceptable risk and an embarrassment," he said and seemed happy to explain himself. "You ruined an investigation years in the works."

"Don't give me that shit," she shot back at him. "You are protecting those vermin, keeping them in business. You're worse than they are."

"Think what you want. It doesn't make any difference. Now before we take you away, where did Freddy Carlson go?" He turned to Mr. Smith whose eyes became very wide. "He took off early this morning before we had the chance to catch him. I don't know how he managed what he did at the hotel, but we know he was the one who helped you get your daughter back."

Mr. Smith looked at Sadi with hopelessness in his eyes, and she felt the same despair. Her hands were shaking. Under her shirt, she squeezed the gun, and the cold metal helped her feel a little more confident. *Do I dare? It might work.* She needed to pull it out, shoot Farley, then hopefully, aim it at Anderson before he grabbed his gun off the table or lunged for her. Mr. Smith's voice made her pause.

"Freddy has nothing to do with this, just like Sadi," he said. "I don't know where he went."

"It's your choice," Agent Anderson said to both of them. "You can either tell us now where he went, or we can make you tell us. So I'll give you one more chance. Where did Freddy go?"

Sadi met Agent Anderson's gaze and saw an excitement or hope that they would still refuse to answer him. She slipped her trembling index finger on the trigger.

"I, I, don't know where he went," Sadi said.

Now's the time, she thought. *It's now or never.*

While drawing a deep breath, she slowly began pulling the gun away from the bare skin of her stomach. But then a strange sensation made her stop. She felt a warning in her head, almost like a voice, and then she heard a distinct noise from the direction of the kitchen.

No, no, no, she thought in a panic, thinking the noise came from the girls. *I told them to stay in the closet.*

"Hmm, who could that be?" asked Agent Anderson, glancing at the doorway. "Your daughter decided to see all the fun. Farley, go bring her in here."

In terror, Sadi watched Agent Farley leave the room, holding his gun in the air as if ready to use it. After he left, she looked from Mr. Smith to Agent Anderson and finally to his gun lying on the table between them.

The next events unfolded as if Sadi sat in an audience, watching a play. Without thinking, she pulled her gun out from its hiding place under the table, and in one swift motion, pointed it directly at Anderson's face. She ordered her index finger to squeeze, but it shook on the trigger instead.

The look in his eyes changed from mirth to surprise but not fear as she had hoped.

"Let me see your hands," she said quietly. With her other hand, she reached across the table and slid Anderson's gun to Mr. Smith then returned both hands to her gun.

The look in Agent Anderson's eyes changed back to mirth, but he held his hands up anyway. "What are you going to do now, *Sadi*?" he asked with a sneer. "My partner has your daughter."

"I don't want to hurt you, but I will. Go to the corner over there and turn to the wall."

"Put my nose in the corner?" he laughed and made no indication of obeying her command. "I don't think so. You're too smart to shoot me. Farley will come and take care of you, and I don't think that's what you want. Just put down the gun, and we'll keep your daughter out of this. She can stay with old Bill here."

"I can deal with your partner," she said as confidently as she could.

Mr. Smith stared at the gun in front of him and slowly picked it up. Perspiration glistened on the wrinkled skin of his forehead. Sadi could see his physical distress, but she worried more about Farley going after her daughter.

He held the gun and pointed it at Anderson.

"What do you want me to do?" Mr. Smith asked.

"Shoot him if he moves," Sadi said and stood from the table. "I'll deal with Farley when he comes back. There's two of us and only one of him." Sadi surprised herself by how confident she felt with the gun. She began to have hope of getting out of this situation.

FIFTY-FOUR

Sadi

Sadi walked slowly to the open door of the study and then stood with her back to the wall, facing Mr. Smith and Agent Anderson. Mr. Smith held the gun up with trembling hands. Agent Anderson still had his hands in the air and a disturbing smile on his face, a look that nearly broke her recent burst of confidence.

She took a brief moment to turn from them and look toward the hallway. A noise from behind her made her bring her attention back to the room. When Sadi turned back to the study, she watched as Anderson leaped toward Mr. Smith and deftly removed the gun from the old man's grasp. He quickly moved behind him with the gun pointed at his head. Sadi felt as though frozen in time.

"Drop the gun, or the old man gets a bullet to the head," Agent Anderson said. His eyes were angry now.

Mr. Smith appeared to struggle for breath and fell forward to catch himself with his hands on the table. He steadied himself with one hand and held the other to his chest as he coughed and gasped. Anderson kept one hand on his chest and partly kept him from falling to the ground.

"I'm sorry," Mr. Smith said while choking and coughing. He attempted to say something else but failed.

Instinctively, Sadi lowered her gun and ran to him as a new panic took hold of her. At that moment, she shut out everything else from her thoughts, even fear for her daughter, and concentrated on Mr. Smith. Her nurturing instincts took control.

"Don't worry," she said and rubbed his back with her free hand while also trying to support him. She felt her gun ripped from her grasp.

"Everything's going to be alright," she said as he struggled for breath. She felt a new panic growing. "Do you have any medication that will help?"

Agent Anderson stepped back from them and let Sadi lower Mr. Smith to his chair. He watched them for a moment and then stepped away to the open door.

"In my drawer," Mr. Smith said through ragged breathing. "Pills, by my bed."

"You're not going anywhere," Agent Anderson said.

Sadi looked at Agent Anderson with pleading in her eyes.

"He needs his medication."

"He looks fine to me," Anderson said absently while switching his gaze from them to the dark hallway. He exhaled, and Sadi thought he sounded irritated as if the decision caused him pain—shoot Mr. Smith or help him. "I'll send Farley to get the goddamned pills."

Anderson opened his mouth to say something else, but a noise from the hallway stopped him. Agent Farley appeared in the doorway, alone. He just stood there, motionless, and looked at the people in the room with a strange expression. He appeared uncertain about what he wanted to do. The gun hung lazily in his hand.

"We should let her get the pills," he said finally, and silence answered him while Agent Anderson considered his words.

"What the hell are you talking about," said Anderson angrily. "She's not going anywhere. Where's her daughter?"

"Couldn't find her," Farley said in confusion. "I followed a noise to the basement but found nothing. We don't want that old man dying on us."

He took a step toward the desk, toward Sadi and Mr. Smith.

With her hand still on Mr. Smith's shoulder, Sadi stood and looked from Farley to Anderson in confusion. Farley looked calm and non-threatening, but Anderson's dark eyes were strained in anger and confusion. Sadi noticed a swollen blood vessel in the middle of his forehead.

"She's not going anywhere, you idiot. You can go get his pills."

Instead of obeying his partner, he stepped between Sadi and his companion and gently pushed her toward the door. "Go get the old man's pills."

While Mr. Smith struggled for breath, Sadi looked in confusion from Anderson to Farley and back again. After a moment, she decided to take a couple of steps toward the door. After neither man attempted to stop her, she ran out of the room, down the hall, and up the stairs.

From behind her, she heard the two men arguing.

"What's she going to do?" said Farley calmly. "We've got her friend, and he needs his medication. She's not going to abandon him."

"What the hell is wrong with you?"

As she ascended the stairs, the sound of the two men arguing became fainter. When she reached the top, she felt a great temptation to abandon Mr. Smith and run to the girls' room to check on them and maybe get them out of the house through the windows. A slight movement at the entrance to Mr. Smith's room caught her attention, and she peered closely to notice the door slowly closing.

"Helen, Daryn," Sadi whispered while fighting to hold back the tears.

Why had they gone into Mr. Smith's room?

"I told you to stay in the closet," she whispered after arriving at the room and putting her hand on the door handle.

When she pushed the door open enough to enter, she almost screamed in fright when she saw the dark figure standing by the bed in the early morning light. It was Freddy. After recovering her senses and looking behind her, she slipped completely into the room and pushed the door nearly closed. Freddy extended his hand, and she saw a prescription bottle half-full of white oblong pills.

"I knew you wouldn't leave us," she said after releasing the door and wiping the tears from her eyes. Sadi had no idea how, but she knew Freddy would take care of the situation, just as he had with the kidnapping. She accepted the pills with one hand and threw her other arm around his neck, hot tears sliding down her cheeks.

"I am sorry to make you feel abandoned, but I needed to come up with a plan."

"What are you going to do?" she asked. The hope she felt was beginning to be replaced by a sudden sense of urgency.

"Mr. Smith must go to the hospital, and you need to take him," he said and gently forced her away from their embrace. He turned away from her and took a glass of water from off the nightstand by the bed then handed it to her. The angry look in Freddy's eyes scared her. He seemed stronger, older, colder. "Take the water too. I will attempt to take care of those two men."

"I can't leave my girls," Sadi said resolutely.

"No you cannot," he said then walked to the door. He opened it just enough for her to fit through it. "You need to take these pills to Mr. Smith. I will get the girls."

Sadi remained at the spot while she tried to comprehend his directions. *He will get the girls?*

"Please tell me what's going on," she pleaded. "I don't know if I can go back down there. I need to get my girls. I need to get out of here."

"You need to trust me, Sadi," Freddy said while approaching her and putting his hand on her shoulder. For a brief moment, the anger in his eyes abated, and he became the Freddy she remembered. He waited for her to answer.

"Okay," she said.

"I will take the girls to the car and then come to the study," he continued, speaking more slowly. "You will get out of here with the girls and Mr. Smith, but please, I need you to take care of him. He needs medical assistance."

The confidence in his tone gave her the courage to consider her next action—going back down the stairs alone to face those two monsters, but she also knew that Mr. Smith needed her to bring his medication.

"Alright," she said after the brief internal struggle. She could either put faith in herself to fix her problems, or she could trust Freddy.

Freddy put his hand on her shoulder and walked her to the bedroom door and pulled it open more. As she quietly left the room and started walking toward the stairs, she felt like a robot. Before quietly placing her foot on the first step, she turned behind her and saw the door to the girls' room was now slightly open.

Sadi slowly descended the stairs and stopped at the bottom before proceeding farther toward the study. She took a moment to take a deep breath and mentally prepare for her re-entry into the room. She still had no explanation for Agent Farley's strange behavior. Why had they let her go alone? They should have sent one of them with her as Agent Anderson requested.

"I'm coming with the water and the pills," she said loud enough for them both to hear before she showed herself. She did not want to surprise two men with guns who looked as though they wanted to use them.

When she noticed Mr. Smith, concern for his welfare momentarily replaced her anxiety. He sat in the chair, putting pressure on his chest with one hand and the other hand on the table. When he looked up and made eye contact with her, she saw panic and relief in his eyes. She rushed to him with his pills and the cup of water.

"Two," he said and coughed.

He swallowed the two tablets with the water and then resumed his former position.

"Thank you, Sadi," he managed to whisper after swallowing them.

"Okay, what else do you need to do for him?" Agent Farley asked in a sincere tone.

"The pills will give me enough time to take him to the hospital," she said without thinking and heard the faint sound of walking down the stairs, a sound she had hoped to hear.

Sadi watched for any signs that the two men also noticed the sound. To help provide cover, she rubbed Mr. Smith's back and whispered how they would be alright. The two men made no indication that they heard Freddy leading the girls to the garage, in the opposite direction of the study. Sadi hoped the girls would keep from talking.

Agent Anderson looked at Agent Farley with obvious anger and disbelief.

"He just got his pills," he snarled. "That's all we're doing for him. The only person going anywhere is Sadi."

"We can follow them to the hospital," Agent Farley explained calmly. "How is she going to get away from us there?"

Agent Anderson shot an icy glare at his companion and opened his mouth to speak, but a sudden noise caused everyone to turn their heads toward the sound. Sadi instantly knew the source of the sound, the inner door to the garage slamming shut. Did Freddy intend to make such a loud noise, or did one of the girls cause it? All faith in Freddy momentarily vanished.

Agent Anderson moved to the door in an instant, his gun held at eye level and pointed to the ceiling. His smile made Sadi shudder.

"Is that our Mr. Carlson's return?" he asked with anticipation. After quickly surveying the room, he looked at his companion. "Stay here and don't let them leave the room and snap out of whatever is wrong with you!"

After taking a quick breath, Anderson left the room with his gun pointed directly ahead of him. Sadi wanted to yell Freddy's name in warning but stopped herself, and listened in horror to the sound of Agent Anderson walking down the hallway.

After a long five seconds, Anderson yelled, "Stop right there, Mr. Carlson!"

Sadi's heart stopped beating for the longest second of her life, and it only resumed after she heard Freddy's voice in response.

"Who are you?" he asked, as though unaware of current events.

"What are you doing in my house?"

"That way, to the study," Agent Anderson said. "You'll discover what I want when we get there."

All hope that Sadi felt when she found Freddy upstairs seemed to melt away in an instant. Freddy entered the room with his hands in the air, followed by Agent Anderson, who wore a smile of triumph and sick pleasure at the others' mental anguish.

Freddy looked first to Sadi, then to Mr. Smith with an unreadable expression. He seemed devoid of emotion, without fear, excitement, or understanding, almost as if in shock. The look in his eyes changed the next instant to one of concern, and he stepped toward Mr. Smith and then put his hand on the old man's shoulder.

Sadi felt instant confusion and lost further confidence that Freddy would successfully handle the situation. Was this his plan, pretend to come home unaware of their presence and give himself up?

"He's having heart problems," Freddy said and turned to the two men with guns pointed at him. He looked them in the eyes and not at the guns, unlike Sadi who could not take her eyes off the cold metal. "I am the one you want. Mr. Smith needs medical assistance, and Sadi needs to take him to the hospital."

"I won't say this again," Anderson said through clenched teeth. "The old man is going nowhere. Sadi can take him upstairs to his bed if you want. Farley, make sure that's where she goes."

He pointed to Freddy.

"You, sit down there, next to your boss."

Agent Farley looked around the room before responding, as if not sure what to say or do.

"Okay," he said and then waved his gun in her direction. "Sadi, help him stand, and we'll take him to the car."

"Farley, what the hell is going on with you?" Anderson barked. "I said take him to his room."

"That's what I said I was going to do," he answered, appearing severely confused.

"No you didn't," he said in irritation as if repeating instructions to a child. "You said you were taking him to his fucking car!"

"Well, that's not what I meant," Farley snorted. "Show me some respect! I don't want this old guy dying on us."

Sadi decided to start moving without waiting for them to finish arguing. She helped Mr. Smith stand from his chair and had to use all her strength to steady him. Gravity seemed to take a very strong hold on the frail old man who ordinarily seemed light enough for a breeze to blow away. As she started walking to the door, Agent Anderson spoke to her, but she thought he was still arguing with Farley.

"Don't fool yourself, Miss Jacobsen, concerning my companion's apparent ineptitude. Try and take advantage of it and we'll have to involve your daughter."

"Agent Farley will take you to the car," Freddy said as she passed him. In his eyes, she recognized the same confidence he showed upstairs.

Farley made no indication of hearing that statement.

"Down the hall and then up the stairs," he said, his gun pointed at the back of Sadi's head.

Without looking back, Sadi left the room with Mr. Smith at her side and Agent Farley in front of them. She could feel Agent Anderson's eyes on her back as she walked away. The threat to involve her daughter felt unreal and failed to frighten her.

In the hallway, Agent Farley moved ahead of Sadi and Mr. Smith and started walking without looking back at them. When he reached the bottom of the stairs, he took his first step without a pause and then continued slowly step by step, never once checking if they were following.

In confusion, Sadi paused at the base of the stairs, afraid of Farley looking behind him and realizing they were not following. She felt like a deer in a spotlight, unable to decide to stay or move, but the pull of Mr. Smith on her arm helped snap her out of the trance. She slowly followed him down the hallway toward the entrance of the garage.

The journey to the garage reminded Sadi of those dreams where she could not run fast enough to escape a chasing phantom. No one interrupted them on their way to the car, but she felt extreme panic during the entire trip. Only after quietly shutting the door to the garage and seeing her girls, did she begin to feel hope for escape. She found the girls patiently waiting in the back seat, and in her excitement, almost let go of Mr. Smith.

During the walk through the hallway, he had remained silent and seemed to be concentrating on simply walking. When Sadi opened the door to the car for Mr. Smith, his strength came to an abrupt end, and he almost fell into the seat. She looked at the girls in the back and noticed Helen with tears running down her cheek and Daryn's arm around her. A sense of relief washed over her like a tsunami.

"Miss Jacobsen," said Daryn tentatively as Sadi helped put Mr. Smith's legs inside the car. "Where's Freddy? He told us not to worry. Isn't he coming with us?"

"Not right now, Daryn," she said. "He'll meet us later."

FIFTY-FIVE

Sadi

As soon as they left the neighborhood, Sadi felt free for the first time in what seemed an eternity even though she had been in danger for only an hour. The bright sunlight from the horizon flooded the car, and the warmth began to heal her former panic. She experienced a moment of guilt for feeling so liberated after abandoning Freddy, and knowing that Mr. Smith was on the verge of death. At least she could better handle the situation now that she and her girls were temporarily out of danger.

Sadi recognized Mr. Smith's medication, Propranolol, which helped people with heart issues. After driving for a few minutes, the drug finally seemed to be taking effect at calming his heart, and he became more responsive than in his study. She wondered if he'd come close to dying.

Sadi drove to the nearest and best hospital available for heart conditions, Legacy Good Samaritan Medical Center, only a fifteen-minute drive from the house. On the way, Mr. Smith recovered enough of his strength to ask about the conversation she had with Freddy in his room. After she recited their conversation, he asked no questions and seemed to relax.

"I knew Freddy would get you out of that," he said with relief. "I'm sorry to be so weak and unable to help you."

"Try to relax, Mr. Smith," she said. "I hate to admit it, but you gave a pretty good excuse to leave."

"Well," he said and tried taking a deep breath but winced in pain. He put pressure on his chest and had to wait before finishing. "Perhaps we would have gotten away sooner if I would not have let him take the gun."

"We got out. That's all that matters. Just sit and relax, we'll be at the hospital soon."

As they pulled into the hospital emergency lane, Sadi realized that they would have to get out of the car. She immediately felt like a mouse being dropped onto a beach with eagles soaring overhead and nowhere to hide. It would be the first time since arriving at Mr. Smith's home, to be so exposed.

If the two men came after them, they would know where to look. The thought should have frightened Sadi, but somehow she knew Freddy would not let them go after her.

After parking at the emergency entrance, she made the two girls accompany her inside while walking with Mr. Smith. She shuddered at the thought of leaving them in the car. The girls held hands as they followed her, and Sadi thought they looked less frightened than during the short car ride. Their natural curiosity at being in a new place helped relieve the stress of the horrible morning. Seeing their reactions helped Sadi feel better too.

"Mr. Smith, sit down while I go talk to them," Sadi said while helping him sit in the waiting area. The girls sat next to him. "Don't worry about a thing. The heart specialists here are the best."

"I know."

She explained to the emergency room staff about what Mr. Smith had taken, a beta blocker to slow down his heart after it became too accelerated. They assured her that they would do their best to get him in a stable condition. After the emergency room staff took him away in a wheelchair, Sadi took the girls and parked the car. For a brief moment, she felt tempted to drive away and never stop.

Sadi led the girls quickly through the parking lot and back to the emergency room, glancing suspiciously at everyone they passed. Every car, she feared, contained a potential government agent looking for her.

"Is he going to be okay?" asked Helen after they reached the waiting area.

"He's going to be fine."

Helen clung to her mother, afraid of separation. Daryn sat on the other side of her. Each girl rested their hand on Sadi's thigh. The longer they waited, the more secure she felt. After a few minutes, she stopped feeling panic whenever a new face appeared.

Eventually, the girls' state of curiosity and wonder began to replace Sadi's paranoia. She loved the feeling of being somewhere other than Mr. Smith's house, their lavish prison palace. Her nerves seemed to find refuge in the emergency room waiting area.

She used the time in the waiting area to more objectively replay what happened back at the house, without the elevated levels of adrenaline and panic. The look in Freddy's eyes added special emphasis to his assurance that she would never have to worry about those men again. Maybe she could get her life back.

Eventually, a nurse came and escorted them to the room where they had taken Mr. Smith. When she shut the door and left them, even more relief swept through her. She told the girls to be quiet so that Mr. Smith could remain asleep, but she knew the girls would be unable to break the effects of the drugs.

They had several hours of waiting, and the girls seemed content to stay in the room and look through all the cupboards. Sadi watched them with pleasure, seeing their curiosity being satisfied.

Even though she trusted Freddy, the thought of returning to the house felt like the wrong action to take. That option seemed too dangerous, but the thought of returning to her own home or Brian's, or anyone else she knew in the Portland area also seemed wrong. She would have to wait for Freddy. At the moment, he held the key to her future.

When two hours had passed, she began to wonder if Freddy would appear at all, and then she remembered Gerald and imagined how he must be panicking about the lack of communication. *Is it safe to call him?* If she could use the hospital phone, the call could not easily be traced back to her, but if law enforcement officials were monitoring his phone, they might be alerted to her location. After a short deliberation, she decided to take that risk.

She made the girls accompany her to the phone at the nurse's station. Would she ever recover from the anxiety she felt at having them out of her sight?

After her first experience with Agents Farley and Anderson, Sadi decided to commit important phone numbers to her memory. She remembered the state of helplessness she'd felt when Detective Zimmerman had offered her phone, and she could not use it.

Sadi quickly dialed Gerald's phone number.

"Gerald Foster speaking," he answered with some formality and a hint of apprehension.

"Hi, Gerald," she said quietly, then waited for him to recognize her voice. He knew her identity instantly.

"Oh my God, Sadi," he said loudly, and she covered the phone with her hand to muffle the sound. "Where have you been? I was worried sick. Why are you calling from a hospital?"

"I'm fine," she said with immense relief at hearing his voice. "Physically fine at least. I'm here with Mr. Smith. They've got him in stable condition now. You should come see him *today*!"

"Of course," he said without hesitation. "I'll leave in the next few minutes. Is *he* back?"

"We can talk when you get here."

"Okay, I'll see you as soon as I can."

After she cut the connection, the next phase of waiting began.

—✳—

The time passed slowly, leaving Sadi to her thoughts. Her imagination ran wild with visions of what Freddy might have seen and what the other world was like. She tried avoiding thoughts of moving there, but the idea of finding more freedom pervaded every thought, especially after escaping another possible incarceration.

Was the temptation of escaping to the other world similar to the lure of the American West in the early days of the United States? If she had lived back then, would she have followed that path?

"I'm hungry," Daryn said after another hour passed, breaking Sadi from her thoughts.

"I am too," Sadi said, an insatiable hunger suddenly materializing. "We can go to the cafeteria."

"They have a cafeteria?" Helen asked. "Cool!"

After returning from a short visit to the cafeteria, they found Gerald talking to a nurse at the nurse's station. He saw them as they approached and Sadi surprised herself by throwing her arms around him.

At that moment, Sadi realized how much she craved physical contact with another adult. She closed her eyes, barely keeping her tears from making an emotional appearance.

"What's going on?" he asked once she let go of him, but he kept one hand on her upper arm. "Is Mr. Smith okay?"

Usually, Sadi hated the thought of anyone, other than her brother, seeing her emotional vulnerability, but she lacked the strength to hide it from Gerald or care. For the past several weeks, she'd needed to be the strong one for Helen and Daryn.

The embrace lasted only a moment before the girls pulled on his suit and drew his attention away. After tearing his eyes away from Sadi, he greeted them with a genuine smile.

"Hello, Helen," he said. "Hello, Daryn. Have you two been taking care of your mother?"

"What was your name again, mister?" Helen asked, acting as the spokeswoman.

"I remember both your names," he said as if insulted. "And you can't even remember one?"

"Mom," Helen said, turning to Sadi in excitement. "Tell him what happened, about the two men who came to our house and—"

Sadi put her hand over Helen's mouth and looked suspiciously at the two nurses sitting at their desks. They seemed too preoccupied to notice.

"Hey," Helen said in protest, but Sadi made a silent shushing with her lips.

"I'll tell him everything when we get back in with Mr. Smith."

After closing the door to Mr. Smith's room, Sadi began her explanation of Mr. Smith's condition and what the hospital staff had told her. While watching the old man sleep, Sadi began telling the rest of the story, starting from when Freddy returned the previous evening. She neglected to mention anything about his extraterrestrial experiences, just that he returned from his trip.

Daryn began pulling on Sadi's shirt.

"Tell him about how you made us hide in the closet."

"Yeah," Helen continued, "and how they yelled at you and Mr. Smith to put your hands in the air, but you didn't, did you? You got away."

"Yes, we got away," Sadi said. When she turned to Gerald, she noticed how his smile had vanished. His eyes became almost completely hidden behind half-opened eyelids.

Helen continued.

"Freddy took us to the car and said he was going to get Mom and Mr. Smith away from the bad men."

"What happened after that?" Gerald asked, looking from one girl to the other.

"Mom says he's going to be alright, and they can't hurt him."

While Sadi and Gerald sat in silence, the two girls shared their accounts of what happened that morning, using their active imaginations to explain what they didn't know. They added a brief summary of how they had arrived at Mr. Smith's house and all their fun exploring it, unintentionally confessing to playing with Freddy's scientific toys. Helen ended the story by complaining about how her mother and Mr. Smith had never let them go outside.

"It was too *dangerous*," Helen said dramatically.

With one hand on each of their shoulders, Gerald pulled the girls closer to him.

"You girls are so brave. Thanks for taking such good care of your mother."

"They were very brave girls," Sadi said in agreement then turned to them. "Helen and Daryn, can you give Mr. Foster and me a minute to talk please?"

Daryn quickly took Helen's hand and started to pull her away.

"Come on, Helen."

Before Helen allowed herself to be pulled away, she had one question for Gerald.

"Are you a liar?"

Sadi put her hand to her mouth in shock. Did she hear Helen correctly? Gerald just laughed.

"Yes, I am a *lawyer*."

"Can you make the bad guys stop bothering us?"

"I can't promise anything, Helen, but I will try."

The girls sat quietly in their seats, and let Sadi and Gerald talk by themselves. Gerald listened without asking questions. Twenty minutes later, before Sadi had finished explaining everything, the door opened and Freddy walked calmly into the room. Without a pause, he stepped to the bed and placed his hand on the old man's arm.

"The doctor says he will be okay," Freddy said without turning to face them, "but he will need rest. Thank you, Sadi, for bringing him here. Hi, Mr. Foster."

Sadi almost forgot that Freddy could know about the people in the room before entering it. She had to remind herself that he could also know her feelings, so she did not even bother attempting to hide her immense relief at seeing him.

"What happened?" she asked and waited several seconds while he deliberated on his answer.

"You do not have to worry about those two agents anymore," he said finally, still not looking at her.

Freddy's words sent a chill through Sadi's chest. Would she ever want to know what happened? Only the outcome mattered, she supposed.

"So those men won't be after Mom anymore?" asked Helen.

Freddy finally turned from the bed and crouched down to get eye level with the girls. He smiled, and his eyes seemed to relax.

"They are gone, and you will never have to worry about them again."

Daryn's eyes glistened with the formation of suspended tears. She threw her arms around Freddy's shoulders.

"They'll never try to take me away again?"

"That is right," he said. After getting back to his feet, he turned to Gerald. "It would be a good idea for Sadi to leave town for a while."

"They can come to my house," Gerald said without any hesitation.

Sadi felt like a commodity traded on Wall Street, as though Gerald and Freddy had met beforehand and agreed on the exchange.

"What did you find out from them?" she asked but then paused and turned to Gerald. "Will you take the girls out into the hall for a few minutes?"

Gerald paused briefly before responding.

"Come on girls," he said after turning to them. "Let's go see what the nurses are doing."

Sadi waited until they left the room.

"How many people do they have looking for me?"

"It is hard to say how many people are involved," Freddy answered. "Other than the lady who rescued you, I think that Farley and Anderson were the only ones with your name. With you away from here and safe, I can better assess the situation. It will not be long before their employers become aware of their disappearance."

Before Sadi could stop herself, she asked the question she planned to keep to herself.

"What did you do with them?"

"They are gone," he said and looked back to the bed.

"I'm sorry, Freddy, for putting you in this situation." Sadi put her hand on his arm.

"It is not your fault," he said quickly and then continued before she could say anything else. "I need to know the name of the detective who helped you escape."

"You're not going to do anything to her, are you?"

"I will need her help," he said reassuringly. "That is all."

"Her name is Zimmerman, Detective Zimmerman." After mentioning her name, Sadi felt a deep sense of debt to the woman. "I owe her my life. If you get to talk to her, will you please thank her for me?"

"Of course," he said.

Just then, Sadi noticed Mr. Smith's eyes open, just a crack at first, but then they closed again. For the next minute, they watched for further signs of movement. Only his steady breathing filled the silence.

"If you want to get to Seattle before it is too late, you should leave soon."

Sadi felt unsatisfied with how she had expressed her gratitude to Freddy. She would have hugged him, but they stood side by side, so she awkwardly placed her hand on his shoulder.

"Thank you, Freddy, for saving me again. I don't know how I can repay you, or Mr. Smith."

"You do not owe me," he said, stiffening slightly at her touch.

FIFTY-SIX

Sadi

Freddy told Sadi to take the car she used to drive to the hospital and then stuffed a huge wad of cash in her hand. She tried protesting, but he insisted, and she lacked the strength to argue. She hugged him goodbye and held on for a long time. To her surprise, he returned the gesture. Gerald, Sadi, and the girls left Freddy alone in the hospital room with his boss.

Although she wanted to get far away from Portland and drive to Seattle that night, Gerald said they should find a hotel and finish the drive in the morning. Her mental exhaustion prevented her from arguing again. The thought of a four-hour drive seemed to bring more fatigue than she already felt.

"The girls will have fun in a hotel room," he said. "It'll be exciting for them. They can go swimming!"

Sadi only had one condition, getting away from Portland, so they crossed the Columbia River and chose a hotel in Vancouver, Washington. But before going to the hotel, they stopped for supplies, since Sadi left everything at Mr. Smith's house. They stopped at a Fred Meyer where she could buy some items she and the girls needed.

Her paranoia had worn off just enough for her to feel comfortable leaving the girls in the car with Gerald while she went shopping on her own. For the first time in weeks, she almost felt free. The short time alone helped seal some of the cracks in her psyche. She wished for more time but thought Gerald might need rescuing from the two little girls who filled their surroundings with endless chatter. At checkout, she used some of the cash Freddy had given her.

After returning to the car that Freddy let her borrow, and snapping her seat belt back in place, she rolled down the window to speak with Gerald. He looked at the girls in the back seat.

"Are you two hungry?"

"Yes, I'm *starving*," Helen said with exaggerated desperation, and Daryn nodded her head expectantly.

"I'm going to take you out to eat. Does that sound fun?"

Both girls looked at each other in excitement. Helen spoke first.

"Can we go to Chuck E. Cheese? Please?"

"Let's save that for another time," Sadi said, rolling her eyes for Gerald to see.

"You always say that," Helen answered in disappointment.

To Sadi's great relief, Helen refrained from further begging.

They ate at a restaurant next to the hotel. The girls hardly touched their food until the waitress brought the dessert, cake, and pie, and then they ate like hyenas at a carcass. Gerald ordered a glass of wine for them both, saying it would help clear her head of unwanted anxiety. In a normal situation with the girls, Sadi would not have chosen to have any alcohol, but it did help.

After dinner and walking to the hotel, Sadi and the girls got one room, and Gerald got the one next door. He helped Sadi put the girls to bed and even gave each a hug before pulling the covers over them.

"I've got to take a shower and get to bed," she said after they left the girls.

Gerald looked at his watch.

"I can only imagine how tired you must be."

They stood in awkward silence for a moment, and then she walked him to the door. After grasping the handle, he turned, put his arms around her, and held her tight. At first, she hesitated to return the affection, but then she hugged him back.

"I'm glad you called me, Sadi. Sorry, our meeting has to be under such horrible conditions."

Sadi wanted nothing more than to hold him longer, but she imagined Freddy watching her with sadness in his eyes, so she began to pull away.

"I'm glad you came too," she said, his arms still around her.

"I'll see you in the morning," he said with a smile, finally pulling away.

"Have a good night."

After closing the door, Sadi stood for a moment and thought of Freddy again and all that he had done for them. She owed him her life, two times over now. If he still loved her, the only way she could imagine to ever pay him back would be to return the affection. Until Sadi could sort all of her emotions, she would stop thinking about Gerald.

—※—

Sadi let Helen and Daryn sleep in until eight the next morning. Then after breakfast, the girls went swimming while she and Gerald watched. Normally, Sadi would have joined them, but she had only purchased swimming suits for the girls the night before. She would have also felt uncomfortable swimming while he watched.

They followed Gerald's car to Seattle, and both girls fell asleep about twenty minutes into the drive. While Sadi watched the scenery, she inspected every other car on the road for suspicious characters who might be spying on them.

After finally arriving at Gerald's house, Sadi exited the vehicle and stretched. Both girls remained peacefully asleep in the backseat. She didn't want to wake them.

"Freddy said we should be safe, and that no one knew where I was," Sadi said as Gerald approached her. "You didn't see anyone following us, did you? I looked several times but noticed nothing out of the ordinary."

Gerald's lips spread into a wide smile.

"The FBI put a GPS tracker on my car several months ago, and Franklin made it send an erroneous signal. But since then, I think the FBI has forgotten me. I haven't noticed anything lately."

Sadi soon discovered how spotless and tidy Gerald kept his ultra-modern home. Upon first inspection, the house looked like no one even lived there, except for the books and filing cabinets. Sadi had a larger home but only by one room. She wondered how he would react when the girls messed everything up. Contrary to her expectations, the thought made her smile.

"Consider this your home for as long as you need," Gerald said. "Can the girls share a room?"

"Yes, they share a room."

"Good," Gerald said with an embarrassed smile. "I have an additional spare one, but unfortunately, it's unprepared for inhabitants. You can sleep in my room, and I can take my study."

"I can take the study," Sadi quickly responded. "It's no trouble, really."

"Well, the truth is that I often fall asleep in my study. Taking that room would be more of an inconvenience, not that you're an inconvenience."

Gerald changed the sheets on his bed, and then Sadi helped him prepare the girls' room. After about an hour of rearranging everything, he told her of an appointment he had to make. He would return a few hours later and then they would spend the rest of the day together.

After he left, Sadi felt as though she was beginning to start life all over again. Could she call her boss, or Zoya, and tell them what had happened to her? They were probably expecting a call from the police instead, informing them of her death. After a moment, she decided against making the call. No one knew her location, except for Freddy and Gerald. For the moment, she finally felt safe. Everything would return to normal. Then she could go back to her old life. Her company would be glad to see her.

"Here we are again, girls," she said after putting their meager belongings in their rooms. "But this time we don't have to stay cooped up all day. What do you say we go out and explore the town?"

Both girls looked at each other.

"Can we go out for pizza?" Helen asked in excitement.

"And then ice cream?" Daryn asked.

"That sounds great," Sadi answered.

For the first time after rescuing the girls with Freddy, Sadi felt no fear of going out into public. The usual warning voice in her head remained silent.

"After we eat, we're going to get some new clothes," she said after remembering all the cash Freddy had given her. She would feel better with it spent, rather than it sitting around, silently calling out to all the thieves in the area.

After returning to the house from shopping and eating, they found Gerald waiting for them. He stood at the door and opened it before her hand touched the door handle.

"How are you feeling?" he asked.

"I'm feeling rejuvenated," she said while holding two bags in each hand. "We had fun, didn't we girls?"

"Look at my new shoes," said Daryn, holding up a box of shoes from Target. When she opened the box, the sunlight glistened off the pink and purple sparkles.

"They are very pretty!"

"She picked them out," said Sadi, rolling her eyes. She hated glitter.

"I was planning to take you all out to dinner again," he said. "Are you up for it?"

"How about we stay here tonight. I'd like to make dinner if that's okay? We've been out shopping for quite a while."

Gerald laughed.

"Well, that's a relief because I don't cook, not well at least."

After a simple dinner of baked chicken, rice, and steamed broccoli, Sadi made the girls take baths. Gerald asked if he could put them to bed. Sadi thought it was a nice gesture and went to relax in the living room. When Gerald returned a few minutes later, he found Sadi sitting on his sofa with two empty wine glasses and a bottle of wine on his antique oak coffee table. Sadi wore the pajamas she had purchased that day.

"Did they give you any trouble," she asked.

Gerald sat down opposite her and picked up the bottle.

"Putting two little girls to bed by myself. Another of my checklist items completed."

"What else is on that checklist of yours?"

"After rescuing a woman and her two kids, there's nothing else on my list."

"I really appreciate you letting us come and stay with you," she said, and her tone became more serious, "but, the credit for saving us goes to Freddy and Detective Zimmerman. I wouldn't be here if it weren't for them."

"Of course," he replied while pouring the red wine. "So Freddy thinks he can clear this up for you? I sure would love to know how."

"Hopefully," Sadi began, "he didn't just say that because that's what I wanted to hear. Even with his new ability to know what others are thinking, I don't see how he can thwart a government investigation."

Gerald shook his head and took a deep breath.

"If we were in any kind of normal situation, I would think the same thing. To be honest, this is too much for me. I can't imagine how you're getting through it."

"Right now, Freddy is my only hope of getting my life back."

"Can I ask you a question about when we encountered the alien probe?"

Sadi would rather delay talking about aliens for as long as possible, but she felt indebted to him. She nodded.

"Sure."

"The experience didn't change you like it did Freddy, did it?"

Sadi got the impression that he was afraid of the answer. His question also made her pause to think. It had never even crossed Sadi's mind. Had Gerald acquired Freddy's psychic abilities, and he knew what she was thinking?

"I feel the same," she said. "Not normal after all this, but the same as I've always felt. I don't have any special abilities like Freddy. Do you?"

"No," he said.

"It is kind of scary how he can read our thoughts," she continued after a sigh, "but out of anyone I've ever met, Freddy is the only one who would not abuse that ability. Is that why the alien chose all of us because we all are somehow tied to Freddy?"

"Seems possible," Gerald said. "What does Freddy know?"

"He said he didn't know the alien's motivations and I believe him, but I think he's not telling us the whole story."

"Maybe it's something we don't want to hear," Gerald said in a slightly dark tone.

She spent the next few minutes repeating all that Freddy had told her, about going to the other world and meeting the alien on the spacecraft, and how the alien had enhanced the BMW. She enjoyed seeing his excitement at the news.

"Can I ask a personal question?" she asked and waited for his acknowledgment.

"Go for it."

"When the alien probe put us in that trance at the barn, what was your experience? I told you mine, but you never told me about yours. What happened to you?"

His smile disappeared, and he put the glass down, staring at it for several seconds. Finally, he looked into her eyes.

"That was an unpleasant experience. Can we talk about something else?"

From the uncomfortable look in his eyes, she suddenly wondered about the reason for his hesitation.

"It wasn't about me, was it?"

After a long pause, he answered but attempted to regain his usual whimsical disposition. "You were in it, yes, but it wasn't all about you. If I told you, you probably wouldn't like me anymore."

"But I don't like you already," she said, trying her best not to smile.

He picked up the wine bottle and refilled his glass.

"Maybe this will help loosen my tongue. I just don't like remembering that experience."

She suddenly regretted asking the question.

"You don't have to talk about it now. Just promise me that you will tell me one day."

He sat back on the couch and held the glass in front of him.

"In the vision, I was a soldier in Afghanistan," he began, and sarcasm laced his words like a glistening film of oil. "Imagine me as a soldier? Huh!"

Sadi smiled but remained silent.

"We were patrolling some godforsaken street in a part of a city unfit for human habitation. We were searching for an insurgent who had no hope of escape."

"By insurgent, do you mean someone trying to fight off the foreign invaders, or was it some criminal?"

"He was just some guy who joined the resistance."

"Got it, sorry to interrupt."

As Sadi listened, she realized his experience felt as real to him as her experience had been to her. He spoke as though his actions and feelings came from real memories. When she remembered her vision from the probe, the tunnel, it seemed real as well. The experience still burned in her memory, but at least hers had ended pleasantly.

"We were pulling so many people out of their homes, looking for this guy. Never mind that we had no right to treat them the way we did, but after a while, I became numb to it. I could hardly think of that anymore. I felt like a robot until we came to the last house. Somehow we knew the man lived in that house. We had checked all the others, so he had to be there. When we kicked in the door, I saw you."

"Was it an Afghan version of me, or was it my Norwegian ancestry me?" Her attempt at being lighthearted contrasted sharply with his sardonic tone. To lighten the mood a bit, she tried imagining how she would look as a native of Afghanistan.

"It was you, just like you are now," he spoke more to himself than to Sadi. "When I looked into your eyes, it was like falling into ice water. You woke me up in a sense, tore me out of the numb cushion surrounding and protecting me from my moral code. You forced me to remember what I was really doing, what I needed to be doing, and how I could never do that to people, no matter the reason. When I looked into your eyes, I saw pure hatred. I wanted to run away. I couldn't face you anymore."

He gave Sadi no time to interject. She felt chills wrack her whole body, almost as though she could see what he had seen.

"The next thing I remember, we forced you outside, then some of my fellow soldiers stormed your house. They pulled out Helen and your husband, the one we were looking for. If the look in your eyes caused me pain, the fear in Helen's eyes was a thousand times worse. She was crying hysterically for you and her father, but one of the soldiers held her back."

"What did you do?"

Sadi asked the question out of morbid curiosity, fearing the answer. Imaging her daughter restrained by soldiers with guns almost overwhelmed her. It brought the unwanted memory of her kidnappers to her mind, and she regretted asking Gerald to share his experience.

He continued as if uninterrupted.

"I had my machine gun. I could have gunned down all my fellow soldiers, to protect the innocent. I could have at least threatened them to leave the man and his family alone and let you all go back to your lives. I yelled at one of them to let your little girl go, I mean Helen, but they ignored me. At that moment, time stopped, as if the probe had only wanted to see my reaction."

"I knew what I was supposed to do, protect my fellow human beings, do whatever was required to make it right, but I did nothing, nothing substantial at least. I knew I had failed whatever test the alien had intended for me, and that's when I came back to my senses. If only I could have had a few minutes more, perhaps I would have found the courage to think of a plan. That's life though, no second chances."

He sat back on the couch and avoided eye contact with Sadi, staring at the glass. After an uncomfortable silence of about thirty seconds, he looked up.

"Do you think I would have found the courage to do the right thing? I usually avoid thinking about this, but sometimes I can't help but wonder."

Sadi had to think for a moment.

"Hindsight is always twenty-twenty, right? That was a tough spot to be in. Kind of makes me feel sorry for the soldiers put in that situation."

"Whenever I think about it, that's where my thoughts always lead. It makes me so angry, angry at the people pushing the game pieces around, never considering that those pieces have lives, thoughts, dreams, loved ones. It keeps me wanting what I've always wanted, to be free of it."

"Whenever you see Helen or me, are you reminded of it?" she asked and tried to empathize with him. "My God, how you must hate seeing us!"

"It's funny," he said, and his smile returned, "but it's actually a relief to see you, especially Helen. Putting her to bed, safe and sound has been therapeutic."

"Why do you suppose I was in your dream?" she asked.

"I don't know why the alien put all that in our heads. Like you said before, it was probably a test of some sort. You passed, and I failed."

"Don't be so hard on yourself," she said sincerely. "You did try to do something. That's more than most people. It takes more than one person to make a change. By protesting the crime you were being forced to commit, you took a stand. The probe or alien or whatever it is, maybe it wanted you just to feel what it would be like. It's not about failing or passing. Did you ever think of that?"

"Huh," he said, draining the last of the wine in his glass. "Maybe you're right."

She put her glass of wine down on the table and watched him process her words. While listening to his story, she felt the bond strengthen between them. She could feel a growing desire to sit closer to him, for physical contact. Gerald sat so close, the act would have been all too easy. Then she remembered Freddy and how she owed him her life.

"Thanks for telling me, but sorry it was painful," she said and stood. "I need to get to bed."

He looked up at her but remained seated. She noticed his glance at her neck and she knew what he was thinking. Her heart rate suddenly accelerated.

"I'm sorry if it scared you, but I guess it was good to get it out of my head."

"There was no reason for me to be scared," she said, thinking of nothing else to say.

He put his glass down on the table and ran his right hand through his hair.

"I'm tired too."

She hated herself for possibly hurting him, for leaving him alone when he wanted her to stay, but thoughts of Freddy being hurt filled her head. She could not hurt the one who had saved her. After saying good night and walking away, she could feel Gerald watch her go.

When she got to her room, Gerald's room, it reminded her of the look he'd given her from the couch and how she had enjoyed the thought of him wanting her, even if it had only been for a moment. After lying down, she realized that she'd forgotten to brush her teeth, but she felt too tired to rise. After a few minutes, sleep entirely consumed her.

—※—

At midnight, her eyes shot open in surprise at the image in her mind. In the vanishing memory of a dream, Freddy's face had hovered over her bed with his mouth moving in silent speech.

In her dream, the eyes were mirrors, just a reflection of herself. As the memory of the dream dissipated, she remembered when Gerald came to the hospital, how she had seen no sign of jealousy in Freddy's eyes. Her mind had been too preoccupied with other things to notice the lack of sadness there.

In the low light of the room, she decided to stand and step into the hallway to shake the memory of the dream, and perhaps check on the girls and get a drink of water. On her way through the living room, she noticed a lump on the couch and immediately recognized Gerald's unconscious form. He had fallen asleep with a book lying beside him.

His exposed shorts and t-shirt contrasted sharply with the suit and tie she was accustomed to seeing him wear. His blanket had fallen to the ground, so she bent over to pick it up and replace it over him, but she hesitated before putting it back in place. He stirred in his sleep, and the movement reminded her of all the times when she'd checked on the girls at night. By some strange impulse, she reached down and brushed hair from his forehead.

At her touch, his eyes slowly opened and for several seconds, he just looked at her. And then before Sadi could respond, he took her hand and pressed it against his forehead. He put his other hand on her shoulder and gently pulled her downward. Without protest, she let him.

FIFTY-SEVEN

Sadi

Sadi awoke to the sound of pounding on the front door. In a panic, she turned in bed to find the other half unoccupied. Conflicting memories and emotions of their midnight encounter evaporated as another fist slammed against the door. She heard muffled voices from men standing outside and required less than a second to realize who they were coming to take.

The same horribly familiar questions raced through her head. *How did they find me? What happened to Gerald? What happened to Freddy? I need to reach the girls!*

She had to find Helen and Daryn and hide them. Helping herself was not on the checklist. She could lament the loss of her freedom later, once the girls were safe. Hopefully, Gerald could stall them, and she trusted that was the reason for his absence. As quickly and quietly as she could, she jumped out of bed and ran to the door. While listening for movement in the hallway, she heard soft footsteps, too soft for grown men.

She opened the door and saw Helen and Daryn walking down the hallway away from her room.

"Girls! Girls!" she whispered in a panic.

When they saw her, she put her finger to her mouth and spoke too quietly for them to hear.

"Come here."

"What's going on?" asked Helen after they ran to her. Daryn hung onto Helen's arm, and Sadi could see terror in their eyes.

Their fright made Sadi angry. Angry was good. She would rather be angry. Sadi pulled her nightgown more tightly around her. For the girls' sake, she attempted to look calm and confident.

"Let's go back to your room for a bit," she said as she rushed them back to the room next to hers. "Gerald's dealing with some guests, and when they leave, he can tell us what happened."

As they waited in their room, Sadi heard the front door open. Gerald spoke loudly enough for her to hear every word.

"Why are you pounding on my door at seven in the morning?"

Sadi could not understand the response from the other side of the front door.

"Quickly, get in the closet, behind the hanging clothes," Sadi demanded after she opened the door to their room. After stepping partly inside the closet with them, she made both girls sit on the ground and then put a blanket on top of them. "I don't want to hear you. No matter what? Got it? And no crying!"

"Are those the bad police again?" Daryn whispered through the blanket to Helen while Sadi arranged the blanket over them.

"No talking," Sadi said impatiently. "I don't know who they are, but just in case they're bad men, we need to be quiet. Gerald should be able to get rid of them, as long as they don't know we're here. Remember, be quiet, even if I leave the room."

As Sadi closed the door to the closet, she felt guilty for talking so impatiently to them but would apologize later. She quickly made the bed and scattered some books over it, in an attempt to make the room look as though no one had been in it for a long while.

During her brief rearrangement of the room, she heard the front door open and Gerald's voice mingling with the voices of at least two other men. They were talking too quietly for her to make out any words. After surveying the room and determining the deception as adequate, she joined the girls in the closet and closed the door.

"Be very quiet, okay? I'm going to be listening for signs of movement." She put her ear to the door and listened. Several seconds later, she heard the front door close rather loudly, then nothing but silence.

After listening in complete silence for about two minutes, Sadi began to wonder how much longer she could bear the growing tension or how long she could expect the girls to keep quiet. The longer she listened for any sound of another human, the more her imagination worked to fill the silence.

Her imagination began taking control. Was someone walking down the hallway? Did she just hear the door handle begin to turn? Were people in the room, listening for any sound from the closet?

Every second felt like a nightmare. Sadi's heart beat so fiercely she thought someone must be able to hear it through the door. Any second, one of the girls would cough or start crying, and they would be caught and hauled away like a bunch of stray dogs.

Sadi stood motionless for another two minutes. Then the girls started whispering.

"I don't hear anything, Miss Jacobsen."

"Are they still here?"

Sadi waited before responding, and when no one opened the door, she started breathing again. The sound of their tiny voices had given her courage.

"I'm going to go check," she said and slowly turned the door handle. "You two stay here and stay quiet!"

Hearing the girls speak helped Sadi distinguish between real noises and those from her imagination. When she peeked through the crack and into the room, she imagined seeing someone sitting on the bed but found the room empty. Out in the hall, she also saw no one and heard no noise either. Tentatively, she gained enough courage to walk toward the living room and the front door, all devoid of any other humans.

It only took a minute to search the entire house and conclude that she and the girls were all alone. The realization brought instant relief for her girls' safety, but fear for Gerald. Judging by the noises she heard and failed to hear, the men at the door had made no search of the house and had come to take Gerald.

Sadi searched the entire house for clues of what had happened. Gerald left no notes and nothing intentionally out of place. She found a pot of coffee brewing, but no cups had been filled, so she assumed he had just barely gotten out of bed when the people came to the door.

As she sat in the living room, with her last two possessions that mattered, she assessed her situation. All the events since meeting Gerald Foster seemed to lead to this moment. The entire time, she could only think of her problems, but now the group Gerald had assembled could be in danger. Surprisingly, the connection between herself and the group brought her some peace of mind and transformed her personal problems into the group's problems.

Sadi no longer felt alone. She needed to contact Cesar Sanchez and let everyone else know about the recent events. If they were after Gerald, they would eventually want the rest of the group.

Sadi planned to log onto Gerald's computer and send a message to the group, but she was unable to find Gerald's laptop. Had his kidnappers taken his laptop too? What could they learn from it?

She considered going to the neighbors but decided to wait for later in the day. That action might arouse suspicion and result in a phone call to the police. Mainly due to that possibility, she felt compelled to leave as soon as possible and try to find Cesar. She would leave Gerald's car in his garage and take Freddy's car.

As Sadi loaded the girls and all of their possessions into the car, she felt as though their refugee status would never end. She also had to finalize a new plan, solve the mystery of what had happened that morning, and tackle the encounter with Gerald in the middle of the night. The disturbing mixture of emotions, both amazing and horrible, became a concoction that only physical exertion could boil away. If she spent too much time sitting and driving, her emotional stew would cook her from the inside out.

To continue down a romantic path with Gerald, she needed sincere motivation with no interference from other issues. *Do I want Gerald, or do I see him as just an escape from the nightmare my life has become?* After driving away from his house, she decided one thing. If nothing horrible had happened to her, she would still have had feelings for him.

She would worry about that issue if she ever saw him again. Helen and Daryn needed their mother now.

PART IV

PROGRAMMING

Spiders build lovely webs
They weave and creep
And wait to suck some heads

FIFTY-EIGHT

Gerald

Gerald awoke twenty minutes after four AM and returned to his study to sleep for the remainder of the morning. Before leaving, he looked beside him on the bed, at Sadi who had fallen asleep next to him. He failed to think of any other experience in his entire life that could compare with what had happened just a few hours earlier.

At midnight, when Gerald opened his eyes to find Sadi standing over him, he stared at her in confusion and excitement and assumed her to be just a figment of his imagination. He often woke in the middle of the night after dreams involving Sadi Jacobsen. He only comprehended the reality of the situation when their hands touched. That moment tore him completely from sleep and made him feel more awake and alive than ever. He considered the possibility of letting go of her hand but at the last moment decided to pull her toward him and see if she would resist. He could always claim confusion or the influence of sleep.

Before it went too far, they had mutually decided to throw a figurative bucket of ice water over themselves. Sadi wanted to move slower and see how they felt in the morning, once she had more time to assimilate the situation. If their relationship accelerated, she wanted to prepare Helen and Daryn properly. They had too many traumatic experiences lately, and any other significant changes in their life might put them into shock.

Despite what his hormones were telling him, Gerald had agreed with her. He would be stupid to try and pressure her into taking their physical relationship too fast. Their initial slide down the passion slope had ended before falling off the cliff. Despite putting on the brakes, he felt like the luckiest guy in the world and would gladly let her take the helm. After getting control of themselves, they spent the next two hours talking and revealing their repressed feelings for each other.

After arising for the second and final time that morning, he found himself in a silent house with all of his guests still asleep. Before going to the kitchen, he peeked into his room and stared at the beautiful woman sleeping in his bed. After shutting the door again, he had to take a deep breath to convince himself of reality. He suddenly felt overwhelmed by what they had all experienced, but he looked forward to taking care of them.

While walking to the kitchen, he wondered what he could make for breakfast. Unfortunately, he only ever cooked for one and his usual diet of fiber cereal and butter toast seemed unfitting for two little girls. He hoped the eggs and bacon in his refrigerator had not expired, but before he could check their expiration date, he heard a knock at the door.

At first, Gerald was afraid for Sadi, but when the men on the other side of his door said they wanted to talk to a Gerald Foster, he knew they had come for him and might be unaware of Sadi and the girls. The men knocked so hard and vehemently, he feared they would break down the door and storm the house. If he opened the door, perhaps he could stall them and give Sadi enough time to awaken and hide somewhere. One of his visitors yelled his name, and Gerald replied just as loudly, hoping for Sadi to hear.

"Who are you? What do you want?"

After opening the door, he found three men on his front porch.

Two of the men in front wore suits, with the shorter of the two wearing dark sunglasses. Another man in soldier fatigues stood behind them with a face of stone. He held a machine gun and seemed to be looking for signs of resistance, perhaps even wanting some.

"Gerald Foster," the man in sunglasses said. He tapped one of his feet slowly as if to the beat of some music and seemed very anxious to get on with the business. "You need to come with us."

While the man was speaking, the taller one standing next to him stepped into the house, pulled Gerald's hands together roughly behind his back, and cuffed them. Legal instincts reminded Gerald not to resist a police arrest or to say much of anything, but he felt unprepared for this breach of his rights.

"What is your legal authority?" he asked as they clicked the handcuffs into place over his wrists.

"You'll understand everything soon enough."

Without saying anything further, the man who cuffed him pushed him gently but forcefully through the door and closed it softly. The soldier and taller man escorted him down his walkway toward the street with the shorter man following them, the man's hand on Gerald's back the whole way.

A dark blue SUV with its engine running waited for him on the street. Behind the tinted windows, Gerald could see another man in the driver's seat. The shorter man stepped quickly ahead of them. With a glance back at the house, up at the sky, and then up and down the street, he opened the back door, and the man behind him shoved Gerald inside then sat down next to him.

"We'll explain everything when in a more secure location," he said, "but for now, you need to keep quiet."

"I demand to know who you are and why you are breaking the law," Gerald said after the soldier opened the other passenger door and sat in the vehicle next to him. "You do know this is breaking the law, don't you? I am a citizen!"

Instead of answering or getting in the vehicle with Gerald, the spokesman of the three took out a phone and spoke loudly into it. He kept glancing in all directions, especially at the sky.

"Yes, we got him. Keep the sky clear and tell me if you see anything that you cannot positively identify."

No one spoke to Gerald until the man with sunglasses entered and the vehicle lurched forward, momentarily pinning Gerald's head to the back of the seat. In the front passenger seat, the man with the sunglasses turned to face Gerald.

"When national security is involved, usual protocols can be superseded."

"National security, what do you mean?"

Oh shit! This is not good.

While waiting for their answer, he took a deep breath and attempted to bring himself back under control. The implications of those two words sent chills down his spine. *National Security* shattered his initial assumption and his hope that they were from the FBI and had finally invented some excuse to arrest him. The FBI was angry that he had successfully eluded their previous attempt to indict him. Since then, they had been trying to come up with something else.

These men came from the military, at least the soldiers did. That implied one thing. They might have discovered the activities of his friends. He hoped they had different suspicions, but he failed to think of any likely alternatives.

"We know about you and your friends, Mr. Foster," he said as if reading his thoughts. Gerald could see his reflection in the mirrored sunglasses.

"What friends?" Gerald asked as if confused. "What are you talking about?"

"I am not authorized to share any details with you," he said and sounded disappointed, "or attempt to interrogate you. Our job is to acquire and deliver. You are free to talk. That is up to you."

"All right," Gerald answered and decided against asking any other questions. Since they intended to keep him ignorant, speaking seemed a waste of time. The man waited a moment, to see if Gerald would continue, then turned back to face the direction of the vehicle.

After leaving his neighborhood and entering the freeway, they rode in silence through traffic. Gerald noticed a tension in the air from the men with him as if something other than capturing him concerned them. He remembered the phone call from front-seat man and wondered why he mentioned identifying something in the air. Their tension seemed like a bad omen.

The journey from his house to the vehicle had happened too fast and gave Gerald no time to assimilate his situation. With his hands uncomfortably cuffed behind his back, he took a moment to get more comfortable while at the same time inspecting his abductors.

Four men accompanied him in the car, one on either side of him and two in the front seats. Both soldiers, the one sitting to his left and the one driving the vehicle, wore camouflage hats so that Gerald could only distinguish them by their faces. Over the headrest in front of him, Gerald could see the man's short blond hair sticking straight out from his head and the possible beginning of a receding hairline. He looked like a shorter version of the singer, Sting. The taller man sitting on his left had the same short hairstyle but thick dark hair.

After a few minutes of driving, he finally found a position for his hands to be the most comfortable behind his back. He fought to control his odd mixture of feelings, anger for losing his freedom, curiosity about his destination, and relief for Sadi's safety. For the moment, he had successfully avoided fear. His usual positive attitude helped him imagine only happy endings to his present condition.

If they knew of Sadi's presence, they had intentionally ignored her. They seemed like the type of people who would be aware of all the occupants of a house before attempting to abduct one of them. They had probably assumed a mother with two small girls would avoid attempting to interfere with armed men.

For the present, they seemed to have no interest in Sadi, but after finishing with him, she might also become a target. If at all possible, he needed to divert their investigation away from his friends, especially her. He focused on that goal and avoided darker thoughts.

Gerald hoped Sadi would be able to tell Cesar what had happened, and then he could tell the rest of the group. He did not want to accept the possibility that Cesar or any of the others were also taken.

His thoughts kept returning to the same questions. Had either of their inventions been discovered or had they merely connected him with the two space flights? Did they only know of the test flight or Freddy's journey to Mercury? If the latter, Freddy would probably be the other target, but he failed to imagine that they would be successful in capturing him. That gave him hope.

He knew two things for certain. They would interrogate him, and he should not accept anything they told him as the complete truth. He knew the game. They would twist the truth to manipulate him. Even though he took some comfort in knowing their tactics, he also knew they had the means to extract information from him, and he only hoped to give the others time to avoid capture.

Gerald's thoughts drifted from his encounter with Sadi in the night to Freddy and his experience with the alien, and then to the other planet. The military must have spotted Freddy on some radar and then traced it back to Gerald. Would the alien help them, he wondered. Unless he saw evidence to the contrary, he would assume the alien did not intend for the military to squash them. There had to be some greater plan. If not the alien, then Freddy might be able to help the situation, but his extrasensory abilities seemed useless against the military. Gerald wished he would have talked with Freddy more. He thought there would be more time.

"Never procrastinate anything important," he whispered to himself, shaking his head with frustration.

Gerald knew his way around the Seattle area, so he was able to easily trace their path. With each turn they made, his mind provided a possible destination. He felt as though he was watching a movie, always trying to predict the next turn of the plot. He rarely watched movies. They were too predictable.

They drove west, and Gerald imagined being taken to some open field, shot, and left for dead with a suicide note in his hand. Would he be forgotten?

Once out of the city, they turned into a private airport he did not know existed. After parking, the man with sunglasses turned and looked at Gerald with an expression of resignation, as if dreading the next course of action.

"Here's where it gets a bit complicated," he said, looking at his watch. He pressed a couple of buttons, accompanied by beeps.

Gerald's heart began beating faster.

"I'm sorry if this sounds too cliché," the man said, "but here's what's going to happen. You get to decide on the level of difficulty."

"Ha," Gerald grunted. "I don't seem to have any choices. You're the ones who abducted me. Remember?"

"True," he said, raising his eyebrows. Gerald could see that his words had made no impact.

The man on Gerald's left removed a syringe from the side of his seat, and Gerald stared at the needle as if the man held a gun to his face. Gerald imagined himself struggling and eventually overpowered by the men around him.

If they were going to kill him through injection, he would rather die fighting, not allow himself to be led willingly like a cow to the slaughterhouse. After a moment, his fears quickly subsided. Maybe he could stall.

"What is it?" he asked as calmly as possible.

"Vitamins," the man said with a smile. "They will help you feel less anxiety. We don't want to make an embarrassing scene, do we?"

A scene in the car, or out? The answer seemed irrelevant.

"Whatever you want," he said in resignation.

He sounded pathetic. These men had complete power over his body and soon might have complete power over his mind. Would he have felt like this when the German stormtroopers came to his door and said to get in the wagon?

"Wise decision."

The man on his left injected him with the clear solution, and Gerald closed his eyes in anticipation of a painful reaction. After a few seconds, his head began to feel lighter and seemed to pull his body up into the air. He suddenly felt silly with his eyes closed and opened them to see the men looking at him strangely. The tension of the morning dissipated like steam. He took a deep breath and smiled.

"These guys aren't that bad," he said quietly. "Sadi and the girls are safe, what else matters?"

The man put his syringe away and placed a large pair of headphones over Gerald's head, completely covering his ears and muffling the noise of the car. When the man energized a digital music player, voices began speaking to him, and the noise helped him forget about everything.

Gerald struggled to understand the content of the recording. A pleasant yet complex Beethoven piano concerto played in the background, continually breaking his concentration and preventing him from connecting the words into anything meaningful. He understood each word individually, just not what they meant strung together. After two minutes of listening, he was finally able to distinguish the voices as a dialogue between two participants, an older woman and a younger man around his age. He felt an unexpected burst of pride when he finally understood what was happening. When the conversation ended, he wanted to hear it again and discover the overall meaning.

The man with the sunglasses exited the car, and the rest of the men waited inside with Gerald. He took out his phone and started talking into it. Gerald could not hear what was said, but he only cared about listening to his headphones, to the conversation between the man and the older woman.

They all waited for several minutes until Sunglass Man outside had finished with his phone call. After everyone had finally gotten out of the car and made it onto the tarmac, Gerald's handcuffs were removed. The men seemed more relaxed and began treating him as they would a child. As they escorted Gerald, he saw three other men waiting at a mid-sized plane. Two of them wore military fatigues and the other one dressed in a suit. Gerald could see them talking, and he thought the action looked like chewing food. It made him hungry and want to laugh.

The sight of the plane mesmerized him. Waves of heat rising off its surface gave the appearance of the aircraft shimmering in and out of existence, partly in this world and partly in the next, and both at the same time. By tilting his head and view, he could make the whole plane twist and contort. He hoped the aircraft would remain an aircraft after he boarded it.

Before they reached the plane, one of the army guys standing next to it approached and greeted them with a polite smile, but Gerald could not hear what they said. The large pistol hanging from the soldier's hip seemed to be looking at Gerald, threatening him. He stared at it, eyes wide.

Gerald wanted to say something, so he removed the earphones.

"Can I see your gun?" he asked the man and slowly reached for it.

The man looked at him with a strange smile but said nothing. The agent at his left took the earphones and placed them back over Gerald's head. He spoke to Gerald politely, as he might speak to a child.

"Let's keep them on, okay?"

"All right," Gerald said indifferently, but he really just wanted to hold the gun.

Somehow, he blinked while staring at the gun, and then the next moment, he was walking up the stairs to the plane. After sitting comfortably in his seat, someone buckled his seatbelt for him. When the aircraft thrust into the sky, Gerald closed his eyes and enjoyed the acceleration.

Comfortably seated and free from distractions, he could finally put all his energy into listening to the voices. With his eyes closed, he soon forgot about the headphones, and the voices felt like they originated from inside his mind. He finally began to understand them. When the dialogue began again, the two participants—Peter and Dr. McGraw—felt like old friends.

—※—

Doctor McGraw: *Are you relaxed, Peter?*

Peter: *Yes.*

Doctor McGraw: *Good. Now listen to me carefully and do what I say. Will you try to do that?*

Peter: *Okay.*

Doctor McGraw: *Close your eyes and imagine yourself in the nightmare that frightened you so much as a child, the one about the witch.*

Peter: *I'm trying to forget it.*

Doctor McGraw: *How long have you been having it?*

Peter: *I don't remember a time when I did not have it.*

Doctor McGraw: *Tell me this, Peter: Can years pass between having this dream, but a previous occurrence feels like it was just a day ago?*

Peter: *Yes.*

Doctor McGraw: *That's common for recurring nightmares and many dreams in general.*

Peter: *What does it mean?*

Doctor McGraw: *Let's look into that. Now close your eyes and take me through the dream.*

Peter: *All right. I'm at my great-aunt's little house, but it's just me there. It always starts upstairs, and I'm eating some of her old candy.*

Doctor McGraw: *One of those great-aunts, I see.*

Peter: *Yeah, the kind with ice cream in the freezer from a previous decade.*

Doctor McGraw: *What do you do next?*

Peter: *I go to her basement.*

Doctor McGraw: *What is her basement like?*

Peter: *It was kind of cozy, with low light and her favorite things. She had lots of souvenirs from her trip to the Hawaiian Islands. I remember the hollow glass ball fisherman floats the most. I remember being fascinated by all the stuff when I was a kid.*

Doctor McGraw: *In your dream, does the basement frighten you?*

Peter: *No, but there's a small closet in it, and I'm terrified of that.*

Doctor McGraw: *What frightens you about the closet?*

Peter: *It goes down, kind of like a chute, to a place deep underground.*

At the bottom, there's a witch!

Doctor McGraw: *Let's backtrack a minute first. So her basement holds semi-pleasant but mysterious associations. Is that right?*

Peter: *Yes, I suppose so.*

Doctor McGraw: *And then the closet, it leads down to an even lower level, and that is what frightens you. How do you know there's a witch down there?*

Peter: *I just know it.*

Doctor McGraw: *And yet you claim never to have seen her?*

Peter: *Like I said, I don't remember ever seeing her, or hearing her.*

Doctor McGraw: *What is your definition of a witch? Don't think too hard. Tell me the first thing you think.*

Peter: *I suppose it is a bad woman who does magic.*

Doctor McGraw: *And what is your definition of magic?*

Peter: *I don't know. Maybe it's something that cannot be understood, a result of an action that cannot be understood or connected?*

Doctor McGraw: *Can you give me an example? I mean, if you are so afraid of what this witch can do, there must be something specific.*

Peter: *I don't know.*

Doctor McGraw: *That's not an acceptable answer. Take your time, until you figure it out.*

Peter: *I, well, I know she's not going to let me leave. She'll never let me leave, and I'll be stuck there forever with her! Maybe she's going to eat me!*

Doctor McGraw: *No need to cry, Peter. You're here with me, in my office. You are safe!*

Gerald loved the compassionate quality of the doctor's voice and how she really cared for her patient. He suddenly wanted to meet her someday.

Peter: *I know, I know. It's just that I want to stay in my great-aunt's basement, but I always go down the chute. It's like following an instinct. Going down the chute scares me so bad, I always wake up before going all the way down.*

Doctor McGraw: *Let me paraphrase what I am hearing. Tell me if*

I am correct.

Peter: *Okay.*

Doctor McGraw: *If you go down the chute, a witch is going to use her magic to prevent you from returning to your old life again, or you'll die, which is basically the same thing. You'll be in a new place forever, but you don't know what's going to happen after that. Am I correct so far?*

Peter: *Yes, I suppose so.*

Doctor McGraw: *See, you're beginning to feel better already. Here, have a tissue. It's not so scary once you walk through it with someone when you step back and learn how to analyze it. You feel better already, don't you?*

Peter: *So, I'm afraid of my life changing? But changing into what? Do you know?*

Doctor McGraw: *I think that's where the witch and her magic come in. By your own definition, her magic is something that cannot be understood, at least not by you. That's why there's a witch down there because only someone with magic can completely change your life. That's your question: What is going to happen to your life? You don't have to fear it.*

The conversation replayed over and over until Gerald had every word memorized. At the end of the conversation, Gerald got the impression that the doctor could solve all of Peter's problems. With her assistance, his healing would begin. When the recording started over again, Gerald listened more closely than the previous time he heard it. Maybe he would catch something new. The patient's experience seemed familiar.

FIFTY-NINE

Gerald

"**W**ake up, Gerald," someone said, gently shaking his shoulder. "Time to take a short drive."

While he slept, someone on the plane had removed Gerald's headphones, and he woke to feel the plane motionless. Intense white light streamed through the windows. Even with the headphones off, he could still hear Doctor McGraw's soothing voice, leading him through his fears. He wanted to listen to the recording again.

After opening his eyes, he noticed Sunglass Man standing over him. He squeezed Gerald's upper arm and pulled him to his feet. Gerald swayed for a moment until the blood delivered the necessary oxygen to his head and things came into focus. He felt as though he had just been awakened from a deep sleep. The effects of the drug had diminished slightly, but his perception of reality still felt strange.

"What happened to the headphones?" he said groggily. "I would really like to hear it again."

"If you're good, you can listen to it again, but first you need to come with us."

Sunglass Man accompanied Gerald in a Hummer, but the other two from his house that morning were replaced by the two soldiers from the airplane, one on his right and the other in the seats behind him. Sunglass Man drove with no one else in the front passenger seat. But on that ride, Gerald rode without handcuffs restraining him.

Gerald lifted his left wrist in the hopes of reading the time from his watch and then kept his arm in the air as he attempted to focus on the watch face. It read thirty-five minutes after six, but the time meant nothing to him. The movement of the hands seemed strange. The second hand on his watch seemed to be moving at twice the usual speed, and he held his hand in the air until the second hand spun around almost twice.

"Okay, that's good," said the soldier next to him and then pushed his hand down. Gerald looked over at him and noticed a small smile.

"Huh," Gerald said curiously. He tried to look at his watch again, but the soldier just pushed his hand down again on his lap. "I need to get a new watch. This one's broken."

"I want what he's on," said the soldier behind them, laughing. The soldier sitting next to Gerald chuckled.

Sunglass Man glanced back through the rear-view mirror with a strange look in his eyes, and the two men went silent. Gerald closed his eyes and took a deep breath. He liked that watch.

When Gerald opened his eyes again, he found himself on a small paved road lined with tall trees on both sides. The Hummer rolled to a stop at a small guardhouse and Gerald could hear the crunch of gravel through the open driver-side window. A gate on a single metal pole blocked their path with a soldier standing in the guardhouse, waiting for them. He looked serious, and Gerald noticed his pistol in a holster at his side. The gun stuck out from his body like an awkward appendage.

Sunglass Man exchanged some secret communication with the guard, and then the soldier turned to inspect all the passengers in the Hummer. Gerald failed to find interest in what the two men said to each other. He listened to the breeze outside and wondered if any wild animals lived in the forest around them. He liked the feeling of isolation from civilization and the sense of protection by United States military personnel.

After passing through the checkpoint, they drove about half a kilometer farther to a large mansion also surrounded by trees. The structure reminded Gerald of an old southern plantation from the movie, *Gone With the Wind*. Sunglass Man stopped the vehicle in a row of gravel parking spaces, directly in front of the building. A large covered porch extended along the entire front of the huge home and Gerald imagined people sitting in lounge chairs on that porch, drinking iced tea on a hot summer afternoon.

At the top of the wide entryway, stood three people, an older woman in the middle with a taller man and woman at each side. The woman on her right seemed slightly overweight or muscular and looked through squinted eyes at the approaching men as if she considered them all as a threat. The man on her right stood just a few centimeters taller than the woman and seemed even more intimidating. He held his weight like an elephant and looked how Gerald imagined an elephant would if it could smile before stomping someone to death.

Only the old woman had a warm and welcoming expression and reminded Gerald of a kind but stern grandmother. She seemed ready to embrace her grandchildren after a long absence from them. When Sunglass Man opened his door, the older woman started walking down the steps while the other two remained at the top.

Sunglass Man met the woman at the bottom of the stairs and greeted her with a polite smile. Gerald watched from the vehicle as she took a folded piece of paper from him and briefly read the contents. She put it in her pocket, and then he came back to the Hummer and opened the door for Gerald. The situation reminded Gerald of the first day of school.

"It's hot out here," Gerald said as the humid air unexpectedly enveloped him. He looked up at the sun just above the tree line and wanted to get back in the air-conditioned Hummer.

"It's nice and cool in the house," Sunglass Man said. "Follow me. I want you to meet Doctor McGraw."

"The one from the recording?" Gerald asked excitedly, failing to hide his emotions. Suddenly, the thought of entering the building seemed much less foreboding.

"That's the one," he answered, his lips stretched into a forced smile. "We're transferring you to her care."

"Where are you going?"

"I'll be around, don't worry."

The woman came up to Gerald and grabbed his shoulder.

"Mr. Foster," she began, and her voice instantly felt familiar to him. "It's good to meet you finally. How are you feeling?"

"Strange," he said in relief, feeling as though he could confide in her.

He turned to look back at the Hummer and saw the two soldiers stretching their legs from the car ride, and he suddenly realized how his legs also felt sore. Standing felt good, but he wobbled a bit.

"You should feel better once you get something in your stomach. I believe you have not eaten since this morning?"

"Yes, I am hungry," Gerald admitted.

"Come on then," she said, then grabbed his shoulder and turned him around, facing the house. She kept her hand on his shoulder the whole way up the stairs as if protecting him from the two imposing humans on either side of the entrance. When they entered the house, the cool and dry air brought instant relief from the heat of the summer sun.

Gerald walked into a huge room. A spiral staircase led upward at the far end and the space on either side was partitioned by office cubicles and an empty front desk. The two assistants followed behind at a close and quiet distance.

Doctor McGraw took him up the stairs and to a room she said would be his while he stayed at the institute. Just before shutting and locking the door, Gerald thought he saw her warm smile disappear.

—※—

Gerald's room reminded him of a moderately priced hotel. The locked doors and bars on the windows seemed to be the only restrictive aspects. Although a pleasant-looking room, the only accommodations were a queen bed, a simple wooden desk, and an old chair in front of the large window. Simple white curtains allowed diffuse light into the room, making the bars behind them easily distinguishable. An open door at the left of the window revealed a small bathroom.

He walked to the window and looked down at a big lawn in the back of the building with a paved path winding around a small pond in the center. The sun had fallen just below the tree line and cast a long shadow across the lawn. No human could be seen, and the view looked like an empty carnival ground.

Gerald paced back and forth several times, from the window to the door. Every time, he would stop at the door and listen for any noises outside. He heard faint sounds of movement far away, possibly on the ground level, but no voices. He went to the bed, sat down, then closed his eyes to focus on breathing. He wanted to feel different. He wanted to care again. A small voice in the back of his mind said he needed to feel normal.

Somehow, they had transformed his mind into clay and were molding that clay against his will, even without any resistance from him. He tried thinking about Sadi and the girls, but he had difficulty concentrating on anything other than his new surroundings, how he had arrived there, and how strange he felt. He could still hear the voices of Doctor McGraw and Peter from the recordings, and that offered the only comfort.

Peter's dream of entering the room with the evil witch, gave Gerald a new desire, a dark desire for the forbidden knowledge only the witch knew. When he finally understood Doctor McGraw's interpretation, the urge to enter that room and meet the witch was even stronger. She felt like a real person to him, and he imagined her speaking to him.

You need to wake up!

Gerald jolted awake when three quick knocks destroyed the silence. He jumped up in bed, his attention fixed to the door. The knocking was followed by the harsh click of the lock, and a short, slender man appeared in the doorway. The male assistant Gerald remembered from the entrance stood behind the new character, a tray of food in one hand and a glass of liquid in the other.

The man's dark brown hair was combed in perfectly straight lines, smooth and flat against his head. He looked at Gerald for a moment before entering the room. He wore slacks with a white shirt, no tie, and a lab coat. The assistant stayed in the hallway, barring the thought of any escape attempt.

"Mr. Foster," the man said as if calling out an attendance roll. "I am Doctor Hirsch and will be working with Doctor McGraw. Our first session will start tomorrow, promptly at seven. Is that understood? We've brought some food. I would advise you to eat and get a good sleep."

"I'm sorry," said Gerald, "but what's starting tomorrow?"

The man took a breath and failed to hide his impatience.

"We're going to talk about your life. Have a good night, Mr. Foster."

After Doctor Hirsch left, the assistant stood in the doorway, looking at Gerald as if he wanted to strangle him. When he walked into the room and set the tray on the desk, Gerald remained on the bed and watched.

"This ain't a motel," he said while shutting the door.

After the door shut and he heard the click of the lock, Gerald listened to the thud of his footsteps until the horrible sound vanished. His empty stomach gave him the strength to stand and walk to the table with the food—a glass of juice, pita bread filled with ham and cheese, and a banana. Usually, the scent of a banana would make him gag, but the smell triggered even more saliva production.

Gerald consumed the entire meal in about three minutes then stood and walked to the small sink in the bathroom. He found a toothbrush, toothpaste, and a small towel. While brushing his teeth, he began to feel faint. He quickly rinsed his mouth and then hurried back to the bed. Immediately after sitting, he looked down and saw the floor begin to move.

I shouldn't have drunk whatever was in that glass.

the floor begin to move.

I shouldn't have drunk whatever was in that glass.

SIXTY

Gerald

Gerald lay on his bed in the fetal position and listened to time flow past him like a river. A quiet swooshing sound seemed to dominate all of his senses. For the longest time, he felt as if he was floating on top of water under a dark sky, heading toward a possible waterfall. He remembered nothing while floating, neither his location nor how he got there.

After an eternity of floating, the river of time exploded into an intense white light, and the abrupt transition forced him to squeeze his eyes shut even further. When his eyes finally adjusted to the light, he slowly opened them to see human forms moving high above him as though he lay at the bottom of a whirlpool. He tried focusing on each of them individually but failed.

When he could see them more clearly, he noticed large claws attached to their outstretched appendages and instead of human faces, they had the faces of gargoyles, smiling and grinding their teeth. Gerald swatted their claws away from his face and yelled for them to leave him alone, but his actions only caused more anger.

After struggling with them for several seconds, they put a cloth over his eyes, and he somehow became unable to move his arms or legs. If he could just follow his instinct to curl into a ball and put his hands over his head, then maybe the sensation of spinning would end, which was almost as bad as the angry gargoyles poking him. When the gargoyles had finally departed, the world still spun around him.

After a long time of silence, Gerald began to hear the sound of people creeping around him, possibly crawling on their hands and knees. The soft noises drifted in and out of his awareness.

"Who's there? Where are you?" Gerald eventually asked, his voice rising to a scream. "I know you're there!"

There was no answer, but an even brighter light exploded into existence high above his head, burning like the sun and causing sweat to form on his forehead. He felt like a chicken strip in a deli display case. Occasionally, a cool breeze would brush his cheek and provide a fleeting moment of comfort.

The light and heat reminded him of the desert, and he remembered his recent experience in the high mountain desert of Utah. That experience somehow seemed different, but he could not think of the reason. Gerald had difficulty thinking of anything other than the miniature sun above his face. How had the gargoyles managed to place the sun above him?

After a while, the many noises surrounding him became more distinct, and he recognized the sounds of scorpions, large spiders, and snakes creeping in the dirt nearby. He wanted to open his eyes to see them, but the intense light kept his eyes shut tight. When the creatures came particularly close, he shrieked in panic and realized how his hands were bound, and he was unable to hit the creatures away.

"Get away from me!"

With his eyes still closed, he noticed a shadow glide across the haze of brightness. Other shadows began dancing across his vision and shifted his attention to the sky from the creatures on the ground with him. He imagined hawks soaring high over his head. They reminded him of clouds, shifting into different forms. The shadows transformed into birds of prey, alien spaceships, and military aircraft. When he eventually identified the pterodactyl flying overhead, he felt its eyes upon him.

He turned his head as though the action would prevent the creature's notice, but too late, the pterodactyl flew down to meet him on the ground.

"What are you doing on the ground?" the pterodactyl asked in a raspy voice.

"I don't know how I got here," Gerald replied. Although he felt afraid, talking to another intelligent creature was exciting and almost normal as if he had previously talked to flying dinosaurs. "I think demons kidnapped me and brought me here."

"I don't see anyone but you," the creature said curiously. "And I've been flying around for a long time."

"I think they left me here to be eaten by something like you."

"You do look rather tasty," the bird said, and Gerald heard the sound of a dry tongue licking a beak. "If I do get hungry and decide to eat you, I promise to do it quickly."

"That's very nice of you," Gerald said with relief. This bird seemed like a decent creature, even if it did intend to eat him.

"I won't spill a drop. That is a promise!"

"That's good because I wouldn't want to go to waste."

The flying reptile stopped talking. Gerald could still see the shadow next to him, but only the wind could be heard. Every moment, he thought, would be the end. If the creature kept its promise, at least his demise would be quick and efficient.

Suddenly, the shadow disappeared and so did thoughts of being eaten. From the distance, the wind brought new voices, sounds not present before. As Gerald listened, he watched the swirls of color through his closed eyelids. The colors and shapes went on forever. He never grew tired of watching them.

After a while, the shadow reappeared, accompanied by a second shadow.

"Why do you think you're here?" a new voice asked.

"I was trying to sleep and then—"

"That was not the question," the voice growled, "not *how did you get here*, but why are you here? Why did the demons take you to my desert? Do they want me to eat you? Are you poison?"

"I don't know why I'm here. Maybe you should just eat me and get it over with."

Gerald wondered how being consumed would feel, to become part of some other creature. Was this new creature another pterodactyl? The voice was different.

"Do you ever wonder what it would be like to fly like I do?"

"I have," he said, afraid of giving the wrong answer.

"But would you like to? I can show you unless you've been flying before. You haven't ever flown before, have you? Don't lie to me! This better not be a trick, because I will eat you if it is, and if you kill me, then I will be very angry and eat you again!"

"I swear," Gerald said. "I've only ever flown in airplanes, never on my own. I promise!"

"Not even on a spaceship?" The voice rose to a crescendo. "Do you promise?"

Gerald felt ready to cry, almost, then he remembered something and the fleeting memory made him stop. He remembered watching a girl he knew and another man ascending high into the atmosphere in a car.

That memory led to another, and then another, and then another. The memories were just images and made no emotional connection to him, until the last. When he thought of Sadi and their magical night together, the flow of memories crashed to a full stop. Nothing else mattered anymore.

In his mind, he returned to that night with her. The bird kept talking, but Gerald could only see Sadi's face hovering above him, swirling colors in the background.

—✳—

Gerald's transition from sleep to consciousness happened gradually, like the night brightening into day. When he briefly opened his eyes, he saw only a diffuse grey light. He attempted to go back to sleep, but the cold hard surface of a metal bed under his back prevented him from finding any comfort.

He lay there for several minutes before discovering his freedom of movement. He could move his arms, legs, and head. After sitting up and allowing some time for the dizziness to dissipate, he could see his surroundings. He found himself in a cell, on a large metal bench in one corner. The room had no window or anything that opened to the outside world, only a grating in the ceiling for airflow and a door with no handle. In one of the corners above the door, he saw a black glass eye, probably a camera to spy on him.

He stood but required several minutes to gain his balance. When he felt ready to move, he took the three large steps necessary to reach the door with no handle. As he had expected, the door would not open.

"Where am I?" he asked in a whisper and tried to remember how he had arrived in his current situation. He expected no reply, but he needed to hear any kind of sound, and his voice would suffice. The physical sensation of talking reminded him of the difference between imagination and the real world. His first recovered memory came to him in a haze, something like being baked alive in an arid desert.

"Just a dream," he said to himself.

Was it a dream?

Slowly, his other recent memories began to return. He remembered being at home, looking at his bed, and seeing Sadi half-covered in his blankets. The memory of two little girls in his guest room made him smile, almost bringing tears to his eyes. Then he remembered hearing the knock on his front door.

The face of Sunglass Man appeared in his mind, then the memory of his ride to the private airport, and then the pathetic surrender of his sanity and will. The injection brought an end to his more recent memories. After that, his memories became fuzzy. He only remembered bits and pieces of the ride in the Hummer, the plane ride, and finally his entrance to the psychiatric hospital in the middle of a humid forest.

Several other thoughts came to his mind, actions he could have taken, but the absurd thoughts initiated a sarcastic smile. His mind usually searched for some way to blame himself for his unfortunate situation.

When he finished attempting to recall everything, he looked down at his clothing. Someone had replaced his clothes with a white hospital gown. Before looking at his wrist to see the time, he could already feel the absence of his watch. He looked at his wrist anyway just in case. He desperately wanted to know the time of day.

How long have I been gone? What else do they know? What did I tell them?

After injecting him, he could not distinguish between reality and hallucination. His fleeting memory of a pterodactyl seemed just as real as Doctor McGraw or Sunglass Man on his doorstep. His rational mind attempted to reassure him of the truth, but he lacked a hundred percent confidence in his ability to think rationally.

Have I ever been fully conscious and rational?

Did they have the ability to hide portions of his memory? It seemed likely. People could go under simple anesthesia and after regaining consciousness still be unable to remember the recovery experience. Gerald did not have to be a genius to follow that logic to the likely conclusion of what happened when intelligence agencies had years to perfect the art of chemical manipulation.

The public always heard about interrogation using language, intimidation, and even torture, but in reality, intelligence agents required only drugs and environmental control. The control system used the threat of violence for another purpose—to intimidate the public— a psychological manipulation to scare anyone who considered the concept of rebellion. When controllers needed real information, they used drugs.

Gerald had no idea how to control himself during states of less than one hundred percent consciousness. He could only trust himself not to betray his friends or their goals. Although he would never willingly betray them, he was human and could be manipulated and had to act carefully. They only needed to create an imaginary scenario where he felt the necessity to offer information to a trusted recipient.

"What is it with these damn lights?" he whispered, suddenly annoyed by the lights in the ceiling.

He wanted to yell for someone to notice him, feel his anger and frustration, but he stopped himself in fear of instigating an unplanned visit. He would be better able to recover with more time in isolation. For the next several minutes, Gerald held his hands over his eyes to receive some stimulating darkness. He felt as though he could sleep for hours, even on the cold metal bed.

After lying down on the bed again and closing his eyes, he tried to sleep, but the bright light kept sleep far away. The light indicated daytime, but his body clock told him it was midnight. He had no way of knowing which one was correct.

Even without sleep, he tried to relax on the hard metal surface and concentrate on pleasant memories. He spent the time thinking about Sadi and Freddy's travels in space. Gerald wished he could have gone to see the other world with him. Then he thought of his job and the clients who would be wondering about his absence.

Despite his effort to keep disturbing memories from appearing, they kept intruding on his thoughts. He remembered being locked in a dark dungeon with a giant talking spider, and how he kept his eyes closed for fear of seeing it. He remembered creatures with claws reaching for him and throwing him into a black hole.

With every passing minute, his state of hunger and thirst began consuming more and more of his thoughts. He knew the purpose of keeping him that way, to wear down his resistance so his mind could more easily be controlled. That might be a good sign, he supposed. Maybe it meant that they had not been successful at extracting all the information out of him. Or, they had already gotten what they wanted but needed to do more investigation for confirmation. If they had gained any contradicting information, then perhaps it meant that they had only tapped into his imagination and not his real memory.

Even in his frightening condition, he consciously chose to remain positive. They were playing a mental game, and he intended to win. Even if they achieved their goals, he would do his best and try to keep his dignity. He defined winning as never quitting.

He refused to accept the possibility that their group mission would fail. To Gerald, their accomplishments seemed to be evidence of their ultimate success. Everything had fallen into place so far, the alien, the money, the connections, everything except for his abduction and Sadi's troubles, but maybe even those could lead to some positive outcome. He had to believe that. He had faith in Freddy and Doroteo keeping the others out of trouble.

For the next two hours, his mind refused to think of anything other than food and drink. Eventually, he felt himself drifting in and out of consciousness. He could finally sleep again. But just before he fell asleep completely, the door opened and the soft creaking sound ripped the anticipated comfort from his grasp.

SIXTY-ONE

Gerald

With bleary eyes, Gerald looked up at his new doctor who was wearing a white lab coat. At first, he failed to recognize the man and thought of him as just a dream, a disturbing memory. Gerald blinked and rubbed his eyes, attempting to determine how much time had passed since they'd first met.

"It's time for your next session," the man said curtly.

"My next session?" Gerald asked groggily. "When was my last one? How long have I been here?"

He rubbed his eyes again to clear away the fuzziness and felt as though they had robbed him of something more important than his freedom—sleep. He noticed movement behind the doctor, and when he looked, a shadow retreated from his sight, a shadow with a face and one gigantic purple eye. Instant fear pulled Gerald to his feet and froze his blood.

"What's wrong?" asked the doctor.

Gerald blinked and shook his head. In the dimly lit hallway, only the large male assistant stood behind Doctor Hirsch.

"What's wrong?" Gerald asked himself. He had no idea.

After taking a moment to recover from fear, Gerald decided not to give them the satisfaction of seeing him suffer from hallucinations, hunger, or thirst.

"I am incarcerated illegally," he said weakly and with indignation. "That is the problem."

"Are we going to be a problem today?" the doctor asked in annoyance.

"Do I look like I'm in the position to be a problem?"

Even if he had his usual strength, Gerald knew the thug behind the doctor could easily subdue him. For as long as possible, he intended on utilizing his only remaining possession, his mental resistance. If they took that away, he would be left with nothing.

Hanging from the assistant's neck was a name tag, but Gerald felt uncomfortable looking at it long enough to read the man's name, so he decided to name him Big Boy. He seemed like the type of man who looked for an excuse for a confrontation, so Gerald also avoided looking into his eyes. Like a gorilla, eye contact probably indicated a challenge.

"I understand your frustration," said the doctor with no sense of compassion. "You're tired and hungry. After our session, we'll get you something to eat."

Doctor Hirsch and Big Boy escorted Gerald through a hallway with no windows to a larger room. The sterile atmosphere in the new room reminded Gerald of a mix between a hospital examination room and a police interrogation room. No windows or clocks lined the walls, nothing to indicate the time of day. A large metal desk sat near the back wall with metal chairs in front of it. An examination table, located in the corner, had straps and a harness for the head and reminded Gerald of an electric chair. Fortunately, he saw no electrical connections. Like everything else in the room, the shiny metal surfaces indicated sterility. Gerald could feel its intended psychological effect.

Never before in his life had he felt a stronger need to know the time, and neither the doctor nor Big Boy had a watch. From the lack of windows, he assumed they were on an underground floor of the building that he remembered entering sometime in the past. He had a vague impression of being in the same room before.

As the doctor set up his computer and adjusted the video camera behind him on the wall, Gerald sat in a chair across the table from him and attempted to get comfortable. When finished with his setup, the doctor nodded to Big Boy, and the man quietly left the room. Gerald felt anger welling up at the thought of being video recorded, but the doctor's first words snapped his attention back to the present.

"Why don't we begin with more of your history with Miss Evans," Doctor Hirsch began. "We previously established the origin of your friendship with her, but tell me more about your personal feelings for her."

The question came as such a surprise, Gerald had no idea how to answer. Did they really have a previous session together where he talked about his relationship with Taylor? His memory felt cut up and glued hastily back together, so the possibility seemed slightly larger than zero that it had actually happened. He also had to consider the possibility the doctor was trying to trick him into revealing information they wanted. He decided to answer and pretend to be unaware of the tactic.

"Are you asking if I feel any physical attraction to her?"

The question seemed like a harmless direction to take.

"Is that the first thing that comes to your mind, sexual attraction?"

"From the way you worded the question, yes that was my impression."

Gerald thought he understood Doctor Hirsch's tactic. He wanted Gerald to think that nothing could be hidden from him. As a lawyer, he knew this type of interrogation.

"Explain it to me then."

"She's a very pretty girl, so I cannot say there is no attraction, but that is not my prime motivation for being her friend."

What am I doing?

Gerald had broken his own advice. Clients must never answer any questions from officials without their lawyer present. That rule applied to lawyers as well.

"If Taylor were to show a sexual interest in you, how would you respond?"

"What has this got to do with anything?" Gerald said, failing to hide his anger. He had asked himself that question many times. The answer made him feel uncomfortable. "Why don't we start by talking about why I'm here?"

"I do not like repeating myself," the doctor said, staring directly into Gerald's eyes. He briefly broke eye contact to look at the computer screen.

"I know you say we've had a session previously, but enlighten me again please."

"It is my job to do a psychological evaluation of you. That is all."

"Can you tell me the purpose of my incarceration?"

"I am not authorized to discuss that with you, nor do I have the desire to do so."

"So what is your goal for this evaluation? What are you trying to show and what has Taylor got to do with it?"

"You seem to be forgetting who is doing the questioning here," the doctor snapped. "We can do this the hard way if you like. I can bring our large and unpleasant friend back into the room?"

Gerald remembered a similar question from the car ride when Sunglass Man threatened the same thing. This time Gerald would not capitulate so easily. The shame of his previous acquiescence prompted more resistance, but before giving his angry reply, he thought of an alternative tactic. He was not obligated to answer truthfully.

"All right," said Gerald in feigned subservience and with a glance at the wireless electric chair across the room to his right. "Let's continue where we left off."

"Now that you've had enough time to think about the answer," the doctor began again with an obvious hint of sarcasm. "How would you respond if Miss Taylor were to show sexual interest in you?"

The man's tone implied disbelief in whatever answer Gerald gave, so he decided to answer with the truth.

"I really don't know how I would respond, but I would be in shock. She's too high-strung for me."

Gerald smiled at the memory of his friend. He knew Taylor would never have a romantic interest in him. She had an intense interest in scientific investigation and would only be satisfied with a man with the same level of interest. She would only be satisfied by someone like herself.

"So you would be interested," Doctor Hirsch said as he typed on the computer. He kept notes on the computer and sometimes typed while talking, but he usually kept his gaze on Gerald.

So far, he still could not understand why they wanted an evaluation. If they planned to take him to court, their results would hardly be admissible testimony since they were illegally acquired. Maybe they were building a case for him being a danger to society so that they could remove him from it. He supposed they could just claim a connection to a terrorist plot. They would not need any substantial evidence against him, even with legal methods.

"Are you presently in any romantic relationship?"

He had to think quickly. If they knew about his relationship with Sadi and he lied, they might think he had some reason to protect her. He had to assume they already knew about Sadi. Most likely, they followed the same rule he did when cross-examining a witness in a courtroom: know the answer to every question you ask, beforehand.

"Not really," he said and stopped.

"So you're interested in someone, but this person might not be interested in you?"

"Yes."

"Where do you want this relationship to go? Marriage, companionship, or just sexual gratification?"

Doctor Hirsch's detached tone made Gerald angry. If asked for the identity of the woman he liked, he prepared to submit the name of an associate of a client.

"It's too early to tell."

"Is it important to you to choose a sexual partner who shares the same political views?"

"Politics can be a major source of contention in a relationship," said Gerald with some relief. "It's smart to avoid any kind of contention."

"So that's a yes," he said as he looked down at the keyboard.

"You have quite a history," the doctor said in a tone of interest. "Some might say you can be considered a political fanatic, an extremist even. Do you still share the views you had when you entered your profession?"

"Is it extremist to disagree with politicians and rich businessmen performing major crimes without prosecution?"

"So do you still feel that the Federal Reserve is one of the largest threats to the United States and that there is a big conspiracy to cover it up?"

"Define conspiracy?"

The doctor seemed shocked by the question, as though Gerald had asked why the sky was red. For the first time during the interview, the doctor had no immediate response. After a moment, he composed himself.

"I define this conspiracy as a group of people conspiring to conceal the Federal Reserve's secret purpose from the public...*that's* what I mean."

Gerald took a deep breath before responding.

"The government controls public education and children are never taught about the most powerful institution affecting the economy. Nothing is being concealed. No one has to hide anything. It's misrepresented, yes but no secret."

"So that's a yes..." More typing followed this statement. "How worried are you that the government is watching you?"

"I usually don't worry too much, unless they put a tracer on my car or a bug in my house," he said with as much sarcasm as he could generate. "Other than that, I don't worry."

"So you think they are spying on you specifically?"

"Not unless they're planting devices on everyone's cars."

Question after question followed in a never-ending stream, and the man usually confirmed them with an answer slightly different than the one given by Gerald. Mostly, the questions concerned the government and what Gerald thought of the government. Some questions seemed benign, and others felt like a trap to depict him as a paranoid conspiracy theorist. After a while, Gerald had difficulty thinking about the correct answer. His state of hunger and thirst kept interrupting his thoughts.

"So you say elected officials aren't really making the decisions but these ultra-intelligent bankers?" Doctor Hirsch continued. "Do you think they're abnormally more intelligent than typical humans?"

"Typical humans?" Gerald said in confusion and thought he detected a subtle change of tone. "What do you mean?"

"Well, to control such an immense system with so many different parties at stake, that would require a group of people with extraordinary capabilities, people with multi-generational plans. According to your own assessment, many of their plans have been in the works for a very long time, but from what we know of typical behavior, humans act in their own best immediate interest, which is on the order of a single lifetime in duration, much shorter than these world-domination plans you mentioned."

Gerald suspected the doctor of putting words in his mouth and twisting them in different directions. He did not remember talking about world domination.

"Are you suggesting they aren't human? Or are you suggesting that I'm saying that?"

"Is that a possibility, in your mind?"

"If they were aliens who lived very long lives, they would probably do things differently. They're exhibiting typical psychopathic behavior."

"So you believe in aliens, but you don't think they have anything to do with the government?"

"I have no reason to believe that aliens are part of the government. I never said that I did."

The doctor paused to turn his attention to the computer screen.

"Have you ever had any experiences that could be considered extraterrestrial in nature, or maybe just something you could not explain?"

The hairs on the back of Gerald's neck stood erect. *Is this what he's been building up to ask?*

"I've never had any contact with aliens."

"Why so certain?" Doctor Hirsch asked. "In several instances during our conversation, you refused to answer with such a definitive response. How do you know this with so much certainty?"

"I would have remembered an experience like that."

"Have you ever dreamed about aliens?"

Gerald paused with the pretense of attempting to remember.

"I seem to vaguely remember one."

"Was this recent?"

"No."

"What do you remember?"

Gerald attempted to remember the dream. Fabricating personal experiences required more energy than telling the truth, and he had little energy to spare.

"I was in an empty city, with no lights," he began, surprised at how clearly the memory returned. "Hiding from aliens that were looking for me, but they never did catch me. I don't remember seeing their faces, just their outlines in the moonlight."

"So they frightened you?"

"As a kid, the dream used to scare me more than it does now."

"If there were aliens visiting Earth, what would their intentions be, do you think? To frighten children?"

Gerald felt a sudden hope. Had the military detected the alien probe and knew his connection to it? Was that their primary concern? If so, the group and their activities could be safe. Perhaps they were really unaware of Sadi's presence when they came to get him. Otherwise, they would have gotten her too.

He suddenly remembered the government agents they encountered at the probe incident, and what Freddy had done to them. Had military psychiatrists been able to recover their memories? Did it mean Freddy and the alien were not as infallible as he had assumed? If military psychiatrists could break through alien mind control techniques, what else were they able to do?

Gerald realized how much he trusted the alien to be almost godlike, omniscient and benevolent. His experience at the barn seemed more like a spiritual experience with the divine, rather than with an alien or demonic force. Freddy's ability to recover Sadi's girls seemed as further evidence of the alien's benevolence.

On the other hand, the alien's involvement in the abduction could not be dismissed. The probability of it being a coincidence seemed ridiculous. Perhaps the alien was not as friendly as he had thought. The alien could have been capitalizing on Gerald's primal human instinct to believe in a higher power, an entity more intelligent than himself. Did his atheistic belief system trigger a subconscious search for God? Then the alien came to fill that need?

What had happened to Freddy on his trip? Did he really travel to another world or was that a lie? Can I trust him now?

Snap, snap, snap!

The sound of Doctor Hirsch's fingers ripped Gerald from his thoughts.

"We're almost done here," he said. "You'll get something to eat and drink, and then you can rest. Don't drift off. It'll just make this longer."

"Sorry," Gerald said. "I'm sorry that my exhaustion and hunger are interfering with what *you* want."

"So you think that if aliens visited Earth, they would be friendly. In what way?"

Did he answer the question already? If so, he could not remember how. He almost did not care anymore.

"I don't know. If aliens spent the time and energy to get here, they would be too intelligent to be barbarians. I mean, if they needed resources, the universe is full of them, and they would have access to far more than we do here on Earth."

"Is there evidence for your hypothesis?"

"I can't think of any, but I also think that if they were intelligent enough to get here in the first place, they'd have no need of humans. They'd have an energy source sufficient to fill all their needs. They wouldn't need us as slaves. We'd be just another species to study."

"You're talking about the popular expectations of alien purposes: human study, slavery, domination, a lust for Earth's resources. What do you think of the possibility that they hate us because of our potential for destruction?"

"Hmmm," he said, pausing to think. "Every sentient creature has the possibility for destruction."

"Yes, but human history would be evidence enough for any intelligent creature to convict us."

"You're speaking like a typical collectivist," Gerald said and then took a second to catch his breath. "Just because some group has done horrible things, doesn't mean that every individual member of that group is responsible, or capable of the same thing."

"Would that matter to an outside observer?" Dr. Hirsch asked calmly. "For example, consider a lion. Would you trust any lion as a pet for a child? Even if you fed it and trained it to be civilized?"

"No, of course not, but I think it's pretty well proven that lions cannot be domesticated."

"And you feel it is safe to condemn every individual lion because of the actions of the majority?"

Gerald wanted to talk about the absurdity of comparing sentient creatures to highly instinctive ones, but he took a moment to consider the consequence of continuing the argument. What did Gerald care if the doctor agreed with him or not? If he let the doctor think he'd won the debate, maybe he could get some food.

"Hmmm," Gerald said in a tone of capitulation as convincingly as he could. "I guess so. Then what?"

They spent the next ten minutes discussing what Gerald would do in an *end-of-the-world* scenario, what he would do to survive. Most of the questions involved extreme situations. Gerald began producing unemotional responses, and he thought the doctor sensed it. Finally, the doctor stopped at the end of a sentence and shook his head while typing.

"I think we're done for now." He moved the mouse and clicked once. A moment later the door opened. Big Boy stepped into the room.

"Done?" asked the big man.

"Yes," he said after logging off the computer. "Take Mr. Foster back to his room and get him something to eat."

Gerald looked at both men in confusion. The place where Gerald slept could hardly be called a room. A cell would more accurately fit the description.

SIXTY-TWO

Gerald

Gerald followed Big Boy back to his cell, attempting to act as inconspicuous as possible. After opening the door, the larger man pushed Gerald firmly inside as though he had refused to enter, invoking the image of livestock being herded into the slaughterhouse.

"Someone will be by in a bit," he said.

After the door closed, Gerald went to his metal bed, sat down, and wondered how long it would be before he could eat. For the next few seconds, he stared at the stainless steel toilet in the corner of the room. He imagined the pool of cold, clear water inside the bowl. How long before his thirst became strong enough for him to consider drinking from it? His throat felt so dry!

Twenty minutes later, Gerald was about to lie down to sleep, but then the door opened. When the older female doctor appeared, Gerald breathed a sigh of relief that it wasn't Big Boy. He attempted to remember her name, but the time he'd met her felt like a different lifetime.

"Mr. Foster," she said after shutting the door. She wore a lab coat and glasses, and her gray hair was pulled back in a bun behind her head. "I do so hate to see you this way, but it should all be over soon.

I brought you something to eat and drink. It's not much, I'm afraid, but it will do."

After inspecting her face briefly, his eyes attached themselves to the tray of food in her hands. With significant concentration, he gathered enough strength to thank her for the food.

She sat down on the bed next to him and put the tray of food between them. He grabbed the glass of water and poured it over his dry tongue, closing his eyes as the cool liquid slid down his throat. He bit one of his two pieces of toast in half and then drained it down with more water.

"I don't remember the last time I ate," he said before putting the other half of the toast in his mouth. "Does toast and eggs mean it's morning?"

"Just eat," she said, ignoring his question.

Even though he desperately wanted to know the time, he failed to find fault in her suggestion. But he finished his little meal in too short of a time. Before swallowing the last few drops of water, he swirled them on his tongue. As the water disappeared down his throat, he finally remembered her name.

Doctor McGraw turned toward him with an uncomfortable twist of her body. She turned completely with her back to the door, from the direction of the security camera. After removing her hand from her lab coat pocket, he noticed her holding something. Then she quickly shoved it into his hand.

"This is for later," she whispered. "Eat it while lying down, with your back to the door and no one will know I gave it to you."

He took the object and put it under his thigh. During the brief transaction, he noticed the identity of the item, a Snickers candy bar. Saliva instantly formed all around his tongue, but he had to wait until she left.

"After you have a little nap, we need to talk," she said after taking the tray.

She spoke in a tone of familiarity as though they knew each other, but he only vaguely remembered meeting her. The drugs they gave him must have severely damaged his memory. Maybe they had talked more in-depth already? He seemed to remember telling her about his dream with the witch in a basement.

"Are you going to tell me what I'm doing here?"

"I'll tell you what I can, but you need to tell me some things too. We're taking it easy on you, for now. It will be in everyone's best interests if you're honest with me."

He attempted to ask more, but she refused to say anything else. She cut the conversation to an abrupt end when she stood and turned to the door.

"Believe me," she said. "You'll need some sleep."

After she left, he lay on his side facing the wall and pulled the Snickers bar from under the blanket, at first just to look. For a few seconds, he stared at the wrapper as if in a trance. He felt like a bird hopping around a bit of cracker, making sure it would not bite him and gathering the courage to eat it.

He felt his eyelids becoming heavy but decided to obey his stomach and allow the saliva pooling in the sides of his mouth to accept the sweet gift. When he took the first bite of the candy bar, he could have died from the endorphins. *These should be illegal*, he thought.

After just a few minutes, he slipped into sleep and held the candy bar wrapper at his chest like a pillow or favorite teddy bear. In his dreams, Gerald wandered through endless parking lots of abandoned cars under a night sky. Huge spaceships and airplanes blocked the starlight, but instead of flying at great speeds and high altitudes, they floated like big balloons at a parade.

One of the spaceships had a bright spotlight sweeping the ground as if in a search for life. Gerald ran frantically from one locked car to the next in the hope of hiding inside one, but all the car doors were locked. While crouching between two SUVs, he heard a female voice barely louder than a whisper.

"Hey," the voice said. "Are you stupid or something? They're gonna find you."

Gerald searched for the source of the voice and eventually saw a manhole lid tilted up from the pavement several cars away. He recognized the faint outline of a small human face. The whites of her eyes appeared to be floating in the darkness of the hole. He looked at the spotlight in the opposite direction and decided to run toward her, crouching low.

The lid lifted higher and swallowed Gerald whole.

Under the concrete, Gerald climbed down a small ladder and found himself in a circular room with one tunnel leading off into the darkness. A group of about eight teenagers sat on a cement ledge surrounding the walls, their ages between eleven and fifteen, he guessed. Two of the teenagers held a small flickering candle, which shed only enough light to illuminate their faces. Most of the kids were talking to each other with hushed laughter.

The girl from the surface, a stocky fifteen-year-old with short brown hair, sat next to Gerald on the concrete ledge, looking at him curiously. Her eyes sparkled in the candlelight.

"What were you doing up there?" she asked curiously. "Don't you know it's not safe to go up top anymore, especially at night."

"I'm sorry," he said. "I forgot."

She continued to stare into his eyes, suspiciously.

"Is there anyone else up there with you?"

Before answering, he decided to keep the knowledge of his friends a secret. Sadi and her two little girls, Taylor, Cesar, and all the others who were hiding in the empty warehouse at the far end of the parking lot. Guilt swept over him again, guilt for abandoning them, but he had no memory of why he left them.

"No," he said finally. "I was by myself."

"It's okay. You can tell us," she said and held onto his arm. "We can help them."

"I'm alone," he said again, this time more forcefully, but before she could challenge him, he continued. "What are you all doing down here?"

The girl looked at her companions with a smile of fake embarrassment. One of them answered for her.

"We're rebelling," a boy said proudly with a chuckle. "Our parents think we're asleep. No tattling, Mister."

"Yeah," said another seriously, "or we'll throw you up top, and give you back to the creeps."

"This guy's lying," said a boy who appeared to be the youngest in the group. He sat on the other side of the girl who had rescued Gerald. They looked like brother and sister.

"Don't be rude! If he says he's alone, then he's alone," his sister said to the younger boy, then turned to face Gerald. "You wouldn't lie to us would you?"

"Listen," Gerald said. "I appreciate you helping me, but I gotta go. Is it okay if I have a quick look up top again?"

Everyone stopped talking to each other and turned to look at him. In the sudden silence, Gerald could hear his own breathing and his heartbeat and something else. The room seemed to have a heartbeat of its own.

Who are these kids?

"We risked our necks to let you down here," said another one.

"Where do you have to go?" asked another, nodding his head in the direction of the dark tunnel opening. "We can probably take you there, through the tunnels."

"Yeah, where do you have to go?"

Gerald turned to look into the darkness of the tunnel opening. The heartbeat seemed loudest from that direction. The thought of going into that darkness seemed more dangerous than returning to the surface and hiding from the spotlight.

All the kids were staring at him, waiting for an answer.

"Sorry, but that's my business," he said apologetically and stood on his feet. "I have to go up top again. I'll be careful."

The little boy tugged at his sister.

"He's got friends in the warehouse, and he doesn't want us to know."

All the kids started talking to each other again, too low for Gerald to hear any of the words. The combined hushed talking sounded like a beehive.

"How did you know that?" Gerald asked.

"He's pretty smart," his sister said.

"You can't fool Tommy," said another girl on the opposite side of the room. "What are you hiding, Mister?"

"There's a tunnel leading to the warehouse," the girl next to him said. "We'll take you there. You don't want to go up top, believe me."

"I'll just go take a look," Gerald said and stepped onto the ledge, preparing to ascend the ladder. Before Gerald could put his foot on the first rung, he felt a hand on his lower leg with a grip too strong for a teenage girl.

"That's too dangerous," the girl said sweetly. "We'll take you through the tunnels."

"Are you sure you know the way?" he asked and then returned to sitting on the cement ledge.

"We know these tunnels like the back of our hands," two girls and a boy said simultaneously.

"Jinx, you owe me a soda!" they all repeated in unison, laughing hysterically.

Gerald laughed nervously with them. Before responding, he noticed the thumping noise from the tunnel getting louder.

"What's that noise?" he asked, trying to sound as unconcerned as possible.

"What noise?" replied one of the boys who nudged the girl next to him. "Scarlett, do you hear anything?"

"I don't hear anything," she replied and laughed. All the kids started laughing again, louder this time. The sound from the tunnel grew louder, and then one of the candles died. The single remaining candle hardly cast enough light to see two kids away from him.

A moment later, the single candle suddenly became two candles, one in the kid's hand and one on the floor, a reflection in the pool of water gathering there. He stood up and picked up one of his feet. Water dripped off his foot and splashed loudly in the growing pool below him.

More laughter erupted from the kids. The last candle died, along with its dark reflection in the water.

"You're not afraid of the dark are you, big guy?"

The girl next to him clutched at his wrist with a grip like a clamp.

"We gotta get out of here," Gerald said in a panic as the water rose past his hips.

He expected the water to feel cold, but his senses contradicted his expectation, and his brain required a moment to recognize the heat. He managed to pull away from her grasp and scrambled for the ladder but failed to find it in the dark.

Suddenly, other hands grabbed him and pulled him down, so that only his head remained on top of the hot water. Gerald felt all the children around him, both above and under the water.

"Let go of me," he said before his head became submerged. The high temperature forced him to close his eyes.

Hands were all over him now, their sharp fingernails digging into his skin. He felt blood flowing from him, from all the piercing fingernails. The next sensation drove a panic through him, so overpowering that he lost conscious control of his body. He felt lips pressed against his wounds and tongues licking.

Pure adrenaline gave him the strength to spin and shake them all off his body. He punched, kicked, and elbowed the creatures away from him. He managed to climb the ladder to the top, pushed the heavy lid open, and slithered outside, water spilling out with him.

On hands and knees, Gerald crawled away from the hole, his eyes still shut from the heat. After reaching nine meters away from the hole, he wiped his eyes and finally opened them. As his vision returned, he attempted to find the hole. The lid lay to the side and water continued gushing out of the hole.

The girl who had rescued him emerged slowly from the water and then rested her head on her hands with her elbows on the ground and her body still submerged in the water. She looked relaxed and wore a sweet smile on her wet face. She licked red blood off her lips.

"You just can't trust anyone these days can you, Gerald!" she said and wiped wet hair from her young face. "Don't get caught in that light."

With a splash, she disappeared.

When Gerald looked up, he could see only the stars and a sliver of the moon, no planes or spaceships. In the distance, he saw the warehouse where his friends were located. If he decided to run, he could reach it in less than a minute, so Gerald took off. While running, the wind began drying his clothes and quickly restored his body temperature to normal. But no matter how long he ran, the building never appeared any closer.

After slowing to a walk, the breeze transformed into a whirlwind, swirling around him. Without looking to the sky, Gerald knew the wind came from a spaceship, but before he could search for it, a spotlight appeared in the distance, cutting through the darkness to meet him.

He started running again, weaving through the parked vehicles in the opposite direction of the warehouse. He could not lead the spaceship to his friends. Their hiding place needed to remain hidden.

Eventually, the light caught up to him, bathing him in a brilliant yellow. Instantly, his muscles stiffened, refusing to obey his command to continue running. The intense yellow light began transmitting a voice, sounding like several voices overlapping each other.

He listened but failed to recognize the language or any distinguishable words. The noise lasted for about ten seconds, then stopped and only the wind could be heard. When the same sequence of noises began again, he recognized the words as English but with a thick accent.

"Where are your friends, Gerry?" the voice asked again.

The words were spoken very slowly as if they caused pain to pronounce and then were followed by more silence, as if waiting for a response. No one ever called him Gerry, except his mother when scolding him, or when abused by a bully in the first few years of grade school. Several decades had passed since anyone had addressed him by that name. The name brought painful memories.

"Tyelll awssss oowhere eeyourr efreindsss arrrrrrr," it said, slowly enunciating each word. He could barely decipher them.

Gerald knew that if he chose to keep the information secret, something terrible would happen. Unconsciously, he thought of the warehouse, where his friends were, two hundred meters behind him. For some reason, he knew the creatures in the spaceship had heard his thoughts. The yellow light quickly shot toward the warehouse, and he felt immediate control over his body again. In horror, he watched as the spotlight reached the warehouse.

A sudden shaking of the earth violently tore his view from the warehouse and the doom of his friends, to the ground. Gerald fell on his butt, and a crack appeared directly beneath his legs. As the crack in the asphalt widened, he held onto the edge. He might have been able to climb back to the surface, if not for the black Hummer rolling down the steep incline toward him.

Gerald let go of the ledge just before the Hummer's immense tires crushed him. As he fell, his view of the sky shrunk until it disappeared completely. He felt as though he was falling down a tunnel.

While falling in the darkness, Gerald waited for the horrible moment of ultimate impact and the end of his terror. After a time, the blackness completely enveloped him, and he could no longer see the falling vehicle above him. But even without seeing it, he imagined its immense weight as an angry Nordic God ready to smash his body with a hammer when he reached the bottom. He prayed for the end to come soon, but the Nordic God refused to answer his prayer.

—※—

Without warning, he landed gently on a soft bed in a room of dim light, his head coming to rest on a fluffy white pillow. Instinctively, he extended his hands as a shield for the Hummer which was about to crash onto him.

When Gerald gained the courage to open his eyes, he found himself alone in a quiet room. A small lamp sat on a desk by a window, casting its soft light onto white curtains. Dark shadows across the room reminded Gerald of a black and white photograph. No light seemed to escape through the white window curtains.

Gerald recognized the room as the first one given to him after he arrived at the psychiatric hospital. As he lay there, he assessed his mental condition. His memories seemed intact. He remembered his last conversation with Doctor McGraw and even the taste of the Snickers candy bar on his tongue. The last meal had rescued him from starvation but not his appetite. At least some of his strength had returned.

Did they put some drugs in the Snickers?

He wanted to sleep again, but the black shadows on the walls looked strange and kept him from closing his eyes. The room felt different, and he wanted to know the reason. He also did not want to dream about that place again, where he ran from spotlights and demon children. With considerable effort, he arose from the bed and walked to the desk with the lamp.

He looked up from the desk at the windows. The white lace curtains seemed too still. He extended his shaking hand to pull the curtains open and stopped breathing at what he saw behind them, a wall of dirt.

While staring at the dirt, the possibility of being buried alive soon became panic. Gerald rushed to the door but hesitated before turning the knob, afraid he would find dirt behind the door as well. When he tried to open the door, he found it locked from the outside.

"If this is the afterlife," he said to himself, taking a deep breath, "it's not so bad. Is this what you get after being crushed by a Hummer?"

Maybe if he returned to the bed and closed his eyes, he would fall asleep and wake in his former prison cell. He would much rather go to that smaller room than stay in his comfortable coffin, surrounded by dirt.

After lying on the bed and closing his eyes, the silence filled him as water in an empty cup. Nothing existed anymore. All troublesome thoughts ended and emotion drifted away. Physical sensations stopped. He finally felt at peace. Nothing remained of him, not even the memory of his friends.

SIXTY-THREE

Audrie

Audrie's plane descended through the low-hanging clouds covering Brasília, Brazil. When she left the New York air of the plane's interior, the humid local air washed over her like a warm wave. Even though her objectives involved unpleasant actions, she loved the feeling of being in a different place. On her way to the car rental area, she grabbed an iced tea in an airport café and closed her eyes while the liquid cooled the lining of her throat.

Before she continued on her journey to Salvador, Brazil, Audrie had arranged a meeting with an old friend from college, the finance minister of Brazil, someone with the resources to give her what she needed. Anselmo Neves had been one of her professors of economics, and he was also a distant cousin on her mother's side. She had two hours before her planned appointment.

Anselmo had offered to have someone get her, but she chose to drive herself. She had only been to Brasilia once and wanted to remember how to navigate in the Brazilian capital. She first drove to her destination, then took a sightseeing drive in the hopes of shaking the feeling of foreboding, which felt like smog from the city.

When she finally exited the car, the physical sensation of standing and using her legs became a sharp reminder of reality. After entering the sterile government offices, she noticed the secretary at a desk and a lone man sitting in the waiting area. He sat stiffly and briefly made eye contact with her. She smiled politely in response, but he looked away before showing any indication of seeing her. His short dark hair and lean appearance gave the impression of someone with a military background.

"He looks fun," Audrie whispered sarcastically to herself.

"Good morning, Miss Garner," the secretary to the finance minister said in confident but fractured English. "Minister Neves should visit with you in a few minutes."

While waiting, Audrie sat two chairs away from the man with the military haircut. The man sat so still, he looked like a robot waiting for its next command. *I hope he's not traveling with me to Salvador.* She suspected that he might.

When she entered the office and shut the door, the finance minister stood from his desk to greet Audrie with an unexpected, if unsurprising, bear hug. Although she had not seen him for over a year, she instantly remembered his thick hair, which had thinned a bit on top.

During her employment, she had become acquainted with several finance ministers but had only visited the Brazilian minister when they first appointed him. She had made an unnecessary excuse to visit him.

"Good to see you, my dear Audrie," he said with a smile. "I am very glad for a more personal visit with you. All this formality in my life is really wearing on me."

He spoke in perfect English and without an accent, just as she remembered in his lectures. She remembered watching recent video interviews of him in English and hearing him speak with a noticeable Portuguese accent to make him appear more Brazilian. The common people liked the concept of local cultures producing their own government officials, those untainted by foreign influences. Audrie only cared about the final product that the United States educational system produced.

"Sorry to inform you, sir," she began with fake formality and a sly smile, "but this is not a personal visit, as I would wish. As I mentioned in my letter, I have a favor to ask, but please don't tell me he's sitting out there in your waiting area. That man looks like a complete bore!"

The minister's smile broadened.

"Sorry, Audrie, but he's all the ABIN could spare at the moment. I'm afraid we don't have the same kind of unlimited budget you have in the States."

"I'm not saying I can't handle him," she said with a dramatic smile, then she changed to a more serious tone. "I just might need some diversion from my troubles. Maybe he can provide some form of entertainment during our time together."

"I doubt it," Anselmo answered and then returned to his desk. "He can provide whatever access you need from the local police department. Have a seat and visit with me for a bit. You don't have to go immediately do you?"

"I can spare some time, but I am in a hurry."

"Good, how's the family? How's work going? I hear you're pretty busy, what with the council and your official position."

They chatted for almost twenty minutes. She usually preferred more control of the conversation, but he showed genuine curiosity about her life and kept her talking about herself the entire time. When he finally asked about her brother, she failed to hide her irritation.

His eyes narrowed with a look of concern.

"Something wrong with Max?"

"Since you brought it up, he's the reason why I'm here."

"Ahhh," he sat back, stretching his arms. He looked pleased with himself. "It always comes back to family doesn't it?"

"Sometimes," Audrie said reluctantly. Although she wanted to give him the satisfaction of agreement, she could not bring herself to agree completely. Audrie spent a lot of effort attempting to minimize her brother's influence in her life.

"So your brother's in trouble, and you want to rescue him somehow? Is he in Salvador?" When he said the name of the city, he reverted to his native accent but then switched back again.

"It might be worse than that," she said with mock concern. "I need to discover if there's any truth to his abuse of public funds before the authorities do. I might be able to do some damage control."

"For your father?" he asked with suspicion in his eyes.

"For the family," she answered and hoped he believed her decoy reason for the visit.

"I don't understand," he said. "So it's an investigation by someone outside your office?"

"I have friends who keep me informed," she said and began to fear getting trapped in deeper and deeper questions. She had only prepared a limited, superficial web of lies. "I don't like to be caught by surprise and neither does my father."

He looked at her with a wide smile.

"Okay, if that's your story."

"That's the situation," she said with finality.

"I guess your high-security clearance has some advantages," he said and shook his head with a short laugh. "The improper use of public funds sounds like something I need to investigate."

She smiled seriously.

"The funds are not local. Don't worry. I would tell you if it were otherwise."

"I'm sure you would," he said. "Just be careful down in Salvador. I really don't know much about your escort, Lasar's his name, but he's the one they sent, per my request. Don't get yourself in anything too deep. I may not be able to be involved, officially. I wish we could talk further, but I have an appointment and need to prepare."

"I understand," Audrie said with some regret about coming to the end of her visit. "Thanks for your help!"

When she left his office, he gave her another bear hug. She felt like a kid again. Half of her enjoyed the sensation, but the other half wanted to get away on her own again and re-establish her non-huggable identity.

When out of the finance minister's office, she took a few steps, stopped, and stared at the man named Lasar, the one who would escort her to Salvador. He appeared to be in the same position as when she saw him earlier. After a moment, he looked up into her eyes, and his mouth instantly widened into a polite but fake smile.

"Are you ready to go, Miss Garner?" He stood and extended his hand. "I am Lasar."

When he took her hand, she had to hold back a grimace at his intense grip. *Is he attempting to impress me with his strength?* In her peripheral vision, she noticed the secretary watching but pretending disinterest.

On their flight, Lasar made only a few comments and asked no questions about their purpose. He either had no real interest in his assignment, or he knew the expectation—do the job without asking questions—or both. To catch everything he said, behind his thick accent, Audrie had to look directly at his face and try to ignore all other noises. She remembered the finance minister saying they had less abundant security resources than she might have expected. If they were going to give her an agent escort, she at least expected a competent English speaker.

Are my expectations too high?

Only after their plane landed in Salvador two hours later did Lasar show any interest in their destination.

"Where do you want first?" he asked, and from the tone of his voice, he seemed perturbed.

"You're not here as my guide," she said with irritation at trying to comprehend his words. She spoke slowly so that he would understand. "I expect to need help from local law enforcement. That's how you are involved. I can find my own way."

He turned to her with a growing smile.

"Understand."

"Do you have any friends in Salvador?" she asked more politely. "We're going to a little airport just north of the city."

"I know the place," he answered but offered no other information.

While driving through the city, they followed the directions from the Garmin GPS unit mounted on the dash. The female voice from the unit grated on Audrie's nerves, but it broke the silence into more manageable bites. When they arrived in the vicinity of their destination, she feared the possibility of seeing her brother's employees on the street and possibly making eye contact. At least with sunglasses covering her eyes and her hair pulled into a ponytail, her identity would be difficult to determine.

After sleeping fitfully on the long plane ride, then meeting with her old professor, and then the other trip to Salvador, Audrie concentrated on staying focused and awake. Did she have the will to wait until the night for some sleep? She could not remember the last time she'd had less rest.

"You will arrive at your destination in 100 meters on the right," said the female voice of her GPS unit.

"Let's drive past it first and don't slow down," she said to Lasar while leaning forward to enhance her view.

As usual, he answered with silence. When they came into view of the building, Audrie could see no activity, just a small warehouse with some high windows. Only two cars sat in the lot, a new black Toyota sedan of some sort and an old red Nissan pickup. Audrie wondered if either one belonged to the people she had come so far to see.

Since Lasar was the surveillance professional, she decided to let him pick a good place to park the car and watch. He chose a spot with a good view, out of sight and far away. She would have parked closer, but they could see just fine with binoculars, so she decided not to complain.

While they sat watching the building and the other cars driving past them, Audrie reviewed the photographs of Mark, Yuri, and Taylor. The photograph of Taylor came from an old college newspaper article from 2007.

What does Max think of this girl? Does he have a sexual interest? Audrie had to consider that possibility. *Trust Max not to stick within his social circle!*

Another question presented itself for the first time. Had Max chosen Taylor for employment, or had Mark? She also wondered if Max even knew about her or the activities of Gerald Foster and his other friends. Could Mark be the cause of the interest in her brother? After all, he was Gerald Foster's friend. Maybe she could shift the investigation to Mark.

The photograph of Mark came from the company website, and Yuri's photograph came from his passport application file. She was confident that the photographs were still good depictions of the targets, although she had doubts about the photograph of Taylor.

"I want to find these people," Audrie said and then handed the pictures to Lasar. He looked at a couple of pictures before speaking.

"Who are these people?" he asked, stopping on the picture of Taylor.

"Employees of the company we're investigating," she said. "We need to see how they spend their day and where they live."

While they waited, Audrie attempted in vain to suppress her feelings of anxiety and restlessness. She hated wasting time. Sitting in a car, waiting for others seemed like the biggest waste of time. Maybe she should have let her PI do more of the work. She had so much work to do at her own job, she could not justify spending more than just a few days delving into her brother's predicaments.

But Audrie refused to accept the option of having another organization uncover her brother's secrets. That outcome left her with no control and truth mixed with lies. Control and power could only come with information. Unless she reached the finish line first, the truth might be buried along with everything else the military uncovered. Failure could lead to embarrassment for the family and disappointment from her father.

Actions set in motion by the government against Max could be halted.

SIXTY-FOUR

Taylor

Taylor thought she heard a noise from behind her in the jet, triggering a strong sense of déjà vu of Max's surprise visit many weeks earlier. Other than the vastly improved condition of the jet, it felt like the exact same situation was happening. She expected to see Max standing behind her, but she found the empty jet and felt a strange mixture of relief and disappointment.

She remembered closing the hangar door but leaving it unlocked, her usual practice. With the jet so close to completion, maybe she needed to act more cautiously. So far, she and Mark were never bothered by anyone. For a few seconds, she returned to work and attempted to shake the uncomfortable feeling. But when she heard footsteps from the hangar, she knew the noise of someone nearby had triggered her sense of warning.

After peeking around the edge of the newly installed stainless steel airlock door, she noticed a tall woman in some official uniform approaching the jet. She wore a baseball cap with some Portuguese writing on it, and her dark blond hair pulled back in a ponytail. The woman looked familiar, but Taylor could not determine the reason.

After exiting the jet, Taylor thought she saw the woman put something into her light purple shoulder bag, possibly a camera.

"Excuse me," Taylor said while descending the stairs. "This is a private hangar."

"I know," the woman said with some apology in her tone. "We like to make our inspections unannounced. Don't worry about being caught off guard. Everyone is."

She smiled warmly, probably intending to disarm the suspects.

Taylor jumped off the final step, then walked briskly toward the woman who was looking curiously at the jet, rather than Taylor. In an attempt to block her view, Taylor positioned herself between the stranger and the jet.

The woman tore her gaze away from the jet to look directly into Taylor's eyes. At the close proximity, the feeling of familiarity returned. The slightly taller woman reminded Taylor of someone, but she did not know who.

"What organization are you with?" Taylor asked.

In an exaggerated Portuguese accent, the woman said the name of her organization and then switched back to English. "The government department responsible for aviation safety," she explained. She reached into her bag and presented Taylor with an ID badge with her picture and unfamiliar Portuguese writing on it. In the title, Taylor recognized only one word, Aviação, which looked like the equivalent of aviation.

"You're here to do what inspection?" Taylor asked with raised eyebrows.

Taylor had no idea about the legitimacy of the visit but planned to make it difficult for the woman to get what she wanted. She and Mark talked only once about the possibility of being inspected by the government. Since they never registered a flight with their aircraft, Mark thought they were not required to contact the government aviation safety department. She focused on breathing slowly and deeply to help control her irritation.

"This is an airport, isn't it?" the woman asked and her smile remained steady, polite. "We need to determine the safety of all aircraft.

Will you please show me that you're up to date with your permits?"

"You're going to have to talk to my supervisor about that." Taylor took one small step closer to the woman, hoping to make her uncomfortable enough to step back in response. The woman remained motionless.

"Does that mean you don't have any permits?" The woman's smile transformed into one of concern. "Or are you refusing to show them to me? Failure to comply with my inspection will involve the authorities."

The woman's threatening tone put Taylor into a higher state of alert. Taylor almost liked the feeling. She worked better with more adrenaline in her blood.

"Here," Taylor said as she pulled a small spiral-bound notebook out of her pocket. She started writing Mark's cell number on it. "I can let you contact my supervisor, and he can get them for you when he returns."

"But you're supposed to have these permits with the aircraft, on the premises, at all times." The woman took a step backward, then stepped to the right and looked back at the jet. "Why don't you call your supervisor and he can tell you where they are, then you can get them for me."

Taylor would have to retrieve the phone from the jet. While away, the woman might take too close of a look and take pictures. Taylor needed to stay with her.

Something felt wrong. She looked at the woman carefully.

"Who can I call to confirm your authority?"

"I can call the police if you would like," she said sweetly. "They can confirm my identity."

The woman's patronizing tone felt like a blood pressure cuff, accentuating her heartbeat. Did she want to call the police? Taylor understood the reason for surprise inspections but not the reason for such rigidity. They were probably used to dealing with employees unaware of documentation requirements.

Usually, Taylor could sense a bluff and loved to expose it. But this woman's tone and body language indicated the opposite of a bluff, almost as if she hoped to perform the threatened action. With Taylor out of the way, her inspection would definitely be easier. In disappointment, Taylor bit her lip, attempting to act more compliant.

"Okay," she said with a patronizing tone of her own. "I'll call my supervisor."

Taylor considered asking the woman to wait outside while she retrieved her phone but knew the action would cause suspicion. She would also look stupid and weak to try and fail, so she turned and walked briskly back to the jet. After reaching the top of the stairs, she glanced back at the woman who began taking a few tentative steps toward one of the jet's wings. Her eyes seemed fixed on the engine and its modifications.

"Shit," Taylor cursed quietly once inside the jet. "This is not good."

Time slowed for the few seconds she had to think. After grabbing the cell phone from the cockpit where she left it, she focused on positive possibilities. She would contact Mark. He would give the woman what she wanted, then she would leave, and they would never see her again.

After exiting the jet, Taylor noticed the woman standing close to the engine and writing in her notebook. If she had come just a few weeks earlier, she would have seen each of the engines on the wings dismantled and on display. She suddenly felt lucky with the timing. With all the parts reassembled, they looked almost like standard aircraft turbines, to the untrained eye.

While descending the stairs, Taylor called Mark on her phone and waited for him to answer it. The woman looked up and smiled again. After the second ring, she began to worry. Mark always answered within three rings. After the fourth ring, she cut the connection and tried again but with the same result. When he saw both her calls and without a message, he would know to call back immediately.

"He should be calling me back any minute," Taylor said when she reached the woman. She expected to wait in silence, but the woman pointed toward the turbine.

"I certainly hope you have a permit for this modification," she said with obvious concern in her tone. "Is it some kind of new design you're working on?"

"My supervisor will be happy to explain everything to you," Taylor replied politely, enjoying the opportunity to be unhelpful.

"While we wait, I'd like to see the inside please," she replied, just as sweetly. The woman turned to walk around Taylor toward the stairs.

Taylor stepped in between the inspector and the stairs.

"I'd rather wait for my supervisor to get here."

The woman kept walking, her eyes on the jet, and stopped just before colliding with Taylor.

"Well then, I suppose we'll wait, but I would think you'd want to get this inspection done as quickly as possible."

Instead of answering the question, Taylor wanted to take control of the conversation.

"This inspection seems strange to me."

"How is it strange?"

"Well, aren't inspections done by more than one person, normally? It makes them appear more authentic."

The woman laughed.

"Are you suggesting that this is not an authentic inspection?"

"It's just that I'm not accustomed to taking everything at face value," Taylor replied, hoping that her belligerent attitude had an intimidating effect, rather than an offensive one.

"You may be comparing us to a government agency in the United States," the woman's tone retained the obvious amusement as if she often looked for opportunities to compare Brazil with the United States. "One person is more efficient. Don't you think?"

"I suppose," Taylor said, wondering why Mark failed to return her call. "Let me make that call again."

This time, Taylor made the call where she stood and felt a little awkward while his phone rang without an answer. "Looks like you'll have to come back later. My boss should have called back by now. Why don't you come back after lunch or you can call him and arrange a more agreeable time?"

The woman frowned and shook her head slightly.

"I'm afraid we need to complete the inspection at the time of arrival. You'll need to show me those permits, and let me look inside your aircraft."

Taylor took a deep breath before responding, her pulse rising in anger.

"Since I don't have the authority to let anyone in here, you'll either have to wait for my supervisor or make whatever call you need to make."

"I see," the woman said.

When they made eye contact, Taylor thought she saw amusement. Was she enjoying Taylor's uncomfortable predicament?

To avoid losing her temper, Taylor imagined holding a voodoo doll of the woman and holding it over hot coals, but the image helped only a little. The woman walked a few steps out of Taylor's audible range and talked quietly on her phone. Just a few minutes later, Taylor heard police sirens and a car stop just outside the hangar.

SIXTY-FIVE

Gerald

Gerald woke to the sound of someone turning the doorknob, but he pretended to be asleep. He opened his eyes when he felt the tapping on his shoulder.

"Gerald, it's me, Sadi! Gerald, it's Sadi! Gerald, it's Sadi, wake up. It's Sadi," she repeated his name in panic. "Oh my God! I thought you were dead. Get up, get up. We've got to get you out of here."

The lamp threw black shadows across the room, casting half of Sadi's face in darkness. If he had not already heard her voice and name, he would have had difficulty recognizing her. At first, Gerald's voice felt locked, as if he'd forgotten how to speak.

"Huh," he said, rubbing his eyes. "How did you get here?"

"There's no time," she said and then pulled him into an upright position. "Can you walk?"

"I think so," he said, standing from the bed. When he looked at her more closely, he noticed that she had shorter hair. "Where's the girls?"

"They're safe with Cesar," she said and then turned back to the open door. Shadows slid across her face like they were living creatures. "I can tell you everything once we get out of here."

She held onto Gerald's arm while leading him to the open door and into the dark hallway beyond. He followed her down the hallway, and his eyes required several seconds to adjust to the darker conditions.

"Where are the others?" he asked, but she moved ahead silently without looking back.

Following her relieved his burden of having to think for himself. Sadi could do the thinking. After turning the corner, they found the next hallway just as dark as the previous one. The only light came from a small window on top of each door. As they passed the rooms, Gerald wondered if they should stop to rescue the people in them, if any. Sadi moved quickly past them, giving him no time to consider the possibility. She stopped at a doorway with a picture of stairs next to it.

"We've got to take the stairs because the elevators are out," she said as she opened it for him.

"How are we going to get past everyone?" he asked, then imagined how Sadi must have gotten there. Freddy must have killed them all. The thought brought a shiver. "Are they dead?"

"They're not dead, just unconscious, but it won't last much longer. We've only got a few more minutes."

After ascending two flights of stairs, she stopped at the exit door and looked through the small window. When she turned, Gerald noticed the gas mask in her hand and the other one hanging at her hip. She handed it to him and put her gas mask over her face. How did he not see them before?

"You used gas?"

Without answering, Sadi opened the door and pulled him through, her hand wet with sweat. After placing the gas mask over his face, he could not ask her any more questions. Why had Sadi risked her own safety and her girls' future to rescue him? Doroteo, Cesar, or Freddy should have done it, not her. He could not imagine them letting Sadi take such a great risk, especially after her own horror story. Did something happen to them? Endless questions began filling the empty parts of his mind.

They moved through an office area and wove between several rows of cubicles. No one was in sight, and he heard no noise. As they walked, Gerald searched in vain for windows to let him view the outside, but he could see only bare cubicle walls.

They came to another door, and Sadi opened it without pausing. As they entered the main entrance of the facility, his memory of the place felt as though it existed only in a dream. The large open area represented another life, a life forever lost to him.

When Gerald noticed the darkness of night through the glass entrance door, he felt an immense rush of relief. Knowing the time of day filled a basic, psychological need. He felt as though he had been walking through mud in a cave with no light and then suddenly on dry ground, bright stars above him.

Before exiting, he noticed the only other humans on their journey through the facility, a woman lying across the front desk and Big Boy on the ground by the front door. When they had first entered the large open room, he had failed to notice them, but now he could not tear his eyes off them as if they were the only objects. How did he not see them?

"Good, they're still out," Sadi said.

Sadi let go of his hand and hurried to the front door. Gerald followed without encouragement. When he felt the humid and warm outside air, he breathed as deeply as he could.

"Oh my God," he said in amazement. "How did you pull this off, Sadi?"

"It wasn't just me," she said and took hold of his hand again. She led him down the stairs. "Doroteo did the hard part, but I insisted on being the one to get you."

His legs were terribly stiff, and he almost tripped going down the stairs.

"How long have I been here?"

"Never mind about that."

While Sadi helped Gerald descend the stairs, he noticed two regular cars and an army Humvee in the parking area but no sign of human life.

"Where's Doroteo?"

"He's out dealing with the guards," she said, leading him down the road. "Freddy used the Beamer to get in here, but the plan changed when the helicopter confronted us."

As they walked, Gerald attempted to accept her explanation. The story made sense, but he had difficulty believing how regular people could subjugate a military facility. But despite his doubts, the experience felt real, and he had to trust his instincts to go along with it. Sadi could explain all the details later.

His lack of exercise had left him in a weakened physical state, and the exertion of their quick pace was covering his entire body with a thin film of sweat. After walking down the road for a couple of minutes, Sadi took a sudden turn into the woods, and they stopped behind the thick trunk of an oak tree. They could not see the road from behind the tree.

"We'll wait here for Doroteo," she said. "Unless something else goes wrong."

Gerald noticed the higher humidity in the underbrush compared to that of the road. Small insects buzzed around his ears, and the absence of a breeze added only slightly to his discomfort. He enjoyed hearing all the sounds, annoying and pleasant, and listening to Sadi was the best prize of all.

She took one last glance around the tree trunk and then stood with her back against the bark. Before speaking, she sighed.

"I know you have a million questions, but I need to know some things first. All right?"

"All right."

"Did you tell them anything?" she asked quickly. "What do you remember? Doroteo said they had ways to get information out of you without you being aware of it."

"I have no memory telling them any damaging information."

"Doroteo said they could also hypnotically reprogram you, through drugs and psychological conditioning. I don't expect you to be aware of anything, but try to remember all that happened to you."

She looked directly into his eyes as if searching for some hidden secret. "They can plant unconscious triggers, like suicide, murder, and sabotage, set off by certain environmental conditions."

"I don't think they did anything like that," he said in an attempt to convince her of his mental health. "I've only been gone for a couple days, right? They can't reprogram people in that short of a time! Hypnosis only works on a very small percentage of the population."

She grabbed his shoulder.

"Gerald, you've been missing for over two weeks, and hypnosis can work on most people with the help of certain drugs."

"What?" he asked, shocked by the information.

"According to Doroteo and Cesar," she continued, "they've had plenty of time to program you. It could be something simple. You could wake up one night to get a glass of water, and on the way, you unconsciously stop at the medicine cabinet and swallow twenty pills. Escaping is not the end of the problem. Once we're clear, we need to erase whatever they did to you."

Sadi's words hit Gerald like slaps across the face, and a sudden paranoia took hold of him. He closed his eyes and took several deep breaths to calm himself.

With his eyes closed, random fragments of memory flickered through his conscious thoughts. He remembered moving the tip of a sharp knife slowly toward his eye and wondering how much pressure he could use before the blade plunged through his pupil. He remembered standing at the edge of a cliff with Freddy and wondering if the alien had given him the ability to fly. When the faces of Daryn and Helen appeared, he opened his eyes to stop the rest of the memory from playing.

Suddenly, his current situation seemed impossible. It was impossible!

"What if all this is just a ruse?" he whispered. "They might be watching us, waiting for us to lead them to the others. We could be doing just what they want us to do. We'll be leading them to the others! To your daughter and Daryn! Can't you see? There's no way you could have gotten me out of there like this!"

"Calm down, Gerald," she said, taking his arm. "Doroteo will be back to get us. He won't let us down, and no one is following us yet. You saw them with your own eyes. They're all back at the facility, unconscious."

Without her hand firmly holding onto his arm, Gerald would have started running through the forest like a madman, away from her so that they could escape. But despite his paranoia, Gerald chose to trust her and let her words comfort him.

Gerald concentrated on breathing and thinking about escaping successfully.

"What happened when they came to get me?" he asked. Talking felt better than letting his thoughts run wild. "I'm assuming you went to Cesar's house?"

"Shhh," she said, holding up a hand. "I think that's Doroteo approaching."

They listened to the sound of approaching wheels on gravel. As the vehicle came closer, he could hear the sound of rocks crunching into the road then the sound stopped just on the other side of the tree. A door opened.

While keeping her hand on his shoulder so that Gerald remained crouched on the ground, Sadi quietly rose to her feet then stepped around the tree and vanished from his sight. After a moment, he heard a familiar voice.

"Is that you, Sadi? It's Doroteo. The way is clear."

"Hi, Doroteo," Sadi answered a moment later then addressed her voice back toward the tree. "Gerald, it's safe to come out."

After leaving the safety of the trees and stepping onto the road, Gerald came face to face with Sadi and Doroteo. Before speaking, Doroteo grasped Gerald's shoulder and inspected him from head to foot.

"It's good to see you, my friend," he said in a thick Spanish accent. "You appear unbroken. Are you okay?"

"I'm better out in the fresh air again," Gerald said with a forced smile. The sight of Doroteo and Sadi together again made him feel a little better but not totally. He would feel better once they got past the guard post. "Sadi said you took care of the guard post. Can we go that way?"

Doroteo went to the dark SUV on the road next to them and held open the back door for Gerald.

"I'll explain on the way. We'll make it past the guard post, no problem, but we've got some driving to be totally clear."

"Freddy's waiting for us a few miles away," Doroteo said. "I don't know if Sadi told you or not, but we had some problems when a helicopter arrived."

"Yes, she told me," he said and entered the back seat. While readjusting his hospital gown to flow smoothly over his legs, he reviewed his journey from the room to the car. The entire escape sequence felt unreal, too fast. "I think I just need to sit down."

"Just try to relax while we drive," Doroteo said.

Sadi took the front passenger seat next to Doroteo, but Gerald wished she would have sat next to him. He wanted to talk to her, hold her hand. When they lurched forward, the sound of grinding gravel under the tires filled the silence. While Doroteo drove through the forest in the dark, Gerald felt like a child traveling with his parents. Maybe he should just follow their advice, so he closed his eyes and tried to relax. When the first tentacles of sleep started reaching toward him, he welcomed their cool embrace.

The sound of an opening door nudged Gerald from sleep but failed to wake him completely. He was only slightly aware of hands pulling him out of the vehicle and helping him into another one. During the transition, someone spoke to him, but the sound felt like a wind far away, and he just listened without response. Sadi's beautiful eyes burned in his lingering dream as twin blue suns.

The sensation of heavy thrust hit him like a rock, preventing blood from entering his brain. When his vision returned, he looked out the window and saw the dark Earth beneath him becoming farther and farther away.

"Where are we?" he asked.

"We already told you," Sadi said from the front passenger seat of the BMW, smiling at him as if he were a child. "Freddy's taking us to the hideout, the cave. Just try and relax."

"A cave," he said to himself and tried to determine what the word meant. He looked at the back of Freddy's seat in front of him, then out the window again. They flew a hundred meters above the trees and Gerald watched the sea of green branches flow below them. Far away, he saw lights from civilization.

"Freddy found a cave where we can be safe."

"The alien probe is there," Freddy said. "It will help you recover, reverse what they've done to your mind. Everything will be fine but be prepared for more acceleration. It'll be just a little while longer."

"How can we escape the military?" Gerald asked. "They've got satellites and those drones that fly at high altitude. They can see everything. They'll know where we're going."

"Close your eyes and try to relax," they said together, their voices blending in harmony.

"Freddy knows what he's doing. They won't see where we're going."

Their reassurance failed to comfort him, but instead of arguing, he closed his eyes and tried to relax. Sadi would not put her daughter or Daryn in jeopardy, so he chose to trust their escape plan, even if he felt uncertain about their success.

While Taylor's NMG engines quickly pulled the BMW through the air, sleep began pulling again on Gerald's senses. Explosions of color started filling his vision, and the light show put him into a trance, away from the surroundings of the spaceship and into the world of his imagination.

A sudden sensation of free-fall replaced his dreams and ripped Gerald from sleep, but he kept his eyes closed in fear of what he might see. Either they lost control of the vehicle, or they were descending fast on purpose. Since no one was screaming, he opened his eyes and turned to look through the window to see Earth rushing up to meet them.

The forest below them stretched as far as he could see, with no visible roads and only a few lights far off in the distance. While getting closer to the land, the steep hills became more apparent and seemed to grow as though alive.

The landscape reminded him of the hills in Kentucky and West Virginia, and the sight brought mixed emotions. He remembered passing through those states with his parents as they drove across the country to the East Coast. His father described the place as the home of the hillbillies.

Very quietly, Gerald started to sing the words of the song he remembered his father singing, some tune from a forgotten television show.

Come and listen to a story 'bout a man named Jed
Poor mountaineer, barely kept his family fed
"What was that Gerald?" asked Sadi from the front seat.
"Oh, nothing."

SIXTY-SIX

Gerald

Freddy maneuvered the vehicle so that it descended gently into the thick trees on the side of a large hill. Once they came under the dark canopy, Freddy energized the headlights, the bright lights momentarily overpowering Gerald's vision. The cave came into view when he could see again, a large hole in the steep hill.

They landed on the flattest ground available with the headlights illuminating the cave entrance from about twenty meters below it. The ground fell steeply behind the car. The headlights illuminated only the area in front of the car, making the appearance of being in a tunnel with the dark cave entrance as the exit.

Freddy extinguished the headlights and then used a bright flashlight to lead them on their short walk to the cave. While struggling through the undergrowth, an irrational fear of the unknown began to grow inside Gerald's mind. He stopped at the cave entrance and took a deep breath before following Sadi into it. Freddy walked behind them, shining the way forward.

They walked through a long and artificial tunnel sloping downward and the farther they walked, the brighter the tunnel ahead of them became. Freddy eventually turned off the flashlight, and they walked the last few meters before the artificial tunnel opened into an enormous natural cavern. The still air smelled damp, but the walls and ground appeared dry.

On the far wall before them, the alien probe was shining brightly. Gerald extended his hand to shield his eyes.

The probe hovered in the air between two stalactites, one large and one small. Several smaller stalactites extended from the wall between them but none as large as the one by the probe. The probe hovered so devoid of motion the cave appeared in motion around it. Just looking at it made Gerald feel dizzy, and he held onto Sadi to steady himself.

"We're safe here, Gerald," she said with a smile, then started leading him toward the probe. "In this place, you can relax."

Normally, a smile from Sadi would have blown away the darkest cloud over Gerald, but after seeing her smile, he shivered from the cold. Why did the cave suddenly feel so cold?

Without Sadi's firm grasp on his upper arm, he might have fallen and impaled himself on one of the stalagmites growing up from the floor. He tried in vain to keep his eyes focused and his balance steady. His vision remained blurry.

"It's so exciting!" she said, staring at the probe with wide eyes as they walked. "Another form of life on the other side of the probe!"

Since entering the tunnel, Gerald felt as if they were traveling to another dimension, with imaginary rock walls, air composed of time and a billion years of emptiness. He felt like a child entering a new world with Sadi and Freddy as his parents.

Sadi stopped him when they arrived below the shining probe. The alien object hovered directly above them, casting their shadows on the floor. When he looked up to see the probe more closely, it looked exactly as he remembered from the barn. It resembled a large bullet with strings of light extending from the open end and moving in the still air as if in an ocean current. After looking up, his dizziness intensified and he was suddenly exhausted.

"Look at the ground, Gerald," Sadi said, pulling firmly on his arm.

When he tore his eyes away from the beautiful light of the probe, he found a large slab of rock at his feet, extending from the ground. The massive stone slab had a smooth surface, contoured to the form of a human. The stone bed appeared to have grown out of the rock, like the other natural rock formations.

"Lie down," she said while sliding her hand across the rock. "I'll stay right beside you."

When Sadi stopped talking, complete silence filled the cave, and his head suddenly felt empty, ready to be filled. She helped him lie on the stone, and he shifted position until he fit the mold perfectly. Lying back became an instant cure for his vertigo, and his vision returned to normal. The tendrils of light from the probe shined as bright as the sun, but despite its intensity, the entire object remained in focus.

As he stared at the probe, he felt Sadi's reassuring hand on his arm, and then a slight vibration of the stone slab. Freddy suddenly appeared to his right, and Sadi looked at him. A silent communication passed between them.

"What's happening?" Gerald asked.

"Do you know what lies in the nucleus of a cell?" Freddy asked, finally looking down.

"The nucleus contains our genetic code," he answered, feeling like a child in grade school. "Our genetic code defines us."

"It is a container," Sadi said, gently wiping hair from his forehead. "For many, it is merely an empty container, but it can become a cage for creatures like you. Walls have been written into the code, to prevent your escape."

"Escape to where? How did walls get written into the code?"

Sadi put her index finger over his mouth.

"Our state is defined," she said quietly, "by what we believe, what we think is possible, and what we are willing to seek. Think of it more like a maze."

She removed her finger from his lips and turned to look at Freddy. He stared at the woman with an unreadable expression.

"Who are you?" Gerald asked them, keeping his focus on the probe.

She continued as if uninterrupted.

"Most humans like you spend all their time wandering in the center of the maze, always assuming they've seen everything, never seeking the exit or even knowing it exists. Fear keeps them in the center. Keeps them from—"

"Ascension," Gerald said as if reading mechanically from a script.

Religious definitions of ascension began filling his mind. Rising from the grave! Ascending into the sky with a horde of angels! Kneeling before the throne of a god!

Gerald had dismissed the idea of ascension as just another religious myth, but then he experienced a moment of doubt. *Was I misled?* Had religious organizations intentionally warped the concept to discourage people from seeking it, while the rest of humanity searched in the wrong places? The association with religion would cause instant rejection by those who despised religion, people like Gerald. He had always thought of himself as too intelligent for blatant trickery, but maybe the trick had more levels of subtlety.

"Your information environment can alter your thoughts and build traps," Freddy said after a long pause. "The damage can be dismantled consciously, but that will take too long. You don't have the time right now."

"What have they done?" he asked. "They've only interrogated me."

"They don't want you to remember the rest," Freddy answered. "They are putting a lot of effort into you, and not only to learn what you know. They're setting a trap for you and your friends!"

"You said that they are putting a lot of effort into me as if they're still doing it? You took me away from them, didn't you?"

In his peripheral vision, Gerald noticed something different. Sadi now had a glass vial in her hand, full of liquid.

"This will begin the restoration," she said and moved it very close to his lips. "All you have to do is swallow."

"Restoration of my genes?"

"Back to its original form," Sadi said, "what was originally intended. Think of this as a software patch. But you have to decide. We won't make that decision for you."

"Who are you?" he asked, feeling overwhelmed with information.

How could he trust anyone to reset his genetic code? *No code is flawless. What will I become?*

"We're here to help," the strange female said. She only resembled Sadi now.

"I choose not to drink it," Gerald answered with determination.

Her smile transformed into an expression Gerald had difficulty interpreting. Her mouth became a thin line, and her eyes opened wide. She pulled the vial away from his lips and looked at Freddy on the other side of the slab.

Gerald turned the probe again and noticed the light from the flowing strings beginning to diminish. The tendrils of light flowed back and forth and slowly disappeared as if they had never existed.

After all the light had vanished, Gerald felt utterly alone. He listened for the sound of breathing or movement from the two standing above him, but he heard nothing. The silence was as dense as the dark.

"Are you still there?" he asked.

He waited for several seconds. No answer. Impulsively, he extended his hand into the air, hoping for one of them to grasp it and remind him of their existence. After several seconds, he realized the cave was devoid of any other life form. But he did feel the presence of the probe, hovering somewhere above him in the darkness.

When he put his hands back down at his side on the stone slab, they fit like a glove, each finger resting in its own groove. He felt at peace again.

Am I still asleep in my cell?

Were Sadi and Freddy just a part of his imagination? What about the probe? His former life? What was real? Maybe he should stop thinking.

After spending several minutes just breathing, he felt air flow gently over his face, tickling his nose. Without understanding how, Gerald knew the probe hovered just above him.

Tiny strings reached out to him and gently brushed his skin. Each touch felt like a tiny shock, an electrical connection devoid of light or pain. Hundreds of strings were touching him simultaneously, and the electrical sensation quickly transformed into waves of dizziness.

The shock of the next experience put Gerald into a panic. The stone slab started to vibrate, and he began sinking into it. The rock suddenly felt like a thick fluid material and quickly covered his arms and legs. After just a few seconds, Gerald could not move. He remembered stories of men falling into cement and being trapped there. Right before the rock covered his face, he took his last breath.

In his world of darkness, he could not move or breathe. The liquid stone perfectly conformed to every part of him. He felt its touch most distinctly on his lips, ears, head, and neck, without pressure or pain. The rock even touched his closed eyelids and prevented him from opening his eyes.

He no longer felt the urge to breathe, so his panic stopped. The electrical treatment left him feeling numb. Other than the cool rock pressed against his skin, he felt no other sensation.

Was this the end?

Unexpectedly, he felt secure and untouchable. When explorers visited the cave in the future, they would be oblivious to his existence. He had become a part of the rock, encased in a new matrix.

The sudden eruption of heat from the rock all around him caused all of his remaining physical sensations to disappear into oblivion, along with his sense of time. He no longer felt connected to anything, not even the rock. The memory of his body, his physical location, and even his identity were lost, leaving him floating in an empty abyss.

A simulation of physical light suddenly appeared in the abyss, more dazzling and beautiful than his natural eyes had ever beheld. The light coalesced into a string, motionless and pulsating in a million different wavelengths. The path of light seemed to stretch forever, sometimes looping back on itself, sometimes heading in a single direction, sometimes spiraling. He soon found himself traveling along the path of light, and then he noticed the movement of another light.

The source of movement materialized in the form of a shining

moth with wings of bright blue, red, and yellow. Two fuzzy white an-
tennae stuck out of its white head and short hair covered its long
cylindrical body. Even the black of its obsidian eyes and feet shined
like a color of its own.

The moth flapped its beautiful wings and followed the path of
light in front of him. With each flap of its wings, glowing dust sprayed
in all directions like mist from a crashing wave. Every movement became an artistic masterpiece no artist could ever recreate. Gerald had
no other desire than to watch.

SIXTY-SEVEN

Audrie

When Audrie entered the hangar, she had a good feeling about what she would find. The jet in front of her seemed to hold the answers to all of her questions. If she could just look inside, she might be able to find the information she wanted. Audrie only needed to remove Taylor Evans from blocking her way. Just a few more minutes and she would be alone in the hangar, and the determined girl in front of her would be gone. She needed to focus on what she had to do and ignore the small guilt from thwarting her brother's activities.

Audrie had to consciously suppress her amusement of the girl's hopeless predicament. She had intentionally put Mark's little helper in an awkward position, waiting in vain for her boss to return a phone call while an angry government inspector threatened to call the police. If Taylor only knew the truth, her pretty face would lose that confident smile.

At that very moment, Taylor's supervisor was sitting in an interrogation cell at the local police station, waiting to be questioned by Lasar. Taylor would soon be joining them. Usually, Audrie would consider it cruel to find delight in causing another person's frustration, but in the end, she was inflicting no real harm.

"I certainly hope you have a permit for this modification," Audrie said, hiding her curiosity with fake concern for compliance with engine design code. For a moment, interest in the aircraft's engines replaced her desire to be rid of the girl. "Is it some kind of new design you're working on?"

From the few seconds she had to see, Audrie noticed something strange about the turbine. If her senses could be trusted, the turbine seemed completely sealed so that no air could pass through it, thus providing the necessary thrust. While not an aviation expert, Audrie at least knew the basics. She had to have a closer look and see the inside of the jet.

"My supervisor will be happy to explain everything to you," Taylor said with a smile as if enjoying the chance to parry the question.

In just a short while, the police would come and take her for questioning by Lasar. Audrie needed an excuse to accuse her of impeding the inspection and have her taken away. The excuse did not necessarily need to be good. The flimsier the better, which would cause even more frustration for the poor girl.

"While we wait, I'd like to see the inside please," Audrie pressed further, taking a step toward the stairs. The girl blocked her path.

"I'd rather wait for my supervisor to get here."

"Well then, I suppose we'll wait," Audrie answered, realizing that Taylor would oppose her every step. "But I would think you'd want to get this inspection done as quickly as possible."

"This inspection seems strange to me," the girl said abruptly. Audrie thought about her tone and tried to determine if she was stalling or challenging the inspection's validity. In the end, she concluded Taylor was stalling. For the moment, Audrie would have to humor her.

"How is it strange?"

"Well, aren't inspections done by more than one person, normally? It makes them appear more authentic."

Before answering, Audrie acted as if the question had been amusing. Did Taylor see through the act? Maybe the girl saw something

Audrie had neglected to consider.

"Are you suggesting that this is not an authentic inspection?"

"It's just that I'm not accustomed to taking everything at face value," the girl said, her eyes widening in expectation of an enlightening response.

Audrie took a deep breath to stall while inventing an answer. Ultimately, whether the girl accepted Audrie's act or not, it would not matter. The plan remained the same. Audrie had local law enforcement at her command, and they would answer when beckoned. She knew the unfairness of the situation, but she had to use the tools available. In her position, Taylor had little power.

"You may be comparing us to a US government agency," Audrie said finally. "One person is more efficient. Don't you think?"

"I suppose," she replied but with a tone of disbelief. "Let me make that call again."

While Taylor made another futile phone call, Audrie looked back at the aircraft, the engine first and then the body. In addition to the modifications of the external turbines, she noticed several other modifications to the aircraft. The windows looked different, nearly black and completely opaque. No light passed through them that Audrie could see. On the surface of the aircraft, Audrie noticed several tinted glass domes covering attached components not usually part of an aircraft.

When Taylor returned, her smile had disappeared.

"Looks like you'll have to come back later," she said. "My boss should have called back by now. Why don't you come back after lunch or you can call him and arrange a more agreeable time?"

"I'm afraid we need to complete the inspection at the time of arrival. You'll need to show me those permits, and let me look inside your aircraft."

"Since I don't have the authority to let anyone in here, you'll either have to wait for my supervisor or make whatever call you need to make."

"I see," Audrie said, intentionally pausing as if she had to consider her next action. Even in defeat, the girl remained confident and reso-lute. Audrie could see why Max or Mark had chosen her. If given any kind of leverage, Taylor would have been a formidable opponent.

Audrie called the police station and while waiting for Lasar to an-swer, she peered into the girl's eyes, suddenly appreciating the spirit behind them. After a moment, she had to turn away from the anger there. A few minutes later, they heard the police sirens.

"She'll recover," Audrie said to herself as she watched the police put Taylor in their car. After they drove out of sight, Audrie walked back to the aircraft and ascended the steps, then disappeared inside.

SIXTY-EIGHT

Taylor

At the police station, Taylor and Mark were interrogated separately. When Taylor later described the appearance of her interrogator to Mark, he said the same man had interrogated him. She was relieved to learn how they both had confessed identical stories, the same story they first told Yuri.

Taylor had acknowledged her feelings of anxiety at being held against her will, but she refused to feel helpless or terrified. Instead, she attempted to focus on the present and not let all the horrible possibilities ruin her ability to think. She never remembered feeling so scared, but at the same time, she felt more in control of herself than in her whole life.

During their entire stay with the police, only their interrogator showed any interest in them. At least to Taylor, he seemed like an outsider in a position of higher authority than the other people at the station. He wore no uniform and walked her and Mark from their individual cells to the interrogation room by himself. No one talked to him, and everyone obeyed his commands.

After being released from the police station, Taylor felt some concern for Mark's emotional state. Although he likely shared her feelings—a total loss of control—the experience seemed to have disturbed him more than her. She felt mostly angry, but he seemed almost in a panic. Would she have reacted the same if she had little children and a spouse depending on her?

On their return trip to the hangar, Mark insisted on driving. It didn't bother her, but she usually drove and he never seemed to care. Maybe he needed the feeling of being in control of something, she wondered.

"That was not a coincidence," he said after they turned a corner, and the station disappeared from their view. His words echoed her thoughts.

"Do you mean how you were taken in for questioning at the same time as the so-called inspector came?"

"Exactly!"

While talking on the drive, Mark kept his eyes fixed on the road and never once made eye contact with her. Although she wanted him to drive faster to increase the distance from the police station, he drove the speed limit to stay off the police radar.

"From the very start, that inspector acted like she wanted me gone," Taylor said. She needed to keep talking. Her imagination kept trying to fill the silence with the worst possible scenes they might find at the hangar.

Would the jet be missing?

Would the hangar entrance have a lock on it and police signs posted?

Would her NMG engines be stolen?

Fortunately, the fusion reactors were at the shop for a small modification, but what if the shop had also been raided? The possibilities almost overwhelmed her. Taylor had little success keeping the anger from her voice when she talked about the inspector.

"That bitch knew you couldn't answer the phone," she said and took a deep breath. "It's so obvious now, that goddamned smile on her face while your phone was ringing!"

When they arrived at the hangar, they saw no sign of disturbance, no evidence of police presence, or any other inspectors. Taylor had to wait several minutes for her heart rate to drop below a hundred.

To her surprise, they found Yuri waiting for them inside the hangar. Taylor rushed past him and up the stairs to the jet. To her relief, she found it the same as she left it.

"Everything seems fine," she said after coming back into view. Both Mark and Yuri looked up at her, pausing their conversation.

"Yuri just got here a while ago," Mark called up to her. "He found the door closed but unlocked."

"I saw no one," he said. "I was about to call you."

While Mark explained the situation to Yuri, Taylor replayed all of the events in her mind, searching for an explanation and more clues she had not yet noticed. She wished she could call the government aviation authority department and ask about that inspector, but the action would bring unwanted attention to them.

She suspected that they would know nothing about any inspection anyway. After talking with that woman for just a few minutes, Taylor thought of the whole scene as highly suspicious. The woman had an English accent and seemed unfamiliar with Portuguese despite her attempt at an accent. The authenticity of the woman's position, however, seemed to have no impact on the situation. Fake or real, the police had come when she called them.

Should Taylor have interrogated the woman more aggressively? She decided to do that next time. Acquiring more information was always a good idea.

"So it's agreed," Mark said at the end of their discussion. "The inspection was bogus."

"I will look into it," Yuri said.

He agreed to make a discreet investigation and keep their names out of any discussion he might have. Taylor had little confidence he would discover anything substantial, but at least he might learn when and how official inspections should take place.

"We've got to call Max and—"

"No," Taylor said before Mark could finish the sentence. "That lady had the power to use the local police, and she was no local. We have to assume she has the authority to access our phone records too, maybe even listen to our conversations. They probably want to see how we react. I think we should wait before calling anyone."

"There's got to be a way we can communicate?" he asked but continued before she could answer. "As a last resort, we can use the website."

"I suppose so," Taylor said reluctantly, "but I don't like it."

As expected, Gerald responded on the website before anyone else. Gerald had no idea what to do but said he would get back to them. The current predicament of the microbiologist woman, Sadi, had kept him preoccupied.

At first, Taylor convinced herself that the corrupt government agency chasing Sadi and the abduction of her daughter were unrelated to the activities of the group, but now she could not ignore the possible connection. Sadi's troubles had become an extra load on Taylor's growing list of concerns. The implications of the woman's predicament seemed too horrible to consider.

Max responded later that night and told them to hire a local security firm to guard their hangar and for Yuri to make the arrangements. Taylor found little comfort in the extra precaution.

"We can't outsource our security," Taylor said after reading the response from Max. "We can't assume the NMG engines will be safe on-site, fully assembled."

"Okay, so we do the same thing we did with the fusion reactors."

"Agreed."

Their plan to keep the NMG devices off-site seemed more substantial than hiring a private security firm and gave her a bit more confidence in their safety. They worked long that night making the NMG engines inoperable by removing key components as they did with the nuclear fusion generators. When finished, they slept in the jet and then in the morning took the parts to the shop and locked them with the catalyst modules from Cerametrics, a place where even the two shop assistants were unaware of their presence.

"What do you think we should do now?" Taylor asked. She wanted Mark to give her instructions. If she pushed herself any harder, she felt as though her brain synapses would melt together. Her extreme physical and mental exhaustion felt almost like they could destroy her. She did not want to stop working until they could do actual testing of the entire system, but she knew her body and mind needed a break.

"Well," he said after a deep breath, his calm tone helping her feel more at ease. "If they come and look at the jet, they're just going to find some strange modifications right? Our story's plausible—high altitude flight. What can they do?"

"I don't know," she answered while wiping the sweat from her forehead. She never did get accustomed to the humidity. "I just feel like we're in France waiting for Hitler to invade. I think we need to get out of here."

"I feel the same, but we can't work any faster."

"We need someone to help us finish," she said, staring directly into Mark's eyes. A familiar face materialized in Taylor's imagination, causing an instant smile. Mark nodded, and his lips also began stretching into a smile.

"We need Cesar," he said.

—※—

They worked for the next twenty hours without a break longer than a bathroom visit, and they snacked while working. Thoughts of Cesar arriving helped provide the energy to keep going and kept Taylor smiling. She was so excited to see him.

Cesar had more extensive experience with engine design and had performed the critical task of designing the retrofit to the existing engine dimensions, while also designing key components for Taylor to assemble into the final products. Without his remote help, they would be weeks behind their current schedule. With him on-site, she and Mark hoped to get ready within two weeks.

She had recently finished the structural mounting for the fusion reactors. With just a couple of hours' notice, they could be installed and connected to the power system of the aircraft. She currently worked, however, on the more daunting task of finishing the power distribution control system, a job usually performed by several people working many thousand man-hours. If Taylor let her mind relax and consider the enormity of the task, despair would have overcome her.

Mark had the responsibility of installing and testing the life support systems, an easier task in her opinion. They had already assembled all the modules and just needed to install and incorporate them into the overall control system. Although Mark's responsibility required less innovation, he worked with the same feverish devotion, and Taylor respected him for his impenetrable determination. She understood why Max had promoted him.

His most difficult task involved applying the same life support systems to the three isolated sections of the jet. If one section lost the ability to maintain atmospheric pressure, occupants could retreat to the other main section. But if both of the main sections' atmospheric integrity failed, only two or three people could escape to the third isolated section, the cockpit.

In those dire circumstances, they relied solely on their last line of defense, the vacuum suits, but they were not intended for protection from complete vacuum, just a minor pressure loss situation. Although the suits could provide the necessary environment, the solution was very temporary. If they needed to use the suits, they would have to return to Earth as soon as possible. In the case of a complete pressure loss, they would be dead.

When Cesar arrived the next evening, he lifted Taylor in a great bear hug and his eyes welled up with tears. Her eyes had the same response. She could only remember a handful of times in her whole life when she'd felt so glad and relieved to see someone. He brought a feeling of safety and security. She missed her mother and Dominga, and Doroteo even, but they could not help her as much as Cesar could. She let that feeling wash over her like a cold waterfall.

Instead of spending time discussing the dangers of their situation,

Taylor, Mark, and Cesar focused all of their resources on finishing the jet. They were working so hard on the jet, the bad news threw them from their hot sauna into a lake at the bottom of a glacier.

Through the website, Franklin sent a brief text message.

The military took Gerald!

SIXTY-NINE

Gerald

Gerald was afraid to open his eyes, so he tried to relax and concentrate on the gray light filling his mind and vision. Would he find himself still encased in rock? When he moved his arms and turned his head, he knew his surroundings had changed. After a long while of lying still and listening, he heard a familiar voice.

"What the hell happened?" Gerald heard the older woman ask, but she did not address him. Her voice sounded far away. "What have you two been doing this whole time? Look at his pulse! He's awake and probably listening to us. Why didn't you come and get me?"

"We don't know what happened," said an unfamiliar voice. "We lost resonance and couldn't get it back."

Gerald attempted to determine the source of the sounds that followed, then after several seconds, he felt cold fingers grip his arm and then a sharp pain. After the pain, came a warm sensation. His eyes burst open to see a shimmering black snake coiled around his arm with fangs and half-moon eyes. When Gerald pulled his arms against the restraints, the snake tightened its grip and started moving up his arm a centimeter at a time.

After moving past his shoulder, the snake squeezed past his neck to arrive at his face. Gerald turned his head to throw the serpent off but felt the side of his head hit something hard and cold. While coiled around his neck, the snake raised its head, exposing wet fangs. Its ice-blue eyes froze Gerald's body, and when the sharp fangs penetrated both of his eyes, he could not even scream.

—※—

Gerald regained consciousness slowly, feeling numb and hungry. The memory of a snake disappeared from his mind, along with the cave, the probe, the kids in the sewer. Those memories were now a part of his real life, the life stolen from him.

Unintentionally, he started thinking about his childhood and one instance in particular, his first crush. He forgot the girl's name, but her dark hair and beautiful brown eyes made the need to remember her name seem unnecessary. Brunettes always attracted him the most. For the most part, he enjoyed thinking about her, except for when she had tried to drown him in boiling water and drink his blood.

Why did he never tell anyone about that? They would not have believed him, he supposed.

When he opened his eyes, he recognized the room at the hospital before being transferred to the prison cell. A small lamp by the window glowed harshly, casting dark shadows across the room like a black-and-white photograph.

No light escaped through the white window curtains, and their stillness reminded him of an ancient tomb, undisturbed for centuries. He wanted to return to sleep, but the strangeness of the black shadows on the walls prevented him from closing his eyes. He arose from the bed and walked to the desk with the lamp.

He extended his hand to pull the curtains open and stared in confusion at what he saw behind them, a wall of dirt. He felt as though it should have frightened him more, but he almost expected it. For a long while, he held the curtain open and stared at the dirt, wondering what it meant.

When he heard the faint noise behind him, his heart froze. After looking, he saw the doorknob slowly turning. He ran to the door in a panic and held the handle so that the alien entity on the other side could not enter. Somehow, he knew that an alien wanted to enter the room and take him. If he allowed it to enter, that would be the end. He wanted to call for help, but the alien would hear him. The handle suddenly stopped moving, and Gerald waited.

After listening for at least a minute and hearing no other noises, Gerald returned to the bed and sat down. He watched the door and wondered what would happen next. Had he imagined it all? Did any of it matter anymore? He closed his eyes and tried to focus on how he had arrived in the room. After a minute, he quit trying to remember and went to sleep.

When he awoke later, he opened his eyes to find the door open. He froze and hoped to appear asleep. If there were an intruder, maybe it would ignore him. After a moment, he noticed something in his peripheral vision. Two very tall and thin forms stood on either side of his bed. At first, they looked like statues, but then they moved.

You're not real! You're not real!

He repeated that thought in an attempt to change reality. If he closed his eyes again, the two entities at his side would disappear. But somehow, he lost the will to close his eyes, so he was forced to obey his curiosity and keep them open.

The creatures had four appendages like a human, stood erect, and had a single head. Their resemblance to humans ended there. They were so tall, their heads almost hit the ceiling. Their clothes, or skin, reminded Gerald of the white bark of a birch tree. Other than their general form, he failed to see any specific features. He wanted to turn his head to see them better, but fear kept him paralyzed. His heart beat so loudly, he knew they could hear his terror.

After a few more seconds, a low humming shattered the silence of the room. It started quickly and remained steady, and Gerald's entire body instantly resonated with the vibration. His eyes shot open wider, and his body stiffened as he began lifting off the bed toward the ceiling. His eyes looked upward so that the creatures could only be seen in his peripheral vision.

He wanted to scream, but his vocal cords were no longer under his control. One of the creatures moved toward the open door, and it opened wider. The other creature stayed with Gerald and pushed his body through the air toward the open doorway. With his heart beating so violently he only had the strength to breathe. The humming almost felt like a liquid underneath him, keeping him afloat.

Outside the room, they entered a large open area the size of a soccer field. He could only see darkness above him and had the feeling of being underground. In his peripheral vision, he saw the door to his room shut. After it closed, all the other doors lining the large open area looked the same and he could no longer determine which had been the door to his room.

The creatures transported Gerald through the air and over a floor composed of large tiles. Each of the tiles had thousands of small holes drilled in them, and the light in the room originated from the holes.

When the humming began to fade, he felt himself descending until he came to rest on a marble table. Then the vibrations stopped completely. His whole body immediately relaxed, but his heart still beat loudly, and he started panting as if he'd just finished a race. One of the creatures stood over him while the other walked out of sight. Gerald thought about jumping off the table but forgot about that option when he noticed how nonhuman the creature looked.

Its oval head stuck out from its long neck at a twenty-degree angle from its body. Instead of two eyes, it had seven in total, one large eye in the center with three more on either side, going halfway around the head. The farther back the eyes were located, the smaller they became. Two skinny appendages reminded Gerald of a mantis but ended with long sharp fingers.

Just below the eyes, a long slit for a mouth was slowly opening and closing and gave the impression of breathing. Behind the thin white lips were the sharp teeth of a carnivore, an opaque grey. If not for the terrifying head and arms, Gerald would have marveled at its beautiful birch tree skin.

"What are you?" Gerald asked, hoping to hear a response. Any intelligible answer would make the situation feel less threatening. He wanted to feel understanding and empathy. Gerald felt an alien voice respond in his mind.

Be at peace!

The telepathic words had the opposite effect of their meaning. An overpowering intruder was opening the door to his mind and forcing its way inside without any resistance. He could feel it slithering around his memories, discovering all his secrets.

Despite his emotional anxiety, his heartbeat slowed and his breathing soon came under control. After thirty seconds, his body seemed to fall asleep, leaving his mind totally awake. He felt like an insect after a wasp sting, alive but waiting for the thing to suck his blood.

When the next movement caught his attention, he lacked the power to move his head, but he could still move his eyes. Five more of the creatures came within view all around him, each one about two meters away. They all looked the same, except for slight differences in height. For about three minutes, Gerald felt all forty-two eyes focused on him. When he felt the humming begin again, the table began to descend. He tore his gaze away from the creatures to the darkness above him.

Gerald descended into the floor of light and soon found himself in a cylindrical chamber capped at both ends. He lay in the center still paralyzed, but with the creatures out of sight, he began to feel a little relief, despite his unfamiliar surroundings. The white walls seemed to glow with their own light and nothing was visible beyond them. For the third time in his recent memory, he lay in a tomb.

The space appeared too clean for a torture chamber, and he could not imagine his blood splattering on the clean walls. He heard a soft sound behind him, and after a few seconds, two slightly curved mirrors moved from the end of the cylinder to stop around his head, one in front of his face and one behind his head. A small green ball, like polished topaz the size of a marble, extended from the center of each mirror. When he looked closely at his reflection behind the green ball, he noticed his image shimmering like a ghost.

When the mirrors began rotating around his head, his reflection came in and out of focus until his eyes began to hurt. But as they increased speed, the mirrors appeared as one continuous mirror with a blurry topaz line in the center.

At first, he only noticed his head and face, but while watching for a while, he could see his eyes from different angles. Never before had he been able to see his face in the mirror without looking directly back at himself. After a short time, he felt as if he was watching someone else.

At first, Gerald failed to notice the next transition. His skin slowly became translucent and he could see his muscles and blood flowing through his veins. When he saw his skull and brain, the image frightened him, but he could not look away or close his eyes. After a few more minutes, his head started to disappear, and he could see the mirror behind him. His vision soon stretched into eternity, and then the next nightmare began.

If he had been sleeping and had this nightmare, the experience would have torn him out of sleep and left him with a cold sweat. But this vision of horror could not be stopped. The machine forced Gerald to witness horrible things, tremendous pain inflicted on his friends, on Sadi and her two girls, his mother, Cesar, Dominga, Taylor. While he watched, he imagined the same experiences on himself, almost as if he could also feel their pain.

After a long time, the horrible scenes became less and less shocking and disturbing. His pain transformed into anger and rage. It warped his senses and twisted his memories until he forgot his own identity and became some kind of wild animal with only instinct as his guide. All his blood vessels prepared to burst. Only then did the machine allow his vision to turn black.

—※—

When he awoke, he found himself on the floor of a cage with three white walls, a white ceiling, and a transparent glass wall in front of him. Large tiles with holes covered the floor and allowed light from below to fill the room. On the other side of the glass stood three of the tall aliens with white birch tree skin. When he saw the creatures, a rage replaced all thought, including his awareness of the glass barrier separating him from them.

He jumped up from the floor and ran toward the creatures, intending to rip off their heads and bite into their necks with his teeth. He had no room in his thoughts to fear them, and when the skin on his forehead cracked open from hitting the glass, anger at the pain gave him the strength to do it again.

After the second impact into the glass, he stopped and rested against the glass wall with the hope that it might disappear while he waited. With his hand, he wiped the blood from his forehead and made a bloody handprint on the transparent material then moved from the blood splattering so that he could see them clearly. As he gulped the air into his burning lungs, he just stared at them.

"Die, die, die," he screamed and pounded his fist against the glass to relieve his intense craving to taste their blood. "Going to kill you! Kill you! Kill you! Kill you!"

After a few seconds, he turned away and paced back and forth in his cell. Whenever the creatures moved, he ran to the glass wall and pounded on it with his fists. All the while, the creatures stood still, watching him calmly.

When Gerald heard a noise from behind him, he turned and noticed a piece of the back wall sliding upward. In the shadows of the opening hole, he heard breathing. He took a few tentative steps toward the sound and stopped, waiting to see its identity. When the black Labrador retriever came into his sight, it stopped, and they made eye contact. At first, the dog seemed happy to see Gerald, but it soon started snarling and backing away from him. The wall closed behind the dog and left it trapped in the room.

Two new thoughts passed briefly through Gerald's mind. First, he remembered the affable nature of dogs in general and how this one probably meant him no harm. But his instinct to defend his new territory overpowered rational thought, and he saw the dog as a threat. The dog continued barking at him in warning and pressing against the wall, toward the corner. For the following brief moment, Gerald just watched, and then he attacked. In less than a minute, he captured the dog and killed it.

Gerald wiped the blood from his face and turned back to the creatures behind the transparent wall. One of them faced the others, and Gerald noticed its long slit of a mouth ripple like the vibration of a string. Its center eye blinked, but the three smaller ones facing his direction remained focused on him.

Gerald was angry and sad at what he'd done to the dog, but he blamed the creatures on the other side of the glass, so he picked up the remains of the dog and threw it at the glass. The impact splattered more blood on it and obscured some of the creatures from his view. He wanted to yell at them, but no words could express what he felt, so he ran to the wall again and continued pounding on it with his fists. After a few seconds, blood had completely covered the glass, and Gerald could no longer see the creatures.

He backed up and started running toward the glass in a final attempt to crash through it and tear them to pieces. But Gerald never experienced an impact. The glass wall became a pool of thick red gas. As he dove into it, the world transformed back into darkness.

SEVENTY

Simon

Simon lived at the same estate as his friend and employer, Max Garner. When Max started his company, TerraWatch, he appointed Simon as head of security. As an additional honor, Max recently charged Simon with the task of keeping him safe. Simon liked the arrangement, but his job had begun to get more complicated.

"I've started a new side-project," Max said, "and knowledge of the activities needs to be kept away from certain military interests. For your own safety, not even you will know the specifics."

"Does it have anything to do with Mark's recent correspondence with Gerald Foster?"

Max shook his head and shrugged, pretending ignorance. Even when they were undergraduates together, that look annoyed Simon.

"I'm flying out to meet with them next week."

"Let me guess. I'm coming with you," Simon said in resignation. He had too much work to do at TerraWatch to go with his boss on one of his adventures.

In the months that followed, Simon had to shift more of his responsibility to his subordinates for the security of the company. He spent more time than he wanted keeping track of the side group—

Gerald, Cesar, Taylor, and their other friends. If he wanted to discover exactly what they had developed, he could have done so, but he wanted to honor Max's desires not to pursue their secrets. He would be content just to know the military would want whatever they had developed.

Simon spent some time running background checks on each individual associated with Gerald Foster. He found Doroteo's history particularly interesting and looked forward to an opportunity to meet him. Not only were they in the same line of work, but something in the old Mexican's face intrigued Simon, like an esoteric piece of knowledge to help Simon with his work.

He learned about the kidnapping of Sadi's daughter only after her miraculous rescue and then about her subsequent escape from the homeland security agents. Although the incident seemed unrelated to the group, he knew it was somehow connected. He planned to learn more about the kid who had supposedly performed the rescue, but Simon had not found the time yet.

—※—

A few minutes before five in the morning, the guard at the gate announced the arrival of the military personnel into the gated community. The intruders refused to identify their intended target, but Simon had to assume the worst. He ran across the yard from his cottage to the main house Max occupied. Adrenaline cleared the sleep from his eyes, but he still swayed after standing too fast.

"Get to the room in the cellar," said Simon as he hurried Max out the bedroom door. He stayed behind to make the bed look like no one had slept in it for a while. "Let's hope they're not coming here."

"I have a bad feeling that they are," Max said with a tone of calm acceptance.

After shutting the door to the cellar with his boss inside, Simon went to the kitchen to get a cup of coffee. While pouring the hot liquid, a loud knock on the front door shattered the silence. Simon waited several seconds before he heard the maid's Ukrainian accent.

"What do you want?" she asked through the door intercom.

After her conversation at the door, Simon met the woman in the hallway on her way to Max's room. She looked more angry than scared.

"Several men are at the front door and wanting to see Max."

"I'll take care of it," Simon said. "Stay out of sight."

On his walk to the door, Simon's heart raced, urging him to run away from the danger, rather than toward it. The men at his door had come without his knowledge, and that accentuated his feeling of failure. He should have known they were coming. Before opening the door, he took a long, deep breath to slow his heartbeat. He instantly recognized two of the three men as CIA agents. They stood in front of a soldier with a machine gun. The shorter agent did the speaking, his fake smile saying more than his words.

"Good morning, Mr. Thatcher," he began. "We would like to speak with Max."

Despite his anxiety, Simon answered with perfect calmness. He knew their reaction before he finished his answer.

"He's not here."

The smile on the shorter man grew wider, and Simon wanted to reach out and strangle him.

"Mr. Thatcher," he began as though explaining to a child. "You don't want to interfere with us, believe me. I understand your position, but we know he's here."

"I do not consent to a search," Simon answered.

"We're beyond the need for your consent," he snorted. "This is a military matter."

Simon smiled, hoping to appear confident that they would fail to find Max at home.

"Well then. Where does that leave us?"

The man turned to address the soldier behind him. The soldier stood with an expressionless face as though bored and ready to take a break.

"Don't let him get in our way."

When the shorter man turned back to face Simon, they held eye contact for a moment. Simon knew he could overpower each of the two CIA agents one at a time but not both of them, and he would certainly have an uphill battle with the tall and muscular soldier behind them. The other agent tentatively stepped into the house and slowly walked past Simon, his eyes scanning the area before him.

"You know I can't help you," Simon said while maintaining his smile.

"I respect that," said the man as he walked past Simon and into the house.

Simon closed the door behind the group of armed men and watched the two CIA agents walk through the house. Simon thought they looked like a group of men getting ready for an enjoyable hunting expedition. He held onto the fantasy that they would quit their search before finding Max, but his hope withered despite his efforts. While they searched, the maid appeared from the hallway and came to stand by him. She did not want them to catch her hiding.

"It's okay," Simon said. "You'll be fine."

"No, Max," she replied sadly.

Simon exhaled slowly. She understood.

The men performed their search for only a short while. They refrained from breaking anything but could be heard shouting at each other and hastily opening and closing doors. After ten minutes, Simon heard a familiar voice from the basement.

"Excuse me," Max said loudly. "But what are you doing in my home?"

"Got him," said one of the other men.

While waiting for them to appear, Simon listened to their conversation.

"Where is your warrant?" Max asked.

"National security matters override civilian protocol," the man answered. "Once we get to a secure location, you can contact a lawyer."

Simon waited for a very long minute for them to reappear at the front door. Standing there and waiting felt like waiting to start a fist-fight. When he and Max finally exchanged looks, Simon felt some relief to see his boss calmly walking in front of the two men.

When he noticed the fear in Max's eyes, Simon had the sudden urge to grab one of the man's guns and shoot them all. When the spokesman turned to him, his clenched teeth helped contain his anger.

"Looks like you were mistaken," said the shorter man as the soldier opened the door for him. "Max was home."

Simon and the housemaid stood on the front porch watching as the government agents loaded their employer into a Humvee. He noticed the morning getting brighter, the sun illuminating the underside of the clouds on the horizon. The beautiful sight seemed like a cruel joke from nature.

While keeping his eyes on the men, Simon turned to the maid and spoke quietly.

"Walk calmly to the garage and get the Land Rover ready, but stay out of sight until they're gone. Go!"

Simon leaned against the door and casually pulled his cell phone from his pocket. Before the night security manager at TerraWatch answered his phone, the soldier glanced briefly back at Simon and held eye contact for just a moment.

"Luke," Simon said when the familiar voice answered. "No time to explain now, but I need you to get a lock on a vehicle leaving Max's place ASAP."

"Which bird should I use?" he asked.

"Which ones are within contact?"

"Just a second," he said while typing. "Both Jefferson and Monroe are available."

"Jefferson then. Just hurry. I can explain later when I see you."

"Is something wrong with Max?"

"Yes," Simon responded. "Just get that satellite lock."

"Almost there."

While the military Humvee began turning onto the street, Simon started walking down the private drive toward the garage. He resumed speaking to the man on the phone.

"I'm going to follow them until you get it. Call me back when you get that lock. I need to make another call."

Simon called the guard at the front neighborhood gate and asked him to stall the Humvee on its way out, if possible. Although he expected no significant delay, a few seconds might be all he needed.

"Make sure you take notice of the way they go. I'm going to follow them."

"Got it, sir," said the guard, and then he cut the connection.

The maid drove the Land Rover to the front gate and waited to meet Simon.

"Are you going to get him back?" she asked. She exited the driver's seat and held the open door for him.

Simon noticed tears ready to fall from her eyes.

"He'll be back. I just need to find out where they're taking him."

Before driving onto the road, Simon took a deep breath and gripped the gear stick, his knuckles turning white. He hated tailing people. Trying to keep up with them in traffic and stay out of sight wore on his nerves. To make the situation worse, he had no experience following government intelligence agents who did that sort of thing for a job. Did they have a backup vehicle, out of sight? He would have to watch for one. If they caught him, he might get in deep trouble and then how could he help Max? He needed that satellite link to follow the vehicle.

When his phone rang, Simon answered it during the first ring.

"They just got through and took a right on Pearl," the guard at the front gate said. "They had Mr. Garner, sir!"

"Thanks," Simon said and cut the connection.

He drove through the gate and pulled onto Pearl Street. When he found no other vehicle on the empty street, he slowed his speed. The Humvee could be seen speeding several blocks away.

Light from the sun behind him reflected from his rearview mirror directly into his eyes, blinding him. While reaching for his sunglasses, the phone rang again.

"Okay, I'm looking at Max's house," Luke said. "Where is Max?"

Simon briefly explained the situation. Together they located the Humvee and started following it. Luke stayed on the line for the next thirty minutes, directing Simon. He stayed out of sight and mostly followed their exact route except when he knew of a shortcut. Simon knew of a military base to the northwest and expected them to drive in that direction, but they drove south into the country. He didn't know of any military installations that way.

Following Max and his abductors seemed like the right course of action to take, but what good would it do them? If the military circumvented usual civil procedures to apprehend a high-profile person like Max, what would they do to a man without connections like himself? Once secure at a military facility, they would discover all of the group's activities. Simon did not doubt it.

PART V

BLACKOUT

After she rips the aether apart
And you enter the void
You might not feel so smart

SEVENTY-ONE

Agent Pratt

"Uh-huh," John Pratt said quietly, nodding his head as an obedient dog. He was sitting with his girlfriend, Carla, at her favorite café in Seattle. While attempting to listen to her and at the same time give the impression of listening, his phone vibrated. At first, he ignored the annoying sensation but knew he would eventually need to answer it. That eventuality would be his excuse to end the conversation.

He usually seized upon any plausible excuse to avoid lunch with her, but the warning look in her eyes that morning had prevented him from declining. Along with the other things he disliked about Carla, her eating habits probably annoyed him the most, especially the sound of her chewing.

Right before his phone rang, she suspected how he felt about the conversation, so he had to prove his sincere interest even more. He would have to wait for a better moment to answer his phone.

"They just can't go anywhere with Keri," she said, referring to the daughter of her friend. Before continuing, she looked directly into his eyes again and dared him to answer his phone.

"She throws terrible fits, and Erika ends up taking her home. I tried convincing her to schedule a time when I could take her to the park with me and Susan. Sometimes it just takes a non-family member to discipline a child to get them to behave. They spoil her, you know."

Yes, Pratt knew.

"I bet I can help turn her around, but she probably knows it and is afraid of me being too harsh. I'm not harsh, am I?"

"Haven't you done enough for her?" he asked and snorted. Agent Pratt never knew why his girlfriend bothered with her friend Erika, one of the most annoying people he knew.

"She's just stressed because her husband's a jerk. You remember Jared don't you?"

"Yeah, I remember him, but I wouldn't call him a jerk." Pratt failed to gather enough resolve to agree with her. "He lets her walk all over him."

For some reason that Pratt could not understand, Erika's husband had commitment issues and failed to see how all his problems would be solved if he just left the annoying woman. Pratt had some respect for the guy, however, for his ability to endure the relationship for whatever he extracted from it. For the sake of their daughter and to keep the peace, he put up with a lot of shit. Pratt shuddered when he imagined himself in the same position.

"She needs his help," she continued. "She has to beg for his help all the time. It's the only way she can get him to do anything."

"I bet you anything that the root cause of the problem is her nagging." Pratt felt compelled by his dislike for Carla's friend and by gender loyalty to defend the man. "Nagging never helped anything."

Carla paused and looked at him as if trying to see inside his mind.

"You're not saying I'm a nag, are you?"

Oh shit!

"Not much," he said and smiled. To his relief, she smiled too.

That was close. He needed to get her thoughts focused back on her friend, not him.

"I'm just suggesting that maybe his timescale is not the same as hers, or maybe he has a different strategy than his wife."

"Ha-yeah," she snorted. "Sitting on your ass on the sofa is not a strategy."

"Devil's advocate," Pratt said, shrugging and taking another bite of his sandwich.

"I'm gonna give her a call later today. When are you coming home tonight, or are you?"

"Don't know," he said and felt more vibrations from his phone. Since he no longer sensed the need to prove his interest in their conversation, he decided to answer the phone. "Sorry, I gotta get this."

When he looked at his phone, he noticed the text message from his boss. The message was simple enough, but Pratt disliked the implication. His boss only used *please* when he had an important message.

My office at one-thirty, please...

—※—

Pratt entered the office of his boss, Jason Smithson, at twenty seconds after one-thirty. Both of their watches showed the same time.

"Sit down please, John."

"What's going on, sir?"

"I've got interesting news," he began. "You might find it more annoying than interesting, but first tell me where we are with Gerald Foster?"

Pratt's heart rate increased as he quickly updated Director Smithson about the Foster case. He carefully included only the official investigation and not what he had acquired personally. If he said too much, his boss would become suspicious and demand to know everything. Pratt felt unprepared to fabricate a believable story that would alleviate all concerns.

He explained Foster's associations with a possible girlfriend, and the Mexicans and Taylor. He neglected to mention Gerald's secret meetings with the old man, Mr. Smith, and the failed intercept in the forest. He especially avoided the topic of his suspicion of being drugged and questioned. During the narrative, Pratt exaggerated personal feelings of anger at the man so that his boss would not suspect fake disinterest. The act reminded him of the reason for his more intense anger.

"I've been pretty busy with my other activities," he concluded. "As you know."

"Okay, here's the news," his boss said and looked straight at Agent Pratt as if inspecting him for some deceit. He gave Pratt the impression of not caring about anything in his report. "The military has taken Gerald Foster into custody, and he's been officially declared off-limits, he and a man named Max Garner. Do you know him at all? I did not see his name in your report."

"The name sounds familiar, but I don't know him." Pratt searched his memory for how he recognized the name. His boss's tone indicated that he should know. Pratt attempted to hide his shock at the news.

"Max Garner is the son of Henry Garner, the—"

"The bank executive?"

"That's the one," Director Smithson said, sounding relieved to hear that Pratt knew the man's name. "Max and Gerald are both involved. When the CIA is done with them, they won't be any problem at all to anyone, at least not Max. He's too high profile."

"Do you know any of the details?"

"You know the military," the director answered, still staring intently at Agent Pratt who felt the man's eyes, like the heat from red coals in a fire. "That's all I've got, but from the way that the information was delivered, it looks like Mr. Foster may never be seen above ground again. How do you feel about that? I was curious about how you would take it."

"That's a weight off my shoulders," Pratt said, attempting to sound genuine, but he felt cheated as if he'd spent several hours with a great fish on his hook and it suddenly escaped. But in this case, someone else had acquired the fish instead, someone who would not get nearly as much satisfaction with it as Agent Pratt would.

"Do you expect me to believe that?" his boss asked. "That's not how I would feel."

"I'm trying to look on the bright side right now," Pratt said, then transformed his sarcastic smile into one of irritation. "The only way to do that is to get back to work. I've got plenty of other criminals to bake."

"You know what this means, don't you?"

"What?" Pratt asked, trying to hide his annoyance.

He needed to be in a less homicidal mood to determine the answer. He needed to go home, do some cocaine, ravage Carla, and finish with a hot shower. While his boss asked the next question, Agent Pratt imagined the many different ways he could inflict damage on Gerald Foster. He was still Agent Pratt's case, and the military had no right to interfere.

"It means that everything to do with Gerald Foster is off limits, his friends, enemies, or associates of any kind. Do you understand me, John?"

Pratt picked up his head from his view of the desk.

"Of course," he lied. "I understand."

"To be honest, I'm disappointed we didn't find out what he was doing, but I don't blame you. He managed to fall into burning oil, and you can't come out of that without pulling a good layer of skin with it. Console yourself on that."

"It is pleasant to think about," Pratt admitted sincerely and knew his boss understood how he felt.

But the director's smile disappeared.

"I don't want any interference from our department. If they even suspect any, it's my ass in the same deep fryer."

—※—

Pratt went home that night, fuming over the news, and his boss's disappointment only made his mood worse. When his boss had said, "I'm disappointed we," he meant, "I'm disappointed in you." He blamed Pratt entirely for the lack of progress with Foster.

He had to take the situation to a higher level. As he slept that night, he could feel the military removing the last remains of his dinner from the table. If he delayed any longer, there would be no scraps left for him. Fortunately, he recently acquired Gerald's internet records for the past month from a friend who had access to them.

Going through the tremendous amount of electronic communication required gallons of coffee. The next morning, he fought a hangover while searching through the list of websites Gerald had visited. Many of them were benign like *amazon.com*, *forbes.com*, and *judicialwatch.org*, but many of them like *reason.com* and *wired.com* made Pratt shake his head in disgust. He detested those types of *alternative* news sources even though he knew many were projects of other intelligence agencies. In his opinion, the people who visited them were more likely to cause trouble. They tended to justify playing outside the boundaries of the law. When he found all the end-the-fed sites, he laughed out loud.

"Like a dog to his vomit," he said.

Gerald often visited a site that was unfamiliar to Pratt, and the frequency caught his attention. The site topic of astronomy also seemed unsuited to his interests. When Pratt visited the site, all he could see were some graphics about a rocket going into the sky and some information about a NASA space program. From what he knew of Gerald, an interest in astronomy failed to fit with his profile.

When Pratt began researching Max Garner and his company, TerraWatch, he instantly suspected the connection to the strange website Gerald kept visiting. The connection between the two men, however, did not make sense. What could they possibly be doing together? Gerald usually worked with lower net-worth individuals and not billion-dollar companies. For the present, he would assume the website linked the two men in a way that interested the military.

Due to his very limited time and proprietary constraints, he only had a few options. Standard procedure called for a backdoor path through the web hosting company. He could get the information, and the law forbade the hosting company from notifying the website owner, but now that the military claimed exclusive jurisdiction over the investigation, he could not follow standard procedure in case the military discovered his activities.

Even if he found the right person to do it covertly for him, the process could ultimately be traced back to him. The military worked quickly, and they could justify almost any action, so he had insufficient time before they completely removed all of the food from the table.

He needed to find the website administrator or the owner, and hopefully, they were the same person. After going to *whois.net*, he typed in the astronomy website address, but the search only found the hosting company and not the owner. Although not the information he wanted, it at least showed something not that uncommon. They paid the small fee to keep their identity a secret. Fortunately, he had a close friend who owed him a favor and could discover the identity himself.

The next afternoon after lunch, Pratt's friend repaid his debt and provided the requested information, neatly encased in a manila folder. After dumping the papers onto his desk, he found the name of the website administrator, a kid named Franklin Harvey. In addition to providing the name, his friend had also performed a basic background check on the guy.

The kid's profile looked like many of the kids Pratt tried to entrap, a typical computer geek and conspiracy theorist. Pratt especially hated that kind of deviant. His growing appetite for enticing one of them to commit some crime needed satisfying, but Franklin seemed too smart to fall for their typical operation.

From the profile alone, Pratt still lacked sufficient evidence linking a personal association with Gerald. But on the next pages of phone records, Pratt found a reason to smile. Franklin and Gerald communicated often. Agent Pratt was now in debt to his friend who had acquired the information.

Another name on the phone record caught his attention and seemed to be highlighted with fluorescent yellow, although the name only appeared once. Franklin had also called the strange kid, Freddy Carlson, who also happened to know Gerald Foster. Pratt had already reviewed Freddy's background and discovered his employment with the former Secretary of Agriculture William Smith. His paperwork also indicated deficient mental and social abilities.

Now he had a link to them all. If he had access to their website activities, he would probably find that they all visited the website.

While thinking about what he had discovered, Pratt remembered the failed intelligence operation with Mr. Smith and that kid when those agents came back with nothing. Even though the agents executing that operation showed ineptitude, their blunder also reflected poorly on him. It reinforced the lesson he had to learn over and over again.

Trust no one with something important to you!

With a feeling of satisfaction but also impatience, Agent Pratt decided on his next course of action. He planned to make a little visit to see his new friend, Franklin Harvey.

SEVENTY-TWO

Agent Pratt

Pratt left the office late that night and headed to Franklin's address, a single-story apartment building in the shape of a U with an open courtyard in the middle. The building sat in a row of three other apartment buildings, two in the same shape and the last one in the shape of an L and next to a small café. Only single-family homes lined the other side of the street. With any luck, apartment number 4 would be near the entrance to the open area in the middle and not in the row of apartments deep within.

While driving slowly past the apartments, Pratt noticed something strange. He saw another set of people monitoring the place, a man and woman in a car, posing as a couple on a date. Although he saw no blatant evidence exposing the fraud, he immediately saw the reality of the situation.

A sudden mixture of emotions assaulted him, relief to arrive at the scene while still a scene but also disappointment and frustration as if arriving after another kid punctured the piñata, and he had to compete with all the other little shits for the candy. He was instantly angry at the man and woman in the black Subaru Legacy.

They had also parked in the place Pratt would have taken, across the street from the neighboring apartment building next to several other cars. A row of large maple trees gave an added layer of concealment.

"Damn it," he swore softly while driving past. "They stole my spot."

The game had changed, and he had to accommodate the new players. If the watchers were any good at their job, they would definitely notice if he drove past again, so he only had one chance to find a good place to park. He turned the corner and parked on the side street with a good view of the back of Franklin's apartment. From his parking place, the other surveillance couple could not see him. A spot in the back would be best for him to escape unnoticed.

He sat in the car and spent some time verifying that no other intelligence agents watched the place from behind. From his brief view of the other surveillance team, he had difficulty determining their identity. Since the military had commandeered the investigation, they were either CIA or DHS, and he hoped to deal with DHS agents rather than those from the CIA. He felt more confident outmaneuvering the idiots from the DHS.

Pratt felt a great urgency to hurry. For all he knew, they could be preparing to take the kid that night. If he wanted to discover anything about their activities, this could be his only chance. With acknowledgment of his desperation, he decided to take more risks than usual and maybe even act a little recklessly. But like all successful operations and magic acts, his plan depended on an effective diversion.

In many of his previous operations, he had experienced similar and more dangerous risks to himself and others, but this one meant more. This situation involved his job. If news of his activities reached his boss, he might lose his position, or worse, be indicted for interfering with a military operation. Those risks weighed more heavily on him than any physical danger. After a moment of reflection, he concluded that he possessed the skills necessary to succeed.

"This'll be fun," he said while reaching under the seat and gripping his gun. Holding it felt good. As he attached the silencer to the end, he thought about the irony of already being the secondary surveillance agent. He liked the idea of having a new experience.

After getting out of the car and casually glancing up and down the quiet street, he experienced a sudden paranoia. He no longer felt like the watcher but the watched. When he attempted to attribute the feeling to anger or a sense of insubordination, he failed. Someone was watching him. The spy could be someone just looking out their window, so he had to follow standard procedure and act inconspicuously.

"No one knows who I am or what I'm doing," he said quietly to himself, then paused to look up at the clear sky and stars. He never really noticed the stars, but he now had to tear his eyes away. One star, in particular, looked brighter than the others.

"Keep 'em out of your head, John!"

After starting to walk in the cool night air, he felt good, and the sensation of being watched started to fade. When he turned the corner and came within view of the apartment entrance, he took a swift glance in the direction of the car with the watchers and smiled when they showed no evidence of paying attention to him. He felt like the leading actor in a play, making his first appearance on stage.

He looked down at his hand as if he held a piece of paper with an address written on it then pretended to look up at the street sign to get his orientation. Garbage cans and yard debris containers sat on the sidewalks on the other side of the street waiting for the morning pickup, with yards just large enough for a small patch of grass. As he walked casually down the street, he heard the muffled noises of parents trying to get kids ready for bed. He stopped when he found an acceptable spot for his plan.

When a group of teenagers passed him, headed for one of the apartment buildings, he smiled and nodded but kept his plain brown baseball cap just above his eyes. Only one girl made eye contact with him before turning back to their conversation. They would be unable to recognize him later.

Pratt walked past the L-shaped apartment building, then past Franklin's apartment building next to it, and then to the end of the street. He stopped next to a tree located between the last apartment building and the back of the café. The tree made a fitting boundary between the two buildings and provided him with what he wanted, limited visibility.

He lit a cigarette and leaned comfortably against the wall of the café, facing the wall of the last apartment building, just a man taking a smoke break. The branches of the tree helped shield him from view. For the next few seconds, he held the cigarette at his side and watched the smoke drift upward past his face.

From his position, he could see the back car window of the surveillance team and the side of Franklin's apartment building. Down the short alley, he heard the noise from a loud TV set through an open window. For a few seconds at least, he had sufficient cover for what he wanted to do.

But before executing his plan, he reviewed it one last time in his head and found no problem. While holding the cigarette between his lips, he would grab his gun and shield the view of it with his hat. Then the fun would begin.

After taking one final breath of fresh air, he initiated the sequence.

With the cigarette held tight between his lips, Pratt drew the smoke into his lungs, and while exhaling, he casually looked down the barrel of his gun and concentrated on his target, a medium-sized home at the end of the other side of the street. Only the silencer on the end of his gun extended out from his hat.

In five evenly spaced intervals, he pulled the trigger. The sound of shattering glass and the impact from the bullets muffled the faint sound of his gun. The bullets soared almost directly above the vehicle of the watchers.

Immediately after Pratt stopped shooting, a woman's scream and the crying of a child became the only sounds. He put his gun away and took one last drag on his cigarette then threw it on the ground in front of him. In a few seconds, the screaming stopped, and lights started illuminating the windows on the street. Then the people started filling the sidewalks to investigate the frightful sounds. Pratt joined them.

In twenty more seconds, he heard the faint sound of approaching police sirens.

"Faster than expected," he whispered to himself and smiled. "Serve and protect."

He loved putting the police to work for him. They now became the servants of the higher law enforcement.

While casually walking across the street, Pratt focused on the actions of the two watchers. Like everyone else, they looked up and down the street in confusion, trying to assess the situation. When they looked in his direction, he had already started approaching the nearest person, a woman in her late fifties who stood on the sidewalk with a cigarette hanging from her fingers. After coming close enough, he noticed the smell of alcohol.

"What's going on?" she asked when he arrived close enough to her.

"I heard a broken window and a scream, down that way." He pointed toward the house he had shot. Two police cars were slowing to a stop in front of the victim's house, and their flashing lights filled the street with a strobe effect, just as he had hoped.

She looked at where Agent Pratt had pointed, taking another drag on her cigarette.

"Oh my God, the Johnson's window's broken."

"I heard someone over there say something about the sound of a gunshot coming from that direction," he said and casually pointed to the people just down the street from them. "But I don't see anyone other than those two in the car over there."

The woman looked at where he pointed and put her hand over her mouth.

"I saw them earlier," she said in more surprise. "They've been there for over an hour, just sitting there."

She started walking away from him toward the surveillance car.

"Perfect," he said to himself with satisfaction. "The town busybody!"

"Where are you going?" he asked while she walked away from him.

"Someone's got to tell the cops," she said, turning slightly to look at him. "I don't trust those two. That's suspicious, that is."

"Hey," he said with feigned shock and concern. "I'm not accusing anyone. Don't get me involved."

"Don't worry," she said. "I'll keep you out of it."

He nodded and watched her walk away down the street toward the police. When she passed the unknown surveillance car, she glanced at them suspiciously without trying to hide her accusatory emotions. Pratt thought she looked extremely pleased with herself, the look of a patriotic citizen doing her duty.

While keeping his attention focused on the new police crime scene, Pratt crossed the street and walked casually toward Franklin's apartment. With every passing moment, more people joined him on the street to watch the spectacle he had created. Pratt took notice of one dark-haired kid in particular and immediately recognized him.

Franklin stood in front of his apartment courtyard with a small group of his fellow residents. He wore a dark cap, shorts, sandals, and a black and white t-shirt with the name of *Ron Paul* on the front. Usually, seeing the name of Ron Paul on something made Pratt sneer in disgust. But nothing could ruin his joy of seeing the kid at that moment. Franklin coming out of his apartment made Pratt's plan a lot easier.

He approached the small group and looked at where some of them pointed. Two of the police were walking to the car of the other surveillance team. With a smile, Pratt slipped discreetly past the group into the apartment courtyard. Pratt was a little disappointed at not being able to watch as one of the cops knocked on the window of their car.

As Pratt had hoped, Franklin neglected to lock his apartment. While shaking his head at his continued good luck, he quietly slipped inside and shut the door behind him. The only lights in the apartment came from a room down the hall and through the front blinds.

He only had a short amount of time to assess his new surroundings and check for bugs. The kid kept his apartment like he kept his matted mess of dark hair. Shirts, socks, and pants seemed to have carefully landed in piles on every piece of furniture. In contrast, the spotless floor appeared recently steam-cleaned and vacuumed.

Pratt instantly noticed his own footprints on the floor. They contrasted sharply with the kid's footprints. He had to assume that Franklin would notice, so he decided to change his plan and wait in the front room, instead of waiting in the room down the hall.

A single cup of instant ramen noodles sat in the center of the coffee table, a spoon beside it and steam drifting upward. Pratt breathed in the salty beef broth and wondered if he had time for a bite. He loved ramen noodles but decided against the diversion.

While waiting for Franklin to return, Pratt spent the time enjoying the blinking police lights from outside and how they made the room seem to pulsate with his own anticipation. When he heard the soft footsteps and the squeaking of the doorknob, he felt the familiar rush of adrenaline enter his bloodstream.

Before the door had finished swinging closed, Agent Pratt put Franklin in a choke hold, and he was unable to breathe or move.

SEVENTY-THREE

Helen

Waking up to someone pounding on the front door had reminded Helen of the previous incident at Mr. Smith's house. That had frightened her more than she could express. The fear of separation from her mother had destroyed her sense of security and all possibility of remaining calm. If she did not have to act bravely for Daryn, she would have run in a panic to her mother and to the bad men who had captured her.

Since they had successfully escaped the last ordeal, she felt more confident in her present circumstance. Her mother seemed more in control of herself and less crazy. Helen could feel it too.

Helen felt as though she had a new purpose in life now, her new sister Daryn. Ever since her abduction, she always thought of how Daryn had lived her whole life in that nightmare. Helen promised herself to give her new best friend a better life, like the one she remembered having. She tried her best to push the bad memories away and focus on the good ones, but recent memories still felt too painful. She hoped the feeling would stop one day.

She unconsciously decided to stay away from all adult men unless her mother knew them. The new man in her mother's life acted kind to her, but so had the man who wanted to take care of her at the hotel. He talked nicely and said he wanted to send her back home. When he held her hand in the hotel room, she remembered wanting to pull away but feeling afraid to do it. She doubted Gerald could make her feel as uncomfortable.

"What are you looking for," Helen asked as she followed her mother around the house.

"We need to get out of here," her mother said, only a hint of patience in her voice. "But first I need to find something. Please go keep Daryn company. I need to concentrate."

Helen worried about leaving her mother alone to herself. Going away would make her mother feel worse, more alone. She needed company. If Helen stayed close, her mom would feel better and would thank her in the end. She seemed ready to explode if anything else went wrong and Helen could only help if she stayed. If she really wanted Helen to leave she would have kept asking.

Later, when Sadi loaded them into the new car that Freddy had given to them, Helen wondered where they would stop next. Instead of asking, she just watched out the window, searching for suspicious people. Since her mother had to concentrate on driving, Helen would help keep them safe from all the evil men in the world.

"Where are we going now?" Daryn asked after they pulled onto the road.

"A very nice place," Sadi said with a fake smile but moist eyes. "I don't know where they took Gerald, but we need to wish him luck. Can you do that for me?"

Helen thought she knew what the look meant. Her mother was sad about leaving Gerald's house. Helen was too. Before they drove away, Sadi took one last look.

They traveled only a short while before arriving at their next destination, another house with a private drive, similar to where Mr. Smith lived. A beautiful dark-haired woman waited in the large half-circle driveway, the same woman Helen remembered when they visited last. The woman was holding her hand above her eyes, shielding them from the bright sunlight.

An older man stood next to her, and his face looked strained from scowling too much. Before her mother could exit the car, the dark-haired woman grasped the door handle and opened it for her.

"Oh my dear woman," she said and embraced her as soon as Sadi stood from the car. "What happened to you? You have been through too much, way too much. Come inside, have something to eat, and we'll talk about it when you're ready. We will take care of everything."

"Thank you," Sadi said, and her eyes began glistening with tears. The woman's strong embrace must have prevented her mother from saying anything else.

SEVENTY-FOUR

Sadi

During the first night at Cesar's house, Sadi had a new nightmare. She weaved through the graves in the cemetery where the body of her son rested, searching for his headstone. For endless hours, she wandered through the mist, reading name after name in search of Jacob Jacobsen. After searching in vain, she came upon a trail leading into a grove of trees, and she knew her son rested there. But the mere sight of the dark grove turned her blood into honey, forcing her heart to increase the pressure, almost breaking in the process.

After walking into the middle of the dark grove, she found the familiar headstone of her son's grave but at the head of a hole with a big pile of moist dirt beside it. As happened in most dreams, she ignored her instincts and walked to the edge of the hole to see the closed casket several meters below the surface of the earth. Soon the casket would open to reveal her son's body. She was close enough to hear his voice.

"Mommy?"

"I'm here, Jacob!"

After the casket opened, Sadi saw two lifeless bodies, her son and Gerald, both long dead. Her heart stopped beating, and she closed her eyes, expecting and hoping for the darkness to consume her.

After a moment, a blue light penetrated through her closed eyelids. When she opened her eyes again, dirt had filled the grave, and a bright light illuminated the whole grove. She looked up to see the alien probe from the barn, hovering above her with its long pulsating tendrils of light. The probe hung motionless, but the long tendrils flowed with the light breeze. They slowly stretched out to her and pulled her away from the grave.

As the strings pulled her away from the earth, she extended both hands to the grave and sobbed.

"Jacob, Jacob..."

—※—

"There there," said a familiar voice from the darkness of her room. Sadi opened her eyes to see Dominga sitting on the edge of her bed. "It's just a dream. It's just a bad dream. You're safe."

Waking in the darkness to find another adult sitting above her would usually have given Sadi a heart attack. But Dominga had a soothing quality to her voice and could only bring comfort. In the darkness of the night, Sadi wondered if she possessed some kind of ancient Mexican magic.

"Hi," she replied and slowly sat up. After sitting, she noticed her matching silk pajama shirt and pants. "I'm sorry if I woke you."

"Don't worry about that," Dominga said with a dismissive laugh. "I don't get much sleep these days anyway. I'm sorry to admit my selfishness, but having you here helps remind me of my insignificant problems, and with Cesar gone to Brazil, I can talk to someone other than Doroteo."

Sadi loved hearing the word *insignificant* spoken with such a strong Spanish accent.

"Well," she said while putting her legs over the bed and stretching her muscles. "I'm glad my problems are benefiting someone."

Even with her eyes open, Sadi could still see the image of Gerald lying in the grave with her son, and the memory made her wish never to sleep again. Maybe she could find a nice tall cliff and throw herself off it. Would that end the pain of the dream? If she had no children depending on her, she might have considered that option.

Sadi forced herself to smile. Being with her friends gave her the strength to act cheerful. For the girls' sake, she had to keep strict control of her emotions.

"It's almost five," Dominga said and stood from the bed. "You don't really want to go back to sleep, after your night vision, do you? Let's go get some coffee."

"That sounds great," Sadi said.

On their way to the kitchen, Sadi stopped at the door of the room with her sleeping girls. The soft glow of the night light covered their innocent faces like a blanket. Both she and Dominga smiled at the sight of them, and Sadi felt a bond begin to form with the older woman who could also appreciate the beauty of sleeping children.

"When Doroteo heard of your visit," Dominga whispered and then started laughing, "he ran to the store to buy a night-light for the girls. He pretended to be bothered by it, but I could see the excitement on his face. Ha!"

Sadi remembered the previous night when Doroteo presented the night light to Helen. She had refused to take it from his hand and tried hiding behind Sadi. He had laughed hard and patted her on the head. The memory made Sadi smile too.

They shut the door to the girls' room and then walked to the kitchen.

"You're going to be safe here," Dominga said as she poured the coffee. "Even if they come to take us. They'll never find the secret room in the basement. It's full of food and everything you'll need until we can get back."

Sadi smiled in return but had little faith in her suggestion.

"You sound pretty confident about getting out of this."

"Cesar and Doroteo will not fail us," she said and laughed. "They have been through worse things than this."

While sipping her coffee, Sadi looked into Dominga's eyes, trying to detect any indication of fake confidence. She saw none.

"I wouldn't mess with them, Doroteo especially."

"You're a smart girl," Dominga said, and Sadi suddenly felt their age difference. Dominga could have been her mother's age but still appeared very young, perhaps in her late forties.

"Thanks!"

"It would not be pretty if someone came to take Doroteo," she continued. "Will you tell me something? How did you escape the people following you? How did you get to Gerald's house? Yesterday, I did not want to make you tell it again, but now my curiosity is getting the better of me."

"Freddy rescued us," Sadi answered without hesitation. Thinking of Freddy reminded her of another reason for hope. "The two agents following me found me at Mr. Smith's house. For the second time since they took Helen, I thought my life was over."

The angry look in Dominga's eyes made Sadi pause, and the older woman said something in Spanish. The words sounded unpleasant.

"I'm sorry," Dominga said. "This whole thing makes me so angry. Continue with your story. How did Freddy get you out of there? Did he kill them? That kid scares me."

"There was no violence," she said while trying to remember what happened. "It was strange, like a dream. The memory feels fuzzy, but probably because I was scared to death. Freddy came in the house, and they just did what he said."

"He told them what to do?" Dominga said in surprise.

"I don't know how he did it, but he took the girls to the car, and then they let me leave with Mr. Smith to the hospital. We left Freddy there at the house with them, but then he came to the hospital later. He didn't tell me what he did with the men, but he said they would never bother me again. I didn't really want to know."

"Mr. Smith was in the hospital?" Dominga asked almost in a panic. "Is he okay? Where is he now?"

"I don't know," Sadi answered and felt guilty for not knowing Mr. Smith's status. The memory filled her with anger. "Those bastards came into the house, and I think Mr. Smith's heart just couldn't handle the stress. The doctors thought he would be okay. Freddy was with him."

Before replying, Dominga thought for a moment.

"I will pray for him, but I'm glad you're here with us. What can you tell me about Freddy? You've known him for a long time, haven't you? Has he always been able to do things like this? What is he?"

Sadi briefly explained her relationship with Freddy and his past. While relating Freddy's traumatic childhood, Dominga put her hand over her mouth and shook her head.

"That poor boy. How can people be so mean to children? Oh, I am sorry to bring that up. This life can be so cruel!"

Sadi explained how she had lost contact with Freddy after she went to college and how Mr. Smith had rescued him and made Freddy responsible for all of his affairs. After she finished with the story, Dominga breathed deeply and sighed in relief. She reminded Sadi of going to a movie that ended well.

"When he visited me," Sadi continued and became lost in the memory. "When he showed me that crystal with the spider, it was the first time I'd seen him in many years. He used to be in love with me, but I don't know if he is still. I hope not."

"Is he the same person you used to know?"

"I think, deep down he's the same person I knew but now? I don't know what's happened to him, what that alien thing did to him."

"Well, I never trusted him," Dominga said in apology. "But you should be able to trust someone simply because they've earned the trust of those you do trust. That should have been enough for me, but when I looked into his eyes, I don't know what I saw. Maybe I just fear what I don't understand. If you tell me he can be trusted, I will trust him."

"Yes, I trust him," she answered, but when Dominga kept looking at her, Sadi continued. "How can I not trust him? I owe him my life, and so do the girls."

Several questions escaped from the back of her mind, where she usually kept them hidden. To ask the questions might make the answers real.

Did the alien arrange everything so she would trust Freddy? Was he the same person who traveled in Taylor's convertible into space? What had happened to him on his journey?

SEVENTY-FIVE

Agent Pratt

"When I let you go, don't scream," Pratt said. "I'm just here to talk to you. That's all."

When he felt Franklin's muscles begin to relax, Pratt injected a small dose of Midazolam into his arm, his drug of choice for interrogation. He always kept a small vial of it for emergencies, and he used only a fraction of the dose necessary for sedation. The drug would impair the kid's memory of the event and also make him more compliant.

Franklin opened his mouth to speak, but Agent Pratt covered his mouth again.

"Just something to calm your nerves," he said in answer to the unspoken question. "That's all. Can I let you go now?"

Franklin nodded, and Pratt let him go. Normally, he would have blindfolded his victim to make him feel more helpless and disoriented, but he wanted the kid to trust him as much as possible.

"Who are you and what did you put into me?"

Franklin turned to face his attacker and rubbed his forearm where a small pool of blood began to form. He took a tentative step backward, then began to sway.

"You better take a seat," Agent Pratt said with fake concern, "before you fall down."

Pratt turned away from the kid and created a small opening in the blinds. While looking outside, he removed his gun and pointed it at the ceiling. Just as expected, he could feel the kid staring at the gun.

"Okay, who are you?" Franklin asked, sitting down and leaning back, his hand pressed to his forehead. He kept his eyes focused on Agent Pratt. The steaming cup of noodles lay on the coffee table in front of him.

"Did you know two people are watching your apartment? They're outside right now."

"Thanks for the information," Franklin answered with exaggerated sarcasm, his hand still on his forehead. He spoke slowly and a bit slurred but controlled. "Now who are you?"

Pratt already disliked Franklin, but he felt impressed by the kid's stamina to remain belligerent with the drug in his system. That would soon change.

"I don't expect you to believe me," Pratt began, trying to make his tone more friendly, "but I want to help you. We know that Gerald Foster and his friend Max Garner were taken recently by the military. It's only a matter of time before they learn all about your operation, but there's still hope to get out of this mess, for you at least."

The kid lowered his hand from his face and tilted his head away from the couch to face Pratt more directly.

"Only a matter of time?" Franklin asked and paused to search for his next words. The drug was beginning to take a stronger hold of him.

"Yes," Pratt interrupted and leaned forward. He picked up the noodles and took a bite. "Taylor and Cesar and the others are still safe. You don't mind, do you?"

Franklin took a deep breath and rubbed his eyes. He began speaking quietly to himself, and Pratt recognized only one word.

"Alien."

Alien? Pratt's eyes narrowed as he tried convincing himself that he heard a different word. *Did the kid just say alien?* Pratt decided to keep the flow going.

"When did you see the alien last?"

"I've never seen it. What do you know about it?"

For a brief moment, Franklin's eyes opened wider.

"That's why the military is interested in you?" Pratt said in exasperation.

Kids like Franklin often fell victim to stupid conspiracy theories about aliens and the military. Pratt was disappointed at having to deal with another stupid kid. Couldn't he deal with people more intelligent, people who posed more of a challenge or threat?

While waiting for Franklin to respond, Pratt recognized the signs of drowsiness. Franklin could not be allowed to fall asleep. Once he lost consciousness, he would lose all memory of the previous conversation, and Pratt had no time to start the conversation again.

"Let's get to your room," Pratt said, knowing the walk would help keep him conscious. "You need to lie down."

"Okay," he agreed.

With his hand on the kid's shoulder, Pratt walked a semi-conscious Franklin to his room. He used the time to plan his next line of questions. As Pratt suspected, the kid used his bedroom as a workroom. A home-assembled desktop computer and a large server sat on a table on one side of the room with a laptop on a small desk by his bed. Only the LEDs and glowing monitors lit the room.

"We've been tracking the movements of this alien for a while now," he said as Franklin leaned against the headboard of his bed. "The damn military's trying to cover it up as usual."

Pratt paused and let silence work its effect on Franklin. Most people felt awkward during long pauses in conversation. Franklin's next words made Pratt change his strategy.

"So they're only interested in the alien," Franklin said bluntly. He spoke with his eyes closed as if suffering from exhaustion. "And not the fusion reactor?"

—※—

Through the slow and laborious process of interrogation, Pratt eventually extracted all the information he wanted. In the end, Pratt had difficulty processing all of it. Not only did Gerald's group have some kind of secret propulsion technology, but their clever engineers had also developed a fusion reactor.

He almost failed to believe the story but trusted in his technique. People could not lie convincingly with the right drugs in their system. Although he instantly dismissed the part about the alien, he knew the kid believed in its existence. The military must have incorporated the idea to entrap them.

Pratt thought he understood the military's interest in their group. Civilians had no justification for trying to keep technology like that to themselves. They should have taken their inventions to the military as soon as they were developed, the fools. They acted typical of deviants like Gerald Foster. He also understood the connection between their group, Max Garner, and his satellite company.

Pratt smiled when he imagined what the CIA would do to extract information from Gerald. Unfortunately, Pratt also knew it might be the only satisfaction he would get from the situation. Foster had gotten himself into quite a mess, one even he could not escape. Pratt needed to let that knowledge satisfy him. Once he accepted the possibility that he would never hear of Gerald Foster again, he felt some relief, the loss of a heavy burden. But for his own curiosity, he needed to follow the case to its conclusion.

Still, knowing that the fucking CIA had taken Gerald and not Agent Pratt. That stung the most. He spent a moment fantasizing about how he could be a thorn in their side.

After finally allowing Franklin to fall asleep on his bed, Pratt considered the option of searching the computers to discover more information, but it would be a long and arduous task, and he did not have the time.

He exited the apartment through the back screen door. Just in case he wanted to return that night, he left the door unlocked. After checking on his car, he walked to where he could see the scene of his crime.

Only a few people remained on the street. A single police vehicle was parked in front of the house with broken windows and bullet holes. An officer sat in the driver's seat while another officer leaned over the hood writing on some papers. For a moment, Agent Pratt watched as Miss Busybody spoke with someone near the house of the victims.

As he'd hoped, Pratt found the car of the two watchers empty. He instinctively scanned the scene without moving his head but did not see them. Without a pause, he turned and started walking away.

Just as a precaution, he decided to walk past his car to make sure no one followed him before driving away from the scene. He was pretty sure the police had taken the watchers in for questioning, but he had to be extra cautious. If he was wrong and they noticed him, it would lead to a lot of trouble.

As he walked down the street, he realized the feeling of being watched from above never went away. In all of the excitement, he just hadn't noticed. Now that he had finished with the operation, the sensation returned with twice the intensity.

After finally returning to his car, he looked up and a single star caught his attention. Other stars shined brighter, but that one looked different for some reason. Was that the same star he'd noticed before all the fun began?

"Stupid alien conspiracy shit!"

Pratt laughed uncomfortably, opened his car door, and then drove away.

SEVENTY-SIX

Franklin

The next morning, Franklin awoke fully clothed and on top of his covers. Pain from a headache seemed to originate from all over his head, unlike the occasional migraine emanating from one specific location. While lying in bed, he wondered if he'd had too much alcohol the previous evening, but he failed to remember having even one drink.

For at least thirty minutes, he stayed in bed while his head throbbed and strange thoughts flashed across his mind like watching a bike race. After a while, he sat up and tried retracing the events of the previous evening. He remembered hearing glass breaking outside and going to investigate. He'd seen nothing very interesting, just a bunch of people looking at each other and the police car, so he went back inside his apartment. After that, his memory became fuzzy.

When he attempted to remember opening the front door, his memory snapped into place like a puzzle piece. He shook his head in disbelief at the confusing story unfolding in his mind. Although the entire story felt dreamlike, each piece of the puzzle was clear: a hand over his mouth, a sting in his arm, a man with dangerous eyes, a gun.

Did someone really break into his apartment and did he talk to that person? What did he say? Was he remembering a dream?

Franklin jumped out of bed, but dizziness almost pulled him back down. After a few seconds, his vision returned and he peered suspiciously around his room.

He was searching for evidence of the truth he did not want to see. All the equipment in his room appeared intact and undisturbed. Fortunately, he'd remembered to log off everything before going outside to investigate the noise. He sometimes forgot to lock his door, but he never forgot to log off from his computers. Ever since Gerald had asked him to join the group, his habit of taking security seriously blossomed into a full-blown schizophrenic paranoia.

The living room remained the way he left it with a cold cup of noodles sitting on the coffee table, only partially consumed. While looking at the cup, he remembered a man asking about it and the memory of the intruder slowly began to materialize into something real, not just imagination.

"Oh my God," Franklin said to the still air. He walked to the couch where the man had been sitting. "He was right here. The shooting in the street was probably just a diversion."

He went to the window and peeked at the street, and then to the empty parking space where the two people had been watching his house. Gone! Franklin sat down and picked up the noodles, staring at them as if in a trance.

"I can't stay here," he said quietly, afraid his voice carried through the walls to the ears of some government agent. With the cup of broth and noodles in his hands, he tried remembering their conversation. Franklin vaguely recalled talking about the alien and maybe mentioning the fusion reactor.

"What the hell did I tell him?" he asked then placed the cup on the table, "and why?"

He touched his shoulder and felt the tenderness from the injection. Although the pain failed to add any new information, it seemed to bring the reality of the experience into focus.

"Shit!" he said loudly. "Damn it!"

He wanted to run to his car and drive until he ran out of money to pay for more gas. But after taking a deep breath, he forced himself to create a moment of peace. He could see two options: no time to escape or enough time to escape. The speed of his next move might affect the outcome, so he must not act in a panic.

He needed a shower.

The warm water flowing over his face helped to calm his nerves and slow the firing of his neurons, but it failed to keep the paranoid images from flowing through his mind. Every time he closed his eyes to rinse soap away, he imagined the door bursting open and armed men taking him away, dripping, naked, and handcuffed into the street. What would the blond from apartment ten think? The irrational fear made him laugh.

Even though the man had assaulted Franklin and then injected him with some drug, at least he'd been friendly. If he worked with the people who took Gerald and Max, would he go to all the trouble to create a diversion, to interrogate him? Probably not. That thought offered some comfort.

What if they expected him to run and planned to follow him? Would he be leading them to someone in the group? Franklin had to assume the worst, but since he might already know about their plans, he could stay one step ahead of them.

With regret and even a little pain, Franklin decided to dismantle the website. Destroying it would be easy, but he imagined the action would feel like killing a child. He had raised the site from nothing. He spent so much time perfecting the security infrastructure. Had he left a crack in the security wall? He could not imagine any weakness, and that scared him. Someone else in the group must have made a mistake, he concluded.

He already wrote a program to do the job. It would send a notification email to all the members of the site, then randomly change all the passwords and keys. Then it would do the same thing on the server dedicated to the group. All the data would be encrypted, and no amount of torture could help decipher it. Not even Franklin could recreate the keys.

After only a moment of hesitation, he clicked the execute command and felt physically sick to see all his hard work burn to smoke in the wind. When completed, he unplugged the computers and then began stuffing his backpack with everything he'd need on the road.

While getting ready to leave, he wondered how long before they would be alerted to the website's destruction. They would know that he knew and would probably come for him.

When he felt ready to open his door and enter the dangerous world outside, he first looked through the window to check for anyone watching. After noticing no one, he took a deep breath, stepped onto his porch, and started walking through the courtyard toward his car. He glanced to where the sun hid just below the horizon. He could not remember the last time he got up before sunrise.

His heart stopped when he saw the girl but not from fear.

When the blond from apartment ten appeared and he noticed her eyes on him, he was instantly paralyzed. He came within her view just in time to see her stop running and begin to walk. Sweat glistened on her pale skin and soaked her white tank top. While watching her approach, he realized that she was going to confront him. With considerable effort, he pulled his eyes away from their instinctive placement on her breasts. Fortunately, her pretty brown eyes helped him stay focused.

"Oh my God!" he whispered to himself before she was close enough to hear.

The irony of the situation seemed tangible. Why now? Why now! Ever since the previous fall when she'd moved into the apartments, he dreamed of an excuse to confront her. So far, he had only ever seen her getting home late at night. When she stopped a meter away, he remembered his frozen, physical state. She smiled, and he tried to return the gesture, but the tension in his cheeks made him feel awkward. He probably looked like a freak.

"You're up early," she said while still breathing heavily. "I've never seen you outside before noon."

While waiting for him to respond, she stretched her hands and arms above her head and bent her back a little bit, as if intentionally tempting him to look at her breasts again. By some miracle of will, he kept his gaze on her face.

"I, um, yeah," he said. She smiled and waited. His mind went blank. Without knowing what his lips would do, he opened his mouth. "I um, need to get out of town."

The sound of his voice seemed to put him back on track. *What did I just say?* Did he just tell someone his intention to leave? The memory of his dangerous situation returned like a swift slap across the face. He imagined the police or FBI asking his neighbors if they had seen him and what he said.

"*Oh, yeah,*" she would say. "*I ran into him this morning, and he said he had to leave town. He seemed worried about something.*"

"That's cool," she said, glancing at his backpack and then bending down to stretch her legs. "Going on vacation somewhere?"

With another burst of superhuman strength, he pulled his eyes away from her bent form to scan the street in search of the watchers. From his viewpoint, he could see only a small section of the street. The watchers or their car could not be seen.

"Yes, actually," he said after slowly exhaling. The fresh oxygen in his blood helped restore his thought process. He had the start of a plan. "Could you do me a favor?"

"Maybe," she said, squinting her eyes suspiciously and wiping sweat from her forehead. "But I don't even know your name. Mine's Christine."

When Christine smiled and said her name, a dormant set of neural pathways burst into life, and he had a new priority—the girl in front of him. Avoiding capture and going to military prison moved to second place on his list.

For the first time in his life, Franklin was aware of an opportunity with a female while it was taking place. He usually noticed opportunities with girls after they took place, and then he'd promise himself to be less oblivious during the next occasion if it ever came. Did the girl in front of him justify the risk? The future would be filled with even more regret if he failed to try.

"I'm sorry," he said, his lips relaxing into a natural smile. Having nothing to lose helped alleviate the pressure. "The name's Franklin and I'm in a bit of trouble. That's why I'm leaving, why I'm out so early."

"Really," she said, and her smile disappeared, replaced by a look of concern, "and I can help somehow?"

He looked around quickly and still saw no one.

"If anyone comes asking about me will you tell them I went to my sister's for a couple days, and then I'm coming back?"

"Who's going to be looking for you?" she asked, more interested now.

"I can't say anything more specific. Will you do that little thing for me?"

"I can," she said with hesitation. "But only if you give me more in-formation. I'm not an answering machine."

"It's actually better if you don't know the details." Her expression of doubt remained, so he continued. "People will be looking for me but because of some friends. They're the ones in trouble, and by asso-ciation, they drug me into it."

While considering his answer, she pursed her lips together and squinted. He shifted the heavy backpack on his shoulder, and it began digging into his skin again. He had to give her something else before she rejected his request, which would remove his only chance with her. It felt really good not to quit like he usually did.

"I know this sounds like a really stupid scheme to get your number, but do you think I can maybe call in a few days to see if anyone came looking, or if you saw anything? Would that be okay?"

"It does sound like a stupid scheme," she said, laughing, "but I've heard worse. Let me guess. You can't give me your number because then it will compromise your situation. Am I right?"

He smiled but could not bring himself to laugh. If he forced it, she would notice.

"Something like that, but I'm really not making this up."

"I know," she said seriously. "I can tell. I'm ready to give you my number. What are you going to write it on? Have a pen in your backpack?"

"You can just tell me. I'll remember." If his memory could hold anything in the world, it would retain her number, even if it contained a hundred digits. "I'll write it down later."

After she gave her number, he repeated it out loud, and then his panic returned from hiding behind his hormones, and he had to force himself to stay and ask some customary questions about her life. In just a few short minutes, he learned the basics of her present situation. She attended college, majoring in special education, and had at least three more years before she could complete her teaching certifications.

She had recently moved into the same apartment with her sister, and he lied about knowing her sister's identity when he could not recall ever seeing her. When he told her about his life, he neglected to mention how he'd dropped out of college and had no desire to return. Most people saw that as a sign of laziness, so he avoided the topic and focused on telling her about his work. She showed interest in his programming and web development work. She even asked for his technical assistance at some future time, and he promised to help her with anything she might need.

People always asked him for technical assistance, from complicated programming issues to simple entertainment systems setup. Knowing how electronic equipment worked seemed to make him an omniscient genius. Several minutes later, he found a good opportunity to end the conversation.

"I'm sorry, but I really have to get going." He shifted awkwardly to walk past her. "I really do plan to call you."

"Did you see what happened last night?" she asked while effectively blocking his path. "I saw the police down the street when I came home, but they were wrapping everything up."

For a split second, a new fear crept into his mind. *Is she intention-*

ally stalling me? Preparing for my apprehension? Disappointment at her possible betrayal outweighed his fear of getting caught.

"There was a shooting, I think, but I only heard glass breaking." He pretended to keep smiling. "No one was hurt, I don't think."

"Wait a second," she said suspiciously. "Were you involved with that?"

"No," he said quickly, a little too quickly. She squinted her eyes even more. The look on his face betrayed his anxiety.

"Wow," she said, looking around in fear. "You really are in trouble. I'm not going to be in trouble, am I? If I help you?"

"I really don't know," he said, relief flooding back into his system. She seemed genuinely concerned. "I don't think doing what I asked can get you into trouble, since I really didn't tell you anything."

"Well, Franklin." She said his name slowly, possibly to entrench it into her memory. "You should probably go. I'll try to do what you say, even if it's the police. They can't prove I lied about anything. I am sorry for your trouble. Call me when you can, you know, to let me know how you're doing."

She took a step out of his way.

"Thank you, Christine," he said.

"I'll wait for your call."

"It was good to meet you, finally."

When Franklin exited the small courtyard and got a better view of the entire street, he instantly noticed the two watchers in their car, which was parked on the other side of the street and farther down than the previous day. The sight of the man and woman erased his excitement from talking to Christine. He casually walked the ten remaining meters to his car and calmly put the heavy backpack in the back seat then closed the door.

Before turning to walk back to his apartment, he spent a moment stretching, hoping the action would make him appear relaxed and not paranoid. If he appeared to be in a hurry, they would probably take action sooner.

While walking back to his apartment, he expected Christine to be gone, but before entering the courtyard, he noticed her peeking around the end of the building. Her eyes switched between him and the surveillance vehicle. As Franklin continued walking, he could feel them all watching him. When he entered the courtyard and exited their view, he felt a momentary relief.

Christine silently joined his side and walked down the path with him, all the way to his apartment door. With the beautiful girl by his side, his pulse quickened even further.

"I saw those two people last night talking with the police," Christine said with concern. "They were being questioned, so they're definitely not with the police. They were in a different car too. I notice those sorts of things. They're the ones after you?"

"Yes," he said but more to himself than to her.

They were in a different car? How could he miss that? What else did he miss?

"If I leave now," he continued, "they're just going to follow me. But maybe I'll be able to lose them, eventually."

His overall plan remained the same, get out of there, but he doubted his ability to escape someone tailing him. He could outrun them maybe for a while but not their phone calls for backup. Now that he had time to think, the situation made sense. Of course, they would still be out there, watching him.

"You can't leave now. They're sure to catch you," Christine said while looking down at the ground at his apartment door. "I've got a plan, but it will involve others. Can you get at least two friends over here?"

He looked up from the ground, from his thoughts, and into her eyes. He should refuse to involve her, but his need for survival superseded his sense of social propriety.

"I can't ask you to help me, but thank you."

"You can thank me later," she said with a smile. "This is going to sound selfish, but before your friends get here, I need to take a shower. How long before they can arrive?"

"Maybe twenty minutes," he said, attempting to think of potential candidates. He refused to tell her about the shortage of his local friends. Franklin had many friends, but only a handful consisted of flesh and blood types within a short driving distance. The rest were digital bits of information, people who lived all over the world. He knew their online names and only some of their faces. He lived in an electronic world and only ventured out into the physical one when he needed something.

"That should give my sister some time to have a look around."

"What do you mean?"

"I'm going to have my sister take a short walk and look for any other people spying on you."

Her smile was a dare for him to argue, and for a moment, Franklin started to worry about the wisdom of involving her. Now her sister would be involved, another unpredictable variable. Christine still felt well worth the risk.

He nodded, and they separated. While away from her, his paranoia started to grow again. The situation seemed too improbable, receiving help just when he needed it the most, and originating from such a beautiful creature. When did providence ever smile upon Franklin Harvey?

—✳—

When back in the safety of his apartment, Franklin emailed the two people he thought most likely to help him. If it was during their usual awake time, his friends would have responded within twenty seconds. When three minutes passed without a response, he knew they were still asleep, and he had to act more aggressively by actually calling them.

"Hello?" his first victim answered with a groggy voice.

"Hey, Victor," Franklin said with fearful optimism.

"Franklin," his friend responded, the anger nearly making the phone resonate with the sound. "What the hell is wrong with you? I just fell asleep, well, ahh, just two hours ago."

"I was wondering if you could come to my apartment and help me stop a leaky faucet?" Franklin spoke in the most relaxed voice he could manage as if Victor had answered cheerfully. "I was going to visit my sister but can't until this damn faucet is fixed. My water bill's going to be through the roof. I need you to come and bring your *tool*."

Franklin waited in silence as his friend began to assess the anomalies in the information being conveyed. In any other situation, Franklin would fear to call before noon. His friend owned no plumbing tools and probably had no idea how to identify one. If Franklin ever did make the mistake of calling too early, he would be apologizing for the intrusion and not acting as though he'd just downloaded the unreleased version of the next *Diablo* video game and just had to tell someone. That offense would be easily forgiven.

The last anomaly involved Franklin's sister. Victor knew how Franklin would never of his own accord visit his sister. They hated each other.

"Do you mean, *The Screwdriver*?" his friend asked tentatively after the long silence. His friend's anger had vanished, and Franklin breathed a sigh of relief.

His friend seemed to understand. Franklin needed help and wanted Victor to bring his roommate who liked to refer to himself as the *Screwdriver*. His roommate thought the name surrounded him with an aura that would be mysteriously attractive to females, and while playing their first-person shooter games, the name did seem to work with females composed of pixels and other players who claimed to be females.

In their circle of gaming friends, the Screwdriver usually took the lead and rarely lost. In real life, he weighed almost three hundred pounds and wore thick glasses. To pay for his rent and food, he operated a respected gaming network.

Like many of his other friends, Victor and the Screwdriver lived in a fantasy world of video games, monsters, and other enemies unable to inflict real harm, enemies easy to eliminate. They longed for real-life action and would jump at the chance to help Franklin. But he regretfully doubted their ability to do so and would soon discover the truth. He crossed his fingers and hoped for the best since he had no other choice.

While waiting for his two friends, Franklin began to worry about the social situation. Would his friends hurt Christine's opinion of him? He hoped they had taken a shower, at least in the last three days. Franklin was the only one who took a shred of pride in his appearance, but if not for the guy who drugged him the previous night, Franklin would have hurried out of the apartment that morning without showering, and Christine would have probably walked right past him, which was another inexplicable sign of good luck.

"Thank you, evil government agent!" Franklin said to himself in an attempt to raise his morale.

When he looked through the blinds after the person began knocking on his door, he expected to see his friends, but instead, he found Christine and her older sister. The sister had darker blond hair and stood maybe a centimeter shorter. Franklin opened his door and stared at the two pretty girls standing there. Christine smiled politely while her sister had a look of distrust and hesitancy.

Without waiting for an invitation to enter, Christine stepped into the apartment followed by her sister who avoided eye contact with him. The sisters wore matching blue jeans. Christine wore a white shirt with her wet hair pulled into a ponytail. The sister looked recently torn out of bed, probably wearing clothes from the previous day.

The sight of the two beautiful girls in his apartment took his breath away for several seconds, even after shutting his door.

"My friends aren't here yet," he said while attempting to restore his breath.

"I know," Christine said, turning to her sister. "This is my sister Francis."

"Hi," the older girl said curtly and nodded slightly.

Franklin stopped himself from extending his hand when she showed signs of keeping her hand stiffly at her side. He wondered why he had never previously noticed her and then realized that he had seen her but thought she lived elsewhere.

Christine raised her hand in warning and stopped Franklin from returning the greeting. She held up a piece of paper for him to read. As he focused on her large and sloppy handwriting, he noticed the older sister roll her eyes slightly. The note had only four words.

Is your apartment bugged?

"I highly doubt it," he whispered and instantly felt silly as if he'd asked her to play cops and robbers with him. "I've inspected the place several times lately. Every time I leave, I check."

Christine turned the piece of paper over and set it down on the coffee table. The other side contained drawings like the plans of a football maneuver. She had a plan.

"I had Francis walk around the block, while I took a shower," she began and looked at her sister. "The two people watching you are still there, but Francis didn't notice any others."

When Christine mentioned the shower, Franklin spent all his energy focusing on the present situation, and not the sudden images of her showering.

"Thank you," he said finally, making eye contact with Francis. The corners of her mouth twisted slowly into a polite smile.

"I'm sorry," the sister said suddenly with a tone of suspicion, almost as an afterthought. "But this isn't some game to get my sister involved with you?"

Franklin was shocked at her abruptness, but Christine came instantly to his defense.

"I've told you, France. We ran into each other by chance, just at the same time as those two—"

"I know," her sister said, cutting Christine short. "I just need to hear it from him."

During the brief interlude, Franklin found interest in her reaction. The older sister seemed more concerned about her sister being manipulated romantically than the danger of the situation.

"I swear," he began. "I was on my way out and ran into her by chance. I've never planned to approach her before now, but yes, I have wanted to, um, talk to her, but this is not some scheme."

Francis looked directly into his eyes for half of a second, though the duration felt much longer.

"I'll believe you for now," she said. "Why are you in trouble? Who are they? Undercover police?"

"I don't know who they are, and I really don't think it's a good idea to tell you all the details." While attempting to explain, he fought the desire to reveal everything. "I mean, it's safer if you don't know. They've already taken one of my friends, and we don't know what's happened to him."

"While in the shower, I started thinking," Christine began.

Jesus! Why did she keep referring to her shower? He was having a difficult time ignoring his imagination of that activity.

"You mentioned your work with web development," she continued, "and that involves security. From what I see, you seem ready to take your server over there with you."

She nodded toward the corner of the room where a laptop sat on a server. All the wires were disconnected and coiled on the table next to them. As she spoke, her smile reminded Franklin of when he had successfully programmed his first microcontroller.

"Don't worry, you don't have to tell us the specifics, but I am willing to bet that you're safeguarding illegal activities for some organization. Am I right?"

"It's not illegal," he said, then stopped himself from saying more. "But it does involve web security. How do you know so much?"

"My sister," Francis said and cleared her throat, "is obsessed with, um, mystery novels, among other things."

"Guilty," Christine said, shrugging her shoulders. "I like to figure things out."

While waiting for his friends to arrive, they sat in his living room around the coffee table, and Christine explained her tentative plan. To his surprise, she took control of the situation, acting as a coach of a football team. As she spoke, she referred to her drawing on the paper, and Franklin began to feel a substantial hope of successfully escaping.

Before she was finished, Franklin saw a pair of shadows pass in front of the window by the door. He ran to the door and opened it before they could knock. As he had feared, he smelled them at the same time he could see them.

SEVENTY-SEVEN

Sadi

The first few days passed very slowly and felt like weeks. They waited impatiently in between website updates. Cesar kept the website updated on the status of the jet and their progress. Then late one night, Franklin posted a cryptic message about being followed. When Sadi woke up the next morning, Doroteo told her the website had disappeared.

"What the hell is going on?" asked Sadi.

"I need to go, but I'll be back, possibly tonight or tomorrow," Doroteo said and then left in his truck.

"He's worried," Dominga said. "I can hear it in his voice."

While waiting for Doroteo to return, Sadi pulled the girls aside and told them of possibly having to hide again in a secret room. She expected a reaction of fear and anxiety, but the girls reacted without much emotion.

"Cool, I want to see it," Helen said.

Doroteo returned that night and told how he had visited Franklin's apartment and found no sign of him, but it did not mean anything suspicious had happened. The next day Doroteo left the house again, only to return a short while later. He went in and out several times the following days. Sadi stopped counting how many trips he made. He seldom spoke to her or even Dominga.

"Where does he go?" Sadi asked when he left for the second time that day.

"He's probably visiting his friends and planning, talking with his web of informants, you know, feeding the network."

Sadi thought of a mafia network, a group of people offering protection to everyone in the neighborhood for a hefty price. Was Doroteo the neighborhood thug? When Sadi mentioned her concerns, Dominga laughed and had to wipe tears out of her eyes before responding.

"No need to worry about his friends," Dominga said once she regained control of her emotions. "He doesn't associate with the violent ones, although you wouldn't be able to tell the difference."

While Doroteo worked on his defense plan, Sadi and Dominga tried to relax in front of the TV while the girls played video games and watched movies. Earlier the previous day, Dominga had visited the movie rental store and brought home ten DVDs for the girls to watch.

Helen wanted to show the movie *Wall-E* to Daryn. Sadi remembered taking Helen to the movie theater to watch it. They had really enjoyed the movie, but while watching it with them and seeing the humans return to Earth, the scene reminded her of their own plight, except the Earth had become too dangerous for them.

While they watched the little robot fly through space with a fire extinguisher, Sadi noticed their eyes. She could see the movie reflected in them. Pure joy and amazement seemed to shine from their tiny faces, the excitement of exploration. At that moment, the dangers of space travel seemed trivial compared to the beauty and wonder above the atmosphere of Earth.

Doroteo returned home in the middle of the next movie, but the girls kept their attention on the high-definition screen. The two grown women turned instantly. From the look in his eyes, even Sadi knew something had changed.

"What's wrong?" Dominga asked.

"I need to show you something," he replied and walked out of their sight, into the hallway. They found him in Cesar's study bringing the desktop computer to life. He opened the Firefox web browser and typed something into the search box. Sadi watched him without looking at the screen. While he typed, Sadi stared at the large tattoo covering the back of his neck, some elaborate Spanish writing. The words looked sinister and reminded her of a video game that her brother loved, but that she had never played—Diablo.

He clicked on the link to a video from a list on YouTube.

"Watch this," he said as a news video of a female reporter began playing.

"Federal investigators are calling the explosion an accident," the voice said from the pretty reporter with blond hair. Above her on the right, a small video box showed a smoldering set of demolished buildings. Black plumes of smoke rose into the air from them.

"Officials are not yet saying what caused the fire, or what was burning, but they assure us that there is no danger to public health. Any environmental concern, if there is any, should be minimal. A spokesman from the local fire department assured us they could bring the blaze under control by morning. Until then, we won't know the full extent of the damage to human life or property."

While the video continued to play, Sadi turned from the female reporter to look intently into the camera view.

"Official statements from the Utah high technology company Cerametrics, are saying that as many as ten employees are unaccounted for, but other sources claim that as many as thirty people could be injured or killed. This may be the worst disaster the state of Utah has seen for a hundred years. Governor Huntsman has called for an investigation into the company's safety precautions to determine if this tragedy could have been prevented. Our affiliate station acquired the following amateur video."

The small video in the upper right of the screen expanded and switched to the view of the same group of buildings before they were destroyed, light gray smoke ascending to the sky from one of them. At first, hardly any flames could be seen, but after a few seconds, one of the buildings exploded in a ball of fire. Dominga jumped in surprise. After the explosion, gigantic flames soared higher into the sky.

When the video of the explosion had finished, the screen zoomed back to the reporter. The woman's eyes widened in obvious amazement then she shook her head and finished her report. "Judging from the video, this reporter has little hope for survivors."

"Oh my God!" Sadi said in amazement after the video stopped. The sight of the explosion made her forget her question of why Doroteo wanted to show them. The company name stuck in her mind.

"Cerametrics," Dominga said with her hand over her mouth. "Is that the company Gerald visited?"

"Yes, Gerald visited Ceramatrics," Doroteo said gravely. He replayed the video, starting just before the explosion. He put his finger on the screen. "See there. Those are high-grade military explosives, which need a very specific detonation. That was no accident!"

"What does it mean?" Sadi asked, not really wanting to know the answer. The sight of the explosion almost made her feel numb, and the implication felt unreal. She answered her own question before Doroteo could. "They're going to blow us up? I mean, they already would have done it, right?"

The thought of being detonated seemed too merciful of an end to her uncertain life.

"No," he said. "They're not going to blow us up, but we can assume one thing. They probably know everything, from Gerald."

Sadi felt instant betrayal but soon realized that if Gerald provided the information, they would have had to remove it from him forcibly. A renewed fear for her girls soon replaced her sorrow for Gerald and the two people huddled around the computer with her.

Dominga said something in Spanish to Doroteo, and he replied so fast it sounded like one long word. Sadi felt as though they were trying to hide information from her. While they spoke to each other, she could see anxiety in their faces.

"I am sorry," Dominga said after finishing with Doroteo.

For an unknown reason, Sadi felt a small twinge of hope. After seeing her new friends with distressing emotions so close to her own, she felt the need to be strong for them. Despite all the bad things she had escaped lately, she held onto hope.

"We'll get out of this," she said.

Doroteo's cell phone rang while Sadi spoke. After putting the phone to his ear, he raised his hands to silence them. He spoke in Spanish for ten seconds, and Dominga looked at Sadi in confusion.

After cutting the connection, Doroteo pulled a gun from the back of his pants.

"We have a visitor," he said, then stood and headed toward the door. "Stay with the girls."

As they walked back to join the girls, Dominga held onto Sadi's arm in an apparent attempt to provide emotional support. Sadi appreciated the gesture but could only think of Gerald answering the door at his house and finding his abductors. She tried focusing on Freddy and Doroteo finding a solution.

Sadi smiled when they found the girls laughing at the movie and having a good time together. When Helen turned and saw her mother, her face turned somber, as if she could see behind the act, to her mother's hidden fears. She paused only for a moment before turning back to the movie. Sadi and Dominga sat on the opposite couch and pretended to watch the movie with them.

"Why did he get a phone call?" Sadi asked quietly. "Someone's watching the house, aren't they?"

"Of course, my dear. Like I said, Doroteo knows how to take care of things, but after what's happened…"

Dominga stopped talking when they heard the door open, followed by the sound of a quiet conversation. While listening and attempting to catch the words, Sadi worried that they would hear a gunshot at any moment and then strangers storming into the house. Perhaps she should have taken the girls to the hiding place, but her curiosity kept her sitting still.

Doroteo appeared a few seconds later, his gun back in his holster.

The frown on his face seemed like a bad sign.

"Freddy is here," he said and sounded angry. "They stopped him at the gate. He's driving the damned BMW."

"Doroteo," said Dominga and nodded toward the girls. "Watch your language!"

Sadi would never have dreamed of scolding the man. He showed no sign of apology, but he seemed unwilling to meet the challenge in the older woman's eyes. He motioned for them to follow him toward the garage entrance.

She had last seen Freddy at the hospital with Mr. Smith. She suddenly felt excited and frightened to see him again. What information did he bring? He possibly held the key to their entire future, and for some reason, she wanted to delay discovering it.

"Why is he here now?" asked Dominga before they reached the door. "The timing can't be good!"

"He is putting us all in danger by bringing that damn car here," Doroteo said.

"He wouldn't be here unless it's important," Sadi said in Freddy's defense, ignoring the temptation to look away from the dangerous black eyes. Doroteo's response of silence said more than any words could.

They opened the door of the garage to find the BMW coming to a slow stop. Sadi stared mesmerized at the car as if seeing a living creature. Any previous doubts she held about Freddy going to another world disappeared when she saw the shiny surface of the vehicle. The car had a quality to it that made the whole story as real as the video of the Cerametrics building explosion. The vehicle almost looked alien to her.

"Let's go to the kitchen," Doroteo said and shut the door to the garage after Freddy entered the house.

Without a word, Freddy led them to the kitchen and leaned against one of the counters. Sadi waited for either Dominga, Doroteo, or Freddy to say something.

"You saw what happened at Cerametrics?" Freddy addressed all of them but kept his eyes on Sadi.

"Yes, we just saw it. Horrible!" Sadi said and tightened her muscles to stop herself from shivering. "You look exhausted. You should sit."

"There's not much time," he said. "It's not safe here anymore."

"It was safer before you arrived," Doroteo said with restrained anger.

Freddy turned to Doroteo with a look of weariness. Sadi would have melted under Doroteo's angry stare, but Freddy just sighed.

"I do apologize for that. Yes, I have hastened their arrival, and they will be coming, but they were preparing anyway. I have news and instructions from Cesar and Taylor."

Dominga's eyes widened.

"What do they say? Are they all right? Oh, please tell me they are okay!"

"They escaped and are safe for now," he answered. "They were almost captured, but the jet worked fine and should be good enough for our escape."

"Escape to where?" Doroteo asked, but Sadi interrupted him.

She grabbed Freddy's shoulder. He looked mentally and physically exhausted.

"Sit down first."

Freddy let her take him to the island in the middle of the kitchen and sit on a stool. He took a deep breath before continuing.

"There is nowhere safe for you anymore," he began. "And you only have a couple of hours to get ready at the most, before they come. Cesar has arranged a meeting place and wants all of you to go there."

He turned to Dominga and then Doroteo.

"Your friends will not be able to stop them!"

After a short moment of silence, Dominga spoke first.

"We can talk about what can and cannot happen later. First, you must tell us everything. What else has happened?"

"Right after the military took Gerald, they also took Max."

"Where did—" Doroteo began, but Freddy held up his hand.

"There is more bad news. Franklin and Gerda are also missing.

Franklin was being watched at his apartment, but his neighbors and friends helped him escape. Then he went to Bellingham to meet with Gerda, but I could not find them there."

"God help us," Dominga said, but her words resonated with empty faith and horror.

"What about Mr. Smith?" Sadi asked. "Is he okay?"

"He is still in the hospital," Freddy said in despair. "The police are guarding him, and I cannot visit him. His son is there too."

"Okay," Sadi said, attempting to think clearly. She kept imagining herself traveling through space via a luxurious corporate jet. "After we all join Cesar, how are you going to get Gerald and Max?"

Freddy made steady eye contact with her, and she saw his answer before he spoke.

"Even if I knew where they were—"

"They're in a military base, for God's sake," Doroteo finished. "We'd have to break through the whole US military. They're beyond our reach."

Sadi looked at Doroteo and then back at Freddy.

"Freddy, that alien gave you the ability to rescue my daughter and me. Can't it lead you to Gerald, and, and Max? We can't go anywhere without them. They've given everything for this whole mess."

Dominga put her hand gently on Sadi's shoulder.

"We need to get you and the girls away safe. We won't leave them forever."

Sadi understood the logic, but the intense pumping of her heart told her to reject the option of abandoning Gerald. She took several deep breaths. The action failed to calm her, and she allowed her frustration to show.

"They might not have that much time!"

"What is Cesar's plan?" Doroteo asked Freddy, ignoring Sadi. "If we make it into space, where does he intend to go?"

Freddy paused before responding then looked at the kitchen door just as Helen pushed it open and entered the room. She walked quickly to Freddy, and the distress on his face melted into a smile.

"Hi, Freddy," she said in excitement. In her approach, she made sure to remain out of Doroteo's reach.

"Hi, Helen," he said, "and you too, Daryn. Come in."

Daryn stood motionless at the kitchen entrance, holding the door. Helen hugged Freddy, and he put one hand on her shoulder. The sight of them together helped bring Sadi's emotions back under control.

"Guess what, Freddy, we saw *WALL-E*. It was awesome. I want to go into space and fly around with a fire extinguisher."

"Really," Freddy said in genuine surprise. When he turned to Sadi, she recognized the true shock on his face. "That does sound fun."

Sadi pulled Helen gently to her.

"We need to finish talking about something serious, so you should go back to your movie."

"I want to stay," Helen said defiantly.

"Go on," Sadi said. "We'll be done in just a few minutes."

"We have to go, don't we?" Helen said in disappointment.

"Well, we can't stay here forever," Sadi replied with sarcasm and pointed her finger to the door. The distraction of the girls helped Sadi feel more in control. "Go on. We'll come and join you in just a few minutes."

Both girls left the kitchen grumbling, and Sadi chuckled at the irony. Her desire to protect the girls from information felt more important than protecting them from physical danger. When the door closed again, Doroteo repeated his question in perfectly enunciated English.

"So where does Cesar say he wants us to go?"

"We cannot stay long enough in space before it is safe to return," Freddy said in a tone of capitulation. Sadi doubted Doroteo or Dominga recognized the subtle intonation. "We can successfully escape the Earth in the ship they built, but the craft is incapable of sustaining life under vacuum for long. The radiation shielding is insufficient, and there are very limited supplies. We need to go to the other planet, where they cannot touch us."

After the plan escaped his lips and entered the real world, Sadi's heart sank. The thought of leaving her home planet filled Sadi with anxiety, overpowering all other concerns. On a superficial level, the option seemed too dangerous. Once off the ground, they were at the total mercy of hasty human engineering. No matter how intelligent the designers, one little mistake could easily translate to death for them all.

How could she possibly have put her girls in so much danger? Up until that moment, the idea had only existed in her imagination, in another dimension. On a deeper level, the thought of leaving Earth felt wrong. She was made of Earth! She belonged to Earth! How could she leave her home?

"I will help you all," said Doroteo, breaking Sadi out of her thoughts. "But I will not be going with you."

Dominga said something in Spanish, but Doroteo replied by just shaking his head. For the first time, Sadi thought she saw the older man experience a normal human emotion—fear. Dominga looked betrayed and sad. Maybe under the facade of disliking the man, she actually would miss him.

"I'm not gone yet," he said softly in English. "I will not abandon you."

"What about the alien?" Sadi asked. "It didn't come all this way to watch us get captured did it?"

Freddy considered his answer before responding.

"It is passive. We cannot count on it. I do not even know where it is."

Dominga turned to Sadi.

"I do not have one rational thought. Are there any other options? Can we really go to this other planet?"

"All I can say," began Freddy and he focused on Sadi, "is that you have to trust me. Sadi, you have known me longer than anyone here. You know I would not lie to you. If we can escape the atmosphere, I promise that you will make it safely to this other place. The girls will be safe there, and we can return when it is safe to do so. Did I not come back? Do you trust me?"

Three pairs of eyes staring back at Sadi felt like a heat lamp on her skin. Her response would change the course of her life, and the lives of her girls. When she looked at Freddy, Sadi saw a different person from the one she once knew. Those same eyes had saved Helen and Daryn from a horror that made Sadi tremble. Those same eyes had delivered her from the men at Mr. Smith's house. They were the only eyes she could hope to save her again.

No matter how much she felt for Gerald, she had to let Freddy lead her away from him.

"Yes, of course, I trust you," she said after a deep breath.

What choice did they have? She could choose a life in some remote part of the Earth, trying to hide from millions of searching eyes, a life of constant fear. She doubted their chances of finding a successful hiding place from the CIA. Maybe they would find peace, so far away on a distant planet. After her decision, a flood of fresh oxygen entered her blood, along with a new focus. She had been thinking too far into the future. They needed to make it out of the house to the rendezvous point.

"You said we have a couple hours before they come to get us," Doroteo said with skepticism in his voice. "How do you know this?"

"I can sense their feelings, do not ask me how. I just can." Freddy looked at all of them in turn, ending on Doroteo. "Before I arrived, the federal agents found out about your friends watching the house. Your friends are good at concealing themselves, so the agents do not know how many are helping you. At the moment, they are trying to assess the situation and plan how to get past them. They are not accustomed to having any real resistance. If you had not prepared like this, you might all be in custody right now."

Even though Doroteo kept frowning, he looked pleased with the compliment.

SEVENTY-EIGHT

Franklin

"Hey, guys," Franklin said to his friends and stepped aside for them to enter. "Sorry, it's so early."

"They broke through, didn't they?" said the thinner one, Victor. "You should have let me check your security protocols."

"No one broke through anything," Franklin said with slight irritation, but Victor no longer seemed to be listening to him.

Before they had fully entered the apartment, both of his friends stopped. To shut the door, Franklin had to push the fat one out of the way with it. They acted like two deer staring at a bright light, at the two girls shining on them from his living room. When Franklin turned to the girls, he noticed a different reaction. Instead of shock, the two girls looked at the intruders as though wasps had flown into the apartment. Franklin should have warned his friends about the two pretty girls. Then maybe they would have attempted to look more presentable.

To his relief, the offensive body odor only originated from one of them, the fat one who referred to himself as Screwdriver. His long, shaggy, and greasy brown hair was parted down the middle so that he could see. He wore black sweatpants and a long black shirt, which stretched at his belly. It had the faded picture of the red dragon from the old *Mortal Kombat* video game, and the word "Fatality" written under it. Behind the persona of a guy without a social clue, his penetrating black opal eyes showed intelligence.

His other friend, Victor, had replaced Franklin as the tallest in the apartment, and also the thinnest who probably weighed as much as one of the girls. He wore a plain brown baseball cap, backward, with his hair neatly tucked under it. Like Franklin, he wore jeans and a t-shirt. His shirt had a picture of the wizard, Gandalf, from *The Lord of the Rings* movies.

Franklin had no pictures or words on his clothes. While looking at his friends and how the girls looked at them, he felt glad to have kept his favorite shirt in his drawer, the one with Eowyn from *The Lord of the Rings*. His new friend from apartment ten reminded him of Eowyn or the actress who played her in the movies.

"I was hoping, Franklin," Christine said, breaking the silence. She stood and looked at his two friends with disappointment. "Hoping to pass off one of your friends as you, but that's not going to happen. No matter, plans change. Hi, I'm Christine, and this is my sister, Francis, and we're all going to help Franklin."

"I'm, uh, Victor," said the tall one and he looked from one girl to the other, then to his shorter companion with the hope that he would take the attention away from him.

Both girls looked at the fat one who stood with an open mouth. Franklin waited a moment for him to say something, then decided to introduce him instead, to break the silence.

"And this is Victor's roommate."

Victor and Franklin looked at each other, not wanting to use his real name. Screwdriver usually became angry if people called him something else. After another uncomfortable second of silence, he finally spoke.

"I'm sorry," he said as if coming out of a trance. "My parents call me Charles, but you can call me Chuck or Charles or whatever feels comfortable. I'll answer to almost anything, I can't tell you how many different names I've had. Sometimes, people like to call me—"

"Chuck sounds good," Christine said with a polite smile.

"Why don't we all sit down and go over the plan," Franklin said before Christine could say anything else. From the short time knowing her, he knew she would take the lead, but he wanted to appear more in control of the situation, more in control than he felt. "I didn't want to say anything over the phone, but there's a car outside with people watching me. Christine's come up with a plan to get me away from them, and I think it just might work."

"I knew it," said Chuck with a serious smile. The excitement helped him to recover from his shock of seeing the girls. "What are they, FBI, CIA, MI6? Let's hope to God they're not the Israelis. If Mossad's out there, you are fucked!"

Franklin suddenly wondered if the Screwdriver thought they were in some video game. Despite how ridiculous the idea seemed, Franklin considered the possibility of a foreign intelligence service, and his situation suddenly felt more hopeless. How could he hope to escape? Would his friend scare the girls away?

"I don't know who it is, but I doubt they're Mossad," said Franklin trying to assuage the group. "They're probably from our government."

"Dude," his friend replied quickly, "Israel controls our government. I've told you a million times."

"No they don't," said Christine without trying to hide her irritation. "That's just disinformation. Israel's just a tool. Where do you think they get all their money? If the US government didn't like what they were doing, their money supply would stop. The CIA would let the Arabs obliterate Israel if they ever crossed the line. They're in an ideal position to control."

Usually, a similar rebuttal would provide Chuck with enough fuel for hours of argument, but the alien creature, a human female, sitting across from them made him pause. Beautiful brown eyes were inspecting his copious surface area and had transformed into a threat he did not understand. In a less stressful set of circumstances, Franklin would have liked to see the battle between them, but his growing impatience urged him to move forward.

But before Franklin could say anything, Chuck responded slowly, almost timidly.

"That's an excellent argument, but they—"

"I would love to argue with you about this," Christine said, nodding her head, "but we might not have much time with the people out there. Let's go over what we've come up with so far."

For the next few minutes, Christine explained the plan, which involved three cars and changing drivers. While she talked, Franklin inspected his friends' reactions. Chuck smiled and seemed entranced and kept looking from her diagram on the paper to her lips. Franklin hoped he was paying more attention to the plan than her. Victor's eyes drifted between each girl and the paper. For most of the conversation, he remained uncharacteristically silent.

"So," Victor began hesitantly when Christine stopped talking and looked up at them. "If they call for backup, um, how do we know if they call for backup?"

"We have to assume that they are going to call for backup," Christine answered and pointed to the paper. While explaining her plan to them, she added more details to the flow chart on the paper. Fortunately, her audience consisted of three guys who drew similar diagrams for their programming and gaming structures. After she and Franklin answered a few more questions from Victor, he seemed satisfied.

"Okay," Victor said. "I think I get it."

"What about you, Chuck?" Christine asked.

Before answering, Chuck's eyes drifted between Francis and Christine's mouth, then he smiled smugly.

"Got it."

During the following moment of silence, Franklin felt his heart beating harder, much harder than when he first saw Christine that morning. His heartbeat seemed to push him to his feet. Christine stood then and stepped next to him by the door. They waited as Francis put Franklin's laptop and server in her large shoulder bag.

"Don't worry," said Chuck while he put both hands on the couch, to push himself up from it. "If there's a tracking device on his car, I'll find it. I know all about tracking devices. A few years ago, I even put one on my little brother's car. It was hilarious. He never figured out how I kept finding him all over the city. You should have seen him when—"

"Okay, thanks guys," Franklin interjected while Christine opened the door for him. Before leaving Francis with his two friends, he noticed the two sisters exchange mysterious glances.

SEVENTY-NINE

Christine

When Christine awoke that morning, she knew the day would be different. Her recent recurring dreams of being chased by an unknown assailant had filled the entire night and left her with more anxiety than usual. She felt a powerful urge that morning to run her regular ten-kilometer route. Only exertion and sweat would successfully erase the stinging memory of her dreams. At the end of her run when she saw Franklin heading to his car, a familiar impulse clicked in her chest and she obeyed the urge to approach him. When he confessed his troubles to her, she felt no surprise.

"Thanks for letting me help you with this," she said after they left his apartment.

While walking to her car, a twelve-year-old blue Honda Accord, she breathed in the crisp morning air, allowing her lungs to expand until the pain forced her to stop. She felt better after leaving the stuffy air of his apartment and his two awkward friends.

"Don't mention it," he said and laughed. "Any time you want to save me, feel free."

"No worries. We'll get you away. Despite how my sister appears, she's really glad to help."

"My god," he said after a few steps and inhaled deeply. "I think it might actually work. I'm feeling good about this. Your plan is better than my idea of just driving away."

"Yeah, we're just going out for coffee. They shouldn't get suspicious yet."

"Oh, I think they'll be suspicious that you're with me," he said, laughing nervously.

He smiled wider, and the tension she noticed in the expression intensified her feeling of empathy. Rescuing a human felt many times more exhilarating than all the hurt animals she had rescued in her life and more exciting than her favorite novels. His forced smile seemed too exaggerated.

"Remember, you're excited to go with me for coffee but not that excited. Or are you?"

She laughed.

"I'm thrilled actually," he said.

He seemed to take the hint and relaxed his smile into a more natural expression. For an additional test, she grabbed his upper arm and gently squeezed. As she expected, he flexed his muscles very slightly. When had he last talked to a normal girl, she wondered. Was she a normal girl?

From her appearance, Christine seemed like a typical, twenty-three-year-old female college student. Only a couple of close friends and her family knew how well she kept her obsessive-compulsive personality hidden from public view. Now Franklin had a glimpse behind the curtain she kept between herself and the rest of the world. Only her sister Francis seemed to care about who knew the secret.

From his body language, Christine knew that Franklin felt a physical attraction to her. She expected the reaction from a guy like him and his two friends. To her extreme relief, Franklin had exhibited the expected sexual relation protocol by attempting to hide his true feelings. But his friends had made no attempt to hide how they looked at her. When his fat friend regurgitated the common disinformation about Jews controlling the government, she almost lost control and laughed. If they'd had more time, she would have enjoyed seeing how he answered her rebuttal.

Once in the car, she immediately engaged the engine and then opened her purse, pretending to search for some object. He spent the time pretending to look out the window at the trees and sky. She thought he made a convincing effort to act inconspicuously.

"I can see them," he said with his eyes on the license plate in front of them. "The guy's in the passenger seat with his head back against the headrest. The girl glanced in our direction, I think."

"Do you normally drink coffee?" he asked.

She kept her eyes focused on her purse.

"Yes, but not this soon after a run," she said and smiled again. She rarely drank coffee and wondered how the caffeine would affect her. "Here we go. Come on, you two, come and get us."

While clipping her seat belt into place, she quickly pulled onto the street, driving in the opposite direction of the watchers' car. The speed of their escape pushed Franklin's head against the headrest, and she smiled at his look of surprise. With one eye, she looked in the rearview mirror and noticed both watchers looking in their direction but making no other movement. She soon turned the corner, and they were out of sight. On the next street, she slowed to a more normal pace, and they watched behind them for signs of pursuit.

"You're an adrenaline junkie, aren't you!" Franklin said while waiting for the watchers to appear in the mirror.

"Not really," she said absently. "Adrenaline's awesome, sure, but I prefer mental challenges. Not really a gambler with my life. Escaping difficult predicaments is more my thing."

The Darth Vader theme from her cell phone suddenly filled the car, the ringtone for her sister. She originally assigned the theme from Star Wars as a joke, but the music reminded her of their perilous situation. Christine hoped the music would fail to increase her passenger's anxiety. She quickly stopped the music and waited for her sister to speak.

"They're gone," a voice whispered in her ear, as if afraid of being overheard.

"Thanks, France," Christine said, then put her phone between her legs. She turned to Franklin and smiled. "They're following us."

"That's good," he said and breathed a sigh of relief. "We don't have to follow the flowchart path of them not following us."

"Yes," she agreed. "That was the more difficult option."

In anticipation, they looked in the rearview mirror, expecting to see the car appear, but they only saw a few other vehicles on the road. Every passing second seemed shorter than the last.

"Shit," he said. "Where are they? Shouldn't we see them by now? Sorry."

"Shit sounds about right," she said. "Maybe they called for backup to follow us."

"Or they've switched to watching by satellite?" Franklin said with uncertainty. "What do you think?"

"If they had a satellite view, they wouldn't need anyone in a car watching you." She shifted her eyes between the road ahead and the rearview mirror.

"Good point," he said, appearing satisfied. "Maybe they split up and got into separate cars?"

"Possibly," she said absently, then noticed far behind, the watchers' white Ford Escort pull into the street. She failed to include the possibility of the watchers separating in her flowchart. "There they are!"

"Good," Franklin said. "Victor should be able to keep track of them. I trust him despite how disoriented he seemed at my apartment."

"What was wrong with him," she asked, thinking she knew the answer.

"He's not used to seeing girls like you," Franklin explained hesitantly.

"What do you mean?" she asked in feigned shock. "Girls like me?"

"You know what I mean," he replied and kept his eyes on the road ahead. "We're not used to pretty girls like you. It was probably like jumping into a swimming pool and seeing a shark."

"A shark huh," she said, smiling at the comparison, and then pushed harder on the accelerator. "Not exactly how I would describe myself."

After arriving at the small shopping center of her favorite café, she parked, stopped the engine, and then they waited. From the outside, she saw only two occupants in the café. When devising the plan, she expected to see more people there. People made good cover. Two would have to be sufficient.

Before exiting the car, they waited until the Ford Escort passed them on the street. Christine opened her door first and stood to watch the car turn and disappear around the corner. When she saw Victor drive past next in an old Toyota Camry, she smiled with satisfaction.

"So far, so good," Christine said while looking down at her watch. In about fifteen minutes, they would arrive at their next decision point. They entered the café, got their drinks, and waited.

—※—

While sipping her iced tea, she asked Franklin a barrage of benign questions about himself. She planned to keep him talking to decrease his anxiety. Under better circumstances, she would take the usual route of a more relaxed conversation, but she might never see him again and would have to extract as much information about him as possible. Secretly, she was enjoying the opportunity to commandeer the situation.

He talked mostly about his employment but refrained from saying anything specific about his current predicament. He had several sources of income. From what she could understand, he mostly worked on a contract basis, customizing websites for a build-your-own website company and some small programming jobs for a company in Germany that she failed to recognize. Nothing he told her seemed even remotely controversial or illegal.

What kind of organization could cause so much trouble? She assumed the reason was either drugs or some terrorist affiliation. Although she desperately wanted to know the cause of his problems, she accepted the wisdom of his decision to keep her in ignorance.

When he finally looked at his watch, she knew they needed to continue with the plan. They had spent enough time talking. She hoped the watchers had settled into their new surveillance position.

"Are you ready?" he asked after looking at his watch.

"Yeah," she said almost regretfully. She wanted to talk longer. "It's been enough time."

They left the café, and instead of walking to her car, they walked down the street in the opposite direction from where the surveillance car had disappeared. While walking, they looked anxiously for the Ford Escort but failed to locate it. She looked up at Franklin and noticed the tension in his eyes and suddenly felt sympathy for him. Their situation no longer seemed like a game. When they reached the little convenience store two blocks away, they stopped.

"Where the hell did they go?" she asked.

"They're good at hiding," he said and laughed nervously.

The plan included the possibility of being followed on foot rather than being watched from a car. She had to know their location. If she failed to locate them soon, she would have to call his friend Victor. She had left that option as a last resort. If the CIA or FBI followed them, they might have the ability to listen to their conversation.

"Is that your sister?" Franklin asked while keeping his eyes on the ground.

She looked down the street at the oncoming traffic and noticed Francis in her black Nissan pickup. Without knowing the location of the surveillance team, she could not let Franklin get in the car with her sister. She had to make a decision, fast.

As her sister drove toward them, Christine reached up and scratched her head, the signal for her sister to continue to the alternate checkpoint. Itching her nose meant Francis could pull to the curb and get Franklin. For a very brief moment, she made eye contact with Francis then looked away. Due to the available turns on that street, it would take her sister about three and a half minutes to arrive at the next checkpoint. She had that much time to find the watchers.

"Okay, we keep walking, and then come," began Christine, but her cell phone rang and stopped her in mid-sentence. She resisted the urge to answer it too quickly. Instead, she pushed the talk button and pulled the phone calmly to her ear. She instantly recognized the voice of his friend Victor.

"You guys don't see them do you?" the voice said with some concern. "We're on the other side of the street, behind you and they're sitting in their car, parked behind the black Ford Truck, the one with dirt all over the tires. They have a perfect view of you."

"I see them. Thanks," she said in relief then clicked end.

She doubted they could hear her phone conversations, but minimizing communication seemed best. She turned to Franklin and took hold of his arm, changing his direction. She finally felt safe to proceed to the next stage of his escape.

"Was that Victor?" Franklin asked.

"Yep," she said excitedly.

A rush of adrenaline entered her bloodstream, and she felt an elevated alertness. She hoped he felt the same. They were one block away from where her sister was going and would arrive first by taking a shortcut through an alley. While walking to their escape route, she held onto his arm and felt as though she was rescuing a baby from a raging river.

"They're parked just down the street, behind that huge black truck," she said and nodded in the direction of the Ford Escort. "When we get to the other street, there's no way they'll be able to get to us in time."

"Unless they get out of their car and chase us," he said gravely.

"That's why we're going to hurry."

With her hand still on his arm, they turned into a parking area for a small grocery store and began walking quickly toward the entrance. After leaving the view of the street and the Ford Escort, they turned and began running to the left of the building, heading for a large delivery truck waiting there.

"When we get behind that," she said as they started running. "They won't be able to see us, and we can run all the way to the other street."

"I can't believe it," he said in excitement. "I think this will actually work."

"They'll think we went into the store," she said as they approached the truck.

Just before reaching the safety of the space behind the truck, Christine felt a moment of dread. In her dream that morning, she remembered running from a monster, feeling it behind her. The memory brought a shiver and a rush of excitement. Maybe Franklin was right about her being an adrenaline junkie.

So far, the plan had gone well. They found the area behind the truck devoid of the driver or any of the store employees. Inside the truck, she noticed the shelves of snack items, bread, and pastries. Slowly, she stepped to the edge of the truck and peeked around the corner. For a few seconds, she watched the cars pass on the street. They were so close to freedom.

"They're not there. We probably have a few minutes before they come to check on us."

"I have a bad feeling that you're going to be in trouble. They know you're with me. They'll know you helped me escape."

"I already told you," she said while still watching the street. "I'm helping you escape the drug dealers or the terrorists. And if they don't believe that, I'll say, I thought it was a game. What are they going to do to me? I don't know anything. I'm just a victim of your lies."

She turned to him and smiled. Before he could respond, her phone rang. She noticed Victor's cell number again and handed her phone to Franklin.

"Victor," he said and then listened. "Okay, we're almost there. I'll talk to you soon."

"They've pulled onto the street," Franklin said. "Probably going to park right over there. When this is all over, I think Victor's gonna disappear for a while. He sounds scared."

"Excuse me," said an angry voice behind Franklin.

They turned toward the sound. A man appeared, walking toward them, a big man wearing a gray baseball cap. Probably the delivery driver.

"What are you doing?" he asked.

"Just taking a shortcut," she answered and then began walking down the alley behind the truck. Franklin followed behind her.

"We didn't take anything," he said while passing the man. As a show of innocence, Franklin held up his hands.

The man got between them and the truck but said nothing. If she had been just another guy, the delivery man might have been more confrontational. Being a girl had its advantages. As they left the area, she felt his eyes on her butt.

They soon reached the other street, then turned to the left and began walking again. She had to prevent herself consciously from running. She did not want to attract any more attention. While walking and watching for her sister, the time passed slowly and reminded her again of her dreams. Her pursuers kept getting closer and closer, and no matter how fast she ran, the monsters were always just behind her.

Without warning, a memory of the previous night burst into her mind, accompanied by a feeling of dread. She remembered waking from her disturbing dreams around midnight. While trying to fall back asleep, she remembered seeing a bright light in her room through her closed eyelids, but when she opened her eyes, she saw nothing but the darkness.

For a brief moment, she doubted her decision to help him. His identity and the identity of his enemies were a complete mystery to her. If the people tracking him were drug dealers or terrorists, they would probably care little about her claims of ignorance. Was Franklin worth the risk? Was her need for excitement worth the risk?

When she looked up at Franklin, her momentary doubt vaporized. Seeing his anxiety almost instantly reignited her instinct to help a fellow traveler escape from danger. Besides, she could distinguish a bad actor when she ran into one.

A movement caught her attention and made them both turn to

face the street. Her sister's black Nissan truck had come from behind them and made a U-turn after passing. Her sister parked several meters ahead of them.

Christine fought the urge to run the last few steps to her sister. When she eventually opened the passenger door to let him inside, she noticed Francis nervously looking up and down the street.

"Hurry, hurry," her sister said. "If they're on the move already, you've got only a few minutes. Traffic's not as bad as you thought."

Instead of entering the truck, Franklin remained standing. He looked from Francis to her, probably trying to decide how to say goodbye. He was probably experiencing a strange mixture of emotions, sadness and relief.

"I don't know how to thank you," he said. "If I'm ever able to come out of hiding and enter society again, I'll do anything for you."

She put her arms around him, tightly pulling him against her. She hoped the physical contact would transfer some comfort. Like her three-year-old nephew, he reluctantly allowed her to hug him. He tentatively pressed one hand on her back.

"Okay," she said after letting him go. "Come see me when you think it's safe."

After they drove away and left her view, Christine turned and began walking in the opposite direction. She extracted a pair of sunglasses and a hat from her purse and took the long way back to her car.

EIGHTY

Franklin

After leaving Christine on the side of the road, Franklin felt like a fool, like a package being delivered secretly across a border. Although grateful for the help and amazed by it even, he could not wait to get in his car and drive. While Francis drove her small pickup truck, he lay on the seat next to her with his head against the door. She narrated their trip as if they were on a tour bus. For the first few minutes, he anxiously waited for her to say they passed the Ford Escort, but they never did.

"I think you can sit up now," she said after fifteen minutes of driving. "We're almost there. No call from your friends should be a good sign, right?"

"Yeah, we should be in the clear," Franklin said doubtfully.

"Your friend Chuck wouldn't forget to call if he ran into trouble would he?" she asked. "Sorry to say this, but he just might be the weak link in our chain."

For the first time since Christine had hugged him goodbye, the muscles in his face relaxed into a natural smile.

"We're definitely not in his comfort zone. He's the guy you want on your team in a game, or if you want to build a leak-proof network, but the real world is not his game. Your sister gave him the perfect job."

"Christine's good at manipulating people," Francis said, almost apologetically. "I'm more of a watcher. Sorry for giving you such a hard time. If you haven't noticed, she needs someone to watch her back."

"She seems capable of taking care of herself," Franklin said, feeling the need to come to Christine's defense.

"She has a hard time controlling her impulses," Francis began slowly as if searching for the right words. "And almost no sense of fear. I've had to get her out of some sticky situations and didn't want this to be another one."

"Hopefully, you'll be able to go home and forget this all happened," he said. "We were lucky. I don't think they planned on me trying to get away."

"Let's hope so, but don't worry. We won't forget you." She glanced at him and smiled, for the first time. "Here's our exit."

They took the next exit from the highway and entered the parking area of a rest stop. Franklin instantly noticed his car parked close to the ramp back to the highway and the two other vehicles with no occupants, next to the restrooms. Chuck sat in his car, with his shaggy head just visible above the seat headrest. When Francis parked next to him, he looked up, and she watched his two black blinking eyes as she might look at an animal in a zoo.

Franklin showed Chuck the palm of his hand. In response, he nodded, the signal that they were alone.

"Well, here we are," Francis said. Before Franklin could respond, she continued. "I know it's probably a bad idea to know about your problems, but it would be nice to know why we're putting our necks out there for you."

"I was running a secure website for a friend of mine," he said, then turned to check for cars entering the rest stop. "They developed some things that other people wanted, nothing dangerous, just... You really don't want to know. I was lucky this time, thanks to you, but I feel like my time's going to run out."

Her light brown eyes reminded him of Christine. She stared at him with concern on her face and appeared to be internally deliberating on asking for more information.

"I'm sorry," she said at last. "I understand."

"Thank you," he said, forcing himself to smile. He opened the door just a crack and paused before exiting. "I am worried about your drive home though."

She smiled with a questioning look on her face, unsure of his tone. "Why is that?"

"You've got to drive back with Chuck."

—※—

Franklin drove in the slow lane on Interstate Five, heading north and purposely letting everyone pass him in the fast lanes. No car seemed to be following him. Only after about twenty minutes of driving did he finally begin to feel safe. While driving, he replayed his time with Christine. The memory felt like a pleasant dream but brought a sharp pain of regret. He failed to imagine a future where he would meet her again, and it was beginning to make him depressed, so he focused on his destination and what he had to do.

But his thoughts kept returning to Christine, her sister, and his friends. Did they get home safely? Christine and Francis would probably meet somewhere and stay for a while before going home. He hoped they were careful but trusted their safety to being ignorant of his situation. Victor would probably go to his parents' house for the night, and Chuck might do something stupid. Would Chuck attempt to follow the Ford Escort and determine their identity? Franklin hoped not.

Before leaving the rest stop, he had installed a new license plate and now had to be extra careful to obey all traffic laws. If the police stopped him, they might take his car VIN and notice that it did not match with the license plates anymore. While keeping his eyes on the road, he pulled out his wallet and removed his driver's license, credit card, and everything else with the name of Franklin Harvey on it. He stuffed the items beneath the carpet under his seat and pulled out his new set of identity cards.

After taking the next exit, he drove about ten kilometers away from the highway where he found a convenience store with a teller machine. He withdrew four hundred dollars from his alternate identity account and then headed back to the highway.

That night he stayed in a cheap motel in Bellingham near the Canadian border. In his dreams, after eventually falling asleep, he replayed his escape. Instead of his apartment, the dream took place in a video game at a castle full of evil creatures who looked like orcs from the Lord of the Rings movies. Christine held a machine gun and led the group through dark hallways, obliterating the monsters trying to eat them. Everyone else had a gun but Franklin, and he felt like an important politician being escorted by his security detail in a fantasy land.

At the end of the dream, he and Christine got separated from the rest of the group. They hid in a dark room while monsters passed by them in the hallway. He woke and the memory of the dream left him with a dark and empty feeling.

How long would he be dreaming of Christine?

"What has my life turned into?" he asked in the darkness of his hotel room. The sound of his voice helped light the darkness in his mind. He often talked to himself as a method of validation. If the thoughts in his head remained credible in the real world, then he could proceed with them. But when entering the air, his thoughts often crashed and burned to ash.

"I'm a renegade!"

The life of a renegade would have been tolerable, perhaps exciting, but without Christine, it seemed lonely and far less romantic. While thinking of Christine and his escape that morning, he suddenly recognized the situation as very improbable. How could he have been so lucky?

No matter how many ways he considered the situation, he could not accept the root cause being luck or chance. Girls like Christine and Francis were rare creatures and to encounter them for the first time on the morning of his planned escape could not be explained by chance. He could think of only two possibilities. They either worked for the government and wanted him to feel as if he got away so that he would lead them to his friends. If that were the case, then people would probably be watching his next moves.

He liked the other alternative. Some benevolent creature wanted to help him, perhaps the alien. Franklin had no experience with religion unless his mother's views on nature could be considered religious. But he did want to believe in benevolent beings other than humans inhabiting the universe. In the motel, he came as close to praying as he ever did, but the action felt simply as if asking himself questions and waiting for someone else to answer them. In some ways, he was relieved at hearing no response. He liked his independence and a sense of privacy.

"It's got to be the alien," he said and shook his head. "Christine and Francis are not working with them."

He opened his backpack by the bed and removed his laptop then watched it for a few seconds before bringing the machine to life. He wanted to send an email to the group to let them know of his status, but that thought never got far enough for a verbal test. Franklin did not need to repeat the option aloud to know that communication was not an option. For some strange reason, the laptop reminded him of what the damned government had done to them all.

In some ways, he seemed to have traveled back in time, before communication evolved beyond the mailbox. He now had to depend almost entirely on physical contact to communicate. Even with his new identity, he still had to act carefully and would only use email in emergencies. Maybe he would write a letter.

He wanted to follow his instincts and join the others at Cesar's house, but he chose to follow his mental conclusions instead. If he joined Cesar and the others, he might be leading their enemies there. He would not be responsible for leading their enemies to that poor woman Sadi and her little girls.

Several days before his escape, right after hearing about Gerald's abduction, he had sent a communication to Gerda, hinting about his plans and desire to stay away from Cesar's home. Gerda responded positively. She felt the same and wanted to stay away from the main group and meet with him. Freddy had sent him a cryptic response about meeting elsewhere but had failed to respond when Franklin asked for clarification.

After his experience in space, his new friend Freddy had become even more distant. Franklin asked for an account of his experience on the other planet, but he received the same information as the rest of the group and his requests for more details were not answered. He only knew the other world existed and in the future, they might be able to make the same journey.

But no matter how much he trusted or liked Freddy, doubts always lingered. The other world story always failed his personal credibility test. Sometimes, he even wondered if Freddy had hallucinated the whole experience. Maybe the alien or the government was manipulating them. Despite his doubts, the possibility of going to another world excited Franklin, more than he could comprehend, but the option seemed like an impossibility now with the founder of the group captured.

Poor Gerald. Franklin wished him the best but could think of no way to help him.

Franklin's thoughts returned to Freddy and how he needed a friend, someone other than an eighty-year-old man. Franklin remembered when they had first met. When he looked the guy in the eyes, he felt as if he was staring into a dark abyss. What lay hidden in the darkness? An alien entity seemed buried somewhere in Freddy's troubled past, and Franklin wanted to discover all of his secrets.

On a higher level, Freddy's intelligence had immediately impressed Franklin. He felt strangely drawn toward other intelligent creatures, like Gerald and that hot-tempered girl, Taylor. From a social perspective and their shared interest in computers, Freddy seemed more on

Franklin's level. The guy had very little formal training in programming and computer science in general, but he had impressive skills, and Freddy was self-taught.

Franklin had acquired his skills with computers from a mix of traditional hard work in school and on his own, and more importantly from a teacher's assistant in college who had taught Franklin more than all of his classes combined. Franklin even worked with him on some of his graduate projects. Unfortunately, he lost contact with the guy after he graduated. Most likely, he went to work for the government to help spy on their citizens.

Franklin used a physical map he'd bought at the local Chevron station to find Gerda's house in Bellingham. Usually, he would have used Google Maps on the internet or a GPS unit, but he knew those methods could give his exact location. When he opened the map in the car, he felt as if he was traveling back in time again. If any event ever destroyed the internet infrastructure, even if just for a few weeks, Franklin knew several individuals who would die from starvation from being lost on the highways and unable to find a grocery store or the phone number for their favorite pizza delivery place.

When he found the neighborhood where Gerda lived, he searched for evidence of another surveillance team and found none. He drove through again just to be sure.

"Shit," he said on his second drive through. "Now someone's going to call the cops because of this creepy guy driving through the neighborhood."

When he drove past her house, he found the driveway empty and the garage door closed. It looked as though no one had been there for weeks. He pulled into the driveway and acted as if planning to change direction.

"Come on," he said, glancing at her house and pretending to be looking through his maps. "Look out the window. Come on!"

After a minute, an old lady from the neighboring house came through her front door and walked toward the sidewalk. She glanced over at him, and he pulled up his map higher. He looked over to make eye contact, then smiled. When he looked back at the window of Gerda's house, he noticed two pairs of eyes looking at him. She smiled and nodded her head, then disappeared.

He pulled out of the driveway and slowly headed out of the neighborhood where he waited at the end of her street, acting like a lost traveler again. When she appeared in her car in his rearview mirror, he began driving to his motel.

Would he ever have a woman follow him to a hotel again? On the drive, he imagined Christine following him for a sexual rendezvous. He laughed then cringed at the thought of meeting Gerda there for the same reason. He entered his apartment and sat in the living room where he stared at the door. After twenty-four hours of being on his own, it felt good to expect friendly company and talk freely.

"Hi," she said when he opened the door. Her relaxed smile felt like sunshine. After a quick check for people with her in the hallway, he shut the door. "It is so good to see you!"

"Likewise," he replied as she embraced him. "Sit down and make yourself comfortable. Well, as much as you can get in this little hovel."

"It's absolutely lovely," she said, desperation saturating her German accent. "What have you heard since Gerald went missing?"

"That was my question," he said and snorted sarcastically. "I don't know much, but he didn't just go missing, the CIA or military or some other shitbag agency came to get him, guys with machine guns. Somehow they spared that poor woman with the two little girls."

"Sadi's safe," she said with relief then sat back and shook her head. "Well, at least we know that much. Did you have trouble getting here?"

"I was lucky," he said, feeling excitement at the chance to talk about what had happened to someone who would understand. "They were staked out on the street, watching my apartment. I barely escaped. Some friends of mine helped divert their attention."

"Oh my God," Gerda said and put her hand on his knee. She suddenly reminded him of his mother. "I bet it shook you up. They won't make that mistake again, I am sure of it. You are lucky."

"I know," he said. "What about you? Have you noticed anyone suspicious?"

"No one was following me," she said with confidence. "Though I would not have been able to get away if they were, I think. I would love to hear about how you did it, but tell me about whatever else you know first."

"Things were going pretty good in Brazil, with the plane, but they ran into trouble with an inspection. The police even came and took them back to the station for interrogation. Fortunately, the police showed no further interest in them."

She paused to consider his words. "Another bit of luck."

"Do you believe in luck?"

"Not really," she answered and smiled again.

She appeared calm and only a little concerned. But the longer they talked, the more his feeling of relief dissipated. *How can she be so calm?* He could feel anger begin to grow. Anger felt good.

"After they were released," he said, "Cesar went down there to help speed things up. Of course, that was before the shit hit the floor. I don't know if they'll have enough time to complete the plan now. We can't run forever."

"I can't believe I am asking this," she said, "but what about the other planet? Do you think it is real? Is it an option?"

"This whole thing is crazy!" he said without trying to hide his frustration. When she mentioned the other planet, the idea failed his validation test again. "I don't think Freddy was lying. I just can't imagine that jet getting anyone that far. The jet was never intended to transport us a long distance. If we could just get enough time, I think the original plan is still sound. We can escape into orbit for a week, and then the world will know about everything, and they won't be able to touch us when we get back."

"Yes yes," she said as if trying to console him. "I know that was the plan, but if we can go to this other planet, we may have no other choice."

"But without Gerald?"

"There's no way we can help him if we're captured as well," she said with a tone of regret. She looked ready to continue speaking, but a noise from the hallway interrupted her. They looked at the door.

After the door crashed open, Franklin and Gerda had only a moment to look at each other. In the next fifteen seconds, they found themselves lying flat on the floor with submachine guns hovering a few centimeters above their necks.

"Thought you could give us the slip?" said the lead man from the SWAT team.

EIGHTY-ONE

Sadi

Sadi and Dominga returned from the conversation in the kitchen to the entertainment room where the girls were watching another movie. Sadi walked to the seventy-inch television set and put her finger over the red *Power* button, threatening to press it. Four eyes quickly turned to look at Sadi's finger.

"Girls," Dominga said sweetly. "You can watch the movie later. Right now, you need to help get your things together. You're going with Freddy, in the car."

Sadi recognized the movie, *City of Ember*, and paused a moment before turning it off. She remembered wanting to watch that movie with the girls. *Will I ever see another movie again? Another movie produced on Earth?*

"We'll take these movies with us," Sadi said, quietly laughing to herself.

"We're going in the car that can go into space?" Daryn asked, and her frown showed panic.

Helen smiled.

"The bad men are coming again, aren't they? Will Freddy take us into space?"

"He's not taking you into space, not yet." Sadi decided to stop hiding the truth from her daughter since it seemed to provide so much pleasure. The girls needed pleasant thoughts and space travel appeared to do the trick for Helen. Sadi wished space travel would have the same effect on her.

"Oh my," said Dominga as she nudged the girls to stand from the comfortable couch. "What brave little girls."

"The bad men aren't trying to get us this time," Sadi said specifically to Daryn. "The men who want to get us this time are just people working for the government. They're just doing their jobs and don't want to hurt us. Freddy's here, and he can keep them away from you."

Daryn looked up into Dominga's eyes.

"As long as we stay with him, we'll be safe right?"

"Freddy will get them," Helen said and turned to her new best friend. She sliced the air with her hand. "Hi-yah!"

The two girls put all their new clothes that Dominga had bought them, into their new backpacks, their second set of new clothes in a month. Mr. Smith had purchased their first new set after they arrived at his house, but they had to leave them. Sadi spent no time feeling guilty about Dominga's and Doroteo's generosity. She could have afforded it if she could access her own money again.

"I'll help the girls," Dominga said. "You go get your things."

Sadi hurried to her room and threw all her belongings into a bag. It took less than a minute. So many thoughts swirled in her head with concern for the girls' future floating to the top of the mix. When she thought of leaving Gerald at the military hornet's nest, only the adrenaline in her blood prevented the tears from falling.

When finished gathering her things, she found Freddy and Doroteo arguing in the kitchen.

"If you go straight up, you'll be too easy of a target," Doroteo said, concern lining his voice, not anger.

Sadi found little comfort in his use of the word, *Up*.

"Trust me," Freddy said confidently. "It will draw attention from you so that you can escape."

"I'm not going to let you use the others for me to escape," he said in frustration. "I don't need that kind of help!"

"Doroteo," Freddy said calmly, "my strategy will work, as it has before, and it will not be putting them in danger, even with their air-support helicopters."

When Dominga returned to the kitchen with the girls, Doroteo stopped arguing and explained the plan to them all. When finished, Dominga laughed in derision.

"Don't be ridiculous," she said, focusing an angry stare at Doroteo. "There is no room for me in the car. I am going with you."

They argued in Spanish for the next full minute, reminding Sadi of a Hispanic soap opera. Helen and Daryn looked at the two dark-haired adults in surprise and a hint of fear. From the moment of their arrival, they had fallen in love with the older woman and treated her as a grandmother. But she had suddenly transformed into a tiger with claws.

At the end of the argument, Sadi heard Cesar's name mentioned. Whatever Doroteo had said made the Mexican goddess surrender. In an apparent attempt to return her dignity, Doroteo spoke his final words in English.

"Cesar would never forgive me."

Two minutes later, Dominga and Freddy sat in the front seat of the BMW with Sadi and the two girls in the back seat. The seating felt cramped, but at least they each had a set of seat belts. Before closing the door, Doroteo pushed a shiny pistol into Freddy's hand. He accepted it without a word.

From the back seat, Sadi watched as Doroteo dialed a number on his phone. He held it to his ear and said something in Spanish, then turned to Freddy.

"Ready when you are. Good luck my friend!"

Freddy shut the car door and turned to face the two little girls. He wore a genuine smile without any evidence of anxiety. His confidence somehow seemed cold to Sadi, but she returned the smile.

"Are you girls ready for the ride of your lives?"

"Aye, Aye, captain!" Helen said and saluted him. Daryn looked much less excited about the situation.

Sadi grasped her seat with white knuckles and watched the back of Freddy's head. He took a deep breath before knocking on the window as the final signal. Sadi had a hard time seeing through the dark windows but could see the outline of Doroteo with his phone in one hand, and a pistol in the other. He said a few words into his phone, then hung up.

As the garage door opened, so did the barrage of lights and noise.

EIGHTY-TWO

Audrie

After her visit to Brazil, the mix of emotions Audrie Garner experienced resulted in a single dominant emotion—anger—and she unconsciously attempted to direct it all at her brother. Although she was acutely angry at him, she knew he did not deserve it. Could she blame a tiger for eating a hiker after they wandered haphazardly into its territory? Max lacked the will to reject the prize of new technology and space travel, especially when wrapped in such an alluring package as a beautiful and intelligent creature like Taylor Evans. The temptation seemed specifically tailored to his interests and desires.

If presented with a similar set of temptations related to her interests, she also would have seized them with both hands. But her understanding of the true causes did not affect their potential to derail her life.

While Yi-Min drove her 2007 silver Range Rover, Audrie reviewed their plans. She focused on cultivating her anger at the whole situation instead of her brother. The anger was helping prepare her for the dangerous decisions they would have to make. They had been driving for several hours, and the recent lull in the conversation seemed to have extracted all of her dark and disturbing thoughts. With every minute of silence, the mood in the vehicle intensified.

Ever since Yi-Min had delivered the news of her brother's incarceration, she had kept in constant contact with Audrie. Together, they uncovered many of Max's secrets, exposing the dark pit that had swallowed him. Their journey to the secret military psychiatric hospital seemed like stepping close to the edge of that pit. If they stepped too close, would they also fall into it?

Unfortunately, Yi-Min and her contacts lacked the clearance to access Max's location. The military closely guarded that secret and Audrie knew she would also have difficulty acquiring the information. Although she had many contacts with the necessary clearance, calling on those kinds of favors could only be used as a last resort.

"Make sure to seal this leak," she remembered her father saying when she'd revealed the fate of his son. "When they eventually let him go, don't let your eyes off him again."

His rebuke had helped fuel the fire of her anger, but his apathy toward what might be happening to her brother was like the sting of a wasp. Would she ever lose favor with her father, as Max did? After she visited Brazil, she contemplated the option of waiting until the military released Max. Whatever damage was done to his mind could be addressed later. Could they successfully break his dangerous tendencies without breaking him entirely? That idea failed to comfort her and only caused more anxiety.

When her surprise visitor made contact, the option of waiting vanished. She found Simon Thatcher, the TerraWatch chief of security, waiting for her one morning in the lobby of her New York office. They met later that day at a park where he asked for her help. With unfeigned disbelief, she listened to the story of how he'd found where they took his boss. The man's tenacity for daring to follow the military impressed her. Simon's obvious concern for her brother almost made Audrie reveal her own concern, but she pretended to have little interest in his information.

"What do you want me to do about it?"

"You're going to tell me what the hell you know about it!"

When his tone of concern turned to anger at her, she cringed.

After separating in the park, the anger in his eyes was burned in her memory. She knew that look, unbelief at the coldness of a fellow human being. Like the other pains she often had to endure, she swallowed his disdain like the mixture of sugar and crushed aspirin her governess used to make.

—※—

They arrived at the guard station as the last rays of the sun stopped filtering through the thick trees. When the direct sunlight had disappeared, the shadows felt like a rising dark tide ready to consume them. Neither of them had the necessary clearance for the visit, but both Audrie and Yi-Min thought they knew the system well enough to circumvent it.

When they came within sight of the guard station, Yi-Min slowed the vehicle and then turned to Audrie with a familiar look that chilled her blood. They had passed the point of no return. Audrie nodded in resignation.

Yi-Min wore a tight black skirt with a white shirt and an open turquoise vest, which hung from her breasts like a waterfall, several centimeters away from her abdomen. In the darker interior of the SUV, her vest looked almost black and covered the white underneath as a shadow. The darkness clothed her petite figure in mystery. Audrie knew she looked a little less-than-professional for a visit to a top-secret psychiatric hospital, but she was sugar for the males they would most certainly meet. Audrie tried to be a little less conspicuous and wore a knee-length dress of dark gray and white. Her blond hair was pulled back in a ponytail, while Yi-Min's black hair fell over her shoulders.

"Good evening," Yi-Min said in an exaggerated Chinese accent. She was looking across Audrie to the guard who stepped to the side of her vehicle. No gate blocked their path, but the man's machine gun was an effective substitute. She waited for him to comprehend her words. Audrie smiled politely and let her Asian friend talk.

Before answering, the guard on the side of the car inspected them both. His eyes stopped on Audrie as he spoke, his mouth in a perfectly straight line.

"Identification please."

The soldier wore a full battle suit of camo, including the hat, and possessed only one distinguishing characteristic, a sharp nose. Another man sat in the guardhouse and watched from the tinted glass. Audrie smiled at them politely.

Yi-Min reached over Audrie and handed the man two sets of identification papers. Audrie could see down her shirt and watched the soldier's eyes for signs of noticing. He made no indication of having any interest and then took the papers to the guardhouse. While waiting for the man to return, Audrie and Yi-Min exchanged glances. Before he returned, they both knew what the soldier's reaction would be.

"You're not on the list of expected visitors, Agent Zhang," he said after returning. He looked from them to the ID papers in his hands. "What is the purpose of your visit? I'm going to have to call this in."

"We are here to see one patient, name is Max Garner," said Yi-Min in the same thick accent. She nodded to Audrie beside her. "This is Audrie Garner, his sister, and I am to accompany her, but her visit was last minute. General Henry Franks probably just hasn't called in yet. You can have your CO call him."

While patiently waiting for his reaction, Yi-Min maintained direct eye contact. The timing of their arrival meant the soldiers would have to call their commanding officer during his off-duty hours when he was probably enjoying time with his family. In turn, their CO would have to call a four-star general at the same time, one of her father's close friends.

Audrie hoped they would not call the general. Even if the soldiers did call him, he would probably give permission, but she wanted to avoid the risk of unwanted attention. After another deep exhale through his nose, the soldier stepped back into the enclosure and turned to his companion. While talking, they kept their faces concealed. Audrie could almost hear their thoughts. Letting a sister visit her brother in such a secure facility seemed like a safe bet.

After a few seconds of discussion between the two men, the one with the sharp nose picked up a phone and spoke into it. At the end of the conversation, he nodded and then hung up. "You've been given permission for the visit, but I'm afraid one of us will have to accompany you."

"Very well," Yi-Min said with an exaggerated sweet smile.

The other soldier exited the guardhouse and stood in front of the vehicle with his submachine gun held in front of his stomach. Unlike his more stoic companion, the second soldier smiled when he had a closer look at the two women. The first soldier opened the door for Yi-Min.

"We need to inspect your vehicle," he said and waited for them both to exit. "And we'll need your weapons if you have any."

Yi-Min silently pulled the pistol from the holster under her vest and handed it to the man. He put it in a small bag from his pocket then opened all the doors of the vehicle and casually looked inside.

"Are these all your weapons?" he asked and paused as if trying to decide whether or not to follow the rule and frisk them.

Audrie understood his internal struggle and smiled. Their feminine presence often had useful effects, but she usually wanted to avoid using them. She preferred to rely on her mental capacities and detested women who had only one weapon in their arsenal, the debilitating male reaction to the female. Alternately, she admired men with the strength to overcome its influence. She thanked whatever god was responsible that neither of the men was a homosexual.

"Yes," Audrie said with a look of impatience. "We have no other weapons." She glanced at Yi-Min to see if she showed any signs of anxiety. Her friend looked completely calm.

After the quick and less-than-thorough vehicle inspection, they returned to their seats with the second soldier taking the backseat behind Audrie. For the next two minutes, they drove in silence the remaining distance to the facility. Audrie could feel the soldier's eyes on the back of her neck.

When they came within view of the facility and the three cars parked in front of it, she wondered about her brother's reaction when he had first arrived. She crossed her arms tightly over her abdomen to offset the sudden chill.

As they exited the vehicle, another soldier appeared from the side of the building, holding a rifle. Audrie noticed the silent exchange between him and the one standing behind her. Yi-Min took the lead up the stairs, and Audrie followed with the soldier from the guardhouse directly behind her. She could almost feel his eyes travel from her feet to her head and back again.

The soldier who had appeared out of nowhere disappeared in the same manner. Without a pause, Yi-Min led them to the front desk where a woman sat. As they approached, the woman watched with narrow eyes through her thick glasses.

"These women are here to visit one of the residents," said the soldier. He turned to Yi-Min and let her finish.

"We are here to see Max Garner," she said sternly with the same thick Chinese accent. The woman squinted in concentration, pausing long enough to translate the words into intelligible English.

"Max Garner is my brother," Audrie added with annoyance.

Audrie shot the woman with her most formidable glance. She turned to the computer in front of her, quietly gulped, and then clicked twice with the mouse. After a questioning look at the soldier standing beside them, the woman picked up the phone.

"Please have a seat," she said before dialing. "I will process your request, but he may not be immediately available."

After Audrie sat in the waiting area, she drew a deep breath and attempted to relax. As Yi-Min took the seat next to her, she silently placed her hand on Audrie's shoulder. The brief touch sent chills down her spine, having the opposite of the intended calming effect. Physical contact reminded Audrie of their plans, extracting them from imagination and into reality.

They waited for about fifteen minutes, but the time felt like an hour. During their wait, the woman at the desk spoke twice on the phone in hushed tones. After the wait, an older woman appeared, coming from behind the front desk.

The woman gave Audrie the immediate impression of a friendly grandmother from a fairytale. After finally escaping from the evil monster, the grandchild would run into her loving arms, but a polite coldness behind her eyes betrayed the practiced friendly smile. When her face relaxed from the strain of smiling, shadows filled the wrinkles in her old face.

"I'm Doctor McGraw," she said and extended her hand. "I am told you are Mister Garner's sister?"

"I am," Audrie said while getting to her feet. "I need to see him for a short while, alone. I trust that he is not being abused?"

"Abused," the old woman said with a shake of her hand in the air. "We do not abuse people, Miss?"

"Audrie Garner."

"We do not abuse people. We treat them. Now, I'm sorry to have to tell you, but your brother is in no condition to see anyone, even his sister. I can have him ready tomorrow."

"Don't be ridiculous," Audrie said using the same tone of disregard the old woman had used. "I insist on seeing him in his present state."

"But he is in between sessions at the moment, under the influence of medication. You will find it too difficult to communicate with him."

"Doctor McGraw," Audrie said as if the woman's concerns could be swept into the corner of the floor and left there. "I was not given all the required security clearances to visit my brother, not to mention your confidential location, just to be turned away from one of the staff. Now take me to Max. I don't care if he's naked and uncon-scious."

The final words escaped her lips with a bit more anger than she had intended, but Audrie felt proud of her tone just the same. The old woman's polite smile finally vanished, leaving only the shadowed wrinkles. At that instant, she transformed from a friendly grandmother into a monster waiting to eat the children.

"Wait here," she said impatiently, "until I can get him presentable. It will be less than ten minutes."

"Thank you," Audrie said politely, bringing her anger back under control. She ignored her instinct to sneer at the old woman in triumph, knowing the act would only instill more hostility. If at all possible, Audrie preferred to prevent hostility.

Audrie felt a sudden panic, followed by an urge to find her brother before the old woman had the chance to make him *presentable*. She imagined him simmering in a concoction of drugs used to dissolve his resistance, preparing him for more information extraction. She knew the military could extract whatever information the patients thought they had successfully hidden.

After learning about her brother's confiscation, Audrie wanted to learn more about what they might do to him, so she and Yi-Min visited Harvard to access the classified documents located there. Audrie already knew about several mind control studies sanctioned by the government such as the infamous *Project Paperclip*, when the CIA brought Nazi doctors to America after World War II and gave them immunity for their war crimes in exchange for their expertise.

From the classified information they'd found, she had doubts about the ability of her brother to completely recover. She imagined the scandal of getting Max returned to them as a mindless vegetable with unknown impulses buried in his psyche. What had they done to him already?

Before she visited Harvard, Audrie had investigated all the disinformation and misinformation about mind control available to the public. The amount of information had almost overwhelmed her. The intelligence community had done an excellent job of surrounding the truth with lies, distraction, and exaggeration. The typical US citizen, stupefied by the public education system, was unlikely to discriminate fact from fiction.

If they knew her brother as she did, they would have easily understood all of his motivations. She had no evidence supporting the idea that any mind control program, foreign or domestic, had influenced his behavior, but she knew he was not antagonistic to the United States. None of that would have mattered to the doctors at the institute. They would have to assume the worst, that some foreign influence had psychologically tampered with him. She understood the military's reasons for his incarceration, but she could not approve of it.

Before the military had taken her brother, she'd held no reservations about their methods. But since his disappearance, her anger toward them had begun to grow almost out of control. During internal reflection, however, she had difficulty distinguishing the true source of her anger. How much of her anger did she direct toward her brother and how much to the system that had caught him in its web?

Ten minutes later, the old woman reappeared with a smile on her face again as if no uncomfortable social confrontation had taken place. With the soldier walking casually behind them, Doctor Mc-Graw led them through a side door into a maze of hallways. As they walked, the soldier's footsteps consumed all other sounds.

They reached an elevator and went down one level. When the doors opened, the dark hallway caught Audrie by surprise. She felt as if they were entering an abandoned hospital. The white brick walls looked ancient, and the air smelled damp. When they made eye contact, Yi-Min just shrugged her shoulders.

They walked in the darkness for about twenty meters then turned the corner into a lighter hallway. Rooms lined both sides of the hall, spaced evenly apart by about two meters. Each door looked the same and had a small narrow window higher than Audrie's eye level. To see inside the rooms, she would have had to stand on the tips of her toes. A bright light shot eerily through a few of them, probably from the occupied rooms.

Doctor McGraw led them to the end of the hallway to a door without a window, which led to another hallway. When she opened that door, Audrie and Yi-Min had to shield their eyes from the bright light. The temperature was about fifteen degrees warmer too. Audrie could easily imagine the effect on any poor soul incarcerated in the facility.

"Sorry," she said. "I should have warned you. The light levels can be quite a shock."

Did the woman find pleasure in their momentary discomfort?

"No problem," said Yi-Min. "With no windows or clocks, the patients probably find it difficult to know what time of day it is. Does your staff experience the intended disorientation as well?"

"Sometimes," she answered.

After Doctor McGraw opened the next door, Audrie's eyes focused instantly on her brother who was sitting in what looked like a metal pool lounge chair. His body was inclined at a forty-five-degree angle and he appeared unconscious. A simple blue hospital gown covered him. Even while unconscious, Audrie thought he looked exhausted.

When Dr. McGraw shut the door behind her, Max opened his eyes and slowly turned to look at them. Audrie paused on her approach, momentarily paralyzed by the dreamy and glazed look in his eyes.

Max was located in front of a stainless steel desk with two black metal chairs on his left. Doctor McGraw took a seat behind the desk and then motioned for them to sit. The soldier stood in front of the door with his eyes shifting between Max and the three women.

"How is he doing?" Yi-Min asked, directing her question to Audrie who sat next to Max.

"Of course you know," Doctor McGraw interjected, "that he is here at the request of the authorities. If you disagree with anything you find concerning him, try and remember that. Don't complain to me."

"I understand," Audrie said without looking at the woman. She attempted to focus all her attention on her brother who seemed to have fallen back asleep. "Max, it's Audrie, your sister. Can you hear me?"

He slowly opened his eyes again and stared at her.

"Audrie?" he whispered then looked from her eyes, to her nose, to her mouth, then her chin. After a moment, his eyes opened wider, almost as if frightened.

"Yes, I'm here," she said. "I've come for a visit."

Max turned to Doctor McGraw, placing both hands on his chair as if to push himself up from it.

"She's back?"

With apparent physical strain, he attempted to sit all the way forward but fell back in his chair. He took a deep breath before trying to speak again.

"Where are the others? Don't let them come back here. Oh, why did you come back here?"

Max started crying and spoke with tears streaming down his cheeks. He turned so that he could see both Doctor McGraw and his sister. "They're not going to let you out again. I'm sorry!"

"Max," Audrie said, trying to redirect his attention and not let his pathetic emotional state soften her resolve. "Look at me. I'm right here. Everything will be fine. You'll get out of here before you know it."

In his delusional state, would she be able to learn what she needed to know? With enough time, yes, but they might not have enough time. How many seconds remained to them? She glanced at her watch and saw two seconds quickly vanish into the past. Time seemed like a car rushing to hit her. Her digital watch face said nine thirty-six.

"You aren't real," he said, wiping tears from his eyes. "Just a dream. This is just a dream."

"Max, look at me," she said, and the anger in her voice forced him to face her, away from Doctor McGraw. Audrie wanted to shake him, but the tension between them still felt like an impenetrable wall. "I am no dream."

"This is real?" he asked suspiciously.

"Yes, Max, I am real, so listen to me. Father sent me to see you. We want to know some things, but you've got to pull yourself together. Can you do that?"

"Know what?" he asked and fresh tears fell out of his eyes. "Know what? I don't know anything anymore. They have everything. I don't know anything. For god's sake! I don't know anything."

Audrie looked at her friend in desperation, but Yi-Min just shook her head.

Audrie turned to the doctor.

"I need to talk with my brother alone now. Your presence seems to have a negative effect on his ability to speak freely."

"That is out of the question, Miss Garner," Doctor McGraw said. "Any information you may learn from him belongs to the United States government. I need to be here."

"Fine," Audrie said with a sigh, then nodded toward the soldier by the door. "I doubt that soldier has the clearance to know about anything Max might say. He and Miss Zhang should wait in the hallway."

Doctor McGraw held Audrie's gaze for a moment then looked at the soldier and nodded. He opened the door and held it for Yi-Min. As she stood to leave with him, Audrie noticed the anxiety in her eyes. Audrie drew a deep breath through her nose and then looked at her watch again. Time seemed to be accelerating even further. Her watch said nine forty-five.

When the door closed, she turned back to her brother. His attention appeared to be focused on the ceiling.

"Max," she said and waited for his eyes to drift lazily back to her face. "We know about the new reactor and drive system. What were you thinking? Did you think you could keep that to yourself? Did you think that kind of technology belongs to you? What if it fell into the wrong hands? Did you consider any of that?"

His eyes widened in horror and Audrie backed away, momentarily startled. He pushed back into his chair as if trying to separate himself from some invisible enemy. In between silent sobbing, he struggled to maintain enough airflow to his lungs.

"Taylor and Mark and the others," he said as memories began flooding his vision. When he turned to look at Doctor McGraw, he spoke slowly and in a whisper. His eyes grew uncomfortably wide again. "The creatures took them. Everyone's gone!"

Audrie looked across the desk at Doctor McGraw without trying to hide her anger. The older woman met her gaze almost as if to remind Audrie of the futility of reasoning with him and her. After turning back to her brother, she managed to speak without showing the sudden dread she felt. The way he'd whispered the word *creatures* sent chills through her heart.

"They're not gone, Max. No creatures took them."

Although he was looking at her again, he still seemed lost in an imaginary world. Her words failed to soften the terrified look in his eyes. She needed a new strategy. Reluctantly, she accepted her failure to reach him.

As she looked into his pathetic, tear-stained cheeks, she imagined herself in the same position. For the first time in her life, she realized how easily humans could be broken. Through her thin dress, the cold metal chair suddenly felt like ice and seemed to suck the heat from her bones.

With more strength than she had intended, she grasped her brother's shoulder and pulled him away from his seat so that their eyes were just centimeters apart. His warm skin under the thin cloth reminded her of his helplessness. For a moment, the image of Max as a little boy replaced his terrified face. Her anger transformed into empathy for him, but she did not relax her grip.

"Is this all because of Taylor? You don't have plans with her, do you?"

When she mentioned Taylor's name, his eyes narrowed to slits, and he seemed to see Audrie for the first time, but in the next moment, he was looking through her again.

"What did you say? What did you say about Taylor?" With each word, his voice grew stronger. "They just gave her back? Don't believe them. It's all just an illusion."

Even though she'd failed to extract Max from his mental abyss, she could see part of the truth in his eyes and the sorrow on his face. His primal motivations seemed focused on Taylor. Audrie felt forced to sanction the path he had chosen.

Did she need to dig any deeper? No, she was out of time. At least she'd seen his concern for the girl and it helped dissipate her anger toward him. She could now apply all of her anger to the woman on the other side of the desk, to the soldier in the hall, and to the system responsible for ensnaring them all.

But did she have the courage to take the next step?

At the moment, courage seemed to make little difference. She had no other choice. After walking into the facility, they had already passed the point of no return.

Before disconnecting from her brother, she took a deep breath and then turned to Doctor McGraw. When she spoke, she erased emotion from her voice.

"If they let you release him eventually, will I get my brother back?"

"Your brother is in a very susceptible state right now," she began. "Seeing him the way he is now is giving you the wrong impression. Over time, he will recover to a more recognizable state."

Audrie put her left hand on the desk and pretended to look at her watch. The time was nine fifty-eight. She had less than two minutes.

"Let's be honest with each other," she said casually then reached down with her right hand and adjusted her skirt. With her hand out of sight, Audrie gripped her inner thigh, and her cold fingers felt like a wake-up call. "What else have you done to him? I mean, you're not just going to let him out of here with what he knows, without some hidden control mechanism. Are you?"

"Miss Garner," the doctor said with blatant impatience. She pushed her seat back and stood while Audrie remained seated. "I have not seen any legitimate reason for your visit, other than maybe personal. I'm afraid the military doesn't accept personal visits, no matter how rich your father is, or how many generals you know. You've seen your brother, and we're done here!"

Audrie looked up at the old woman, her eyes wide in sudden fear. For the first time, she felt as though a real monster confronted her. Before standing, she glanced at her wrist and watched as the seconds changed from fifty-four to fifty-five. Audrie began silently counting.

She quickly removed her hand from under her skirt, revealing a small injection gun Yi-Min had given her. Before Doctor McGraw could respond, Audrie jumped out of her seat and punched the old woman in the chest three times with the needle. According to Yi-Min, only one shot would have been sufficient.

"Yes, we are done," Audrie answered as the old woman fell back in her seat, a look of surprise in her clear eyes.

When Audrie heard the loud explosion from the floor above them, she ignored her immediate reaction of shock and kept her focus on the old woman. With their eyes locked, the doctor put both hands on the desk to help keep herself steady. Audrie watched with pleasure as the woman's eyes started to droop and the color drained from her face. A moment later, her arms lost all of their strength, and her head fell forward to crash on her desk. When the woman had become still, Audrie turned her attention to Max.

Max began looking around the room with the same panic in his eyes. After making eye contact with him, all of Audrie's other emotions dissipated, replaced by sympathy. For the first time since they were children, she put both arms around him in a warm embrace and then helped him to his feet.

EIGHTY-THREE

Audrie

"What's going on?" Max asked during their first few steps. When he turned to the desk, the sight of Doctor McGraw lying unconscious on the table stopped his movement, and he almost fell over from dizziness.

"This isn't real!" he barked, shaking his head. "Where are you taking me?"

"Yes, Max, this is real," she said as she got him moving again. He walked slowly and uncertainly. Audrie hoped he would not hinder their escape. He weighed too much for her to carry, but somehow she managed to escort him to the door.

She stopped after noticing the door open a crack and then saw Yi-Min peeking inside the room. When she opened the door farther, Audrie noticed the soldier lying on the side of the hallway, with Yi-Min holding his gun.

"Did you have any trouble?" Audrie asked before Yi-Min could ask the same question.

"No," she said. "He looked away when we heard the explosion."

"This juice works fast," Audrie said after bringing the injection up to eye level.

"I told you," Yi-Min answered with an uneasy smile. "Come on, we need to help them find Gerald."

At the mention of his friend's name, Max looked down at Yi-Min, his eyes becoming slits. He spoke in a whisper.

"Foster is here?"

Before Audrie could answer, she heard the sound of a door handle turning. Both women looked down the hallway where it ended in another corner. Yi-Min quickly placed herself between the direction of the sound and Audrie and Max with her gun pointed at the floor.

"Get back in the room," she whispered to Audrie then put her finger to her lips for Max.

Audrie pulled her brother back through the doorway with her and then held the door open just a crack so that she could open it quickly if needed. Max's eyes instantly became focused on the doctor's unconscious body, and he froze, staring at her. Audrie hoped he would stay that way.

With one hand on her brother and one hand on the door handle, Audrie leaned close to listen. For several seconds, she heard only silence, and the time felt like hours. When she felt a slight pressure pulling the door open, she resisted the instinct to shut it. After a moment, she sensed Yi-Min's presence on the other side.

"It's me," she said softly. "Simon's coming, and he's bringing a guest."

After opening the door, Audrie noticed two men approaching them: a masked man with a black baseball cap accompanied by a taller, much larger man dressed in a hospital smock walking in front of him, slightly to the left. A blindfold covered the larger man's eyes, and his hands appeared either handcuffed or tied behind his back.

She instantly recognized the masked man as Simon. He held a gun in one hand, pressed into the larger man's upper arm, almost in his armpit. After coming within a few steps of them, Simon stopped and pushed the larger man against the wall.

"Stay right here, big guy," said the voice behind the mask. Simon held the man against the wall for a moment then turned to look at his boss. Audrie saw anger in his eyes.

"Is he alright?"

"Only if we get them out of here," Audrie said, her eyes fixed on their captive against the wall. When she noticed the cut on his upper lip, she imagined several ways that Simon might have subdued him.

"We've got to hurry," Simon said. He pressed his gun again in the man's back. "This guy will be our blind guide to Mr. Foster's cell. Right?"

"I already told you the room number," the man said, confidence in his deep voice and a bit of amusement. "But you idiots aren't getting out of here with anyone!"

"We'll see," Simon said.

They all followed as Simon and their big captive led them toward the darker hallway. Audrie focused on keeping her brother moving and on his feet. He seemed oblivious to their surroundings and kept looking in every direction as if he saw a hallway full of people, or other creatures. Audrie shuddered at what he might be imagining.

After opening the door to the darker hallway, Audrie noticed a man lying on the floor just two meters away from them. He appeared asleep with no visible trace of blood or other physical trauma. He wore the same hospital smock as their captive. Simon led the blind-folded man around his coworker on the floor.

They turned in the opposite direction from where Doctor Mc-Graw had led them, into an even darker hallway. Light shined from the high windows above only two of the doors, casting an eerie glow on the opposite wall. Yi-Min went ahead of them and stood close to the door to see the number.

"This is it, room L23," Yi-Min said while the others approached. She moved so that Simon could stand in front of her, the big man on his other side.

Simon removed a card from his jacket and held it close to a black pad by the door handle. Audrie heard a soft click, and the door opened. Light from inside made the entire corridor brighter but seemed to frighten Max. He backed away from the cell, and Audrie had to keep him from running away down the hall. He extended his right hand to shield the light from the room and started shaking his head.

"Please don't put me back in the light," he begged. "Not the light."

Audrie ignored her brother while Simon entered the cell, pushing their captive in front of him. Yi-Min blocked the entrance and glanced nervously down the hall.

"We're getting Gerald, your friend," Audrie said to Max, her eyes fixed on the cell. "You don't have to go back there."

"Gerald?" he whispered and seemed to relax a little.

He removed his hand to look into the cell with her, and together they waited for what might happen next. She was relieved to let Yi-Min and Simon take control of the operation. Taking care of Max would require all of her concentration.

When Simon exited, pulling the half-conscious Gerald Foster into the hallway with him, Audrie looked for the first time at the man responsible for their dangerous predicament. She hardly recognized Gerald from his picture. He looked thinner and even more mentally disturbed than Max. When he emerged from the intense light of his cell, he looked at each of them with no sign of recognition. During his brief eye contact with her, he seemed to look right through her. She had expected to be angry at him, but she felt only sympathy at seeing him in a worse condition than her brother.

After Simon and Gerald got out of the way, Yi-Min disappeared into the cell. Two seconds later, Audrie heard the same sound as when she incapacitated the doctor, two shots from the injection gun.

"What the hell?" said a deep voice from inside the cell.

"Just something to help you sleep," Yi-Min said, still out of Audrie's view, "and forget!"

A moment later, Yi-Min stepped out of the cell and then shut the door on the soon-to-be sleeping giant. With the hallway darker, her brother's trepidation seemed to lessen. He reverted to a more withdrawn state, looking at the elusive shadows again.

Both Simon and Yi-Min helped Gerald walk down the hallway.

With their support, he walked evenly, but if they let go of him, he would have collapsed. Max held tightly onto Audrie's arm. She liked the feeling of his dependence on her. The experience reminded her of being children together.

They walked past the elevator to the end of the dark corridor. They stopped at a closed door with a picture of stairs on it.

"Okay," Simon said. "These stairs lead up to the ground floor, to the side of the building. It should be all clear, but I'll check first."

Simon used the stolen access card to open the door and then held it open as they all entered the stairwell. Just inside, stairs only went up and another door led to the next floor down. When Audrie saw the graphic of descending stairs, she shuddered at the thought of what might lie below them. The door seemed to separate them from an unknown enemy.

After a long two minutes of maneuvering the two drugged prisoners up the stairs, they reached the next floor. As Simon extended his hand toward the door, it opened from the outside, and Audrie's heart almost stopped. Another man wearing a mask stood in their path, blocking their exit.

EIGHTY-FOUR

Audrie

When Simon first contacted Audrie, he revealed his desire to rescue her brother from the psychiatric hospital. Audrie remembered laughing in his face. At the time, his idea seemed preposterous, a waste of time, the risks far outweighing any benefit. The military would be releasing him on their own eventually, so why go to all the trouble? Once the intelligence community got their desired information, he would be free and then she could pick up the pieces. The military could keep Gerald Foster.

After her trip to Brazil, Audrie mistakenly believed she had discovered all the information about her brother's activities. When Simon told her more of the story, she could not believe it, at first. The part about the alien and another world seemed like a fantasy. Then she watched the explosion at the company in Salt Lake City, Cerametrics.

Such a blatant act of destruction meant that directors in the national security agencies and the energy industry were afraid. The invention of a fusion reactor would turn the world upside down and cause too much uncertainty. They had to destroy the Mormons who had secretly developed the fusion energy source.

Their ostentatious destruction would send a powerful message to anyone who interacted with them. Disinformation agents were in full force, flooding the internet with wild conspiracy theories intended to prevent serious investigators from discovering the true objectives of the attack. As expected, the major media outlets declared the root cause as an accident and quickly returned their attention to the latest controversy in the world of sports.

After Audrie had more of the facts, she had to accept the possibility of a worse situation for her brother. The event would be more than just a dark mark on her family. She now had to worry about his life and future.

When Yi-Min told her about what they could do to Max, she almost had a panic attack. The intelligence community had spent billions of dollars on mind control research programs such as Bluebird, MK Ultra, and Paperclip. Psychiatrists at the CIA had also learned how to plant suicide and murder programs in a target's psyche, among other horrors. Max needed to escape from their influence, and Audrie felt obligated to help. Her high status in society would help ensure her absolution of any indictment.

At first, she had failed to share Simon's optimism, but then he told her of a young man from Gerald's group who could help. When she had met Freddy, much of her disbelief vanished. Not only could the young man sense her thoughts, but something in his eyes frightened her.

She vividly remembered when Simon had introduced her to the young man, and how he looked at her, as though he knew her already. She saw the clear recognition in his eyes. His age appeared early twenties, but Audrie sensed more to him than age could have produced. When he shook her hand, she felt a shock to her entire system.

—※—

After arriving at the top of the stairs and remembering the identity of this second masked man, Audrie attempted to calm herself and rid her mind of all personal thoughts. Freddy looked at each of them, and when his eyes met hers, she stopped breathing. What else did he see?

"Freddy," Simon said as the door closed, and Freddy stepped inside the stairwell. "Is everything okay? What's the status?"

Freddy tore his gaze away from Audrie and their two rescued captives.

"Everyone in the building is subdued, but we might not have much time. The guard at the gate escaped and is running for help. When he finds a way to get a message to his superiors, they will be sending a full assault team and helicopters. I do not know how much time we have."

With unexpected speed, Gerald Foster broke free from Simon's grasp and took hold of Freddy's shoulder. His sudden movement made Audrie tighten her grip on Max. Freddy waited patiently for Gerald to speak.

"Freddy, Freddy," he said in a loud whisper. "The alien! Don't let it take you! It's not what we thought!"

Before responding, Freddy took a deep breath and grabbed Gerald's arm.

"Everything is going to be fine, Gerald. You are getting out of here tonight. You and Max need to go with Simon. Okay?"

Both Gerald and Max looked at Simon and then at the door with fear apparent in their eyes. Max strengthened his grip on her arm.

"I'm not leaving Audrie."

"I can't go with you now," she said, and tears threatened to blur her vision. With some effort, Audrie disengaged his hand from her arm. "Simon and Freddy will take you to safety. We'll see each other again soon. I promise. I promise!"

The fear in his eyes seemed to reflect her own anxiety at the next part of the plan. In her heart, she wanted to believe her promise of seeing him again, but would she be able to keep it?

"Are you sure you can handle both of them by yourself?" Yi-Min asked as Simon took hold of Max's arm.

"Don't worry about me," he said then turned to open the door. "I'll get them to the car."

The door closed and her brother disappeared with Gerald and

Simon. Immediately afterward, she and Yi-Min led Freddy down the stairs and back into the maze of hallways. On their journey back to Doctor McGraw's office, Freddy walked behind them and asked no questions. Without having to help the two escapees, they arrived at the office in less than a minute.

Audrie and Yi-Min walked past the unconscious guard on the floor without looking at him. They found the room just as Audrie remembered, with the doctor's body slumped over the table. Audrie pulled out her injection gun and extended it to Freddy. For a moment, he just stared at it.

"Take care of my brother," she said.

"I will," he said then took the gun out of her hand and it disappeared in his jacket. Yi-Min gave him her injection gun next. "I am sorry to leave you both like this. I feel like I am abandoning you to a pack of wolves."

"We'll be okay," Yi-Min said.

Audrie put her hand on his shoulder.

"It's the only way," she said.

At her touch, his whole body stiffened, and she realized what should have been obvious at their introduction. She could now see his physical attraction to her. With her hand on his arm, he almost seemed paralyzed. At that moment, his eyes revealed that he knew what she had just realized.

"I am afraid they will do to you what they did to Max and Gerald." He took a step backward, out of her grasp.

"Yi-Min and I will be okay," Audrie said, letting her hand fall to her side. "Our story is pretty tight. You followed us, remember? After you convinced me to visit him, to see if he was okay? I'm blaming it all on you."

She tried smiling but failed. She felt guilty for blaming the entire incident on him.

They returned to the hallway and stood next to the unconscious soldier on the floor. Audrie watched as Freddy injected Yi-Min once in the upper right shoulder. As she began to lose consciousness, Audrie and Freddy gently lowered her body to the floor. Audrie held her hand and looked into her eyes until they closed. After arranging Yi-Min comfortably on the floor near the guard, they walked back into the office. Audrie concentrated on breathing.

"Will you remember me?" Freddy asked when they reached Doctor McGraw's desk.

The old woman looked so still, she seemed almost dead. Audrie felt just a little guilty for overdosing her.

"Yes, I'll remember," Audrie answered, putting her hand on his to steady herself. "Just not the last several hours."

Freddy shot her with the injection gun, and her vision soon began to fade. As he guided her gently to the floor, she realized with sadness that she would never remember the look in his eyes.

EIGHTY-FIVE

Taylor

Taylor sat in front of the campfire with her hands held toward the flames for warmth. The late summer Canadian weather was uncomfortably cold to her, especially after her recent hot stay in Brazil. Light from the flames cast shadows of Sadi, Cesar, and Mark on the tent behind them. In the darkness, she watched their shadows dance on the tent wall.

For several hours, they waited by the fire and filled the silence by discussing any available topic. Judging by their expressions, Taylor imagined the others shared her emotions. She feared the silence. If they let the silence linger too long around the campfire, dark thoughts might begin creeping into their imaginations, thoughts of the rescue mission Simon and Freddy were attempting and the possibility of them never returning. Dark thoughts also included the chance of being discovered before they could escape.

So far, the group had escaped detection in the Canadian forest, but Taylor knew that government agents would eventually find them. Agents from the United States military were probably able to track Freddy's escape in the convertible. They probably knew about the jet and would be looking for it via satellite.

During a short lull in the conversation, she concentrated on memories of camping trips with her father and brother. She missed them. If she left the planet, she would miss her mother.

"Are you sure they're not going to wake up on us?" Taylor asked for the second time, nodding toward the tent. Doroteo had captured two forest rangers near their camp by the lake. After sedating them, he put them in the tent where they were sleeping peacefully. If all went according to plan, their captives would wake after they all had departed.

Cesar looked at her from across the fire and nodded his head. He did not even attempt to smile. She wanted a verbal answer but was not surprised at his silent one. When he learned of Sadi and Dominga's narrow escape, his mood changed and his level of verbal communication dropped almost to zero. He felt responsible for all of them.

With Doroteo guarding their camp from the darkness, Taylor and the others could relax a little by the fire. Taylor had come to trust in Doroteo's abilities, especially after providing the cover for Freddy's rescue the previous night. She almost wished she could have been there to see the feat. If there was a movie with a scene like that, she'd want to see it.

"I'll check on them," Sadi said a moment later, getting to her feet and lifting the tent flap. As the woman poked a flashlight inside, Taylor watched the tent glow like a Chinese paper lantern. A moment later, Sadi zipped the flap closed again.

"No movement," she said and returned to her seat between Cesar and Mark.

Taylor watched the woman for a moment then returned her gaze to the fire. At the moment, Sadi's two daughters and Mark's two sons were asleep in the plane, just twenty meters away from them, behind a wall of trees. Dominga and Mark's wife took turns with Sadi to help watch the kids and guard the plane.

Taylor recalled when Mark's wife, Susan, had met them at the lake with her two sons. During their emotional reunion, Taylor could see a mixture of anger and relief in the woman's eyes. When Mark had introduced her to the group, she had looked at Taylor with instant suspicion. Taylor saw the questions in her eyes. How had her husband spent so much time with a single girl like Taylor? What had they done together? Fortunately for Taylor, the woman's anxiety about the entire situation had prevented any awkward interrogation.

"Come on, you guys," Taylor said with a smile. "We made it safe so far, didn't we? They'll be here with Max and Gerald soon. Freddy hasn't failed yet, has he? It's like an adventure."

"I wish we had your optimism," Sadi replied with a sneer directed at herself. "I'll feel better when we get off this stupid rock."

The bitterness in Sadi's voice surprised Taylor and reminded her of similar emotions she was holding back like a mountain of water behind a dam. How much pressure could she handle before the dam broke and the flood swept over them all? If they did successfully escape, it would not matter. For the moment, she had to keep certain thoughts from her mind, like Freddy failing to rescue Max and Gerald.

If Freddy did not return that night, he'd instructed her to get the others to safety and abandon them. Freddy said there would still be hope, but how could Taylor leave Gerald, the man who stood by her from the beginning? Gerald had become the driving force behind everything.

She hoped the military had failed to steal his optimism, Gerald's most defining trait. He would not be the same without it. If she never saw Gerald again, she would honor his memory by taking that part of him with her.

Taylor had only one justification for abandoning her friends. They could help no one if they were caught. They had already lost two others from their group, Franklin and Gerda. Taylor could not fail them as well. When safe, they would have to return and attempt to rescue them.

Taylor always hated internal reflection and stopped herself from continuing down the path of asking more questions about unpleasant possibilities. In the end, her answers might not even matter. Her father always told her to stop wasting time worrying about a result that might never occur. Unless she took control of her imagination, it could become her worst enemy.

While watching the flames, she focused on her memories of their arrival into the Canadian forest. After they had eluded the authorities in Brazil and finally flew into space in their plane, Taylor nearly had a panic attack. With the BMW, they'd had time to test and prove its spaceworthiness before attempting a flight. And even then, they'd experienced problems. But with the plane, they were forced to test it before she had greater than eighty percent confidence in survival.

The silence was becoming uncomfortable again, so Taylor looked up from the hot coals at the base of the fire, focusing on Cesar. He was poking the fire with a stick.

"I was never so afraid in my life," Taylor said, quietly laughing. "Descending on this lake. Remember, Cesar? You had to pry my hands off the controls."

"Seeing your face didn't help me remain calm," Cesar said, making eye contact with her through the flames.

The memory of losing her composure in front of Cesar would probably never fail to bring embarrassment, and she hoped the reminder would help lighten his mood. Even though they'd already had a similar conversation, Cesar made no mention of the long list of obscenities she had used and how he had to shake her physically from hysteria.

"Was it hard to come back?" Mark asked.

"For more than one reason," she answered, grateful for his assistance in keeping the conversation alive. "Returning to Earth meant possible death, but it was also beautiful. You'll all see very soon. Once we've left the atmosphere, nothing else will matter."

"It's funny, you know." Mark spoke more to himself than anyone else. "It's always been my dream, but I never thought it would happen, and especially like this."

"Mine too," Taylor said, opening her mouth to continue, but Sadi's sudden movement stopped her.

"Something's coming," Sadi said, pointing to a light from the other side of the lake, behind Taylor. She remained sitting and seemed afraid to move.

"It's a car," Taylor said after turning.

Cesar stood from his seat and began walking toward the lake.

"Stay here."

As if hypnotized, everyone stared at the headlights gliding across the water toward them. Taylor squinted and held her breath as the lights intensified. But in the next instant, the bright light vanished, and her eyes required a moment for the BMW to materialize.

"Holy shit," Taylor said, putting her hand to her mouth and feeling her heart pounding in her chest. She imagined Gerald and Max in the vehicle, and her eyes suddenly became moist. "It's them!"

Light from the moon reflected off the shiny surface of the water.

"It's Freddy," Sadi said, rising from her chair and starting to walk toward Cesar on the shore of the lake.

Taylor could feel a large volume of blood pumping through her heart. For the second time that day, she forgot to breathe. The sight of the flying vehicle reminded her of when she and Max had made her first trip into space. While waiting, Taylor could not decide who she wished to see more, Max or Gerald.

All four adults stood on the shore and watched as the car landed next to them and then gently rolled to a stop. Freddy stepped out first, followed by Simon. They looked exhausted.

Taylor could see the outline of two men in the back seat. Before she recognized them, she had to take a couple of steps around the front of the car. They gave her the impression of two children waiting for the signal from their parents to exit.

Freddy stood motionless for a moment with his eyes focused on the four people there to greet him. While Simon opened the door to the back seat, Sadi threw her arms around Freddy and held him tightly, her glistening tears reflecting the moonlight.

"Oh my God, Freddy. You did it! Somehow, I knew you would." She turned her head to look at the back of the BMW. "How's Gerald, and Max? Did anyone get hurt?"

"We escaped," Freddy said after she released him. "But we need to get out of here. I do not know how much time we have."

"Yeah," Simon said. "We need to get these two to the plane."

They all watched as Simon opened the door and helped Max stand on his feet then tried to balance him. Mark stepped over to help his fellow employee. He looked up at his boss and seemed ready to ask a question but remained silent.

Cesar glanced at Taylor with a look of concern then opened the door for Gerald.

"Gerald," Taylor said, placing her hand on his shoulder. "Are you okay? What did they do to you?"

Gerald just looked up at Taylor without recognition, so she gently shook his shoulder. The physical sensation had no effect. Both men looked like the ghosts of their former selves.

"What the hell is wrong with them?" she asked and turned to Freddy, then Simon.

"They're on some pretty strong drugs," Simon said.

Sadi came to stand by Taylor, and together they helped Gerald stand. When Sadi took hold of his arm, Gerald looked into her eyes and seemed to recognize her. But instead of smiling, his eyes narrowed in distrust. As they walked with him, he never stopped looking at her. Of the two escaped convicts, he seemed the most unstable and required the most support to move. Sadi stood on one side and Taylor on the other.

"How's Max's sister?" Taylor asked when they got close to the fire.

Freddy turned to Taylor as if she was interrupting his thoughts. Their eyes met briefly, then he looked back to the ground.

"She and her friend were fine when we left them."

When Taylor first learned about Max's sister, who had disguised herself as the fake airplane inspector and sent them to jail, she laughed almost hysterically. She remembered hating the woman and thinking she looked familiar. Taylor could not believe she had missed the family resemblance to Max.

Before continuing to the plane, Freddy made Max and Gerald stop at the fire to rest. Freddy and Simon spent the next few minutes sharing a brief version of their escape. Simon spoke the most. While listening, Taylor became angry again and began fantasizing about vengeance, eliminating those responsible for torturing her friends and anyone else who would threaten their freedom.

"We should get out of here as soon as possible," Freddy said suddenly. "I do not like this feeling."

"What is it?" Simon asked, standing with him.

"There are many people out there looking for us, some very close," he responded. "We need to go."

EIGHTY-SIX

Taylor

As they prepared to leave, Taylor thought of Doroteo out in the forest somewhere. Hopefully, he would change his mind and come with them, but he seemed determined to stay. She would feel better if he went with them on their journey.

Before joining the others on their way to the plane, Taylor extinguished the fire and made one final check on the occupants of the tent.

"Sleep tight, guys," she whispered to the sleeping forest rangers.

While approaching the wall of trees separating the camp from the plane, Taylor heard a twig snap behind her. Instinctively, she turned, expecting to see Doroteo. Instead, she saw a man in dark, indistinct clothing step out from behind the tent. The red coals of the dying fire reflected off the whites of his eyes and teeth. She failed to recognize him but could see his smile. Her heart seemed to stop.

"Hello there," the man said happily.

"Hi," Taylor said, attempting to appear calm. To keep her racing heart under control, she had to focus on breathing. While waiting for him to continue, she noticed his right hand was held behind his back.

"Where do you think you're going?" he asked politely.

The man wore a leather jacket, unzipped, and dark jeans with several pockets. He had a pistol attached to his hip, and his dark hair blended into the darkness of the night. When Taylor saw the weapon, she knew he was not just another forest ranger checking on campers.

Taylor suddenly felt paralyzed, fear and frustration rooting her feet to the earth. Instinctively, she expected Doroteo to spring from the darkness and throw the man to the ground, but the silence was menacing, incapable of offering aid.

"Who are you?" she asked, hoping to give Doroteo more time if he was out there.

"Just start walking," the man answered, pulling his hand from behind his back and pointing a pistol at her head.

For several seconds, her body became even more rigid.

He recognized her state of fear and waved his gun toward the trees as a reminder to move. The action broke the hypnotic spell and she took a step backward.

"Come on. Let's go meet your friends. We'll have plenty of time to make conversation."

Taylor felt a burning between her eyes as if the weapon had a powerful laser sight. She took another step back, trying to decide what to do and not wanting to lead him to the others. She'd always imagined having a gun pointed at her and liked to think she'd have more courage. Instead, she lost all rational thought. She felt like a thoughtless machine, a large blood pump.

When she failed to move farther, the man lowered the gun. Her eyes followed the movement.

"Don't like it when I do that, do you?"

With his weapon lowered, she regained some of her cognitive ability. She would try to lead him in the wrong direction.

But then without warning, he lunged forward, grabbed the back of her head with his left hand, and then forcefully spun her around to face the trees. At his quick movement, her heart stopped again, and she squealed in pain at his firm grip on her hair.

"Okay, okay, I'm going," she managed to say, humiliated by his complete control over her body. No one had ever made her feel so powerless. His speed and strength surprised her.

"That's a good girl," he said.

In contrast with his cheerful voice, he pushed her roughly forward. If not holding onto her, she would have fallen. While being forced to walk, her emotions changed from fear to anger and indignation.

"Simon," she yelled, then drew a quick breath. "Simon!"

In a flash, the man's hand released her shoulder and then closed around her mouth.

"Now we're having fun!"

With his hand over her mouth and his gun pressed against her back, he pushed her forward through the trees until they reached the jet, about thirty seconds later, and found Simon and Cesar in front of Gerald, Max, and Sadi. Taylor required a moment to recognize the other weapon pointed in her direction, a gun in Simon's hand. Instead of being stricken with fear, she was relieved, and she hoped Simon would just eliminate the man, even if he also hit her. The man stopped pushing her and stood still.

Shoot him, she wanted to say, but the man's hand prevented her. *Shoot him!*

"Drop the gun, Mr. Thatcher," the man said from behind her head. Taylor felt his warm breath on her hair and recognized the confidence in his voice, indicating extensive training in handling precarious conflict situations. "Not even I am that good of a shot, Simon. You're just going to end up hurting your friend."

For the next few seconds, Simon just held the weapon, silently and steadily pointed at her. In his eyes, she saw the struggle of indecision but a determination not to yield. Taylor closed her eyes, gulped, and wondered if she would ever open them again. After what felt like an eternity of darkness, she opened her eyes just as Simon lowered his arm and dropped the gun to the ground. After the thud of his gun striking the dirt, Simon raised his hands in the air.

In disappointment and anger, Taylor elbowed the man in the ribs and tried hitting the gun from his grip. In response, he laughed with a sneer and pushed her violently away from him, toward her friends. By some miracle, she managed to keep herself from falling to the ground.

With his hand off her mouth, she drew in a deep breath and turned to face him. She had never felt so angry in her entire life. With supreme self-control, she stopped herself from ramming her shoulder into him. He aimed his weapon at her face again, the look in his eyes stopping her from lunging. She almost started growling at him.

She slowly stepped backward until she reached her friends and felt Sadi's warm hand grasp her shoulder. Her soothing touch helped erase the residual pain from where the man had held her.

Gerald turned to her, panic in his eyes. But a moment later, he turned back to the man as if he could see through him to the trees beyond.

"It's okay, Taylor," Sadi whispered. "Freddy and Doroteo are still out there. Freddy took off when you were at the tent."

"So this is what we've all been trying to find, is it?" the man asked, and Sadi stopped talking. While inspecting the plane, he stepped closer to the group.

"Who are you?" Simon asked.

The man ignored him and continued talking to himself.

"I was beginning to think all this was just another training exercise. I thought they had us out here chasing ghosts!" He spoke with excitement and kept shaking his head. "This really is amazing. When they told us that you recovered Max Garner and Gerald Foster, I didn't believe it. But here they are. I'm looking right at them, and I still don't believe it! When they get the details of what happened out of you, I hope to read about it."

The man looked back at the jet and shook his head in mock regret.

"You deserve the Nobel prize in physics, you really do. Too bad no one will ever know about this. It really is a shame. Now, where is that interesting friend of yours? The one who talks with our friends from the sky?"

Did Freddy sense these guys and go to get Doroteo?

The possibility of Freddy abandoning them never crossed her mind. She felt a twinge of hope again.

During the next few seconds, a series of noises stole everyone's attention. Taylor heard scuffling in the woods beyond the man and to her left, followed by a muffled gunshot in the same direction, maybe sixty meters away. They all turned in the direction of the sound, even the man with the gun. Taylor squinted to see what lay out in the dark woods.

"Damn it," a new male voice said from the direction of the noise.

Taylor winced when she heard the distinct sound of someone falling on the ground and getting hit with a hard object. Somehow, she knew the source.

The sudden stillness lasted only a second, replaced by the sounds of movement in the woods—the snapping of small sticks and undergrowth pushed out of the way. Freddy emerged from the thick wall of trees first, staggering forward and barely able to keep from falling. Taylor gulped and held her breath. Blood was trickling down his forehead, glistening red in the moonlight. Then the taller man appeared behind him.

"The bastard shot me!" said the new man angrily.

He held one hand at his side, under his armpit, and a gun in the other hand pointed at Freddy. The new man dressed like the first, but a dark military hat covered his head. The man who had accosted Taylor laughed and then turned back to the group.

"They're very interested in your friend here. I'm glad he decided to stick around."

During their short walk to join the group, Taylor watched in horror. Her second-to-last hope had just disappeared.

The man with the hat put a bag over Freddy's head and cuffed his hands behind his back then walked the last few meters to stand by his comrade. He pushed Freddy to the ground and held his shoulder, forcing him to stay on his knees. Freddy groaned in pain.

"He's gonna stay right here," the man said, also wincing from pain. "We don't need this guy's voodoo."

"Don't hurt him," Sadi said, mustering enough courage for one step forward.

"He'll be okay," Taylor whispered without turning her head.

"I asked you a question," said Simon. "Who are you?"

"All you need to know," said the man without a hat, "is that *we* are the United States government. We're here to serve you and take you to safety before anyone gets hurt. Now, before we continue here, I'm going to need..."

The sound of approaching footsteps interrupted him. The man released his grip on Freddy and sidestepped deftly to the right, with his gun pointing in the direction of the noise on the path behind them. The man without a hat was no longer smiling.

Doroteo materialized from the dark, walking slowly and his lips pressed tightly together. When Taylor recognized him, it triggered a deep breath of relief. He would know how to handle the situation. But when she saw the anger in his eyes, she held the next cold breath inside her lungs.

When the next man appeared behind him, her heart sank to a new low. The man was much taller so that his entire head showed above Doroteo. Taylor felt a strange familiarity with the man, but she could not identify him.

When she heard the man speak, even his voice sounded familiar.

"Hold it there, shithead."

Doroteo stopped.

"Identify yourself!" demanded the man without a hat. "I recognized Mister Ortiz."

"No need for alarm, gentlemen," said the newcomer. While he stepped slowly to the side, Taylor saw one hand holding a gun, pointed at Doroteo's head. In the other hand, he held a shiny ID displayed in his open wallet. "I'm Agent Pratt from the Seattle FBI office."

The man with a hat looked at his companion.

"FBI? Aren't you a bit out of your jurisdiction, Agent Pratt? I think you need to hand over your gun."

When Taylor heard the FBI agent's name, she and Cesar looked at each other in surprise. A distant memory burst into her mind, the image of an unconscious man on a cot, in a foreclosed home. In another situation, she would have laughed. At the moment, she felt as though karma had finally caught up with them.

"Gerald Foster is my case," he said casually. "I've been tracking his friends. I stopped this son of a bitch from shooting you two in the head. If you don't mind, I will keep the gun with me. Oh, and by the way, you're welcome."

Agent Pratt stepped farther away from Doroteo and slid his gun inside his jacket. Taylor squinted to see Agent Pratt's face more clearly. His eyes seemed to challenge either of the two men to confiscate his weapon.

In the next instant, the man without a hat recovered from his initial shock at the surprise visit. He focused on Doroteo then back on Agent Pratt, spending a few seconds for consideration of the new situation.

"Agent Pratt huh," he said finally, smiling. "Gerald Foster is no longer your concern, *Agent*, but I guess that since you're here, you can wait with us until our backup arrives."

"Go join your friends," said the man with a hat and then stepped behind Doroteo. He aimed his gun at Doroteo's face while his comrade pointed his gun at the ground between himself and Taylor. Doroteo stood still, and the man with the hat stepped closer.

"Don't get too close to this bastard," Agent Pratt said in a strangely jovial tone. He extended his hand in warning and the man with the hat stopped to look at him. "He can be hard to handle."

"When I need your advice, *FBI*, I'll ask for it." The man returned his attention to Doroteo and paused.

"Come on, Doroteo," Cesar called out to his friend. "Don't get yourself killed."

Doroteo paused with apparent indecision, and Taylor saw his ultimate acceptance of their impossible predicament. Then he silently joined his friends, dangerously silent. Cesar placed his hand on Doroteo's shoulder and whispered something too soft for Taylor to hear.

—※—

The three armed men stood several meters apart from each other, and the man with a hat pulled out a black cell phone and made a call. He spoke loud enough for all to hear.

"We have them secured."

When the man put his phone away, Taylor noticed a blank expression on Sadi's face as her last hope died. Taylor tried imagining the woman's emotions and shuddered. *She's got kids!* Taylor's pulse accelerated even faster than before the man had grabbed her hair. She could not accept the idea of their plan coming so close to completion, just to fail at the end.

When she noticed the tear sliding down Sadi's cheek, Taylor put her arm around the woman. The sight of the woman's single tear produced an emotion more hopeless than Taylor had ever experienced. All the anger, hope, and anxiety from her whole life welled up inside her, and she felt ready to collapse.

"This is not the end," said Freddy's muffled voice from his kneeling position on the ground, his first words since being captured. "If you let them go, we will spare you."

The man with the hat kicked Freddy in the ribs, and he fell the rest of the way to the ground. Then without pause, he turned to Agent Pratt, standing eye to eye with him.

"I'm surprised you want to stick around, FBI," he said with thick sarcasm. "When my superiors learn that you failed to divulge this location to the *proper* authorities, you might lose your job, or maybe even join your friends here. But I suppose that since you did help us, I guess we could leave your participation out of the official report. You've only got about twenty minutes to get the hell out of here!"

"Like I said, you're welcome." Agent Pratt casually took two more steps away from them and looked up at the back of the jet. Their threat did not seem to affect him. He focused on the aircraft as if in admiration. "Of course, you wouldn't be worried about your superiors learning how the *FBI* just saved your asses?"

The man without a hat narrowed his eyes in anger then turned to the people at the base of the jet's ladder. Taylor felt his eyes sweep over them all.

"Don't look so goddamned unhappy," he said with a sneer and a smile. Mockery and triumph saturated his tone. "In just a few minutes, you can all go on a nice and comfortable helicopter ride."

Taylor grabbed Sadi's hand tightly, and the older woman returned the sentiment. For a moment, she closed her eyes and concentrated on the physical pressure on her hand. Maybe some strength could flow from her to Sadi and vice versa. Without knowing how or when, she would make sure that Sadi and her daughters escaped, even if she died as a result. If she could just kill any of the three men in front of them, she would feel satisfied. She especially hated the one who had pulled her hair and shoved her.

After opening her eyes again, she stared at the man without a hat. Their eyes made contact for a brief moment that seemed to stretch forever. With hate swelling inside her, she imagined inflicting severe pain on him. She would wipe that smug smile from his face.

In the next instant, her mind experienced difficulty interpreting the sensory information from her eyes and ears, and she attempted to determine if her imagination had come to life or if she was dreaming. The scene seemed to freeze in time after half of the man's face exploded in a red-and-white mess.

The next gunshot explosion ripped Taylor from her trance, and her whole body shuddered as if awoken from a nightmare. The harsh burst turned her attention from the man with only half a face, now lying on the ground, to the man with a hat standing a few meters away. He fell to his knees, grabbing his neck in pain.

Taylor and all of her companions turned to Agent Pratt, his gun still pointed at the man with a hat. For the next few seconds, the kneeling man just stared at the FBI agent, making a horrible gurgling sound from choking on his own blood. Then he collapsed to the ground and fell peacefully silent.

While everyone waited for Agent Pratt's next action, the silence of the forest covered the violent scene like a blanket. But the serenity lasted only a moment before a child began crying inside the jet. Agent Pratt finally turned away from his victims, glancing at Gerald and then focusing on Doroteo.

"If there's one thing I despise more than Mr. Foster here," Agent Pratt said, waving his gun absently in Gerald's direction. "It's the fucking CIA!"

The next few seconds felt like an eternity, the violent deaths repeating in Taylor's mind until they became her only thoughts. Everyone, including her, just stared at the dead men on the ground, even Doroteo appeared as shocked as everyone else. When Taylor finally turned to Agent Pratt, he looked up from the man he'd just killed to meet her gaze. She expected him to aim the pistol at them next, but he kept it pointed at the ground.

Doroteo became the first to break the stillness by taking a few steps closer to the FBI agent until he stood within the man's reach.

"What now?" Doroteo asked.

Agent Pratt's next quick action made Taylor jump in surprise. He flipped the gun in the air, caught it by the barrel, and extended the weapon to Doroteo.

"You can have the murder weapon back," he said with a sneer. "They'll probably never link this to you, but at least it won't be me. God that felt good! Stupid bastards."

While maintaining eye contact, Doroteo took the weapon and deftly slipped it inside his jacket. Taylor was extremely confused and stood like a statue, staring at the two men. Her heart rate slowed, and she took a couple of deep breaths.

Sadi left Taylor's side and ran to Freddy, carefully removing the bag from his head. While kneeling on the ground, she held her hand on his shoulder to steady him.

"Are you okay, Freddy?"

"I need a minute before I can stand."

Agent Pratt and Doroteo turned to watch them.

Taylor looked back at the FBI agent, not knowing whether to thank him or grab Simon's gun from the ground and shoot him. The bloody memory of the two deaths seemed to chase away all rational thought.

"I want a closer look at our friend here," Agent Pratt said then stepped confidently toward the several pairs of eyes looking at him.

After glancing at Simon, the FBI agent turned to Gerald. Taylor stepped closer toward him, ready to throw herself in the way of any attack. She did not like the look in the agent's eyes.

As if trying to assess the physical condition of a burn victim, the FBI agent scanned Gerald from his face down to his hospital gown. In response, Gerald leaned back, his eyes opening uncomfortably wide. He stepped backward and almost hit the ladder leading up to the jet.

"What did they do to you?" Agent Pratt asked himself quietly. While speaking, he maintained eye contact with Gerald but spoke loudly enough for the whole group to hear. "I expected some satisfaction when I heard they took you in, but I was just pissed they got you first. Now that I'm looking at you..."

He sneered and shook his head as though sincerely disappointed. After drawing a deep breath of the crisp night air, he sighed and turned to Taylor, the next closest person. He stared at her as though in recognition, squinting. During the awkward silence, she wondered if he was remembering his abduction and interrogation.

Does he recognize my voice?

Agent Pratt suddenly broke eye contact, turning to face the jet.

"What the hell are you all still doing here?"

After strapping herself in the pilot's seat, Taylor looked outside again. Agent Pratt was standing where they had left him, watching the jet with a curious mixture of amusement and disappointment. The two dead CIA agents lay on either side of him, their red blood just barely visible in the moonlight. He shook his head as though from some personal irritation, then he returned to the shadow of the trees.

EIGHTY-SEVEN

Sadi

While Mark and Taylor piloted the jet from the cockpit, Cesar monitored the bank of sensors at the front of the plane. When he told everyone the news of the approaching helicopters, they were already ascending into the sky, the BMW flying close by their side. Sadi was sitting with her two girls, talking about what they might see in space. The lively conversation shifted their attention away from the military pursuit and helped ease Sadi's nerves.

Instead of flying at an incline and gaining altitude slowly, they ascended straight into the sky. At the start of their ascent, Sadi made the mistake of looking out a window at the fast-retreating ground. The sensation of vertigo felt so much different than a plane ride, making her grateful for an empty stomach. In only three minutes, they left the military helicopters far below them and out of firing range.

Light from the sun soon replaced the darkness of night.

During the heaviest acceleration, Sadi's nearest neighbors clutched her hands, Gerald on her left and Daryn on her right, terror evident in their tight grips. Mark's ten-year-old boy nearly went into shock. The blood almost drained entirely from his little face. His youngest child, a five-year-old boy, held on to his mother's hand and cried. From

Sadi's viewpoint, Helen and Simon were the only ones smiling, but she imagined Taylor thoroughly enjoying herself.

Sadi experienced their flight through the atmosphere and into space as if it were a disjointed dream. At first, the terrifying experience on the ground left her feeling numb, her mind refusing to accept anything other than a horrible fate for them all. In one possible scenario, she imagined the jet losing power and then falling like a shooting star through the atmosphere—everyone cooked alive in a burning fireball. But the horrors in her mind and the bloody events at the lake began to fade like the Canadian forest below them, replaced by stillness and the silence of space.

For the first time since Helen's abduction, Sadi began to feel truly safe. The space above the atmosphere became a place where no evil influence from Earth could touch her or those she loved. Except for the cold, unfeeling universe, fewer creatures held power over them. Her children and Gerald sat safely by her side, and her new friends would help ease the anxiety of leaving her home planet and all she ever knew.

—※—

After nearly forty minutes of ascending into the sky, Taylor decreased the acceleration so their weight felt like normal gravity. The lower pressure unexpectedly alleviated Sadi's remaining anxiety, letting her finally relax in her seat, and all the children began to show normal types of activity. Helen was the first to react to the mood of the other children, sharing her excitement about their situation.

"I wonder what the aliens will look like," she said to Daryn by her side. "I bet they'll be super tiny. Mom said their probe was little, so they have to be tiny to fit inside it. Right, Mom?"

"Maybe," Sadi answered, smiling. She considered offering her own opinion but decided she would rather hear Helen's next uninfluenced thoughts.

"Little wouldn't be that scary, I guess," Daryn said, consoling herself. She turned to Sadi, probably hoping for confirmation from an adult. But Helen did not give her mother time to respond.

"Unless they look like a cockroach!"

"Helen," Sadi said, placing her hand comfortingly on Daryn's shoulder. "I highly doubt they're cockroaches."

"Or a praying mantis!"

Sadi shuddered at the horror suddenly appearing in her imagination, the alien probe filled with cockroaches and praying mantises. She opened her mouth to protest, but Mark interrupted her by speaking from the cockpit.

"You can take your seatbelts off now and move about the cabin."

"You couldn't wait to say that," Taylor said, laughing.

When the children escaped from their seats, they began showing even more signs of emotional recovery, even the youngest of the children, Mark's five-year-old boy. They spoke with excitement and took turns showing each other different views from the windows. Sadi and the other two women enjoyed watching them. Simon and Max also watched but with a mixture of curiosity and suspicion.

When Taylor stepped from the cockpit a few minutes later, she looked at the kids for a moment and smiled. For the first time that horrible night, she appeared almost happy, though still tense. She looked at Sadi with a mysterious glint in her eyes.

"Freddy's established a communication link and wants to talk to you, Sadi."

Once in the cockpit, Mark motioned for Sadi to sit in the copilot's chair, then extended a headset in his hand. After following his direction to look out the window, Sadi noticed the top of the BMW about fifty meters away. Earth filled half the view and stars filled the other half.

For several seconds, the beauty and immensity of the scene consumed her entire attention, and she just stared. After refocusing on the BMW, she could faintly see through the windshield and noticed Freddy and Doroteo looking back at her. Since Freddy was still a bit dizzy from being hit in the head, Doroteo had decided to accompany him in the BMW. Seeing the two men again reminded her of the activity in the forest. The memory already seemed like a dream from another life.

"Hello, Sadi," Freddy said, waving. His voice felt like an echo.

"Hi, Freddy and Doroteo," she answered. "Can you both hear me?"

"We can hear you," Doroteo said, bluntly.

For the first time since meeting him, Sadi heard uncertainty in his voice, or maybe fear. While waving, tears began to form in her eyes.

"We did it, didn't we?" she said, wiping the single tear falling down her cheek. "We made it."

"Yes, we did," Freddy answered in a more somber tone. "I wanted to tell you something. I will not be going with you at this time. We are returning to Earth."

"What are you talking about? We barely got away." The thought of them returning almost made her sick inside. "You need to come with us. Can't you go back later?"

"I need to return for Mr. Smith. We also have to help find Franklin, Gerda, and Audrie. We cannot abandon them."

When he mentioned Audrie's name, Sadi thought she heard something more than worry in his voice. She wanted to keep arguing but knew the futility of the effort. She would be unable to change his mind.

"I understand," she said after the long pause.

"The military is preparing to send EMP missiles to disable you," he said. "They want to stop you from communicating with anyone. You need to go."

"What—" she began but a flash of light suddenly stopped her.

The alien probe had appeared between them, forcing Sadi to shield her eyes from the reflected sunlight. She focused on the open end of the probe and didn't even notice when Taylor joined Mark behind her.

As she remembered at the barn the previous winter, tentacles of light extended from behind the chrome object as though flowing in a gentle ocean current. Their slow, rhythmic swaying made her forget the jet's tremendous speed and even the beautiful scene behind it. Taylor and Mark, she realized, were looking for the first time at the probe, probably experiencing the same sensation of anxiety and awe.

Freddy's voice reminded her of his presence.

"Do not be afraid, Sadi. The probe will guide you. You *will* see us again."

With her gaze still fixed on the probe, Freddy's words floated somewhere in the space between them, barely registering. She recalled her vision of the cave when she and Helen had escaped the darkness.

While lost in her memories, the BMW turned and vanished from sight.

—※—

After recovering from the trauma of their narrow escape, Sadi began wondering more about what had happened to Max and Gerald, since neither of them would say much about it. She secretly discussed the issue with Taylor and Simon, and they agreed to wait and see. Like everyone else, Max and Gerald needed rest, just more of it.

Sadi spent the majority of her time trying to relax and listening to the children talk excitedly about what awaited them. The more they traveled in the extreme light of the sun, the brighter her thoughts became. Eventually, most of her worries shriveled to nothing, and she focused almost completely on their next destination, a brighter future.

As the hours passed, Earth slowly shrank to a small blue dot against the sea of black and white dots. While seeing her home planet retreat farther and farther away, Sadi thought of her son and how his remains lay in its cold embrace, remembered only by his family and a few others. Surprisingly, the increased distance failed to make her feel any worse about the situation. Her son still seemed as far away as when she last stood at his grave.

When they finally arrived near Mercury, the globules of blackness began forming around them. Sadi held her two girls tightly, the warmth of their hands and the light in their eyes helped expel the fear and anxiety from the dark.

After passing through the dark tunnel, Sadi slowly opened her eyes to a new light.

Continues in Book 3

About the Author

Hyrum is the product of a large family and the Utah desert. He's an Eagle Scout, has degrees in chemistry and chemical engineering, and spent a few years as the Libertarian Chairman of his county. After he and his wife raised their family in the Pacific Northwest, they all moved to Kentucky, where they now reside. Other than the people in his life, he loves exploring the world and creating things.